THE COMPLETE SHORT STORIES OF

JAMES PURDY

WORKS BY JAMES PURDY

NOVELS

Malcolm

The Nephew

Cabot Wright Begins

Eustace Chisholm and the Works

Jeremy's Version

I Am Elijah Thrush

The House of the Solitary Maggot

In a Shallow Grave

Narrow Rooms

Dream Palaces: Three Novels

Mourners Below

On Glory's Course

In the Hollow of His Hand

Garments the Living Wear

Reaching Rose

Gertrude of Stony Island Avenue

SHORT STORIES AND PLAYS

Don't Call Me by My Right Name and Other Stories

63: Dream Palace and Other Stories

Color of Darkness

Children Is All

A Day After the Fair

Proud Flesh

The Candles of Your Eyes

Out with the Stars

In the Night of Time and Four Other Plays

Dream Palace: Selected Stories, 1956–1987

Epistles of Care

Moe's Villa and Other Stories

James Purdy: Selected Plays

POETRY

Collected Poems

The Brooklyn Branding Parlors

The Oyster Is a Wealthy Beast

The Blue Room

The Running Sun

I Will Arrest the Bird That Has No Light

Don't Let the Snow Fall

Sunshine Is an Only Child

Lessons and Complaints

THE COMPLETE SHORT STORIES OF

JAMES PURDY

Introduction by John Waters

LIVERIGHT PUBLISHING CORPORATION

A Division of W. W. Norton & Company

New York • London

Printed in the United States of America
First Edition

For information about permission to reproduce selections from this book, write to Permissions, Liveright Publishing Corporation, a division of W. W. Norton & Company, Inc., 500 Fifth Avenue, New York, NY 10110

For information about special discounts for bulk purchases, please contact W. W. Norton Special Sales at specialsales@wwnorton.com or 800-233-4830

Manufacturing by Courier Westford
Book design by Chris Welch
Production manager: Anna Oler

Library of Congress Cataloging-in-Publication Data

Purdy, James, 1914–2009.
[Short stories]
The complete short stories of James Purdy / James Purdy ;
introduction by John Waters. — First edition.
pages cm
Includes bibliographical references.
ISBN 978-0-87140-669-9 (hardcover)
1. Short stories, American. I. Waters, John. II. Title.
PS3531.U426C66 2013
813'.54—dc23

2013013992

Liveright Publishing Corporation
500 Fifth Avenue, New York, N.Y. 10110
www.wwnorton.com

W. W. Norton & Company Ltd.
Castle House, 75/76 Wells Street, London W1T 3QT

1 2 3 4 5 6 7 8 9 0

CONTENTS

INTRODUCTION

by John Waters

Think of *The Complete Short Stories of James Purdy* as a ten-pound box of poison chocolates you keep beside your bed—fairy tales for your twisted mind that should never be described to the innocent. Randomly select a perfectly perverted Purdy story and read it before you go to sleep and savor the hilarious moral damage and beautiful decay that will certainly follow in your dreams. James Purdy writes gracefully disquieting stories for the wicked and here they *all* are at last. Together. Every single damned one of them!

Many of Purdy's characters are terribly sad. So distressed they "want to be dead like a bug." So lonely that they call the prerecorded weather or time message on the phone for company or go to the doctor every single day for social contact. One man is so filled with sorrow in his old age that he retreats to a phone booth and speaks into the dial tone coming from the receiver about the dead: "They are all gone. All of them." In towns so small (one is described as having a "population about four hundred people including the dead"), isolation is everywhere. "There isn't anything to say about such private sorrow," one of Purdy's characters announces, but yes there is, and James says it with wit, incredible sympathy, and elegant understanding.

His people are angry, too. They "never feel satisfied." One heroine (if you could possibly call her that) is described as "like every damned thing in the world had been permanently screwed for her, like it had all been planned wrong before she even got here." Many of his characters are defenseless against their own evil and suffer a tragic guilt no one will punish. Purdy loves being a shit-stirrer and can depict hate better than any writer (except perhaps Christina Stead). One fictitious husband is so overcome with fury at his wife's tirade against him that he only "saw her mouth and throat moving with unspoken words." In another story, a son wants his father's love so badly, he hisses black foam from his mouth. Diseased bodies explode onto horrified loved ones. Even inanimate objects can add to the grief of living in Purdy's fiction, like a refrigerator with an agonizing hum that exaggerates the pain of a couple's divorce battles. Nature is treacherous too: the wind steals valuable possessions, even spreads gossip. Birds are dangerous creatures who pilfer precious jewelry from hidden places. Money is the root of all hell, a burden, a curse you can purposely leave to your despised heirs. Purdy's lunatics are out of their minds, but unfortunately not enough so to be oblivious to their own despair.

Yet with all this literary turmoil, Purdy can write about common sense. "Well, when there ain't nothin' else," one damaged optimist reasons, "you got to stoop down and pick up the rotten." His creatures are "crazier than the devil on Christmas," as one announces, but Purdy has the same absurdist sympathy for a clueless dowager as he does for a homeless murderer. There's even crackpot happy endings to some of his stories although the unadventurous reader may not initially understand how Purdy's mismatched partners could possibly describe what they have as any kind of relationship, much less a successful one.

The rewards of tiny sexual attractions and the intense secrets that most can never reveal are Purdy's poetic strength. Erotic tension is always brewing and no one is spared the inner agonizing of frustration and desire. Desperate people, sometimes so horny they "touched you as though to determine if you were flesh or not," do despicable things to one another. Longing is an agony you can't avoid in Purdy's world; searching, always searching for that one sexual being you lost. My favorite damaged soul? The hustler in "Some of These Days" who unsuccessfully hunts his onetime sugar daddy in every porno theater in Manhattan until he gives up, moves into a twenty-four-hour Times Square grind house to live forever, and is finally dragged away by the authorities to a mental institution. This is just one of Purdy's love stories.

Purdy can be as funny as Jane Bowles when he writes about inappropriate attractions, always fractured from reality. His prose may seem old-fashioned at first; a couch is a "davenport," or "Madame Sobey looked at her TV machine a great deal of the time," but when he uses "The End" after the final line of a story it seems so transgressive you can imagine a copy editor today getting nervous. He uses words you seldom hear in real life; a real vocabulary lesson in unpleasantness. "A kind of hoarfrost came over her mouth." What the hell is a hoarfrost? Or "a bad odor, what a fellow I know called fetor." I'm still trying to use the word "fetor" in a sentence and sound as well-spoken as Purdy. Are his pernicious words like one of his characters, written down so shockingly "even flames" will not be able to burn them?

Can Purdy be bad? Well, in a box of chocolates this large, there's bound to be a few left at the bottom that time has made stale. Purdy can be a misogynist. Women are often evil gossips, some even emit fetor (there I go!). A man brutally beats his wife after she endlessly nags she will leave him just because she suddenly finds her married last name ridiculous. Yet when a woman in her sixties shows up completely naked at a male neighbor's front door in another story, Purdy writes about this man's understanding and kindly reaction. His black characters may seem a little sexualized and cartoonish and he does use the N-word, but isn't that a true portrait of how his characters would see things at the time they were written? Isn't Purdy, a "prisoner of decision" himself, just like the flawed humans he writes about?

James is not for everyone. I'm still surprised that brilliant literary critic and novelist Edmund White is not a fan, claiming to be "allergic" to Purdy's work. But for some readers, the special ones who delight in wickedly funny feel-bad books, James Purdy has never been on the "fringes of American literary mainstream," as the *New York Times* has claimed. No, he's been dead center in the black little hearts of provocateur-hungry readers like myself right from the beginning. Now we are ready to feel the exhilaration of devouring this exhausting new volume of literary treats. Yes, James Purdy *is* too much! But he's like a drug one can never get enough of. He makes us light-headed. High. Even sick. Overdosing on James Purdy's stories is a new kind of excitement. And not a bad way to die, either.

—2013

THE COMPLETE SHORT STORIES OF

JAMES PURDY

A GOOD WOMAN

Maud did not find life in Martinsville very interesting, it is true, but it was Mamie who was always telling her that there were brighter spots elsewhere. She did not believe Mamie and said so.

Mamie had lived in St. Louis when her husband was an official at the head office of a pipeline company there. Then he had lost his job and Mamie had come to Martinsville to live. She regretted everything and especially her marriage, but then she had gradually resigned herself to being a small town woman.

Mamie was so different from Maud. "Maud, you are happy," she would say. "You are the small town type, I guess. You don't seem to be craving the things I crave. I want something and you don't."

"What is it you want?" Maud asked.

The two women were sitting in Hannah's drug store having a strawberry soda. Mamie was reminded, she said, of some old-fashioned beer parties she and her husband had been invited to in Milwaukee when they were younger.

Mamie did not know what it was she wanted. She felt something catch at her heart strings on these cool June days and she would purposely remind herself that summer would soon be over. She always felt the passing of summer most keenly before it had actually begun. Fall affected her in a strange way and she would almost weep when she saw the falling maple leaves or the blackbirds gathering in flocks in deserted baseball parks.

"Maud, I am not young," Mamie would say, thinking of how bald and whitish and grubby her husband was getting.

Maud put down her ice-cream spoon, the straw hanging half out of the dish, and looked at her. Maud was every bit three years younger than Mamie, but when her best friend talked the way she did, Maud would take out her purse mirror and stare wonderingly through the flecks of powder on the glass. Maud had never been beautiful and she was getting stout. More and more she was spending a great deal of money on cosmetics that Mr. Hannah's young clerk told her were imported from a French town on the sea coast.

"If I could only leave off the sweets," Maud said, finishing her soda.

"Maud, are you happy?" Mamie sighed. But Maud did not answer. She had never particularly thought about happiness; it was Mamie who was always reminding her of that word. Maud had always lived in Martinsville and had never thought much about what made people happy or unhappy. When her mother died, she had felt lonely because they had always been companions. For they were not so much like mother and daughter as like two young women past their first youth who knew what life was. They had spent together many a happy afternoon saying and doing foolish young things, in the summer walking in the parks and fairgrounds and in the winter making preserves and roasting fowl for Thanksgiving and Christmas parties. She always remembered her mother with pleasure instead of grief. But now she had Mamie for a friend and she was married to Obie.

Her marriage to Obie had been her greatest experience, but she did not think about it much anymore. Sometimes she almost wished Obie would go away so that she could remember more clearly the first time she had met him when he was an orchestra leader in a little traveling jazz band that made one-night stands near the airport in Martinsville. Obie had been so good-looking in those days, and he was still pretty much the same Obie, of course, but he was not Obie the bandleader anymore. But once he had quit playing in orchestras and had become a traveling salesman, Maud's real romance had ended and she could only look out her window onto the muddy Ohio River and dream away an afternoon.

Obie and Mamie had talks about Maud sometimes. "We spend too much," Obie would say to her. He said he lived on practically nothing on the road. They both agreed she was not very practical. And she spent too much on cosmetics and movies. Mamie did not say so much about the movies because she knew she was the cause there of Maud's spending more than her income allowed, but then it was not Mamie surely who advised her the night of the carnival to buy that imported ostrich plume fan with the ruby jewels in the center and a good many other things of the same kind. And how could Maud give up the pleasure of the movies, or the ice cream or perfumes she got at Mr. Hannah's drug store? And what would Mr. Hannah do for star customers, for that was what Mamie said she and Maud were. They were actually out of all Martinsville his star customers, though they never purchased anything in his pharmaceutical department.

"Maud," Mamie said, "what do we get out of life anyway?"

Maud was not pleased with Mamie's taking this turn in the conversation. She did not like to get serious in the drug store as it spoiled her enjoyment of the ice cream and she had to think up an answer quickly on account of Mamie's impatience or Mamie would not be pleased and would think she was slow-witted, and she was sure Mamie thought she was slow-witted anyhow.

When Maud left Mamie that day she began to think it over. She walked slowly down the street, going north away from Mr. Hannah's drug store.

Mr. Hannah was standing by his green-trimmed display window, watching her as she walked to her yellow frame house over the river.

"What do we get out of life anyway?" Mamie's words kept humming about in her mind but she was so tired from the exhaustion of the warm dusty day that she did not let herself think too much about it. She did not see why Mamie had to keep thinking of such unpleasant things. It depressed her a little, too, and she did not like the feeling of depression. She did not want to think of sad things or whether life was worth living. She knew that Mamie always enjoyed the sad movies with unhappy endings, but she could never bear them at all. Life is too full of that sort of thing, she always told Mamie, and Mamie would say, pouting and giving her a disappointed look, "Maud, you are like all small town housewives. You don't know what I am feeling. You don't feel things down in you the way I feel them."

As she sauntered along she saw Bruce Hauser in front of his bicycle shop. Bruce was a youngish man always covered with oil and grease from repairing motorcycles and machines. When he smiled at Maud she could see that even his smile was stained with oil and car paint and she found herself admiring his white teeth.

She heard some school boys and girls laughing and riding over the bridge on their bicycles and she knew that school was out for the summer and that was why they were riding around like they were. It had not been so very long since she had gone to school, she thought, and for the second time that day she remembered her mother and the warm afternoons when she would come home from school and throw her books down on the sofa and take down her red hair, and her mother and she would eat a ripe fruit together, or sometimes they would make gooseberry preserves or marmalade. It was all very near and very distant.

The next day she felt a little easier at finding Mamie in a better humor and they went to a movie at the Bijou. It was a comedy this afternoon and Maud laughed quite a lot. On the way home Mamie complained that the movie had done nothing to her, had left her, she said, like an icicle, and she felt like asking for her money back.

When they sat down in Hannah's drug store, they began reading the *Bill of Fair with Specialties*—for though they had sat in the same booth for nearly five years and knew all the dishes and drinks, they still went on reading the menu as if they did not know exactly what might be served. Suddenly Mamie said, "Are you getting along all right with Obie, Maud?"

Maud raised her too heavily penciled eyebrows and thought over Mamie's question, but instead of letting her answer, Mamie went on talking about the movie, and when they were leaving the drug store, Maud told Mr. Hannah to charge her soda.

"Why don't you let me pay for yours?" Mamie said, pulling her dress which had stuck to her skin from the sticky heat of the day.

Maud knew that Mamie would never pay for her soda even if she happened to be flat broke and hungry. She knew Mamie was tight, but she liked her anyway. Maud owed quite a bill at Mr. Hannah's and nearly all of it was for strawberry sodas. If Obie had known it, Maud would have been in trouble all right, but she always managed to keep Obie from knowing.

"I know," Mamie said on the way home, "I know, honey, that you and Obie don't hit it off right anymore."

Maud wondered how Mamie knew that, but what could she say to deny it? She said, "Obie has to work out of town too much to be the family man I would like him to be."

When Maud got home that night she found that Obie had arrived. He was a little cross because she had not prepared dinner for him.

"I was not sure you was coming," Maud said.

She prepared his favorite dinner of fried pork chops and French fried potatoes with a beet and lettuce salad and some coffee with canned milk and homemade preserves and cake.

"Where was you all day?" Obie asked at the table, and Maud told him she usually went to a movie with Mamie Sucher and afterwards she went to the drug store and got a soda.

"You ought to cut down on the sweets," Obie said, and Maud remembered having caught a reflection of herself that day in the hall mirror, and she knew she was a long way from having the same figure she had had as a girl. For a moment she felt almost as depressed as Mamie said she was all the time.

While Maud was doing the dishes, Obie told her that he had some good news for her, but she knew from the first it was not really good news. Obie told her that he had quit his traveling job and was going to sell life insurance now. He said he was getting too old to be on the road all the time. He wanted to have a little home life for a change, and it wasn't right for Maud to be alone so much.

Maud did not know what to say to him. The tears were falling over her hands into the dishwater, for she knew Obie would never make as much money selling life insurance as he had made on the road as a traveling salesman, and she knew there wouldn't be any more money for her for a long while. And all of a sudden she thought of the time when she had first begun getting stout and the high school boys had quit asking her for dances at the Rainbow Gardens and didn't notice her anymore.

The next time Maud saw Mamie was a week later, and Mamie was curious to know everything and asked how Obie was getting along these days.

"He quit his sales work," Maud said, and she felt the tears beginning to come, but she held them back by breathing deeper.

"I'm not a bit surprised," Mamie said. "I saw it coming all the time."

They walked over to the movie, and it was a very sad one. It was about a woman who had led, as Maud could see, not a very virtuous life. She had talked with three or four such women in her lifetime. The woman in the picture gave up the man she was in love with and went away to a bigger town. Mamie enjoyed it very much.

On the way home Mamie wanted Maud to come and have a soda.

"A strawberry soda?" Maud said, putting on some more lipstick and looking in at the green display windows with their headache ads and pictures of cornplasters. "I can't afford it."

"What do you mean, you can't afford it?" Mamie said.

"Obie has to make good at his insurance first," Maud told her.

"Come on in and I will buy you one," Mamie said in a hard firm voice, and though Maud knew Mamie did not want to spend money on her, she couldn't bear to go home to an empty house without first having some refreshment, so she went in with her.

As soon as they had finished having their sodas, Mr. Hannah came over to Maud and said he would like to have a few words in private with her.

"I am paying for this," Mamie said as if she suspected trouble of some sort.

Maud made a motion with her hand and started to walk with Mr. Hannah toward the pharmacy room.

"Do you want me to wait outside?" Mamie said, but she got no reply.

An old woman with white gloves was sitting in a booth looking at Maud and Mr. Hannah. Maud knew her story and kept looking at her. She was to have married a young business man from Baltimore, but the day before the wedding the young man had died in a railroad accident. Ever since then, the old woman had not taken off her white wedding gloves.

"Well, Maud," said Mr. Hannah, his gray old eyes narrowing under his spectacles, "I've been meaning to talk over with you the little matter of your bill and have been wondering whether or not . . ."

Maud could feel the red coming up over her face. She knew the old woman with the white gloves was hearing all of it. Maud feared perhaps she had put on too much rouge, for Mr. Hannah was giving her peculiar looks.

"How much is the bill?" she managed to say.

Mr. Hannah looked over his books, but he did not need to look to know how much Maud owed.

"Thirty-five dollars," he said.

Maud moved slightly backwards. "Thirty-five?" she repeated without believing, and she looked over on the books where her account was listed in black purplish ink. "Surely," Maud said, "that must be a mistake."

"Well, you have been having sodas on credit for more than six months," Mr. Hannah said, grinning a little.

"Not surely thirty-five dollars' worth," Maud told him working the clasp on her purse, "because," she said, "I can't pay it, Obie isn't making full salary and I can't give it to you now at all."

"No hurry to collect yet," Mr. Hannah said and there was a little warmth coming into his voice. "Ain't no hurry for that," he said.

Suddenly Maud could not control her tears. They were falling through her fingers into a small handkerchief embroidered with a bluebird and a rosebush.

"Now, Maud," Mr. Hannah said, "I will be real easy on you. Maybe you would like to talk it all over in the pharmacy room," he said taking her arm, and before she knew her own mind he had led her into the back room.

"Don't in any case," Maud begged him, sobbing a little, "don't in any case, Mr. Hannah, tell my husband about this bill."

"No need at all, no need at all," he said, turning on the light in the pharmacy room. Mr. Hannah was staring at her. Maud was not beautiful, really. Her powder-spotted mirror told her that, and she had a receding chin and large pores. But Mr. Hannah was looking. She remembered now how he had led a singing class at the First Presbyterian Church and he had directed some girls to sing "America the Beautiful" in such a revised improper way that the elders had asked him to leave the church, and he had, and soon after that his wife had divorced him.

As Mamie Sucher was not there to prompt her, Maud did not know what more to say to him. She stood there looking at the bill. She knew it could not be thirty-five dollars. She knew she was being cheated and yet she could not tell him to his face he was lying. It was the only drug store in town where she could get sodas on credit. All the other stores made you pay on leaving or before you drank your soda. Maud stood there paralyzed, looking at the bill, and her face felt hot and sticky.

Then Mr. Hannah said something that pleased her. She did not know why it pleased her so much. “Maud, you beautiful girl, you,” he said.

He was holding her hand, the hand with her mother’s ruby ring. “Why don’t you ever come into the pharmacy room,” he said. “Why do you have to wait for an invitation, good friends like us?” And he clasped her hand so tightly that the ring pressed against her index finger, painfully. She had never been in the pharmacy room before but she did not like the whiffs of drugs and the smell of old cartons of patent medicines that came from there. “Maud, you beauty,” he said.

Maud knew that she should say something cold and polite to Mr. Hannah, but suddenly she could not. She smiled and as she smiled the rouge cracked a little on her lips. Mr. Hannah was saying, “Maud, you know you don’t have to stand on form with an old friend of the family like me. You know, Maud, I knowed you when you was only a small girl. I knowed your mother well, too.”

She laughed again and then she listened to the flies on the screen, the flies that were collecting there and would be let in.

She tried to take the bill from his hand. “I will give it to my husband,” she said.

“He will be very mad,” Mr. Hannah warned her.

“Yes,” Maud breathed hard. It wasn’t possible for a man like Obie to believe that she could come into this drug store of Mr. Hannah’s and buy only strawberry sodas and make that large a bill, and she knew Obie would never believe her if she told him.

“Well, give me the bill, Mr. Hannah,” she said, but Mr. Hannah was still muttering about how dangerous such little things were to the happiness of young married people. Maud thought right then of a time when her mother had gone walking with her and Maud had a new pink parasol and all of a sudden a dirty alley cur had jumped on her as if to spoil her new parasol, not purposely but only in play, and she had said, “Oh, hell,” and to hear her swear for the first time had given her mother a good laugh. And now she said so that Mr. Hannah could scarcely hear, “Oh, hell,” and he laughed suddenly and put his arm around her.

She had thought everything like that was over for her and here was Mr. Hannah hugging her and calling her "beauty."

She knew it was not proper for her to be in this position with an old man like Mr. Hannah, but he wasn't doing anything really bad and he was so old anyhow, so she let him hug her and kiss her a few times and then she pushed him away.

"I ain't in no hurry to collect, you know that, Maud," Mr. Hannah said, and he had lost his breath and was standing there before her, his old faded eyes watering.

"Of course, my husband ought to see this bill," Maud said, but she just couldn't make the words have any force to sound like she meant it.

"You just go home and forget about it for a while, why don't you, Maud," he said.

She kept pushing a black imitation cameo bracelet back and forth on her arm. "You know how my husband would feel against it," she said.

Then Mr. Hannah did something that was even more surprising. He suddenly tore up the bill right in front of her.

Maud let out a little cry and then Mr. Hannah moved closer to her and Maud said, "No, Mr. Hannah, no, you let me make this right with you because Obie will soon be getting a check." She became actually frightened then with him in the dark, stale-smelling pharmacy room. "Some day," she said, "some day I will make this right," and she hurried out away from Mr. Hannah and she walked quickly, almost unconsciously, to the screen door where the flies were collecting before a summer thunder shower.

"I will make this right," she said, and the old druggist followed her and shouted after her, "You don't need to tell him, Maud."

"Don't call me Maud," she gasped.

She stopped and looked at him standing there. She laughed. The screen door slammed behind her and she was in the street.

It was getting a little late and Mamie was gone and the street was almost empty. She felt so excited that she would have liked to talk to Mamie and tell her what had happened to her, but she was too excited to talk to anyone and she hurried straight toward her house near the river.

Just as she got to the bridge she saw Bruce Hauser. She said, "Good evening, Bruce, how are you?" She could not say any more, she was that excited, and without waiting a minute to talk to Bruce, she took out her key and unlocked the door. As she was about to go up the stairs, she caught a reflection of herself in the hall mirror. She stared into it. Maud felt so much pleasure seeing herself so young, that she repeated Mr. Hannah's words again, "Maud, you beauty, you beauty." She was as pretty and carefree this June day as she had been that time when she and her mother had walked with the new pink parasol—long before she had met Obie—and they had joked together, not like mother and daughter, but like two good girl chums away at school.

YOU REACH FOR YOUR HAT

People saw her every night on the main street. She went out just as it was getting dark, when the street lights would pop on, one by one, and the first bats would fly out round Mrs. Bilderbach's. That was Jennie. Now what was she up to? everyone would ask, and we all knew, in company and out. Jennie Esmond was off for her evening walk and to renew old acquaintances. Now don't go into details, the housewives would say over the telephone. Ain't life dreary enough without knowing? They all knew anyhow as in a movie they had seen five times and where the sad part makes them cry just as much the last showing as the first.

They couldn't say too much, though. Didn't she have the gold star in the window, meaning Lafe was dead in the service of his country? They couldn't say too much, and, after all, what did Jennie do when she went out? There wasn't any proof she went the whole hog. She only went to the Mecca, which had been a saloon in old World War days and where no ladies went. And, after all, she simply drank a few beers and joked with the boys. Yes, and well, once they told that she played the piano there, but it was some sort of old-fashioned number and everybody clapped politely after she stopped.

She bought all her clothes at a store run by a young Syrian.

Nobody liked him or his merchandise, but he did sell cheap and he had the kind of things that went with her hair, that dead-straw color people in town called angel hair. She bought all her dresses there that last fall and summer, and they said the bargain she got them for no one would ever believe.

Then a scandalous thing. She took the gold star out of the window. What could it mean? Nobody had ever dreamed of such a thing. You would have thought anyone on such shaky ground would have left it up forever. And she took it down six months after the sad news. It must mean marriage. The little foreign man. But the janitor said nobody ever called on her except Mamie Jordan and little Blake Higgins.

She went right on with her evening promenades, window-shopping the little there was to window-shop, nodding to folks in parked cars and to old married friends going in and out of the drug store. It wasn't right for a woman like Jennie to be always walking up and down the main street night after night and acting, really acting, as if she had no home to go to. She took on in her way as bad as the loafers had in front of the court house before the mayor ordered the benches carried away so they couldn't sit down. Once somebody saw her in the section around the brewery and we wondered. Of course, everyone supposed the government paid her for Lafe's death; so it wasn't as if she was destitute.

Nobody ever heard her mention Lafe, but Mamie Jordan said she had a picture of him in civilian clothes in her bedroom. He wasn't even smiling. Mamie said Jennie had had such trouble getting him to go to Mr. Hart's photography studio. It was right before his induction, and Jennie had harped on it so long that Lafe finally went, but he was so mad all the time they were taking him he never smiled once; they had to finish him just looking. Mamie said Jennie never showed any interest in the picture and even had toilet articles in front of it. No crepe on it or anything.

Mamie didn't understand it at all. Right after he was reported missing in action she went down to offer her sympathy and Jennie was sitting there eating chocolates. She had come to have a good cry with her and there she was cool as a cucumber. You'd never have known a thing had happened. It made Mamie feel so bad, because she had always liked Lafe even if he never would set the world on fire, and she had burst out crying, and then after a little while Jennie cried too and they sat there together all evening weeping and hugging each other.

But even then Jennie didn't say anything about Lafe's going really meaning anything to her. It was as though he had been gone for twenty years. An old hurt. Mamie got to thinking about it and going a little deeper into such a mystery. It came back to her that Lafe had always gone to the Mecca tavern and left Jennie at home, and now here she was out there every night of her life.

Mamie thought these things over on her way to the movie that night. No one had ever mentioned Jennie's case lately to her, and, truth to tell, people were beginning to forget who Lafe was. People don't remember anymore. When she was a girl they had remembered a dead man a little longer, but today men came and went too fast; somebody went somewhere every week, and how could you keep fresh in your memory such a big list of departed ones?

She sighed. She had hoped she would run into Jennie on her way to the movie. She walked around the court house and past the newspaper office and she went out of her way to go by the drygoods store in hopes she would see her, but not a sign. It was double feature night; so she knew she would never get out in time to see Jennie after the show.

But the movie excited her more than ever, and she came out feeling too nervous to go home. She walked down the main street straight north, and before she knew it she was in front of the Mecca. Some laboring men were out front and she felt absolutely humiliated. She didn't know what on earth had come over her. She looked in the window and as she did so she half expected the men to make some underhanded move or say something low-down, but they hardly looked at her. She put her hands to the glass, pressing her nose flat and peering in so that she could see clear to the back of the room.

She saw Jennie all right, alone, at one of the last tables. Almost before she knew what she was doing, she was walking through the front door. She felt herself blushing the most terrible red ever, going into a saloon where there were no tables for ladies and before dozens of coarse laboring men, who were probably laughing at her.

Jennie looked up at her, but she didn't seem surprised.

"Sit down, Mamie." She acted just as cool as if they were at her apartment.

"I walked past," Mamie explained, still standing. "I couldn't help noticing you from outside."

"Sweet of you to come in," Jennie went on. Something in the dogged, weary quality of her voice gave Mamie her chance. She brought it right out: "Jennie, is it because you miss him so that you're . . . here?"

The old friend looked up quickly. "Dear Mame," she said, laughing, "that's the first time I've heard you mention him in I don't know how long."

Jennie simply kept on looking about as if she might perhaps find an explanation for not only why she was here but for the why of anything.

"I wish you would let me help you," Mamie continued. "I don't suppose you would come home with me. I suppose it's still early for you. I know my 'Lish always said time passed so fast with beer."

Jennie kept gazing at this frowsy old widow who was in turn gazing at her even more intently. She looked like her dead mother, the way she stared.

"I understand," Mamie repeated. She was always saying something like that, but Jennie didn't weigh her friend's words very carefully. She wasn't quite sure just who Mamie was or what her friendship stood for, but she somehow accepted them both tonight and brought them close to her.

"You may as well drink. May as well be sheared for a sheep as a lamb."

"I believe I will," Mamie said, a kind of belligerence coming into her faded voice.

"Charley," Jennie called, "give Mamie some bottle beer."

The "girls" sat there laughing over it all.

The smile began to fade from Jennie's mouth. She looked at her old friend again as if trying to keep fresh in her mind that she was really sitting there, that she had come especially. Mamie had that waiting look on her face that old women always have.

The younger woman pulled the tiny creased photograph from her purse. Mamie took it avidly. Yes, it was coming, she knew. At last Jennie was going to pour herself out to her. She would know everything. At last nothing would be held back. In her excitement at the thought of the revelation to come, she took several swallows of beer. "Tell me," she kept saying. "You can tell old Mamie."

"He wasn't such a bad looker," Jennie said.

The friend leaned forward eagerly. "Lafe?" she said. "Why, Lafe was handsome, honey. Didn't you know that? He was." And she held the picture farther forward and shook her head sorrowfully but admiringly.

"If he had shaved off that little mustache, he would have been better looking. I was always after him to shave it off, but somehow he wouldn't. Well, you know, his mouth was crocked. . . ."

"Oh, don't say those things," Mamie scolded. "Not about the dead." But she immediately slapped her hand against her own mouth, closing out the last word. Oh, she hadn't meant to bring that word out! We don't use that word about loved ones.

Jennie laughed a little, the laugh an older woman might have used in correcting a little girl.

"I always wondered if it hurt him much when he died," she said. "He never was a real lively one, but he had a kind of hard, enduring quality in him that must have been hard to put out. He must have died slow and hard and knowing to the end."

Mamie didn't know exactly where to take up the thread from there. She hadn't planned for this drift in the conversation. She wanted to have a sweet memory talk and she would have liked to reach for Jennie's hand to comfort her, but she couldn't do it now the talk had taken this drift. She took another long swallow of beer. It was nasty, but it calmed one a little.

"I look at his picture every night before I climb in bed," Jennie went on. "I don't know why I do. I never loved him, you know."

"Now, Jennie, dear," she began, but her protest was scarcely heard in the big room. She had meant to come forward boldly with the "You did love him, dear," but something gray and awful entered the world for her. At that moment she didn't quite believe even in the kind of love which she had seen depicted that very night in the movies and which, she knew, was the only kind that filled the bill.

"You never loved him!" Mamie repeated the words and they echoed dully. It was a statement which did not bear repeating; she realized that as soon as it was out of her mouth.

But Jennie went right on. "No, I never did love Lafe Esmond."

"Closing time!" Charley called out.

Mamie looked around apprehensively.

"That don't apply to us," Jennie explained. "Charley lets me stay many a night until four."

It was that call of closing time that took her back to her days at the cigar factory when fellows would wait in their cars for her after work. She got to thinking of Scott Jeffreys in his new Studebaker.

She looked down at her hands to see if they were still as lovely as he had said. She couldn't tell in the dim light, and besides, well, yes, why not say it, who cared about her hands now? Who cared about any part of her now?

"My hands were lovely once," Jennie said aloud. "My mother told me they were nearly every night and it was true. Nearly every night she would come into my bedroom and say, 'Those lovely white hands should never have to work. My little girl was meant for better things.'"

Mamie swallowed the last of the bottle and nodded her head for Jennie to go on.

"But do you think Lafe ever looked at my hands? He never looked at anybody's hands. He wasn't actually interested in woman's charm. No man really is. It only suggests the other to them, the thing they want out of us and always get. They only start off by complimenting us on our figures. Lafe wasn't interested in anything I had. And I did have a lot once. My mother knew I was beautiful."

She stopped. This was all so different from anything Mamie had come for. Yes, she had come for such a different story.

"Lafe married me because he was lonesome. That's all. If it hadn't been me it would have been some other fool. Men want a place to put up. They get the roam taken out of them and they want to light. I never loved him or anything he did to me. I only pretended when we were together.

"I was never really fond of any man from the first."

Mamie pressed her finger tightly on the glass as if begging a silent power in some way to stop her.

"I was in love with a boy in the eighth grade and that was the only time. What they call puppy love. Douglas Fleetwood was only a child. I always thought of forests and shepherds when I heard his name. He had beautiful chestnut hair. He left his shirt open winter and summer and he had brown eyes like a calf's. I never hardly spoke to him all the time I went to school. He was crippled, too, poor thing, and I could have caught up with him any day on the way home, he went so slow, but I was content to just lag behind him and watch him. I can still see his crutches moving under his arms."

Mamie was beginning to weep a little, a kind of weeping that will come from disappointment and confusion, the slow heavy controlled weeping women will give when they see their ideals go down.

"He died," Jennie said.

"When Miss Matthias announced it in home economics class that awful January day, I threw up my arms and made a kind of whistling sound, and she must have thought I was sick because she said, 'Jennie, you may be excused.'

"Then there were those nice boys at the cigar factory, like I told you, but it never got to be the real thing, and then Lafe came on the scene."

Here Jennie stopped suddenly and laughed rather loudly. Charley, who was at the other end of the room, took this for some friendly comment on the lateness of the hour and waved and laughed in return.

Mamie was stealthily helping herself to some beer from Jennie's bottle.

"Drink it, Mame," she said. "I bought it for you, you old toper." Mamie wiped a tear away from her left eye.

"As I said, I was tired of the cigar factory and there was Lafe every Friday at the Green Mill dance hall. We got married after the big Thanksgiving ball."

"Why, I think I remember that," Mamie brightened. "Didn't I know you then?"

But Jennie's only answer was to pour her friend another glass.

"He went to the foundry every morning after I had got up to cook his breakfast. He wouldn't go to the restaurants like other men. I always had such an ugly kimono to get breakfast in. I was a fright. He could at least have given me a good-looking wrapper to do that morning work in. Then there I was in the house from 4:30 in the A.M. till night waiting for him to come back. I thought I'd die. I was so worn out waiting for him I couldn't be civil when he come in. I was always frying chops when he come."

She took a big drink of beer.

"Everything smelled of chops in that house. He had to have them."

Charley began again calling closing time. He said everybody had to clear the place.

"It ain't four o'clock, is it?" Mamie inquired.

"No, not yet. I don't know what come over Charley tonight. He seems to want to get rid of us early. It's only one-thirty. I suppose some good-lookin' woman is waiting for him."

Yes, the Mecca was closing. Jennie thought, then, of the places she had read about in the Sunday papers, places where pleasure joints never closed, always open night and day, where you could sit right through one evening into another, drinking and forgetting, or remembering. She heard there were places like that in New Orleans where they had this life, but mixed up with colored people and foreigners. Not classy at all and nothing a girl would want to keep in her book of memories.

And here she was all alone, unless, of course, you could count Mamie.

"I was attractive once," she went on doggedly. "Men turned around every time I went to Cincinnati."

Mamie, however, was no longer listening attentively. The story had somehow got beyond her as certain movies of a sophisticated slant sometimes did with her. She was not sure at this stage what Jennie's beauty or her lack of it had to do with her life, and her life was not at all clear to her. It seemed to her in her fumy state that Jennie had had to cook entirely too many chops for her husband and that she had needed a wrapper, but beyond that she could recall only the blasphemies against love.

"My mother would have never dreamed I would come to this lonely period. My mother always said that a good-looking woman is never lonely. 'Jennie,' she used to say, 'keep your good looks if you don't do another thing.' "

The craven inattention, however, of Mamie Jordan demanded notice. Jennie considered her case for a moment. Yes, there could be no doubt about it. Mamie was hopelessly, unbelievably drunk. And she was far from sober herself.

"Mamie Jordan," she said severely, "are you going to be all right?"

The old friend looked up. Was it the accusation of drink or the tone of cruelty in the voice that made her suddenly burst into tears? She did not know, but she sat there now weeping, loudly and disconsolately.

"Don't keep it up anymore, Jennie," she said. "You've said such awful things tonight, honey. Don't do it anymore. Leave me my little mental comforts."

Jennie stared uncomprehendingly. The sobs of the old woman vaguely filled the great empty hall of the drinking men.

It was the crying, she knew, of an old woman who wanted something that was fine, something that didn't exist. It was the crying for the idea of love like in songs and books, the love that wasn't there. She wanted to comfort her. She wanted to take her in her arms and tell her everything would be all right. But she couldn't think of anything really convincing to say on that score. She looked around anxiously as if to find the answer written on a wall, but all her eyes finally came to rest on was a puddle of spilled beer with Lafe Esmond's picture swimming in the middle.

No, you can't really feel sorry for yourself when you see yourself in another, and Jennie had had what Mamie was having now too many times, the sorrow with drink as the sick day dawned.

But the peculiar sadness evinced by Mamie's tears would not go away. The sore spot deep in the folds of the flesh refused to be deadened this time, and it was this physical pang which brought her back to Lafe. She saw him as if for a few illumined seconds almost as though she had never seen him before, as though he were existing for her for the first time. She didn't see exactly how the dead could know or Lafe could be in any other world looking down on her, and yet she felt just then that some understanding had been made at last between them.

But it was soon over, the feeling of his existing at all. Lafe wasn't coming back and nobody else was coming back to her either. If she had loved him she would have had some kind of happiness in looking at his photograph and crying like Mamie wanted her to. There would be consolation in that. Or even if they had brought him home to her so she would be able to visit the grave and go through the show and motions of grief. But what was him was already scattered so far and wide they could never go fetch any part of it back.

Clasping Mamie by the arm, then, and unfolding the handkerchief to give to her, she had the feeling that she had been to see a movie all over again and that for the second time she had wept right in the same place. There isn't anything to say about such private sorrow. You just wait till the lights go on and then reach for your hat.

SOUND OF TALKING

In the morning Mrs. Farebrother would put her husband in the wheelchair and talk to him while she made breakfast. As breakfast time came to an end he would sink his thumb into the black cherry preserves or sometimes he would take out an old Roman coin he had picked up from the war in Italy and hold that tight. In the summertime it helped to watch the swallows flying around when the pain was intense in his legs, or to listen to a plane going quite far off, and then hear all sound stop. There was a relief from the sound then that made you almost think your own pain had quit.

This morning began when Mrs. Farebrother thought of her trip to the city the day before, how she stared at the two young men on the bus, for they reminded her of two brothers she had known in high school, and of course her visit to the bird store.

As her husband's pain grew more acute, which happened every morning after breakfast, she would talk faster, which she knew irritated him more, but she felt that it distracted him more from his pain than anything else. Her voice was a different kind of pain to him, and that was diversion. For a while he held on to an iron bar when he had suffered, then he had pressed the Roman coin, and now he dabbed in the cherry preserves like a child.

"You know what I would like?" Mrs. Farebrother said. "I almost bought one yesterday in the bird store."

She moved his wheelchair closer to the window before telling him. "A raven."

"Well," he grunted, not letting his pain or anger speak this early. He hated birds, even the swallows which he watched from the kitchen were not silent enough for him.

"Ever since I was a little girl those birds have fascinated me. I never realized until the other day that I wanted one. I was walking down the intersection and I heard the birds' voices being broadcast from that huge seed store, all kinds of birds broadcasting to that busy street. I thought a bird might be a kind of amusement to us."

Here Mrs. Farebrother stopped talking as she moved him again, her eyes trying to avoid looking at his legs. Many times she did not know where to look, she knew he did not like her to look at him at all, but she had to look somewhere, and their kitchen was small and what one saw of the outdoors was limited.

"Do you need your pill," she said with too great a swiftness.

"I don't want it," he answered.

"I have plenty of nice ice water this morning," she said, which was a lie. She didn't know why she lied to him all the time. Her anguish and indecision put the lies into her mouth like the priest giving her the wafer on Sunday.

"Tell me about the bird store," he said, and she knew he must be in unusual pain and she felt she had brought it on him by telling about her outing. Yet if she had made him begin to suffer, she must finish what had started him on it, she could not let him sit in his wheelchair and not hear more.

"I went up two flights to where they keep the birds," she began, trying to keep her eyes away from his body and not to watch how his throat distended, with the arteries pounding like an athlete's, his upper body looking more muscular and powerful each day under the punishment that came from lower down. But his suffering was too terrible and too familiar for her to scrutinize, and in fact she hardly ever looked at him carefully: all her glances were sideways, furtive; she had found the word in the crossword puzzles one evening, *clandestine*; it was a word which she had never said to anybody and it described her and haunted her like a face you can't quite remember the name for which keeps popping up in your mind. When they lay together in bed she touched him in a clandestine way also as though she might damage him; she felt his injuries were somehow more sensitive to her touch than they were to the hand of the doctor. She slept very poorly, but the doctor insisted that she sleep with him. As she lay in the bed with him, she thought of only two things, one that he could not approach her and the other when would he die.

Thinking like this, she had forgotten she was telling a story about the bird store. It was his contemptuous stare that brought her back to her own talking: "It was a menagerie of birds," she said, and stopped again.

"Go on," he said as though impatient for what could not possibly interest him.

"Vergil," she said looking at his face. "Verge."

She did not want to tell the story about the raven because she knew how infuriating it was to him to hear about pets of any kind. He hated all pets, he had killed their cat by throwing it out from the wheelchair against a tree. And all day long he sat and killed flies with a swiftness that had great fury in it.

"The men up there were so polite and attentive," she said, hardly stopping to remember whether they were or not, and thinking again of the young men on the bus. "I was surprised because in cities you know how people are, brusque, never expecting to see you again. I hadn't gone up there to see anything more than a few old yellow canaries when what on earth do you suppose I saw but this raven. I have never seen anything like it in my life, and even the man in the shop saw how surprised and interested I was in the bird.

What on earth is that? I said, and just then it talked back to me. It said, *George is dead, George is dead.*"

"George is *what?*" Vergil cried at her, and for a moment she looked at him straight in the face. He looked as though the pain had left him, there was so much surprise in his expression.

"George is dead," she said and suddenly by the stillness of the room she felt the weight of the words which she had not realized until then. Sometimes, as now, when the pain left his face all her desire came back for him, while at night when she lay next to him nothing drew her to him at all; his dead weight seeming scarcely human. She thought briefly again about the hospital for paraplegics the doctor had told her about, in California, but she could never have mentioned even *paraplegic* to Vergil, let alone the place.

"What was the guy in the bird shop like?" he said, as though to help her to her next speech.

"Oh, an old guy sixty or seventy," Mrs. Farebrother lied. "He said he had clipped the bird's tongue himself. He started to describe how he did it, but I couldn't bear to hear him. Anything that involves cutting or surgery," she tried to stop but as though she had to, she added, "Even a bird . . ."

"For Christ's sake," Vergil said.

"I have never seen such purple in wings," Mrs. Farebrother went on, as though a needle had skipped a passage on the record and she was far ahead in her speech. "The only other time I ever saw such a color was in the hair of a young Roumanian fellow I went to high school with. When the light was just right, his hair had that purple sheen. Why, in fact, they called him the raven; isn't that odd, I had forgotten. . . ."

"Let's not start your when-I-was-young talk."

She thought that when he grunted out words like this or when he merely grunted in pain he sounded like somebody going to the toilet, and even though it was tragic she sometimes almost laughed in his face at such moments. Then again when sometimes he was suffering the most so that his hair would be damp with sweat, she felt a desire to hit him across the face, and these unexplained feelings frightened her a great deal.

But today she did not want him to suffer, and that is why she did not like to tell about the raven; she knew it was hurting him somehow—why she did not know, it was nothing, it bored her as she told it, and yet he insisted on hearing everything. She knew that if he kept insisting on more details she would invent some; often that happened. He would keep asking about the things that went on outside and she would invent little facts to amuse him. Yet these "facts" did not seem to please him, and life described outside, whether true or false tortured him.

"Oh, Verge, I wished for you," she said, knowing immediately what she had said was the wrong thing to say; yet everything was somehow wrong to say to him.

"Then I said to the man in charge, doesn't the raven ever say anything but George is . . ." She stopped, choking with laughter; she had a laugh which Vergil had once told her sounded fake, but which somehow she could not find in her to change even for him.

"Then the man gave me a little speech about ravens," Mrs. Farebrother said.

"Well?" he said impatiently. His insistence on details had made her tired and gradually she was forgetting what things had happened and what things had not, what things and words could be said to him, what not. Everything in the end bore the warning FORBIDDEN.

"He said you have to teach the birds yourself. He said they have made no effort to teach them to talk." Mrs. Farebrother stopped trying to remember what the man had said, and what he had looked like.

"Well, he must have taught the bird to say *George is dead*," Vergil observed, watching her closely.

"Yes, I suppose he did teach him that," she agreed, laughing shrilly.

"Had there been somebody there named George?" he said, curious.

"I'm sure I don't know," she said abstractedly. She began dusting an old picture-frame made of shells. "I imagine the bird just heard some-one say that somewhere, maybe in the place where they got it from."

"Where did they get it from?" he wondered.

"I'm sure nobody knows," she replied, and she began to hum.

"*George is dead*," he repeated. "I don't believe it said that."

"Why, Verge," she replied, her dust rag suddenly catching in the ruined shells of the frame. Tired as her mind was and many as the lies were she had told, to the best of her knowledge the bird had said that. She had not even thought it too odd until she had repeated it.

"Maybe the old man's name was George," Mrs. Farebrother said, not very convincing. A whole whirlwind of words waited for her again: "I asked him the price then, and do you know how much he wanted for that old bird, well not old, perhaps, I guess it was young for a raven, they live forever. . . . Fifty dollars!" she sighed. "Fifty dollars without the cage!"

He watched her closely and then to her surprise he drew a wallet out from his dressing gown. She had not known he kept a wallet there, and though his hands shook terribly, he insisted on opening it himself. He took out five ten-dollar bills, which oddly enough was all that was in it, and handed them to her.

"Why, Verge, that isn't necessary, dear," she said, and she put her hands to her hair in a ridiculous gesture.

"Don't talk with that crying voice, for Christ's sake," he said. "You sound like my old woman."

"Darling," she tried to control her tears, "I don't need any pet like that around the house. Besides, it would make you nervous."

"Do you want him or don't you," he said furiously, pushing up his chest and throat to get the words out.

She stopped in front of the wheelchair, trying to think what she *did* want; nearly everything had become irrelevant or even too obscure to bear thinking about. She fingered the five ten-dollar bills, trying to find an answer to please both of them. Then suddenly she knew she wanted nothing. She did not believe anybody could give her anything. One thing or another or nothing were all the same.

"Don't you want your raven," he continued in his firm strong male voice, the voice he always used after an attack had passed so that he seemed to resemble somebody she had known in another place and time.

"I don't really want it, Vergil," Mrs. Farebrother said quietly, handing him the bills.

He must have noticed the absence of self-pity or any attempt to act a part, which in the past had been her stock-in-trade. There was nothing but the emptiness of the truth on her face: she wanted nothing.

"I'll tell you what, Verge," she began again with her laugh and the lies beginning at the same time, as she watched him put the money back in his wallet. Her voice had become soothing and low, the voice she used on children she sometimes stopped on the street to engage in conversation. "I'm afraid of that bird, Vergil," she confessed, as though the secret were out. "It's so large and its beak and claws rather frightened me. Even that old man was cautious with it."

"Yet you had all this stuff about ravens and Roumanians and high school," he accused her.

"Oh, high school," she said, and her mouth filled with saliva, as though it was only her mouth now, which, lying to him continually, had the seat of her emotions.

"It might cheer things up for you if something talked for you around here," he said.

She looked at him to determine the meaning of his words, but she could find no expression in them or in him.

"It would be trouble," she said. "Birds are dirty.

"But if *you* want him, Verge," and in her voice and eyes there was the supplication for hope, as if she had said, If somebody would tell her a thing to hope for maybe she would want something again, have desire again.

"No," he replied, turning the wheel of the chair swiftly, "I don't want a raven for myself if you are that cool about getting it."

He looked down at the wallet, and then his gaze fell swiftly to the legs that lay on the wheelchair's footrest. She had mentioned high school as the place where life had stopped for her; he remembered further back even than Italy, back to the first time he had ever gone to the barbershop, his small legs had then hung down helplessly too while he got his first haircut; but they had hung *alive.*

"Of course you could teach the bird to talk," she said, using her fake laugh.

"Yes, I enjoy hearing talk so much," and he laughed now almost like her.

She turned to look at him. She wanted to scream or push him roughly, she wanted to tell him to just *want* something, anything for just one moment so that she could want something for that one moment too. She wanted him to want something so that she could want something, but she knew he would never want at all again. There would be suffering, the suffering that would make him swell in the chair until he looked like a god in ecstasy, but it would all be just a man practicing for death, and the suffering illusion. And why should a man practicing for death take time out to teach a bird to talk?

"There doesn't seem to be any ice after all," Mrs. Farebrother said, pretending to look in the icebox. It was time for his medicine, and she had quit looking at anything, and their long day together had begun.

CUTTING EDGE

Mrs. Zeller opposed her son's beard. She was in her house in Florida when she saw him wearing it for the first time. It was as though her mind had come to a full stop. This large full-bearded man entered the room and she remembered always later how ugly he had looked and how frightened she felt seeing him in the house; then the realization it was someone she knew, and finally the terror of recognition.

He had kissed her, which he didn't often do, and she recognized in this his attempt to make her discomfort the more painful. He held the beard to her face for a long time, then he released her as though she had suddenly disgusted him.

"Why did you do it?" she asked. She was, he saw, almost broken by the recognition.

"I didn't dare tell you and come."

"That's of course true," Mrs. Zeller said. "It would have been worse. You'll have to shave it off, of course. Nobody must see you. Your father of course didn't have the courage to warn me, but I knew something was wrong the minute he entered the house ahead of you. I suppose he's upstairs laughing now. But it's not a laughing matter."

Mrs. Zeller's anger turned against her absent husband as though all error began and ended with him. "I suppose he likes it." Her dislike of Mr. Zeller struck her son as staggeringly great at that moment.

He looked at his mother and was surprised to see how young she was. She did not look much older than he did. Perhaps she looked younger now that he had his beard.

"I had no idea a son of mine would do such a thing," she said. "But why a beard, for heaven's sake," she cried, as though he had chosen something permanent and irreparable which would destroy all that they were.

"Is it because you are an artist? No, don't answer me," she commanded. "I can't stand to hear any explanation from you. . . ."

"I have always wanted to wear a beard," her son said. "I remember wanting one as a child."

"I don't remember that at all," Mrs. Zeller said.

"I remember it quite well. I was in the summer house near that old broken-down wall and I told Ellen Whitelaw I wanted to have a beard when I grew up."

"Ellen Whitelaw, that big fat stupid thing. I haven't thought of her in years."

Mrs. Zeller was almost as much agitated by the memory of Ellen Whitelaw as by her son's beard.

"You didn't like Ellen Whitelaw," her son told her, trying to remember how they had acted when they were together.

"She was a common and inefficient servant," Mrs. Zeller said, more quietly now, masking her feelings from her son.

"I suppose *he* liked her," the son pretended surprise, the cool cynical tone coming into his voice.

"Oh, your father," Mrs. Zeller said.

"Did he then?" the son asked.

"Didn't he like all of them?" she asked. The beard had changed this much already between them, she talked to him now about his father's character, while the old man stayed up in the bedroom fearing a scene.

"Didn't he always," she repeated, as though appealing to this new hirsute man.

"So," the son said, accepting what he already knew.

"Ellen Whitelaw, for God's sake," Mrs. Zeller said. The name of the servant girl brought back many other faces and rooms which she did not know were in her memory. These faces and rooms served to make the bearded man who stared at her less and less the boy she remembered in the days of Ellen Whitelaw.

"You must shave it off," Mrs. Zeller said.

"What makes you think I would do that?" the boy wondered.

"You heard me. Do you want to drive me out of my mind?"

"But I'm not going to. Or rather it's not going to."

"I will appeal to him, though a lot of good it will do," Mrs. Zeller said. "He ought to do something once in twenty years at least."

"You mean," the son said laughing, "he hasn't done anything in that long."

"Nothing I can really remember," Mrs. Zeller told him.

"It will be interesting to hear you appeal to him," the boy said. "I haven't heard you do that in such a long time."

"I don't think you ever heard me."

"I did, though," he told her. "It was in the days of Ellen Whitelaw again, in fact."

"In *those* days," Mrs. Zeller wondered. "I don't see how that could be."

"Well, it was. I can remember that much."

"You couldn't have been more than four years old. How could you remember then?"

"I heard you say to him, *You have to ask her to go.*"

Mrs. Zeller did not say anything. She really could not remember the words, but she supposed that the scene was true and that he actually remembered.

"Please shave off that terrible beard. If you only knew how awful it looks on you. You can't see anything else but it."

"Everyone in New York thought it was particularly fine."

"Particularly fine," she paused over his phrase as though its meaning eluded her.

"It's nauseating," she was firm again in her judgment.

"I'm not going to do away with it," he said, just as firm.

She did not recognize his firmness, but she saw everything changing a little, including perhaps the old man upstairs.

"Are you going to 'appeal' to him?" The son laughed again when he saw she could say no more.

"Don't mock me," the mother said. "I will speak to your father." She pretended decorum. "You can't go anywhere with us, you know."

He looked unmoved.

"I don't want any of my friends to see you. You'll have to stay in the house or go to your own places. You can't go out with us to our places and see our friends. I hope none of the neighbors see you. If they ask who you are, I won't tell them."

"I'll tell them then."

They were not angry, they talked it out like that, while the old man was upstairs.

"Do you suppose he is drinking or asleep?" she said finally.

"I THOUGHT HE looked good in it, Fern," Mr. Zeller said.

"What about it makes him look good?" she said.

"It fills out his face," Mr. Zeller said, looking at the wallpaper and surprised he had never noticed what a pattern it had before; it showed the sacrifice of some sort of animal by a youth.

He almost asked his wife how she had come to pick out this pattern, but her growing fury checked him.

He saw her mouth and throat moving with unspoken words.

"Where is he now?" Mr. Zeller wondered.

"What does that matter where he is?" she said. "He has to be somewhere while he's home, but he can't go out with us."

"How idiotic," Mr. Zeller said, and he looked at his wife straight in the face for a second.

"Why did you say that?" She tried to quiet herself down.

"The way you go on about nothing, Fern." For a moment a kind of revolt announced itself in his manner, but then his eyes went back to the wallpaper, and she resumed her tone of victor.

"I've told him he must either cut it off or go back to New York."

"Why is it a beard upsets you so?" he wondered, almost to himself.

"It's not the beard so much. It's the way he is now too. And it disfigures him so. I don't recognize him at all now when he wears it."

"So, he's never done anything of his own before," Mr. Zeller protested suddenly.

"Never done anything!" He could feel her anger covering him and glancing off like hot sun onto the wallpaper.

"That's right," he repeated. "He's never done anything. I say let him keep the beard and I'm not going to talk to him about it." His gaze lifted toward her but rested finally only on her hands and skirt.

"This is still my house," she said, "and I have to live in this town."

"When they had the centennial in Collins, everybody wore beards."

"I have to live in this town," she repeated.

"I won't talk to him about it," Mr. Zeller said.

It was as though the voice of Ellen Whitelaw reached her saying, *So that was how you appealed to him.*

SHE SAT ON the deck chair on the porch and smoked five cigarettes. The two men were somewhere in the house and she had the feeling now that she only roomed here. She wished more than that the beard was gone that her son had never mentioned Ellen Whitelaw. She found herself thinking only about her. Then she thought that now twenty years later she could not have afforded a servant, not even her.

She supposed the girl was dead. She did not know why, but she was sure she was.

She thought also that she should have mentioned her name to Mr. Zeller. It might have broken him down about the beard, but she supposed not. He had been just as adamant and unfeeling with her about the girl as he was now about her son.

Her son came through the house in front of her without speaking, dressed only in his shorts and, when he had got safely beyond her in the garden, he took off those so that he was completely naked with his back to her, and lay down in the sun.

She held the cigarette in her hand until it began to burn her finger. She felt she should not move from the place where she was and yet she did not know where to go inside the house and she did not know what pretext to use for going inside.

In the brilliant sun his body, already tanned, matched his shining black beard.

She wanted to appeal to her husband again and she knew then she could never again. She wanted to call a friend and tell her but she had no friend to whom she could tell this.

The events of the day, like a curtain of extreme bulk, cut her off from her son and husband. She had always ruled the house and them even during the awful Ellen Whitelaw days and now, as though they did not even recognize her, they had taken over. She was not even here. Her son could walk naked with a beard in front of her as though she did not exist. She had nothing to fight them with, nothing to make them see with. They ignored her as Mr. Zeller had when he looked at the wallpaper and refused to discuss their son.

"YOU CAN GROW it back when you're in New York," Mr. Zeller told his son.

He did not say anything about his son lying naked before him in the garden but he felt insulted almost as much as his mother had, yet he needed his son's permission and consent now and perhaps that was why he did not mention the insult of his nakedness.

"I don't know why I have to act like a little boy all the time with you both."

"If you were here alone with me you could do anything you wanted. You know I never asked anything of you. . . ."

When his son did not answer, Mr. Zeller said, "Did I?"

"That was the trouble," the son said.

"What?" the father wondered.

"You never wanted anything from me and you never wanted to give me anything. I didn't matter to you."

"Well, I'm sorry," the father said doggedly.

"Those were the days of Ellen Whitelaw," the son said in tones like the mother.

"For God's sake," the father said and he put a piece of grass between his teeth.

He was a man who kept everything down inside of him, everything had been tied and fastened so long there was no part of him anymore that could struggle against the stricture of his life.

There were no words between them for some time; then Mr. Zeller could hear himself bringing the question out: "Did she mention that girl?"

"Who?" The son pretended blankness.

"Our servant."

The son wanted to pretend again blankness but it was too much work. He answered: "No, I mentioned it. To her surprise."

"Don't you see how it is?" the father went on to the present. "She doesn't speak to either of us now and if you're still wearing the beard when you leave it's me she will be punishing six months from now."

"And you want me to save you from your wife."

"Bobby," the father said, using the childhood tone and inflection. "I wish you would put some clothes on too when you're in the garden. With me it doesn't matter, you could do anything. I never asked you for anything. But with her . . ."

"God damn *her*," the boy said.

The father could not protest. He pleaded with his eyes at his son.

The son looked at his father and he could see suddenly also the youth hidden in his father's face. He was young like his mother. They were both young people who had learned nothing from life, were stopped and drifting where they were twenty years before with Ellen Whitelaw. Only *she*, the son thought, must have learned from life, must have gone on to some development in her character, while they had been tied to the shore where she had left them.

"Imagine living with someone for six months and not speaking," the father said as if to himself. "That happened once before, you know, when you were a little boy."

"I don't remember that," the son said, some concession in his voice.

"You were only four," the father told him.

"I believe this is the only thing I ever asked of you," the father said. "Isn't it odd, I can't remember ever asking you anything else. Can you?"

The son looked coldly away at the sky and then answered, contempt and pity struggling together, "No, I can't."

"Thank you, Bobby," the father said.

"Only don't *plead* anymore, for Christ's sake." The son turned from him.

"You've only two more days with us, and if you shaved it off and put on just a few clothes, it would help me through the year with her."

He spoke as though it would be his last year.

Why don't you beat some sense into her?" The son turned to him again.

The father's gaze fell for the first time complete on his son's nakedness.

BOBBY HAD SAID he would be painting in the storeroom and she could send up a sandwich from time to time, and Mr. and Mrs. Zeller were left downstairs together. She refused to allow her husband to answer the phone.

In the evening Bobby came down dressed carefully and his beard combed immaculately and looking, they both thought, curled.

They talked about things like horse racing, in which they were all somehow passionately interested, but which they now discussed irritably as though it too were a menace to their lives. They talked about the uselessness of art and why people went into it with a detachment that would have made an outsider think that Bobby was as unconnected with it as a jockey or oil magnate. They condemned nearly everything and then the son went upstairs and they saw one another again briefly at bedtime.

The night before he was to leave they heard him up all hours, the water running, and the dropping of things made of metal.

Both parents were afraid to get up and ask him if he was all right. He was like a wealthy relative who had commanded them never to question him or interfere with his movements even if he was dying.

He was waiting for them at breakfast, dressed only in his shorts but he looked more naked than he ever had in the garden because his beard was gone. Over his chin lay savage and profound scratches as though he had removed the hair with a hunting knife and pincers.

Mrs. Zeller held her breast and turned to the coffee and Mr. Zeller said only his son's name and sat down with last night's newspaper.

"What time does your plane go?" Mrs. Zeller said in a dead, muffled voice.

The son began putting a white paste on the scratches on his face and did not answer.

"I believe your mother asked you a question," Mr. Zeller said, pale and shaking.

Ten-forty," the son replied.

The son and the mother exchanged glances and he could see at once that his sacrifice had been in vain: she would also see the beard there again under the scratches and the gashes he had inflicted on himself, and he would never really be her son again. Even for his father it must be much the same. He had come home as a stranger who despised them and he had shown his nakedness to both of them. All three longed for separation and release.

But Bobby could not control the anger coming up in him, and his rage took an old form. He poured the coffee into his saucer because Mr. Zeller's mother had always done this and it had infuriated Mrs. Zeller because of its low-class implications.

He drank vicious from the saucer, blowing loudly.

Both parents watched him helplessly like insects suddenly swept against the screen.

"It's not too long till Christmas," Mr. Zeller brought out. "We hope you'll come back for the whole vacation."

"We do," Mrs. Zeller said in a voice completely unlike her own.

"So," Bobby began, but the torrent of anger would not let him say the thousand fierce things he had ready.

Instead, he blew savagely from the saucer and spilled some onto the chaste white summer rug below him. Mrs. Zeller did not move.

"I would invite you to New York." Bobby said quietly now, "but of course I will have the beard there and it wouldn't work for you."

"Yes," Mr. Zeller said, incoherent.

"I do hope you don't think I've been . . ." Mrs. Zeller cried suddenly, and they both waited to hear whether she was going to weep or not, but she stopped herself perhaps by the realization that she had no tears and that the feelings which had come over her about Bobby were likewise spent.

"I can't think of any more I can do for you," Bobby said suddenly.

They both stared at each other as though he had actually left and they were alone at last.

"Is there anything more you want me to do?" he said, coldly vicious.

They did not answer.

"I hate and despise what both of you have done to yourselves, but the thought that you would be sitting here in your middle-class crap not speaking to one another is too much even for me. That's why I did it, I guess, and not out of any love. I didn't want you to think that."

He sloshed in the saucer.

"Bobby," Mr. Zeller said.

The son brought out his *What?* with such finished beauty of coolness that he paused to admire his own control and mastery.

"Please, Bobby," Mr. Zeller said.

They could all three of them hear a thousand speeches. The agony of awkwardness was made unendurable by the iciness of the son, and all three paused over this glacial control which had come to him out of art and New York, as though it was the fruit of their lives and the culmination of their twenty years.

DON'T CALL ME BY MY RIGHT NAME

Her new name was Mrs. Klein. There was something in the meaning that irritated her. She liked everything about her husband except his name, and that had never pleased her. She had fallen in love with him before she found out what his name was. Once she knew he was Klein, her disappointment had been strong. Names do make a great difference, and after six months of marriage she found herself still not liking her name. She began using more and more her maiden name. Then she always called herself on her letters Lois McBane. Her husband seldom saw the mail arrive so perhaps he did not know, and had he known she went by her old name he might not have cared enough to feel any particular hurt.

Lois Klein, she often thought as she lay next to her husband in bed. It is not the name of a woman like myself. It does not reflect my character.

One evening at a party when there had been more drinking for her than usual, she said offhand to him in the midst of some revelry: "I would like you to change your name."

He did not understand. He thought that it was a remark she was making in drink which did not refer to anything concrete, just as once she had said to him, "I want you to begin by taking your head off regularly." The remark had meant nothing, and he let it pass.

"Frank," she said, "you must change your name, do you hear? I cannot go on being Mrs. Klein."

Several people heard what it was she said, and they laughed loudly so that Lois and Frank would hear them appreciating the remark.

"If you were all called Mrs. Klein," she said turning to the men who were laughing, "you would not like to be Mrs. Klein either."

Being all men, they laughed harder.

"Well, you married him, didn't you," a man said, "and we guess you will have to keep his name."

"If he changed his name," another of the men said, "what name would you have him change it to?"

Frank put his hand on her glass, as though to tell her they must go home, but she seized the glass with his hand on it and drank quickly out of it.

"I hadn't thought what name I did want," she said, puzzled.

"Well, you aren't going to change your name," Frank said. "The gentlemen know that."

"The gentlemen do?" she asked him. "Well, I don't know what name I would like it changed to," she admitted to the men.

"You don't look much like Mrs. Klein," one of the men said and began to laugh again.

"You're not friends!" she called back at them.

"What are we, then?" they asked.

"Why don't I look like Mrs. Klein?" she wanted to know.

"Don't you ever look in the mirror?" one of the men replied.

"We ought to go, Lois," her husband said.

She sat there as though she had heard the last of the many possible truths she could hear about herself.

"I wonder how I will get out of here, Frank," she said.

"Out of where, dear?" he wondered. He was suddenly sad enough himself to be dead, but he managed to say something to her at this point.

"Out of where I seem to have got into," she told him.

The men had moved off now and were laughing among themselves. Frank and Lois did not notice this laughter.

"I'm not going to change my name," he said, as though to himself. Then, turning to her: "I know it's supposed to be wrong to tell people when they're drunk the insane whim they're having is insane, but I am telling you now and I may tell the whole room of men."

"I have to have my name changed, Frank," she said. "You know I can't stand to be tortured. It is too painful and I am not young anymore. I am getting old and fat."

"No wife of mine would ever be old or fat," he said.

"I just cannot be Mrs. Klein and face the world."

"Anytime you want me to pull out is all right," he said. "Do you want me to pull out?"

"What are you saying?" she wanted to know. "What did you say about pulling out?"

"I don't want any more talk about your changing your name or I intend to pull up stakes."

"I don't know what you're talking about. You know you can't leave me. What would I do, Frank, at my age?"

"I told you no wife of mine is old."

"I couldn't find anybody now, Frank, if you went."

"Then quit talking about changing our name."

"*Our* name? I don't know what you mean by *our* name."

He took her drink out of her hand and when she coaxed and whined he struck her not too gently over the mouth.

"What was the meaning of that?" she wanted to know.

"Are you coming home, Mrs. Klein?" he said, and he hit her again. Her lip was cut against her teeth so that you could see it beginning to bleed.

"Frank, you're abusing me," she said, white and wide-eyed now, and as though tasting the blood slightly with the gin and soda mix.

"Mrs. Klein," he said idiotically.

It was one of those fake dead long parties where nobody actually knows anybody and where people could be pushed out of windows without anybody's being sure until the morrow.

"I'm not going home as Mrs. Klein," she said.

He hit her again.

"Frank, you have no right to hit me just because I hate your name."

"If you hate my name, what do you feel then for me? Are you going to act like my wife or not."

"I don't want to have babies, Frank. I will not go through that at my age. Categorically not."

He hit her again so that she fell on the floor, but this did not seem to surprise either her or him because they both continued the conversation.

"I can't make up my mind what to do," she said, weeping a little. "I know of course what the safe thing is to do."

"Either you come out of here with me as Mrs. Klein, or I go to a hotel room alone. Here's the key to the house," he said, and he threw it on the floor at her.

Several of the men at the party had begun to notice what was really going on now. They thought that it was married clowning at first and they began to gather around in a circle, but what they saw had something empty and stiff about it that did not interest and yet kept one somehow watching. For one thing, Mrs. Klein's dress had come up and exposed her legs, which were not beautiful.

"I can't decide if I can go on with his name," she explained from the floor position to the men.

"Well, it's a little late, isn't it, Mrs. Klein," one of the men said in a sleepy voice.

"It's never too late, I don't suppose, is it?" she inquired. "Oh, I can't believe it is even though I feel old."

"Well, you're not young," the same man ventured. "You're too old to be lying there."

"My husband can't see my point of view," she explained. "And that is why he can't understand why his name doesn't fit me. I was unmarried too long, I suppose, to suddenly surrender my own name. I have always been known professionally and socially under my own name and it is hard to change now, I can tell you. I don't think I can go home with him unless he lets me change my name."

"I will give you just two minutes," Mr. Klein said.

"For what? Only two minutes for what?" she cried.

"To make up your mind what name you are going out of here with."

"I know, men," she said, "what the sensible decision is, and tomorrow, of course, when I'm sober I will wish I had taken it."

Turning to Frank Klein, she said simply, "You will have to go your way without me."

He looked hurriedly around as though looking for an exit to leave by, and then he looked back to her on the floor as though he could not come to a decision.

"Come to your senses," Frank Klein said unemphatically.

"There were hundreds of Kleins in the telephone directory," she went on, "but when people used to come to my name they recognized at once that I was the only woman going under my own special name."

"For Jesus Christ's sake, Lois," he said, turning a peculiar green color.

"I can't go with you as Mrs. Klein," she said.

"Well, let me help you up," he said.

She managed to let him help her up.

"I'm not going home with you, but I will send you in a cab," he informed her.

"Are you leaving me?" she wanted to know.

He did not know what to say. He felt anything he said might destroy his mind. He stood there with an insane emptiness on his eyes and lips.

Everyone had moved off from them. There was a silence from the phonograph and from the TV set, which had both been going at the same time. The party was over and people were calling down to cabs from all the windows.

"Why won't you come home with me?" she said in a whisper.

Suddenly he hurried out the door without waiting for her.

"Frank!" she called after him, and a few of the men from the earlier group came over and joked with her.

"He went out just like a boy, without any sense of responsibility," she said to them without any expression in her voice.

She hurried on out too, not waiting to put her coat on straight.

She stood outside in the fall cold and shivered. Some children went by dressed in Hallowe'en costumes.

"Is she dressed as anybody?" one of the children said pointlessly.

"Frank!" she began calling. "I don't know what is happening really," she said to herself.

Suddenly he came up to her from behind a hedge next to where she was standing.

"I couldn't quite bring myself to go off," he said.

She thought for a minute of hitting him with her purse which she had remembered to bring, but she did nothing now but watch him.

"Will you change your name?" she said.

"We will live together the way we have been," he said not looking at her.

"We can't be married, Frank, with that name between us."

Suddenly he hit her and knocked her down to the pavement.

She lay there for a minute before anything was said.

"Are you conscious?" he said crouching down beside her. "Tell me if you are suffering," he wanted to know.

"You have hurt something in my head, I think," she said, getting up slightly on one elbow.

"You have nearly driven me out of my mind," he said, and he was making funny sounds in his mouth. "You don't know what it means to have one's name held up to ridicule like this. You are such a cruel person, Lois."

"We will both change our names, if you like," she said.

"Why do you torture me?" he said. "Why is it you can't control your power to torture?"

"Then we won't think about it, we will go home," she said, in a cold comforting voice. "Only I think I am going to be sick," she warned.

"We will go home," he said in a stupid voice.

"I will let you call me Mrs. Klein this one evening, then tomorrow we will have a good talk." At the same moment she fell back on the walk.

Some young men from the delicatessen who had been doing inventory came by and asked if there was anything they could do.

"My wife fell on the walk," he said. "I thought she was all right. She was talking to me just a moment ago."

"Was it your wife, did you say?" the younger man leaned down to look at her.

"Mrs. Klein," Frank replied.

"You are Mr. Klein, then?"

"I don't understand," the older of the two young men said. "You don't look somehow like her husband."

"We have been married six months."

"I think you ought to call a doctor," the younger man said. "She is bleeding at the mouth."

"I hit her at a party," Frank said.

"What did you say your name was?" the older man asked.

"Mr. Klein. She is Mrs. Klein," Frank told them.

The two men from the delicatessen exchanged looks.

"Did you push her?" the one man asked.

"Yes," Frank said. "I hit her. She didn't want to be Mrs. Klein."

"You're drunk," the one man ventured an opinion.

Lois suddenly came to. "Frank, you will have to take me home," she said. "There is something wrong with my head. My God," she began to scream, "I am in awful pain."

Frank helped her up again.

"Is this your husband?" the one man asked.

She nodded.

"What is your name?" he wanted to know.

"It's none of your business," she said.

"Are you Mrs. Klein?" he asked.

"No," Lois replied. "I don't happen to be Mrs. Klein."

"Come on, J.D., we can't get mixed up in this," the younger man said. "Whatever the hell their names are."

"Well, I'm not Mrs. Klein, whoever you are," she said.

Immediately then she struck Frank with the purse and he fell back in surprise against the building wall.

"Call me a cab, you cheap son of a bitch," she said. "Can't you see I'm bleeding?"

EVENTIDE

Mahala had waited as long as she thought she could; after all, Plumy had left that morning and now here it was going on four o'clock. It was hardly fair if she was loitering, but she knew that certainly Plumy would never loiter on a day like this when Mahala wanted so to hear. It was in a way the biggest day of her whole life, bigger than any day she had ever lived through as a girl or young woman. It was the day that decided whether her son would come back to live with her or not.

And just think, a whole month had rolled past since he left home. Two months ago if anyone had said that Teeboy would leave home, she would have stopped dead in her tracks, it would have been such a terrible thing even to say, and now here she was, talking over the telephone about how Teeboy had gone.

"My Teeboy is gone." That is what Mahala said for a long time after the departure. These words announced to her mind what had happened, and just as an announcement they gave some mild comfort, like a pain-killer with a fatal disease.

"My Teeboy," she would say, like the mother of a dead son, like the mother of a son who had died in battle, because it hurt as much to have a son missing in peacetime as to have lost him through war.

The room seemed dark even with the summer sunshine outside, and close, although the window was open. There was a darkness all over the city. The fire department had been coming and going all afternoon. There were so many fires in the neighborhood—that is what she was saying to Cora on the telephone, too many fires: the fire chief had just whizzed past again. No, she said to Cora, she didn't know if it was in the white section of town or theirs, she couldn't tell, but oh it was so hot to have a fire.

Talking about the fires seemed to help Mahala more than anything. She called several other old friends and talked about the fires and she mentioned that Teeboy had not come home. The old friends did not say much about Teeboy's not having returned, because, well, what was there to say about a boy who had been practicing to leave home for so long. Everyone had known it but her blind mother love.

"What do you suppose can be keeping my sister Plumy?" Mahala said to herself as she walked up and down the hall and looked out from behind the screen in the window. "She would have to fail me on the most important errand in the world."

Then she thought about how much Plumy hated to go into white neighborhoods, and how the day had been hot and she thought of the fires and how perhaps Plumy had fallen under a fire truck and been crushed. She thought of all the possible disasters and was not happy, and always in the background there was the fresh emotion of having lost Teeboy.

"People don't know," she said, "that I can't live without Teeboy."

She would go in the clothes closet and look at his dirty clothes just as he had left them; she would kiss them and press them to her face, smelling them; the odors were especially dear to her. She held his rayon trousers to her bosom and walked up and down the small parlor. She had not prayed; she was waiting for Plumy to come home first, then maybe they would have prayer.

"I hope I ain't done anything I'll be sorry for," she said.

It was then, though, when she felt the worst, that she heard the steps on the front porch. Yes, those were Plumy's steps, she was coming with the news. But whatever the news was, she suddenly felt, she could not accept it.

As she came up the steps, Plumy did not look at Mahala with any particular kind of meaning on her face. She walked unsteadily, as if the heat had been too much for her.

"Come on in now, Plumy, and I will get you something cool to drink."

Inside, Plumy watched Mahala as if afraid she was going to ask her to begin at once with the story, but Mahala only waited, not saying anything, sensing the seriousness of Plumy's knowledge and knowing that this knowledge could be revealed only when Plumy was ready.

While Mahala waited patiently there in the kitchen, Plumy arranged herself in the easy chair, and when she was once settled, she took up the straw fan which lay on the floor.

"Well, I seen him!" Plumy brought the words out.

This beginning quieted the old mother a little. She closed her mouth and folded her hands, moving now to the middle of the parlor, with an intentness on her face as if she was listening to something high up in the sky, like a plane which is to drop something, perhaps harmless and silver, to the ground.

"I seen him!" Plumy repeated, as if to herself. "And I seen all the white people!" she finished, anger coming into her voice.

"Oh, Plumy," Mahala whined. Then suddenly she made a gesture for her sister to be quiet because she thought she heard the fire department going again, and then when there was no sound, she waited for her to go on, but Plumy did not say anything. In the slow afternoon there was nothing, only a silence a city sometimes has within itself.

Plumy was too faint from the heat to go on at once; her head suddenly shook violently and she slumped in the chair.

"Plumy Jackson!" Mahala said, going over to her. "You didn't *walk* here from the white district! You didn't walk them forty-seven blocks in all this August heat!"

Plumy did not answer immediately. Her hand caressed the worn upholstery of the chair.

"You know how nervous white folks make me," she said at last.

Mahala made a gesture of disgust. "Lord, to think you walked it in this hot sun. Oh, I don't know why God wants to upset me like this. As if I didn't have enough to make me wild already, without havin' you come home in this condition."

Mahala watched her sister's face for a moment with the same figuring expression of the man who comes to read the water meter. She saw everything she really wanted to know on Plumy's face: all her questions were answered for her there, yet she pretended she didn't know the verdict; she brought the one question out:

"You did see Teeboy, honey?" she said, her voice changed from her tears. She waited a few seconds, and then as Plumy did not answer but only sank deeper into the chair, she continued: "What word did he send?"

"It's the way I told you before," Plumy replied crossly. "Teeboy ain't coming back. I thought you knowed from the way I looked at you that he ain't coming back."

Mahala wept quietly into a small handkerchief.

"Your pain is realer to me sometimes than my own," Plumy said, watching her cry. "That's why I hate to say to you he won't never come back, but it's true as death he won't."

"When you say that to me I got a feeling inside myself like everything had been busted and taken; I got the feeling like I don't have nothing left inside of me."

"Don't I know that feeling!" Plumy said, almost angrily, resting the straw fan on the arm of the chair, and then suddenly fanning herself violently so that the strokes sounded like those of a small angry whip. "Didn't I lose George Watson of sleeping sickness and all 'cause doctor wouldn't come?"

Plumy knew that Mahala had never shown any interest in the death of her own George Watson and that it was an unwelcome subject, especially tonight, when Teeboy's never coming back had become final, yet she could not help mentioning George Watson just the same. In Mahala's eyes there really had never been any son named George Watson; there was only a son named Teeboy and Mahala was the only mother.

"It ain't like there bein' no way out to your troubles: it's the way out that kills you," Mahala said. "If it was goodbye for always like when someone dies, I think I could stand it better. But this kind of parting ain't like the Lord's way!"

Plumy continued fanning herself, just letting Mahala run on.

"So he ain't never coming back!" Mahala began beating her hands together as if she were hearing music for a dance.

Plumy looked away as the sound of the rats downstairs caught her attention; there seemed to be more than usual tonight and she wondered why they were running so much, for it was so hot everywhere.

Her attention strayed back to Mahala standing directly in front of her now, talking about her suffering: "You go through all the suffering and the heartache," she said, "and then they go away. The only time children is nice is when they're babies and you know they can't get away from you. You got them then and your love is all they crave. They don't know who you are exactly, they just know you are the one to give them your love, and they ask you for it until you're worn out giving it."

Mahala's speech set Plumy to thinking of how she had been young and how she had had George Watson, and how he had died of sleeping sickness when he was four.

"My only son died of sleeping sickness," Plumy said aloud, but not really addressing Mahala. "I never had another. My husband said it was funny. He was not a religious man, but he thought it was queer."

"Would you like a cooling drink?" Mahala said absently.

Plumy shook her head and there was a silence of a few minutes in which the full weight of the heat of evening took possession of the small room.

"I can't get used to the idea of him *never* comin' back!" Mahala began again. "I ain't never been able to understand that word *never* anyhow. And now it's like to drive me wild."

There was another long silence, and then, Mahala suddenly rousing herself from drowsiness and the heat of the evening, began eagerly: "How did he look, Plumy? Tell me how he looked, and what he was doing. Just describe."

"He wasn't doin' nothin'!" Plumy said flatly. "He looked kind of older, though, like he had been thinking about new things."

"Don't keep me waiting," Mahala whined. "I been waitin' all day for the news, don't keep me no more, when I tell you I could suicide over it all. I ain't never been through such a hell day. Don't you keep me waitin'."

"Now hush," Plumy said. "Don't go frettin' like this. Your heart won't take a big grief like this if you go fret so."

"It's *so* unkind of you not to tell," she muffled her lips in her handkerchief.

Plumy said: "I told you I talked to him, but I didn't tell you where. It was in a drinking place called the Music Box. He called to me from inside. The minute I looked at him I knew there was something wrong. There was something wrong with his hair."

"With his hair!" Mahala cried.

"Then I noticed he had had it all made straight! That's right," she said looking away from Mahala's eyes. "He had had his hair straightened. 'Why ain't you got in touch with your mother,' I said. 'If you only knowed how she was carryin' on.'

"Then he told me how he had got a tenor sax and how he was playing it in the band at the Music Box and that he had begun a new life, and it was all on account of his having the tenor sax and being a musician. He said the players didn't have time to have homes. He said they were playing all the time, they never went home, and that was why he hadn't been."

Plumy stopped. She saw the tenor sax only in her imagination because he had not shown it to her, she saw it curved and golden and heard it playing far-off melodies. But the real reason she stopped was not on account of the tenor sax but because of the memory of the white woman who had come out just then. The white woman had come out and put her arm around Teeboy. It had made her get creepy all over. It was the first time that Plumy had realized that Teeboy's skin was nearly as light as the white people's.

Both Teeboy and the woman had stood there looking at Plumy, and Plumy had not known how to move away from them. The sun beat down on her in the street but she could not move. She saw the streetcars going by with all the white people pushing one another around and she looked around on the scorched pavements and everyone was white, with Teeboy looking just as white as the rest of them, looking just as white as if he had come out of Mahala's body white, and as if Mahala had been a white woman and not her sister, and as if Mahala's mother and hers had not been black.

Then slowly she had begun walking away from Teeboy and the Music Box, almost without knowing she was going herself, walking right on through the streets without knowing what was happening, through the big August heat, without an umbrella or a hat to keep off the sun; she could see no place to stop, and people could see the circles of sweat that were forming all over her dress. She was afraid to stop and she was afraid to go on walking. She felt she would fall down eventually in the afternoon sun and it would be like the time George Watson had died of sleeping sickness, nobody would help her to an easy place.

Would George Watson know her now? That is what she was thinking as she walked through the heat of that afternoon. Would he know her—because when she had been his mother she had been young and her skin, she was sure, had been lighter; and now she was older looking than she remembered her own mother ever being, and her skin was very black.

It was Mahala's outcries which brought her back to the parlor, now full of the evening twilight.

"Why can't God call me home?" Mahala was asking. "Why can't He call me to His Throne of Grace?"

Then Mahala got up and wandered off into her own part of the house. One could hear her in her room there, faintly kissing Teeboy's soiled clothes and speaking quietly to herself.

"Until you told me about his having his hair straightened, I thought maybe he would be back," Mahala was saying from the room. "But when you told me that, I knew. He won't never be back."

Plumy could hear Mahala kissing the clothes after she had said this.

"He was so dear to her," Plumy said aloud. It was necessary to speak aloud at that moment because of the terrible feeling of evening in the room. Was it the smell of the four o'clocks, which must have just opened to give out their perfume, or was it the evening itself which made her uneasy? She felt not alone, she felt someone else had come, uninvited and from far away.

Plumy had never noticed before what a strong odor the four o'clocks had, and then she saw the light in the room, growing larger, a light she had not recognized before, and then she turned and saw *him*, George Watson Jackson, standing there before her, large as life. Plumy wanted to call out, she wanted to say *No* in a great voice, she wanted to brush the sight before her all away, which was strange because she was always wanting to see her baby and here he was, although seventeen years had passed since she had laid him away.

She looked at him with unbelieving eyes because really he was the same, the same except she did notice that little boys' suits had changed fashion since his day, and how that everything about him was slightly different from the little children of the neighborhood now.

"Baby!" she said, but the word didn't come out from her mouth, it was only a great winged thought that could not be made into sound. "George Watson, honey!" she said still in her silence.

He stood there, his eyes like they had been before. Their beauty stabbed at her heart like a great knife; the hair looked so like she had just pressed the wet comb to it and perhaps put a little pomade on the sides; and the small face was clean and sad. Yet her arms somehow did not ache to hold him like her heart told her they should. Something too far away and too strong was between her and him; she only saw him as she had always seen resurrection pictures, hidden from us as in a wonderful mist that will not let us see our love complete.

There was this mist between her and George Jackson, like the dew that will be on the four o'clocks when you pick one of them off the plant.

It was her baby come home, and at such an hour.

Then as she came slowly to herself, she began to raise herself slightly, stretching her arms and trying to get the words to come out to him:

"George Watson, baby!"

This time the words did come out, with a terrible loudness, and as they did so the light began to go from the place where he was standing: the last thing she saw of him was his bright forehead and hair, then there was nothing at all, not even the smell of flowers.

Plumy let out a great cry and fell back in the chair. Mahala heard her and came out of her room to look at her.

"What you got?" Mahala said.

"I seen *him*! I seen *him*! Big as life!"

"Who?" Mahala said.

"George Watson, just like I laid him away seventeen years ago!"

Mahala did not know what to say. She wiped her eyes dry, for she had quit crying.

"You was exposed too long in the sun," Mahala said vaguely.

As she looked at her sister she felt for the first time the love that Plumy had borne all these years for a small son Mahala had never seen, George Watson. For the first time she dimly recognized Plumy as a mother, and she had suddenly a feeling of intimacy for her that she had never had before.

She walked over to the chair where Plumy was and laid her hand on her. Somehow the idea of George Watson's being dead so long and yet still being a baby a mother could love had a kind of perfect quality that she liked. She thought then, quietly and without shame, how nice it would be if Teeboy could also be perfect in death, so that he would belong to her in the same perfect way as George Watson belonged to Plumy. There was comfort in tending the grave of a dead son, whether he was killed in war or peace, and it was so difficult to tend the memory of a son who just went away and never came back. Yet somehow she knew as she looked at Plumy, somehow she would go on with the memory of Teeboy Jordan even though he still lived in the world.

As she stood there considering the lives of the two sons Teeboy Jordan and George Watson Jackson, the evening which had for some time been moving slowly into the house entered now as if in one great wave, bringing the small parlor into the heavy summer night until you would have believed daylight would never enter there again, the night was so black and secure.

MAN AND WIFE

"How could it happen to you in good times if you didn't do nothing wrong?" Peaches Maud said.

"Peaches, I am trying to tell you," Lafe replied. "None of the men in the plant ever liked me." Then as though quoting somebody: "I am frankly difficult."

"Difficult? You are the easiest-to-get-along-with man in the whole country."

"I am not manly," he said suddenly in a scared voice, as though giving an order over a telephone.

"Not manly?" Peaches Maud said and surprise made her head move back slightly as though the rush of his words was a wind in her face.

"What has manly got to do with you being fired?" She began walking around the small apartment, smoking one of the gold-tipped cigarettes he bought for her in the Italian district.

"The foreman said the men never liked me on account of my character," Lafe went on, as though reporting facts he could scarcely remember about a person nearly unknown to him.

"Oh, Jesus," Maud said, the cigarette hanging in her mouth and a thin stream of smoke coming up into her half-closed eyes. "Well, thank God we live where nobody knows us. That is the only thing comes to mind to be grateful for. And for the rest, I don't know what in hell you are really talking about, and my ears won't let me catch what you seem to be telling."

"I have done nothing wrong, Peaches Maud."

"Did you ever do anything right?" She turned to him with hatred.

"I have no character, Maud," he spoke slowly, as though still quoting from somebody.

It was true, Maud thought, puffing vigorously on the Italian cigarette: he had none at all. He had never found a character to have. He was always about to do something or start something, but not having a character to start or do it with left him always on the road to preparation.

"What did the men care whether you had a character or not?" Maud wanted to know.

For nearly a year now she had worn corsets, but this afternoon she had none, and, it being daylight, Lafe could see with finality how fat she was and what unsurpassed large breasts stuck out from her creased flesh. He was amazed to think that he had been responsible so long for such a big woman. Seeing her tremendous breasts, he felt still more exhausted and unready for his future.

"They told me in the army, Peaches, I should have been a painter."

"Who is this *they*?" she inquired with shamed indignation.

"The men in the mental department."

Lafe felt it essential at this moment to go over and kiss Maud on the throat. He tasted the talcum powder she had dusted herself with against the heat, and it was not unwelcome in his situation. Underneath the talcum he could taste Maud's sweat.

"All right, now." Maud came down a little to him, wiping his mouth free of the talcum powder. "What kind of a painter did these mental men refer to?"

"They didn't mean somebody who paints chairs and houses," Lafe said, looking away so that she would not think he was criticizing her area of knowledge.

"I mean why did they think you was meant for a painter?" Maud said.

"They never tell you those things," he replied. "The tests test you and the mental men come and report the findings."

"Well, Jesus, what kind of work will you go into if it ain't factory work?"

Lafe extracted a large blue handkerchief dotted with white stars and held this before him as though he were waiting for a signal to cover his face with it.

"Haven't you always done factory work?" Peaches Maud summarized their common knowledge in her threatening voice.

"Always, always," he replied in agony.

"Just when you read how the whole country is in for a big future, you come home like this to me," she said, suddenly triumphant. "Well, I can tell you, I'm not going back to that paint factory, Lafe. I will do anything but go back and eat humble pie to Mrs. Goreweather."

"I don't see how you could go back." He stared at her flesh.

"What meaning do you put in those words?" she thundered. Then when he stared at her uncomprehending: "You seem to lack something a husband ought to have for his wife."

"That's what everything seems to be about now," he said. "It's what I lack everywhere."

"Stop that down-at-the-mouth talk," she commanded evenly.

"All the way home on the streetcar I sat like a bedbug." He ignored her.

"Lafe, what have I told you?" She tried to attract his attention now back to herself.

"I have always lacked something and that lack was in my father and mother before me. My father had drink and my mother was easily recognized as . . ."

She pulled his arm loosely toward her: "Don't bring that up in all this trouble. She was anyhow a mother. . . . Of course, we could never afford for me to be a mother. . . ."

"Maybe I should go back and tell the men all the things I lack they still don't know about."

"You say things that are queer, all right," Maud said in a quieter voice, and then with her old sarcasm: "I can kind of see how you got on the men's nerves if you talked to them like you talk at home."

"You're beginning to see, you say, Peaches?" Lafe said, almost as though he were now the judge himself, and then he began to laugh.

"I wish you would never laugh that way," Maud corrected him. "I hate that laugh. It sounds like some kid looking through a bathroom window. Jesus, Lafe, you ought to grow up."

He continued to laugh for a few moments, giving her the chance to see he had already changed a little for her. It was his laughing that made her pace up and down the room, despite the heat of July, and listen with growing nervousness to the refrigerator make its clattering din.

"I can see what maybe the men meant," she said in her quiet-triumph-tone of voice, and at the same time putting rage into her eyes as they stared at the refrigerator.

"Chris, I hated every goddamn man."

"You can't afford to hate nobody! You can't go around hating men like that when you earn your bread with them."

"You hated Mrs. Goreweather."

"Look how unfair! You know Mrs. Goreweather had insanity in her family, and she pounced on me as a persecution target. You never even hinted there was any Mrs. Goreweather character at the factory."

"I was *her*!"

"Lafe, for Jesus' sake, in all this heat and noise, let's not have any of this mental talk, or I will put on my clothes and go out and get on the streetcar."

"I'm telling you what it was. The company psychiatrist told me I was the Mrs. Goreweather of my factory."

"How could he know of her?"

"I told him."

"No," she said stopping dead in the room. "You didn't go and tell him about her!" She picked up a large palm straw fan from the table and fanned with angry movements the large patches of sweat and talcum powder on her immense meaty body. As Lafe watched her move the fan, he thought how much money had gone to keep her in food these seven peculiar years.

"I am not a normal man, Peaches Maud," he said without conviction or meaning. He went over to her and touched her shoulder.

"I'll bet that psychiatrist isn't even married," Maud said, becoming more gentle but suddenly more worried.

"He wasn't old," Lafe said, the vague expression coming over his face again. "He might be younger than me."

"If only that damn refrigerator would shut up," she complained, not knowing now where to turn her words.

She went over to the bed and sat down, and began fanning the air in his direction, as though to calm him or drive away any words he might now say.

"You have no idea how the refrigerator nags me sometimes when you can be gone and away at work. I feel like I just got to go out when I hear it act so."

"Maud," he said, and he stopped her arm from fanning him. "I have never once ceased to care for you in all this time and trouble."

"Well, I should hope," she said, suddenly silly, and fanning her own body now more directly.

"You will always attract me no matter what I am."

"Jesus, Lafe!" And she beat with the fan against the bedpost so that it shook a little.

Then they both noticed that the refrigerator was off.

"Did I jar it still?" she wondered.

But the moment she spoke it began again, louder and more menacing.

"I am not a man to make you happy." Lafe touched her shoulder again.

"I thought I told you I couldn't stand that mental talk. I have never liked having you say you felt like a bug or any other running of yourself down. Just because you lost your job don't think you can sit around here with me in this heat and talk mental talk now."

"Maud, I feel I should go away and think over what it is I have done to myself. I feel as though everything was beginning to go away from me."

"What in Jesus' name would you go away on?" she exclaimed, and she threw the fan in the direction of the refrigerator.

"I realize now how much of me there is that is not right," he said, as though he had finally succeeded in bringing this fact to his own attention.

"Jesus! Jesus!" she cried. "How much longer do I, an old married woman, have to listen to this?"

"Peaches Maud!" he said, standing up and looking down at her squatting bulk on the bed. "There's no point me postponing telling you. Why I am without a job should be no sort of mystery for you, for you are after all the woman I married. . . . Have you been satisfied with me?"

"Satisfied?" she said, becoming quiet again, and her hand rising as though still in possession of the fan. "Lafe, listen a moment." Peaches spoke quickly, holding her finger to her face, as though admiring a strain of music. "Did you ever hear it go so loud before? I swear it's going to explode on us. Can they explode, do you suppose?"

He stood there, his face and body empty of meaning, not looking where she pointed to the refrigerator.

Maud broke a piece of chewing gum in two and, without offering him the other piece, began to unfold the tin foil and then to chew the gum industriously but with a large frown between her eyes as though she could expect no pleasure from what she had put into her mouth.

"You never let me show you nothing but the outside," he said, his face going white and his eyes more vacant.

"Well, that's all anybody human wants to hear," she shouted, but she felt a terrible excitement inside, and her mouth went so dry she could hardly chew the gum.

"Peaches Maud, you have to listen to what I am trying to tell you." He touched her jaws as though to stop her chewing. "First of all you must answer my first question. Have you been satisfied with me?"

Peaches Maud felt welling up within her for the first time in seven years a terrible tempest of tears. She could not explain why or from where these tears were coming. She felt also, without warning, cold and she got up and put on her kimono.

"Don't tell me no more now." She faced him, drawing the kimono sash about her.

The refrigerator clattered on in short unrhythmic claps as though to annihilate all other sound.

"Answer my question, Peaches." He took her hand up from the folds of the kimono.

"I bought this for you in Chinatown." He made an effort to raise his voice.

"I don't want to hear no memory talks, Lafe, for the love of Christ!" And she looked down at him suddenly as though she had gone up above him on a platform.

"Maud," he coaxed, putting a new and funny hopeful tone into his voice, "I can forget all that mental talk like you say. I did before anyhow. The men in the army tried to make me feel things too, with their tests, and here I went and married you."

"Stop it now," she began to make crying sounds. "I can't bear to hear no more of that talk, I tell you. Put it off for later. I don't feel up to hearing it, I tell you."

"We both quick change and make up our minds, don't we?" he said, briefly happy. He kissed her on the face.

"Don't kiss me when I feel like I do," she said peevishly.

Then without any warning, shouting as though something had stung her: "What did the company psychiatrist tell you?"

"You got to answer my first question first," Lafe said, a kind of mechanical strength coming to him.

"I can't answer until I hear what he told you," she said.

"Peaches," he pleaded with her.

"I mean what I said now." She began to sob a little.

"No, don't tell me after all, Lafe." Her face was open now and had a new empty weak quality he had never seen on it before. "I feel if it's what I am fearing I'd split open like a stone."

"How could it be that bad?" he seemed to ask himself this question.

"I can tell it is because you keep making it depend on me being satisfied. I know more than you think I know."

Then she began to scream at him again as though to stop any tears that might have force enough to fall.

"What did you do at the factory that wasn't human? Oh, I thank Jesus we don't live in the same neighborhood with them men that work for you. This apartment may be hell with nothing but foreigners around us and that busted refrigerator and no ventilation but heat from the roof, but thank Jesus nobody don't know us."

"You won't answer me, then?" he said, still as calm and empty in his movements as before.

"You're not a woman," she told him, "and you can't understand the first question can't be answered till I know what you done."

"I asked the psychiatrist if it was a crime."

"Well, what did he tell you?" Peaches Maud raised her voice as though she saw ahead some faint indication of escape.

"He said it depended. It was what the men thought where you had to work."

"Well, what in the name of Christ did the men think?"

"They thought it was a crime."

"Was it a boy you were stuck on?" Peaches Maud said, making her voice both empty and quiet, and at the same time all the tears came onto her face as though sprayed there by a tiny machine, in one second.

"Did the psychiatrist call you up, Peaches?" he said, and he took hold of the bedpost and stared away from her.

Then, when she did not answer, he went over to her: "Did he, Peaches?" He took her by the hands and waited for her to answer.

"You leave loose of me, Lafe Krause. Do you hear? Leave loose of my hands."

"Peaches," he called in a voice that seemed to come from under the floor.

"Don't call me that old love name," she wept. "I'm an old fat woman tied down to a . . ."

She waited before she said the word, listening as though for any sound that might rescue them there both together.

"Did he call you up?" Lafe kept on, but his voice carried now no real demand, and came as though at a still greater distance from under where they stood.

Listening sharply, Maud felt it was true: the refrigerator had stopped again, and the silence was high and heavy as the sky outside.

"Did he call you, Maud, did he?"

"No," she answered, finally, still feeling he had to be addressed at some depth under where she was standing. "It was your mother. She told me before we got married. I said I would take a chance."

"The old bitch told you," he reflected in his exhausted voice.

"Considering the way the son turned out, the mother can hardly be blamed," Maud said, but her voice was equally drained of meaning.

"Peaches," he said, but as if not addressing the word to her at all, and going rapidly over to the refrigerator and opening up the door.

"The little light is out that was on here," he said dully.

"There ain't no point in fussing with it now," she remarked.

"Maybe I could fix it," he said.

"I doubt that. I doubt you could, Lafe Krause. I don't think I would want you to fix it anyhow, even if you could. . . ."

"Don't you want me to do nothing for you then anymore?" He turned with a slight movement toward her, his eyes falling on her breasts.

"I can't stand the pressure, I can't," she shouted back at him. "Why did you have to go and do it?"

"I didn't do nothing," he explained, as though trying to remember what had been said and what had not. "That's why it's so odd. They just felt I looked like I was going to, and they fired me."

"Jesus, I don't understand," she said, but without any tears on her face now. "Why did this have to happen to me when I can't bear to hear about anything that ain't human."

But her husband was not listening to her words or noticing whether she had tears or not. He was looking only at what was she, this fat, slightly middle-aged woman. She looked as though she had come to her permanent age, and he knew then that though he was but twenty-eight, he might as well be sixty, and the something awful and permanent that comes to everybody had come at last to him. Everything had come to an end, whether because he had looked at boys, or whether because the men had suddenly decided that yes, there was something odd in his character.

"Peaches," he said, and as he paused in his speech, the name he had always called her seemed to move over into the silence and vacancy of the broken refrigerator. "I will always stand by you anyhow, Peaches Maud."

PLAN NOW TO ATTEND

Fred Parker had not seen Mr. Graitop since college days and yet he recognized him at once. Mr. Graitop's face had not changed in twenty years, his doll-small mouth was still the same size, his hair was as immaculately groomed as a department story dummy. Mr. Graitop had always in fact resembled a department store dummy, his face wax-like, his eyes innocent and vacant, the doll-like mouth bloodless and expressionless, the body loose and yet heavy as though the passions and anguish of man had never coursed through it.

Fred on the other hand felt old and used, and he was almost unwilling to make himself known to Mr. Graitop. The fact that he remembered him as Mr. Graitop instead of by his first name was also significant. One did not really believe that Mr. Graitop had a first name, though he did and it was Ezra. Fred had remembered him all these years as Mister. And now here he was like a statue in a museum, looking very young still and at the same time ancient, as though he had never been new.

"Mr. Graitop!" Fred cried in the lobby of the hotel. The hotel was said to be one of the world's largest, perhaps the largest, and Fred felt somehow the significance of his meeting the great man here where they were both so dwarfed by physical immensity, their voices lost in the vastness of the lobby whose roof seemed to lose itself in space indefinitely.

Mr. Graitop's face broke into a faint but actual smile and his eyes shone as though a candle had been lighted behind his brain.

"You are *him*," Fred said with relief. He was afraid that perhaps there was another man in the world who looked like Graitop.

"Yes, you are not deceived in me," Mr. Graitop said, pale and serious.

Fred was going to say *twenty years*, but he decided this was not necessary. He was not sure that Graitop would know it was twenty years, for he had always denied facts of any kind, changing a fact immediately into a spiritual symbol. For instance, in the old days if Fred had said, "It has been twenty minutes," Graitop would have said, "Well, *some* time has passed, of course." He would have denied the twenty because they were figures.

"You are just the same, Mr. Graitop," Fred said, and almost at once he wished he had not called to him, that he had hurried out of the world's largest hotel without ever knowing whether this was the real Graitop or only his twenty-year-younger double.

As they were at the entrance of the Magnolia Bar, Fred ventured to ask him if he would have a drink, although it was only ten o'clock in the morning.

Mr. Graitop hesitated. Perhaps because he did remember it was twenty years, however, he nodded a quiet assent, but his face had again emphasized the bloodless doll expression, and one felt the presence of his small rat-terrier teeth pressed against the dead mouth.

"Mr. Graitop, this is unbelievable. Really not credible."

Mr. Graitop made odd little noises in his mouth and nose like a small boy who is being praised and admonished by the teacher at the same time.

Fred Parker already felt drunk from the excitement of having made such a terrible mistake as to renew acquaintance with a man who had been great as a youth and was now such a very great man he was known in the movement as the great man.

"What is your drink now, Mr. Graitop?" Fred spoke as though on a telephone across the continent . . . "After twenty years," he explained, awkwardly laughing.

Mr. Graitop winced, and Fred felt that he did so because he did not like to be called by his last name even though he would not have liked to be called by his first, and perhaps also he did not like the twenty years referred to.

As Graitop did not answer immediately but continued to make the small-boy sounds in his nose and throat, Fred asked in a loud voice, "Bourbon and water, perhaps?"

"Bourbon and water," Mr. Graitop repeated wearily, but at the same time with a somewhat relieved note to his voice as though he had recognized his duty and now with great fatigue was about to perform it.

"I can't tell you how odd this is," Fred said nervously emphatic when they had been served.

"Yes, you said that before," Mr. Graitop said and his face was as immobile as cloth.

"But it is, you know. I think it's odd that I recognized you."

"You do?" Mr. Graitop sipped the drink as though he felt some chemical change already taking place in his mouth and facial muscles and perhaps fearful his changeless expression would move.

Then there was silence and strangely enough Mr. Graitop broke it by saying, "Your name is Fred, isn't it."

"Yes," Fred replied, paralyzed with emotion, and with his drink untouched. He suddenly noticed that Graitop had finished his.

"Graitop, won't you have another?" Fred asked, no invitation in his voice.

Graitop stared at him as though he had not understood actually that he had already finished one.

"Don't you drink, sir?" Fred said, surprised at once to hear his own questions.

"No," Graitop replied.

"Another bourbon and water," Fred told the bartender.

"You know," Fred began, "this reminds me of one semester when we were roommates and we neither of us went to the football game. We could hear the crowd roaring from our room. It sounded like some kind of mammoth animal that was being punished. It was too hot for football and you tried to convert me to atheism."

Mr. Graitop did not say anything. Everybody had heard of his great success in introducing "new Religion" to America so that when many people thought of "new Religion" they thought immediately of Graitop.

It was a surprise to Fred to remember that Graitop had been a practicing atheist in the college quadrangles, for he remembered it only this instant.

"You were one, you know," Fred said almost viciously.

"We are always moving toward the one path," Graitop said dreamily, drinking his second drink.

Although Fred was a hard drinker, he had swiftly lost all his appetite for it, and he knew that it was not the early hour. Very often at this hour, setting out as a salesman, he was completely oiled.

"Is it the new religion that keeps you looking so kind of embalmed and youthful," Fred said, as though he had had his usual five brandies.

"Fred," Mr. Graitop said on his third drink, with mechanical composure, "it is the only conceivable path."

"I liked you better as an infidel," Fred said. "You looked more human then, too, and older. I suppose you go to all the football games now that you're a famous man."

"I suppose I see a good many," Graitop said.

"Fred," Mr. Graitop said, closing his eyes softly, and as he did so he looked remarkably older, "why can't you come with us this time?"

Fred did not know what to say because he did not exactly understand the question.

"There is no real reason to refuse. You are a living embodiment of what we all are without *the* prop."

"I'm not following you now," Fred replied.

"You are, but you won't let yourself," Graitop said, opening his eyes and finishing his third drink. He tapped the glass as though it had been an offering for Fred.

Fred signaled for another drink for Graitop just as in the past he would have for himself. His own first drink remained untouched, which he could not understand, except he felt nauseated. He realized also that he hated the great man and had always hated him.

"Well, what am I?" Fred said as he watched Graitop start on his fourth drink.

"The embodiment of the crooked stick that would be made straight," the great man replied.

"You really do go for that, don't you. That is," Fred continued, "you have made that talk part of your life."

"There is no talk involved," Mr. Graitop said. "No talk, Fred."

I wonder why the old bastard is drinking so much, Fred nearly spoke aloud. Then: "Graitop, nobody has ever understood what makes you tick."

"That is unimportant," his friend replied. "It, too, is talk."

"Nobody ever even really liked you, though I don't suppose anybody ever liked St. Paul either."

"Of course, Fred, you are really with us in spirit," Graitop said as though he had not heard the last statement.

Fred looked at his drink which seemed cavernous as a well.

"Graitop," he said stonily, "you discovered Jesus late. Later than me. I'd had all that when I was twelve. . . ."

"You're part of the new movement and your denying it here to me only confirms it," Mr. Graitop informed him.

"I don't want to be part of it," Fred began and he tasted some of his drink, but Graitop immediately interrupted.

"It isn't important that you don't want to be part: you are part and there is nothing you can do about it. You're with us."

"I couldn't be with you," Fred began, feeling coming up within him a fierce anger, and he hardly knew at what it was directed, for it seemed to be larger than just his dislike, suspicion, and dread of Graitop.

Then Mr. Graitop must have realized what only the bartender had sensed from the beginning, that he was not only drunk but going to be sick. Fred had not noticed it at all, for he felt that he had suddenly been seized and forced to relive the impotence and stupidity of his adolescence.

With the bartender's help, he assisted Mr. Graitop out of the bar. In the elevator, Graitop grew loud and belligerent and shouted several times: "It's the only path, the only way."

"What is your room number?" Fred said hollow-voiced as they got out of the elevator.

"You are really part of our group," Graitop replied.

Fred took the key out of Graitop's pocket and nodded to the woman at the desk, who stared at them.

"You are completely oiled," Fred informed Graitop when the latter had lain down on the bed. "And yet it doesn't convince me any more than your preaching."

"I wonder if I had appointments," Graitop said weakly. "I was to speak to some of our people. . . ."

"I wonder which of us feels more terrible," Fred replied. "This meeting after twenty years [and he shouted the number] has been poison to both of us. We hate one another and everything we stand for. At least I hate you. You are probably too big a fraud to admit hate. I'm saying this cold sober, too, although I guess just the inside of a bar oils me up."

"You are a living embodiment of sin and sorrow and yet you are dear to us," Graitop said, looking at the ceiling.

"What the hell are you the living embodiment of, what?" Fred said and he began loosening his friend's clothing. Before he knew it, he had completely undressed Mr. Graitop as mechanically as he undressed himself when drunk. As his friend lay there, a man of at least forty, Fred was amazed to see that he looked like a boy of sixteen. Almost nothing had touched him in the world. So amazed and objective was Fred's surprise that he took the bed lamp and held it to his face and body to see if he was not deceived and this forty-year-old man was not actually a palimpsest of slightly hidden decay and senility. But the light revealed nothing but what his eye had first seen—a youth untouched by life and disappointment.

He looked so much like God or something mythological that before he knew what he was doing Fred Parker had kissed him dutifully on the forehead.

"Why did you do that?" Mr. Graitop said, touching the place with his finger, and his voice was almost human.

Fred Parker sat down in a large easy chair and loosened his necktie. He did not answer the question because he had not heard it. He felt intoxicated and seriously unwell.

"How in hell do you live, Graitop?" he said almost too softly to be heard. "Are you married and do you have kids?"

"Yes, yes," Graitop replied, and he began to drivel now from his mouth.

Fred got up and wiped off his lips, and put the covers over him.

"A missionary," Fred Parker said. "But of what?"

"Don't be a fool," Graitop said sleepily. Suddenly he was asleep.

Fred Parker watched him again angrily from the chair.

"Who in hell are you, Graitop?" he shouted from the chair. "Why in hell did I run into you, Why in hell did I speak to you. . . . Why don't you look and act like other men?"

Fred called room service for ice, whiskey, and water. He began immediately the serious drinking he should not have been without all morning.

"When the bastard is conscious, I will ask him who he is and what he means to do."

"It's all right, Fred," Mr. Graitop said from time to time from the bed. "You are really with us, and it's all all right."

"I wish you wouldn't use that goddamn language, Graitop," he said. "You don't have the personality for a missionary. Too young and dead-looking. Too vague."

From the bed there came sounds like a small boy sleeping.

WHY CAN'T THEY TELL YOU WHY?

Paul knew nearly nothing of his father until he found the box of photographs on the backstairs. From then on he looked at them all day and every evening, and when his mother Ethel talked to Edith Gainesworth on the telephone. He had looked amazed at his father in his different ages and stations of life, first as a boy his age, then as a young man, and finally before his death in his army uniform.

Ethel had always referred to him as *your father*, and now the photographs made him look much different from what this had suggested in Paul's mind.

Ethel never talked with Paul about why he was home sick from school and she pretended at first she did not know he had found the photographs. But she told everything she thought and felt about him to Edith Gainesworth over the telephone, and Paul heard all of the conversations from the back stairs where he sat with the photographs, which he had moved from the old shoe boxes where he had found them to two big clean empty candy boxes.

"Wouldn't you know a sick kid like him would take up with photographs," Ethel said to Edith Gainesworth. "Instead of toys or balls, old photos. And my God, I've hardly mentioned a thing to him about his father."

Edith Gainesworth, who studied psychology at an adult center downtown, often advised Ethel about Paul, but she did not say anything tonight about the photographs.

"All mothers should have pensions," Ethel continued. "If it isn't a terrible feeling being on your feet all day before the public and then having a sick kid under your feet when you're off at night. My evenings are worse than my days."

These telephone conversations always excited Paul because they were the only times he heard himself and the photographs discussed. When the telephone bell would ring he would run to the backstairs and begin looking at the photographs and then as the conversation progressed he often ran into the front room where Ethel was talking, sometimes carrying one of the photographs with him and making sounds like a bird or an airplane.

Two months had gone by like this, with his having attended school hardly at all and his whole life seemingly spent in listening to Ethel talk to Edith Gainesworth and examining the photographs in the candy boxes.

Then in the middle of the night Ethel missed him. She rose feeling a pressure in her scalp and neck. She walked over to his cot and noticed the Indian blanket had been taken away. She called Paul and walked over to the window and looked out. She walked around the upstairs, calling him.

"God, there is always something to bother you," she said. "Where are you, Paul?" she repeated in a mad sleepy voice. She went on down into the kitchen, though it did not seem possible he would be there, he never ate anything.

Then she said *Of course*, remembering how many times he went to the backstairs with those photographs.

"Now what are you doing in here, Paul?" Ethel said, and there was a sweet but threatening sound to her voice that awoke the boy from where he had been sleeping, spread out protectively over the boxes of photographs, his Indian blanket over his back and shoulder.

Paul crouched almost greedily over the boxes when he saw this ugly pale woman in the man's bathrobe looking at him. There was a faint smell from her like that of an uncovered cistern when she put on the robe.

"Just here, Ethel," he answered her question after a while.

"What do you mean, *just here*, Paul?" she said going up closer to him.

She took hold of his hair and jerked him by it gently, as though this was a kind of caress she sometimes gave him. This gentle jerking motion made him tremble in short successive starts under her hand, until she let go.

He watched how she kept looking at the boxes of photographs under his guard.

"You sleep here to be near them?" she said.

"I don't know why, Ethel," Paul said, blowing out air from his mouth as though trying to make something disappear before him.

"You don't know, Paul," she said, her sweet fake awful voice and the stale awful smell of the bathrobe stifling as she drew nearer.

"Don't, don't!" Paul cried.

"Don't what?" Ethel answered, pulling him toward her by seizing on his pajama tops.

"Don't do anything to me, Ethel, my eye hurts."

"Your eye hurts," she said with unbelief.

"I'm sick to my stomach."

Then bending over suddenly, in a second she had gathered up the two boxes of photographs in her bathrobed arms.

"Ethel!" he cried out in the strongest, clearest voice she had ever heard come from him. "Ethel, those are my candy boxes!"

She looked down at him as though she was seeing him for the first time, noting with surprise how thin and puny he was, and how disgusting was one small mole that hung from his starved-looking throat. She could not see how this was her son.

"These boxes of pictures are what makes you sick."

"No, no, Mama Ethel," Paul cried.

"What did I tell you about calling me Mama?" she said, going over to him and putting her hand on his forehead.

"I called you Mama Ethel, not Mama," he said.

"I suppose you think I'm a thousand years old." She raised her hand as though she was not sure what she wished to do with it.

"I think I know what to do with these," she said with a pretended calm.

"No, Ethel," Paul said, "give them here back. They are my boxes."

"Tell me why you slept out here on this backstairs where you know you'll make yourself even sicker. I want you to tell me and tell me right away."

"I can't, Ethel, I can't," Paul said.

"Then I'm going to burn the pictures," she replied.

He crawled hurrying over to where she stood and put his arms around her legs.

"Ethel, please don't take them, Ethel. Pretty please."

"Don't touch me," she said to him. Her nerves were so bad she felt that if he touched her again she would start as though a mouse had gotten under her clothes.

"You stand up straight and tell me like a little man why you're here," she said, but she kept her eyes half closed and turned from him.

He moved his lips to answer but then he did not really understand what she meant by *little man*. That phrase worried him whenever he heard it.

"What do you do with the pictures all the time, all day when I'm gone, and now tonight? I never heard of anything like it." Then she moved away from him, so that his hands fell from her legs where he had been grasping her, but she continued to stand near his hands as though puzzled what to do next.

"I look is all, Ethel," he began to explain.

"Don't bawl when you talk," she commanded, looking now at him in the face.

Then: "I want the truth!" she roared.

He sobbed and whined there, thinking over what it was she could want him to tell her, but everything now had begun to go away from his attention, and he had not really ever understood what had been expected of him here, and now everything was too hard to be borne.

"Do you hear me, Paul?" she said between her teeth, very close to him now and staring at him in such an angry way he closed his eyes. "If you don't answer me, do you know what I'm going to do?"

"Punish?" Paul said in his tiniest child voice.

"No, I'm not going to punish this time," Ethel said.

"You're not!" he cried, a new fear and surprise coming now into his tired eyes, and then staring at her eyes, he began to cry with panicky terror, for it seemed to him then that in the whole world there were just the two of them, him and Ethel.

"You remember where they sent Aunt Grace," Ethel said with terrible knowledge.

His crying redoubled in fury, some of his spit flying out onto the cold calcimine of the walls. He kept turning the while to look at the close confines of the staircase as though to find some place where he could see things outside.

"Do you remember where they sent her?" Ethel said in a quiet patient voice like a woman who has endured every unreasonable, disrespectful action from a child whom she still can patiently love.

"Yes, yes, Ethel," Paul cried hysterically.

"Tell Ethel where they sent Aunt Grace," she said with the same patience and kind restraint.

"I didn't know they sent little boys there," Paul said.

"You're more than a little boy now," Ethel replied. "You're old enough. . . . And if you don't tell Ethel why you look at the photographs all the time, we'll have to send you to the mental hospital with the bars."

"I don't know why I look at them, dear Ethel," he said now in a very feeble but wildly tense voice, and he began petting the fur on her houseslippers.

"I think you do, Paul," she said quietly, but he could hear her gentle, patient tone disappearing and he half raised his hands as though to protect him from anything this woman might now do.

"But I don't know why I look at them," he repeated, screaming, and he threw his arms suddenly around her legs.

She moved back, but still smiling her patient, knowing, forgiving smile.

"All right for you, Paul." When she said that *all right for you* it always meant the end of any understanding or reasoning with her.

"Where are we going?" he cried, as she ushered him through the door, into the kitchen.

"We're going to the basement, of course," she replied.

They had never gone there together before, and the terror of what might happen to him now gave him a kind of quiet that enabled him to walk steady down the long irregular steps.

"You carry the boxes of pictures, Paul," she said, "since you like them so much."

"No, no," Paul cried.

"Carry them," she commanded, giving them to him.

He held them before him and when they reached the floor of the basement, she opened the furnace and, tightening the cord of her bathrobe, she said coldly, her white face lighted up by the fire, "Throw the pictures into the furnace door, Paul."

He stared at her as though all the nightmares had come true, the complete and final fear of what may happen in living had unfolded itself at last.

"They're Daddy!" he said in a voice neither of them recognized.

"You had your choice," she said coolly. "You prefer a dead man to your own mother. Either you throw his pictures in the fire, for they're what makes you sick, or you will go where they sent Aunt Grace."

He began running around the room now, much like a small bird which has escaped from a pet shop into the confusion of a city street, and making odd little sounds that she did not recognize could come from his own lungs.

"I'm not going to stand for your clowning," she called out, but as though to an empty room.

As he ran round and round the small room with the boxes of photographs pressed against him, some of the pictures fell upon the floor and these he stopped and tried to recapture, at the same time holding the boxes tight against him, and making, as he picked them up, frothing cries of impotence and acute grief.

Ethel herself stared at him, incredulous. He not only could not be recognized as her son, he no longer looked like a child, but in his small unmended night shirt like some crippled and dying animal running hopelessly from its pain.

"Give me those pictures!" she shouted, and she seized a few which he held in his fingers, and threw them quickly into the fire.

Then turning back, she moved to take the candy boxes from him.

But the final sight of him made her stop. He had crouched on the floor, and, bending his stomach over the boxes, hissed at her, so that she stopped short, not seeing any way to get at him, seeing no way to bring him back, while from his mouth black thick strings of something slipped out, as though he had spewed out the heart of his grief.

63: DREAM PALACE

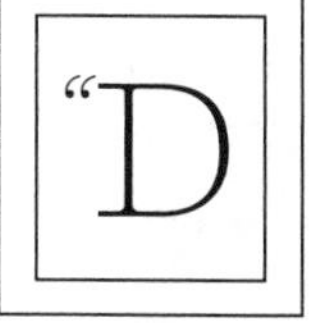

o you ever think about Fenton Riddleway?" Parkhearst Cratty asked the greatwoman one afternoon when they were sitting in the summer garden of her "mansion."

Although the greatwoman had been drinking earlier in the day, she was almost sober at the time Parkhearst put this question to her.

It was a rhetorical and idle question, but Parkhearst's idle questions were always put to her as a plea that they should review their lives together, and she always accepted the plea by saying nearly the same thing: "Why don't you write down what Fenton did?" she would say. "Since you did write once," and her face much more than her voice darkened at him.

Actually the eyes of the greatwoman were blackened very little with mascara and yet such was their cavernous appearance they gaped at Parkhearst as though tonight they would yield him her real identity and why people called her great.

"Fenton Riddleway is vague as a dream to me," the greatwoman said.

"That means he is more real to you than anybody," Parkhearst said.

"How could it mean anything else?" she repeated her own eternal rejoinder. Then arranging her long dress so that it covered the floor before her shoes, she began to throw her head back as though suffering from a feeling of suffocation.

It was her signal to him that he was to leave, but he took no notice of her wishes today.

"I can't write down what Fenton did because I never found out who he was," Parkhearst explained again to her.

"You've said that ever since he was first with us. And since he went away, a million times."

She reached for the gin; it was the only drink she would have since the days of Fenton.

"Not that I'm criticizing you for saying it," she said. "How could *I* criticize you?" she added.

"Then don't scratch and tear at me, for Christ's sake," he told her.

Her mouth wet from the drink smiled faintly at him.

"What Fenton did was almost the only story I ever really wanted to write," Parkhearst said, and a shadow of old happiness came over his thin brown face.

Grainger's eyes brightened briefly, then went back into their unrelieved darkness.

"You can't feel as empty of recollection as I do," Grainger mumbled, sipping again.

Parkhearst watched the veins bulge in his hands.

"Why are we dead anyhow?" Parkhearst said, bored with the necessity of returning to this daily statement. "Is it because of our losing the people we loved or because the people we found were damned?" He laughed.

One never mentioned the "real" things like this at Grainger's, and here Parkhearst had done it, and nothing happened. Instead, Grainger listened as though hearing some two or three notes of an alto sax she recalled from the concerts she gave at her home.

"This is the first time you ever said you were, Parkhearst. Dead," she said in her clearest voice.

He sat looking like a small rock that has been worked on by a swift but careless hammer.

"Are you really without a memory?" she asked, speaking now like a child.

He did not say anything and she began to get up.

"Don't get up, or you'll fall," he said, almost not looking in her direction.

The greatwoman had gotten up and stood there like some more than human personage at the end of an opera. Parkhearst closed his eyes. Then she advanced to a half-fall at the feet of her old friend.

"Are those tears?" she said looking up into his face.

"Don't be tiresome, Grainger. Go back and sit down," he said, with the petulance of a small boy.

Pushing her head towards his face, she kissed him several times.

"You're getting gray," she said, almost shocked. "I didn't know it had been such a long time."

"I try never to think about those things," he looked at her now. "Please get up."

"Do you think Fenton Riddleway would know you now, Parkhearst?" the greatwoman asked sullenly but without anything taunting in her voice.

"The real question is whether we would know Fenton Riddleway if we saw him."

"We'd know him," she said. "Above or beneath hell."

As evening came on in the "mansion" (*mansion* a word they both thought of and used all the time because Fenton had used it), they drank more and more of the neat Holland gin, but drunkenness did not take: was it after all, they kept on saying, merely the remembrance of a boy from West Virginia, that mover and shaker Fenton, that kept them talking and living.

"Tell me all about what he did again," Grainger said, seated now on her gold carved chair. The dark hid her age, so that she looked now only relatively old; it almost hid the fact that she was drunk, drunk going on to ten years, and her face was shapeless and sexless.

"Tell me what he did all over again, just this last time. If you won't write it down, Parkhearst, you'll have to come here and tell it to me once a month. I had always hoped you would write it down so I could have it read to me on my bad nights. . . ."

"Your memory is so much better than mine," Parkhearst said.

"I have no memory," the greatwoman said. "Or only a grain of one."

She raised her glass threateningly, but it had got so dark in the room she could not see just where Parkhearst's tired voice was coming from. It was like the time she had called Russell long distance to his home town, the voice had wavered, then had grown, then had sunk into indistinguishable sounds. Parkhearst would take another drink of the gin, then his voice would rise a bit, only to die away again as he told her everything he could remember.

"Are you awake?" Parkhearst questioned her.

"Keep going," she said. "Don't stop to ask me a single thing. Just tell what he did, and then write it all down for me to read hereafter."

He nodded at her.

THERE WAS THIS park with a patriot's name near the lagoon. Parkhearst Cratty had been wandering there, not daring to go home to his wife Bella. He had done nothing in weeks, and her resentment against him would be too heavy to bear. Of course it was true, what he was later to tell Fenton himself, that he was looking for "material" for his book. Many times he had run across people in the park who had told him their stories while he pretended to listen to their voices while usually watching their persons.

In this section of the park there were no lights, and the only illumination came from the reflection of the traffic blocks away. Here the men who came to wander about as aimless and groping as he were obvious shades in hell. He always noticed this fact as he noticed there were no lights. Parkhearst paid little attention to the actual things that went on in the park and, although not a brave or strong young man, he had never felt fear in the park itself. It was its atmosphere alone that satisfied him and he remained forever innocent of its acts.

It was August, and cool, but he felt enervated as never before. His marriage pursued him like a never-ending nightmare, and he could not free himself from the obsession that "everything was over."

Just like children, he and the greatwoman Grainger longed, and especially demanded even, that something should happen, or again Parkhearst would cry, "A reward, I must have a reward. A reward for life just as I have lived it."

It was just as he had uttered the words *a reward* that he first saw Fenton Riddleway go past, he remembered.

In the darkness and the rehearsed evil of the park it was odd, indeed, as Parkhearst now reflected on the event, that anyone should have stood out at all that night, one shadow from the other. Yet Fenton was remarkable at once, perhaps for no other reason than that he was actually lost and wandering about, for no other reason than this. Parkhearst did not need to watch him for more than a moment to see his desperation.

Parkhearst lit a cigarette so that his own whereabouts would be visible to the stranger.

"Looking for anybody?" Parkhearst then asked.

Fenton's face was momentarily lighted up by Parkhearst's cigarette: the face had, he noted with accustomed uneasiness, a kind of beauty but mixed with something unsteady, unusual.

"Where do you get out?" the boy asked.

He stood directly over Parkhearst in a position a less experienced man than the writer would have taken to be a threat.

Parkhearst recognized with a certain shock that this was the first question he had ever had addressed to him in the park which was asked with the wish to be answered: somebody really wanted out of the park.

"Where do you want to go?"

Fenton took from his pocket a tiny dimestore notebook and read from the first page an address.

"It's south," Parkhearst replied. "Away from the lagoon."

Fenton still looked too unsure to speak. He dropped the notebook and when he stooped to pick it up his head twitched while his eyes looked at the writer.

"Do you want me to show you?" Parkhearst asked, pretending indifference.

Fenton looked directly into his face now.

Those eyes looked dumb, Parkhearst saw them again, like maybe the eyes of the first murderer, dumb and innocent and getting to be mad.

"Show me, please," Fenton said, and Parkhearst heard the Southern accent.

"You're from far off," Parkhearst said as they began to walk in the opposite direction from the lagoon.

Fenton had been too frightened not to want to unburden himself. He told nearly everything, as though in a police court, that he was Fenton Riddleway and that he was nineteen, that he had come with his brother Claire from West Virginia, from a town near Ronceverte, that their mother had died two weeks before, and that a friend of his named Kincaid had given him an address in a rooming house on Sixty-*three* Street . . .

"You mean Sixty-*third*," Parkhearst corrected him, but Fenton did not hear the correction then or when it was made fifty times later: "A house on Sixty-three Street," he continued. "It turns out to be a not-right-kind of place at all. . . ."

"How is that?" Parkhearst wondered.

They moved out of the middle section of the park and into a place where the street light looked down on them. Fenton was gazing at him easily but Parkhearst's eyes kept to his coat pocket, which bulged obviously.

"Is that your gun there?" he said, weary.

Fenton watched him, moving his lips quickly.

"Don't let it go off on yourself," Parkhearst said ineffectively as the boy nodded.

"But what were you saying about that house?" the writer went back to his story.

"It's alive with something, I don't know what. . . ."

Fenton's thick accent, which seemed to become thicker now, all at once irritated Parkhearst, and as they drew near the part of the city that was more inhabited and better lighted, he felt himself surprised by Fenton's incredibly poor-fitting almost filthy clothes and by the fact that his hair had the look of not ever perhaps having been cut or combed. He looked more or less like West Virginia, Parkhearst supposed, and then Parkhearst always remembered he had thought this, he looked not only just West Virginia, he looked himself, Fenton.

"What's it alive with, then?" Parkhearst came back to the subject of the house.

"I don't mean it's got ghosts, though I think it maybe does." He stopped, fishing for encouragement to go on and when none came he said: "It's a not-right house. There ain't nobody in it for one thing."

"I don't think I see," Parkhearst said, and he felt not so much his interest waning as his feeling that there was something about this boy too excessive; everything about him was too large for him, the speech, the terrible clothes, the ragged hair, the possible gun, the outlandish accent.

"All the time we're alone in it, I keep thinking how empty it is, and what are we waiting for after all, with so little money to tide us over, if he don't show up. Claire cries all the time on account of the change. The house don't do *him* any good."

"Can you find your way back now, do you think?" Parkhearst asked, as they got to a street down which ordinary people and traffic were moving.

A paralysis had struck the writer suddenly, as though all the interest he might have had in Fenton had been killed. He was beginning to be afraid also that he would be involved in more than a story.

Fenton stopped as if to remind Parkhearst that he had a responsibility toward him. His having found the first person in his life who would listen to him had made him within ten minutes come to regard Parkhearst as a friend, and now the realization came quickly that this was only a listener who having heard the story would let him go back to the "not-right house."

"Here's fifty cents for you," Parkhearst said.

He took it with a funny quick movement as though money for the first time had meaning for him.

"You won't come with me to see Claire?"

Parkhearst stared. This odd boy, who was probably wanted by the police, who had come out of nothing to him, had asked him a question in the tone of one who had known him all his life.

"Tomorrow maybe," Parkhearst answered. He explained lamely about Bella waiting for him and being cross if he came any later.

The boy's face fell.

"You know where to find the house?" Fenton said, hoarse.

"Yes," Parkhearst replied dreamily, indifferent.

Fenton looked at Parkhearst, unbelieving. Then: "How can you find it?" he wondered. "I can't ever find it no matter how many times I go and come. How can you then?"

The sorrow on Fenton's face won him over to him again, and he felt Bella's eyes of reproach disappear from his mind for a moment.

"Tomorrow afternoon I'll visit you at the house," he promised. "Two o'clock."

A moment later when Fenton was gone, Parkhearst looking back could not help wait for the last sight of him in the street, and a new feeling so close to acute sickness swept over him. It was the wildness and freedom Fenton had, he began to try to explain to himself. The wildness and freedom held against his own shut-in locked life. He hurried on home to Bella.

BELLA LISTENED VAGUELY to the story of Fenton Riddleway. There had been, she recalled mechanically, scores, even hundreds, of these people Parkhearst met in order to study for his writing, but the stories themselves were never put in final shape or were never written, and Parkhearst himself forgot the old models in his search for new ones.

"Is Fenton to take the place of Grainger now?" Bella commented on his enthusiasm, almost his ecstasy.

There was no criticism in her remark. She was beyond that. Bella Cratty had resigned herself to her complete knowledge of her husband's character. There was, furthermore, no opposing Parkhearst; if he were opposed he would disintegrate slowly, vanish before her eyes. He was a child who must not be crossed in the full possession of his freedom, one who must be left to follow his own whims and visions.

She had married him without anyone knowing why, but everyone agreed she had done so with the full knowledge of what he was. If she had not known before, their married life had been a continuous daily rehearsal of Parkhearst's character; he was himself every minute, taking more and more away from what was *her* with each new sorrow he brought home to her. He became more and more incurable and it was his incurable quality which made him essential to her.

She was not happy a second. Had she seen the wandering men in the park after whom Parkhearst gazed, she might have seen herself like them, wandering without purpose away from the light. And though she tried to pretend that she wanted Parkhearst to have friends no matter what they were, no matter what they would do, she never gave up suffering, and each of the "new" people he met and "studied" cost her an impossible sacrifice.

There was something at once about the name Fenton Riddleway that made her feel there was danger here in his name as Grainger was in hers. Only there was something in the new name more frightening than in Grainger's.

As two o'clock approached the following day (an evil hour in astrology, Parkhearst had noticed covertly, for Bella objected to his interest in what she called "the moons"), both of them felt the importance of his departure. He had tried to get her "ready" from the evening before so that she would accept this as Fenton's day, when as a writer he must find out all there was to know about this strange boy. Parkhearst used the word *material* again, though he had promised himself to give up using the word.

"I suppose in the end you will let Grainger have Fenton," Bella remarked, a sudden hostility coming over her face as she sat at the kitchen table drinking her coffee.

Parkhearst stopped his task of sewing on a button on his old gray-green jacket.

It was only when his wife said that that he understood he did not wish to share Fenton with anyone, until, he lied to himself, he had found out everything Fenton had done. And then he corrected this lie in his own mind: he simply did not want to share Fenton with anybody. Grainger would spoil him, would take him over, if she were interested, and he knew of course that she was going to be.

"Grainger won't get him," he said finally.

Bella laughed a very high laugh, ridden with hysteria and shaky restraint. "You've never kept anybody from one another as long as you've been friends," she reviewed their lives. "What would happen," she went on bitterly, "if you couldn't show one another what you take in, what you accomplish. If there was no competition!"

"Fenton is different," Parkhearst said, pale with anger. Then suddenly, so shaken by fear of what she said, he told her a thing which he immediately realized was trivial and silly: "He has a gun, for one thing."

Bella Cratty did not go on drinking coffee immediately, but not due to anything Parkhearst had said except his pronouncing of Fenton's name. There had, of course, in their five years of marriage and in their five years of Grainger, been people with guns, and people whom he had found in streets, in parks, in holes, who had turned out to be all right, but now she suddenly felt the last outpost of safety had been reached. Their lives had stopped suddenly, and then were jerked ahead out of her control at last. She felt she was no longer *here.*

"Maybe Grainger *should* meet him," she said in a tone unlike herself, because there was no hysteria or pretending in it, just dull fear, and then she finished the coffee at the same moment her husband finished sewing the button on his coat.

Still holding his needle and thread, he advanced to her and kissed her on the forehead. "I know you hate all this," he said, like a doctor or soldier about to perform an heroic act. "I know you can't get used to all this. Maybe you aren't used to what is me."

Bella had not waited this time for the full effect of the kiss. She got up and quickly went into the front room and began looking out the window with the intensity of one who is about to fly out into space. He followed her there.

"Do you hate me completely?" Parkhearst asked, happy with the sense she had given him permission to go for Fenton.

It was nearly two o'clock, he noted, and she did not give him goodbye and the word to leave.

"Just go, dear," she said at last, and it was not the fact she had put on a martyr's expression in her voice, the voice was the only one that could come from her having chosen, as she had, the life five years before.

"I can't go when you sound like this," he complained. His voice told how much he wanted to go and that it was already past two o'clock.

Yet somehow the strength to give him up did not come to her. He had to find it in her for himself and take it from her.

"Go now, go," she said when he kissed the back of her neck.

"I will," he said, "because I know I'm only hurting you by staying."

Bella nodded.

When he was gone, she watched for him onto the street below. From above she could see him waving and throwing a kiss to her as he moved on down toward Sixty-third Street. He looked younger than Christ still, she said. A boy groom . . . Sometimes people had half-wondered, she knew, if she was his very young mother. She stood there in that stiff height so far above him and yet felt crawling somewhere far down, like a bug in a desert, hot and sticking to ground, and possibly not even any more alive.

AS NECESSARY AS Bella was to his every need for existence, his only feeling of life came when he left her, as today, for a free afternoon. And this afternoon was especially free. There was even the feeling of the happiness death might give. It was only later that life was to be so like death that the idea of dying was meaningless to him, but tonight, he remembered, he had thought of death and it was full of mysterious desirability.

It was one of those heavy days in the city when a late riser is not certain it is getting light or dark, an artificial twilight in which the sounds of the elevated trains and trucks weight darkness the more. Parkhearst hurried on down the interminable street, soon leaving the white section behind, and into the beginning of the colored district. People took no notice of him, he was no stranger to these streets, and besides he was dressed in clothes which without being too poor made him inconspicuous.

He was not looking at the street anyhow today, whose meanness and filth usually gave his soul such satisfaction. His whole mind was on Fenton. Fenton was a small-town boy, and yet all his expression and gestures and being made it right that he should live on this street, where no one really belonged or stayed very long.

It was difficult, though, to see Fenton living in a house, even in the kind of house that would be near Sixty-third Street. There must be some kind of mistake there, he thought.

He went on, pursued by the memory of Fenton's face. Was there more, he wondered out loud, in that face than poverty and a tendency to be tricky if not criminal? What were those eyes conveying, then, some meaning that was truthful and honest over and above his deceit and rottenness?

He was late. He hurried faster. The dark under the elevated made him confuse one street for another. He stopped and in his indecision looked back east toward the direction of the park where he had met Fenton: he feared Fenton had played a trick on him, for there was nothing which resembled a house on the street. He stood in front of a fallen-in building with the handwritten sign in chalk:

THE COME AND SEE RESURRECTION PENTECOSTAL CHURCH.
REVEREND HOSEA GULLEY, PASTOR.

Then walking on, he saw near a never-ending set of vacant lots the house he knew must contain Fenton. It was one of those early twentieth-century houses that have survived by oversight but which look so rotten and devoured that you can't believe they were ever built but that they rotted and mushroomed into existence and that their rot was their first and last growth.

There was no number. It was a color like green and yellow. Around the premises was a fence of sharp iron, cut like spears.

He began knocking on the immense front door and then waiting as though he knew there would be no answer.

As nobody stirred, he began calling out the name of his new friend. Then he heard some faint moving around in the back and finally Fenton, looking both black and pale, appeared through the frosted glass of the inner door and stared out. His face greeted Parkhearst without either pleasure or recognition, and he advanced mechanically and irritably, as though the door had blown open and he was coming to close it.

"No wonder you had trouble finding it," Parkhearst said when Fenton unlocked the door and let him in.

"He's having a bad spell, that's why I'm in a hurry," Fenton explained.

"Who?" Parkhearst closed the door behind him.

"Claire, my brother Claire."

They went through a hallway as long as a half city block to a small room in which there was a dwarflike cot with a large mattress clinging to it and a crippled immense chest of drawers supported by only three legs. The window was boarded up and there was almost no light coming from a dying electric bulb hung from the high ceiling.

On the bed lay a young boy dressed in overall pants and a green sweater. He looked very pale but did not act in pain.

"He says he can't walk now," Fenton observed. "Claire, can't you say *hello* to the visitor?" Fenton went over to the bed and touched Claire on the shoulder.

"He keeps asking me why we can't move on. To a real house, I suppose," Fenton explained softly to Parkhearst. "And that worries him. There are several things that worry him," Fenton said in a bored voice.

"Look," Claire said cheerfully and with energy, pointing to the wall. There were a few bugs moving rather rapidly across the cracked calcimine. "Sit down in this chair," Fenton said and moved the chair over to Parkhearst.

"Do you really think," Fenton began on the subject that was closest to him too, "that we're *in* the right house maybe?"

Parkhearst did not speak, feeling unsure how to begin. For one thing, he was not positive that the small boy who was called Claire was not feebleminded, but the longer he looked the more he felt the boy was reasonably intelligent but probably upset by the kind of life he was leading with Fenton. He therefore did not reply to Fenton's question at once, and Fenton repeated it, almost shouting. He had gotten very much more excited since they had met in the park the evening before.

Parkhearst was noticing that Claire followed his brother with his eyes around the room with a look of both intense approval and abject dependence. It was plain that between him and nothing there was only Fenton.

"We've come to the end of our rope, I guess," Fenton said, almost forgetting that Parkhearst had not replied to his question.

"No," Parkhearst said, but Fenton hardly heard him now, talking so rapidly that his spit flew out on all sides of his mouth. He talked about their mother's funeral and how they had come to this house all because Kincaid had known them back in West Virginia and had promised them a job here. Then suddenly he picked up a book that Claire had under the bedclothes and showed it to Parkhearst as though it was both something uncommon and explanatory of their situation. The book, old and ripped, was titled *Under the Trees*, a story about logging.

"Doesn't anybody else live here?" Parkhearst inquired at last.

"We haven't heard nobody," Fenton replied. "There's so many bugs it isn't surprising everybody left, if they was here," he went on. "But Claire says there is," he looked in the direction of his brother. "Claire feels there is people here."

"I hear them all the time," Claire said.

"No, there is nobody here," Parkhearst assured both of them. "This is a vacant house and you must have made a mistake when you came in here. Or your friend Kincaid played a joke on you," he finished, seeing at once by their expression he should not have added this last sentence.

"Anyhow," Parkhearst continued awkwardly while Fenton stared at him with his strange eyes, "it's no place for you, especially with Claire sick. I think I have a plan for you, though," Parkhearst said, as though thinking through a delicate problem.

Fenton walked over very close to him as though Parkhearst were about to hand him a written paper which would explain everything and tell him and Claire what to do in regard to the entire future.

"I think Grainger will give you the help you need," he explained. He had forgotten that Fenton knew nothing about her.

Fenton turned away and looked out the boarded window. Evidently he had expected some immediate help, and Parkhearst had only spoken a name like a matchbox, Grainger, adding later that was the last name of a wealthy woman that nobody ever called by her first name. This was discouraging because of course Fenton knew he could never do anything to please anybody with such a name.

"Grainger will like you," Parkhearst went on doggedly, knowing he was not moving Fenton at all.

"You would be interested in going to her mansion at least," he said.

Claire, following Fenton's example, showed likewise no interest in the "great woman."

"If you promise me you will go with me to the house of the 'great woman,'" Parkhearst said (using that phrase preciously and purposely just as he had mentioned Grainger without explaining who she was or that she was a woman), "I assure you we'll be able to help you between us. Really help."

He had not finished this speech when he remembered what Bella had told him about his handing over Fenton to Grainger.

Fenton turned now from the boarded window and faced him. His whole appearance had grown surprisingly ominous as though Parkhearst had destroyed some great promise and hope.

"We don't have no choice," Fenton said, his words more gentle than his expression, and he looked at Claire, although he addressed his words to no one.

"I don't know what I'll do in the house of a greatwoman," Fenton went on. "Why do you call her *great*?"

"Oh I don't know," Parkhearst replied airily. "Of course she isn't, really. But is anybody? Was anybody ever?"

"I never did hear anybody called that," Fenton said. He looked at Claire as though he might have heard someone called that.

"Why is she great?" he wondered aloud again.

Parkhearst felt flustered despite his years of looking and collecting the "material" and talking with the most intractable of persons.

"If you come tomorrow, I feel you'll understand," Parkhearst told him, getting up. "I don't see why you act like this when you're in trouble." Then: "Where's your gun," he said irritably.

Fenton put his hand quickly to his pocket. "Fuck you," he said, feeling nothing there.

"Don't think I can get offended," Parkhearst said. "Neither your talk nor your acts. You just seemed a bit young to have any gun."

"Young?" Fenton asked, as though this had identified his age at last. His face flushed and for the first time Parkhearst noticed that there was a scar across his lip and chin.

"Please come, Fenton, when we want to help you," he said, almost as soft as some sort of prayer.

"I don't like to go in big houses. You said she was rich, too. Claire and me don't have the clothes for it. . . . Say, are you trying to make us a show for somebody?" Fenton asked, as though he had begun to understand Parkhearst. His face went no particular color as this new thought took hold of him. "Or use us? You're not trying to *use* us, are you?"

When he asked that last question, Parkhearst felt vaguely a kind of invisible knife cut through the air at him. He could not follow the sources of Fenton's knowledge. At times the boy talked dully, oafish, and again he showed a complete and intuitive knowledge of the way things were and had to be.

"I want to help you," Parkhearst finally said in a womanish hurt voice.

"Why?" Fenton said in an impersonal anger. Then quickly the fight in him collapsed. He sat down on the cheap kitchen chair occupied a moment before by Parkhearst Cratty.

"All right, then, I'll come for your sake. But Claire has to stay here."

"All right, then, Fenton. I'll be here for you."

They argued a little about the hour.

Fenton did not look at Parkhearst as he said goodbye, but Claire waved to him as though seated in a moving vehicle, his head constantly turning to keep sight of the visitor.

"WHO IS THAT, Fenton?" Claire asked as soon as his brother had returned from closing the front door.

"He's a man who writes things about people," Fenton said. "He wants me to tell him things so he can write about me."

Fenton looked up at the high sick ceiling; the thought of the man writing or listening to him in order to write of him was too odd ever to be understood.

"Like you write in your little note papers?"

"No," Fenton answered, and turned to look at Claire. "I only put things down there to clear up in me what we are going to do next. Understand?"

"Why can't I see them, then, Fenton?"

"Because you can't, hear?"

"I want to read your little note papers!"

Fenton began to slap Claire, rather gently at first, and then with more force. "Don't mention it again," he said, hitting him again. "Hear?"

Claire's weeping both hurt Fenton deeply and gave him a kind of pleasure, as though in the hitting the intense burden of Claire was being lightened a little.

He had written once in the "note papers" a thought which had caused him great puzzlement. This thought was that just as he had wished Mama dead, so that he felt the agent of her death, so now he wanted Claire to be dead, and despite the fact that the only two people in the world he had loved were Mama and Claire.

Then he had to realize that the thing which stung him most about Claire when they were with strangers was his brother's not being quite right and that when he had been with the writer he had not felt this pain. There was this about the man who had turned up in the park, you did not feel any pain about telling him things, things almost as awful as those he had put down in the note papers.

"Why is it?" Fenton asked, raising his voice as though addressing a large group of people, "when I am so young I am so pissed-off feeble and low?"

Claire shook his head as he was accustomed to when Fenton put these questions to him. He had never answered any of them, and yet Fenton asked more and more of them when he knew that Claire did not know the answers.

Then Claire, seeing his chance, watching his brother narrowly, said, without any preparation: "I heard God again in the night."

Fenton tried to quiet himself in the tall room. It was always much easier to calm yourself outdoors or in a farmhouse, but in a small but high room like this when sorrow is heard it is hard to be quiet and calm. Fenton nevertheless made his voice cool as he said, "Claire, what did I tell you about talking like that?"

"I did." Claire began to cry a little.

"Are you going to quit talking like that or ain't you?" Fenton said, the anger welling up in him stronger than any coolness he had put into his voice.

"Don't hit me when I tell you, Fenton," Claire cried on. "Don't you want to know I hear Him?"

Fenton's hands loosened slightly. He felt cramps in his insides.

"I told you those was dreams," Fenton said.

"They ain't! I hear it all day when I don't dream. . . ."

"Maybe somebody lives here, that's all." Fenton waited as though to convince himself. "I could forgive you if you dreamed about Mama and she come running to you to say comforting things to you. But you always talk about God. And I strongly doubt . . ."

"Don't say it again, Fenton, don't say it again!" Claire sat up in bed.

". . . not only strongly doubt but know He's not real. . . ."

Claire let out a strange little cry when he heard the blasphemy and fell back on the bed. Claire fell so awkwardly it made Fenton laugh.

After this, Fenton felt the cramps again and he knew he must go out and get a drink. Yet because neither of them had had anything to eat since morning he feared that if he began drinking now he would not remember to get Claire anything to eat.

He began to rub Claire's temples gently. If only they were safe from trouble he would always be kind to Claire, but trouble always made him mean.

"It's so crappy late out!" he began again, moving away from Claire.

"Why does it have to feel so late out everywhere?" This was one of the things which he had written on the note papers so he wouldn't feel so burned up and dizzy. "Even the writer says I am so young," Fenton muttered on, "yet why do I feel I only got two minutes more to do with?"

"It's late, all right," Claire said, still weeping some, but with a happy look on his face now. The small boy had gotten up out of bed and was walking over to where Fenton now stood near the window.

"You heard me tell you to stay in bed, didn't you. . . . Didn't you hear, crapface?"

The boy paused there in the middle of the room, his mouth open disgustingly. But he had already turned his mind away from Claire. He whirled out of the room and was gone.

"He forgot his gun," Claire said looking out into the awful night of the hall. "He don't know how to use it anyhow," he finished and went back to the little bed.

Everything had changed so much since he had been Mama's son, nothing as little as forgetting a gun was remarkable.

"He's gone, he's gone," Claire kept repeating to himself. "Fenton's gone," he repeated on and on until he had fallen asleep again.

FENTON HAD SOON found the taverns where his existence aroused no particular interest or comment. People occasionally noticed his accent or his haircut, but generally they ignored him. There was such an endless row of taverns and the street itself was so endless he could always choose a different tavern for each day and each drink. In the end he went to the places that served both colored and white. It would have been unreal of him to Mama had she known, but this kind of tavern made him feel the easiest, perhaps it was more like home.

He knew now (he began all over again) that Kincaid was not coming to find them in the house. And as he went on with his drink he knew that nobody was ever coming to the house because it was the "latest" time in his life and maybe the "latest" in the world.

"Then where will we end up?" he said quickly, aloud. He felt that some of the customers must have looked at him, but when he said nothing more nobody came over to him or said anything. He got out a pencil stub and wrote something on the note papers.

"Things don't go anywhere in our lives," he wrote. "Sometimes somebody like Mama dies and the whole world stops or begins to move backwards, but nothing happens to us, even her dying don't get us anywhere except maybe back. Yet you have to go on waiting, it's the one thing nobody lets up on you for. Like now we're doing for Kincaid and for what?"

Someone had left a newspaper on the bar, open to the want ad section. Fenton began reading these incomprehensible notifications of jobs. Someone once had told him, perhaps Kincaid, that nobody was ever hired this way, they were only put in there because the employers had to do it, and actually, this somebody had told him, they were really all hired to begin with, probably when you read about them.

Fenton remembered again that he did not know how to do anything. He had no skills, no knowledge. That was why the big old house with tall rooms was getting more ghosty for him, it was so much like the way he was inside himself, the house didn't work at all, and he was all stopped inside himself too just like the house. That was why it was like a trap, he said.

As he drank a little more he decided he must move on to another drinking place because the bartender had begun to watch him write in the note papers too much and it scared him.

He went on in search of the next place, but before he reached it he saw the All Night Theater, a movie house that never closed. Instead of choosing another drinking place, he decided to choose this, for the price of admission was nearly the same as that of a beer.

There was the same sad smell inside, a faint stink from old men and a few boys who had been out in the open, standing or lying on the pavement during part of the night. The seats did not act as though they were required to hold you off the floor. Faces twisted around to look at you, or somebody's hand sometimes came out of the dark and touched you as though to determine whether you were flesh or not.

Fenton did not notice or care about any of these things. He scarcely looked at the picture, and half the audience must have been sleeping or looking at the floor, at nothing.

HE DID NOT know what time he woke up in the All Night Theater. The audience had thinned out a little. The screen showed a horse and a man crossing a desert, walking as though they were not going to go much longer if they didn't find some water or perhaps just a cool place to stop.

It was then that Fenton remembered Parkhearst Cratty and the greatwoman. For the first time he began to think about them as having some slight meaning, some relationship to himself. That is, they knew about him, and he existed for them. He had gotten as far down in the dumps as possible and still be alive, and now he began to come up a little out of where he was and to think about what Parkhearst Cratty was jawing about.

The thought that anybody called the greatwoman should want to see him struck him suddenly as so funny that he laughed out loud. Then he stopped and looked around him, but nobody was looking at him. The dead world of the shadows on the screen seemed to look at him just then more than the men around him.

Fenton sat a little while longer in the All Night Theater holding his notebook down to a little of the light at the end of the aisle so that he might write down some more of what he was thinking. Then having written a little more, he gazed at the want ads again that he had carried along with him and saw the words MEN MEN MEN under the difficult light.

Finally he got hungry and walked out into the gray street. It was six o'clock in the morning and it would be a long day until night came and brought Parkhearst Cratty and his plans.

Fenton went into a cafe called Checker where some colored men were drinking orange pop. He ordered a cup of black coffee, and then drinking that, he ordered another. Then he ordered some rolls and ate part of those. After that he ordered some coffee and rolls to take out, and started home to Claire.

Just before getting to the house, he went back to a small tavern he had missed before and had a whiskey.

It was funny, he reflected, that before coming here to the city with its parks and vacant houses he had almost never had a drink, and now he had it, quite a bit.

CLAIRE STARED AT him, his face red and swollen from bites. Fenton had him get up and they began going through the mattress looking for the bugs.

"Where was you?" Claire wanted to know.

"All Night Movie."

This answer perfectly satisfied Claire.

"Why don't you drink the coffee I brought you and eat those rolls?"

"I ain't hungry, Fenton."

"Drink the coffee like I tell you."

Fenton kept looking at the mattress. "I don't see any of the bastards," he said. "They must be inside the fucking mattress."

"Fenton," Claire soothed him. "I didn't dream last night at all or hear anything."

"So?" Fenton spoke crossly. He set the mattress down and then lazily began eating the rolls Claire had not touched.

"I didn't even feel the bugs biting," Claire said, pushing his face close to Fenton to show him, but his voice trailed off as he saw Fenton's heavy lack of interest in what he had done and thought.

Then all at once Fenton saw his brother's face, which was almost disfigured from the bites. Fenton's own fear and amazement communicated themselves frightfully to Claire.

"You look Christ awful," Fenton cried.

"Don't scare me now, Fenton," Claire began to whimper.

"I don't aim to scare you," Fenton said with growing irritability. "Have you been crying over Mama or is your face just swelled from bugs?"

"I don't know," Claire said, and he quit whimpering.

There was something terribly old and pinched now in Claire's small face.

Fenton took him by the hands and looked at his face closer.

"Ain't you well or what?" he said, the irritation coming and going in his voice, but finally yielding to a kind of sadness. "Why don't you tell me what is bothering you?" he went on.

He put his mouth on the top of Claire's head, and half-opened his lips noticing the funny little boy smell of his hair.

"You can tell me if you have been thinking about God now, if you want to, Claire."

"I ain't been thinking about Him," he said.

"Well," Fenton said, "you can if you want to. It don't matter anyhow."

"I don't think about Him," Claire said, as if from far off.

"I think I'll go to bed now," Fenton complained, looking at the cruelly narrow cot. "You slept some, didn't you, Claire."

"Yes," Claire said, a tired sad duty in his voice.

"Can I walk around outdoors now?" Claire asked, watching Fenton's oblivious brooding face.

"Yes," Fenton replied slowly. "I guess it's all right if the house is open when it's daylight. Nobody ain't coming in anyhow.

"Don't get lost, though," Fenton went on quietly as Claire began to go out.

"What's going on inside the little thing's mind?" Fenton said to himself. He loosened his heavy belt and lay down on the cot.

Fenton thought about how Claire thought about Mama. He himself thought a lot about her when actually he wasn't very aware even that he was thinking about her. Maybe he thought about her all the time and didn't even know it. But he never thought she was waiting for him on some distant star as Claire did.

"Claire," he said, beginning to sleep, "why is it one of us is even weaker than the other. When West Virginia was tough why did we come clear over here? . . ."

Even though it was day it was night really, always, in this city and night like night in caves here in the house.

Fenton lay thinking of the long time before Parkhearst Cratty would come. He thought of Parkhearst as a kind of magicman who would show different magic tricks to him, but he knew not one would take on him.

"No damn one," he said, becoming asleep.

IT WAS EVEN darker somehow when he awoke, and he knew at once that Parkhearst Cratty was there, shaking him.

"Wake up, West Virginia," Parkhearst was saying.

Fenton's mouth moved as though to let out laughter but none came, as though there were no more sound at all in him now.

"She's waiting for us," Parkhearst said.

Fenton said quiet obscene words and Parkhearst waited a little longer, situated as though nowhere in the dark.

"Where's Claire?" Parkhearst wondered vaguely.

"Ain't he here?" Fenton said.

"No," Parkhearst said, a kind of uneasiness growing in him again.

"Claire went out, but he'll be back," Fenton said, remembering.

Then when Parkhearst did not say anything in reply, Fenton said rather angrily: "I said he'd be back."

"Well, let's go, then," Parkhearst said lightly. "She gets cross when people are late," he explained.

Fenton held on to his belt as though that were what was to lift him out of bed, then got up, and turned on the light.

"You're dressed up!" He looked at Parkhearst and then down at himself.

They suddenly were both looking at Fenton's shoes, as though they couldn't help it, and as they both saw they were so miserable and ridiculous, they had to look at them objectively as horrors.

"I'm not really dressed up," Parkhearst said weakly, feeling the weakness come over him again which he always felt in Fenton's presence. "But come on, Fenton," he said, thinking of the boy's toes slightly coming through the shoes. "She's sent a taxi for us, and it's waiting."

Fenton threw a look back at the room. "So long, house," he said, and he actually waved at the room, Parkhearst noted.

They said almost nothing on the way to the greatwoman's house. Fenton kept his head down as though he were praying or sick in his stomach. He did not look out even when Parkhearst pointed out things that might have had a personal interest to him: the sight of the park where they had met, or the police station.

At last the taxi came to the house. Fenton hesitated, as though he might not get out after all. "Is this a mansion?" he asked.

Parkhearst looked at him closely. Fenton's words always had an ambiguousness about them, but there could be no ambiguousness when you studied his face: he meant just what he said, and perhaps that made the words odd.

They could hear the music from the outside.

"That is the new music the musicians are playing," Parkhearst explained. "Grainger doesn't really listen to it, but she has the musicians come because there is nothing else left to do, and it draws her circle of people to her."

Without knocking, they entered what was the most immense room Fenton had ever seen. It was almost as dark, however, as the house where he and Claire had been waiting, and the ceiling was no taller. There were a number of people sitting in corners except for one large corner of the room where some colored musicians were playing.

At the far end of the room on a slightly raised little platform, in a mammoth chair, Grainger, the greatwoman, sat, or rather hung over one side of the arm.

"My God, we're late after all," Parkhearst exclaimed. "She's too drunk to know us, I'm afraid."

Fenton began to feel a little easier once he was inside the mansion. No one had paid him the least attention. It was, in fact, he saw with relief, not unlike the All Night Theater, for whatever the people were doing here in the mansion, they were paying absolutely no attention to him or Parkhearst or perhaps to anything. Yet they must have seen him, for he could see their heads move and hear their voices as they talked softly among themselves. And again like the All Night Theater, they were about half colored and half white.

Parkhearst was not doing anything as Fenton's attention returned slowly to him. They were in the middle of the great room, and his guide merely stood there watching Grainger. Finally, as though after a struggle with himself, he took Fenton's hand angrily and said, "Come over here, we have to go through with this."

They went up to the woman in the chair. She was possibly forty and her face was still beautiful although her mouth was slightly twisted and her throat was creased now and fat. Her eyes, although not focused on the two young men who were standing in front of her, were extremely beautiful and would have been intelligent had they not been so vacant. Whenever Parkhearst addressed her, she would immediately turn her head in the other direction.

"Grainger, I have brought Fenton Riddleway here to see you, just as you told me to do."

She did not say a word, although Parkhearst knew that she had heard him.

"She's angry," Parkhearst said, like a radio commentator assigned to a historical event which is hopelessly delayed. He sighed as though he could no longer breathe in this atmosphere.

"Everything is getting to be more difficult than anything is really worth," he pronounced.

"Please look at Fenton at least and we will leave then," he addressed Grainger.

Suddenly the greatwoman laughed and took Parkhearst's hands in her very small ones. Parkhearst gave a sound expressing relief, though his face did not lose the agonized look it had assumed the moment he recognized she was drunk.

"Are you going to be good now?" he inquired in a calmer voice.

She laughed cheerfully, like a young girl.

Fenton thought that she looked beautiful at that moment and he looked at her dress which was the kind he felt a princess in old books might have worn; it was so frighteningly white and soft and there was so much of it, it seemed to fill the little platform on which they were now all standing.

Then as Grainger's eyes moved away from Parkhearst they settled slowly and gloomily upon Fenton. They immediately expressed hostility or a kind of sullen anger. Then looking away from both of them, she picked up a drink she had placed on the floor by the chair and took a swallow so deep that she seemed to be talking to someone in the end of the glass.

"Haven't you had enough, tonight?" Parkhearst said gently. "It's that Holland stuff, too, and you promised me you wouldn't ever take that again."

"Cut that, Parkhearst, cut that," she said suddenly. "You've been boring me for a year now and I'm not listening to any more."

This was said in a tone that was tough and which was hard to connect with the soft long dress and the fine eyes.

"Well, give us something to drink then," Parkhearst retorted. "If you're sobered up enough now to be ugly, you can remember your duties as the hostess."

Grainger pointed contemptuously to a table where there were bottles and glasses. Then her gaze returned to Fenton, and the same hostility and suspicion crossed her face.

"Who is this?" she said, putting her hand on his face as one might touch what is perhaps a door in a dark house.

Fenton could only stand there, allowing her hand to be on him and looking down at her dress. He found that her gaze and touch were not unlike the soft glances that the characters on the screen of the All Night Theater had given him last night, looking down while he wrote what he had to write in the note papers.

His meekness and his quiet partially calmed the anger of her expression.

"Don't you like Fenton, Grainger?" Parkhearst said, returning with drinks for himself and Fenton.

"Why didn't you fill mine up too?" she said, turning bitterly to Parkhearst.

"Because you've had enough. And I'm taking the drink you now have away from you," he said, reaching for her glass.

Grainger smiled at this and put the glass into his hand.

"Now, Grainger, wake up, clear awake, and look at this boy I brought to meet you. You're always wanting to meet new people and then when I bring them to you, you get into a state like this and don't even know me when I come in. This is Fenton Riddleway."

"I saw him," the greatwoman said. She kept eyeing her drink, which Parkhearst had set on the table near her.

"How do you feel about the musicians tonight?" she inquired suddenly.

"I've heard them when they sounded more advanced," Parkhearst said. "But I wasn't listening to them at all. . . . Anyhow, the new music sounds only like its name to me now. It was only new that first night."

"So you brought Fenton to see me," she said, looking now for the first time without hostility at the guest.

Fenton had finished half his drink and both he and Parkhearst had sat down on the floor at the feet of Grainger.

She began to grow quiet now that they were both with her and both drinking. *If everything*, she had said once a long time ago, *could be a garden with the ones you always want and with drinking for ever and ever.*

"Do you think you're going to like Fenton?" Parkhearst began again.

"If you want me to, I guess I can," Grainger answered. She looked at her drink on the table but then evidently gave up the struggle to have it.

"He looks a little like Russell," Grainger said without any preparation for such a statement.

The remark made Parkhearst go a little white because Russell had been everything. Russell had been her first husband, the one who when he died, people said, made her go off the deep end and drink for ten years, to end up the way she was now.

"Only he's *not*," Grainger added. But she added this only because she saw Parkhearst change color. "Nobody could quite be Russell again," she said.

When Parkhearst did not reply, holding his face in a wounded quivering expression, the greatwoman flared up. "I said, could they, Parkhearst?"

"Just nobody could resemble Russell," Parkhearst said.

"Well, all right, then, why didn't you say that before?" she scolded.

She ignored his contemptuous silence and acted happy. "Russell was the last of any men that there were," she began, turning to Fenton. "He didn't love me, of course, but I couldn't live without him, every five minutes having to touch him or see him coming somewhere near me. . . ."

"That isn't true, Grainger, and you know it. Why do you lie to this boy, making out that Russell wasn't crazy about you? . . ." Then he stopped as he realized how deadly it was going to be ever to get started on Russell all over again.

Upstairs, he wanted to tell Fenton, there was that memorial room to him everybody has heard about somewhere but never seen, a shrine to his being, with hundreds of immense photographs, mementos, clothes, and everywhere fresh flowers every day. Grainger herself never went into the shrine, and Negro women kept the flowers fresh and the holy places dusted.

"Crazy . . . about *me*?" Grainger shot at him and a look of unparalleled meanness came over her face, so that she resembled at that moment a stuffed carnivore he had once seen in a museum. "Nobody was ever crazy about me. The only reason anybody's here now is I have more money than anybody else in town to slake them."

Parkhearst looked up at the word *slake*; he could not ever remember hearing her use it before.

"Look at them!" she shouted, pointing to the dim figures in the next room. "Nobody was ever crazy about me."

Both Fenton and Parkhearst gazed back at the people in the next room as though to see them, in the greatwoman's word, being *slaked*.

Then her anger subsided, and she gave Fenton a brief oversweet smile. Growing a bit more serious and commanding, she said: "Come over here, Fenton Riddleway."

Parkhearst gave a severe nod with his head for Fenton to go to her.

Fenton had hardly gotten to her chair when she reached out and took his hand in hers and held it for a moment. She laughed quietly, kissed his hand in so strange a manner that the action had no easy meaning, and then released it.

Parkhearst had risen meanwhile and poured himself and Fenton another shot of gin.

"You think I should have more?" Fenton said in a way that recalled Claire.

"Well naturally, yes," Parkhearst said, and trembled with nervousness. The comparison of Fenton with Russell did not augur too well. He felt a kind of throbbing jealousy as well as fear. It was the biggest compliment that Grainger had ever given to any of the men he had brought to her house. He felt suddenly that he had given Grainger too much in giving her Fenton and Fenton too much in giving him to her.

Parkhearst realized with a suddenness which resembled a break in his reason that he needed both Grainger and Fenton acutely, and that if he lost them to each other, he would not survive this time at all.

In the midst of his anguish, his eye fell upon both of them coolly, almost as though he had not seen either of them before. It was outrageous, rather sad, and frightening all at once; not so much because she had a dress that was too fine for royalty and Fenton looked somehow seedier than any living bum, but because something about the way they were themselves, both together and apart, made them seem more real and less real than anybody living he had ever known.

"He's Russell!" Grainger said finally, without any particular emphasis.

"No, he's not," Parkhearst replied firmly but with the anger beginning to come to make his words shake in his mouth.

"He is," she said, louder.

"No, Grainger, you know these things don't happen twice. Nothing does."

"Just for tonight he is," Grainger replied, staring at Fenton.

"Not even for tonight. He just isn't Russell, Grainger. Look again."

"I'm going to have a drink now," she threatened him. Half to her own surprise she saw Parkhearst make no attempt to prevent her. She walked rigidly, balancing herself with outstretched hands, over to the little table, filled her glass with a tremendous drain of the bottle, and drank half the draught: at once.

"Grainger!" Parkhearst was frightened, forgetting he had permitted her to get up at all.

"All right, he isn't Russell, then. Or he is Russell. What difference! He can stay here, though. . . . Does he need anything?"

The drink, Parkhearst thought, perhaps has sobered her.

She sat down in the great chair and began staring at Fenton again. Then his clothes at last caught her attention.

"Would you accept a suit?" she began. "One of Russell's suits," the greatwoman said, turning her face away from Parkhearst as though to shield her words from him and give them only to Fenton.

Fenton in turn looked at Parkhearst for a clue, and Parkhearst could only look down, knowing that Fenton would never understand the generosity that was being offered, the giving away of the clothes of the dead young Christ.

"Why don't you go upstairs?" She turned in rage now on Parkhearst. "Why don't you go upstairs with your jealous eyes and give him one of Russell's suits?"

As her face lay back in the chair, burning with rage, Parkhearst saw how mistaken he had been about her ever being sobered up by a drink. At that very moment the musicians stopped playing the new music for the evening, the hostess fell over, slightly, upsetting her drink, and then with almost no noise slipped to the floor and lay perfectly still, her drinking glass near her hand, without even a goodnight, lying there, as Parkhearst observed, looking a little too much like Hamlet's mother.

WE MAY AS well go to my house now," Parkhearst said, after they had got one of Russell's suits on Fenton.

"What shall we do with my old clothes?" Fenton wondered, looking at them with almost as much wonder now as other people had.

Parkhearst hesitated. "We'll take them," he said. "This way."

They went downstairs away from the "shrine" and walked past the room where Grainger was lying on an immense silver bed with red coverings. She had her clothes still on. Parkhearst hesitated near the bed.

"I suppose we should say goodnight to her, in case she's conscious."

They both stood there in dead silence while Parkhearst tried to make up his mind.

"Grainger!" he called. Then he suddenly laughed as he saw the serious expression on Fenton's face.

"She's just out, she won't be up and around for God knows when," Parkhearst explained in his bored tone. "When she gets in these states she lies till she gets up or until they find her. I will have to come over here tomorrow and see how things are. . . ."

Then for the first time since they had been in the "shrine," Parkhearst gave Fenton a more critical look. Russell's suit had been a close enough fit all right; the greatwoman had not been too drunk to understand the relative sizes of the two men, although the trousers were a bit too short in the legs. The suit made a tremendous change, of course, and yet the boy who looked out from this absurdly rich cloth seemed to belong in it, despite the expression of pain mingled with rage imprinted on his mouth. He was a Russell of some kind in the clothes.

Parkhearst gave him a last look directly in the eye.

"My wife will be asleep," Parkhearst told him in a rather cross voice, "but if we speak low, she won't hear us. Anyhow we have to have coffee."

PARKHEARST'S HOME WAS an apartment on the fifth floor of a building that leaned forward slightly as if it would bend down to the street.

"I forgot you had a wife," Fenton remarked, looking at him vaguely. "I never thought of you as married."

"A lot of people can't," Parkhearst admitted. "I suppose it's because I never had a job, never worked."

Parkhearst observed with some satisfaction that this made no impression on Fenton. He believed that if he had said he had murdered someone, for instance, Fenton would have accepted this statement with the same indifferent air.

That, as Parkhearst was beginning to see more and more, was the main thing about Fenton, his being able to accept nearly anything. For one so young it was unusual. He accepted the immense dreariness of things as though there were no other possibility in the shape of things.

A cat came out of the door as they entered the apartment. They proceeded down a long hallway to a kitchen.

"I'll throw your old clothes on this bench," Parkhearst said. Then he began to fumble with the coffee can.

Before he began to measure out the coffee he stopped as though he thought somebody was calling to him from the front of the apartment. Then when he did not hear his wife's voice, he began to boil the water for the coffee.

Fenton put his head down on the tiny kitchen table before which he sat.

"Don't go to sleep, Fenton. You can't spend the night here. My wife would die. . . . And Claire must be worrying about you."

"Not Claire," Fenton mumbled. "I thought I told you that we sleep at different times, on account of the bed being so small, and the bugs and all. There are hundreds of bugs." He began to think of the anguish they cause. "They crawl up and down, sometimes they go fast, and you can never find them when they bite. They stink like old woodsheds."

"Bugs are awful," Parkhearst agreed. "But," he went on, "about Claire. He may not miss you, but is he safe alone?"

"I'm too sick to care," Fenton said, his head on the table now.

"How are you sick?" Parkhearst wondered.

"Inside," Fenton replied, still not taking his head off the table and talking into the wood like a colored fortune teller Parkhearst had once known. "Where your soul's supposed to be," he spoke again.

Parkhearst stared at him.

"If there was a God," Fenton said quickly, raising his head from the table and giving Parkhearst an accusing look, "none of this would happen."

"Oh, it might, Fenton," Parkhearst answered. "You don't think He's all-powerful, do you?"

"Do you believe in Him?" Fenton wondered.

"I don't believe but I'm always thinking about it somehow."

"Do you believe Claire is dying?" Fenton said quickly.

"No," Parkhearst answered.

"I keep seeing him dead," Fenton said.

Parkhearst handed Fenton a cup of coffee. Then he sat down, facing Fenton. They both drank their coffee without continuing the discussion. Parkhearst from time to time would listen intently to see if Bella called to him, but there was no sound, no matter how many times he stopped to listen.

"I want to be dead like a bug," Fenton said and laid his head down on the table again.

"Drink all of that coffee and then I'll get you some more."

Parkhearst watched the thick hair come loose from the head and creep over the table's edge like a strange unfolding plant.

"Is this the first time you've ever been drunk?" Parkhearst's voice came from far away.

"I drink nearly all the time," Fenton said, and some coffee began to trickle down the side of his mouth. "When I go home," he went on, "Claire will be dead. I will be happy, like a great load has been taken off my neck, and then I will probably fly into a thousand pieces and disappear. I am sick of him just the same, dead or alive. He makes it too hard for me, just like Mama did. Both him and her talked too much about God and how we would all meet at His Throne on the Final Day. . . . Do you disbelieve in the Throne too?" he looked up at Parkhearst.

The writer watched him, silent.

Fenton was watching him also, almost as though from behind his thick disheveled hair.

"Keep drinking the coffee," Parkhearst said in a soft voice. He felt weak lest Bella should get up and see this. Then he began to feel irritated seeing Fenton in Russell's clothing.

"Grainger is an idiot," Parkhearst said.

"Are you in love with me too?" Fenton asked Parkhearst, but the writer merely sat there drinking, as though he had not heard.

Fenton did not say any more for a long time. Perhaps ten minutes passed this way in the silence of the city night; that is a silence in which although one cannot really say *this is a sound I am hearing now*, many little contractions and movements like the springs of a poorly constructed machine make one feel that something will break with a sudden crash and perhaps destroy everyone.

Fenton knocked his cup off the table and it broke evenly in two at Parkhearst's feet.

"What did you think of the *church* Grainger has for Russell?" Parkhearst said, getting up for another cup.

He poured coffee into the cup and handed it to his friend. "Drink this."

Fenton half sat up and gulped down some more of the coffee.

"Did you hear what I asked about her *church* for him?" Parkhearst began again.

"Why did she love Russell so?" Fenton asked, and the whites of his eyes suddenly extinguished his pupils so that he looked like a statue.

"He was nothing," Parkhearst said. "Rather beautiful. His mind worked all right, I guess. He was nothing. He had so little personality he looked all right in all kinds of clothes. I think he had millions of life insurance policies. He was a blank except for one thing. He loved Grainger. I think maybe he was the one started calling her by her last name, and now nobody calls her by her first. Grainger didn't love him, but he told her he loved her every ten minutes. It was funny, I could never figure it out, why he loved her. I used to stare at him to try to understand who he was. I think I know who Grainger is, but not Russell. Then he died in his car one night. Nobody knows what from. They said his heart. And he had all these life insurance policies. He was rich though before, owned factories and mines and patents and things. After that Grainger never had to think about work. But I think she's spent nearly all she has. When she has spent the last of it she will have to die too. . . ."

Parkhearst's voice ended with a little sound like an old phonograph record stopping but still running. He had not given the speech for any reason except the pleasure he took in telling it. "The way they found him in the car is so beautiful. He had been out drinking all night, and of course he and Grainger together. He said goodbye to her from that car he had from Italy, and she went dragging into her bedroom, not very much like Shakespeare but like the girl in Shakespeare, they threw kisses into and out of the balcony, and then

Grainger fell down dead drunk on her bed, and Russell still sat out there in the Italian car, trying to call somebody because he suddenly, I suppose, felt sick; the coroner said he had felt sick, Russell had opened his vest, and had blown the horn that only sounded like a small chime (the neighbors told about that), and the next morning there he sat in the sun under her house, dead as time. Grainger never mentioned how he died to anybody we know. She doesn't even drink any more than she did then, but there's something different about her, I guess, because after he died she could never change but always had to go on acting herself.

"The *church*," Parkhearst began again, getting up and looking out into the black windows. "What do you think of the *church*?"

"All those photographs of rich people?" Fenton said.

"Yes," Parkhearst nodded seriously. "And those fake poses of her. She knows she is not the woman in those photos, of course, because she wasn't the woman in her own mind Russell said she was.

"Grainger knows the truth about herself," Parkhearst continued, "but it only makes things more impossible for her. And it's really only money that keeps her alive, and it's going, nearly gone."

"You make me sicker than I was," Fenton said suddenly. "Why do you find out all these things about people when they are so sad?"

"I don't know," Parkhearst said softly.

"How do you know all these things?" Fenton said almost desperately. "Do you know about me like that too?" He laid his head down on the table and didn't wait for Parkhearst's answer.

Parkhearst said nothing.

Then Fenton got up. "I got to go back."

"Where?" Parkhearst was curious and anxious.

"The All Night Theater."

"Why don't you tell me about the All Night Theater some time?" Parkhearst asked.

"There ain't nothing to tell. It's what it says, it goes on all night."

"It's like the park then." Parkhearst had a very quiet voice.

Fenton did not say anything, drinking his coffee from the saucer.

"It's morning," Parkhearst announced more cheerfully.

"You can't tell when it's morning in a city place," Fenton said.

"You told me that before," Parkhearst said, "but that is only because you're Fenton that you think that."

THE NEXT DAY, Parkhearst woke up with a headache and the feeling of rags on his tongue. He knew without looking that Bella had gone to work.

He thought of the greatwoman almost at once and before he thought of Fenton. He would have to go to see her at once. She would still be unconscious, the wreck of her evening undisturbed yet by the maids.

His face looked old and thin and brown in the looking glass, old for twenty-nine. Yet how old did that look, except older than Fenton Riddleway?

Then all the part about Grainger and Russell and Russell's resembling Fenton or Fenton's resembling Russell came back.

"I suppose in Grainger's mind," he said aloud to himself, "she thinks she has already taken him over, away from me. Of course it's true. I've given her everybody she ever had."

He had forgotten Russell only because he had never counted him.

A NOT UNUSUAL thing was to smell flowers in front of Grainger's house. Today their perfume was stronger than usual. There was the silence of early day inside of the house, but there was evidence that the maids had come and gone, and noiselessly enough to have left her still sleeping in the front parlor.

The flowers, he noticed, were only roses. Grainger lay on the divan, a queer frayed coverlet over her. A tiny smile covered her mouth.

"Is the Queen of Hell conscious?" he said in a voice that struggled with both eagerness and contempt.

He began kissing her on the eyelids. "Open those big blue eyes."

Grainger opened her eyes, her smile vanished, and the accusing frown returned. "You cheap son of a bitch," she said groggily. "You never loved Russell. You never even would talk about him. You didn't understand his greatness. His going never even moved you."

"Shall I make you some breakfast now?" he wondered.

"You hated Russell."

He kissed her fingers.

"You make me sick. You cheap son of a bitch," she said, looking at him kiss her fingers. "I ought to hate you. Russell hated you. He said you were lacking in the fundamental. That boy you dragged here last night, what's his name? . . ."

Parkhearst told her.

". . . he hates you too. You know so damn much. You sit around seeing things so that you can write them down in a hundred years."

Parkhearst went on holding her fingers as though he were giving her the energy to go on.

He looked longingly at some hot coffee on a nearby table, then letting her hands fall slowly, he got up and went over to the table and poured himself a cup and began sipping.

"And why do we all love you, though, when you stink with cheapness, dishonor, not having probably one human hair on your body. Maybe I love you the most. . . ."

"Don't forget my wife," he said, and the expression *my wife* as he said it had a different quality than that of any other husband who had ever said the words.

"*Your wife!*" she said, getting up and staring at him. "She owns you, but I wouldn't call that loving. Anyhow, she's overpaid. . . ."

"Overpaid?" he said, his mouth dropping slightly.

They were both silent, as though even for them frankness had overstepped itself.

"What was I saying to you when we ran into this quiet period?" she began again.

"About my wife getting too much for her money," he said exhaustedly.

"Who is this Fenton?" she changed topics. "What did you bring him here for?"

"I thought he would be a change for you. You really ordered him anyhow, and have forgotten it."

"I never ordered *him*," she said carefully, drawing the silk coverlet up to her eyebrows. "Did you think he would remind me of Russell?" she put the question with coy crafty innocence, and he felt he would laugh.

"No, Grainger, it didn't occur to me at the time."

"Don't lie to me as though I were your wife!" she lashed at him. "If he hadn't looked a *little* like Russell would you have brought him here then?"

"Yes, I would, Grainger." He smarted now under her attack. "I brought him here because he was so much just himself. This boy is better than Russell," he took final courage to throw at her.

"I'm glad you said *boy*." Grainger was quiet under his blasphemy. "He's a child, really. And I'm an old woman."

Parkhearst waited for her.

"How did you find him?" she went on, muttering now, less irritation in her voice.

"How do I find everybody?" he said, a kind of dull bitterness in his voice.

"I never find anybody at all," she said. "Are you jealous because I did something for him?" she wanted to know suddenly.

"Yes, I suppose," he said. "But after all I wanted to bring him here. I was willing to take the risk."

She saw the flowers for the first time.

"Do you know why I buy all these flowers?" she asked him.

"Of course," he said, impatient at her always changing the subject so abruptly.

"No, you don't," she said with a ridiculous emphasis. "Tell me why I have them then, if you know. . . ."

"Why do you have that church upstairs?" he said.

"Church?" she said, somewhat distracted and looking at him with her back to the window. He had forgotten that this was his private word and that he had not ever used it for her; and yet he had employed it with such force of habit, she knew it was his word and that he must say it all the time when out of her presence.

Recovering from her shock over the word, she began to talk about the flowers again: "I can see now you don't know everything after all."

"If there hadn't been any Russell, of course you wouldn't have flowers," he raised his voice as he would have had he lived an ordinary domestic life with ordinary people.

"Should I go to see him?" She changed to a new line of thought.

He stared at her with almost real anger.

"Should I return his call or not?" she roared. "Don't start being Christ with me again or something will happen."

"It's too silly even for you to say," he told her. "Returning a call to Fenton." His voice, though, softened a bit.

"He is very beautiful, isn't he?" she said. "More than Russell was."

"Grainger, you know we never agree with one another about who is beautiful or who is anything."

"He's more beautiful than Russell," she went on, both musing and commanding. "But there's something not right with him that Russell never had. There was nothing really wrong with Russell."

He looked up briefly at her as though something important had finally been said.

"When should I go visit him?" she asked him eagerly.

"We can't go today." Parkhearst acted bored. "Bella's coming home this afternoon from work."

"I wish you would quit mentioning Bella," she complained. "It's all you talk about . . . You get me involved with this new boy, and then you go off with your wife, and leave me without anything."

"Grainger, don't be a complete idiot all the time."

"*I'll* go," she said. "You'll stay home and entertain that Bella and

I'll go. And every minute," she vituperated, "you'll be thinking of me and him together."

Parkhearst laughed a little, and then the pain of the scene which she had just presented to his imagination bore down with unaccustomed weight.

"You don't even know where he lives," he said. "I can just see you going in there in your finery."

He laughed such a nasty laugh that Grainger found herself listening to it as attentively as one of the "concerts."

THE NEXT THING Fenton remembered was standing in front of a wrestling arena known as Fair City. He was in front of a little wooden gate with his hands put through the partitions as though asking somebody for an admission ticket. It was still early morning, almost no one was on Sixty-third Street; and so, removing his hands from the partitions at last, he began walking in the direction of the house.

Right in front of the house he stopped. He heard several voices singing something vaguely sacred. "It's niggers," he said peevishly, rubbing the back of his neck. He raised his eyes to the Come and See Resurrection Church. He leaned his head then gently over onto the pavement so that it was within a few inches of the curb and some of the coffee he had drunk came up easily. Then he got up and unlocked the door to the house and went inside.

He felt he must look creased and yellow as he opened Claire's door.

Claire was sitting on the kitchen chair but hardly glanced up at Fenton and only nodded in answer to his brother's greeting.

The sound of the colored spiritualists was just faintly audible here.

"How can they shout when it's morning?" Fenton asked, and then as Claire did not say any more, he asked, "I don't suppose anybody called?"

Claire merely stared at him.

"Ain't you all right?" Fenton said, going over to the chair and touching him.

"Dooon't," the boy cried, as though he had touched him on a raw nerve.

"Claire! Are you sick?" Fenton wanted to know.

"Don't touch my head," Claire told him, and Fenton took his hand away.

"Let me get you into bed, and I'll go for coffee and rolls," Fenton told him and he helped him into the cot.

"I don't want none," Claire said and he closed his eyes.

"You didn't notice my new clothes," Fenton complained.

"Yes, I did," Claire replied without opening his eyes.

"Do you like them?" Fenton said, looking around, as though to find some part of the room that would reflect his image.

"Kind of, yeah," Claire answered.

"I'll go for something for you now," Fenton encouraged him, but he didn't go. He kept staring at the deep pallor of Claire. He looked around the room as though there might be something there that would extend help to them.

Fenton looked at himself as he sat there on the chair in his new clothes. He wondered if he was changing; there was something about the wearing of those clothes that made him feel almost as if his body had begun to change, that his soul had begun to change into another soul. A new life was beginning for him, he dimly recognized. And with the new life, he knew, Claire would be less important. He knew that Claire would not like Grainger or Parkhearst and would not go to visit them or be with them. He knew that Claire actually never wanted to leave this room again. He had come to the last stages of his journey. Fenton tried not to think of this but it was too difficult to avoid: Claire had come as far now as he could. . . . There could be no more journeying around for him. And Fenton knew that as long as Claire was Claire he would not let him lead the "new life" he saw coming for him. There would be trouble, then, a great deal of trouble.

He wanted desperately to be rid of Claire and even as he had this feeling he felt more love and pity for him than ever before. As he sat there gazing at Claire, he knew he loved him more than any other being. He was almost sure that he would never feel such tenderness for any other person. And then this tenderness would be followed by fury and hatred and loathing, so that he was afraid he would do something violent, would strike the sick boy down and harm him.

"Claire," he said looking at him in anguish. "What are we going to do about this?"

Claire moved his closed eyes vaguely. "Don't know," Claire replied.

Fenton smiled to think that Claire did not ask what *this* was. Well, the boy was past caring, and it was plain enough what *this* was: *this* was everything that faced and surrounded them. It was plain, all right, what it was. Their trouble had made them both one.

"What do you want me to do?" Fenton said, his desperation growing. "Tell me what to do."

"We can't go away now, can we?" Claire said, and his voice was calmer but weaker.

Fenton considered this, taking out from his pants cuff a cigarette butt which he had begun in the greatwoman's house, lighting it swiftly with a kitchen match, and inhaling three powerful drags all at once.

Claire opened his eyes slowly and stared at his brother, waiting for the answer.

"No, we can't go away anywhere," Fenton said.

"Isn't there any place to go but here?" Claire asked.

"This is as far as we can get. Anyhow for the winter. . . . We have to stick in here now."

Claire closed his eyes again.

"Unless, of course, you want to go and live at Grainger's with me," Fenton said.

"What would I do there in her big house?" Claire said angrily, his eyes opening and closing.

"She would get a special room for you, where you could do anything you want. She could buy you anything you want, take you anywhere and show you anything. You would never know how happy you could be."

"What are *you* going to do there?" Claire wondered with surprise. . . .

"I'm going to marry her."

"Marry?" Claire sat up briefly in bed, but his strength could not hold him up, and falling back flat, he uttered: "You're not old enough."

"I'm more than old enough," Fenton laughed. "You've seen me enough times to know that. I got to make use of what I have, too. She thinks I look like her old husband."

"I ain't going to go there. . . . I ain't going to leave this house," Claire said.

"Well, suit yourself," Fenton said. "But I'm going over there. . . . The only thing is I don't believe any of it. It's a dream I keep having. Not one of those real pleasant dreams you have when you open a package and something beautiful falls out. In this dream even bigger more wonderful things seem like they're going to happen, getting married to a rich woman and living in a mansion and dressing up like a swell and all that, but at the same time it's all scary spooky and goddamned rotten. . . ."

"It's rotten, all right," Claire said. "You don't have to tell nobody that twice."

"Well, when there ain't nothing else you got to stoop down and pick up the *rotten*. You ought to know that."

"Not me. I don't have to pick it up if I don't want to."

"Well, then you can stick here till you choke to death on it," Fenton said passionately.

They both stopped as if listening to the words he had just said. They contained enough of some sort of truth and the truth was so terrible they had to listen to it as though it were being repeated on a phonograph for them.

"When do you aim on going?" Claire said suddenly, his voice older and calmer.

"In a day or so," Fenton warned him.

"Well it could be sooner. . . . You don't mind if I just stay here, do you?" Claire implored him.

"There's nothing to stop you staying here, of course," Fenton said irritably, twisting the hair around his ear. "This house don't have no owner, no tenants, nobody going to bother you but the spooks." He hurried on, talking past the pain that registered on Claire's face when he heard the words. "But I ain't coming dragging my ass over here every day just to see how you are when you could be living like a king."

"You don't need to come over and see me on account of I ain't asking you to," Claire said.

"Well, then don't be sorry if something happens to you. . . ."

"Nothing ain't going to happen and you know it," Claire shouted. "Why would anything happen to *me*?"

"Well, that's because you don't know nothing about cities is all," he said. "Do you know how many murders are done right in this one town?"

Claire did not answer for a moment and then said, "Those are rich people they murder. Like that old woman you're going to move in with. She's a likely murder person now. And you too if you get to be her husband."

"That's where you're wrong," Fenton said. "Most of the murders they do in this town are on bums, young boys and men that don't have no home and come from nowhere, these they find with their throats cut and their brains mashed out in alleys and behind billboards. Damned few rich people are ever found murdered in this town."

"You think you can scare me into moving into your old woman's house, don't you?" Claire said. "Well, you can do to her all you want to, but I ain't going to be there to watch you . . . fuck her."

"Now listen to that dirty-mouthed little bugger talk, would you. What would Mom think if she knew her religious little boy talked like a cocksucker?" He slapped Claire across the face. ". . . after all I done for you," Fenton finished.

"Go be with that old woman, why don't you, and leave me alone," Claire warned him. "I don't need you nor her. I don't need nobody."

"You'll come bellyachin' around trying to get in touch with me, you'll come crawling like you always do some night when you get the shit scared out of you in this house, hearing the sounds that you can't explain and maybe *seeing* something too. . . ."

Claire could not control the look of terror that appeared at Fenton's words.

"Claire," Fenton changed suddenly to a tone of imploring, "you got to listen to reason. You *can't* live in this old house alone. . . . Something *will* happen to you. Can't you see that. . . ."

"Why will it?" Claire said, his terror abating a little, searching in himself for some secret strength.

"Thing happen here. Everybody knows that. Now listen, Claire," Fenton went on. "Grainger would be very good to you and you could be happy there with her, you don't know how happy you would be. You haven't ever been happy or comfortable before so you don't know what you're talking about. Anyhow, Claire, I can't leave you here. I can't leave you here. . . . I'd have to do something else first. . . ."

"I don't see why not," he said. "I would rather be dead than go there."

"You would not rather be dead. You're a tough little bastard and you would rather be alive and you know it. . . . I'm not going to leave you here, Claire. I'm going to take you with me and you may just as well make up your mind to it now. . . . Hear?"

"You won't even get to drag me because I'm not going. . . ."

Fenton's anguish grew. He knew he could not leave Claire and he knew Claire's determination would be hard to break. He felt suddenly an uncontrollable urge of violence against this puny, defiant, impossible little brother. If he had only not taken him from West

Virginia in the first place. Or if he had only died as the doctor had said he would a long time ago. He knew that he *did* want to go on to the "new life" with Grainger and Parkhearst. He wanted to change, he wanted to wear Russell's clothes, he wanted the life that was just in sight and which Claire was now preventing. He knew that as long as there was Claire, whether he went with him or stayed in the house hardly mattered, because he knew that as long as there was Claire there was part of his old life with him, and he wanted to destroy all that behind him and begin all over again. Claire was a part of his old life, part of his disbelief in himself, the disbelief he could ever change and be something different. Claire did not even believe he could be married and love a woman. And though Claire was younger, he could exert this terrible triumph of failure over him.

Whether Claire stayed in the old house or followed him to Grainger's, he would exert a power of defeat over him.

Then suddenly Fenton realized that he did not want Claire to come with him. He preferred him to stay in the old house. And at the same time he knew that if he stayed he would never have a moment's peace. . . .

There was no way out that he could see. He could only stand there staring at Claire with impotence and rage.

"All right for you," Fenton said at the end. "All I can say is watch out, watch out something don't happen now to you."

A TENT PRODUCTION of *Othello* was to take place that night near Sixty-third Street, the young man who had approached Fenton was telling him, and as somebody was following him he would welcome Fenton's company and protection.

"Who is Hayden Banks?" Fenton wondered, looking at the handbill which described the dramatic spectacle about to take place.

"Hayden Banks," replied the young man, "is one of the greatest living actors. You are probably seeing him just before he is to gain his international reputation. London is already asking for him. Few actors can touch him. He is playing, of course, Othello himself. The costumes are by a friend of mine, and I will introduce you to a good many of the cast, if you like."

"I don't know if I want that," Fenton said.

"You *will* go with me to the performance," the young man said.

Fenton did not say anything. He had to go somewhere, of course, there could be no doubt about that.

"I wish you would come with me because I'm afraid of the man who is following me. Don't look back now. You see, I'm in trouble," he explained. "You look like a good kind of bodyguard for me and if you come with me I'm less likely to get into . . . trouble. . . . And I can't disappoint Hayden Banks. This is the last night of *Othello*, but I have been afraid to go out all week because this Mexican is following me. I'm in awful trouble with him."

Fenton half turned around but he saw nobody in particular behind him, a crowd of people who all seemed to be following them.

"I'll go with you," Fenton said. Then he looked at the young man carefully. He was the most handsome young man he had ever seen, almost as beautiful as a girl in boy's clothes. He had never seen such beautiful eyelashes. And at the same time the young man looked like Grainger. He might have been Grainger's brother. He almost wanted to ask him if he was Grainger's brother, but of course Grainger could not have a brother. . . .

"You don't know what it is, being followed."

"What will he do if he catches you?"

The young man stared at him. Fenton could not tell whether he was telling the truth or making this up, but there was a look of fear on his face that must be genuine at least.

"I wish you wouldn't use the word *catch*," the young man said.

"Are you afraid he will . . . hurt you," Fenton changed *kill* to *hurt* before he spoke.

"I'm afraid of the worst," the young man replied. "And you'll be an awfully good boy to come with me."

Fenton nodded.

The young man signalled a taxi and, waiting, said, "Those are awfully interesting clothes you have on. I've never seen clothes like that before. They remind me of some pictures of my father, wedding pictures."

Fenton looked down at himself as though seeing the clothes on himself for the first time. "These are clothes of a friend of mine," he explained.

"Get in," the young man urged as the taxi pulled up beside them. "Get in and don't stare at the crowd like that."

"Was I staring?" Fenton said, like a man awakened from sleepwalking.

"Staring into the crowd like that might incite him. You have an awful look when you stare," the young man said, looking more carefully now at Fenton. "I hope I am going to be safe with *you* now. I don't usually pick up people on the street like this. And maybe you don't like Shakespeare." He began to examine Fenton now more carefully that he felt free of the danger of being followed.

Fenton could see that his anxiety was genuine, but even so the way he said things seemed womanish and unreal, a little like Parkhearst. Both these men said things as though nothing was really important except the gestures and the words with which they said them. When he listened to either this young man or Parkhearst, Fenton felt that the whole of life must be merely a silly trifling thing to them, which bored them, and which they wanted to end, a movie they felt was too long and overacted.

"What is your name?" the young man said suddenly.

Fenton told him and the young man replied, "This is the most interesting name I have ever heard. Is it your own?"

Fenton looked down at his clothes and said it was.

"My name is Bruno Korsawski," he told Fenton.

They shook hands in the dark of the taxi and Bruno held Fenton's hand for many seconds.

"You may have saved my life," Bruno explained.

Soon they reached a vast lot deserted except for a giant circus tent before which fluttered, propelled by a giant cooling machine, banners reading

HAYDEN BANKS THE GENIUS OF THE SPOKEN WORD IN OTHELLO

In addition to the angry puffing face of Hayden Banks on the posters was a picture of a rather old looking young man dressed, as Fenton thought, like a devil you might expect to see in an old valentine, if valentines had devils, but he lacked horns and a tail.

Fenton remembered vaguely having read *The Merchant of Venice* and he had heard from someplace that *Othello* had to do with a black man who tortured a white woman to death. He felt a vague curiosity to see Hayden Banks, however. There was nobody around the huge empty tent tonight, and the whole scene reminded him of the conclusion of a county fair which he had seen in West Virginia.

BRUNO KORSAWSKI WAS the kind of man who introduced all of his new friends to all of his old friends. His life was largely a series of introductions, as he was always meeting new people, and these new people had to be introduced to the old people. His idea of the world was a circle, a circle of friends, closed to the rest of men because of his world's fullness. He had thought that Fenton would be one of his circle. However, the introductions did not go off too well.

They went at once to the star's dressing room. A purple sign with strange heavy tulips drawn on it announced MR. HAYDEN BANKS.

"You dear!" Hayden cried on seeing Bruno. "You look absolutely imperial."

Mr. Hayden Banks did not really look human, Fenton thought, and it was not only the deformity of his makeup.

"This is my friend Fenton Riddleway."

Mr. Banks bowed, and Fenton could not think of anything to say to him. . . .

"Don't you love his name?" Bruno said to Mr. Hayden Banks.

"It's incomparably the best I've heard," Mr. Banks replied. "Uncommonly good. But you've got to forgive me now, I haven't put on my beard yet, and without my beard I'm afraid some of you may mistake me for Desdemona.

"It's been so charming seeing you." Hayden Banks held out his hand to Fenton, and then whispering in Fenton's ear, he said, "You charmer you."

Fenton again could not think of anything to say, and in the hall Bruno said angrily to him, "You didn't open your mouth.

"I guess I'm used to people who talk well and a lot," Bruno explained apologetically as they went to their seats, which were in the first row. "You see what influence can do for you." Bruno pointed. "The best seats: compliments of Hayden Banks."

A small string orchestra was playing, an orchestra which Bruno explained was absolutely without a peer for its interpretation of the Elizabethan epoch. "They stand untouched," he stated, still speaking of the orchestra.

Whether it was the nearness of the actors or the oppressive heat of the tent or the general unintelligibility of both what the actors said and what they did, Fenton became sleepy, and he could not control a weakness he had for breaking wind, which considerably upset Bruno, although nobody else in the small audience seemed to hear. Perhaps Fenton's slumber was due also to the influence of the All Night Theater, and drama for Fenton was a kind of sleeping powder.

When Hayden Banks made his appearance, there was a tremendous ovation from the first few rows of the tent, and for a while Fenton watched this tall bony man beat his chest with complete lack of restraint and such uncalled-for fury that Fenton was amazed at such enormous energy. He could think of nothing in his own life that would have allowed him to pace, strut and howl like this. He supposed it belonged to an entirely different world where such things were perhaps done. The more, however, the great Moor shouted and complained about his wife's whoring, the more sleepy Fenton became. It was, however, something of a surprise to hear him fret so much about a whore and have so many rich-looking people nodding and approving of the whole improbable situation.

"He kills Desdemona," Bruno explained, watching Fenton doze with increasing displeasure.

"Would you buy me a drink now?" Fenton asked Bruno during intermission.

At the bar, the bartender asked Fenton if he was old enough, and Bruno said, "I can vouch for him, Teddy," and exchanged a knowing look with the bartender.

"There is one thing," Bruno began to Fenton after he had nodded to literally scores of friends and acquaintances: "I wonder if you couldn't control yourself a little more during the soliloquies at least."

Fenton knew perfectly well to what Bruno referred but he chose to say, "What are those?"

"During the performance, dear," Bruno went on, "you're making noises which embarrass me since I am among friends who know me and know I brought you as a guest."

"My farts, then?" Fenton said without expression.

"Brute!" Bruno laughed gaily.

"Would you buy me another whiskey now?" Fenton asked him.

When they returned to their seats Fenton immediately dozed off and did not waken until the last act which, whether due to his refreshing sleep or to the fact the actors seemed to talk less and do more, was rather frighteningly good to him. Hayden Banks seemed to murder the woman named Desdemona (Aurelia Wilcox in real life) with such satisfaction and enjoyment that he felt it stood with some of the better murder shows he had seen at the All Night Theater. He applauded quite loudly, and Bruno, smiling, finally held his hand and said, "Don't overdo it."

After the performance, Bruno invited Fenton to meet the entire cast, and as drinks were being served now in the dressing room, Fenton drank four or five additional whiskies to the congratulations of nearly all present. At times Fenton would have sober moments and remember Aurelia Wilcox patting his hair or Hayden Banks giving him a hug and kiss, or the young man who played Iago and who looked even more like a valentine devil off the stage whispering in his ear.

"Hayden says we're to go on to his apartment and wait for him there," Bruno explained finally to Fenton, showing him at the same time a tiny key to the great man's rooms.

"YOU WERE EXTREMELY rude to Hayden Banks. You act like a savage when you're with people. I've never met anybody like you. What on earth *is* West Virginia if you are typical?"

They were in Hayden Banks' apartment and Fenton, instead of replying to Bruno's remarks, was looking about, comparing it with Grainger's mansion. The walls had been painted so that they resembled the ocean, and so skillfully done that one actually thought he was about to go into water. Fenton stared at the painting for a long while, noticing in the distance some small craft, a dwarf moon and the suggestion of dawn in the far distance.

"Arden Carruthers did that painting," Bruno said. "Arden Carruthers is one of the most promising of the younger artists and this mural will be worth a small fortune some day."

Bruno was smoking something strange smelling which Fenton recognized as one of the persistent odors of the All Night Theater. As he smoked, he drew nearer to Fenton, and his expression of critical disapproval of the boy suddenly vanished.

"What are you clenching your fists for, as though you were going into the prize ring?" Bruno said.

Fenton sniffed at the cigarette and then suddenly knew what it must be. It was what had changed Bruno.

"You are very beautiful looking. The Italian Renaissance all over again in your face," Bruno said. He kept standing right over Fenton as though he were a bird that was going to come down on top of his head. He kept staring right into the crown of his head.

Fenton suddenly reached out and with violence seizing Bruno's wrist cried, "Give me some of that," so that the cigarette nearly fell from his fingers.

"Have you ever had any?" Bruno wanted to know.

"Give me some," Fenton said again, remembering now with terrifying insistence the smell in the All Night Theater. He felt that he could really dominate this man now as much as he could Claire. At the same time he was terribly afraid. He felt that something decisive and irrevocable was about to happen.

"Just smoke a little of it and don't inhale as deep as I did," Bruno said nervously. "I don't think you know how."

Fenton took the cigarette and began inhaling deeply.

"Now stop," Bruno said. "I don't have a warehouse of those."

"No wonder somebody was following you," Fenton laughed.

"I wonder which one of us is more scared of the other," Bruno said finally, and he sat down at Fenton's feet.

Fenton was about to say that he was not afraid of anybody, but Bruno began babbling about Fenton's shoes. "Where on earth did you get *those*? They're privately manufactured!" He stared at Fenton with renewed respect and interest. "You didn't get *those* in West Virginia."

Bruno stared at Fenton again.

"You haven't killed anybody, have you?" he said finally.

Fenton stared at him and he went on agitatedly, "Why you've finished that entire cigarette. I hope you know what you've done and what it was. I'm not responsible for you, remember."

"Who the fuck is responsible?" Fenton said.

"Don't use that language," Bruno sniggered, and then got up swiftly and sat down beside Fenton. He began kissing his hair, and then slowly unbuttoning his shirt. He took off all his clothes, as from a doll, piece by piece, without resistance or aid, but left on at the last the privately manufactured shoes. . . .

The next thing Fenton remembered he was standing naked in the middle of the room, boxing; he was boxing the chandelier and had knocked down all the lamps, he had split open Bruno's face and Bruno was weeping and held ice packs to his mouth.

Then the next thing he remembered was Bruno standing before him with Hayden Banks who looked exactly like the murdered Desdemona. Bruno had a gun in his hand and was ordering him to leave.

"Don't you ever come back if you don't want to go to jail," Bruno said, as Fenton went out the door dressed in clothes that did not look like his own.

Morning is the most awful time. And this morning for Fenton was the one that shattered everything he had been or known; it marked the limits of a line, not ending his youth but making his youth superfluous, as age to a god.

He seemed to be awake and yet he had the feeling he had never been awake. He was not even sure it was morning. He was back in the old house, in Claire's room, and though he was staring at Claire he knew that his staring was of no avail, that he already knew what had happened and the staring was to prevent him from telling himself what he saw. He could not remember anything at that moment, he had even forgotten Bruno Korsawski and the production of *Othello* starring some immortal fruit.

Then the comfortable thought that it was breakfast time and that he would go out and get Claire his rolls and coffee. He was so happy he was here with Claire and he realized again how necessary Claire was to him, and how real he was compared to the Parkhearsts and the Brunos and the Graingers.

"Claire," he said softly. He went over to the bed and began shaking him. The room seemed suddenly deadly cold and he thought of the winter that would come and how uninhabitable this deserted old wreck would be. . . . And Claire, he recognized, almost as with previous knowledge, was as cold as the room. And yet he was not surprised. . . .

He sat there suddenly wondering why he was not surprised that Claire was cold. And at the same time he was surprised that he could be so cold. He shook him again.

"Claire," he said.

He began to be aware of a splitting headache.

He got up and turned on the sickly light. He was careful somehow not to get too close to Claire now that he had turned on the light, but stood at a safe distance, talking to him, telling him how he was going to get him some breakfast.

"Some good hot coffee will make you feel like a new boy, Claire," he said.

And then suddenly he began to weep, choking sobs, and these were followed by laughter so unlike his own that he remained frozen with confusion.

"I'm going right now, hear?" he said to Claire. "I'll be right back with the coffee. . . ." Then he laughed again. The silence of the room was complete.

He hurried to the lunch stand and then ran all the way back with the steaming coffee and rolls.

He bent down over Claire but was somewhat careful not to look at his face. His head ached as though the sockets of his eyes were to burst. He kept talking to Claire all the time, telling him how they were going back to West Virginia as soon as he got a little money saved up; they would buy a stock farm later and raise Black Angus cattle, and have a stable of horses. It was not impossible, Claire, he said.

He held Claire's head up but still without looking and tried to pour coffee down his throat. "This coffee's strong enough to revive a stiff," he laughed, ignoring the coffee's running down the boy's neck, ignoring that none of the coffee had even got into his mouth.

"Eat this bread," he said and put some to Claire's mouth. He pressed the small piece of roll heavily against the blue lips, smashing it to the coffee-moistened cold lips.

"Eat this, drink this," Fenton kept saying, but now he no longer tried to administer the bread and coffee. "Eat and drink."

We have to go back, Claire. We want to go back to West Virginia, you know you do.

Then as though another person had entered the room and commanded him, Fenton stood up, and pulled the light down as far as he could to search mercilessly the face and body of Claire.

The light showed Claire's neck swollen and blue with marks, the neck broken softly like a small bird's, the hair around his neck like ruffled young feathers, the eyes had come open a little and seemed to be attempting to focus on something too far out of his reach. The brown liquid of the coffee like blood smeared the paste of the offering of bread around his mouth.

Fenton looked down at his hands.

After that he did not know what happened, or how long he stayed in the room, trying to feed Claire, trying to talk to him, trying to tell him about Black Angus in West Virginia.

Slowly the sound of Fenton's own voice worked him from the stupor he had been in, saying again and again, "You're dead, you little motherfucker. Dead as mud and I don't have no need sitting here staring you down."

FOR A GOOD many days he walked all over the city, riding street cars when they were full so that he could shove his way in without paying, eating in cheap lunch stands when they were full and running out the back door without paying the bill. He found he could steal fruit and candy from grocery stands without much trouble. In the evening he would go to the square in front of a large gray library and listen to the revivalists and the fanatics.

Older men sometimes invited him to a beer, men he met in the crowds in front of the speaker, but as he drank with them his mind would wander and he would say things which chilled further talk, so that after a while absently he would look around and find himself alone looking down at his hands.

There was no respite for his misery during which time he slept in hallways, covering himself with newspapers he collected in alleys. By day he would go down to the docks and watch crews unload cargo, or he would go into a large museum where they kept the bones of prehistoric animals which he knew never existed. These big-boned monsters calmed some of his crushing grief.

But at last there came to him an idea which gave him some solace, if not any real hope or restoration. It was that Claire must be put in a sheltered place. He must have a service, a funeral. The thought did not occur to him that Claire was really dead until then; before he had only thought how he had killed him. And the thought that anybody *knew* he had killed Claire or was looking for him never occurred to him. What had happened to both him and Claire was much too terrible and closed in for the rest of the world to know or care about.

It was night when he returned to the house. He had vaguely remembered going upstairs weeks before and finding an old chest up there, an old cedar chest, perhaps, or merely an old box. He walked up the stairs now, using matches to guide his way. He heard small footsteps scamper about or it might have been only the echo of his own feet.

He stood in the immense vacant attic with its suffocating smell of rotting wood, its soft but ticklingly clammy caress of cobwebs, the feeling of small animal eyes upon him and the imperceptible sounds of disintegration and rot. How had he known there was a chest up here? As he thought of it now he could not remember having seen it. Yet he knew it was here.

He put himself on hands and knees and began groping for the presence of it. He came across a broken rocking chair. His kitchen matches lit up pictures on the wall, one of a girl in her wedding dress, another of a young man in hunting costume, one of Jesus among thieves. Another picture was a poem concerning Mother Love. At the extreme end of the attic and in a position which must have been directly above the room where he and Claire had lived and where Claire now lay dead was a chest; it was not a fragrant cedar chest, such as he had hoped, but an old white box with broken hinges and whose inside lid was covered with a filthy cloth.

But even more disappointing was that inside was a gauzy kind of veil, like a wedding veil and his eye turned wearily to the picture of the girl in her wedding costume as though this veil might be the relic of that scene. But whatever the veil was, it might serve this cause. It was not a fit resting place for Claire, but it would have to do.

He hurried now downstairs and into the room, with the sudden fear that Claire might have disappeared. He sat down beside him, and his agony was so great he scarcely noticed the overpowering stench, and at the same time he kept lighting the kitchen matches, but perhaps more to keep his mind aware of the fact of Claire's death than to scare off the stink of death.

It took him all night to get himself ready to carry Claire up, as though once he had put him in the chest, he was really at last dead forever. For part of the night he found that he had fallen asleep over Claire's body, and at the very end before he carried him upstairs and deposited him, he forced himself to kiss the dead stained lips he had stopped, and said, "Up we go then, motherfucker."

ABOUT JESSIE MAE

"I don't visit Jessie Mae's any more because of her untidiness," Myrtle said to Mrs. Hemlock as the two women walked through the garden, where they had been talking, toward Mrs. Hemlock's kitchen, where Myrtle was going to copy down a special recipe for the older woman.

"But I didn't know it had gone so far," Mrs. Hemlock said with mild disbelief.

"I didn't say it had gone *too* far now," Myrtle told her. "Nothing is under any order or control, that's all."

"And that I can believe," Mrs. Hemlock agreed.

"You see, Jessie Mae's never had to do anything for herself," Myrtle explained.

Mrs. Hemlock stared at her friend's youthful face, in the late morning Florida light, the desire for *more* written on her own expectant mouth and heavy double chin.

"You know Jessie Mae was *twice* an heiress," and Myrtle hit the word as hard as possible in order to begin at the beginning of her knowledge.

"I knew she had everything, of course," Mrs. Hemlock said in somewhat hushed tones now, as though a matter of considerable delicacy had been disclosed. She looked down at her apron suddenly and removed a long ravelling which had come to rest there.

Myrtle looked quickly at Mrs. Hemlock's apron and said, "That's cunning."

"It's Portuguese or Spanish or something," Mrs. Hemlock smiled, opening the back screen to her kitchen.

"You know, you have beautiful things, Mrs. Hemlock," Myrtle said.

Mrs. Hemlock laughed pleasantly.

"I love to come to *your* house," Myrtle told her.

"But I can't understand Jessie Mae's being *untidy*," Mrs. Hemlock seemed very surprised, and she pointed quickly to a large easy chair which she had brought into her kitchen specially for her many visitors. Myrtle sat down with a great sigh of pleasure.

"This chair!" Myrtle groaned loudly and pretended to collapse from their long earlier talk in the garden.

Mrs. Hemlock smiled at this compliment, too, and chuckled mildly, her double chin moving slightly as if she were singing a lullaby.

"I'm Jessie Mae's distant cousin, you know," Myrtle said suddenly.

Mrs. Hemlock paused a second because she was not sure she knew this or not. But dimly, from many years back in certain St. Augustine circles, a faint recollection stirred in her brain.

"I remember," Mrs. Hemlock nodded, and opening the refrigerator she moved swiftly for such a stout woman to hand Myrtle a tall cool glass of fruit punch, thickly frosted, and non-alcoholic.

"You jewel!" Myrtle almost squealed. "You think of everything. And you *have* everything."

Mrs. Hemlock could not conceal her pleasure again. Her heavy, healthy face flushed slightly from the additional praise.

"I'm alone and I have to keep busy at something," Mrs. Hemlock glanced at her kitchen.

"But most women wouldn't bother," Myrtle said. "You're *always* cooking. And so generous in sending around things to we neighbors. Why you're making us all fat, too!" Myrtle laughed loudly.

Mrs. Hemlock started at this, but then she laughed pleasantly also.

"I suppose eating is a sin," Mrs. Hemlock pretended seriousness.

"Nothing that gives one pleasure like this is," Myrtle was firm on this point, and Mrs. Hemlock could see Myrtle was thinking of Jessie Mae again.

"Well!" Mrs. Hemlock exclaimed, drinking now some of her own fruit punch and hoping Myrtle would go back to her first subject, "It's nice we're all a bit different."

"It's wonderful," Myrtle said, referring to the drink. "And I suppose it's a secret recipe . . ."

"No, no," Mrs. Hemlock deprecated this, but acted abstracted now, almost as if tasting something in the drink which she had not remembered putting there. Then suddenly she broke out: "I didn't know, as a matter of fact, you *were* Jessie Mae's distant cousin."

Myrtle put down her glass of juice on the kitchen table, which was provided with a handsome imported linen tablecloth, fresh and spotless.

"I really had forgotten, that is," Mrs. Hemlock said in a kind of apology.

"I'm really one of the last of her own people," Myrtle spoke indifferently, but with a certain tone which implied that the relationship might be important for others to remember.

"Jessie Mae is of course basically a fine person," Mrs. Hemlock stated, fearful now that she had perhaps stressed the untidiness too much, even though Myrtle had brought the whole subject up in the garden.

"Mrs. Hemlock, Jessie Mae's in terrible shape!" Myrtle suddenly changed any direction toward or need for apology, and she stared at her drink as if she had promised herself not to touch it again.

Mrs. Hemlock moistened her lips critically, as if she, too, did not require the refreshment now of the punch.

"Is Jessie Mae *worried* or something?" Mrs. Hemlock felt her way in the break which had come into the conversation.

"Worried, my foot," Myrtle sprang suddenly at this suggestion, and she picked up her glass again and tasted the punch.

"She lives to worry other people, if you want to know. . . . Or if you really think about it, too much money and not enough to do. . . . Do you know she has a maid to *dress* her now!"

Mrs. Hemlock's heavy face was suffused with the flush of pleasure. And although she had stood until now in her professional guise as hostess, she decided to sit down. She sat directly in front of Myrtle and said: "She *doesn't*!"

Myrtle looked almost cross at Mrs. Hemlock, for she felt the latter's exclamation was hardly necessary even in a rhetorical sense.

"I don't think Jessie Mae does a thing for herself any more," Myrtle was definite on this. "She has, you know, eight servants."

"And yet her house remains so—" and Mrs. Hemlock was going to describe the untidiness again but Myrtle had already gone ahead with:

"Jessie Mae orders everything there is to be done. And you can bet your bottom dollar that if there's untidiness she orders that too!"

Mrs. Hemlock gasped quietly and lowered her head as if to take in all the meaning of the statement, but Myrtle did not see fit to let her contemplate anything at that moment.

"She keeps these eight servants busy, let me tell you. For every one of the rooms in her house, and there must be twenty if there's one—they're all in *use*!"

Mrs. Hemlock's eyes came open wide and then closed, and her mouth closed hard too like one who had found more put in it than she had been ready for.

"That's only the beginning!" Myrtle cried.

Mrs. Hemlock's eyes came open now and there was such a look of perfect satisfaction on her face that Myrtle's own expression softened and glowed with the reflected pleasure from her older friend.

"You *don't* know about her!" Myrtle intoned with happiness, sure at last of Mrs. Hemlock's ignorance.

"I was only at her house in the old days, when she entertained

General Waite so much," Mrs. Hemlock said, coolly matter-of-fact, a hint of total abdication in her tone. "Jessie Mae's brother was more or less head of the house then."

"Well, Corliss liked to act like he was," Myrtle took this statement up. "But Jessie Mae was running the whole place even then, and running him too. He died of her bossing, many people think."

"Then, of course, I've been there several times to tea, and to her art fairs," Mrs. Hemlock put in rather firmly before stepping down altogether.

"Oh, those are nothing, my dear, I'm sorry to say. You see you have to spend the night to know how it really is!" Myrtle was suddenly indignant now, but Mrs. Hemlock could see that her indignation was over the principle of Jessie Mae's behavior.

For just a second Mrs. Hemlock looked at her large red recipe book lying open to the place where Myrtle was to fill in the instructions for baking Bavarian cookies. But then she moved her eyes away from the book back directly into Myrtle's face. She wanted Myrtle to know now that she didn't know anything about Jessie Mae, and that she wanted more than anything else to find out all there was.

Myrtle saw this expression on Mrs. Hemlock's face, and put her hands in her lap as a signal they could begin in earnest.

"Jessie Mae's trouble is she won't have anything planned or in order, until she wants it. And she doesn't know what she wants until the moment she does want it!"

Myrtle suddenly stopped there like one who has not quite caught the meaning of her own words. Mrs. Hemlock stared at her and her mouth came open again, and it was this openmouthed expression and the immense interest on Mrs. Hemlock's face, together with the wonderful health and cleanliness of the latter, and the wonderful comfort and luxury of her kitchen that made Myrtle want to stay on here, perhaps indefinitely. She did not know when things had been better for a talk.

"More punch?" Mrs. Hemlock said in her most encouraging tone.

"I'd love more!"

"And some of my ice box fudge bars with it!" Mrs. Hemlock coaxed, almost a bit hysterical with the pleasure which the Jessie Mae story was giving her.

"I'd love some fudge bars too," Myrtle said, absentmindedly, still hesitating, it was obvious, whether to give all she knew about their common acquaintance now, or perhaps hold some last bit still back, for another time, or forever.

"As I say," Mrs. Hemlock spoke in her matter-of-fact voice, afraid whatever she said would spoil the "more" that might come, "as I say, I was never a *friend* of Jessie Mae's, but I've known her for twenty-five years."

Myrtle did not even consider this but thanked Mrs. Hemlock for the fudge bars and the second glass of punch.

"I could eat these all day," Myrtle said chewing softly, not to be hurried or budged. She made a sound of pleasure.

"I wonder you don't win prizes with your culinary genius, Mrs. Hemlock," Myrtle purred, deliberating. "You should be famous."

The older woman bowed her head in pleasure and the blush of her health and good living covered her face and throat.

But both women waited for the signal to begin again, calmly now, but with tremendous expectation.

"I know everything about her," Myrtle said suddenly.

One would not have known Mrs. Hemlock had broken their talk by going to the icebox for the fudge bars. It was almost as though Jessie Mae herself were there before them on the TV screen, helpless and exposed for all their comments.

"I lived with her for a month!" Myrtle said after she had quit chewing on the fudge bars. "In 1952!"

Mrs. Hemlock waited.

"A month, mind you!"

"Then of course you do know," Mrs. Hemlock said in a voice close to awe.

"I was afraid every minute," Myrtle said.

Mrs. Hemlock showed a slight lack of comprehension.

"You spoke of her untidiness, Mrs. Hemlock," Myrtle swept on. "Well," she laughed, "you wouldn't think that that was largely connected with her leaving her jewels everywhere. She left thousands and thousands of dollars' worth of diamonds in my room."

Mrs. Hemlock shook her head.

"Then one evening I discovered in the top bureau drawer of my room enough other jewels for the Queen herself!"

Mrs. Hemlock began to say something but Myrtle hardly paused long enough to allow her friend to tense her mouth.

"I couldn't stand that kind of untidiness, if you please, and besides I'm not so sure her untidiness, as we call it, wasn't purposeful."

"Well!" Mrs. Hemlock managed to cry.

"It's part of her way of getting even!"

"But what would she want to get even for when she's got everything!" Mrs. Hemlock propelled the question into the room and beyond into the garden.

"You don't know everything," Myrtle cautioned again. "She hates me, she hates women even more. And she's not only untidy. You started to use the right word when we were outside. She's *dirty*!"

Mrs. Hemlock let out a moan of weak remonstrance.

"I could tell you things," Myrtle said, "but we're here in a beautiful tidy house with such wonderful things to eat. I won't."

Myrtle had suddenly stopped talking, and she lay back in her chair, leaving Mrs. Hemlock with a look of complete and unexpected emptiness on her red face.

Then, perhaps of a second mind, Myrtle said: "Her whole life is to get back at everybody. Hence the servants. Hence the parties at which nothing is quite right. Hence the jewels strewn everywhere to make everybody feel they are suspected of stealing. Who wants to go to a house where jewels are strewn everywhere. Why it makes the closest of us to her wince! And don't think she doesn't accuse people of taking them. And not just the servants!"

"Why, she sounds . . . *gone*," Mrs. Hemlock had groped for the word but did not look satisfied when she had got it.

"No," Myrtle corrected politely, smiling quickly, "Jessie Mae is just hateful . . . She's not *gone* as you say. A man, a strong old-fashioned type over her would have gone a long way to getting the house tidied up and the jewels either sold or put in a vault. But she's never had a strong hand over her, and since the day her old father died, she's done just as she pleased every second . . ."

"Really, I never!" Mrs. Hemlock began.

"But the thing nobody seems to know," Myrtle said, sitting up still more straight, and her face a peculiar shade, "and the thing nobody can believe even when you tell them, is that the whole house is nothing but an excuse for dogs!"

Mrs. Hemlock's chin trembled but she said nothing.

"Jessie Mae has thirty pedigreed dogs in those rooms upstairs if she has one!"

Mrs. Hemlock closed her eyes again, but she could not conceal the pleasure that rested on her mouth and chin.

Myrtle waited until her friend opened her eyes and then she said: "Jessie Mae sleeps downstairs, where she made her brother sleep before her. The dogs live upstairs, and there's a servant on duty for every room of them."

"You're funning!" Mrs. Hemlock used an old word and an old tone that sounded like *Amen*.

"And when I stayed there that month," Myrtle said, her mouth dry from the exertion, "she let me see the whole performance, since I had to sleep downstairs with her in any case. After all the visitors and the bores had left, she let the dogs out of their upstairs rooms, and then they would romp and tear and romp and tear, and that old woman ran and romped right along with them, laughing and shouting at them, and the dogs all yelping and carrying on like a pack of wild animals after her until you wouldn't know which acted the nuttier, she or the dogs."

"Good God!" Mrs. Hemlock turned a deep orange now, and she fanned her face with her fat hand.

"I usually never talk about Jessie Mae to anybody," Myrtle intoned.

"Of course," Mrs. Hemlock nodded, a tone of firm moral philosophy in her voice.

"But you've been so kind and considerate, to all of we neighbors," Myrtle almost scolded, "and especially to me, that I think of you, Mrs. Hemlock, as a confidante."

"Thank you, Myrtle. I'm touched," Mrs. Hemlock managed to get out.

"It's the truth. You've been an angel. Why you've baked for us and sent us things. This could be another Delmonico's!" she waved with her hand. "I've never tasted such cooking. And the comparison between your wonderful generosity and neatness and normal ways always comes as such a distinct contrast with Jessie Mae, who is, after all, my cousin, but who never does anything for anybody, and who just isn't anyhow the kind of person you want to visit."

Myrtle stopped, perhaps in realization she had told more than she had ever known she knew.

"But the poor old thing," Mrs. Hemlock ventured.

"Well, with all her wealth why doesn't she try to straighten herself out, for pity's sake. She could help so many people if she cared about anybody but herself."

Myrtle waited now finally for Mrs. Hemlock to speak, but the older woman sat there quietly, a fudge bar still untasted in her hand, thinking about Jessie Mae's running up and down with the dogs.

"I'm not surprised now the house looked so bad," Mrs. Hemlock said at last, but with a kind of dreamy expression that lacked conviction.

Myrtle was so tired she just lay back in the chair.

"Would you like a nice home-made devilled ham sandwich with a good cup of strong coffee?" Mrs. Hemlock said invitingly. "You look *awfully* tired, Myrtle."

"Why, I'd love one, of course . . . But shouldn't I fill in that recipe for you first," Myrtle said, and she took out of her apron pocket a piece of paper which contained her directions for baking Bavarian cookies.

"I think you deserve a sandwich first. Copying is awfully tiring too."

"Well, you know me and your cooking," Myrtle giggled.

"Why, I would have *never* known that about Jessie Mae if you hadn't just happened to be walking through the garden today," Mrs. Hemlock said, and she began to boil the water for the coffee.

"I know you won't tell anybody," Myrtle said. "Because as you know, she *is* part of my family, though you'd never know it the way she acts."

"I understand, of course," and Mrs. Hemlock smiled from above her pink chin. "But it *does* explain at last the . . . *untidiness.* My stars, yes."

Mrs. Hemlock was firm on that point.

Myrtle nodded abstractedly and both women were silent now waiting for the coffee to be ready.

YOU MAY SAFELY GAZE

"Do we always have to begin on Milo at these Wednesday lunches," Philip said to Guy. Carrying their trays, they had already picked out their table in the cafeteria, and Philip, at least, was about to sit down.

"Do I *always* begin on Milo?" Guy wondered, surprised.

"You're the one who knows him, remember," Philip said.

"Of course, Milo is one of the serious problems in our office, and it's only a little natural, I suppose, to mention problems even at one of our Wednesday lunches."

"Oh, forget it," Philip said. Seated, he watched half-amused as Guy still stood over the table with his tray raised like a busboy who would soon now move away with it to the back room.

"I don't dislike Milo," Guy began. "It's not that at all."

Philip began to say something but then hesitated, and looked up at the cafeteria clock that showed ten minutes past twelve. He knew, somehow, that it was going to be Milo all over again for lunch.

"It's his attitude not just toward his work, but life," Guy said, and this time he sat down.

"His life," Philip said, taking swift bites of his chicken à la king.

Guy nodded. "You see now he spares himself the real work in

the office due to this physical culture philosophy. He won't even let himself get mad anymore or argue with me because that interferes with the development of his muscles and his mental tranquility, which is so important for muscular development. His whole life now he says is to be strong and calm."

"A muscle ascetic," Philip laughed without amusement.

"But working with him is not so funny," Guy said, and Philip was taken aback to see his friend go suddenly very pale. Guy had not even bothered to take his dishes off his tray but allowed everything to sit there in front of him as though the lunch were an offering he had no intention of tasting.

"Milo hardly seems anybody you and I could know, if you ask me," Guy pronounced, as though the final decision had at last been made.

"You forget one of us *doesn't*," Philip emphasized again, and he waved his fork as though they had finally finished now with Milo, and could go on to the real Wednesday lunch.

But Guy began again, as though the talk for the lunch had been arranged after all, despite Philip's forgetfulness, around Milo.

"I don't think he is even studying law anymore at night, as he was supposed to do."

"Don't tell me that," Philip said, involuntarily affecting concern and half-resigning himself now to the possibility of a completely wasted hour.

"Oh, of course," Guy softened his statement, "I guess he goes to the law library every night and reads a little. Every waking hour is, after all, not for his muscles, but every real thought, you can bet your bottom dollar, *is*."

"I see," Philip said, beginning on his pineapple snow.

"It's the only thing on his mind, I tell you," Guy began again.

"It's interesting if that's the only thing on his mind, then," Philip replied. "I mean," he continued, when he saw the black look he got from Guy, "—to know somebody who is obsessed . . ."

"What do you mean by that?" Guy wondered critically, as though only he could tell what it was that Milo might be.

"You said he wanted to devote himself to just this one thing." Philip wearily tried to define what he had meant.

"I tried to talk to Milo once about it," Guy said, now deadly serious, and as though, with all preliminaries past, the real part of his speech had begun. Philip noticed that his friend had still not even picked up his knife or fork, and his food must be getting stone cold by now. " 'Why do you want to look any stronger,' I said to Milo. He just stared at me, and I said, 'Have you ever taken a good look in the mirror the way you are now,' and he just smiled his sour smile again at me. 'Have you ever looked, Milo?' I said, and even I had to laugh when I repeated my own question, and he kind of laughed then too . . . Well, for God's sake, he knows after all that nobody but a few freaks are going to look like he looks, or will look, if he keeps this up. You see he works on a new part of his body every month. One month he will be working on his pectorals, the next his calf muscles, then he will go in for a period on his latissimus dorsi."

Philip stopped chewing a moment as though seeing these different muscle groups slowly developing there before him. Finally, he managed to say, "Well at least he's interested in something, which is more than . . ."

"Yes, he's interested in *it*, of course," Guy interrupted, "—what he calls being the sculptor of his own body, and you can find him almost any noon in the gym straining away while the other men in our office do as they please with their lunch hour."

"You mean they eat their lunch then." Philip tried humor.

"That's right," Guy hurried on. "But he and this Austrian friend of his who also works in my office, they go over to this gym run by a cripple named Vic somebody, and strain their guts out, lifting barbells and throwing their arms up and around on benches, with dumbbells in their fists, and come back an hour later to their work looking as though they had been in a rock mixer. They actually stink of gym, and several of the stenographers have complained saying they always know when it's exercise day all right. But nothing stops those boys, and they just take all the gaff with as much good humor as two such egomaniacs can have."

"Why egomaniacs, for God's sake," Philip wondered, putting his fork down with a bang.

"Well, Philip," Guy pleaded now. "To think of their own bodies like that. These are not young boys, you know. They must be twenty-five or so, along in there, and you would think they would begin to think of other people, other people's bodies, at least." Guy laughed as though to correct his own severity before Philip. "But no," he went on. "They have to be Adonises."

"And their work suffers?" Philip wondered vaguely, as though, if the topic had to be continued, they might now examine it from this aspect.

"The kind of work young men like them do—it don't matter, you know, if you're good or not, nobody knows if you're really good. They do their work and get it out on time, and you know their big boss is still that old gal of seventy who is partial to young men. She sometimes goes right up to Milo, who will be sitting at his desk relaxed as a jellyfish, doing nothing, and she says, 'Roll up your sleeves, why don't you, and take off your necktie on a warm day like this,' and it will be thirty degrees outside and cool even in the office. And Milo will smile like a four-year-old at her because he loves admiration more than anything in the world, and he rolls up his sleeves and then all this bulge of muscle comes out, and the old girl looks like she'd seen glory, she's that gone on having a thug like that around."

"But you sound positively bilious over it," Philip laughed.

"Philip, look," Guy said with his heavy masculine patience, "doesn't it sound wrong to you, now seriously?"

"What in hell do you mean by wrong, though?"

"Don't be that way. You know goddamn well what I mean."

"Well, then, no, I can't say it is. Milo or whatever his name."

"You know it's Milo," Guy said positively disgusted.

"Well, he is, I suppose, more typical than you might think from the time, say, when you were young. Maybe there weren't such fellows around then."

"Oh, there were, of course."

"Well, now there are more, and Milo is no exception."

"But he looks at himself all the time, and he has got himself tattooed recently and there in front of the one mirror in the office, it's not the girls who stand there, no, it's Milo and this Austrian boy. They're always washing their hands or combing their hair, or just looking at themselves right out, not sneaky-like the way most men do, but like some goddamn chorus girls. And oh, I forgot, this Austrian fellow got tattooed too because Milo kept after him, and then he was sorry. It seems the Austrian's physical culture instructor gave him hell and said he had spoiled the appearance of his deltoids by having the tattoo work done."

"Don't tell me," Philip said.

Guy stared as he heard Philip's laugh, but then continued: "They talked about the tattoo all morning, in front of all the stenogs, and whether this Austrian had spoiled the appearance of his deltoid muscles or not."

"Well, it *is* funny, of course, but I couldn't get worked up about it the way you are."

"They're a symbol of the new America and I don't like it."

"You're terribly worked up."

"Men on their way to being thirty, what used to be considered middle age, developing their bodies and special muscles and talking about their parts in front of women."

"But they're married men, aren't they?"

"Oh, sure," Guy dismissed this. "Married and with kids."

"What more do you want then. Some men are nuts about their bowling scores and talk about that all the time in front of everybody."

"I see you approve of them."

"I didn't say that. But I think you're overreacting, to use the phrase . . ."

"You don't have to work with them," Guy went on. "You don't have to watch them in front of the one and only office mirror."

"Look, I've known a lot of women who griped me because they were always preening themselves, goddamn narcissists too. I don't care for narcissists of either sex."

"Talk about Narciss-uses," said Guy. "The worst was last summer when I went with Mae to the beach, and there *they* were, both of them, right in front of us on the sand."

Philip stiffened slightly at the prospect of more.

"Milo and the Austrian," Guy shook his head. "And as it was Saturday afternoon there didn't seem to be a damn place free on the beach and Mae wanted to be right up where these Adonises or Narcissuses, or whatever you call them, were. I said, 'We don't want to camp here, Mae,' and she got suddenly furious. I couldn't tell her how those birds affected me, and they hardly even spoke to me either, come to think about it. Milo spit something out the side of his mouth when he saw me, as though to say *that for you*."

"That was goddamn awful for you," Philip nodded.

"Wait till you hear what happened, for crying out loud. I shouldn't tell this during my lunch hour because it still riles me."

"Don't get riled then. Forget them."

"I have to tell you," Guy said. "I've never told anybody before, and you're the only man I know will listen to a thing like this. . . . You know," he went on then, as though this point were now understood at last between them, "Mae started staring at them right away. 'Who on earth are they?' she said, and I couldn't tell whether she was outraged or pleased, maybe she was a bit of both because she just fixed her gaze on them like paralyzed. 'Aren't you going to put on your sun tan lotion and your glasses?' I said to her, and she turned on me as though I had hit her. 'Why don't you let a woman relax when I never get out of the house but twice in one year,' she told me. I just lay back then on the sand and tried to forget they were there and that she was there and that even I was there."

Philip began to light up his cigarette, and Guy said, "Are you all done eating already?" and he looked at his own plate of veal cutlet and peas which was nearly untouched. "My God, you are a fast eater. Why, do you realize how fast you eat," he told Philip, and Philip said he guessed he half-realized it. He said at night he ate slower.

"In the bosom of your family," Guy laughed.

Philip looked at the cafeteria clock and stirred unceremoniously.

"But I wanted to finish telling you about these boys."

"Is there *more*?" Philip pretended surprise.

"Couldn't you tell the way I told it there was," Guy said, an indeterminate emotion in his voice.

"I hope nothing happened to Mae," Philip offered weakly.

"Nothing ever happens to Mae," Guy dismissed this impatiently. "No, it was them, of course. Milo and the Austrian began putting on a real show, you know, for everybody, and as it was Saturday afternoon, as I said, nearly everybody from every office in the world was there, and they were all watching Milo and the Austrian. So, first they just did the standard routine, warm-ups, you know, etc., but from the first every eye on the beach was on them, they seemed to have the old presence, even the lifeguards were staring at them as though nobody would ever dare drown while they were carrying on, so first of all then they did handstands and though they did them good, not good enough for that many people to be watching. After all somebody is always doing handstands on the beach, you know. I think it was their hair attracted people, they have very odd hair, they look like brothers that way. Their hair is way too thick, and of course too long for men of our generation. . . ."

"Well, how old do you think I am?" Philip laughed.

"All right, of *my* generation, then," Guy corrected with surliness. He went on, however, immediately: "I think the reason everybody watched was their hair, which is a peculiar kind of chestnut color, natural and all that, but maybe due to the sun and all their exercising had taken on a funny shade, and then their muscles were so enormous in that light, bulging and shining with oil and matching somehow their hair that I think that was really what kept people looking and not what they did. They didn't look quite real, even though in a way they are the style.

"I kept staring, and Mae said, 'I thought you wasn't going to watch,' and I could see she was completely held captive by their performance as was, I guess, everybody by then on the goddamn beach.

"'I can't help looking at freaks,' I told Mae, and she gave me one of her snorts and just kept looking kind of bitter and satisfied at seeing something like that. She's a great woman for sights like that, she goes to all the stock shows, and almost every nice Sunday she takes the kids to the zoo. . . ."

"Well, what finally did come off?" Philip said, pushing back his chair.

"The thing that happened, nobody in his right mind would ever believe, and probably lots of men and boys who saw it happen never went home and told their families."

"It should have been carried in the papers then," Philip said coolly and he drank all of his as yet untouched glass of water.

"I don't know what word I would use to describe it," Guy said. "Mae has never mentioned it to this day, though she said a little about it on the streetcar on the way home that afternoon, but just a little, like she would have referred to a woman having fainted and been rushed to the hospital, something on that order."

"Well, for Pete's sake now, what did happen?" Philip's ill humor broke forth for a moment, and he bent his head away from Guy's look.

"As I said," Guy continued quietly, "they did all those more fancy exercises then after their warm-ups, like leaping on one another's necks, jumping hard on each other's abdomens to show what iron men they were, and some rough stuff but which they made look fancy, like they threw one another to the sand as though it was a cross between a wrestling match and an apache dance, and then they began to do some things looked like they were out of the ballet, with lots of things like jumping in air and splits, you know. You know what kind of trunks that kind of Narciss-uses wear, well these were tighter than usual, the kind to make a bullfighter's pants look baggy and oversize, and as though they had planned it, while doing one of their big movements, their trunks both split clear in two, at the same time, with a sound, I swear, you could have heard all over that beach.

"Instead of feeling at least some kind of self-consciousness, if not shame, they both busted out laughing and hugged one another as though they'd made a touchdown, and they might as well both been naked by now, they just stood there and looked down at themselves from time to time like they were alone in the shower, and laughed and laughed, and an old woman next to them just laughed and laughed too, and all Mae did was look once and then away with a funny half-smile on her mouth, she didn't show any more concern over it than the next one. Here was a whole beach of mostly women, just laughing their heads off because two men no longer young, were, well, exposing themselves in front of everybody, for that's all it was."

Philip stared at his empty water glass.

"I started to say something to Mae, and she nearly cut my head off, saying something like *why don't you mind your own goddamn business* in a tone unusually mean even for her. *Don't look damn you if you don't like it* was what my own wife said to me."

Suddenly Philip had relaxed in his chair as though the water he had drunk had contained a narcotic. He made no effort now to show his eagerness to leave, to hurry, or to comment on what was being said, and he sat there staring in the direction of, but not at, Guy.

"But the worst part came then," Guy said, and then looking critically and uneasily at Philip, he turned round to look at the cafeteria clock, but it showed only five minutes to one, and their lunch hour was not precisely over.

"This old woman," he continued, swallowing hard, "who had been sitting there next to them got out a sewing kit she had, and do you know what?"

"I suppose she sewed them shut," Philip said sleepily and still staring at nothing.

"That's exactly correct," Guy said, a kind of irritated disappointment in his voice. "This old woman who looked at least eighty went right up to them the way they were and she must have been a real seamstress, and before the whole crowd with them two grown men laughing their heads off she sewed up their tights like some old witch in a story, and Mae sat there as cool as if we was playing bridge in the church basement, and never said boo, and when I began to really let off steam, she said *Will you keep your big old ugly mouth shut or am I going to have to hit you over the mouth with my beach clogs.* That's how they had affected my own wife.

"So," Guy said, after a pause in which Philip contributed nothing, "this country has certainly changed since I grew up in it. I said that to Mae and that was the final thing I had to say on the subject, and those two grown men went right on lying there on the sand, every so often slapping one another on their muscles, and combing their hair with oil, and laughing all the time, though I think even they did have sense enough not to get up and split their trunks again or even they must have known they would have been arrested by the beach patrol."

"Sure," Philip said vacantly.

"So that's the story of Milo and the Austrian," Guy said.

"It's typical," Philip said, like a somnambulist.

"Are you sore at me or something," Guy said, picking up his and Philip's checks.

"Let me pay my own, for Christ's sake," Philip said.

"Listen, you *are* sore at me, I believe," Guy said.

"I have a rotten headache is all," Philip replied, and he picked up his own check.

"I hope I didn't bring it on by talking my head off."

"No," Philip replied. "I had it since morning."

COLOR OF DARKNESS

Sometimes he thought about his wife, but a thing had begun of late, usually after the boy went to bed, a thing which *should* have been terrifying but which was not: he could not remember now what she had looked like. The specific thing he could not remember was the color of her eyes. It was one of the most obsessive things in his thought. It was also a thing he could not quite speak of with anybody. There were people in the town who would have remembered, of course, what color her eyes were, but gradually he began to forget the general structure of her face also. All he seemed to remember was her voice, her warm hearty comforting voice.

Then there was the boy, Baxter, of course. What did he know and what did he not know. Sometimes Baxter seemed to know everything. As he hung on the edge of the chair looking at his father, examining him closely (the boy never seemed to be able to get close enough to his father), the father felt that Baxter might know everything.

"Bax," the father would say at such a moment, and stare into his own son's eyes. The son looked exactly like the father. There was no trace in the boy's face of anything of his mother.

"Soon you will be all grown up," the father said one night, without ever knowing why he had said this, saying it without his having even thought about it.

"I don't think so," the boy replied.

"Why don't you think so," the father wondered, as surprised by the boy's answer as he had been by his own question.

The boy thought over his own remark also.

"How long does it take?" the boy asked.

"Oh a long time yet," the father said.

"Will I stay with you, Daddy," the boy wondered.

The father nodded. "You can stay with me always," the father said.

The boy said *Oh* and began running around the room. He fell over one of his engines and began to cry.

Mrs. Zilke came into the room and said something comforting to the boy.

The father got up and went over to pick up the son. Then sitting down, he put the boy in his lap, and flushed from the exertion, he said to Mrs. Zilke: "You know, I am old!"

Mrs. Zilke laughed. "If you're old, I'm dead," she said. "You must keep your youth," she said almost harshly to the father, after a pause.

He looked up at her, and the boy suddenly moved in his father's arms, looking questioningly at his father. He kissed his father on the face.

"He's young yet," the boy said to Mrs. Zilke.

"Why, of course. He's a young man," she said. "They don't come no younger for fathers."

The father laughed and the boy got up to go with Mrs. Zilke to his bed.

The father thought about Mrs. Zilke's remark and he listened as he heard her reading to the boy from a story-book. He found the story she read quite dry, and he wondered if the boy found anything in it at all.

It was odd, he knew, that he could not remember the color of his wife's eyes. He knew, of course, that he must remember them, and that he was perhaps unconsciously trying to forget. Then he began to think that he could not remember the color of his son's eyes, and he had just looked at them!

"WHAT DOES HE know?" he said to Mrs. Zilke when she came downstairs and sat for a moment with the newspaper. She lit a cigarette and blew out some smoke before she replied to him. By then he was looking out the window as though he had forgotten her presence and his question.

"He knows everything," Mrs. Zilke said.

The father came to himself now and looked at her gently.

"They all do now, don't they," the father said, meaning children.

"It seems so," the woman said. "Yes," she said, thinking. "They know everything."

"Everybody seems forty years old to me," the father said. "Even children maybe. Except they are complete mysteries to me. I don't know what to say to any of them. I don't know what they know, I guess."

"Oh, I understand that. I raised eight kids and I was always thinking the same thing."

"Well, that relieves me," he told Mrs. Zilke.

She smiled, but in her smile he thought he saw some thought reserved, as though she had not told everything.

"Of course we never know any other human being, do we?" he told Mrs. Zilke, hesitating as though to get the quotation right.

She nodded, enjoying her cigarette.

"Your son is lonely," she said suddenly.

The father did not look at her now.

"I mean by that," she went on, "it's too bad he's an only child."

"Doesn't he have other children over here, though. I thought—"

"Oh, it's not the same," Mrs. Zilke said. "Having in other youngsters like he does on Saturday and all. It's not enough."

"Of course I am gone a good deal."

"You're gone all the time," she said.

"That part can't be helped, of course. You see," he laughed, "I'm a success."

Mrs. Zilke did not return his laughter, he noticed, and he had noticed this before in plain strong old working women of her kind. He admired Mrs. Zilke tremendously. He was glad she had not laughed with him.

"No one should have just the one child," she told him.

"You know," he said, confidentially, "when you have just your work, as I do, people get away from you."

He looked at the bottle of brandy on the bookshelf.

"Would you have a pony of brandy with me, Mrs. Zilke."

She began to say no because she really didn't like it, but there was such a pleading look on his young face, she nodded rather regally, and he got up and poured two shots.

"Thank you for drinking with me," he said suddenly, as though to brush away something that had come between his words and his memory.

"Quite a bouquet," she said, whiffing first.

"You are really very intelligent," he told Mrs. Zilke.

"Because I know the bouquet," she said coldly.

"Oh, that and a lot of other things."

"Well, I don't know anything," Mrs. Zilke said.

"You know everything," he remarked. "All I have is my work."

"That's a lot. They need you," she said.

He sat down now, but he did not touch the brandy, and Mrs. Zilke having smelled the bouquet put her tiny glass down too.

They both sat there for a moment in silence as though they were perhaps at communion.

"I can't remember the color of my wife's eyes," he said, and he looked sick.

Mrs. Zilke sat there as though considering whether this had importance, or whether she might go on to the next topic of their talk.

"And tonight, would you believe it, I couldn't remember the color of his!"

"They're blue as the sea," Mrs. Zilke said rather gruffly, but with a kind of heavy sad tone also in her voice.

"But what does it matter about those little things," she said. "You're an important man!"

He laughed very loud at this, and Mrs. Zilke suddenly laughed, too. A cord of tension had been snapped that had existed between them earlier.

The father lifted his glass and said the usual words and Mrs. Zilke took her glass with a slight bored look and sipped.

"I can taste the grapes in that, all right," she said.

"Well, it's the grapes of course I buy it for," he replied in the tone of voice he might have used in a men's bar.

"You shouldn't care what color their eyes are or were," Mrs. Zilke said.

"Well, it's my memory about people," he told her. "I don't know people."

"I know you don't," she said. "But you have other things!"

"No, I don't. Not really. I could remember people if I wanted to."

"If you wanted to," Mrs. Zilke said.

"Well, why can't I remember my wife's eyes?" he brought the whole thing out. "Can you remember," he wanted to know, "the color of eyes of all those in your family."

"All forty-two of them," she laughed.

"Well, your husband and your sons and daughters."

"Oh, I expect I can," she was rather evasive.

"But you do, Mrs. Zilke, you know you do!"

"All right, but I'm just a woman about the house. You're out in the world. Why should you know the color of people's eyes! Good grief, yes!"

She put her glass down, and picked up some socks she had been darning before she had put the boy to bed.

"I'm going to work while we talk," she said with a firmness that seemed to mean she would be talking less now and that she would probably not drink the brandy.

Then suddenly closing his own eyes tight he realized that he did not know the color of Mrs. Zilke's eyes. But suddenly he could not be afraid anymore. He didn't care, and he was sure that Mrs. Zilke would not care if he knew or not. She would tell him not to care. And he remembered her, which was, he was sure, more important. He remembered her kindness to him and his son, and how important they both were to him.

"HOW OLD *are* you?" Baxter asked him when he was sitting in his big chair with his drink.

"Twenty-eight, I think," the father said vaguely.

"Is that old enough to be dead?" the son wondered.

"Yes and no," the father replied.

"Am I old enough to be dead?"

"I don't think so," the father replied slowly, and his mind was on something else.

"Why aren't we all dead, then?" the son said, sailing a tiny paper airplane he had made. Then he picked up a bird he had made out of brown paper and sailed this through the air. It hit a philodendron plant and stuck there in it, as though it were a conscious addition.

"You always think about something else, don't you?" the boy said, and he went up and stared at his father.

"You have blue eyes," the father said. "Blue as the sea."

The son suddenly kissed his father, and the father looked at him for a long time.

"Don't look funny like that," the boy said, embarrassed.

"Like what?" the father said, and lowered his gaze.

The son moved awkwardly, grinding his tiny shoes into the carpet.

"Like you didn't know anything," the boy said, and he ran out into the kitchen to be with Mrs. Zilke.

AFTER MRS. ZILKE went to bed, which was nearly four hours after the boy had gone, the father was accustomed to sit on downstairs thinking about the problems in his work, but when he was at home like this he often thought about *her*, his wife of long ago. She had run off (this was almost the only term he used for her departure) so long ago and his marriage to her had been so brief that it was almost as though Baxter were a gift somebody had awarded him, and that as the gift increased in value and liability, his own relation to it was more and more ambiguous and obscure. Somehow Mrs. Zilke seemed more real to him than almost anybody else. He could not remember the color of her eyes either, of course, but she was quite real. She was his "mother," he supposed. And the boy was an infant "brother" he did not know too well, and who asked hard questions, and his "wife," who had run off, was just any girl he had gone out with. He could not remember her now at all.

He envied in a way Mrs. Zilke's command over everything. She understood, it seemed, everything she dealt with, and she remembered and could identify all the things which came into her view and under her jurisdiction. The world for her, he was sure, was round, firm, and perfectly illuminated.

For him only his work (and he remembered she had called him a man of importance) had any real meaning, but its relationship to everything else was tenuous.

As he went upstairs that night he looked into his son's room. He was surprised to see that the boy was sleeping with an enormous toy crocodile. The sight of the toy rather shocked him. For a moment he hesitated whether or not to remove the toy and then deciding not to disturb him, he went to his room, took off all his clothes, and stood naked, breathing in front of the opened window. Then he went quickly to bed.

"IT'S HIS FAVORITE DOLL," Mrs. Zilke said at breakfast. "He wouldn't part with it for the world." She referred to the toy crocodile.

"I would think it would give him nightmares," the father said.

"He don't have nightmares," Mrs. Zilke said, buttering the toast. "There you are, sir!" and she brought him his breakfast.

The father ate silently for a while.

"I was shocked to see that crocodile in his bed," he told Mrs. Zilke again.

"Well, that's something in you, is all," she said.

"I expect. But why couldn't it have been a teddy bear or a girl doll."

"He has those too. It just happened to be crocodile night last night," Mrs. Zilke said, restless now in the kitchen.

"All right," the father said, and he opened the newspaper and began to read about Egypt.

"Your boy needs a dog," Mrs. Zilke said without warning, coming in and sitting down at the table with him. Her hands still showed the traces of soap suds.

"What kind?" the father said.

"You're not opposed to it, then?" Mrs. Zilke replied.

"Why would I oppose a dog?" He continued to look at the newspaper.

"He's got to have something," Mrs. Zilke told him.

"Of course," the father said, swallowing some coffee. Then, having swallowed, he stared at her.

"You mean he doesn't have anything?"

"As long as a parent is living, any parent, a child has something. No, I didn't mean *that*," she said without any real apology, and he expected, of course, none.

"I'd rather have him sleeping with a dog now than that crocodile."

"Oh, that," Mrs. Zilke said, impatient.

Then: "All right, then," he said.

He kept nodding after she had gone out of the room. He sat there looking at his old wedding ring which he still wore. Suddenly he took the ring off his finger for the first time since he had had it put on there by the priest. He had left it on all these years simply because, well, he wanted men to think he was married, he supposed. Everybody was married, and he had to be married somehow, anyhow, he knew.

But he left the wedding ring lying on the table, and he went into the front room.

"Sir," Mrs. Zilke called after him.

"Just leave the ring there," he said, thinking she had found it.

But on her face he saw something else. "You'll have to take the boy to buy the dog, you know. I can't walk on hard pavements anymore, remember."

"That will be fine, Mrs. Zilke," he said, somehow relieved at what she said.

THE DOG THEY bought at the shop was a small mongrel with a pitifully long tail, and—the father looked very close: brown eyes. Almost the first thing he did was to make a puddle near the father's desk. The father insisted on cleaning it up, and Baxter watched, while Mrs. Zilke muttered to herself in the kitchen. She came in finally and poured something white on the spot.

The dog watched them too from its corner, but it did not seem to want to come out to them.

"You must make up to your new little friend," the father said.

Baxter stared but did not do anything.

"Go to him," the father said, and the son went over into the corner and looked at the pup.

The father sat down at his desk and began to go through his papers.

"Did you have a dog?" Baxter asked his father.

The father thought there at the desk. He did not answer for a long time.

"Yes," the father finally said.

"What color was it," the son asked, and the father stirred in his chair.

"That was so long ago," he said, almost as though quoting himself.

"Was it gray then?" the boy wanted to know.

The father nodded.

"A gray dog," the son said, and he began to play with his new pet. The dog lifted its wet paw and bit the boy mildly, and the boy cried a little.

"That's just in fun," the father said absentmindedly.

Baxter ran out into the kitchen, crying a little, and the small dog sat in the corner.

"Don't be afraid of the little fellow now," Mrs. Zilke said. "Go right back and make up to him again."

Baxter and Mrs. Zilke came out of the kitchen and went up to the dog.

"You'll have to name him too," Mrs. Zilke said.

"Will I have to name him, Daddy?" the boy said.

The father nodded.

After supper all three sat in the front room. Baxter nodded a little. The father sat in the easy chair smoking his pipe, a pony of brandy near him. They had gathered here to decide what name to choose for the dog, but nobody had any ideas, it seemed, and the father, hidden from them in a halo of expensive pipe smoke, seemed as far away as if he had gone to the capital again.

Baxter nodded some more and Mrs. Zilke said, "Why, it still isn't bedtime and the little man is asleep!"

From below in the basement where they had put the pup they could all hear the animal's crying, but they pretended not to notice.

Finally, Mrs. Zilke said, "When he is housebroken you can sleep with him, Baxter."

Baxter opened his eyes and looked at her. "What is that?" he said.

"When he learns to take care of himself, not make puddles, you can have him in bed with you."

"I don't want to," the boy said.

Mrs. Zilke looked stoically at the father.

"Why don't you want to, sweetheart," she said, but her words showed no emotion.

"I don't want anything," the boy said.

Mrs. Zilke looked at the father again, but he was even more lost to them.

"What's that hanging loose in your mouth," Mrs. Zilke suddenly sprang to attention, adjusting her spectacles, and looking at the boy's mouth.

"This." The boy pointed to his lips, and blushed slightly. "Gum," he said.

"Oh," Mrs. Zilke said.

The clock struck eight.

"I guess it *is* your bedtime," Mrs. Zilke said.

She watched the boy.

"Do you want to go to bed, Baxter," she said, abstractedly.

The boy nodded.

"Say goodnight to daddy and kiss him," she told him perfunctorily.

The boy got up and went over to his father, but stopped in front of the rings of smoke.

"Goodnight," the boy lisped.

"What's that in his mouth," the father addressed his remark to Mrs. Zilke and his head came out of the clouds of smoke.

Mrs. Zilke got up painfully now and putting on her other glasses looked at the boy.

"What are you sucking?" Mrs. Zilke said, and both of them now stared at him.

Baxter looked at them as though they had put a net about him. From his long indifference to these two people a sudden new feeling came slowly into his dazed, slowly moving mind. He moved back a step, as though he wanted to incite them.

"Baxter, sweetheart," the old woman said, and both she and the father stared at him as though they had found out perhaps who he was.

"What do you have in your mouth, son," the father said, and the word *son* sounded queer in the air, moving toward the boy with the heaviness and suggestion of nausea that the dog puddle had given him earlier in the afternoon.

"What is it, son," the father said, and Mrs. Zilke watched him, her new understanding of the boy written on her old red face.

"I'm chewing gum," the boy told them.

"No, you're not now, Baxter. Why don't you tell us," Mrs. Zilke whined.

Baxter went over into the corner where the dog had been.

"That dog is bad, isn't he," Baxter giggled, and then he suddenly laughed loudly when he thought what the dog had done.

Meanwhile Mrs. Zilke and the father were whispering in the cloud of tobacco smoke.

Baxter sat down on the floor talking to himself, and playing with a broken piece of Tinker Toy. From his mouth still came sounds of something vaguely metallic.

Then Mrs. Zilke came up stealthily, a kind of sadness and kindness both in her face, like that of a trained nurse.

"You can't go to sleep with that in your mouth, sweetheart."

"It's gum," the boy said.

Mrs. Zilke's bad legs would not let her kneel down beside the boy on the floor as she wished to do. She wanted to have a close talk with him, as she did sitting by his bed in the nursery, but instead now, standing over him, so far away, her short heavy breathing sounding obnoxiously in the room, she said only, "You've never lied to me before, Baxter."

"Oh yes I have," Baxter said. "Anyhow this is gum," and he made the sounds again in his mouth.

"I'll have to tell your father," she said, as though *he* were already away in Washington.

"It's gum," the boy said in a bored voice.

"It's metal, I think," she said looking worriedly at the boy.

"It's just gum." The boy hummed now and played with the Tinker Toy.

"You'll have to speak to him," Mrs. Zilke said.

The father squatted down with the son, and the boy vaguely realized this was the first time the father had ever made the motion of playing with him. He stared at his father, but did not listen to what he was talking about.

"If I put my finger in your mouth will you give it to me?" the father said.

"No," the boy replied.

"You wouldn't want to swallow the thing in your mouth," the father said.

"Why not," the boy wondered.

"It would hurt you," the father told him.

"You would have to go to the hospital," Mrs. Zilke said.

"I don't care where I go," the boy said. "It's a toy I have in my mouth."

"What sort of toy," the father wondered, and he and Mrs. Zilke suddenly became absorbed in the curiosity of what Baxter had there.

"A golden toy," the boy laughed, but his eyes looked glassy and strange.

"Please," the father said, and he put his finger gently on the boy's lips.

"Don't touch me!" the son called out suddenly. "I hate you!"

The father drew back softly as though now he would return to his work and his papers, and it was Mrs. Zilke who cried out instead: "Shame!"

"I do hate him," the boy said. "He's never here anyhow."

"Baxter," the father said.

"Give your father what's in your mouth or you will swallow it and something terrible will happen to you."

"I want it right where it is," the boy said, and he threw the Tinker Toy at Mrs. Zilke.

"Look here now, Baxter," the father said, but still sleepily and with no expression.

"Shut your goddamn face," the boy spat out at his father.

The father suddenly seized the boy's chin and jaw and forced him to spit out what he had.

His wedding ring fell on the carpet there, and they all stared at it a second.

Without warning the son kicked the father vigorously in the groin and escaped, running up the stairs.

Baxter stepped deliberately from the safety of the upper staircase and pronounced the obscene word for his father as though this was what he had been keeping for him for a long time.

Mrs. Zilke let out a low cry.

The father writhing in pain from the place where the boy had kicked him, managed to say with great effort: "Tell me where he learned a word like that."

Mrs. Zilke went over to where the ring lay now near the Tinker Toy.

"I don't know what's happening to people," she said, putting the ring on the table.

Then, a weary concern in her voice, she said, "Sir, are you hurt?"

The tears fell from the father's eyes for having been hit in such a delicate place, and he could not say anything more for a moment.

"Can I do anything for you, sir?" Mrs. Zilke said.

"I don't think right now, thank you," he said. "Thank you." He grunted with the exquisite pain.

"I've put your ring up here for safekeeping," she informed him.

The father nodded from the floor where he twisted in his pain.

NIGHT AND DAY

"The chestnut man will be here before too long," Cleo said, "and I will buy you a lot of nice chestnuts before bedtime. But you must be a good boy, you must not tell Grandy things Mama says when we're alone together. After lunch tomorrow maybe he will take you out for a walk around the park. Won't that be nice?"

But he just sat there, on the new Persian rug, with his little train and engine, also new like the rug, and also gifts from Grandy, and would not answer her.

There was always the difficulty of his going to sleep, and the best thing was to just let him lie in bed talking to the animals on the wall, talking sometimes half the night.

One night, when Grandy made her tell him she was going to have the animals painted off the walls if he didn't behave, he had put up a fuss and said he was going to tell Grandy what she had called the old man the night he had not given her enough money. After that he got to talk to the kangaroo for an hour and told him what Mama had called Grandy, and then he told his other favorite, the elephant that stood on the weighing machine, and finally he told the South American foxes.

Tonight the chestnut man had not come, and when there was unexpectedly no sound from the little room upstairs, Cleo, once the tension had let up, began crying a little and said to Grandy: "His father will never know what bringing up a child means. And wouldn't care maybe if he knew."

Grandy patted her hand lightly.

"Where do you suppose Bruce is anyhow," she said, coldly angry. "It's going on two years."

"Cleo," Grandy said, "you know as well as I the only thing you can do."

They sat down then to their supper of cold chicken, cheese casserole, and cup after cup of coffee ready to strengthen her.

She had just put some food into her mouth when the door upstairs opened and he screamed.

Going up immediately to his room and sitting down with the perfunctory motions of a sleepwalker, she said: "Why can't you control yourself for just one meal."

"Where is Grandy?" he wondered.

"Grandy is reading the paper," she told him.

"I want to see Grandy."

"Well, he is too old and tired to come up the steps all the time."

"Tell Grandy to come up."

"You go to sleep."

She went down again and sat with Grandy and he began to smooth her hair as was his custom.

"Please, please," Cleo said when he kissed her loudly. "Let's try to be a little more careful now."

"Has he been careful?"

"Bruce?" she said, knowing, of course, that it was Bruce he meant.

Grandy watched her as though commanding her to give the answer he wanted.

"I loved Bruce, Grandy. I really did."

"He deserted *you*," Grandy said.

"Oh, now, father, father." She was weak with him.

"I know my own son," he told her. "Bruce ran out on you."

"There is no proof of that, father." Then: "Oh, *Bruce*, *Bruce*," she said, pretending she was saying this to herself.

"Bruce is no-account, never was, and it's infantile to ever expect his return."

"You shouldn't even think such a thing about your own boy," Cleo said unemphatically.

"Have Grandy come up now!" the small voice from upstairs called.

"He listens to everything we say and do," Cleo told the old man.

"And understands nothing, just like Bruce."

"But you *love* him, don't you," she said, fear in her voice, and her face suddenly red under the lamplight.

"Who?" Grandy roared.

"Who but the boy!" she said rather hotly.

"You know who I love," he told Cleo, and he put his hand on her lap. "And I know who you love."

"Oh, Grandy, Grandy." She was pliant and soft again.

"Why must it always be *Grandy*," the old man said. "Why can't it be . . ."

"Have Grandy come up, Mama; have him do that now. I am so lonesome."

"Talk to the little kangaroo until you go to sleep, lover," she called up. "Tell the little kangaroo your thoughts."

"No, I'm tired of *him*," the child said. "I want a new animal for telling my thoughts to," he called angrily.

"He wants a police dog," Cleo told the old man.

"They want everything," he replied, holding her hand tightly.

"Like some other people in this world," Cleo said, not removing her hand.

"You can't go on like this," Grandy emphasized to her, peremptorily removing his hand from hers and placing it on her cheek, where it stroked back and forth insinuatingly near her ear like a mouth whispering messages.

"What would our lives be like, if I did this terrible thing?" Cleo said.

"You've already gone more than half the way," Grandy said.

"Oh, Grandy," she cried, and she pushed her face into his vest and cried a little.

"If Bruce ever knew, my God, my God." Her voice came muffled and weak from against his chest.

"And what do you think Bruce might be doing tonight?" He was cool and unmoved.

"Well, he's not with my *mother*," she gasped, weakly impetuous, as though this were her last outburst of concern, for immediately after she sank back into his arms, and he kissed her with real feeling.

"Where are you now?" The voice came from upstairs.

"Oh, is he out of his bed, do you think?" Cleo asked, jumping up.

"Sit down, Cleo," the old man commanded. "Nothing is going to surprise us. You're jumpy as a cat. Do sit down, and don't get up again."

"I wish that boy had a nurse sometimes."

"He could have," Grandy told her.

"Oh, dear, dear. What *is* it all about?"

"Don't talk like one of those religious philosophers now," Grandy said to her. "You know and I know what is going to happen." He kissed her on the mouth.

"I don't know, and you can't make me," she said weakly.

He kissed her again.

"What is it, then, my *age*?" he asked ironically.

"Your age?" She laughed. "Have I ever known a younger man?" She touched his mouth, and he clasped her hand tightly at this.

"Younger than Bruce," he said, and his coy, crafty wink made her tense.

"Grandy, we might destroy everything!" she cautioned.

"You forget Bruce has already done that. How long has he been gone?" He began counting with that theatrical manner he so often assumed now.

"I can't helping thinking Bruce loved me," she said ignoring his manner.

"And his supposed love is enough."

"But for God's sake," she said getting up and pacing about the room. "You're his *father*! Grandy, you're Bruce's father!"

"How many times have you seen Bruce in the last two years—do you remember?" he asked now, his theatrical manner stronger than ever.

"He's been gone, of course, a little more than a year this time."

"*This* time!" Grandy stood up now and walked over to her. He embraced her with passion. Everything else he did resembled different people doing different things successively. But his embraces were his own. Perhaps that is what made her go on with them.

"More than a year, Cleo!" he said, almost shaking her. "Do you realize how ridiculous that is. Your own husband. Why a year? Why a month? Why even a fortnight? Why should that be?" He actually shook her now. "Why?"

"Please, please, don't wake the child again now. He's been quiet for nearly half an hour."

"Bruce can take *him*!" he said with great suddenness.

"Grandy!" she cried. "Why, you must know me better than that. Why, Grandy!"

She moved out of his orbit, her mouth trembling with surprise, her face a hot, red moon of hurt and confusion.

"Of course, I didn't mean that just as it sounded."

"You did too." She turned on him. "How dare you! Grandy, how dare you!"

She wept a little and, finding no handkerchief, she accepted the one he handed her.

"Give up that little thing upstairs," she began. "I hate you for that talk." Then softening a little again: "Oh, Grandy, Grandy, what *am* I going to do?"

"Do you want to answer this question," he cleared his throat, the actor playing now the counselor-at-law, closing the case. "Where would you have been this past year without my help? How would the little prince upstairs have eaten and slept, do you think? Who would have had the artist to paint the animals on his bedroom wall?"

"Stop all of this talk at once," she said without conviction. "Oh, Grandy." She collapsed.

He held her hand as though this gesture were the source of his power and her weakness.

"You're not a working-woman type, Cleo," he told her, his mouth to her ear now. He kissed her softly and insistently.

"I'm not very clever, if that's what you mean," she said, wiping her tears on his handkerchief again.

"You're not clever in the world's view. You're not a modern woman, Cleo. You belong at home with a man who can take care of you. You aren't meant to make your own way. . . . But that's right what you're going to be doing, if you go on with Bruce! My patience . . ." He thundered now.

"Oh, no, Grandy," she sobbed. "Don't speak like this. We have to think . . ."

"You've said that for months. What do we have to think about?"

"Maybe there are circumstances we don't understand," she begged him. "Maybe there's something happened to Bruce we don't know about."

"You forget you're talking about my son."

"That doesn't mean anything here," she said, some of her old thoughts awakening suddenly, only to fade to extinguishment under his touch.

"I know Bruce better than anybody in the world," he emphasized.

"You know him as a man," she said.

"I'm his father," Grandy said.

"You're a man." She was implacable.

"All right, you love Bruce then," he told her.

"I didn't say that. I didn't say that at all." A wave of weakness, impotence, idiocy swept over her again.

"Then what do you mean?" He was insistent.

"All I meant," she said, her breath coming heavily and fear changing her voice so that it resembled both a child's and an old woman's, "all I meant is, are we being fair to *them*, are we . . ."

"Tell me this," he said, holding her hand with savage firmness. "Does Bruce love you?"

She drew back, as though this question, never posed before, had swept away everything of the little she had held back for herself.

"Grandy, please, do we have to be so . . . so specific?"

"Yes, Cleo, yes."

"What was your question then?" she said, reaching for her cigarettes.

"Here," he commanded, "take one of mine."

"I'd rather have one of my . . ."

He put the cigarette in her mouth and lit it.

"Now, Cleo, I also can be of another mind. . . ."

"About what?" she said, looking at him with her terrified, young-innocent-girl face.

"There is a limit to *my* time, *my* endurance. And I'm not going to live forever, after all. I want life now. Not tomorrow. And I've waited . . ."

"Grandy, just don't do anything rash yet. Please wait, things will straighten out, I know. . . ."

"Have you ever thought that I might have somebody else, too?" he said.

"Yes," she said, trying to steady the fear that made her voice muffled as though she were speaking to him through a curtain. "I've thought of that, Grandy . . . many times." She lifted her tear-stained face to him.

"Think of it tonight with special clearness," he ordered her.

"I will, Grandy," she said, the tears falling again now, and she noticed that he did not caress her, did not hold out a hand to her. He had given her the question, the final decision; he was not going to do more. She saw that she must answer.

"It's the most difficult thing in the world, Grandy."

"Bawling's not going to help you, not going to get you anywhere." He was like another man now, and she saw something in him at that moment, vague and far away, which must have destroyed happiness for her with his son Bruce.

"I must know *now*," he told her.

"Oh, Grandy, no." She wept now, unashamed, uncontrolled.

"Of course," she said incoherently, "it's you, Grandy."

"And if it's me, then, it can't be him."

"You mean Bruce," she said, looking up from her hands which she had put over her face, hopefully expectant.

"I mean the kid!" He was clear and complete.

"What are you saying," she said, suddenly calm, her tears suddenly gone, a white toneless face, stripped of every emotion, looking at him.

"I want to marry *you*. Let Bruce have the kid."

"He's not a kid," she said.

"Well, what the hell is he?"

"He's still almost an infant." She walked up and down the room.

"And you will go to work to support him then?"

She did not say anything.

"I asked you a question, Cleo. Will you go to work in a factory or office to support him?"

"I never knew before how cruel you really are, and *were*."

"I've waited for you for at least two years, and I can't wait any longer." His voice quieted down slowly.

"I think I am beginning to see how it would be," she said and walked to the other side of the room and sat down.

"What was the meaning of that cryptic remark?"

"There was nothing cryptic in it, and it was more than a remark. I think it was a decision."

"You've made a decision?" He smiled knowingly.

"I think I have," she said.

He laughed.

"I must try to be calm, though," she told him. "I must say only what I mean and no more."

"That would be unusual for you." He used all his bitterness.

"Would it, Grandy?" She looked at him and as he gazed at her he hardly recognized her. She hardly, perhaps, recognized herself.

"What then have I been doing these years?" she said. "My God, yes, what."

"Now, Cleo, what is this?" he said going over to the chair where she was sitting.

"Don't come near me," she ordered him, and there was a strength in the way she motioned to him with trembling, thin hands covered with his rings.

"I see everything, of course, I've always seen it," she told him. "I think I see myself."

"You sound just like Bruce now," he said. "The goddam old preacher in him has come out in you."

"Just words," she said. "Just your old words." She stood up. "Words from an old goat," she cried, looking at his white hair.

"Cleo," he admonished, with gay good humor. "Realize what you are saying, my dear."

"What does that mean, realize what I'm saying. I'm *realizing* you, for the love of God. Don't you know that?"

"And what does that mean?" he said, and his disguise, or disguises, suddenly to her seemed to fall like pieces of cardboard at their feet. She felt she almost heard a sound of collapse in the room.

"An old old goat on his last legs, making a bargain as hard . . . as hard . . ." she said.

"Cleo, you know if you finish saying this, there can be nothing more for the two of us. Consider well what you are going to say."

He held up his hand.

"Oh, the theater of *that*!" She almost spat, her handsome face suddenly ugly.

At that moment they heard the bare feet and saw the child come into the room, or rather they did not see him. They both looked and looked away as though, after all, he had been there from the beginning.

The boy clasped his mother around the waist, but she went on talking, her hand, which had always fallen automatically on his curls when he went up close to her, suddenly now raised at the old man.

"You hit Grandy! Mama you hit Grandy!" the child cried, and he ran between her and his grandfather.

"Stop, don't touch him," she told the child. She went over to where the boy stood and brought him back to her.

"He's not your Grandy any more," she roared at him.

"Cleo, I can and I will make trouble for you if you speak in front of that boy."

"You old goat," she cried, and her hand now fell on the head of her son.

"You whoring old goat!"

THE LESSON

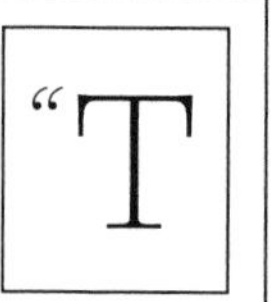

“This is not ladies’ day at the pool,” Mr. Diehl said. “I can’t admit her.”

“But she pleaded so.”

Mr. Diehl was about to give his lesson to a young man and wanted no women in the pool. He knew that if a woman entered the pool during the lesson she would distract the young man, who was already nervous about learning to swim. The young man was quite upset already, as he was going to have to go to a country house where there was lots of swimming and boating, and if he didn’t know how, his hosts would be very put out with him. They might never invite him again. At any rate that was his story, and besides, he was the commander’s son.

“But my grandmother always wants as many people to come into the pool as possible,” the girl said. Her grandmother owned the pool.

“I have worked for your grandmother for a long time,” Mr. Diehl, the swimming instructor said, “and I’m sure that she would not want a woman in the pool at this hour who does not belong to the club and so far as I know doesn’t even know how to swim.”

“Well, I asked her that,” the girl said.

"And what did she say?" the swimming instructor wanted to know.

"She said she could swim."

"Just the same she can wait until the lesson is over. It takes only half an hour."

"I told her that, but she wanted to go in the pool right away. She has gone downstairs to change."

"For Christ's sake," Mr. Diehl said.

His pupil, the commander's son, was already splashing around in the shallow water, waiting for the lesson.

"Go and tell her in a half hour."

The girl looked as though she was not going to tell the woman.

"If your grandmother were here she would back me up on this," Mr. Diehl said.

"But she's not here and my instructions were to do as best I thought."

"As best you thought," Mr. Diehl considered this, looking at the girl. She was sixteen, but he knew she had a slow mind and he wondered what had ever made Mrs. Schuck leave the pool in the hands of such an immature person.

"Look," Mr. Diehl said. "Just go and tell the woman that I can't have her in the pool while I am giving this special lesson."

"Well, I can't forbid her the pool very well, now, can I. If she wants to come in! This club isn't that exclusive and she knows one of the members."

"I don't care if she knows the man who invented swimming, she can't come in. Is that clear?"

"Mr. Diehl, you forget that I am the granddaughter of the owner of the pool."

"I am responsible for what goes on in the water, am I not?"

"Yes, I'll go along with you there."

"All right then," Mr. Diehl said, as though having made his point. "Go tell her I can't have her in the water until after the lesson. Can't you do that?"

"No," the girl said. "I can't tell that to a perfectly good customer."

"You have this pool mixed up with a public dance hall or something. This is not exactly a money-making organization, as your grandmother must have told you. It is a club. Not open to everybody. And this unknown woman should not have been allowed in here anyhow. Not at all."

"I know better," the girl said. "Many nice people come here just for an occasional swim."

"Not unless they are known," Mr. Diehl said.

"But she knows a member," the girl pointed out.

"Who is the member?" Mr. Diehl wanted to know.

"Oh, I can't remember," the girl told him.

"But I know every member by name," Mr. Diehl was insistent. "I've been swimming instructor here now for nine years."

"I know, I know," the girl said. "But this woman has every right to come in here."

"She's not coming in the water."

"Well, I don't know what to tell her. She's already putting on her suit."

"Then she can take it right off again," Mr. Diehl said.

"But not here, though," the girl tried a joke. Mr. Diehl did not laugh.

"What I'm trying to get you to see, Polly," Mr. Diehl said, and it was the first time he had ever called her by name, "is that this is a pretty high-class place. Do you know by chance who that boy is who is waiting for the lesson."

Mr. Diehl waited for the girl to answer.

"I don't know who he is," she replied.

"That is Commander Jackson's son."

"And he doesn't know how to swim?"

"What has that got to do with it?" the swimming instructor said.

"Well, I'm surprised is all."

"Look, time is slipping away. I don't want to have any more argument with you, Polly. But I'm sure your grandmother would back me up on this all the way if she were here. Is there any way we can reach her by telephone?"

"I have no idea where she went."

"Well, this strange woman cannot come into the pool now."

"I am not going down to the locker room and tell her to put her clothes back on, so there," Polly said.

She was very angry, but she had also gotten a little scared.

"Then I'm going to have to tell your grandmother how nasty you've been."

"How nasty *I've* been?"

Mr. Diehl went up to the girl and put his hands on her shoulder as he often did to his students. "Look here now," he said. He did not realize how he was affecting the girl and how the water fell from him on her blouse. She looked at his biceps as they moved almost over her mouth and the way his chest rose and fell. She had always lowered her eyes when she met him in the hall, avoiding the sight of his wet, dripping quality, the many keys held in his hand, his whistle for the days when they practiced champion swimming. He had seemed to her like something that should always remain splashing about and breathing heavily in water.

"Polly, will you please cooperate with me," Mr. Diehl said.

"I don't think I can," she said.

He put down his arms in a gesture of despair. "Will you please, please just this once go down to the ladies' dressing room and tell that woman that you've made a mistake and that she can't come into the pool just now?"

Polly looked out now into the water where the commander's son was floating around by holding on to a rubber tire.

"I just can't tell her," Polly said, turning red.

"You can't tell her," Mr. Diehl observed. Then: "Look, do you know who the commander is?"

"Well, doesn't everybody?" Polly answered.

"Do you know or don't you?" Mr. Diehl wanted to know. Some more water fell from him as he gesticulated, wetting her blouse and her arms a little, and she was sure that water continued to fall from him no matter how long he had been out of the pool. She could hear him breathing and she could not help noticing his chest rise and fall as though he were doing a special swimming feat just for her in this room.

"Polly!" he said.

"I can't! I can't!" she cried.

He could see now that there was something else here, perhaps fear of something, he could not tell, he did not want to know.

"You're not going to run into any difficulty in just telling her, are you, that you didn't know the rules and that she will have to wait until the lesson is over."

"I can't and I won't," Polly said, and she refused to look at him.

The commander's son was watching them from the middle of the shallow part of the pool, but he did not act as though he was impatient for the lesson to begin, and Polly remembered what a severe instructor Mr. Diehl was said to be. Sometimes while she had sat outside in the reception room she had heard Mr. Diehl shout all the way from the pool.

"Look, do we have to go all over this again?" Mr. Diehl said. "You know the commander."

"I know the commander, of course," she said.

"Do you know he is the most influential member of the club here?"

Polly did not say anything.

"He built this pool, Polly. Not your grandmother. Did you know that?"

She felt that she might weep now, so she did not say anything.

"Are you hearing me?" Mr. Diehl wanted to know.

"*Hearing* you!" she cried, distracted:

"All right, now," he said, and he put his hand on her again and she thought some more drops of water fell from him.

"I can't see how anybody would know," she said. "How would the commander know if a young woman went into his pool. And what would his son out there care."

"His son doesn't like people in the pool when he is taking a lesson," Mr. Diehl explained. "He wants it strictly private, and the commander wants it that way too."

"And the commander pays you to want it that way also."

"Polly, I'm trying to be patient."

"I'm not going to tell her she can't come in," Polly said.

She stood nearer now to the edge of the pool away from his moving arms and chest and the dripping water that she felt still came off them.

"Step away from the edge, please, Polly," he said, and he took hold of her arm drawing her firmly over to him, in his old manner with special pupils when he was about to impart to them some special secret of swimming.

"Don't always touch me," she said, but so faintly that it was hardly a reproach.

"Polly, listen to me," Mr. Diehl was saying to her. "I've known you since you were a little girl. Right?"

"Known me?" Polly said, and she felt the words only come vaguely toward her now.

"Been a friend of your family, haven't I, for a good long time. Your grandmother knew me when I was only a boy. She paid for some of my tuition in college."

"College," Polly nodded to the last word she had heard, so that he would think she was listening.

"You'll feel all right about this, Polly, and you will, I know, help me now that I've explained it to you."

"No, I can't," she said, awake again.

"You can't what?" Mr. Diehl said.

"I can't is all," she said but she spoke, as she herself recognized, like a girl talking in her sleep.

The hothouse heat of the swimming pool and the close presence of Mr. Diehl, a man she had always instinctively avoided, had made her forget in a sense why they were standing here before the water. Somewhere in a dressing room, she remembered, there was a woman who in a little while was going to do something wrong that would displease Mr. Diehl, and suddenly she felt glad this was so.

"Mr. Diehl, I am going," she said, but she made no motion to leave, and he knew from her words that she was not going. They were going on talking, he knew. It was like his students, some of them said they could never be champions, but they always were. He made them so. Some of the timid ones said they could never swim, the water was terror to them, but they always did swim. Mr. Diehl had never known failure with anything. He never said this but he showed it.

"Now you listen to me," Mr. Diehl said. "All you have to do is go and tell her. She can sit outside with you and watch television."

"The set isn't working," Polly said, and she walked over close to the edge of the pool.

"Please come over here now," Mr. Diehl said, and he took hold of her and brought her over to where he had been standing. "Polly, I would never have believed this of you."

"Believed what?" she said, and her mind could not remember now again why exactly they were together here. She kept looking around as though perhaps she had duties she had forgotten somewhere. Then, as she felt more and more unlike herself, she put her hand on Mr. Diehl's arm.

"Believed," he was saying, and she saw his white teeth near her as though the explanation of everything were in the teeth themselves—"believed you would act so incorrigible. So bad, Polly. Yes, that's the word. Bad."

"Incorrigible," she repeated, and she wondered what exactly that had always meant. It was a word that had passed before her eyes a few times but nobody had ever pronounced it to her.

"I would never want your grandmother to even know we have had to have this long argument. I will never tell her."

"I will never tell her," Polly said, expressionless, drowsily echoing his words.

"Thank you, Polly, and of course I didn't mean to tell you you didn't have to. But listen to me."

She put her hand now very heavily on his arm and leaned there.

"Are you all right, Polly," he said, and she realized suddenly that it was the first time he had ever really been aware of her being anything at all, and now when it was too late, when she felt too bad to even tell him, he had begun to grow aware.

"Polly," he said.

"Yes, Mr. Diehl," she answered and suddenly he looked down at her hand on his arm, it was pressing there, and he had become, of course, conscious of it.

He did not know what to do, she realized, and ill as she felt, the pleasure of having made him uncomfortable soothed her. She knew she was going to be very ill, but she had had at least, then, this triumph, the champion was also uncomfortable.

"You'll go and tell her then," Mr. Diehl said, but she knew now that he was not thinking about the woman anymore. The woman, the lesson, the pool had all lost their meaning and importance now.

"Polly," he said.

"I will tell her," she managed to say, still holding him tight.

"Polly, what is it?" he exclaimed.

He took her arm off him roughly, and his eyes moved about the room as though he were looking for somebody to help. His eyes fell cursorily upon the commander's son, and then back to her, but it was already too late, she had begun to topple toward him, her hands closed over his arms, and her head went pushing into his chest, rushing him with a strength he had seldom felt before.

When they fell into the water it was very difficult for him to get hold of her at all. She had swallowed so much water, and she had struck at him so hard, and had said words all the time nobody could have understood or believed but him. It was her speaking and struggling, as he said later, which had caused her to swallow so much water.

He had had to give her partial artificial respiration, a thing he had not done really in all his life, although he had taken all the courses in it as befitted a champion swimmer.

"Get out of the pool for God's sake and call somebody," Mr. Diehl yelled to the commander's son, and the boy left off hanging to the rubber tire, and slowly began to climb out of the shallow water.

"Get some speed on there, for Christ's sake," he said.

"Yes, sir," the commander's son replied.

"I can't be responsible for this whole goddam thing," he shouted after the retreating boy.

"Now see here, Polly, for Christ's sake," Mr. Diehl began looking down at her.

She opened her eyes and looked at him.

"You certainly pulled one over me!" he cried, looking at her, rage and fear on his mouth.

She lay there watching his chest move, feeling the drops of water falling over her from his body, and smelling behind the strong chemical odor of the pool the strong smell that must be Mr. Diehl himself, the champion.

"I'll go tell her now," Polly said.

Mr. Diehl stared at her.

"She must never come here at all," Polly said. "I think I see that now."

Mr. Diehl stretched out his hand to her to lift her up.

"Go away, please," she said. "Don't lean over me, please, and let the water fall from you on me. Please, please go back into the pool. I don't want you close now. Go back into the pool."

MRS. BENSON

"I don't know why Mrs. Carlin entertained," Mrs. Benson admitted. "She didn't like it, and she couldn't do it."

"I had to sit an entire hour under one of those potted palms she had in her house," Mrs. Benson's daughter, Wanda, recalled. "There was a certain odor about it—whether from the soil, or the plant, or the paper about the container. I felt terribly uncomfortable."

The two women, Wanda Walters, unmarried and thirty, from Philadelphia, and her mother, who lived in Europe, and had been married many times, and who was now Mrs. Benson, had nearly finished their tea, in an English tearoom within walking distance from the American Express, in Paris.

Mrs. Benson had known the English tearoom for many years, though she could never exactly remember its French name, and so could not ever recommend it to her friends, and she and her daughter, when they had their yearly reunions in Paris, always came to it. Their meeting in Paris this year had been rather a prolonged one, owing to Wanda's having failed to get a return passage to the States, and it had been a summer that was hot, humid, and gray—and not eventful for either of them.

This year, too, they found themselves going less and less anywhere at all, and they were somewhat embarrassed—at least, Mrs. Benson said *she* was—to find that they spent the better part of the day in the English tearoom, talking, for the most part, about people they had both known in Philadelphia twenty-odd years ago, when Wanda had been "little," and when Mrs. Benson—well, as she said, had at least had a different name!

It was the first time in many years, perhaps *the* first, that Mrs. Benson had really talked with her daughter at length about anything (they had always *traveled* before, as the older woman said), and certainly the first time in Wanda's memory that they had talked at all about "back home," as Mrs. Benson now called it with a chilly, condescending affection. And if their French or American friends happened by now, Mrs. Benson, if not Wanda, expressed by a glance or word a certain disappointment that their "talk" must be interrupted.

Mrs. Benson had made it a fixed practice not to confide in her daughter (she had once said to a close friend of hers: "I don't know my daughter, and it's a bit too late to begin!"), but the name *Mrs. Carlin*, which had come into their conversation so haphazardly, as if dropped from the awning of the café, together with the gloominess of their Paris, had set Mrs. Benson off. *Mrs. Carlin* came to open up a mine of confidences and single isolated incidents.

This was interesting to Wanda because Mrs. Benson had always been loath to "tell," to reminisce. Mrs. Benson hated anecdotes, regarding them as evidence of senility in the old, and cretinism in the young, and though there were other people "back home," of course, Mrs. Carlin could easily carry them through for the rest of Paris, and the potted palms, which had so dismayed Wanda, seemingly set Mrs. Benson "right" at last.

"I don't suppose you remember when they were popular," Mrs. Benson referred to the palms. "But they were once nearly everywhere. I've always disliked them, and, I think, perhaps, I even vaguely *fear* them."

"I don't think Mrs. Carlin *liked* them," Wanda said abruptly, so abruptly that Mrs. Benson dropped a long ash from her cigarette into her tea, and then called the waiter.

"How on earth do you know Mrs. Carlin didn't like them?" Mrs. Benson flushed slightly and then paused while the waiter brought her a fresh cup.

Wanda paused also. She felt that her mother did not *want* to know that she knew anything about Mrs. Carlin, and Wanda, in any case, was not very much interested in explaining what she did mean.

"I simply meant this," Wanda felt she must explain, under the *look* her mother gave her. "The part of the house Mrs. Carlin used for *entertainment* could not have reflected *anybody's* taste."

Mrs. Benson opened her eyes wide, and brought her mouth into a kind of cupid's bow. Then, in a voice quieter than her expression, she said: "I'd have to say, Wanda, that you were right!

"But how on earth did you *know*?" Mrs. Benson suddenly brought out, and she looked at her daughter as if a fresh light had been thrown on the latter's character also.

"What I think I meant," Wanda began again tearing apart one of the tiny envelopes of sugar that lay beside her spoon, "Mrs. Carlin was, as we both know, more than a *little* wealthy . . ."

Mrs. Benson cleared her throat, but then decided; evidently, not to speak, and her silence was as emphatic as she could make it.

"That is," Wanda went on slowly, "she could *afford* to entertain rather shabbily."

"Rather *shabbily*?" Mrs. Benson considered this. "That is a terribly queer word for *her*."

"But you yourself . . ."

"I don't like potted palms," Mrs. Benson pushed through to what was, as her face showed, the important matter here, "and I don't like all those original early nineteenth-century landscapes with cattle," she became now as firm as if in court, "but as to her house being *shabby* . . ."

"*Depressing* then," Wanda said. "It was certainly depressing."

Mrs. Benson laughed, guardedly indulgent. "You're so hard on the poor dear," she said in a tone of voice unlike her own.

"But I thought you thought as I did," Wanda cried. "About *her*, at least!" Displeasure and boredom rang in her voice, but there was an even stronger expression there of confusion and doubt.

"I do, and I don't," Mrs. Benson put endearment and confidence now into her voice. Then, unaccountably, she looked at her rings. She had many. They were, without doubt, too genuine, if anything, and as they shone in the later afternoon light, they made her mother look, Wanda felt, both very rich and very old.

"I think you're right, though," Wanda heard Mrs. Benson's voice continuing, "right about Mrs. Carlin's not caring whether she impressed *people* or not."

"I don't know if I quite meant that," Wanda told her mother, but under her breath now. "I mean only she didn't care whether they *enjoyed* themselves or not at her house."

They were both silent for a moment, as if surprised at the difficulties which had suddenly sprung up from nowhere, difficulties that were so obscure in themselves, and yet which offered some kind of threat of importance.

"The potted palms were a fright, of course," Mrs. Benson seemed either conciliatory or marking time. "And even for potted palms, they were dreadful." She touched her daughter's arm lightly. "They looked *dead*."

Going on, Mrs. Benson added: "I always thought of old-fashioned small-town Greek candy-kitchens when I saw those palm trees at Mrs. Carlin's. And her strange little painted-glass player piano, too!"

"I never saw *that*," Wanda admitted. She looked away from her mother's expression.

"Oh, you've forgotten it, is all," Mrs. Benson said. "It played for *all* the guests, that player piano . . . at least once." She laughed. "Mrs. Carlin seldom invited anybody twice."

Mrs. Benson had a peculiar, oblique, faraway look in her eyes, a look Wanda did not remember quite ever having seen on her mother's face before—indeed, on anybody's face.

Then, suddenly clearing her throat, Mrs. Benson coughed ceremoniously, struggling perhaps with a decision.

The one thing, Wanda remembered again, the thing that her mother disliked so much in others, was stories, *anecdotes*—indeed any narration which was prolonged beyond the length of a paragraph. But usually when Mrs. Benson cleared her throat *and* coughed, she was going to tell something which was important and necessary, if not long, or anecdotal.

But then, quickly, as if she had been given a reprieve of some kind, Mrs. Benson cried: "Oh, it's all so *nothing*!" and poured herself some tea.

"But what else was there?" Wanda cried, annoyance and curiosity both in her voice. Mrs. Benson shook her head.

"You did have something special, I believe," Wanda was positive.

"Oh, not actually," Mrs. Benson said. Then, with her faraway look again, she managed to say, "I *was* remembering an afternoon—oh, a long, long time ago at Mrs. Carlin's. . . . But in a *different* part of the house, you see."

Wanda waited, suddenly touched with something stronger than curiosity. But she knew that if she so much as moved now, Mrs. Benson might remember her own horror of anecdotes, and would close up tight.

"I dread to think how long ago that actually was," Mrs. Benson continued carefully, and her eyes then strayed out to the street, where a bus was slowing down to stop for a woman and a small child.

Mrs. Benson waited for the woman and child to board the bus, then commencing again: "I can't believe that it was so long ago as 1935, I mean, or along in there. . . . But, Mrs. Carlin had already begun to entertain her guests in one part of the house . . . and to *live* herself in another! She had begun dividing up her life in that way!"

She smiled at Wanda, almost in the manner of one who had finished her story there.

Wanda nodded only enough to let her mother know she was listening.

"I don't care much for this *tea*, today," Mrs. Benson said suddenly in an unexpectedly loud voice, and she looked up and about the room.

When Wanda said nothing, but showed that she was waiting, Mrs. Benson drank some more of the tea she did not like, and said: "Mrs. Carlin had never, I think, been particularly interested in *me*, as distinct from the others, until your father left me. . . . Evidently, *she* had never been too happy in her marriage, either . . . I gathered that from something she once let drop. . . .

"However," Mrs. Benson said, raising the empty tea cup, and looking up under at the bottom of it hurriedly, "however, she wanted me to see things. I knew that. She wanted me to see the things—the part of the house, you understand, that the *others* never saw."

Wanda nodded, a kind of fleeting awareness in her face.

"That was when she called me, well *aside*, I suppose one would have to say, and said something to me like, *'I want to really have you in some time, Rose.'* "

It came as a sort of shock to Wanda to hear her mother's Christian name. She had not only not heard it for many years—she had actually forgotten it, so separate had their two lives, and their very names, become.

But Mrs. Benson had gone right on now through her daughter's surprise, or shock: "At first I hadn't quite understood what Mrs. Carlin meant, you see. . . . She had taken hold of my arm, gently, and led me out of the room where she had always entertained the *others.* We got into a small gold elevator, and were gone in a minute. . . . When we got out, well—let me assure you, there wasn't a potted palm in the place!

"It was another house, another atmosphere, another place and time!"

A look of something like pain crossed Wanda's face, but her mother missed this in her final decision to "tell."

"It was a bit incredible to me then, and it's more so now," Mrs. Benson anticipated her daughter's possible incredulity, or indifference.

Pausing briefly, it was Mrs. Benson's turn now to study her daughter's face critically, but evidently, at the last, she found nothing on the younger woman's face to stop her.

Still, Mrs. Benson waited, looking at nothing in particular, while the waiter removed the empty cups, wiped the marble swiftly with a small cloth, bowed vaguely, and muttering part of a phrase, left.

Mrs. Benson commented perfunctorily on the indulgence of French waiters and French cafés, pointing out how wonderful it was to be able to stay *forever* when one wanted to.

Outside the light was beginning to fail, and a slight breeze came across to them from the darkening boulevard.

Wanda moved suddenly and unceremoniously in her chair, and Mrs. Benson fixed her with a new and indeterminate expression.

Raising her voice, almost as if to reach the street, Mrs. Benson said: "A week after Mrs. Carlin had showed me the 'real' part of the house, she invited me again, in an invitation she had written in her own hand, and which I must have somewhere, still. . . . I had never had a *written* invitation before from her, nobody had . . . always telephoned ones. . . . It was a dark January afternoon, I recall, and I was feeling, well, at that time, pretty low. . . . In the *new* part of the house—and I couldn't get over this time its *immensity*—tea was never mentioned, thank God, and we had some wonderful ancient Portuguese brandy. . . . But as we sat there talking, I kept hearing something soft but arresting. . . ."

Mrs. Benson stopped now in the guise of one who hears only what she is describing.

"Looking back away from Mrs. Carlin," Mrs. Benson said, "in the furthest part of the room, I was quite taken aback to see some actual *musicians*. Mrs. Carlin had an entire small string orchestra playing there for her. . . . You know, I thought I was mistaken. I thought it was perhaps a large oil, a mural, or something. . . . But Mrs. Carlin touched my hand just then, and said, *'They're for you, Rose.'* "

Mrs. Benson pressed her daughter's hand lightly at that, as if to convey by some touch *part* of the reality of that afternoon.

"I think she wanted to *help* me," Mrs. Benson said in a flat plain voice now, and with a helpless admission of anticlimax. "Your father—as I've said, had just *gone*, and I think she knew how everything stood."

Mrs. Benson avoided her daughter's glance by looking at her hands, which she held before her again now, so that there was the sudden quick scintillation again, and then went on: "When Mrs. Carlin took me to the door that day, I knew she wanted to say something else, something still more *helpful*, if you will, and I was afraid she was going to say what in fact she did."

Wanda's open-eyed expression made her mother suddenly smile.

"It was nothing sensational, my dear, or alarming! Mrs. Carlin was never *that*!"

"Well, for heaven's sake, then," Wanda cried.

"I said it was nothing sensational." In Mrs. Benson's dread of the *anecdote*—the inevitable concomitant of old age—she had so often told people nothing at all, and safety still, of course, lay in being silent. But as Wanda watched Mrs. Benson struggle there, postponing the telling of what she would have liked so much to tell, she realized in part what the struggle meant: Mrs. Benson had invariably all her life told her daughter *nothing*.

But Mrs. Benson had gone on again: "Mrs. Carlin was still beautiful then, and as I see now, *young*. . . . And I rather imagine that when she was very young, and when there had been, after all, a Mr. Carlin . . ."

A look from Wanda sped Mrs. Benson on: "I don't know *why* I treasure what Mrs. Carlin said to me," she hurried faster now. "But it is one of the few things that any other human being ever said to me that I do hold on to."

Mrs. Benson looked at the *addition* which the waiter had left, and her lips moved slightly over what was written there.

"Mrs. Carlin said to me," she went on, still looking at the waiter's bill, although her eyes were closed, " 'You're the only one who could *possibly* be asked in here with me, my dear. . . . I couldn't have the *others*, and I knew I couldn't have them. . . . They're not for *us* . . . And if you should ever feel you would like to *stay on*,' Mrs. Carlin said, '*why don't you, my dear?*' "

"She actually thought so well of you!" Wanda said, and then hearing the metallic hardness of her own voice, lowered her eyes in confusion.

"Of course, that was a long time ago," Mrs. Benson said vaguely, more of a cold edge now in her voice. "She wouldn't want *anyone* there now," she added.

"She is such a recluse then?" Wanda asked. Mrs. Benson did not answer. She had taken some francs out of her purse and was staring at them.

"Some of this money," she pointed out, "have you noticed? It comes to pieces in one's hands. I hardly know what to do with some of the smaller notes."

"These little reunions in Paris are such a pleasure, Mother," Wanda said in a rather loud, bright voice.

"Are they, my dear?" Mrs. Benson answered in her old firm manner. Then, in a sudden hard voice: "I'm so glad if they are."

The two women rose from the table at the same time, Mrs. Benson having deposited some of the notes on the marble-topped table, and they moved toward the front of the café, and into the street.

ENCORE

"He's in that Greek restaurant every night. I thought you knew that," Merta told her brother.

"What does he do in it?" Spence said, wearily attentive.

"I don't go to Greek restaurants and I don't spy on him," she said.

"Then how do you know so certainly he is there every night?"

"How do you know anything? He's not popular at the college. He says he likes to talk to Spyro, the restaurant owner's son, about painting. I don't know what they do!"

"Well, don't tell me if you don't know," her brother said. He got up and took his hat to go.

"Of course," she continued anxiously stepping in front of him to delay his going, "it isn't so much that Spyro is all at fault, you know. There are things wrong with Gibbs, too. As I said, he's not popular at the college. He wasn't asked to join a fraternity, you know. And the restaurant has made up for that, I suppose. It's always open for him day or night."

"Maybe you should make your own home more of a place he could bring his friends to," Spence said, a kind of cold expressionless tone in his voice.

"You would say that," she repeated almost without emotion.

"I don't suppose you ever half considered what it is, I mean this home. It's not a home. It's a flat, and I'm a woman without a husband."

"I know, I know Merta. You've done it all alone. Nobody's lifted a finger but you." His weariness itself seemed to collapse when he said this, and he looked at her with genuine feeling.

"I'm not trying to get your pity. I wanted to tell somebody what was going on at Spyro's is all. I needed to talk to somebody."

"I think Spyro's is the best place he could go," Spence said.

"And Spyro's awful father and grandfather!" she cried as though seeing something from far back of dread and ugliness.

"The Matsoukases?" Spence was surprised at her vehemence.

"Yes, the Matsoukases! With their immense eyes and black beards. Old Mr. Matsoukas, the grandfather, came here one evening, and tried to get fresh with me."

"I can hardly believe it," Spence said.

"You mean I am making it up," she accused him.

"No, no, I just can't visualize it."

"And now," she returned to the only subject which interested her, "Gibbs is there all the time as though it was his home."

"Do you talk to him about it, Merta?"

"I can't. I can't tell him and nag him about not going to the Greek restaurant at night. It's glamor and life to him, I suppose, and I suppose it *is* different. A different sort of place. The old man hasn't allowed them to put in juke boxes or television or anything, and you know Gibbs likes anything funny or different, and there isn't anything funny or different but maybe Spyro's. None of the college crowd goes there, and Gibbs feels he's safe there from their criticism and can drink his coffee in peace."

"Well it sounds so dull, drinking coffee in a seedy Greek restaurant, I don't see why a mother should worry about her son going there. And call me out of bed to talk about it!"

"Oh Spence," she said urgently again, "he shouldn't go there. Don't you see? He shouldn't be there."

"I don't see that at all," Spence said. "And Merta, I wish you would quit calling me up at this hour of the night to talk about your son, who is nearly a grown man by now. After all I have my profession to worry about too. . . ."

She stared at him.

"I had to talk with somebody about Spyro," she said.

"Oh, it's Spyro then you wanted to talk about," Spence said, the irritation growing in his manner.

"Spyro," she said vaguely, as though it were Spence who himself had mentioned him and thus brought him to mind. "I never cared much for that young man."

"Why not?" Spence was swift to hold her to anything vague and indirect because he felt that vagueness and indirectness was her method.

"Well, Spyro does all those paintings and drawings that are so bizarre."

"Bizarre," he paused on the word. "They're nearly *good*, if you ask me."

"I don't like Spyro," she said.

"Why don't you invite him here, if your son likes him?" he put the whole matter in her hands.

"When I work in a factory all day long, Spence. . . ."

"You don't feel like doing anything but working in a factory," he said irritably.

"I thought my own brother would be a little more understanding," she said coldly angry.

"I wish you would be of Gibbs," he told her.

"Oh Spence, please, please."

"Please, nothing. You always have a problem, but the problem is you, Merta. You're old and tired and complaining, and because you can't put your finger on what's wrong you've decided that there's something wrong with your son because he goes, of all places, to a Greek restaurant and talks to Spyro who draws rather well and who is now making a portrait of your son."

"Spence! Don't tell me that!"

"You dear old fool, Merta," he said and he put on his hat now, which she looked at, he thought, rather critically and also with a certain envy.

"That's a nice hat," she forced herself to say at last.

"Well a doctor can't look like a nobody," he said, and then winced at his own words.

"What you should do, Merta," he hurried on with another speech, "is get some sort of hobby, become a lady bowler, get on the old women's curling team, or meet up with some gent your own age. And let your son go his own way."

"You are comforting," Merta said, pretending to find humor in his words.

"WAS THAT SPENCE leaving just now?" Gibbs said, putting down some books.

Merta held her face up to be kissed by him, which he did in a manner resembling someone surreptitiously spitting out a seed.

"And how was Spyro tonight?" she said in a booming encouraging voice whose suddenness and loudness perhaps surprised even her.

He looked at her much as he had when as a small boy she had suddenly burst into the front room and asked him what he was being so very still for.

"Spyro is doing a portrait of me," he told her.

"A portrait," Merta said, trying hard to keep the disapproval out of her voice.

"That's what it is," Gibbs said, sitting down at the far end of the room and taking out his harmonica.

She closed her eyes in displeasure, but said nothing as he played "How High the Moon." He always played, it seemed, when she wanted to talk to him.

"Would you like Spyro to come visit us some day?" she said.

"Visit us?"

"Pay a call," she smiled, closing her eyes.

"What would he pay us a call for?" he wondered. Seeing her pained hurt look, he expanded: "I mean what would he get to see here."

"Oh, me," she replied laughing. "I'm so beautiful."

"Spyro thinks you don't like him," Gibbs said, and while she was saying *Tommyrot!* Gibbs went on: "In fact, he thinks everybody in this town dislikes him."

"They *are* the only Greeks, it's true," Merta said.

"And we're such a front family in town, of course!" he said with sudden fire.

"Well, your Uncle Spence is somebody," she began, white, and her mouth gaping a little, but Gibbs started to play on the harmonica again, cutting her off.

She tried to control her feelings tonight, partly because she had such a splitting headache.

"Would you like a dish of strawberry Jell-O?" Merta said above the sound of the harmonica playing.

"What?" he cried.

"Some strawberry Jell-O," she repeated, a little embarrassment now in her voice.

"What would I want that for?" he asked, putting down the harmonica with impatience.

"I suddenly got hungry for some, and went out there and made it. It's set by now and ready to eat."

There was such a look of total defeat on her old gray face that Gibbs said he would have some.

"I've some fresh coffee too," she said, a touch of sophistication in her voice, as if coffee here were unusual and exotic also.

"I've had my coffee," he said. "Just the Jell-O, thank you."

"Does Spyro always serve you coffee?" she said, her bitterness returning now against her will as they stood in the kitchen.

"I don't know," he said belligerently.

"But I thought you saw him every evening," She feigned sweet casualness.

"I never notice what he serves," Gibbs said loudly and indifferently.

"Would you like a large dish or a small dish of Jell-O?" she said heavily.

"Small, for Christ's sake," he told her.

"Gibbs!" she cried. Then, catching herself, she said, "Small it will be, dear."

"What have you got to say that you can't bring it out!" he suddenly turned on her, and taking the dish of Jell-O from her hand he put it down with a bang on the oilcloth covering of the tiny kitchen table.

"Gibbs, let's not have any trouble. Mother has a terrible headache tonight."

"Well, why don't you go to bed then," he said in his stentorian voice.

"Perhaps I will," she said weakly. She sat down and began eating right out of the Jell-O bowl. She ate nearly all the rubbery stiff red imitation strawberry Jell-O and drank in hurried gulps the coffee loaded with condensed milk.

"Spence gave me hell all evening," she said eating. "He thinks I would be happier if I found a fellow!"

She laughed but her laughter brought no response from Gibbs.

"I know I have nothing to offer anybody. Let's face it."

"Why do you have to say *let's face it*?" Gibbs snapped at her.

"Is there something wrong grammatically with it?" she wondered taking her spoon out of her mouth.

"Every dumb son of a bitch in the world is always saying *let's face it*."

"And your own language is quite refined," she countered.

"Yes, let's face it, it is," he said, a bit weakly, and he took out the harmonica from his pocket, looked at it, and put it down noiselessly on the oilcloth.

"I've always wanted to do right by you, Gibbs. Since you was a little boy, I have tried. But no father around, and all . . ."

"Mom, we've been over this ten thousand times. Can't we just forget I didn't have an old man, and you worked like a team of dogs to make up for everything?"

"Yes, let's do. Let's forget it all. For heaven's sake, I'm eating all this Jell-O," she said gaily.

"Yes, I noticed," he said.

"But I want to do for you," she told him suddenly again with passion, forgetting everything but her one feeling now, and she put out her hand to him. "You're all I have, Gibbs."

He stared at her. She was weeping.

"I've never been able to do anything for you," she said. "I know I'm not someone you want to bring your friends home to see."

"Mom, for Christ's sake," he said.

"Don't swear," she said. "I may not know grammar or English, but I'm not profane and I never taught you to be. So there," she said, and she brought out her handkerchief and wiped her eyes, making them, he saw, even older and more worn with the rubbing.

"Mom," he said, picking up the harmonica again, "I don't *have* any friends."

"No? she said, laughing a little. Then understanding his remark more clearly as her weeping calmed itself, she said, commanding again, "What do you mean now by that?"

"Just what I said, Mom. I don't have any friends. Except maybe Spyro."

"Oh, that Greek boy. We would come back to him."

"How could I have friends, do you think. After all . . ."

"Don't you go to college like everybody else?" she said hurriedly. "Aren't we making the attempt, Gibbs?"

"Don't get so excited. I don't care because I don't have any friends. I wasn't accusing you of anything."

"You go to college and you ought to have friends," she said. "Isn't that right?"

"Look, for Christ's sake, just going to college doesn't bring you friends. Especially a guy like me with . . ."

"What's wrong with you," she said. "You're handsome. You're a beautiful boy."

"Mom, Je-sus."

"No wonder that Greek is painting you. You're a fine-looking boy."

"Oh, it isn't that way at all," he said, bored. "Spyro has to paint somebody."

"I don't know why you don't have friends," she said. "You have everything. Good looks, intelligence, and you can speak and act refined when you want to . . ."

"You have to be rich at that college. And your parents have to be . . ."

"Is that *all* then?" she said, suddenly very white and facing him.

"Mom, I didn't mean anything about you. I didn't say any of this to make you feel . . ."

"Be quiet," she said. "Don't talk."

"Maybe we *should* talk about it, Mom."

"I can't help what happened. What was *was*, the past is the past. Whatever wrong I may have done, the circumstances of your birth, Gibbs . . ."

"Mom, please, this isn't about you at all."

"I've stood by you, Gibbs," she hurried on as if testifying before a deaf judge. "You can never deny that." She stared at him as though she had lost her reason.

"I'd like to have seen those rich women with their fat manicured husbands do what I've done," she said now as though powerless to stop, words coming out of her mouth that she usually kept and nursed for her long nights of sleeplessness and hate.

She stood up quickly as if to leave the room.

"With no husband and no father to boot in this house! I'd like to see *them* do what I did. God damn them," she said.

Gibbs waited there, pale now as she was, and somehow much smaller before her wrath.

"God damn everybody!" she cried. "God damn everybody."

She sat down and began weeping furiously.

"I can't help it if you don't have friends," she told him, quieting herself with a last supreme effort. "I can't help it at all."

"Mom," he said. He wanted to weep too, but there was something too rocklike, too bitter and immovable inside him to let the tears come loose. Often at night as he lay in his bed knowing that Merta was lying in the next room sleepless, he had wanted to get up and go to her and let them both weep together, but he could not.

"Is there anything I could do to change things here at home for you?" she said suddenly wiping away the tears, and tensing her breast to keep more of the torrent from gathering inside herself. "Anything at all I can do, I will," she said.

"Mom," he said, and he got up, and as he did so the harmonica fell to the linoleum floor.

"You dropped your little . . . toy," she said, tightening her mouth.

"It's not a toy," he began. "This is," he began again. "You see, this is the kind the professionals play on the stage . . . and everywhere."

"I see," she said, struggling to keep the storm within her quiet, the storm that now if it broke might sweep everything within her away, might rage and rage until only dying itself could stop it.

"Play something on it, Gibbs darling," she said.

He wanted to ask her if she was all right.

"Play, play," she said desperately.

"What do you want me to play, Mom?" he said, deathly pale.

"Just play any number you like," she suggested.

He began then to play "How High the Moon" but his lips trembled too much.

"Keep playing," she said, beating her hands with the heavy veins and the fingers without rings or embellishment.

He looked at her hands as his lips struggled to keep themselves on the tiny worn openings of the harmonica which he had described as the instrument of the professionals.

"What a funny tune," she said. "I never listened to it right before. What did you say they called it?"

"Mom," he said. "Please!"

He stretched out his hand.

"Don't now, don't," she commanded. "Just play. Keep playing."

EVERYTHING UNDER THE SUN

"I don't like to make things hard for you," Jesse said to Cade, "but when you act like this I don't know what's going to happen. You don't like nothing I do for you anyhow."

The two boys, Jesse and Cade, shared a room over the south end of State Street. Jesse had a job, but Cade, who was fifteen, seldom could find work. They were both down to their last few dollars.

"I told you a man was coming up here to offer me a job," Cade said.

"You can't wait for a man to come offering you a job," Jesse said. He laughed. "What kind of a man would that be anyhow."

Cade laughed too because he knew Jesse did not believe anything he said.

"This man did promise me," Cade explained, and Jesse snorted.

"Don't pick your nose like that," Jesse said to Cade. "What if the man seen you picking."

Cade said the man wouldn't care.

"What does this man do?" Jesse wondered.

"He said he had a nice line of goods I could sell for him and make good money," Cade replied.

"Good money selling," Jesse laughed. My advice to you is go out and look for a job, any job, and not wait for no old man to come to teach you to sell."

"Well nobody else wants to hire me due to my face," Cade said.

"What's wrong with your face?" Jesse wanted to know. "Outside of you picking your nose all the time, you have as good a face as anybody's."

"I can't look people in the eye is what," Cade told him.

Jesse got up and walked around the small room.

"Like I told you," Jesse began the same speech he always gave when Cade was out of work, "I would do anything for you on account of your brother. He saved my life in the goddam army and I ain't never going to forget that."

Cade made his little expression of boredom which was to pinch the bridge of his nose.

"But you got to work sometimes!" Jesse exploded. "I don't get enough for two!"

Cade grimaced, and did not let go the bridge of his nose because he knew this irritated Jesse almost as much as his picking did, but Jesse could not criticize him for just holding his nose, and that made him all the angrier.

"And you stay out of them arcades too!" Jesse said to Cade. "Spending the money looking at them pictures," Jesse began. "For the love of . . ." Suddenly Jesse stopped short.

"For the love of what?' Cade jumped him. He knew the reason that Jesse did not finish the sentence with a swear word was he went now to the Jesus Saves Mission every night, and since he had got religion he had quit being quite so friendly to Cade as before, cooler and more distant, and he talked, like today, about how good work is for everybody.

"That old man at the trucking office should have never told you you had a low IQ," Jesse returned to his difficulty of Cade's finding work.

But this remark did not touch Cade today.

"Jesse," Cade said, "I don't care about it."

"You don't care!" Jesse flared up.

"That's right," Cade said, and he got up and took out a piece of cigarette from his pants cuff, and lit a match to the stub. "I don't believe in IQs," Cade said.

Did you get that butt off the street? Jesse wanted to know, his protective manner making his voice soft again.

"I ain't answering that question," Cade told him.

"Cade, why don't you be nice to me like you used to be," Jesse said.

"Why don't *I* be nice to *you*!" Cade exclained with savagery.

Suddenly frightened, Jesse said, "Now simmer down." He was always afraid when Cade suddenly acted too excited.

"You leave me alone," Cade said. "I ain't interferin' with your life and don't you interfere with mine. The little life I have, that is." He grunted.

"I owe something to you and that's why I can't just let you be any old way you feel like being," Jesse said.

"You don't owe me a thing," Cade told him.

"I know who I owe and who I don't," Jesse replied.

"You always say you owe me on account of my brother saved your life just before he got hisself blowed up."

"Cade, you be careful!" Jesse warned, and his head twitched as he spoke.

"I'm glad he's gone," Cade said, but without the emotion he usually expressed when he spoke of his brother. He had talked against his brother so long in times past in order to get Jesse riled up that it had lost nearly all meaning for both of them. "Yes, sir, I don't care!" Cade repeated.

Jesse moved his lips silently and Cade knew he was praying for help.

Jesse opened his eyes wide then and looking straight at Cade, twisted his lips, trying not to let the swear words come out, and said: "All right, Cade," after a long struggle.

"And if religion is going to make you close with your money," Cade began looking at Jesse's mouth, "close and *mean*, too, then I can clear out of here. I don't need you, Jesse."

"What put the idea into your head religion made me close with my money?" Jesse said, and he turned very pale.

"You need me here, but you don't want to pay what it takes to keep me," Cade said.

Jesse trembling walked over to Cade very close and stared at him.

Cade watched him, ready.

Jesse said, "You can stay here as long as you ever want to. And no questions asked." Having said this, Jesse turned away, a glassy look on his face, and stared at the cracked calcimine of their wall.

"On account of my old brother I can stay!" Cade yelled.

"All right then!" Jesse shouted back, but fear on his face. Then softening with a strange weaknes he said, "No, Cade, that's not it either," and he went over and put his arm on Cade's shoulder.

"Don't touch me," Cade said. "I don't want none of that *brother* love. Keep your distance."

"You behave," Jesse said, struggling with his emotion.

"Ever since you give up women and drinking you been picking on me," Cade said. "I do the best I can."

Cade waited for Jesse to say something.

"And you think picking on me all the time makes you get a star in heaven, I suppose," Cade said weakly.

Jesse, who was not listening, walked the length of the cramped little room. Because of the heat of the night and the heat of the discussion, he took off his shirt. On his chest was tattooed a crouched black panther, and on his right arm above his elbow a large unfolding flower.

"I did want to do right by you, but maybe we *had* better part," Jesse said, crossing his arms across his chest. He spoke like a man in his sleep, but immediately as he had spoken, a scared look passed over his face.

Cade suddenly went white. He moved over to the window.

I can't do no more for you!" Jesse cried, alarmed but helpless at his own emotion. "It ain't in me to do no more for you! Can't you see that, Cade. Only so much, no more!"

When there was no answer from Cade, Jesse said, "Do you hear what I say?"

Cade did not speak.

"Fact is," Jesse began again, as though explaining now to himself, "I don't seem to care about nothing. I just want somehow to sit and not move or do nothing. I don't know what it is."

"You never did give a straw if I lived or died, Jesse," Cade said, and he just managed to control his angry tears.

Jesse was silent, as on the evenings when alone in the dark, while Cade was out looking for a job, he had tried to figure out what he should do in his trouble.

"*Fact* is," Cade now whirled from the window, his eyes brimming with tears, "it's all the other way around. I don't need you except for money, but you need me *to tell you who you are*!"

"What?" Jesse said, thunderstruck.

"You know goddam well *what*," Cade said, and he wiped the tears off his face with his fist. "On account of you don't know who you are, that's why."

"You little crumb," Jesse began, and he moved threateningly, but then half remembering his nights at the Mission, he walked around the room, muttering.

"Where are my cigarettes?" Jesse said suddenly. "Did you take them?"

"I thought you swore off when you got religion," Cade said.

"Yesh," Jesse said in the tone of voice more like his old self, and he went up to Cade, who was smoking another butt.

"Give me your smoke," he said to Cade.

Cade passed it to him, staring.

"I don't think you heard what I said about leaving," Cade told Jesse.

"I heard you," Jesse said.

"Well, I'm going to leave you, Jesse. God damn you."

Jesse just nodded from where he now sat on a crate they used as a chair. He groaned a little like the smoke was disagreeable for him.

"Like I say, Jesse," and Cade's face was dry of tears now. "It may be hard for me to earn money, but I know who I am. I may be dumb, but I'm *all together*!"

"Cade," Jesse said sucking on the cigarette furiously. "I didn't mean for you to go. After all, there is a lot between us."

Jesse's fingers moved nervously over the last tiny fragment of the cigarette.

"Do you have any more smokes in your pants cuff or anywhere?" Jesse asked, as though he were the younger and the weaker of the two now.

"I have, but I don't think I should give any to a religious man," Cade replied.

Jesse tightened his mouth.

Cade handed him another of the butts.

"What are you going to offer me, if I do decide to stay," Cade said suddenly. "On account of this time I'm not going to stay if you don't give me an offer!"

Jesse stood up suddenly, dropping his cigarette, the smoke coming out of his mouth as though he had all gone to smoke inside himself.

"What am I going to offer you?" Jesse said like a man in a dream. "What?" he said sleepily.

Then waving his arms, Jesse cried, "All right! Get out!"

And suddenly letting go at last he struck Cade across the mouth, bringing some blood. "Now you git," he said. "Git out."

Jesse panted, walking around the room. "You been bleedin' me white for a year. That's the reason I'm the way I am. I'm bled white."

Cade went mechanically to the bureau, took out a shirt, a pair of shorts, a toothbrush, his straight razor, and a small red box. He put these in a small bag such as an athlete might carry to his gym. He walked over to the door and went out.

Below, on the sidewalk, directly under the room where he and Jesse had lived together a year, Cade stood waiting for the streetcar. He knew Jesse was looking down on him. He did not have to wait long.

"Cade," Jesse's voice came from the window. "You get back here, Cade, goddamn you." Jesse hearing the first of his profanity let loose at last, swore a lot more then, as though he had found his mind again in swearing.

A streetcar stopped at that moment.

"Don't get on that car, Cade," Jesse cried. "Goddam it."

Cade affected impatience.

"You wait now, goddam you," Jesse said putting on his rose-colored shirt.

"Cade," Jesse began when he was on the street beside his friend. "Let's go somewhere and talk this over. . . . See how I am," he pointed to his trembling arm.

"There ain't nowhere to go since you give up drinking," Cade told him.

Jesse took Cade's bag for him.

"Well if it makes you unhappy, I'll drink with you," Jesse said.

"I don't mind being unhappy," Cade said. "it's *you* that minds, Jesse."

"I want you to forgive me, Cade," Jesse said, putting his hand on Cade's arm.

Cade allowed Jesse's arm to rest there.

"Well, Jesse," Cade said coldly.

"You see," Jesse began, pulling Cade gently along with him as they walked toward a tavern. "You see, I don't know what it is, Cade, but you know everything."

Cade watched him.

They went into the tavern and although they usually sat at the bar, today they chose a table. They ordered beer.

"You see, Cade, I've lied to you, I think, and you're right. Of course your brother did save my life, but you saved it again. I mean you saved it more. You saved me," and he stretched out his trembling arm at Cade.

Jesse seeing the impassive look on Cade's face stopped and then going on as though he did not care whether anybody heard him or not, he said: "You're all I've got, Cade."

Cade was going to say *all right now* but Jesse went on speaking frantically and fluently as he had never spoken before. "You know ever since the war, I've been like I am . . . And Cade, I need you that's why . . . I know you don't need me," he nodded like an old man now. "But I don't care now. I ain't proud no more about it."

Jesse stopped talking and a globule of spit rested thickly on his mouth.

"I'm cured of being proud, Cade."

"Well, all right then," Cade finally said, folding his arms and compressing his mouth.

"All right?" Jesse said, a silly look on his face, which had turned very young again.

"But you leave me alone now if I stay," Cade said.

"I will," Jesse said, perhaps not quite sure what it was Cade meant. "You can do anything you want, Cade. All I need is to know you won't really run out. No matter what I might some day say or do, you stay, Cade!"

"Then I don't want to hear no more about me getting just any old job," Cade said, drinking a swallow of beer.

"All right," Jesse said. "All right, all right."

"And you quit going to that old Mission and listening to that religious talk.'"

Jesse nodded.

"I ain't living with no old religious fanatic," Cade said.

Jesse nodded again.

"And there ain't no reason we should give up drinking and all the rest of it at night."

Jesse agreed.

"Or women," Cade said, and he fumbled now with the button of his shirt. It was such a very hot night his hand almost unconsciously pushed back the last button which had held his shirt together, exposing the section of his chest on which rested the tattooed drawing of a crouched black panther, the identical of Jesse's.

"And I don't want to hear no more about me going to work at all for a while," Cade was emphatic.

"All right, then, Cade," Jesse grinned, beginning to giggle and laugh now.

"Well I should say *all right*," Cade replied, and he smiled briefly, as he accepted Jesse's hand which Jesse proffered him then by standing up.

DADDY WOLF

You aren't the first man to ask me what I am doing so long in the phone booth with the door to my flat open and all. Let me explain something, or if you want to use the phone, I'll step out for a minute, but I am trying to get Operator to re-connect me with a party she just cut me off from. If you're not in a big hurry would you let me just try to get my party again.

See I been home 2 days now just looking at them 2 or 3 holes in the linoleum in my flat, and those holes are so goddam big now—you can go in there and take a look—those holes are so goddam big that I bet my kid, if he was still here, could almost put his leg through the biggest one.

Maybe of course the rats don't use the linoleum holes as entrances or exits. They could come through the calcimine in the wall. But I kind of guess and I bet the super for once would back me up on this, the rats are using the linoleum holes. Otherwise what is the meaning of the little black specks in and near each hole in the linoleum. I don't see how you could ignore the black specks there. If they were using the wall holes you would expect black specks there, but I haven't found a single one.

The party I was just talking to on the phone when I got cut off was surprised when I told her how the other night after my wife and kid left me I came in to find myself staring right head-on at a fat, I guess a Mama rat, eating some of my uncooked cream of wheat. I was so took by surprise that I did not see which way she went out. She ran, is all I can say, the minute I come into the room.

I HAD NO more snapped back from seeing the Mama rat when a teeny baby one run right between my legs and disappeared ditto.

I just stood looking at my uncooked cream of wheat knowing I would have to let it go to waste.

It was too late that evening to call the super or anybody and I know from a lot of sad experience how sympathetic he would be, for the rats, to quote him, is a *un-avoidable probability* for whatever party decides to rent one of these you-know-what linoleum apartments.

If you want something better than some old you-know-what linoleum-floor apartments, the super says, *you got the map of Newyorkcity to hunt with.*

Rats and linoleum go together, and when you bellyache about rats, remember you're living on linoleum.

I always have to go to the hall phone when I get in one of these states, but tonight instead of calling the super who has gone off by now anyhow to his night job (he holds 2 jobs on account of, he says, the high cost of chicken and peas), I took the name of the first party my finger fell on in the telephone book.

This lady answered the wire.

I explained to her the state I was in, and that I was over in one of the linoleum apartments and my wife and kid left me.

She cleared her throat and so on.

Even for a veteran, I told her, this is rough.

She kind of nodded over the phone in her manner.

I could feel she was sort of half-friendly, and I told her how I had picked her name out from all the others in the telephone book.

It was rough enough, I explained to her, to be renting an apartment in the linoleum district and to not know nobody in Newyorkcity, and then only the other night after my wife and kid left me this Mama rat was in here eating my uncooked cream of wheat, and before I get over this, her offspring run right between my legs.

This lady on the wire seemed to say *I see* every so often but I couldn't be sure on account of I was talking so fast myself.

I would have called the super of the building, I explained to her, in an emergency like this, but he has 2 jobs, and as it is after midnight now he is on his night job. But it would be just as bad in the daytime as then usually he is out inspecting the other linoleum apartments or catching up on his beauty sleep and don't answer the door or phone.

When I first moved into this building, I told her, I had to pinch myself to be sure I was actually seeing it right. I seen all the dirt before I moved in, but once I was in, I really *seen*: all the traces of the ones who had been here before, people who had died or lost their jobs or found they was the wrong race or something and had had to vacate all of a sudden before they could clean the place up for the next tenant. A lot of them left in such a hurry they just give you a present of some of their belongings and underwear along with their dirt. But then after one party left in such a hurry, somebody else from somewhere moved in, found he could not make it in Newyorkcity, and lit out somewhere or maybe was taken to a hospital in a serious condition and never returned.

I moved in just like the others on the linoleum.

Wish you could have seen it then. Holes everywhere and that most jagged of the holes I can see clear over here from the phone booth is where the Mama rat come through, which seems now about 3,000 years ago to me.

I told the lady on the phone how polite she was to go on listening and I hoped I was not keeping her up beyond her bedtime or from having a nightcap before she did turn in.

I don't object to animals, see. If it had been a Mama bird, say, which had come out of the hole, I would have had a start, too, as a

Mama bird seldom is about and around at that hour, not to mention it not nesting in a linoleum hole, but I think I feel the way I do just because you think of rats along with neglect and lonesomeness and not having nobody near or around you.

See my wife left me and took our kid with her. They could not take any more of Newyorkcity. My wife was very scared of disease, and she had heard the radio in a shoe-repair store telling that they were going to raise the V.D. rate, and she said to me just a few hours before she left, *I don't think I am going to stay on here, Benny, if they are going to have one of them health epidemics.* She didn't have a disease, but she felt she would if the city officials were bent on raising the V.D. rate. She said it would be her luck and she would be no exception to prove the rule. She packed and left with the kid.

Did I feel sunk with them gone, but Jesus it was all I could do to keep on here myself. A good number of times at night I did not share my cream of wheat with them. I told them to prepare what kind of food they had a yen for and let me eat my cream of wheat alone with a piece of warmed-over oleo and just a sprinkle of brown sugar on that.

My wife and kid would stand and watch me eat the cream of wheat, but they was entirely indifferent to food. I think it was partly due to the holes in the linoleum, and them knowing what was under the holes of course.

We have only the one chair in the flat, and so my kid never had any place to sit when I was to home.

I couldn't help telling this party on the phone then about my wife and *Daddy Wolf.*

I was the one who told my wife about *Daddy Wolf* and the *Trouble Phone* in the first place, but at first she said she didn't want any old charity no matter if it was money or advice or just encouraging words.

Then when thing got so rough, my wife did call *Daddy Wolf.* I think the number is Crack 8-7869 or something like that, and only ladies can call. You phone this number and say *Daddy Wolf, I am a lady in terrible trouble. I am in one of the linoleum apartments, and just don't feel I can go on another day. Mama rats are coming in and out of their holes with their babies, and all we have had to eat in a month is cream of wheat.*

Daddy Wolf would say he was listening and to go on, and then he would ask her if she was employed anywhere.

Daddy Wolf, yes and no. I just do not seem to have the willpower to go out job-hunting any more or on these house-to-house canvassing jobs that I have been holding down lately, and if you could see this linoleum flat, I think you would agree, Daddy Wolf, that there is very little incentive for me and Benny.

Then my wife would go on about how surprised we had both been, though she was the only one surprised, over the high rate of V.D. in Newyorkcity.

You see, Daddy Wolf, I don't hold a thing back, I have been about with older men in order to tide my husband over this rough financial situation we're in. My husband works in the mitten factory, and he just is not making enough for the three of us to live on. He has to have his cream of wheat at night or he would not have the strength to go back to his day-shift, and our linoleum apartment costs 30 smackers a week.

I leave the kid alone here and go out to try and find work, Daddy Wolf, but I'm telling you, the only job I can find for a woman of my education and background is this house-to-house canvassing of Queen Bee royal jelly which makes older women look so much more appealing, but I hardly sell more than a single jar a day and am on my feet 12 hours at a stretch.

The kid is glad when I go out to sell as he can have the chair to himself then. You see when I and his Daddy are home he either has to sit down on my lap, if I am sitting, or if his Daddy is sitting, just stand because I won't allow a little fellow like him to sit on that linoleum, it's not safe, and his Daddy will not let him sit on his lap because he is too dead-tired from the mitten factory.

That was the way she explained to *Daddy Wolf* on the *Trouble Phone*, and that went on every night, night after night, until she left me.

Daddy Wolf always listened, I will give him credit for that. He advised Mabel too: *go to Sunday school and church and quit going up to strange men's hotel rooms. Devote yourself only to your husband's need, and you don't ever have to fear the rise in the V.D. rate.*

My wife, though, could just not take Newyorkcity. She was out selling that Queen Bee royal jelly every day, but when cold weather come she had only a thin coat and she went out less and less and that all added up to less cream of wheat for me in the evening.

It is a funny thing about cream of wheat, you don't get tired of it. I think if I ate, say, hamburger and chop suey every night, I would get sick and tired of them. Not that I ever dine on them. But if I did, I would—get sick and tired, I mean. But there's something about cream of wheat, with just a daub of warm oleo on it, and a sprinkle of brown sugar that makes you feel you might be eatin' it for the first time.

My wife don't care for cream of wheat nearly so much as I do.

Our kid always ate with the old gentleman down the hall with the skullcap. He rung the bell when it was supper time, and the kid went down there and had his meal. Once in a while, he brought back something or other for us.

It's funny talking to you like this, Mister, and as I told this lady I am waiting to get re-connected with on the phone, if I didn't know any better I would think either one of you was *Daddy Wolf* on the *Trouble Phone.*

Well, Mabel left me, then, and took the kid with her.

It was her silly fear of the V.D. rate that really made her light out. She could have stayed here indefinitely. She loved this here city at first. She was just crazy about Central Park.

Newyorkcity was just the place for me to find work in. I had a good job with the Singer sewing-machine people in one of their spare-parts rooms, then I got laid off and was without a thing for over 6 months and then was lucky to find this job at the mitten factory. I raise the lever that sews the inner lining to your mittens.

I don't think it is Mabel and the kid leaving me so much sometimes as it is the idea of that Mama rat coming through the holes in the linoleum that has got me so down-in-the-dumps today. I didn't even go to the mitten factory this a.m., and I have, like I say, got so down-in-the-dumps I almost felt like calling *Daddy Wolf* myself on the *Trouble Phone* like she did all the time. But knowing he won't talk to nobody but ladies, as a kind of next-best-thing I put my finger down haphazard on top of this lady's name in the phone book, and I sure appreciated having that talk with her.

See *Daddy Wolf* would only talk with my wife for about one and a half minutes on account of other women were waiting to tell him their troubles. He would always say *Go back to your affiliation with the Sunday school and church of your choice, Mabel, and you'll find your burdens lighter in no time.*

Daddy said the same thing to her every night, but she never got tired hearing it, I guess.

Daddy Wolf told Mabel she didn't have to have any fear at all of the V.D. rate on account of she was a married woman and therefore did not have to go out for that relationship, but if she ever felt that *desire* coming over her when her husband was gone, to just sit quiet and read an uplifting book.

Mabel has not had time, I don't think, to write me yet, taking care of the kid and all, and getting settled back home, and I have, well, been so goddam worried about everything. They are talking now about a shut-down at the mitten factory so that I hardly as a matter of fact have had time to think about my wife and kid, let alone miss them. There is, as a matter of fact, more cream of wheat now for supper, and I splurged today and bought a 5-pound box of that soft brown sugar that don't turn to lumps, which I wouldn't ever have done if they was still here.

The old gent down the hall with the skullcap misses my kid, as he almost entirely kept the boy in eats.

He never speaks to me in the hall, the old man. They said, I heard this somewhere, he don't have linoleum on his floor, but carpets, but I have not been invited in to see.

This building was condemned two years ago, but still isn't torn down, and the old man is leaving as soon as he can find the right neighborhood for his married daughter to visit him in.

Wait a minute. No, I thought I seen some action from under that one hole there in the linoleum.

Excuse me if I have kept you from using the phone with my talk but all I can say is you and this lady on the phone have been better for me tonight than *Daddy Wolf* on the *Trouble Phone* ever was for my wife.

Up until now I have usually called the super when I was in one of these down-moods, but all he ever said was *Go back where you and Mabel got your own people and roots, Benny. You can't make it here in a linoleum apartment with your background and education.*

He has had his eyes opened—the super. He has admitted himself that he never thought Mabel and me could stick it out this long. (He don't know she is gone.)

But I won't give up. I *will not* give up. Mabel let a thing like the hike in the V.D. rates chase her out. I tried to show her that that was just statistics, but she always was superstitious as all get-out.

I judge when this scare I've had about the Mama rat dies down and I get some sleep and tomorrow if I go back to the mitten factory I will then really and truly begin to miss Mabel and the kid. The old man down the hall already misses the kid. That kid ate more in one meal with him than Mabel and me eat the whole week together. I don't begrudge it to him, though, because he is growing.

Well, Mister, if you don't want to use the phone after all, I think I will try to have Operator re-connect me with that party I got disconnected from. I guess as this is the hour that Mabel always called *Daddy Wolf* I have just automatically caught her habit, and anyhow I sure felt in the need of a talk.

Do you hear that funny clicking sound? Here, I'll hold you the receiver so as you can hear it. Don't go away just yet: I think Operator is getting me that party again, so stick around awhile yet.

No, they cut us off again, hear? there is a bad connection or something.

Well, like I say, anyhow Mabel and the kid did get out of here, even if it was superstition. Christ, when I was a boy I had every one of those diseases and it never did me no hurt. I went right into the army with a clean bill of health, Korea, home again, and now Newyorkcity.

You can't bullshit me with a lot of statistics.

Mabel, though, goddam it, I could knock the teeth down her throat, running out on me like this and taking the kid.

WHERE IS THAT GODDAM OPERATOR?

Hello. Look, Operator, what number was that I dialed and talked so long. Re-connect me please. That number I just got through talking with so long. I don't know the party's name or number. Just connect me back, will you please. This here is an emergency phone call, Operator.

GOODNIGHT, SWEETHEART

Pearl Miranda walked stark naked from her classroom in the George Washington School where she taught the eighth grade, down Locust Street, where she waited until some of the cars which had stopped for a red traffic light had driven on, then hurried as fast as her weight could allow her down Smith Avenue.

She waited under a catalpa tree, not yet in leaf, for some men to pass by on the other side of the street. It was fairly dark, but she could not be sure if they would see her.

Hurrying on down Smith Avenue then, she passed a little girl, who called out to her, though the child did not recognize her.

The house she at last turned into was that of Winston Cramer, who gave piano lessons to beginners, and whom she herself had taught in the eighth grade nearly twenty years before.

She rang the doorbell.

She could see Winston beyond the picture window sitting in an easy chair engaged in manicuring his nails.

She rang and rang, but he did not move from his sitting position.

A woman from across the street came out on the porch and stood there watching.

Pearl rapped now on the door, and called Winston's name softly. Then she saw him get up. He looked angry.

"I discontinued the subscription," she heard his cross high voice. "I don't want the *News*—" and he caught sight of her.

He stood looking at her, immobile behind the glass of the door. Then he opened the door cautiously.

"Miss Miranda?"

"Let me in, for pity's sake," she answered him. "It's all right to open the door."

The woman across the street went on standing on her porch looking over at the Cramer house.

"Miss Miranda," Winston could only go on repeating when she was inside.

"Go and get me a bathrobe or something, Winston. For pity's sake." She scolded with her eyes.

Winston stood on for a minute more, trying to keep his gaze only on her face.

She could hear him mumbling and making other silly sounds as he went upstairs.

Pearl Miranda lowered the shade for the picture window, and then, seeing the shade up on a smaller side window, she lowered it also. She picked up a music album and held this over her.

"For God Almighty's sake," Winston said when he handed her a bathrobe.

She put it on with some difficulty, and Winston did not help her. She sat down.

"What can I get for you?" he wondered.

"Usually they give people brandy in such cases," Miss Miranda said. "Cases of exposure," she spoke with her usual precise culture and refinement. "But I think you remember my views on drinking."

"I don't drink either, Miss Miranda," Winston told her.

"Some hot milk might be all right." She seemed to speak condescendingly now. "In the case of a chill coming on." Looking down at her bare feet, she inquired, "Do you have any house slippers, by chance."

"I have some that were my mother's," Winston told her.

That will be fine she was about to say, but he was already racing up the steps.

When he came back, he acted a bit more like himself, and he helped her on with the tickly, rabbit-lined house slippers.

"What happened to you?" he asked, looking up at her from his kneeling posture before her.

"Get me the hot milk first," she told him.

He turned to go out into the kitchen, then wheeling around he said: "Miss Miranda, are you really all right?"

She nodded.

"Shouldn't I call the doctor?"

She shook her head vigorously.

He came back into the room, his left hand slowly stealing up to his throat. "You were assaulted, weren't you?" he asked.

"No, Winston, I was not," she replied. "Now please fix me my milk." She spoke to him much as she would have twenty years ago in her classroom.

Miss Miranda sank back into the warmth and mild comfort of the bathrobe and slippers while he was in the kitchen. She could hear him muttering to himself out there as he went about the task of warming the milk. She supposed all lonely people muttered to themselves, and it was one of the regrettable habits she could never break in herself.

Waiting, she looked at his Baldwin piano loaded with Czerny practice books. Another stack of music books sat on his piano stool.

She felt depressed thinking of Winston earning his living sitting all day and part of the evening hearing ungifted children play scales. It was not a job for a man.

Then she thought of how her own sister had felt sorry for her having to teach the eighth grade.

"I'm shaking more now than when you walked in," Winston mumbled inaudibly, bringing in a little Mexican tray with a steaming pot of milk and a cup.

"Doesn't that look nice," Miss Miranda said.

"I'll get you a napkin, too." And he left the room again.

"Don't bother," Miss Miranda called out after him, but not vigorously, for she wanted a napkin.

She hiccuped a bit drinking the hot milk.

Winston cleared the exercise books from the piano stool, sat down and watched her drink the hot milk.

"Just a touch of cinnamon maybe?" He pointed to her cup.

She shook her head.

"I just took a pie out of the oven a couple of hours ago," he informed her. "Would you like a piece?"

"What flavor is it, Winston?" Miss Miranda wondered.

"Red raspberry," he told her, "Fresh ones."

She studied his face a second, "I might at that," she spoke as if consulting with a third party.

"Do you do all your own cooking, Winston?"

"Since Mother died, yes," he said. "But even in her day I did quite a bit, you know."

"I bet you're a good cook, Winston. You were always a capable boy." Her voice lowered as she said the second sentence.

"I haven't really talked to you since the eighth grade," Winston reminded her in a rather loud voice.

"I expect not." Miss Miranda drank some more of the milk. "My, that hits the spot."

"Wouldn't you like another hot cup?"

"Yes, I think I would," she replied.

He took the tray and all and went out into the kitchen.

Miss Miranda muttered when he had gone, and held her head in her hands, and then suddenly, as if in pain, she cried out, "God!"

Then she straightened out her face and got calm, her hands folded on her bathrobe, for Winston's return.

He handed her a new cup of milk, and she thanked him.

"You're not hurt now, Miss Miranda," he ventured again. He looked very scared.

"I've had a trick played on me is all, Winston." She opened her eyes at him wide.

Somehow, however, she did not seem to be telling the truth, and as she did not look away, Winston looked down at the floor, an expression of sorrow and disappointment about his mouth and eyes. Then he got up from the piano stool and went over to an easy chain and plumped himself down.

"You gave me a start." He put his hand across his chest.

"Now don't you give out on me," she said.

"You don't want me to call the police or anybody?" he asked, and she could see how upset he was getting.

"Just calm down, now. Of course I don't want the police. We'll handle this our own way."

"You said it was a joke, Miss Miranda."

She nodded.

There was a long silence.

"Ready for your raspberry pie?" he asked weakly.

She wiped her hands carefully on the linen napkin. "You could have just given me a paper napkin, Winston," she told him. "Do you have to do your own laundry, too?"

He mumbled something which sounded like *I'm afraid I do.* "I'll get you that pie." He went out of the room.

He came back, after a rather lengthy absence, with a generous piece of red raspberry pie on a hand-painted plate.

"A pretty, pretty sight," Miss Miranda said.

She bit into her piece of pie and said *Mmmm.*

"I wish you would let me do something for you," he almost whined.

"Now sit down, Winston, and be quiet. Better do nothing than do the wrong thing," she admonished.

"I know you haven't done anything wrong, of course," Winston said, and his voice sounded prophetic of weeping.

"Now, I'll explain everything just as soon as I have eaten your pie here," she told him. "But it's all nothing to be concerned about."

"Did anybody see you come in here?" he wondered.

She chewed on for a few seconds. "I suspect they may have. Who lives across the street from you there?" She pointed with her fork in the direction of the house in question.

"Not Bertha Wilson," Winston exclaimed.

"A woman came out on that porch. I think she saw me. Of course I know Bertha Wilson," Miss Miranda said.

"Oh, gosh." Winston raised his voice. He looked at her now almost accusingly. "It's all so unusual," he cried, thinking something much more extreme than his words gave inkling of.

"Winston, you've got to keep calm," Miss Miranda told him. "I *had* to come in here tonight. You know that."

"I don't begrudge you coming in here," he said, and he was more in possession of himself.

"Then let's both be calm and collected." She handed him the empty pie plate. "What beautiful work people did when they painted their own china." She nodded at the plate.

"My Aunt Lois hand-painted all of Mother's china."

He left the room with the plate, and there was complete silence everywhere for a few minutes. Then she heard the water running in the kitchen, and she realized he was doing the dishes.

"He's a neat one," she said out loud.

She shook her head then, though she did this about something else than his neatness, and she cried, "God!" again.

In about a quarter of an hour, he came on back into the living room, sat down, crossed his legs, and said, "Now."

"I don't think I'm even going to have a chill." She smiled at him.

Winston was looking at her narrowly, and she thought he was less sympathetic. There was a look of irritability on his face. His mouth had set.

"How long has it been since you lost your mother?" Miss Miranda said.

"Two years this April," he replied without expression.

Miss Miranda shook her head. She opened the linen napkin out and put it over the lap of the bathrobe.

"What happened tonight was a joke," she said, and stopped.

"Did many people see you cross over the school playground?" he wondered.

"The school playground?"

"There are the fewest trees there to hide under," he explained.

"I couldn't tell if anybody saw me or not," she said.

"Miss Miranda, if you were . . . *harmed*, you must have me call the doctor."

"You want me to leave?" she inquired. "I will—"

"I didn't mean leave," he protested.

"Please be calm, Winston," she asked him.

"I am calm, Miss Miranda. . . . But gosh almighty, nobody can just sit here and act like nothing happened to you. . . . I never heard of such a thing as tonight!"

She sat thinking how it all must seem to him. At the height of her predicament she had not had time to think.

"I'm unhurt, Winston, except for the exposure, and I told you I can see I'm not going to have a chill."

"I can go over to your house and get your clothes."

She nodded pleasantly. "Tomorrow," she said.

"Tonight!" He was emphatic.

"This young man who looked like one of my own former students came into my classroom at six o'clock tonight," she began her story. "I was cleaning the blackboard."

Winston watched her, his face drained of blood.

"He asked me if I remembered him, and I said I didn't, though his face was familiar. . . . He then asked if I remembered Alice Rodgers. Of course, I remembered her. We just expelled her last term, you know. She had gotten herself and nearly every boy in the eighth grade in all that trouble. You remember reading about it all in the paper . . .

"Do you remember all that about Alice Rodgers?" Miss Miranda asked him.

Winston half-nodded.

"This young man, oh, he couldn't have been more than twenty . . . certainly not more than your age at the most, Winston . . . he said, 'I think you ought to have to pay for what you did to Alice Rodgers, ruining her name and reputation.'

" 'I only wanted to make a real future for Alice Rodgers,' I told him.

" 'In the reformatory?' he asked with an ugly grin."

Miss Miranda stopped, perhaps expecting Winston to help her on, but he did nothing.

"Then," Miss Miranda said, "he asked me to take off my clothes. He had a gun, you see."

Winston got up and walked in the direction of the next room.

"Where are you going?" Miss Miranda cried.

He looked back at her, asked her to excuse him, and then came back and sat down.

"He said he would use the gun if I didn't do exactly as he said," she spoke in a matter-of-fact tone.

Miss Miranda was looking at Winston, for she was certain that he was not listening to what she said.

"He took all my clothes away from me, including my shoes, and keys, and then, saying he hoped I would remember Alice Rodgers for the rest of all our lives, he walked out, leaving me to my plight. . . ."

Winston was looking down at the carpet again.

Miss Miranda's voice continued: "I called out to him from the bannister to come back. 'How will I get home?' I called after him."

Her voice now trailed off. Suddenly she held her head in her hands and cried, "Oh, God! God!"

"Are you in pain?" Winston looked up sleepily from the carpet.

"No," Miss Miranda replied quickly.

"My head's in a whirl," Winston told her.

"I don't remember that young man at all," Miss Miranda went on. "But you know, Winston, after you've taught so many years, and when you're as old as I am, all young people, all old people, too, look so much alike."

"Miss Miranda, let me call somebody! We should inform—"

"No," she told him. "I won't hear of it. Now, please be calm and don't let what has happened upset you. I want to stay here tonight."

"This young man you describe. He didn't harm you in any way?"

"He did not," Miss Miranda said in the voice of one who defends.

She looked at Winston.

Without warning, he began to gag. He rushed out of the parlor to a small room near the kitchen.

He evidently did not have time to close the door behind him. She could hear him vomiting.

"Oh, dear," Miss Miranda said.

She came into the bathroom and watched him. He was straining very hard over the toilet bowl.

"Winston, I am going to hold your head," she advised him. He made no motion.

She held his head while he vomited some more.

When he had stopped, she took a fresh wash cloth off the rack, and wiped his mouth.

"I've had the virus," he explained.

Suddenly he turned to the bowl again and vomited.

"Poor lad," she said, wiping his mouth again with the cloth.

"You must lie down now," she admonished him.

He walked toward an adjoining room where there was a double bed, and lay down on it.

She helped him off with his shoes, and put the covers partly over him.

"I'm afraid it was me who upset you," she apologized.

"No, Miss Miranda, it's the virus. Can't seem to shake it off. I catch it off and on from my pupils. First from one, then the other."

"Just rest quietly," she said.

When he had dozed off, she exclaimed again, "God! God!"

She must have dozed off, too, in her chair by the double bed, for some time later she awoke with a start and heard him vomiting again in the bathroom, and she hurried in to hold his head.

"Winston, poor lad," she said, feeling his hair wet with sweat.

"How could you stand to watch me be sick like that," he wondered later when they were back in the bedroom.

"I've taught public school for thirty years," she reminded him.

"Miss Miranda," he said suddenly, "you were raped tonight, weren't you?"

She stared at him.

"You've got to let me call the doctor." He wiped his mouth.

"I was not . . . raped," she denied his statement.

He watched her.

"That fellow just asked you to take off your clothes?"

She nodded.

"On account of Alice Rodgers." He echoed her story.

"I had testified against Alice in court," she added, "and they sent her to the reformatory."

"Well, if it's your story," he said.

"I wouldn't lie to you," Miss Miranda said.

"Nobody will believe you," he told her.

"Aren't you talking too much, Winston?" Miss Miranda showed concern for his health.

He did not answer.

"Bertha Wilson saw you across the street," he said sleepily.

"She was looking in my direction all right," Miss Miranda admitted.

"She must have seen you then."

"Oh, it was quite dark, Winston, after all."

"Bertha's got real X-ray eyes."

"Well, so she saw me," Miss Miranda said. "I had to come in somewhere."

"Oh, it's all right," Winston said. "Nobody will think anything about *us*."

"Oh, God!" Miss Miranda cried suddenly.

Winston raised himself on his elbows.

"You in pain, Miss Miranda? Physical pain?"

She stifled back her sobs.

"Miss Miranda," Winston began. "That young man that came into your classroom tonight . . . are you listening to me . . . that young man was Fred Rodgers. Alice Rodgers' older brother."

Miss Miranda went on making the stifling sounds.

"Did you hear what I said, Miss Miranda?"

She nodded.

"Alice Rodgers' older brother," he repeated. "I know him. Listen, Miss Miranda, I know he wouldn't stop at just taking away your clothes. Don't you think I have any sense at all?"

He looked away from the look she gave him then.

"Knowing Fred Rodgers the way I do, Miss Miranda, I know he wouldn't stop at what you said he did. He had it in for you for sending his sister to the reform school."

"I'm nearly sixty years old, Winston," Miss Miranda said in the pool of darkness that was her chair. "I'd rather we didn't talk about it, if you don't mind."

"You've got to call the doctor," he said.

Miss Miranda looked down at the long lapel of her bathrobe.

"You had blood on you, too," Winston told her.

A moment later, he screamed and doubled up with pain in the bed.

"Winston, for pity's sake."

"I think I got an attack of appendicitis," he groaned. "Ouch, ouch, ouch." He touched his stomach.

"Do you want a doctor then!" she cried, as if he had betrayed her.

He lay back in the bed and groaned. His face went a kind of green, then yellow, as if suddenly illuminated by a searchlight.

"Dear God. God!" Miss Miranda cried.

"I may get all right," Winston told her, and he smiled encouragement at her from out of his own distress.

"Oh, what shall I do. What *shall* I do," she cried.

"I guess we both will have to have the doctor," Winston told her.

"I can't tell him, Winston. . . . I'm sixty years old."

"Well, you let *him* do the worrying now, Miss Miranda."

"You knew this Fred Rodgers?" She cried a little now.

Winston nodded.

"I never taught him, though." She sighed. Suddenly she cried again, "Dear God. God!"

"You try to be calm, Miss Miranda," he comforted her.

He seemed almost calm now himself.

"Why don't you lay your head down on the bed, you look so bad," he told her.

"Oh, aren't we in the worst situation, Winston," she said.

She cried a little.

She laid her head down on the bed, and he patted her hair a moment.

"I don't know how many people saw me," she said.

Winston lay back, easier now. His pain had quit.

Miss Miranda, suddenly, as if in response to his pain's easing, began to tremble violently.

"Get into bed," he told her. "You've got a chill coming on."

He helped her under the covers.

She screamed suddenly as he put her head down on the pillow.

"Just try to get as quiet as possible, Miss Miranda." He helped her cover up.

She was trembling now all over, crying, "Oh, God! At sixty!"

"If you can just get a good night's rest," he comforted her.

"Dear God. Oh, God!"

"In the morning the doctor will fix you up."

"I can never go back and teach those children," she said.

Winston patted her hand. His nausea had left him, but he had a severe headache that throbbed over his temples.

"What is that woman's name across the street again?" Miss Miranda questioned him.

"You mean Bertha Wilson."

Miss Miranda nodded.

"I taught her in the eighth grade. Way back in 1930, just think."

"I wouldn't think about it, Miss Miranda."

"Wouldn't think about what?"

"Anything."

"I can't believe this has happened," she told Winston.

"The doctor will come and fix us both up."

"I don't see how I can have the doctor or go back to school or anything," she wept.

She began crying hard now, and then after a while she got quiet.

"Go to sleep," he said.

He had thought to go upstairs and sleep in the bedroom that had been his mother's, but he didn't know whether he had the strength to get up there, and in the end he had crawled back under the covers next to Miss Miranda, and they both lay there close to one another, and they both muttered to themselves in the darkness as if they were separated by different rooms from one another.

"Good night," he said to her.

She looked up from her pillow for a moment.

"Good night, sweetheart," he said again, in a much lower voice.

She looked at the wall against which he had said the last words. There was a picture of his mother there, pretty much as Miss Miranda remembered her.

"God," Miss Miranda whispered. "Dear God."

SERMON

Ladies and people, you must realize, or you would not be sitting here before me, that I am the possessor of your ears. Don't speak, I will talk. You have sat here before, and have heard things men, or, in some cases, ladies told you. I have no intention of telling you the same things, but will proceed just as though you were all in the privacy of your own bathhouses. I was not called here to entertain you. You could entertain yourselves if you weren't here. The fact you are here means something. (I will not mention the fact of my being here.) We face one another across the hostile air, you waiting to hear and to criticize, and I half-staring at some of you and not seeing the rest of you, though perhaps wanting to. Some of you are rude. Many of you are old and homely, others are not up to the speech I have in readiness. We *all* of us know *all* of this. It is in the *air* I look through to see you. Yet we all feel we have to go on. You have left the comfort of your living rooms and bathhouses to be here. I have come because I am a speaker and had to. None of us are really happy, none of us are in the place he feels he might want to be. Many of you feel there must be a better place for you than the one you are occupying now. There is a feeling of everything being not quite right. You feel if you only knew more or could do more you would be somewhere else. The fact is, however, you are wrong.

I say this looking at all of you now. You are wrong, and I am powerless to add or subtract from that fact. You came originally wrong, and you have been getting worse in every way since that day. There is, in fact, no hope for you, and there never was. Even if you had never been born there would have been no hope for you. It was hopeless whether you arrived or not. Yet you all arrived, you got here, you are *here*. And it is all so meaningless, because you all know there is a better place for you than here. And that is the trouble.

You will not accept the *hereness*. You will not accept me. Yet I am the only thing there is under the circumstances, but you reject me, and why—well I will tell you why. Because you have nothing better to do or be than the person you are now, occupying the particular chair you now occupy and which you are not improving by occupying. You have improved nothing since you came into this situation. You have tried to improve yourself, of course, or things connected with yourself, but you have only finished in making everything worse, you have only finished in making yourself worse than when you were sent, worse than what you were when you were born, worse even than what you were before you entered this great Amphitheater.

There is, in short, no hope for you, as I said earlier. You are bad off and getting more so, and sadly enough when you get in the worst shape of all so that you think you will not be able to go on for another second, the road ahead is still worse yet. For there is no hope for you even when things get so impossibly terrible that you will kill yourself. For that is no solution. In death you will only begin where you left off, but naturally, in worse shape.

Yet you continue to sit here watching me, like skinned tadpoles whose long-dead brains still send messages to your twitching feet. You twitch as you listen to me but you hear nothing. You have never heard anything.

And now you are waiting for the message, the solution to all my speech. You have been thinking, "What He says is terrible and frightening, but now will come the Good Part, the part with the meaning . . ." Ladies and people, listen to me. I have no Good Part to give you. My only message, if it can be called one, and I do not call it one, I call it nothing, my message to you is there is no message. You have made a terrible mistake in coming to the Amphitheater tonight to hear Me, yet you would have made a mistake no matter what you did tonight for the simple reason that you have no choice but to make mistakes, because you have no plans. You are going somewhere because you think you have to . . . That is what you are doing, and how therefore could you do anything but make mistakes. You continue to act and you have nothing to act with but the actions. Hence you are doomed to lectures and books hoping to save yourselves in the evening. Another attempt at action. You are doomed because you will go on trying to be other than you are and therefore you succeed always in continuing as you have been. There is no choice. You are listening even now with your pathetic tadpole faces because you know you are not getting my words. Give up trying, dear auditors. Be without trying to be. Lie back in your seats and let the air have its way with you. Let it tickle you in the spots where you are always fighting its insistent moisture. Don't let it retreat. Let things be. Don't try to be improved by my speech, because nothing can improve you. Surrender to what you are continuing *against*, and perhaps you will not have to go ahead with everything. And I know how weary you are of going ahead. Oh, don't I know it.

You are beginning to look at the Giant Clocks, meaning you have stood all you can for one night. I do not pity or sympathize with you and at the same time I do, because you do not belong here, as I said earlier. Nobody belongs here. It has all been a mistake your coming here. I, of course, am a Mistake, and how could my coming be a success. Yet in a sense it *is*, ladies and people, for the simple reason that I have prepared no speech and have not thought about what I am saying to you. I knew it would be hopeless. I knew when I saw your faces that you would only listen to what you say to yourself in your bathhouses or your laundry cleanup kitchens. You knew everything anyhow and have continued to improve on what has already been done. Hence you are hopeless.

I have talked here tonight in the hope you would not hear, because if you didn't you might not so thoroughly disgust yourselves, and therefore me. But you have sat in exactly the rapport or lack of it which I expect from the human tadpole. You have been infinitely repulsive to me, and for that I thank you, because by being infinitely repulsive you have continued continuity and what more could any speaker ask. What if you had become while I was talking. The whole world would have changed, of course. You would have all become alive. But the truth of the continuum is that it is continuous. You have not failed History, the continuous error. You have gone on with it, but *continuing*.

And so I say to you, pale and yet red tadpoles, you are hopeless and my words are spoken to tell you not to hope. You have nothing with which to win. It is doom itself that I see your bloated eyes and mouths begging for. How could I say anything to you then but to return to you the stale air which you have been breathing in my face all evening. I return it to you, therefore, not in flatulence, that would be to flatter you, but in air in return. And I thank you. I *mean* this. I thank you one and all, ladies and people. I take pleasure in my activity though I know you do not, are not expected to take any and would be miserable if my pleasure became real to you. And so farewell, or rather good-by, because we will meet again. There is no escape from it. That is why we are all so repulsive to one another: infinitely so. Life is immortal. Its eggs are too numerous for it but to spawn at the mere touch, and therefore with real emotion I say, *So be it*. Come whenever you can, I am always here. Good-by, and yet not good-by.

GOD

HOME BY DARK

Every day his grandfather bought him a new toy of a cheap kind, and a little racing car made out of chocolate. The boy ate the racing car slowly and almost dutifully as he and his grandfather sat on the immense porch and talked about how the birds know when to leave for the South.

"Have we ever been South?" the boy asked his grandfather, after he had finished the chocolate racing car and wiped his hands carefully on his cowboy handkerchief.

"No," the old man said. "Not since your parents died."

"Why don't we go?" the young boy said.

"There would be no reason to," the old man replied.

The birds that had been twittering on the huge lawn that surrounded the great white house in which he lived with his grandfather suddenly rose together in a flock as if hearing an inaudible signal, and disappeared into a clump of trees far off.

"There they all go," the boy told his grandfather.

"There they go," the old man repeated.

"Are you glad they're gone?" the young boy wondered.

"They're not really gone. Not South," the old man told the boy. "It isn't time yet—it's only July."

"Oh, I knowed they hadn't gone South," the boy told his grandfather. "I saw them yesterday do it. They practice like this all day long. They twitter and twitter and twitter, then they all get silent and then *zoom*, they all fly off like they knowed it was time."

"*Knew*," the grandfather corrected.

"Yes, *knew*," the boy nodded, and put his hand gently on his grandfather's hand.

"Birds are really strange creatures," the old man admitted. "They remember always where to go, where to build their nests, where to return to. . . ." He shook his head.

"They know to go South when it's cold," the boy agreed. "Except the sparrows. They stay all winter, poor little fellows. They are tough. They don't have no more feathers than the other birds, yet they stay right on, don't they?"

The grandfather nodded.

"Maybe, though, they *do* have more feathers and we can't see them," the boy added, thinking.

"That could be," the old man told his grandson, and he brought his cane up now painfully, and then pressed down with it with his hand.

The boy waited a little for his grandfather to say something more, and the old man, sensing the boy's need for words, said: "Did you like your chocolate racing car?"

"It was sweet and bitter and sweet all at the same time, and then at the very end it was soapy."

"Soapy?" the grandfather wondered.

The boy nodded.

"Well, then there was something wrong with it," the old man complained faintly.

"No," the boy said airily. "That's the way the sweet and the bitter get after you have them both together. See," he said pulling on his grandfather's cane a little, "after you taste the sweet you taste the bitter and after you taste the sweet again you taste the sweet and the bitter, and it's only soapy for a second?"

"I see," the grandfather nodded.

"And then it's all sweet!" The boy laughed, and he jumped up and down on the porch steps, making strange little sounds imitating nobody knew what.

"And I lost a tooth!" the boy told his grandfather.

"Cook told me," the old man informed him.

"Tonight when I go to bed, I am going to put it under my pillow and when I wake up in the morning do you know what is going to be under where I slept all night?"

The grandfather smiled and shook his head.

"A pot of gold," the boy told him.

"What will you do with it?" the grandfather asked.

"I might turn into a bird and go South then," the boy told him.

"But you wouldn't want to leave your old granddad and Cook," the grandfather chided.

The boy thought a moment and said, "I would fly back for supper."

"Well, it will be interesting to see your pot of gold tomorrow," the old man agreed.

"You really think I will get it then?" the boy asked.

"All wishes like that come true," the grandfather said somewhat gravely. "It's because they're a . . . a *pure* wish."

"A *pure* wish?" the boy wondered, scratching his nose. "What's that?"

"Well, like pure candy; you've had that, you know."

The boy shook his head.

"Your chocolate racing car is pure candy," the grandfather said, unsure this was so, and no conviction in his voice.

"Oh," the boy answered.

"All you really wished for, you see," the grandfather explained, "was to have your wish come true. You really hadn't thought what you would do with your wish and your pot of gold."

"Yes," the boy agreed, but his attention wandered.

"So tonight when you go to sleep you must just think that you want the pot of gold, and that is all you want. And don't wish for it too hard, you know."

"No?" the boy raised his voice.

"Not too hard. That would frighten the good fairy away."

"The good fairy?" the boy wondered.

"Yes. Who did you think brought your pot of gold?"

"I thought," the boy felt his way. "I thought . . . somebody dead."

"What?" the old man said, and he moved his cane again so that now it pointed down to the grass where the birds had gathered in a flock.

"Cook didn't really tell me who did bring it," the boy said, studying the confusion on his grandfather's face.

"Yes," the old man said absently, and then looking at his grandson he said, "well, it's really the good fairy, I expect. Don't you know about her?"

The boy shook his head.

"Well, she is the one who's supposed to bring the gold." And the old man laughed rather loudly.

"Do you believe in her?" the boy asked.

"The good fairy?" the old man said, and he began to laugh again, but stopped. "Yes, I do," he said after a pause and with a sleepy serious expression.

The grandfather fished his heavy gold watch out of his vest pocket and looked at its face.

"Seven P.M.," he said.

"Seven P.M.," the boy repeated. "One hour to bedtime."

"That's right," the grandfather said, and he put his hand on the boy's head.

"Why don't you want to go South?" the young boy wondered, suddenly.

"Well," the old man stirred in his chair. "Memories, I suppose, you know." But then looking at his grandson he knew the boy did *not* know, and he said, "It's a long story."

"You don't remember why?" the boy asked.

"When you're older I will talk about it," the old man began. "You see there's so much explanation to it, and well, I'm very old, and it tires me out when I make long explanations."

"What is *explanation*—just telling everything, then?"

"Yes," the old man smiled. "And if I told you why I don't want to go South why we'd be here for days!"

"But we are anyhow!" the boy exclaimed. "We're always just standing and sitting and standing and talking here or watching the birds."

The old man was silent.

"Ain't we?" the boy said.

"Well, if I was a bird I would *never* go South," the old man spoke almost as if to himself.

The boy waited and then when his grandfather said no more he told him: "I would always come home at dark, I think, if I was a bird."

"Yes, sir, *tomorrow*," the old man's voice sounded, taking on warmth, "you'll have your pot of gold!"

"Hurray!" the small boy shouted, and he ran around the old man's chair making sounds now that were those of a jet.

"What will you buy me tomorrow?" the boy asked his grandfather.

"But tomorrow you will have your own pot of gold!" the grandfather told his grandson. "You'll be rich!"

"Will I, then?" the boy wondered.

"Don't you believe you'll have it?" the old man interrogated.

"No," the boy said softly.

"But you must believe," the grandfather warned him.

"Why?" the boy asked, looking closely into his grandfather's face.

"You must always believe in one thing, that one thing."

"What is *that one thing*?" the boy asked, an almost scared look on his face.

"Oh, it's hard to say," the old man admitted failure again.

"Not like going South now, don't tell me again," the boy complained.

"No, this is even harder to explain than going South, but I will try to tell you."

The old man drew his grandson closer to him and arranged the collar of the boy's shirt. He said: "There is always one thing a person believes and wants to believe even if he doesn't believe it."

"Ahem," the boy said, standing on only one leg.

"Do you see?" the old man asked, his face soft and smiling.

"Yes," the boy replied, his voice hard.

"All right, then," the old man went on. "There is this one thing you want and you want it more than anything in the world. You see?"

"Like the birds knowing where to fly, you mean?" the boy was cautious.

"Yes," the old man doubted this, and then said, "but more like your pot of gold."

"Oh," the boy replied.

"You want this one thing, and you have to go on believing in it, no matter what."

"Well, what is the thing?" the boy smiled broadly now, showing the place in his mouth where he had lost his tooth, which was a front one.

"Only the person who knows can tell!" the grandfather said loudly as though this were a joke now.

"But am I old enough to know?" the boy said, puzzled and surprised.

"You're old enough and you should tell me now," the grandfather encouraged him.

"So," the boy paused, screwing his eyes shut, and he stood first on one foot and then on another. "I would like my father and mother both to be alive again, and all of us, including you, living South."

The old man opened his mouth and closed it again.

"Isn't that the right answer?" the boy said, worried.

"Yes, of course," the old man hurriedly agreed.

"You don't act like it was the right answer," the boy complained.

"Well, it is, anyhow. The only thing was—I was thinking about wishes that are about the future, you see."

"Oh," the boy was disappointed. Then in a kind of querulous voice he said, "My wish wasn't the future?"

"It's so hard to explain," the grandfather laughed, and he roughed up the boy's hair.

"Well," the boy said, "let's talk about things we can tell each other."

The grandfather laughed.

The light was beginning to die slowly in the trees, and a full rounded moon began to show in the near distance.

Suddenly the boy said, *Oh* in a scared voice.

"What is it?" the grandfather was concerned.

"I think I lost my tooth," the boy said.

"You did?" the grandfather was even more alarmed now than the boy.

"I did, I lost it." He felt suddenly in his pockets.

"When we were talking about the birds, you know, I throwed my hand out . . . and the tooth must have been in my hand."

"You *threw* your hand out. Well, then it's in the grass," the grandfather said.

"Yes," the boy agreed.

The old man got out of his chair and his grandson helped him silently down the twelve steps that led to the long walk about which extended the immense lawn where the tooth had been thrown.

They searched patiently in the long grass, which had needed cutting for some time.

"It was such a little tooth," the boy said, as though he realized this fact for the first time.

The old man could not bend over very far, but his eyes, which were still keen, looked sharply about him for the tooth.

"Oh, what shall I ever do!" the boy said suddenly.

"But it will turn up!" the old man cried, but there was the same note of disappointment and fear in his voice, which, communicating itself to the boy, caused the latter to weep.

"You mustn't cry," the grandfather was stern. "It won't do at all!"

"But the pot of gold and all!" the boy cried.

"It doesn't matter at all," the grandfather said, and he touched the boy on the face.

"But you told me it did." The boy wept now.

"I told you *what?*" the old man said.

"You told me there was just that one thing you should want to believe in."

"But you've only lost your tooth," the old man replied. "And we'll find it. It isn't lost forever. The gardener will find it when he comes."

"Oh, I'm afraid not," the boy said, wandering about now picking up the grass by the handfuls, looking and watching about him in the fading light.

"If we only hadn't let Cook take the flashlight we might locate it with that," the grandfather said, a few minutes later, when the light was quite gone.

The boy now just stood in one place staring down at the grass.

"I think we'll have to give up the search for tonight," the grandfather finally said.

"But this is the only night I can have my wish!" the boy cried. "This is the ONLY night."

"Nonsense," the grandfather told him. "Not true at all."

"But it is, it is," the boy contradicted his grandfather, gravely.

"How do you know?" the grandfather wondered.

"My mother told me," the boy said.

"But you don't . . . you don't remember her!" the grandfather stared into the growing dark.

"She told me in my sleep," the boy said, his voice plain, unemphatic.

The grandfather looked at his grandson's face but the dark hid it and its expression from him.

"Let's go up the steps now," the grandfather told him.

The small boy helped the old man up the twelve steps, and at the last one the old man laughed, making fun of his fatigue.

"Don't ever get old now, don't you ever do that," he laughed.

The grandfather sat down heavily in the chair, his cane thrown out as though commanding something, or somebody.

"We'll find your tooth tomorrow, or we'll all be hanged," the grandfather said cheerily. "And we won't let Cook take our flashlight again, will we?"

The boy did not answer. He stood as he stood every night beside his grandfather, looking out over the western sky, tonight half-seeing the red harvest moon rise.

"I will buy you something different tomorrow," the grandfather said, "so that it will be a real surprise. Do you hear?"

The boy said yes.

"You're not crying now," the grandfather said. "That's good."

The boy nodded.

"I'm glad you're brave too, because a boy should not cry, really, no matter even . . . Well, he should never cry."

"But I don't know what to believe in now," the boy said in a dry old voice.

"Fiddlesticks," the old man said. "Now come over here and sit on my lap and I will talk to you some more."

The boy moved slowly and sat down on his grandfather's lap.

"Ouch," the grandfather said playfully when he felt how heavy the boy was.

"Just the two of us," the old man said. "Just the two of us here, but we're old friends, aren't we. Good, good old friends."

He pushed the boy's head tight against his breast so he would not hear the sounds that came out now like a confused and trackless torrent, making ridiculous the quiet of evening, and he closed his own eyes so that he would not see the moon.

SCRAP OF PAPER

I hadn't the slightest intention of pampering Naomi or condescending to her in any way; the wages I paid her were far in advance of their day when she came to me. I allowed her, for example, my own reading material, and many a time I have invited her to a bite of cake in my presence when she served me tea; all these things I repeat now because the rumor she has been circulating that I struck her for having faded my beautiful rose carpets from Portugal is quite beside the point; what I did to Naomi could never, not even in a court of law, be construed as striking. I merely slapped her. She deserved it, she admitted she deserved it. She faded my carpets, and she didn't care. But that was not the real crisis, and it did not cause her to leave. Naomi had changed. She was not a double personality, as some people call it, not a bit of it; Naomi had simply become another woman from the pleasant, efficient, know-her-place, very attractive though black as the ace of spades girl I took in some twenty years ago.

"You're a woman of at least forty, though you lie to your men friends about your age!" I cried to her on that terrible April morning when she smashed the entire china closet before my eyes. "Why, oh why," I went on, nearly beside myself, "did you fade that beautiful pair of carpets from Portugal? . . . You willfully and deliberately exposed them to that pitiless sunlight. . . ." Then she threw the beautiful Dresden teapot straight at me. . . . I was calm. I said, "Naomi, if that had hit me, you would have gone to death row. . . ."

I paid her, of course, and never expected to set eyes on her again, but she returned. Wore a veil, and asked if she could bring her husband to visit. . . .

"What sort of a *young* man did you marry, may I ask?" I said, and she did not evidently like the long stress I had put on the word *young*.

"I married me a man, Mrs. Bankers," she replied.

"Naomi, my dear." I raised my hand as a warning, for my fingers were resting near my emergency telephone. "Remember," I said, "we are friends now."

Stung perhaps by the rudeness in her voice, I cried, "You are no more the Naomi who came to me in 1947 than you're a water buffalo!" I knew I had chosen a poor comparison. I had been reading something about the animal in a picture magazine, and it came unexpectedly to mind.

"Why do you compare me to a vicious Oriental beast of burden?" she inquired, and she stood up.

"Will you sit down, Naomi!" I cried. "And please lift up your veil. In *our* day," I could not help adding, "veils were worn only by Catholic ladies when in mourning. You're not Catholic and you are incapable of mourning for anybody. Besides, you never knew your family. . . . I asked you what sort of a young man you had married, and I wish you'd be civil enough to follow the rules of conversation, or bid me good morning."

Then I heard her words as clear as a gong: "A while back you throwed up to me in your nasty lady-way my age, and now you go into my dress, when these is the points you rest weakest on yourself, for you know as well as I that you are crowding eighty and that you never wore a stitch of clothes yet that couldn't be snapped up by the freak show."

"How dare you," I cried. "Speak so to a woman who provided you with your bread for twenty years!"

"And your advanced age, technically you are a ancient, and your odd getups are the least of it, for I won't mention nobody in and around this suite has ever thought you was anything but harmless-crazy! There!" she cried, and she got up and moved around the room to touch her glove on the windowsill and pretended to find dirt.

"Your house is filthy since I left you and you know it!" Naomi went on after a long wait on my part. "And don't you use the expression how-dare-you to me, 'cause I'm not in the mood for your old-fashioned smooth hellishness," she added.

"All right," I soothed her, for I felt gravely ill, and told her I felt so. "You'll fix me some tea," I informed her, "and you'll stay in case I have an attack. . . . Do you realize," I admonished her, "what you're doing to me? . . . You came here to kill me, in the cleverest way possible, and you know it."

"All you heiresses is tarred to the same stick: a honest day's work with your hands would have told you the difference between loafing-fatigue and heart ailment. . . ."

I sniffed at her words, said nothing more, and waited for her to prepare my tea. Naomi always prepared it so well, in fact she was a born cook, although of course I trained her. When she came to me she couldn't boil water, as they say. I trained her indeed in everything, and I paid for two of her abortions. I was a second mother to her.

"What do you pay this Norwegian charm woman works for you?" Naomi said, pouring me some tea.

"Are you going to kill me if I don't tell you, my dear?" I inquired of her.

"I already know anyhow, Miss Smarty," Naomi said.

"Now, you look here," I replied, getting really angry.

"I seen your Norwegian up the street the other day." Naomi ignored me. "Asked her right out after telling her who I was. She hesitated a minute and then she told me. I says, "That's more than Mrs. Bankers paid me for a month backbreaking work.'"

"You ate a great deal while here, Naomi, don't forget," I reminded her.

"But here you are"—I could no longer contain myself—"at your old tricks of humiliating me in my own home!"

"Don't you work yourself up to that attack now, Mrs. Bankers, and then up and blame me; that's about the size of it; you'd like to work yourself to a stroke here and have the police think I brought it on."

"I want to be your friend, Naomi, and as I said earlier, I'm ready to meet your young husband."

"He ain't no youth, he's over thirty," she snapped at me. "You don't think I want me a youth, do you, after all the trouble I got in with the others, which, as you like to remind the world, you was so good at helping me out in."

"I'll meet him," I said.

"I never said one thing about bringing him." She was as tart as ever.

"Oh, Naomi, Naomi!" I cried.

Then I heard myself saying it, after all the insults the slut had poured on me. I heard myself saying, "Why don't you come back, Naomi?"

Do you know what she did, she laughed so hard you would have thought somebody knocked the wind out of her the way she finally had to gasp for breath.

"Oh, it's not that funny." I felt myself turning red.

"You don't care then I faded the rugs." Naomi started in again on that.

When I looked peaceable, she went on: "Let me tell you, Mrs. Bankers. I think them rugs was faded when you got them from your Great-Aunt Betty, or whoever give them to you. It come from the camels faded."

"How would you know the condition of heirlooms!" I shot at her.

" 'Cause I know myself, and I know when people fib about themselves to me."

"You have no self!" I retorted. "You're a chameleon, and you're color-blind!"

"What did you say?" She became incoherent with rage, shouting at me.

"Oh, forget it, why can't you? I said to her. "I haven't an ounce of prejudice and you know it."

She laughed her terrible put-on nasty laugh.

"Naomi, Naomi," I now appealed to her. "Why can't you come to your senses and come back here to live? . . . That man you married surely can't love you. . . . I'll bet he's living off you. . . . Tell me if I'm not speaking the truth."

She gave me a very queer look, then poured me some more tea.

"Would you like me to fix you some toast, and open you a jar of some preserves. Noticed you had an unopened jar out there."

"Think somebody else with a well-known sweet tooth wants some preserves," I said. "Go ahead, do all the things you just said you'd do, including the opening of the preserves," I told her.

I waited till she brought everything in. "Naomi," I cried, "that is of course a wedding ring on your finger, let's see." She extended her hand and of course that was what it was, very nice gold in it, too.

"I'm very put out you're married," I said.

She laughed pleasantly.

"Naomi, you should never have thrown that china pot at me that day," I told her.

"Now, now, Mrs. Bankers," she cautioned, and she sat down again in that damned costume and veil of hers.

"What nationality is this husband of yours, Naomi?" I ventured.

"Cuban."

"White?" I wondered.

"Oh, he's got several strains in him, Mrs. Bankers, including a dash of Chinese."

"You would," I sighed. "Well, it won't last, and you'll be back," I chided.

She fidgeted.

"Matter of fact, Mrs. Bankers," she began, and her face fell, "I'll let you in on a secret. It ain't lasted. It's over. . . . Now clap your little hands with joy."

"Then, my love, unless my name's not Mrs. Bankers, you're here as a suppliant!"

"As a what?"

"You heard me. You're here to beg your old job back when I no longer need you. When I've learned to get on without you!"

"Beggin'! Hear her! Huh-huh, Mrs. Bankers, Naomi don't have to beg, and you get that straight. I'm givin' you a offer."

Wreathed in pleasurable smiles, happy as I had not been in months, I confess, I drank another cup of tea.

"Tell you what," Naomi said, cautious, sweet. "I'll tell the tea leaves for you."

I hesitated, and she went on: "Bet that Norwegian bitch can't do that. She sure can't clean neither." She looked at the woodwork.

"You'll be mean to me if you come back!" I cried. "And oh, Naomi, God Almighty, can you be mean. You're the meanest woman ever drew breath when you are mean. . . . You've abused me sometimes until I thought I'd die. . . ."

"Mrs. Bankers, stop it."

"Some nights," I went right on, "I was in mortal fear you'd kill me."

"Monkey nuts!" she sneered. "I don't believe you was ever in mortal fear of anything anyhow!"

"Oh, Naomi, you'd persecute me if I let you back here, now you know you would. . . . Besides, maybe you killed your young Cuban husband, how do I know?"

"That little old punk isn't worth killin'," she mumbled.

"But," she went on, getting her ire up perhaps because she saw how I was smiling, "if you don't want me back, Mrs. Bankers, you don't and you know better than me that help like I can give is at a high bid today and scarcer than true love."

"Don't rub it in, Naomi." I felt myself bending. "Don't lord it over me. You will anyhow. But I ask you not to. You're cruel, and you're in control. What more can I say?"

"Honey, the day anybody is in control over you, they'll have the spots took out of leopards."

"Oh, don't be droll. You are anyhow. . . . God, I've missed your talk, Naomi. Sick to death of listening to foreigners. . . . Could your Cuban speak any known tongue outside of his own?"

"We didn't do much talking." Naomi smiled.

I stared at her, then merely said, "I expect not," and sighed.

I went on talking. "I've suffered so cruelly from insomnia since you went away," and I shaded my eyes. "All night long night after night awake listening to the boat whistles."

"Nobody to rub your poor little head." Naomi smiled.

"Nobody to do anything for me! While you lay in the arms of that Cuban . . . Naomi, a thing has occurred to me, knowing your temper. . . . You didn't kill him, did you? I won't keep an escaped murderess in my home! Did you come here because you've killed him?"

"I can see losin' me ain't changed you none, Mrs. Bankers. . . . Now hear my terms, dear heart. I'll come back if you'll sign a paper to the effect I never faded your rose rugs. . . ."

I looked at her to indicate I knew she had gone completely out of her mind.

"A little scrap of paper that I can keep," she went right on, "in case you turn ugly again and bring the subject up at a inopportune time."

"Naomi, child, who put you up to this?" I controlled myself.

"Did you ever know me to have to wait for somebody to put me up to anything, Mrs. Bankers? You must be losing your memory too!"

"Well, then what do you want me to sign a paper for!" I screamed at her.

She folded her arms, and oh the triumph on her mouth!

"Because," she went on, "I want *an* apology, that's why. And without *a* apology, I don't come back."

"Damn you, and damn your methods!" I cried, but I couldn't put any force in my voice, and oh did she observe that.

"What could I do with a old piece of paper that would simply say you, Celia Bankers, was mistaken in accusing Naomi Green of having faded your beautiful Portuguese rose rugs. With regret for having inconvenienced her, and then your signature."

Wiping my eyes, I said, "I'm surprised you wouldn't demand also that I put the date and place of my birth so that I could be further humiliated by a servant! . . . So then this is your reason! You came back here not to apologize yourself and ask for your job back, but to humiliate me in my own home, remind me again, as is your insane habit, of my age, and having insulted me, leave me again to the mercies of these sweating snooty standoffish irresponsible foreigners! Oh, Naomi, why did I ever take you in. Why did I ever set eyes on you, I hate you. . . . Now, get out. You've had your sweet revenge."

"Now, now, sweetheart." She was as cool as a mountain spring, and took my cup out to the kitchen, got a fresh bigger one, filled it with strong hot tea, and put more bread in the toaster.

"Did your Cuban lover send you here to blackmail me?" I inquired, taking the tea.

"Don't try to change the subject, Mrs. Bankers."

"I won't write any absurd note abdicating from my natural rights and dignity so that you can show my statements to your lovers and laugh at me behind my back!"

"Miss Bankers! I'm warning you!"

"I'll never sign, you slut! Never."

"Miss Bankers, I'm going to have to punish you if you don't quit carryin' on like this."

"All the time I needed you and had to trust my person, my affairs, my very health and life to these no-account foreigners, you were lying in bed with a man and having to pay him for his favors to you! Don't interrupt me! That's how old you are now, and don't think I don't know it. You have to pay for it now at your age. You always have acted as if I knew nothing of the world. I know everything, you fool."

"Eat your toast and shut your mouth, Mrs. Bankers. I'm in no need of seeing you in one of your fits of hysterics, and I won't put up with it. You need me, you need me bad, you need me so bad I could make you take all your clothes off and crawl on hands and knees on your old faded carpets and say, 'Naomi! Come home!' "

"Yes, my carpets"—I looked down at them—"which of course I faded myself, or they came from the camels faded."

I began to cry hard then.

"I'm not taken in by your bawlin'," she scoffed.

"I didn't expect you to be." I blew my nose, and got really angry again. "A black whore like you."

Naomi laughed, and began waltzing around the room.

"Don't break anything now because you'll have to stay and work it out for nothing, remember."

"I'll stay as soon as you sign that paper."

Coming over to the little Italian marble-topped table on which her teacup and jam rested, Naomi put down a blank sheet of linen paper, with a quill pen, copiously dipped.

"Take that paper and pen away, you low conniving creature!" I cried, but I'm afraid I showed no force or decision.

"I'll raise your pay," I said suddenly.

"You bet you will, Mrs. Bankers."

"I'll never sign, though."

"I've never told a soul how old you are, and you know it," Naomi said.

"You don't know how old I am." I raised my voice now.

"And I never told nobody you was a bona fide virgin either, and had never been married. I never even told anybody your real name."

I laid my head back against the velvet of the chair and said, "Go ahead, blackmail me."

"I've been faithful to you, Mrs. Bankers, and you know it."

"I won't sign your paper. If I signed it, you'd make me sign more, sign my life away to you."

"I won't let you off the hook just the same. I have my pride about them rugs. You told everybody I faded them. It hurt my standing."

"With whom, pray tell!" I demanded.

"The doormen," she said, after thinking for quite a while.

"Those drunken Irish idiots! A lame excuse coming from you!"

There was a long, terrible silence, and then I said, "Go back to your Cuban lover. . . . I'll stay here and die with foreigners."

"If I go this time, Mrs. Bankers, I ain't never coming back."

I began crying again, and Naomi could see she had scared me good.

"You've humiliated me for twenty years." I had to take the handkerchief she offered me, my own was useless by now.

Naomi folded her arms and sat down.

"You have no respect for me, you've never acted like I was your employer, and you've blackmailed me over the years because you know my correct age and that I was never married. You also know my real name. . . . So what can I do? . . . You and your likes are taking over. I'm a prisoner in my own house and nation!"

"Rotgut! Mrs. Bankers, and you know it."

Then she took my hand, put the pen in it, and held my hand to the paper.

I pretended to scream.

"If you don't sign in two seconds, I'm going out that door and never darken it again, and you can go ahead with your threat to die with them Norwegians and Croats."

"But I don't even know what to write!" I appealed to her.

"Write this," she said: ". . . *I, Celia Bankers, confess I wrongfully accused my maid of twenty years' standing, Miss Naomi Green, of having faded my beautiful rose Portuguese carpets, causing her as a result to lose face with the people who run this building and to look bad in general, whereas my carpets were already faded before Naomi got here.*"

I had written all the words dutifully and then handed the sheet of paper to Naomi.

"God Almighty, you wrote it!" she said.

I looked at the wall. I was very pale.

Suddenly, hearing the tearing sounds, I looked up. Naomi had torn up what I had just written.

"My dear child," I cried, extending my right arm toward her.

Naomi kneeled down, and I caressed her hair in the folds of my skirt.

"I've been just wonderful to you from the start, Mrs. Bankers, and you got to admit it."

"Do you want me to sign a paper to that effect also?" I wondered. "For I may as well while the pen is still wet with ink. . . ."

"Now, now." Naomi stirred under my fingers.

"Oh, Naomi, how I hate foreigners. I never want one of them to touch me again as long as I live. . . . You're so beautiful, after all, child." I patted Naomi's cheek. "You're a black rose." I kissed her hair. "I'd sign anything, I guess, to have you back."

Naomi giggled.

"To think though you got married, and to a Cuban who's of course black," I said. "How inconsiderate you have always been. Naomi, you are a fool."

Naomi jerked her head up from my lap.

"Now what have I said?" I cried, on seeing the look of flashing anger in Naomi's eyes. "I declare you don't know how to behave for more than five minutes at a time. . . . Lie still, and don't get so excited, Naomi. . . . After all, my dear, if you were a big enough fool to come back here, I'm a bigger one to let you."

MR. EVENING

"You were asking the other day, Pearl, what that very tall young Mr. Evening—the one who goes past the house so often—does for a living, and I think I've found out for you," Mrs. Owens addressed her younger sister from her chair loaded with hand-sewn cushions.

Mrs. Owens continued to gaze out the big front window, its heavy shutter pulled back now in daylight to allow her a full view of the street.

She had paused long enough to allow Pearl's curiosity to whet itself while her own attention strayed to the faces of passersby. Indeed Mrs. Owens's only two occupations now were correcting the endless inventory of her heirlooms and observing those who passed her window, protected from the street by massive wrought-iron bars.

"Mr. Evening is in and out of his rooming house frequently enough to be up to a good deal, if you ask me, Grace," Pearl finally broke through her sister's silence.

Coming out of her reverie, Mrs. Owens smiled. "We've always known he was busy, of course." She took a piece of newsprint from her lap, and closed her eyes briefly in the descending rays of the January sun. "But now at last we know what he's busy at." She waved the clipping gently.

"Ah, don't start so, child." Mrs. Owens almost laughed. "Pray look at this, would you," and she handed the younger woman a somewhat lengthy "notice" clipped neatly from the *Wall Street Journal.*

While Pearl put on thick glasses to study the fine print, Mrs. Owens went on as much for herself as her sister: "Mr. Evening has always given me a special feeling." She touched her lavaliere. "He's far too young to be as idle as he looks, and on the other hand, as you've pointed out, he's clearly busier than those who make a profession of daily responsibility."

"It's means, Grace," Pearl said, blinking over her reading, but making no comment on it, which was a kind of desperate plea, it turned out, for information concerning a certain scarce china cup, circa 1910. "He has means," Pearl repeated.

"Means?" Mrs. Owens showed annoyance. "Well, I should hope he has, in his predicament." She hinted at even further knowledge concerning him, but with a note of displeasure creeping into her tone at Pearl's somewhat offhand, bored manner.

"I've telephoned him to appear, of course." Mrs. Owens had decided against any further "Preparation" for her sister, and threw the whole completed plan at her now in one fling. "On Thursday, naturally."

Putting down the "notice" Pearl waited for Mrs. Owens to make some elaboration on so unusual a decision, but no elaboration came.

"But you've never sold anything, let alone shown to anybody!" Pearl cried, after some moments of deeply troubled cogitation.

"Who spoke of selling!" Mrs. Owens tightened an earring. "And as to showing, as you say, I haven't thought that far. . . . But don't you see, poor darling"—here Mrs. Owens's voice boomed in what was perhaps less self-defense than self-explanation—"I've not met anybody in half a century who wants heirlooms so bad as he." She tapped the clipping. "He's worded everything here with one thought only in mind—my seeing it."

Pearl withdrew into incomprehension.

"Don't you see this has to be the case!" Here she touched the "notice" with her finger. "Who else has the things he's enumerated here? He's obviously investigated what I have, and he could have inserted this in the want ads only in the hope it would catch my eye."

"But you're certainly not going to invite someone to the house who merely wants what you have!" Pearl found herself for the first time in her life not only going against her sister in opinion, but voicing something akin to disapproval.

"Why, you yourself said only the other night that what we needed was company!" Mrs. Owens put these words adroitly now in her sister's mouth, where they could never have been.

"But Mr. Evening!" Pearl protested against his coming, ignoring or forgetting the fact she had been quoted as having said something she never in the first place had thought.

"Don't we need somebody to tell us about heirlooms! I mean *our* heirlooms, of course. Haven't you said as much yourself time after time?"

Mrs. Owens was trying to get her sister to go along with her, to admit complicity, so to speak, in what she herself had brought about, and now she found that Pearl put her mind and temper against even consideration.

"Someone told me only recently"—Pearl now hinted at a side to her own life perhaps unknown to Mrs. Owens—"that the young man you speak of, Mr. Evening, can hardly carry on a conversation."

Mrs. Owens paused. She had not been inactive in making her own investigations concerning their caller-to-be, and one of the things she had discovered, in addition to his being a Southerner, was that he did not or would not "talk" very much.

"We don't need a conversationalist—at least not about *them*," Mrs. Owens nearly snapped, by *them* meaning the heirlooms. "What we need is an appreciator, and the *muter* the better, say I."

"But if that's all you want him for!"—Pearl refused to be won—

"why, he'll smell out your plan. He'll see you're only showing him what he can never hope to buy or have."

A look of deep disappointment tinged with spleen crossed Mrs. Owens's still-beautiful face.

"Let him *smell* out our plan, then, as you put it," Mrs. Owens chided in the wake of her sister's opposition, "we won't care! If he can't talk, don't you see, so much the better. We'll have a session of 'looking' from him, and his 'appreciation' will perk us up. We'll see him taking in everything, dear love, and it will review our own lifelong success. . . . Don't be so down on it now. . . . And mind you, we won't be here quite forever," she ended, and a certain hard majestical note in her voice was not lost on the younger woman. "The fact," Mrs. Owens summed it all up, "that we've nothing to give him needn't spoil for us the probability he's got something to give us."

Pearl said no more then, and Mrs. Owens spoke under her breath: "I haven't a particle of a doubt that I'm in the right about him, and if it should turn out I'm wrong, I'll shoulder all the blame."

WHATEVER PARTICLE OF a doubt there may have been in Mrs. Owens's own mind, there was considerable more of doubt and apprehension in Mr. Evening's as he weighed, in his rooming house, the rash decision he had made to visit formidable Mrs. Owens in—one could not say her business establishment, since she had none—but her background of accumulation of heirlooms, which vague world was, he could only admit, also his own. Because he had never known or understood people well, and he was the most insignificant of "collectors," he was at a loss as to why Mrs. Owens should feel he had anything to give her, and since her "legend" was too well known to him, he knew she, likewise, had nothing at all to give him, except, and this was why he was going, the "look-in" which his visit would give him. Whatever risk there was in going to see her, and there appeared to be some, he felt, from "warnings" of a queer kind from those who had dealt with her, it was worth something just to get inside, even though again he had been informed by those in the business it would be doubtful if he would be allowed to mention "purchase" and in the end it was also doubtful he would be allowed even a close peek.

On the other hand, if Mrs. Owens wanted him to tell her something—this crossed his mind as he went toward her huge pillared house, though he could not imagine even vaguely what he could have to tell her, and if she was mad enough to think him capable of entertaining her, for after all she was a lonely ancient lady on the threshold of death, he would disabuse her of all such expectations almost as soon as they had met. He was uneasy with old women, he supposed, though in his work he spent more time with them than with other people, and he wanted, he finally said out loud to himself, that hand-painted china cup, 1910, no matter what it might cost him. He fancied she might yield it to him at some atrocious illegal price. It was no more improbable, after all, than that she had invited him in the first place. Mrs. Owens never invited anybody, that is, from the outside, and the inside people in her life had all died or were incapacitated from paying calls. Yes, he had been summoned, and he could hope at least therefore that what everybody else told him was at least thinkable—purchase, and if that was not in store for him, then the other improbable thing, "viewing."

But Mr. Evening could not pretend. If his getting the piece of china or even more improbably other larger heirlooms, kept from daylight as well as human eyes, locked away in the floors above her living room, if possession meant long hours of currying favor, talking and laughing and dining and killing the evening, then no thank you, never. His inability to pretend, he supposed, had kept him from rising in the antique trade, for although he had a kind of business of his own here in Brooklyn, his own private income was what kept him afloat, and what he owned in heirlooms, though remarkable for a young dealer, did not make him a figure in the trade. His inconspicuous position in the business made his being summoned by Mrs.

Owens all the more inexplicable and even astonishing. Mr. Evening was, however, too unversed both in people and the niceties of his own profession to be either sufficiently impressed or frightened.

Meanwhile Pearl, moments before Mr. Evening's arrival gazing out of the corner of her eye at her sister, saw with final and uncomfortable consternation the telltale look of anticipation on the older woman's face which demonstrated that she "wanted" Mr. Evening with almost the same inexplicable maniacal whim which she had once long ago demonstrated toward a certain impossible-to-find Spanish medieval chair, and how she had got hold of the latter still remained a mystery to the world of dealers.

I

"Shall we without further ado, then, strike a bargain? Mrs. Owens intoned, looking past Mr. Evening, who had arrived on a bad snowy January night.

He had been reduced to more than his customary kind of silent social incommunicativeness by finally seeing Mrs. Owens in the flesh, a woman who while reputed to be so old, looked unaccountably beautiful, whose clothes were floral in their charm, wafting sachets of woody scent to his nostrils, and whose voice sounded like fine chimes.

"Of course I don't mean there's to be a sale! Even youthful you couldn't have come here thinking that." She dismissed at once any business with a pronounced flourish of white hands. "Nothing's for sale, and won't be even should we die." She faced him with a lessening of defiance, but he stirred uncomfortably.

"Whatever you may think, whatever you may have been told"—she went now to deal with the improbable fact of their meeting—"let me say that I can't resist their being admired" (she meant the heirlooms, of course). She unfolded the piece of newsprint of his "notice." "I could tell immediately by your way of putting things"—she touched the paper—"that you knew all about them. Or better,

I knew you knew all about them by the way you left things undescribed. I knew you could admire, without stint or reservation." She finished with a kind of low bow.

"I'm relieved"—he began to look about the large high room—"that you're not curious then to know who I am, to know about me, that is, as I'm afraid I wouldn't be able to satisfy your curiosity on that score. That is to say, there's almost nothing to tell about me, and you already know what my vocation is."

She allowed this speech to die in silence, as she did with an occasional intruding sound of traffic which unaccountably reached her parlor, but then at his helpless sinking look, she said in an attempt, perhaps, to comfort: "I don't have to be curious about anything that holds me, Mr. Evening. It always unfolds itself, in any case.

"For instance," she went on, her face taking on a mock-wrathful look, "people sometimes try to remind me that I was once a famous actress, which though being a fact, is irrelevant, and, more, now meaningless, for even in those remote days, when let's say I was on the stage, even then, Mr. Evening, these"—and she indicated with a flourish of those commanding white hands the munificent surroundings—"these were everything!

"One is really only strictly curious about people one never intends to meet, I think, Mr. Evening," Mrs. Owens said.

She now rose and stood for a moment, so that the imposition of her height over him, seated in his low easy chair, was emphasized, then walking over to a tiny beautiful peachwood table, she looked at something on it. His own attention, still occupied with her presence, did not move for a moment to what she was bestowing a long, calm glance on. She made no motion to touch the object on the table before her. Though his vision clouded a bit, he looked directly at it now, and saw what it was, and saw there could be no mistake about it. It was the pale rose shell-like 1910 hand-painted china cup.

"You don't need to bring it to me!" he cried, and even she was startled by such an outburst. Mr. Evening had gone as white as chalk.

He searched in vain in his pockets for a handkerchief, and noting his distress, Mrs. Owens handed him one from the folds of her own dress.

"I won't ever beg of you," he said, wiping his brow with the handkerchief. "I would offer you anything for the cup, of course, but I can't beg."

"What will you do then, Mr. Evening?" She came to within a few inches of him.

He sat before her, his head slightly tilted forward, his palms upturned like one who wishes to determine if rain is beginning.

"Don't answer"—she spoke in loud, gay tones—"for nobody expects you to do anything, beg, bargain, implore, steal. Whatever you are, or were, Mr. Evening—I catch from your accent you are Southern—you were never an actor, thank fortune. It's one of the reasons you're here, you are so much yourself.

"Now, mark me." Mrs. Owens strode past his chair to a heavy gold-brocaded curtain, her voice almost menacing in its depth of resonance. "I've not allowed you to look at this cup in order to tempt you. I merely wanted you to know I'd read your 'notice,' which you wrote, in any case, only for me. Furthermore, as you know, I'm not bargaining with you in any received sense of the word. You and I are beyond bargaining with one another. Money will never be mentioned between us, papers, or signatures—all that goes without saying. But I do want something," and she turned from the curtain and directed her luminous gray eyes to his face. "You're not like anybody else, Mr. Evening, and it's this quality of yours which has, I won't say won me, you're beyond winning anybody, but which has brought an essential part of myself back to me by your being just what you are and wanting so deeply what you want!"

Holding her handkerchief entirely over his face now so that he spoke to her as from under a sheet, he mumbled, "I don't like company, Mrs. Owens." His interruption had the effect of freezing her to the curtain before her. "And company, I'm afraid, includes you and your sister. I can't come and talk, and I don't like supper parties. If I did, if I liked them, that is, I'd prefer you."

"What extraordinary candor!" Mrs. Owens was at a loss where to walk, at what to look. "And how gloriously rude!" She considered everything quickly. "Good, very good, Mr. Evening. . . . But *good* won't carry us far enough!" she cried, and her voice rose in a great swell of volume until she saw with satisfaction that he moved under her strength. The handkerchief fell away, and his face, very flushed, but with the eyes closed, bent in her direction.

"You don't have to talk"—Mrs. Owens dismissed this as if with loathing of that idea that he might—"and you don't have to listen. You can snore in your chair if you like. But if you come, say, once a week, that will more than do for a start. You could consider this house as a kind of waiting room, let's say, for a day that's sure and bound to come for all, and especially us. . . . You'd wait here, say, on Thursday, and we could offer you the room where you are now, and food, which you would be entitled to spurn, and all you would need do is let time pass. I could allow you to see, very gradually"—she looked hurriedly in the direction of the cup—"a few things here and there, not many at a visit, of course, it might easily unhinge you in your expectant state"—she laughed—"and certainly I could show you nothing for quite a while from up there," and she moved her head toward the floors above. "But in the end, if you kept it up, the visits, I mean, I can assure you your waiting would 'pay off,' as they say out there. . . . I can't be any more specific." She brought her explanation of the bargain to an abrupt close, and indicated with a sweeping gesture he might stand and depart.

II

Thursday, then, set aside by Mrs. Owens for Mr. Evening to begin attendance on the heirlooms, loomed up for the two of them as a kind of fateful, even direful, mark on the calendar; in fact, both the mistress of the heirlooms and her viewer were ill with anticipation. Mr. Evening's dislike of company and being entertained vied with his passion for "viewing." On the other hand, Mrs. Owens, watched over by a saddened and anguished Pearl, felt the hours and days speed precipitously to an encounter which she now could not understand her ever having arranged or wanted. Never had she lived through such a week, and her fingers, usually white and still as they rested on her satin cushions, were almost raw from a violent pulling on and off of her rings.

At last Thursday, 8:30 PM, came, finding Mrs. Owens with one glass of wine—all she ever allowed herself, with barely a teaspoon of it tasted. Nine-thirty struck, ten, no Mr. Evening. Her lips, barely touched with an uncommon kind of rouge, moved in a bitter self-deprecatory smile. She rose and walked deliberately to a small ebony cabinet, and took out her smelling bottle, which she had not touched for months. Opening it, she found it had considerably weakened in strength, but she took it with her back to her chair, sniffing its dilute fumes from time to time.

Then about a quarter past eleven, when she had finished with hope, having struck the silk and mohair of her chair several castigating blows, the miracle, Mr. Evening, ushered in by Giles (who rare for him showed some animation), appeared in his heavy black country coat. Mrs. Owens, not so much frosty from his lateness as incredulous that she was seeing him, barely nodded. Having refused her supper, she had opened a large gilt book of Flaxman etchings, and was occupying herself with these, while Pearl, seated at a little table of her own in the furthest reaches of the room, was dining on some tender bits of fish soaked in a sauce into which she dipped a muffin.

Mr. Evening, ignored by both ladies, had sat down. He had not been drinking, Mrs. Owens's first impression, but his cheeks were beet-red from cold, and he looked, she saw with uneasy observation, more handsome and much younger than on his first call.

"I hate snow intensely." Mrs. Owens studied his pants cuffs heavy with flakes. "Yet going south somewhere"—it was not clear to whom she was speaking from this time on—"that would be now too much in the way of preparation merely to avoid winter wet. . . . At one time traveling itself was home to me, of course," she continued, and her hands fell on a massive yellowed ivory paper-opener with a larger than customary blade. "One was put up in those days, not hurled over landscape like an electric particle. One wore *clothes*, one 'appeared' at dinner, which was an occasion, one conversed, *listened*, or merely sat with eyes averted, one rose, was looked after, watched over, if you will, one was often more at home *going* in those days than when one remained home, or reached one's destination."

Mrs. Owens stopped, mortified by a yawn from Mr. Evening. Reduced to a kind of quivering dumbness, Mrs. Owens could only restrain herself, remembering the "agreement."

A butler appeared wearing green goggles and at a nearly imperceptible nod from Mrs. Owens picked up a minuscule marble-topped gold inlaid table, and placed it within a comfortable arm's reach of Mr. Evening. Later, another servant brought something steaming under silver receptacles from the kitchen.

"Unlike the flock of crows in flight today"—Mrs. Owens's voice seemed to come across footlights—"I can remember *all* my traveling." She turned the pages of Flaxman with critical quickness. "And that means in my case the globe, all of it, when it was largely inaccessible, and certainly infrequently commented or written upon by tradespeople and typists." She concentrated a moment in silence as if remembering perhaps how old she was and how far off her travel had been. "I didn't miss a country, however unrecommended or unlisted by some guide or hotel bursar. There's no point in going now or leaving one's front door when every dot on the map has been ground to dust by somebody's heavy foot. When everybody is *en route*, stay home! . . . Pearl, my dear, you're not looking at your plate!"

Pearl, who had finished her fish, was touching with nearsighted uncertainty the linen tablecloth with a gleaming fork. "Wear your glasses, dear child, for heaven's sake, or you'll stab yourself!"

Mr. Evening had closed his eyes. He appeared like one who must impress upon himself not to touch food in a strange house. But the china on his table was stunning, though obviously brand-new and therefore not "anything." At last, however, against his better judgment, he lifted one of the cups, then set it down noiselessly. Immediately the butler poured him coffee. Against his will, he drank a tablespoon or so, for after the wet and cold he needed at least a taste of something hot. It was an unbelievable brew, heady, clear, fresh. Mrs. Owens immediately noted the pleasure on his face, and a kind of shiver ran through her. Her table, ever nonpareil, might win him, she saw, where nothing in her other "offerings" tonight had reached him.

"After travel was lost to me," Mrs. Owens went on in the manner of someone who is dictating memoirs to a machine, "the church failed likewise to hold me. Even then" (one felt she referred to the early years of another century), "they had let in every kind of speaker. The church had begun to offer thought and problems instead of merging and repose. . . . So it went out of my life along with going abroad. . . . Then my eyes are not, well, not so bad as Pearl's, who is blind without glasses, but reading tires me more and more, though I see the natural world of objects better perhaps now than ever before. Besides, I've read more than most, for I've had nothing in life but time. I've read, in sum, everything, and if there's a real author, I've been through him often more than twice."

Mr. Evening now tried a slice of baked Alaska, and it won him. His beginning the meal backwards was hardly intentional, but he had looked so snowy the butler had poured the coffee first, and the coffee had suggested to the kitchen the dessert course instead of the entrée.

Noting that Mr. Evening did not touch his wine, Mrs. Owens thought a moment, then began again, "Drinking has never been a consolation to me either. Life might have been more endurable, perhaps, especially in this epoch," and she looked at her glass, down scarcely two ounces. "Therefore spirits hardly needed to join travel in the things I've eliminated. . . ." Gazing upwards, she brought out, "The human face, perhaps strangely enough, is really all that has been left to me," and after a moment's consultation with herself, she looked obliquely at Mr. Evening, who halted conveying his fork, full of meringue, to his mouth. "I need the human face, let's say." She talked into the thick pages of the Flaxman drawings. "I can't stare at my servants, though outsiders have praised their fetching appeal. (I can't look at what I've acquired, I've memorized it too well.) No, I'm talking about the unnegotiable human face. Somebody," she said, looking nowhere now in particular, "has that, of course, while, on the other hand, I have what he wants badly, and so shall we say we are, if not a match, confederates of a sort."

Times had passed, if not swiftly, steadily. Morning itself was advancing. Mr. Evening, during the entire visit, having opened his mouth chiefly to partake of food whose taste alone invited him, since he had already dined, took up his napkin, wiped his handsome red lips on it, though it was, he saw, an indignity to soil such a piece of linen, and rose. Both Mrs. Owens and her sister had long since dozed or pretended to doze by the carefully tended log fire. He said good night therefore to stone ears, and went out the door.

III

It was the fifth Thursday of his visits to Mrs. Owens that the change which he had feared and suspected from the start, and which he was somehow incapable of averting, came about.

Mrs. Owens and her sister had ignored him more and more on the occasion of his "calls," and an onlooker, not in on the agreement, might have thought his presence was either distasteful to the ladies, or that he was too insignificant—an impecunious relative, perhaps—to merit the bestowal of a glance or word.

The spell of the pretense of indifference, of not recognizing one another, ended haphazardly one hour when Pearl, without any preface of warning, said in a loud voice that strong light was being allowed to reach and ruin the ingrain carpet on the third floor.

Before Mrs. Owens could take in the information or issue a command as to what might be done, if she intended indeed to do anything about protecting the carpet from light, she heard a certain flurry from the direction of the visitor, and turning saw what the mention of this special carpet had done to the face of Mr. Evening. He bore an expression of greed, passionate covetousness, one might even say a deranged, demented wish for immediate ownership. Indeed his countenance was so arresting in its eloquence that Mrs. Owens found herself, going against her own protocol, saying, "Are you quite all right, sir?" But before she had the words out of her mouth he had come over to her chair without waiting her permission.

"Did you say ingrain carpet?" he asked with great abruptness.

When Mrs. Owens, too astonished at his tone and movement, did not reply, she heard Mr. Evening's peremptory: "Show it to me at once!"

"If you have not taken leave of your senses, Mr. Evening," Mrs. Owens began, bringing forth from the folds of her red cashmere dress an enormous gold chain, which she pressed, "would you be so kind, I might even say, so decent, as to remember our agreement, if you cannot remember who I am, and in whose house you are visiting."

Then, quickly, in a voice of annihilating anger, loud enough to be heard on a passing steamship: "You've not waited long enough, spoilsport!"

Standing before her, jaws apart, an expression close to that of an idiot who has been slapped into brief attention, he could only stutter something inaudible.

Alarmed by her own outburst, Mrs. Owens hastened to add, "It's not ready to be shown, my dear, special friend."

Mrs. Owens took his hands now in hers, and kissed them gently.

Kneeling before her, not letting go her chill handclasp, looking up into her furrowed rouged cheeks, "Allow me one glimpse," he beseeched.

She extricated her hands from his and touched his forehead.

"Quite out of the question." She seemed almost to flirt now, and her voice had gone up an octave. "But the day will come"—she motioned for him to seat himself again—"before one perhaps is expecting it. You have only hope ahead of you, dear Mr. Evening."

Obeying her, he seated himself again, and his look of crestfallen abject submissiveness, coupled with fear, comforted and strengthened Mrs. Owens so that she was able to smile tentatively.

"No one who does not live here, you see, can see the carpet." She was almost apologetic for her tirade, certainly she was consoling.

He bent his head.

Then they heard the wind from the northeast, and felt the huge shutter on the front of the house struggle as if for life. The snow followed soon after, hard as hail.

Tenting him to the quick, Mrs. Owens studied Mr. Evening's incipient immobility, and after waiting to see whether it would pass, and as she suspected, noted that it did not, she rang for the night servant, gave the latter cursory instructions, and then sat studying her guest until the servant returned with a tiny decanter and a sliver of handsome glass, setting these by Mr. Evening, who lightly caressed both vessels.

"Alas, Mr. Evening, they're only new," Mrs. Owens said.

He did not remember more until someone put a lap robe over his knees, and he knew the night had advanced into the glimmerings of dawn, and that he therefore must have slept upright in the chair all those hours, fortified by nips from the brandy, which, unlike the glass that contained it, was ancient.

When morning had well advanced, he found he could not rise. A new attendant, with coal-black sideburns and ashen cheeks, assisted him to the bathroom, helped him bathe and then held him securely under the armpits while he urinated a stream largely blood. He stared into the bowl but regarded the crimson pool there without particular interest or alarm.

Then he was back in the chair again, the snow still pelted the shutters, and the east wind raved like lunatics helpless without sedation.

Although he was certain Mrs. Owens passed from time to time in the adjoining room—who could fail to recognize her tread, as dominating and certain as her resonant voice—she did not enter that day either to look at him or inquire. Occasionally he heard, to his acute distress, dishes being moved and, so it seemed, placed in straw.

Once or twice he thought he heard her clap her hands, an anachronism so imperial he found himself giggling convulsively. He also heard a parrot screech, and then almost immediately caught the sound of its cage being taken up and the cries of the bird retreating further and further into total silence.

Some time later he was served food so highly seasoned, so copiously sprinkled with herbs and spices that added to his disinclination to partake of food, he could not identify a morsel of what he tasted.

Then Giles reappeared, with a sterling-silver basin, a gleaming tray of verbena soap, and improbably enough, looking up at him, his own straight razor, for if it was one thing in the world of manhood he had mastered, it was to shave beautifully with a razor, an accomplishment he had learned from his captain in military school.

"How did they get my own things fetched here, Giles?" he inquired, with no real interest in having his question answered.

"We've had to bring everything, under the circumstances," Giles replied in a hollow vestryman's voice.

Mr. Evening lay back then, while he felt the servant's hands tuck a blanket about his slippers and thighs.

"Mrs. Owens thinks it's because your blood is thinner than we Northerners that the snow affects you in this way." Giles offered a tentative explanation of the young man's plight.

Suddenly from directly overhead, Mr. Evening heard carpenters, loud as if in the room with him, sawing and hammering. He stirred uncomfortably in his stocking feet.

In the hall directly in line with his chair, though separated by a kind of heavy partition, Mrs. Owens and two gentlemen of vaguely familiar voices were doing a loud inventory of "effects."

Preparations for an auction must be in progress, Mr. Evening decided. He now heard with incipient unease and at the same time a kind of feeble ecstasy the names of every rare heirloom in the trade, but these great objects' names were loudly hawked, checked, callously enumerated, and the whole proceedings were carried off with a kind of rage and contempt in the voice of the auctioneer so that one had the impression the most priceless and rarest treasures worthy finally of finding a home only in the Louvre were being noted here prior to their being carted out in boxes and tossed into the bonfire. At one point in the inventory he let out a great cry of "Stop it!"

The partition in the wall opened, and Mrs. Owens stood staring at him from about ten feet away; then after a look of what was meant perhaps to be total unrecognition or bilious displeasure, she closed the sliding panel fast, and the inventory was again in progress, louder, if anything, than before, the tone of the hawker's voice more rasping and vicious.

Following a long nap, he remembered two strangers, dressed in overalls, enter with a gleaming gold tape; they stooped down, grunting and querulous, and made meticulous if furtive movements of measuring him from head to toe, his sitting posture requiring them, evidently, to check their results more than once.

Was it now Friday night, or had the weekend already passed, and were we arrived at Monday?

The snow had continued unabated, so far as his memory served, though the wind was weaker, or more fitful, and the shutters nearly silent. He supposed all kinds of people had called on him at his lodgings. Then Giles appeared again, after Mr. Evening had passed more indistinct hours in his chair, and the servant helped him into the toilet, where he passed thick clots of blood, and on his return to his chair Mr. Evening found himself face to face with his own large steamer trunk and a pair of valises.

While he kept his eyes averted from the phenomenal appearance of his luggage, Giles combed and cut his long chestnut hair, trimmed the shagginess of his eyebrows, and massaged the back of his neck. Mr. Evening did not ask him if there was any reason or occasion for tonsorial attention, but at last he did inquire, more for breaking the lugubrious silence than for getting any pertinent answer, "What was the carpentering upstairs for, Giles?"

The servant hesitated, stammered, and in his confusion came near nipping Mr. Evening's ear with the barber's shears, but at last answered the question in a loud whisper: "They're remodeling the bed."

The room in which he had sat these past days, however many, four, six, a fortnight, perhaps, the room which had been Mrs. Owens's and her sister's on those first Thursday nights of his visits, was now only his alone, and the two women had passed on to other quarters in a house whose chambers were, like its heirlooms, difficult, perhaps impossible, to number.

Limited to a kind of speechless listlessness—he assumed he must be very ill, though he did not wonder why no doctor came—and passing several hours without attendance, suddenly, in pique at being neglected, he employed Mrs. Owens's own queer custom and clapped his hands peremptorily. A dark-skinned youth with severe bruises about his temples appeared and, without inquiry or greeting, adjusted Mr. Evening's feet on a stool, poured him a drink of something red with a bitter taste, and, while he waited for the sick man to drink, made a gesture of inquiry as to whether Mr. Evening wished to relieve himself.

More indistinct hours swam slowly into blurred unremembrance. At last the hammering, pounding, moving of furniture, together with the suffocating fumes of turpentine and paint, all ceased to molest him.

Mrs. Owens, improbably, appeared again, accompanied by Pearl.

"I am glad to see you better, Mr. Evening, needless to say," Mrs. Owens began icily, and one could see at once that she appeared some years younger, perhaps strong sunlight—now pouring in—flattered her, or could it be, he wondered, she had had recourse to plastic surgery during his illness, at any rate, she was much younger, while her voice was harsher, harder, more actresslike than ever before.

"Because of your splendid recovery, we are therefore ready to move you into your room," Mrs. Owens went on, "where, I'm glad to report, you'll find more than one ingrain carpet spread out for you to rest your eyes on. . . . The bed," she added after a careful pause, "I do hope will meet with your approval" (here he attempted to say something contradictory, but she indicated she would not allow it), "for its refashioning has cost all of us here some pains to make over." Here he felt she would have used the word *heirloom*, but prevented herself from doing so. She said only, in conclusion, "You're over, do you realize, six foot six in your stocking feet!"

She studied him closely. "We couldn't let you lie with your legs hanging out of the bedclothes!

"Now, sir"—Mrs. Owens folded her arms—"can you move, do you suppose, to the next floor, provided someone, of course, assists you?"

The next thing he remembered was being helped up the interminable winding staircase by a brace of servants, while Mrs. Owens and Pearl brought up the rear, Mrs. Owens talking away: "Those of us who are Northerners, Mr. Evening, have of course the blood from birth to take these terribly snowy days, Boreas and his blasts, the sight of Orion climbing the winter night, but our friends of Southern birth must be more careful. That is why we take such good care of you. You should have come, in any case, from the beginning and not kept picking away at a mere Thursday call," she ended on a scolding note.

The servants deposited Mr. Evening on a large horsehair sofa which in turn faced the longest bed he had ever set eyes on, counting any, he was certain, he had ever stared at in museums. And now it must be confessed that Mr. Evening, for all the length of him, had never from early youth slept in the kind of bed that his height and build required, for after coming into his fortune, he had continued to live in lodging houses which did not provide anything adequate for his physical measurements. Here at Mrs. Owens's, where his living was all unchosen by him, he now saw the bed perfectly suited for his frame.

A tiny screen was thrown up around the horsehair sofa, and while Mrs. Owens and Pearl waited as if for a performance to begin, Cole, a Norwegian, as it turned out, quietly got Mr. Evening's old business clothes off, and clad him in gleaming green and shell silk pajamas, and in a lightning single stride across the room carried the invalid to the bed, propped him up in a layer of cushions and pillows so that he looked as a matter of fact more seated now than when he had spent those days and nights in the big chair downstairs.

Although food had been brought for all of them, seated in different sections of the immense room, that is for Pearl, Mrs. Owens, and Mr. Evening, only Pearl partook of any. Mr. Evening, sunk in cushions, looked nowhere in particular, certainly not at his food. Mrs. Owens, ignoring her own repast (some sort of roast game), produced from the folds of her organdy gown a jewel-studded lorgnette, and began reading aloud in droning monotone a list of rare antiques, finally naming with emphasis a certain ormolu clock, which caused Mr. Evening to cry out, "If you please, read no more while I am dining!" although he had not touched a morsel.

Mrs. Owens put down the paper, waved it against her like a fan, and having put away her lorgnette came over to the counterpane of the bed.

She bent over him like a physician and he closed his eyes. The scent which came from her bosom was altogether like that of a garden by the sea.

"Our whole life together, certainly," she began, like one talking in her sleep, "was to have been an enumeration of effects. I construed it so, at any rate. . . . I had thought," she went on, "that you would be attentive. . . . I procured these special glasses"—she touched the lorgnette briefly—"and if I may be allowed an explanation, I thought I would read to you since I no longer read to myself, and may I confess it, while I lifted my eyes occasionally from the paper, I hoped to rest them by letting them light on your fine features. . . . If you are to deprive me of that pleasure, dear Mr. Evening, say so, and new arrangements and new preparations can be made."

She pressed her hand now on the bed, as if to test its quality.

"I do not think even so poor an observer and so indifferent a guest as yourself can be unaware of the stupendous animation, movement, preparation, the entire metamorphosis indeed which your coming here has entailed. Mark me, I am willing to do more for you, but if I am to be deprived of the simple and may I say sole pleasure left to me, reading a list of precious heirlooms and at the same time resting my eyes from time to time on you, then say so, then excuse me, pray, and allow me to depart from my own house."

Never one endowed with power over language, Mr. Evening, at this, the most dramatic moment in his life, could only seize Mrs. Owens's pliant bejeweled hand in his rough, chapped one, hold her finger to his face, and cry, "No!"

"No what?" she said, withdrawing her hand, a tiny indication of pleasure, however, moving her lips.

Raising himself up from the hillock of cushions, he got out, "What about the things I was doing out there," and he pointed haphazardly in the direction of where he thought his shop might possibly lie.

Mrs. Owens shook her head. "Whatever you did out there, Mr. Evening"—she looked down at him—"or, rather, amend that, sir, to this; you are now doing whatever and more than you could have ever done elsewhere. . . . This is your home!" she cried, and as if beside herself, "Your work is here, and only here!"

"Am I as ill as everything points to?" He turned to Pearl, who continued to dine.

Pearl looked to her sister for instructions.

"I don't know how you could be so self-centered as to talk about a minor upset of the urinary tract as illness"—Mrs. Owens raised her voice—"especially when we have prepared a list like this"—she tapped with her lorgnette on the inventory of antiques—"which you can't be ass enough not to know will one day be yours!"

Mrs. Owens stood up and fixed him with her gaze.

Mr. Evening's eyes fell then like dropping balls to the floor, where the unobtainable ingrain carpets, unobserved by him till then, rested beneath them like live breathing things. He wept shamelessly and Mrs. Owens restrained what might have been a grin.

He dried his eyes slowly on the napkin which she had proffered him.

"If you would have at least the decency to pretend to drink your coffee, you would see your cup," she said.

"Yes," she sighed, as she studied Mr. Evening's disoriented features as he now caught sight of the 1910 hand-painted cup within his very fingertip, unobserved by him earlier, as had been the ingrain carpets. "Yes," Mrs. Owens continued, "while I have gained back my eyesight, as it were"—she raised her lorgnette briefly—"others are to all practical purposes sand-blind . . . Pearl"—she turned to her sister—"you may be excused from the room.

"My dear Mr. Evening," Mrs. Owens said, her voice materially altered once Pearl had disappeared.

He had put down the 1910 cup, perhaps because it seemed unthinkable to drink out of anything so irreplaceable, and so delicate that a mere touch of his lips might snap it.

"You can't possibly now go out of my life." Mrs. Owens half-stretched out her hand to him.

He supposed she had false teeth, they were too splendid for real, yet all of her suddenly was splendid, and from her person again came a succession of wild fragrance, honeysuckle, jasmine, flowers without names, one perfume succeeding another in enervating succession, as various as all her priceless heirlooms.

"Winter, even to a Southerner, dear Mr. Evening, can offer some tender recompense, and for me, whose blood, if I may be allowed to mention it again, is incapable of thinning." Here she turned down the bedclothes clear to his feet. The length of his feet and the beautiful architecture of his bare instep caused her for a moment to hesitate.

"I'm certain," she kept her words steady, placing an icy hand under the top of his pajamas, and letting it rest, as if in permanent location on his breast, "that you are handsome to the eye all over."

His teeth chattered briefly, as he felt her head come down on him so precipitously, but she seemed content merely to rest on his bare chest. He supposed he would catch an awful cold from it all, but he did not move, hearing her say, "And after I'm gone, all—all of it will be yours, and all I ask in return, Mr. Evening, is that all days be Thursday from now on."

He lay there without understanding how it had occurred, whether a servant had entered or her hands with the quickness of hummingbirds had done the trick, but there he was naked as he had come into the world, stretched out in the bed that was his exact length at last and which allowed him to see just what an unusually tall young man he was indeed.

ON THE REBOUND

"Frankly, gentlemen," Rupert Douthwaite reflected one gray afternoon in January to a few of us Americans who visited him from time to time in his "exile" in London, "no one in New York, no one who counted, ever expected to see Georgia Comstock back in town," and here Rupert nodded on the name, in his coy, pompous, but somewhat charming way, meaning for us to know she was an heiress, meaning she had "everything," otherwise he would not be mentioning her. "She sat right there." He pointed to a refurbished heirloom chair which had accompanied him from New York. "I would never have dreamed Georgia would sue for a favor, least of all to me, for, after all"—he touched a colorful sideburn—"if you will allow me to remind you, it was I who replaced Georgia so far as literary salons were concerned." He groaned heavily, one of his old affectations, and took out his monocle, one of his new ones, and let it rest on the palm of his hand like an expiring butterfly. "Georgia's was, after all, the only bona fide salon in New York for years and years—I say that, kind friends, without modification. It was never elegant, never grand, never *comme il faut*, granted, any more than poor Georgia was. She was plain, mean, and devastating, with her own consistent vulgarity and bad taste, but she had the energy of a fiend out of hot oil and she turned that energy into establishing the one place where everybody had to turn up on a Thursday in New York, whether he liked it or not.

"When the dear thing arrived, then, at my place after her long banishment, I was pained to see how much younger she'd gotten. It didn't become her. I preferred her old, let's say. It was obvious she'd had the finest face-lifting job Europe can bestow. (You know how they've gone all wrong in New York on that. You remember Kathryn Combs, the film beauty. One eye's higher than the other now, dead mouth, and so on, so that I always feel when Kathryn's about I'm looking into an open casket.) But Georgia! Well, she hardly looked forty.

"Now, mind you, I knew she hadn't come back to New York to tell me she loved me—the woman's probably hated me all my life, no doubt about it, but whatever she'd come for, I had to remind myself she had been helpful when Kitty left me." Rupert referred openly now to his third wife, the great New York female novelist who had walked out on him for, in his words, a shabby little colonel. "Yes," he sighed now, "when all the papers were full of my divorce before I myself hardly knew she had left me, Georgia was most understanding, even kind, moved in to take care of me, hovered over me like a mother bird, and so on. I had been ready to jump in the river, and she, bitch that she is, brought me round. And so when she appeared five years to the day after New York had kicked her out, and with her brand-new face, I saw at once she had come on a matter as crucial to her as my bust-up had been with Kitty, but I confess I never dreamed she had come to me because she wanted to begin all over again (begin with a salon, I mean of course). Nobody decent begins again, as I tried to tell her immediately I heard what she was up to. She'd been living in Yugoslavia, you know, after the New York fiasco. . . .

"When she said she did indeed want to begin again, I simply replied, 'Georgia, you're not serious and you're not as young as you look either, precious. You can't know what you're saying. Maybe it's the bad New York air that's got you after the wheat fields and haymows of Slavonia.'

"'Rupert, my angel,' she intoned, 'I'm on my knees to you, and not rueful to be so! Help me to get back and to stay back, dearest!'

"'Nonsense'—I made her stop her dramatics—'I won't hear of it, and you won't hear of it either when you're yourself again.'

"I was more upset than I should have been, somehow. Her coming and her wish for another try at a salon made me aware what was already in the wind, something wicked that scared me a little, and I heard myself voicing it when I said, 'Everything has changed in New York, sweety, since you've been away. You wouldn't know anybody now. Most of the old writers are too afraid to go out even for a stroll anymore, and the new ones, you see, meet only on the parade ground. The salon, dear love, I'm afraid, is through.'

"'I feel I can begin again, Rupert, darling.' She ignored my speech. 'You know it was everything to me, it's everything now. Don't speak to me of the Yugoslav pure air and haymows.'

"Well, I looked her up and down, and thought about everything. There she was, worth twenty million she'd inherited from her pa's death, and worth another six or seven million from what the movies gave her for her detective novels, for Georgia was, whether you boys remember or not, a novelist in her own right. Yet here she was, a flood of grief. I've never seen a woman want anything so much, and in my day I've seen them with their tongues hanging out for just about everything.

"'Let me fix you a nice tall frosty drink like they don't have in Zagreb, angel, and then I'm going to bundle you up and send you home to bed.' But she wouldn't be serious. 'Rupert, my love, if as you said I saved you once' (she overstated, of course), 'you've got to save me now.'

"She had come to the heart of her mission.

"'What did I do wrong before, will you tell me,' she brought out after a brief struggle with pride. 'Why was I driven out of New

York, my dear boy. Why was I blacklisted, why was every door slammed in my face.' She gave a short sob.

"'Georgia, my sweet, if you don't know why you had to leave New York, nobody can tell you.' I was a bit abrupt.

"'But I don't, Rupert!' She was passionate. 'Cross my heart,' she moaned. 'I don't.'

"I shook my finger at her.

"'You sit there, dear Douthwaite, like the appointed monarch of all creation whose only burden is to say no to all mortal pleas.' She laughed a little, then added, 'Don't be needlessly cruel, you beautiful thing.'

"'I've never been that,' I told her. 'Not cruel. But, Georgia, you know what you did, and said, the night of your big fiasco, after which oblivion moved in on you. You burned every bridge, highway, and cowpath behind you when you attacked the Negro novelist Burleigh Jordan in front of everybody who matters on the literary scene.'

"'I? Attacked him?' she scoffed.

"'My God, you can't pretend you don't remember.' I studied her new mouth and chin. 'Burleigh's grown to even greater importance since *you* left, Georgia. First he was the greatest black writer, then he was the greatest Black, and, now, God knows what he is, I've not kept hourly track. But when you insulted him that night, though your ruin was already in the air, it was the end for you, and nearly the end for all of us. I had immediately to go to work to salvage my own future.'

"'Ever the master of overstatement, dear boy,' she sighed.

"But I was stony-faced.

"'So you mean what you say?' she whined, after daubing an eye.

"'I mean only this, Georgia,' I said, emphasizing the point in question. 'I took over when you destroyed yourself' (and I waited to let it sink in that my own salon, which had been so tiny when Georgia's had been so big, had been burgeoning while she was away, and had now more than replaced her. I was *her* now, in a manner of speaking).

" 'Supposing then you tell me straight out what I said to Burleigh.' She had turned her back on me while she examined a new painting I had acquired, as a matter of fact, only a day or so before. I could tell she didn't think much of it, for she turned from it almost at once.

" 'Well?' she prompted me.

" 'Oh, don't expect me to repeat your exact words after all the water has flowed under the bridge since you said them. Your words were barbarous, of course, but it was your well-known tone of voice, as well as the exquisitely snotty timing of what you said, that did the trick. You are the empress of all bitches, darling, and if you wrote books as stabbing as you talk, you'd have no peer. . . . You said in four or five different rephrasings of your original affidavit that you would never kiss a black ass if it meant you and your Thursdays were to be ground to powder.'

" 'Oh, I completely disremember such a droll statement.' She giggled.

"Just then the doorbell rang, and in came four or five eminent writers, all of whom were surprised to see Georgia, and Georgia could not mask her own surprise that they were calling on me so casually. We rather ignored her then, but she wouldn't leave, and when they found the bottles and things, and were chattering away, Georgia pushed herself among us, and began on me again.

"At last more to get rid of her than anything else, I proposed to her the diabolic, unfeasible scheme which I claimed would reinstate her everywhere, pave the way for the reopening of her Thursday salon. I am called everywhere the most soulless cynic who ever lived, but I swear by whatever any of you hold holy, if you ever hold anything, that I never dreamed she would take me on when I said to her that all she'd be required to do was give Burleigh the token kiss she'd said she never would, to make it formal and she'd be back in business. You see, I thought she would leave in a huff when she heard my innocent proposal and that in a few days New York would see her no more—at least I'd be rid of her. Well, say she'd quaffed one too many of my frosty masterpieces, say again it was the poisonous New York air, whatever, I stood dumbfounded when I heard her say simply, 'Then make it next Thursday, darling, and I'll be here, and tell Burleigh not to fail us, for I'll do it, Rupert, darling, I'll do it for you, I'll do it for all of us.'

"The next day I rang to tell her of course that she wasn't to take me seriously, that my scheme had been mere persiflage, etc. She simply rang off after having assured me the deal was on and she'd be there Thursday.

"I was so angry with the bitch by then I rang up big black Burleigh and simply, without a word of preparation, told him. You see, Burleigh and I were more than friends at that time, let's put it that way." Rupert smirked a bit with his old self-assurance. "And," he went on, "to my mild surprise, perhaps, the dear lion agreed to the whole thing with alacrity.

"After a few hours of sober reflection, I panicked. I called Burleigh back first and tried to get him not to come. But Burleigh was at the height of a new wave of paranoia and idol worship and he could do no wrong. He assured me he wanted to come, wanted to go through with our scheme, which he baptized divine. I little knew then, of course, how well he had planned to go through with it, and neither, of course, did poor Georgia!

"Then, of course, I tried again to get Georgia not to come. It was like persuading Joan of Arc to go back to her livestock. I saw everything coming then the way it did come, well, not *everything*." Here he looked wistfully around at the London backdrop and grinned, for he missed New York even more when he talked about it, and he hadn't even the makings of a salon in London, of course, though he'd made a stab at it.

"I didn't sleep the night before." Rupert Douthwaite went on to describe the event to which he owed his ruin. "I thought I was daring, I thought I had always been in advance of everything—after all, *my* Thursdays had been at least a generation ahead of Georgia's in smartness, taste, and éclat, and now, well, as I scented the fume-heavy air, somebody was about to take the lead over from me.

"Everybody came that night—wouldn't you know it, some people from Washington, a tiresome princess or so, and indeed all the crowned heads from all the avenues of endeavor managed to get there, as if they sensed what was to come off. There was even that fat man from Kansas City who got himself circumcised a few seasons back to make the literary scene in New York.

"Nobody recognized Georgia at first when she made her entrance, not even Burleigh. She was radiant, if slightly drawn, and for the first time I saw that her face-lifting job wasn't quite stressproof, but still she only looked half her age, and so she was a howling success at first blush.

"'Now, my lovely'—I spoke right into her ear redolent of two-hundred-dollar-an-ounce attar of something—please bow to everybody and then go home—my car is downstairs parked directly by the door, Wilson is at the wheel. You've made a grand hit tonight, and now go while they're all still cheering.

"'I'm going through with it, love.' She was adamant, and I saw Burleigh catch the old thing's eye and wink.

"'Not in my house, you won't,' I whispered to her, kissing her again and again in deadly desperation to disguise my murderous expression from the invited guests. 'After all,' I repeated, 'my little scheme was proposed while we were both in our cups.'

"'And it's in cups where the truth resides, Douthwaite, as the Latin proverb has it,' and she kissed me on the lips and left me, walking around the room as in her old salon grandeur days, grasping everybody's outstretched hand, letting herself be embraced and kissed. She was a stunning, dizzy success, and then suddenly I felt that neither she nor Burleigh had any intention of doing what they had agreed to do. I was the fool who had fallen for their trap.

"When I saw what a hit she was making, I took too many drinks, for the more accolades she got, the angrier and more disturbed I became. I wasn't going to let Georgia come back and replace me, whatever else might happen.

"I went over to where Burleigh was being worshipped to death.

He turned immediately to me to say, 'Don't you come over here, Ruppie, to ask me again not to do what I am sure as greased lightning I'm going to do, baby,' and he smiled his angry smile at me.

" 'Burleigh, dearest,'—I took him by the hand—'I not only want you to go through with it bigger and grander but megatons more colossal than we had planned. That's the message I have to give you,' and I kissed and hugged him quietly.

"I couldn't be frightened now, and what I had just proposed to him was a little incredible even for me, even for me drunk, I had gone all out, I dimly realized, and asked for an assassination.

"But the more I saw Georgia's success with everybody, the more I wanted the horror that was going to happen. And then there was the size of her diamond. It was too much. No one wore diamonds that big in the set we moved in. She did it to hurt me, to show me up to the others, that whereas I might scrape up a million, let's say, she had so much money she couldn't add it all up short of two years of auditing.

"Time passed. I looked in the toilet where Burleigh was getting ready, and hugged encouragement.

"Then I felt the great calm people are said to feel on learning they have but six months to live. I gave up, got the easiest seat and the one nearest to the stage, and collapsed. People forgot me.

"Still the hog of the scene, Georgia was moving right to where she knew she was to give her comeback performance.

"Some last-minute celebrities had just come in, to whom I could only barely nod, a duchess, and some minor nobility, a senator, a diva, and somehow from somewhere a popular film critic of the hour who had discovered he was not homosexual, when with a boom and a guffaw Burleigh sails out of the john wearing feathers on his head but otherwise not a stitch on him.

"I saw Georgia freeze ever so slightly—you see, in our original scheme nothing was said about nakedness, it was all, in any case, to have been a token gesture, she had thought—indeed *I* had thought, but she stopped, put down her glass, squared her shoulders like a good soldier, and waited.

"Burleigh jumped up on my fine old walnut table cleared for the occasion. Everybody pretended to like it. Georgia began to weave around like a rabbit facing a python. Burleigh turned his back to her, and bent over, and with a war whoop extended his black biscuits to her. She stood reeling, waiting for the long count, then I heard, rather than saw, owing to heads in the way, her kissing his behind, then rising I managed to see him proffer his front and middle to her, everything there waving, when someone blotted out my view again, but I gathered from the murmur of the crowd she had gone through with it, and kissed his front too.

"Then I heard her scream, and I got up in time to see that Burleigh had smeared her face with some black tarlike substance and left a few of his white turkey feathers over that.

"I believe Georgia tried to pretend she had wanted this last too, and that it was all a grand charade, but her screams belied it, and she and Burleigh stood facing one another like victims of a car accident.

"It had all failed, I realized immediately. Everybody was sickened or bored. Nothing was a success about it. Call it wrong timing, wrong people, wrong actors or hour of the evening, oh explain it any way you will, it was all ghastly and cruddy with nonsuccess.

"I stumbled over to the back of my apartment, and feeling queasy, lay down on the floor near the rubber plant. I thought queerly of Kitty, who had, it seemed, just left me, and I—old novelist *manqué*—thought of all those novels I had written which publishers never even finished reading in typescript, let alone promised to publish, and I gagged loudly. People bent down to me and seemed to take my pulse, and then others began filing out, excusing themselves by a cough or nod, or stifling a feeble giggle. They thought I had fainted from chagrin. They thought I had not planned it. They thought I was innocent but ruined.

"I have never seen such a clean, wholesale, bloody failure. Like serving a thin, warm soup and calling it baked Alaska.

"I didn't see anybody for weeks. Georgia, I understand, left for Prague a few days later. Only Burleigh was not touched by anything.

Nothing can harm him, bad reviews, public derision, all he has to do is clap his hands, and crowds hoist him on their shoulders, the money falls like rain in autumn.

"Burleigh has his own salon now, if you can call his big gatherings on Saturday a salon, and Georgia and I both belong to a past more remote than the French and Indian Wars.

"To answer your first question, Gordon"—Rupert turned now to me, for I was his favorite American of the moment—"I've found London quieting, yes, but it's not my world exactly, sweety, since I'm not in or of it, but that's what I need, isn't it, to sit on the sidelines for a season and enjoy a statelier backdrop? I don't quite know where Georgia is. Somebody says it's Bulgaria."

LILY'S PARTY

As Hobart came through the door of Crawford's Home Dinette, his eyes fell on Lily sitting alone at one of the big back tables, eating a piece of pie.

"Lily! Don't tell me! You're supposed to be in Chicago!" he ejaculated.

"Who supposed I was to be?" Lily retorted, letting her fork cut quickly into the pie.

"Well, I'll damn me if—" He began to speak in a humming sort of way while pulling out a chair from under her table and sitting down unbidden. "Why, everybody thought you went up there to be with Edward."

"Edward! He's the last person on this earth I would go anywhere to be with. And I think you know that!" Lily never showed anger openly, and if she was angry now, at least she didn't let it stop her from enjoying her pie.

"Well, Lily, we just naturally figured you had gone to Chicago when you weren't around."

"I gave your brother Edward two of the best years of my life." Lily spoke with the dry accent of someone testifying in court for a second time. "And I'm not about to go find him for more of what he gave me. Maybe you don't remember what I got from him, but I do. . . ."

"But where were you, Lily? . . . We all missed you!" Hobart harped on her absence.

"I was right here all the time, Hobart, for your information." As she said this, she studied his mouth somewhat absentmindedly. "But as to your brother, Edward Starr," she continued, and then paused as she kept studying his mouth as if she found a particular defect there which had somehow escaped scrutiny hitherto. "As to Edward," she began again, and then stopped, struck her fork gingerly against the plate, "he was a number-one poor excuse for a husband, let me tell you. He left me for another woman, if you care to recall, and it was because of his neglect that my little boy passed away. . . . So let's say I don't look back on Edward, and am not going to any Chicago to freshen up on my recollections of him. . . ."

She quit studying his mouth, and looked out the large front window through which the full October moon was beginning its evening climb.

"At first I will admit I was lonesome, and with my little boy lying out there in the cemetery, I even missed as poor an excuse for a man as Edward Starr, but believe you me, that soon passed."

She put down her fork now that she had eaten all the pie, laid down some change on the bare white ash wood of the table, and then, closing her purse, sighed, and softly rose.

"I only know," Lily began, working the clasp on her purse, "that I have begun to find peace now. . . . Reverend McGilead, as you may be aware, has helped me toward the light. . . ."

"I have heard of Reverend McGilead," Hobart said in a voice so sharp she looked up at him while he held the screen door open for her.

"I am sure you have heard nothing but good then," she shot back in a voice that was now if not deeply angry, certainly unsteady.

"I will accompany you home, Lily."

"You'll do no such thing, Hobart. . . . Thank you, and good evening."

He noticed that she was wearing no lipstick, and that she did not have on her wedding ring. She also looked younger than when she had been Edward Starr's wife.

"You say you have found peace with this new preacher." Hobart spoke after her retreating figure. "But under this peace, you hate Edward Starr," he persisted. "All you said to me tonight was fraught with hate."

She turned briefly and looked at him, this time in the eyes. "I will find my way, you can rest assured, despite your brother and you."

He stayed in front of the door of the dinette and watched her walk down the moonlit-white road toward her house that lay in deep woods. His heart beat violently. All about where he stood were fields and crops and high trees, and the sailing queen of heaven was the only real illumination after one went beyond the dinette. No one came down this small road with the exception of lovers who occasionally used it for their lane.

Well, Lily was a sort of mystery woman, he had to admit to himself. And where, then, did the rumor arise that she had been to Chicago. And now he felt she had lied to him, that she had been in Chicago after all and had just got back.

Then without planning to do so, hardly knowing indeed he was doing so, he began following after her from a conveniently long distance down the moonlit road. After a few minutes of pursuing her, he saw someone come out from one of the ploughed fields. The newcomer was a tall still-youthful man with the carriage of an athlete rather than that of a farmer. He almost ran toward Lily. Then they both stopped for a moment, and after he had touched her gently on the shoulder they went on together. Hobart's heart beat furiously, his temple throbbed, a kind of film formed over his lips from his mouth rushing with fresh saliva. Instead of following them directly down the road, he now edged into the fields and pursued them more obliquely. Sometimes the two ahead of him would pause, and there was some indication the stranger was about to leave Lily, but then from something they said to one another, the couple continued on together. Hobart would have liked to get closer to them so that he might hear what they were saying, but he feared discovery. At any rate, he could be sure of one thing, the man walking with her was not Edward, and also he was sure that whoever he was he was her lover. Only lovers walked that way together, too far apart at one time, too weaving and close together another time: their very breathing appeared uneven and heavy the way their bodies swayed. Yes, Hobart realized, he was about to see love being made, and it made him walk unsteadily, almost to stumble. He only hoped he could keep a rein on his feelings and would not make his presence known to them.

When he saw them at last turn into her cottage he longed for the strength to leave them, to go back home to forget Lily, forget his brother Edward, whom he was certain Lily had been "cheating" all through their marriage (even *he* had been intimate once with Lily when Edward was away on a trip, so that he had always wondered if the child she bore him in this marriage might not have been after all his, but since it was dead, he would not think of it again).

Her cottage had a certain fame. There were no other houses about, and the windows of her living room faced the thick forest. Here she could have done nearly whatever she liked and nobody would have been the wiser, for unless one had stood directly before the great window which covered almost the entire width of her room, any glimpse within was shut out by foliage, and sometimes by heavy mist.

Hobart knew that this man, whoever he was, had not come tonight for the purpose of imparting Jesus' love to her but his own. He had heard things about this young preacher Reverend McGilead, he had been briefed on his "special" prayer meetings, and had got the implication the man of the cloth had an excess of unburned energy in his makeup. He shouted too loud during his sermons, people said, and the veins in his neck were ready to burst with the excess of blood that ran through him.

From Hobart's point of observation, in the protection of a large spruce tree, nothing to his surprise he saw whom he believed to be the young preacher take her in his arms. But then what happened was unforeseen, undreamed of indeed, for with the rapidity of a professional gymnast, the preacher stripped off his clothing in a trice, and stood in the clear illumination of her room not covered by so much as a stitch or thread. Lily herself looked paralyzed, as rodents are at the sudden appearance of a serpent. Her eyes were unfocused on anything about her, and she made no attempt to assist him as he partially undressed her. But from the casual way he acted, it was clear they had done this before. Yes, Hobart confessed to himself, in the protective dark of the tree under which he stood, one would have expected certainly something more gradual from lovers. He would have thought that the young preacher would have talked to her for at least a quarter of an hour, that he would have finally taken her hand, then perhaps kissed her, and then oh so slowly and excitingly, for Hobart at least, would have undressed her, and taken her to himself.

But this gymnast's performance quite nonplussed the observer by the spruce tree. For one thing, the gross size of the preacher's sex, its bulging veins and unusual angry redness, reminded him of sights seen by him when he had worked on a farm. It also recalled a surgical operation he had witnessed performed by necessity in a doctor's small, overcrowded office. The preacher now had pushed Lily against the wall, and worked vigorously at, and then through, her. His eyes rolled like those of a man being drawn unwillingly into some kind of suction machine, and saliva suddenly poured out of his mouth in great copiousness so that he resembled someone blowing up an enormous balloon. His neck and throat were twisted convulsively, and his nipples tightened as if they were being given over to rank torture.

At this moment, Hobart, without realizing he was doing so, came out from his hiding place, and strode up to the window, where he began waving his arms back and forth in the manner of a man flagging a truck. (Indeed Lily later was to believe that she thought she had seen a man with two white flags in his hands signaling for help.)

Lily's screams at being discovered broke the peace of the neighborhood, and many watchdogs from about the immediate vicinity began barking in roused alarm.

"We are watched!" she was finally able to get out. Then she gave out three uncadenced weak cries. But the preacher, his back to the window, like a man in the throes of some grave physical malady, could only concentrate on what his body dictated to him, and though Lily now struggled to be free of him, this only secured him the more tightly to her. Her cries now rose in volume until they reached the same pitch as that of the watchdogs.

Even Hobart, who had become as disoriented perhaps as the couple exhibited before him, began making soft outcries, and he continued to wave his arms fruitlessly.

"No, no, and no!" Lily managed now to form and speak these words. "Whoever you are out there, go, go away at once!"

Hobart now came directly up to the window. He had quit waving his arms, and he pressed his nose and mouth against the pane.

"It's me," he cried reassuringly. "Hobart, Edward Starr's brother! Can't you see?" He was, he managed to realize, confused as to what he now should do or say, but he thought that since he had frightened them so badly and so seriously disturbed their pleasure, he had best identify himself, and let them know he meant no harm. But his calling to them only terrified Lily the more, and caused her young partner to behave like someone struggling in deep water.

"Hobart Starr here!" the onlooker called to them, thinking they may have mistaken him for a housebreaker.

"Oh merciful Lord," Lily moaned. "If it is you, Hobart Starr, please go away. Have that much decency—" She tried to finish the sentence through her heavy breathing.

The preacher at this moment tore off the upper part of Lily's dress, and her breasts and nipples looked out from the light into the darkness at Hobart like the troubled faces of children.

"I'm coming into the house to explain!" Hobart called to them inside.

"You'll do no such thing! No, no, Hobart!" Lily vociferated back to him, but the intruder dashed away from the window, stumbling over some low-lying bushes, and then presently entered the living room, where the preacher was now moaning deeply and beginning even at times to scream a little.

"What on earth possessed you." Lily was beginning to speak when all at once the preacher's mouth fell over hers, and he let out a great smothered roar, punctuated by drumlike rumblings from, apparently, his stomach.

Hobart took a seat near the standing couple.

The preacher was now free of Lily's body at last, and he had slumped down on the floor, near where Hobart was sitting, and was crying out some word and then he began making sounds vaguely akin to weeping. Lily remained with her back and buttocks pressed against the wall, and was breathing hard, gasping indeed for breath. After her partner had quit his peculiar sobbing, he got up and put on his clothes, and walked out unsteadily into the kitchen. On the long kitchen table, the kind of table one would expect in a large school cafeteria, Hobart, from his chair, could spy at least fifteen pies of different kinds, all "homemade" by Lily expressly for the church social which was tomorrow.

He could see the preacher sit down at the big table, and cut himself a piece of Dutch apple pie. His chewing sounds at last alerted Lily to what was happening, and she managed to hurry out to the kitchen in an attempt to halt him.

"One piece of pie isn't going to wreck the church picnic. Go back there and entertain your new boyfriend, why don't you," the preacher snapped at her attempt to prevent him eating the piece of pie.

"He's Edward Starr's brother, I'd have you know, and he's not my boyfriend, smarty!"

The preacher chewed on. "This pie," he said, moving his tongue over his lips cautiously, "is very heavy on the sugar, isn't it?"

"Oh, I declare, hear him!" Lily let the words out peevishly, and she rushed on back into the living room. There she gazed wide-eyed, her mouth trying to move for speech, for facing her stood Hobart, folding his shorts neatly, and stark naked.

"You will not!" Lily managed to protest.

"Who says I don't!" Hobart replied nastily.

"Hobart Starr, you go home at once," Lily ordered him. "This is all something that can be explained."

He made a kind of dive at her as his reply, and pinioned her to the wall. She tried to grab his penis, clawing at it, but he had perhaps already foreseen she might do this, and he caught her by the hand, and then slapped her. Then he inserted his membrum virile quickly into her body, and covered her face with his freely flowing saliva. She let out perfunctory cries of expected rather than felt pain as one does under the hand of a nervous intern.

At a motion from her, some moments later, he worked her body about the room, so that she could see what the preacher was doing. He had consumed the Dutch apple pie, and was beginning on the rhubarb lattice.

"Will you be more comfortable watching him, or shall we return to the hall?" Hobart inquired.

"Oh, Hobart, for pity's sake;" she begged him. "Let me go, oh please let me go." At this he pushed himself more deeply inwards, hurting her, to judge by her grimace.

"I am a very slow comer, as you will remember, Lily. I'm slow but I'm the one in the end who cares for you most. Tonight is my biggest windfall. After all the others, you see, it is me who was meant for you. . . . You're so cozy too, Lily."

As he said this, she writhed, and attempted to pull out from him, but he kissed her hard, working into her hard.

"Oh this is all so damned unfair!" She seemed to cough out, not speak, these words. "Ralph," she directed her voice to the kitchen, "come in here and restore order. . . ."

As he reached culmination, Hobart screamed so loud the preacher did come out of the kitchen. He was swallowing very hard, so that he did remind Hobart of a man in a pie-eating contest. He looked critically at the two engaged in coitus.

A few minutes later, finished with Lily, Hobart began putting on his clothes, yawning convulsively, and shaking his head, while Ralph began doggedly and methodically to remove his clothing again, like a substitute or second in some grueling contest.

"Nothing more, no, I say no!" Lily shouted when she saw Ralph's naked body advancing on her. "I will no longer cooperate here."

He had already taken her, however, and secured her more firmly than the last time against the wall.

Hobart meanwhile was standing unsteadily on the threshold of the kitchen. He saw at once that the preacher had eaten two pies. He felt un-understandably both hungry and nauseous, and these two sensations kept him weaving giddily about the kitchen table now. At last he sat down before a chocolate meringue pie, and then very slowly, finickily, cut himself a small piece.

As he ate daintily he thought that he had not enjoyed intercourse with Lily, despite his seeming gusto. It had been all mostly exertion and effort, somehow, though he felt he had done well, but no feeling in a supreme sense of release had come. He was not surprised now that Edward Starr had left her. She was not a satisfier.

Hobart had finished about half the chocolate meringue when he reckoned the other two must be reaching culmination by now for he heard very stertorous breathing out there, and then there came to his ears as before the preacher's intense war whoop of release. Lily also screamed and appealed as if to the mountain outside, *I perish! Oh, perishing!* And a bit later, she hysterically supplicated to some unknown person or thing *I cannot give myself up like this, oh!* Then a second or so later he heard his own name called, and her demand that he save her.

Hobart wiped his mouth on the tablecloth and came out to have a look at them. They were both, Lily and Ralph, weeping and holding loosely to one another, and then they both slipped and fell to the floor, still sexually connected.

"Gosh all get out!" Hobart said with disgust.

He turned away. There was a pie at the very end of the table which looked most inviting. It had a very brown crust with golden juice spilling from fancily, formally cut little air holes as in magazine advertising. He plunged the knife into it, and tasted a tiny bit. It was of such wonderful flavor that even though he felt a bit queasy he could not resist cutting himself a slice, and he began to chew solemnly on it. It was an apricot, or perhaps peach, pie, but final identification eluded him.

Lily now came out into the kitchen and hovered over the big table. She was dressed, and had fixed her hair differently, so that it looked as if it had been cut and set, though there were some loose strands in the back which were not too becoming, yet they emphasized her white neck.

"Why, you have eaten half the pies for the church social!" she cried, with some exaggeration in her observation, of course. "After all that backbreaking work of mine! What on earth will I tell the preacher when he comes to pick them up!"

"But isn't this the preacher here tonight?" Hobart, waving his fork in the direction of the other room motioned to the man called Ralph.

"Why, Hobart, of course not. . . . He's no preacher, and I should think you could tell . . ."

"How did I come to think he was?" Hobart stuttered out, while Lily sat down at the table and was beginning to bawl.

"Of all the inconsiderate selfish thoughtless pups in the world," she managed to get out between sobs. "I would have to meet up with you two, just when I was beginning to have some sort of settled purpose."

Ralph, standing now on the threshold of the kitchen, still stark naked, laughed.

"I have a good notion to call the sheriff!" Lily threatened. "And do you know what I'm going to do in the morning? I'm going back to Edward Starr in Chicago. Yes siree. I realize now that he loved me more than I was aware of at the time."

The two men were silent, and looked cautiously at one another, while Lily cried on and on.

"Oh, Lily," Hobart said, "even if you do go see Edward, you'll come home again to us here. You know you can't get the good loving in Chicago that we give you, now, don't you?"

Lily wept on and on, repeating many times how she would never be able to explain to the church people about not having enough pies on hand for her contribution to the big social.

After drying her tears on a handkerchief which Hobart lent her, she took the knife and with methodical fierce energy and spiteful speed cut herself a serving from one of the still-untouched pies.

She showed by the way she moved her tongue in and out of her mouth that she thought her pie was excellent.

"I'm going to Chicago and I'm never coming back!" As she delivered this statement she began to cry again.

The "preacher," for that is how Hobart still thought of him, came over to where Lily was chewing and weeping, and put his hand between the hollows of her breasts.

"Now don't get started again, Ralph. . . . No!" she flared up. "No, no, no."

"I need it all over again," Ralph appealed to her. "Your good cooking has charged me up again."

"Those pies *are* too damned good for a church," she finally said with a sort of moody weird craftiness, and Ralph knew when she said this that she would let him have her again.

"Hobart"—Lily turned to Edward's brother—"why don't you go home? Ralph and I are old childhood friends from way back. And I was nice to you. But I am in love with Ralph."

"It's my turn," Hobart protested.

"No, no." Lily began her weeping again. "I love Ralph."

"Oh, hell, let him just this once more, Lily," the "preacher" said. Ralph walked away and began toying again with another of the uncut pies. "Say, who taught you to cook, Lily?" he inquired sleepily.

"I want you to send Hobart home, Ralph. I want you to myself. In a bed. This wall stuff is an outrage. Ralph, you send Hobart home now."

"Oh why don't you let the fellow have you once more. Then I'll really do you upstairs." Meanwhile, he went on chewing and swallowing loudly.

"Damn you, Ralph," Lily moaned. "Double damn you."

She walked over to the big table and took up one of the pies nearest her and threw it straight at the "preacher."

The "preacher"'s eyes, looking out from the mess she had made of his face, truly frightened her. She went over to Hobart, and waited there.

"All right for you, Lily," the "preacher" said.

"Oh, don't hurt her," Hobart pleaded, frightened too at the "preacher"'s changed demeanor.

The first pie the "preacher" threw hit Hobart instead of Lily. He let out a little gasp, more perhaps of surprised pleasure than hurt.

"Oh, now stop this. We must stop this," Lily exhorted. "We are grown-up people, after all." She began to sob, but very put-on like, the men felt. "Look at my kitchen." She tried to put some emphasis into her appeal to them.

The "preacher" took off his jockey shorts, which he had put on a few moments earlier. He took first one pie and then another, mashing them all over his body, including his hair. Lily began to whimper and weep in earnest now, and sat down as if to give herself over to her grief. Suddenly one of the pies hit her, and she began to scream, then she became silent.

There was a queer silence in the whole room. When she looked up, Hobart had also stripped completely, and the "preacher" was softly slowly mashing pies over his thin, tightly muscled torso. Then, slowly, inexorably, Hobart began eating pieces of pie from off the body of the smeared "preacher." The "preacher" returned this favor, and ate pieces of pie from Hobart, making gobbling sounds like a wild animal. Then they hugged one another and began eating the pies all over again from their bare bodies.

"Where do you get that stuff in my house!" Lily rose, roaring at them. "You low curs, where do you—"

But the "preacher" had thrown one of the few remaining pies at her, which struck her squarely in the breast and blew itself red all over her face and body so that she resembled a person struck by a bomb.

Ralph hugged Hobart very tenderly now, and dutifully ate small tidbits from his body, and Hobart seemed to nestle against Ralph's body, and ate selected various pieces of the pie from the latter.

Then Lily ran out the front door and began screaming *Help! I will perish! Help me!*

The dogs began to bark violently all around the neighborhood.

In just a short time she returned. The two men were still closely together, eating a piece here and there from their "massacred" bodies.

Sitting down at the table, weeping perfunctorily and almost inaudibly, Lily raised her fork, and began eating a piece of her still-unfinished apple pie.

SUMMER TIDINGS

There was a children's party in progress on the sloping wide lawn facing the estate of Mr. Teyte and easily visible therefrom despite the high hedge. A dozen school-aged children, some barely out of the care and reach of their nursemaids, attended Mrs. Aveline's birthday party for her son Rupert. The banquet or party itself was held on the site of the croquet grounds, but the croquet set had only partially been taken down, and a few wickets were left standing, a mallet or two lay about, and a red and white wood ball rested in the nasturtium bed. Mr. Teyte's Jamaican gardener, bronzed as an idol, watched the children as he watered the millionaire's grass with a great shiny black hose. The peonies had just come into full bloom. Over the greensward where the banquet was in progress one smelled in addition to the sharp odor of the nasturtiums and the marigolds, the soft perfume of June roses; the trees have their finest green at this season, and small gilt brown toads were about in the earth. The Jamaican servant hardly took his eyes off the children. Their gold heads and white summer clothing rose above the June verdure in remarkable contrast, and the brightness of so many colors made his eyes smart and caused him to pause frequently from his watering. Edna Gruber, Mrs. Aveline's secretary and companion, had promised the Jamaican a piece of the "second" birthday cake when the banquet should be over, and told him the kind thought came from Mrs. Aveline herself. He had nodded when Edna told him of his coming treat, yet it was not the anticipation of the cake which made him so absentminded and broody as it was the unaccustomed sight of so many young children all at once. Edna could see that the party had stirred something within his mind for he spoke even less than usual to her today as she tossed one remark after another across the boundary of the privet hedge separating the two large properties.

More absent-minded than ever, he went on hosing the peony bed until a slight flood filled the earth about the blooms and squashed onto his open sandals. He moved off then and began sprinkling with tempered nozzle the quince trees. Mr. Teyte, his employer and the owner of the property which stretched far and wide before the eye with the exception of Mrs. Aveline's, had gone to a golf tournament today. Only the white maids were inside his big house, and in his absence they were sleeping most of the day, or if they were about would be indifferently spying the Jamaican's progress across the lawn, as he labored to water the already refreshed black earth and the grass as perfectly green and motionless as in a painted backdrop. Yes, his eyes, his mind were dreaming today despite the almost infernal noise of all those young throats, the guests of the birthday party. His long black lashes gave the impression of having been dampened incessantly either by the water from the hose or some long siege of tears.

Mr. Teyte, if not attentive or kind to him, was his benefactor, for somehow that word had come to be used by people who knew both the gardener and the employer from far back, and the word had come to be associated with Mr. Teyte by Galway himself, the Jamaican servant. But Mr. Teyte, if not unkind, was undemonstrative, and if not indifferent, paid low wages, and almost never spoke to him, issuing his commands, which were legion, through the kitchen and parlor maids. But once when the servant had caught pneumonia, Mr. Teyte had come unannounced to the hospital in the morning, ignoring the rules that no visits were to be allowed except in early evening, and though he had not spoken to Galway, he had stood by his bedside a few moments, gazing at the sick man as if he were inspecting one of his own ailing riding horses.

But Mrs. Aveline and Edna Gruber talked to Galway, were kind to him. Mrs. Aveline even "made" over him. She always spoke to him over the hedge every morning, and was not offended or surprised when he said almost nothing to her in exchange. She seemed to know something about him from his beginnings, at any rate she knew Jamaica, having visited there three or four times. And so the women—Edna and Mrs. Aveline—went on speaking to him over the years, inquiring of his health, and of his tasks with the yard, and so often bestowing on him delicacies from their liberal table, as one might give tidbits to a prized dog which wandered in also from the great estate.

The children's golden heads remained in his mind after they had all left the banquet table and gone into the interior of the house, and from thence their limousines had come and taken them to their own great houses. The blonde heads of hair continued to swim before his eyes like the remembered sight of fields of wild buttercups outside the great estate, stray flowers of which occasionally cropped up in his own immaculate greensward, each golden corolla as bright as the strong rays of the noon sun. And then the memory came of the glimpsed birthday cake with the yellow center. His mouth watered with painful anticipation, and his eyes again filled with tears.

The sun was setting as he turned off the hose, and wiped his fingers from the water and some rust stains, and a kind of slime which came out from the nozzle. He went into a little brick shed, and removed his shirt, wringing wet, and put on a dry one of faded pink cotton decorated with a six-petaled flower design. Ah, but the excitement of all those happy golden heads sitting at a banquet—it made one too jumpy for cake, and their voices still echoed in his ears a little like the cries of the swallows from the poplar trees.

Obedient, then, to her invitation, Galway, the Jamaican gardener, waited outside the buttery for a signal to come inside, and partake of the birthday treat. In musing, however, about the party and all the young children, the sounds of their gaiety, their enormous vitality, lung power, their great appetites, the happy other sounds of silverware and fine china being moved about, added to which had been the song of the birds now getting ready to settle down to the dark of their nests, a kind of memory, a heavy nostalgia had come over him, recollection deep and far-off weighted him down without warning like fever and profound sickness. He remembered his dead loved ones. . . . How long he had stood on the back steps he could not say, until Edna suddenly laughing as she opened the door on him, with flushed face, spoke: "Why, Galway, you know you should not have stood on ceremony. . . . Of all people, you are the last who is expected to hang back. . . . Your cake is waiting for you. . . ."

He entered and sat in his accustomed place where so many times past he was treated to dainties and rewards.

"You may wonder about the delay," Edna spoke more formally today to him than usual. "Galway, we have, I fear, bad news. . . . A telegram has arrived. . . . Mrs. Aveline is afraid to open it. . . ."

Having said this much, Edna left the room, allowing the swinging door which separated the kitchen from the rest of the house to close behind her and then continue its swing backwards and forwards like the pendulum of a clock.

Galway turned his eyes to the huge white cake with the yellow center which she had expressly cut for him. The solid silver fork in his hand was about to come down on the thick heavily frosted slice resting sumptuously on hand-painted china. Just then he heard a terrible cry rushing through the many rooms of the house and coming, so it seemed, to stop directly at him and then cease and disappear into the air and the nothingness about him. His mouth became dry, and he looked about like one who expects unknown and immediate danger. The fork fell from his brown calloused muscular hand. The cry was now repeated if anything more loudly, then there was a cavernous silence, and, after some moments, steady prolonged hopeless weeping. He knew it was Mrs. Aveline. The telegram must have brought bad news. He sat on looking at the untasted cake. The yellow of its center seemed to stare at him.

Edna now came through the swinging door, her eyes red, a pocket handkerchief held tightly in her right hand, her opal necklace slightly crooked. "It was Mrs. Aveline's mother, Galway. . . . She is dead. . . . And such a short time since Mrs. Aveline's husband died, too, you know. . . ."

Galway uttered some words of regret, sympathy, which Edna did not hear, for she was still listening to any sound which might try to reach her from beyond the swinging door.

At last turning round, she spoke: "Why, you haven't so much as touched your cake. . . ." She looked at him almost accusingly.

"She has lost her own mother. . . ." Galway said this after some struggle with his backwardness.

But Edna was studying the cake. "We can wrap it all up, the rest of it, Galway, and you can have it to sample at home, when you will have more appetite." She spoke comfortingly to him. She was weeping so hard now she shook all over.

"These things come out of the blue," she managed to speak at last in a neutral tone as though she was reading from some typewritten sheet of instructions. "There is no warning very often as in this case. The sky itself might as well have fallen on us. . . ."

Edna had worked for Mrs. Aveline for many years. She always wore little tea aprons. She seemed to do nothing but go from the kitchen to the front parlor or drawing room, and then return almost immediately to where she had been in the first place. She had supervised the children's party today, ceaselessly walking around, and looking down on each young head, but one wondered exactly what she was accomplishing by so much movement. Still, without her, Mrs. Aveline might not have been able to run the big house, so people said. And it was also Edna Gruber who had told Mrs. Aveline first of Galway's indispensable and sterling dependability. And it was Galway Edna always insisted on summoning when nobody else could be found to do some difficult and often unpleasant and dirty task.

"So, Galway, I will have the whole 'second' cake sent over to you just as soon as I find the right box to put it in. . . ."

He rose as Edna said this, not having eaten so much as a crumb. He said several words which hearing them come from his own mouth startled him as much as if each word spoken had appeared before him as letters in the air.

"I am sorry . . . and grieve for her grief. . . . A mother's death. . . . It is the hardest loss."

Then he heard the screen door closing behind him. The birds were still, and purple clouds rested in the west, with the evening star sailing above the darkest bank of clouds as yellow as the heads of any of the birthday children. He crossed himself.

Afterwards he stood for some time in Mr. Teyte's great green backyard, and admired the way his gardener's hands had kept the grass beautiful for the multimillionaire, and given it the endowment of both life and order. The wind stirred as the light failed, and flowers which opened at evening gave out their faint delicate first perfume, in which the four-o'clocks' fragranace was pronounced. On the ground near the umbrella tree something glistened. He stooped down. It was the sheepshears, which he employed in trimming the ragged grass about trees and bushes, great flower beds, and the hedge. Suddenly, stumbling in the growing twilight he cut his thumb terribly on the shears. He walked dragging one leg now as if it was his foot which he had slashed. The gush of blood somehow calmed him from his other sad thoughts. Before going inside Mr. Teyte's great house, he put the stained sheepshears away in the shed, and then walked quietly to the kitchen and sat down at the lengthy pine table which was his accustomed place here, got out some discarded linen napkins, and began making himself a bandage. Then he remembered he should have sterilized the wound. He looked about for some iodine, but there was none in the medicine cabinet. He washed the quivering flesh of the wound in thick yellow soap. Then he bandaged it and sat in still communion with his thoughts.

Night had come. Outside the katydids and crickets had begun an almost dizzying chorus of sound, and in the far distant darkness tree frogs and some bird with a single often repeated note gave the senses a kind of numbness.

Galway knew who would bring the cake—it would be the birthday boy himself. And the gardener would be expected to eat a piece of it while Rupert stood looking on. His mouth now went dry as sand. The bearer of the cake and messenger of Mrs. Aveline's goodness was coming up the path now, the stones of gravel rising and falling under his footsteps. Rupert liked to be near Galway whenever possible, and like his mother wanted to give the gardener gifts, sometimes coins, sometimes shirts, and now tonight food. He liked to touch Galway as he would perhaps a horse. Rupert stared sometimes at the Jamaican servant's brown thickly muscled arms with a look almost of acute disbelief.

Then came the step on the back porch, and the hesitant but loud knock.

Rupert Aveline, just today aged thirteen, stood with outstretched hands bearing the cake. The gardener accepted it immediately, his head slightly bowed, and immediately lifted it out of the cake box to expose it all entire except the one piece which Edna Gruber had cut in the house expressly for the Jamaican, and this piece rested in thick wax paper separated from the otherwise intact birthday cake. Galway fell heavily into his chair, his head still slightly bent over the offering. He felt with keen unease Rupert's own speechless wonder, the boy's eyes fixed on him rather than the cake, though in the considerable gloom of the kitchen the Jamaican servant had with his darkened complexion all but disappeared into the shadows, only his white shirt and linen trousers betokening a visible presence.

Galway lit the lamp, and immediately heard the cry of surprise and alarmed concern coming from the messenger, echoing in modulation and terror that of Mrs. Aveline as she had read the telegram.

"Oh, yes, my hand," Galway said softly, and he looked down in unison with Rupert's horrified glimpse at his bandage—the blood having come through copiously to stain the linen covering almost completely crimson.

"Shouldn't it be shown to the doctor, Galway?" the boy inquired, and suddenly faint, he rested his hand on the servant's good arm for support. He had gone very white. Galway quickly rose and helped the boy to a chair. He hurried to the sink and fetched him a glass of cold water, but Rupert refused this, continuing to touch the gardener's arm.

"It is your grandmother's death, Rupert, which has made you upset. . . ."

Rupert looked away out the window through which he could see his own house in the shimmery distance; a few lamps had been lighted over there, and the white exterior of his home looked like a ship in the shadows, seeming to move languidly in the summer night.

In order to have something to do and because he knew Rupert wished him to eat part of the cake, Galway removed now all the remaining carefully wrapped thick cloth about the birthday cake and allowed it to emerge yellow and white, frosted and regal. They did everything so well in Mrs. Aveline's house.

"You are . . . a kind . . . good boy," Galway began with the strange musical accent which never failed to delight Rupert's ear. "And now you are on your way to being a man," he finished.

Rupert's face clouded over at this last statement, but the music of the gardener's voice finally made him smile and nod, then his eyes narrowed as they rested on the bloodstained bandage.

"Edna said you had not tasted one single bite, Galway," the boy managed to speak after a struggle to keep his own voice steady and firm.

The gardener, as always, remained impassive, looking at the almost untouched great cake, the frosting in the shape of flowers and leaves and images of little men and words concerning love, a birthday, and the year 1902.

Galway rose hurriedly and got two plates.

"You must share a piece of your own birthday cake, Rupert . . . I must not eat alone."

The boy nodded energetically.

The Jamaican cut two pieces of cake, placed them on large heavy dinner plates, all he could find at the moment, and produced thick solid silver forks. But then as he handed the piece of cake to Rupert, in the exertion of his extending his arm, drops of blood fell upon the pine table.

At that moment, without warning, the whole backyard was illuminated by unusual irregular flashing lights and red glares. Both Rupert and Galway rushed at the same moment to the window, and stared into the night. Their surprise was, if anything, augmented by what they now saw. A kind of torchlight parade was coming up the far greensward, in the midst of which procession was Mr. Teyte himself, a bullnecked short man of middle years. Surrounded by other men, his well-wishers, all gave out shouts of congratulation in drunken proclamation of the news that the owner of the estate had won the golf tournament. Suddenly his pals raised Mr. Teyte to their shoulders, and shouted in unison over the victory.

Listening to the cries growing in volume, in almost menacing nearness as they approached closer to the gardener and Rupert, who stood like persons besieged, the birthday boy cautiously put his hand in that of Galway.

Presently, however, they heard the procession moving off beyond their sequestered place, the torchlights dimmed and disappeared from outside the windows, as the celebrators marched toward the great front entrance of the mansion, a distance of almost a block away, and there, separated by thick masonry, they were lost to sound.

Almost at that same moment, as if at some signal from the disappearing procession itself, there was a deafening peal of thunder, followed by forks of cerise lightning flashes, and the air, so still before rushed and rose in furious elemental wind. Then they heard the angry whipping of the rain against the countless panes of glass.

"Come, come, Rupert," Galway admonished, "your mother will be sick with worry." He pulled from a hook an enormous mackintosh, and threw it about the boy. "Quick, now, Rupert, your birthday is over. . . ."

They fled across the greensward where only a moment before the golf tournament victory procession with its torches had walked in dry clear summer weather. Galway who wore no covering was immediately soaked to the skin.

Edna was waiting at the door, as constant in attendance as if she were a caryatid now come briefly to life to receive the charge of the birthday boy from the gardener, and in quick movement of her hand like that of a magician she stripped from Rupert and surrendered back to Galway his mackintosh, and then closed the door against him and the storm.

The Jamaican waited afterwards for a time under a great elm tree, whose leaves and branches almost completely protected him from the full fury of the sudden violent thundershower, now abating.

From the mackintosh, however, he fancied there came the perfume of the boy's head of blonde hair, shampooed only a few hours earlier for his party. The odor came now swiftly in great waves to the gardener's dilating nostrils, an odor almost indistinguishable from the blossoms of honeysuckle. He held the mackintosh tightly in his hand for a moment, then drawing it closer to his mouth and pressing it hard against his nostrils, he kissed it once fervently as he imagined he saw once again the golden heads of the birthday party children assembled at the banquet table.

SOME OF THESE DAYS

What my landlord's friends said about me was in a way the gospel truth, that is he was good to me and I was mean and ungrateful to him. All the two years I was in jail, nonetheless, I thought only of him, and I was filled with regret for the things I had done against him. I wanted him back. I didn't exactly wish to go back to live with him now, mind you, I had been too mean to him for that, but I wanted him for a friend again. After I got out of jail I would need friendship, for I didn't need to hold up even one hand to count my friends on, the only one I could even name was him. I didn't want anything to do with him physically again, I had kind of grown out of that somehow even more while in jail, and wished to try to make it with women again, but I did require my landlord's love and affection, for love was, as everybody was always saying, his special gift and talent.

He was at the time I lived with him a rather well-known singer, and he also composed songs, but even when I got into my bad trouble, he was beginning to go downhill, and not to be so in fashion. We often quarreled over his not succeeding way back then. Once I hit him when he told me how much he loved me, and knocked out one of his front teeth. But that was only after he had also criticized me for not keeping the apartment tidy and clean and doing the dishes, and I threatened him with an old gun I kept. Of course I felt awful bad about his losing this front tooth when he needed good teeth for singing. I asked his forgiveness. We made up and I let him kiss me and hold me tight just for this one time.

I remember his white face and sad eyes at my trial for breaking and entering and possession of a dangerous weapon, and at the last his tears when the judge sentenced me. My landlord could cry and not be ashamed of crying, and so you didn't mind him shedding tears somehow. At first, then, he wrote me, for as the only person who could list himself as nearest of kin or closest tie, he was allowed by the authorities to communicate with me, and I also received little gifts from him from time to time. And then all upon a sudden the presents stopped, and shortly after that, the letters too, and then there was no word of any kind, just nothing. I realized then that I had this strong feeling for him which I had never had for anybody before, for my people had been dead from the time almost I was a toddler, and so they are shadowy and dim, whilst he is bright and clear. That is, you see, I had to admit to myself in jail (and I choked on my admission), but I had hit bottom, and could say a lot of things now to myself, I guess I was in love with him. I had really only loved women, I had always told myself, and I did not love this man so much physically, in fact he sort of made me sick to my stomach to think of him that way, though he was a good-looker with his neat black straight hair, and his robin's-egg-blue eyes, and cheery smile. . . . And so there in my cell I had to confess what did I have for him if it was not love, and yet I had treated him meaner than anybody I had ever knowed in my life, and once come close to killing him. Thinking about him all the time now, for who else was there to think about, I found I got to talking to myself more and more like an old geezer of advanced years, and in place of calling on anybody else or any higher power, since he was the only one I had ever met in my twenty years of life who said he cared. I would find myself saying like in church, *My landlord*, though that term for him was just a joke for the both of us, for all he had was this one-room flat with two beds, and my bed was the little one, no more than a cot, and I never made enough to pay him no rent for it, he just said he would trust me. So there in my cell, especially at night, I would say *My landlord*, and finally, for my chest begin to trouble me about this time and I was short of breath often, I would just manage to get out *My lord*. That's what I would call him for short. When I got out, the first thing I made up my mind to do was find him, and I was going to put all my efforts behind the search.

And when there was no mail now at all, I would think over all the kind and good things he done for me, and the thought would come to me which was blacker than any punishment they had given me here in the big house that I had not paid him back for his good deeds. When I got out I would make it up to him. He had took me in off the street, as people say, and had tried to make a man of me, or at least a somebody out of me, and I had paid him back all in bad coin, first by threatening to kill him, and then by going bad and getting sent to jail. . . . But when I got out, I said, I will find him if I have to walk from one ocean shore to the other.

And so it did come about that way, for once out, that is all I did or found it in my heart to do, find the one who had tried to set me straight, find the one who had done for me, and shared and all.

One night after I got out of jail, I had got dead drunk and stopped a guy on Twelfth Street, and spoke, *Have you seen my lord?* This man motioned me to follow him into a dark little theater, which later I was to know all too well as one of the porno theaters, he paid for me, and brought me to a dim corner in the back, and then the same old thing started up again, he beginning to undo my clothes, and lower his head, and I jumped up and pushed him and ran out of the movie, but then stopped and looked back and waited there as it begin to give me an idea.

Now a terrible thing had happened to me in jail. I was beat on the head by another prisoner, and I lost some of the use of my right eye, so that I am always straining by pushing my neck around as if to try to see better, and when the convict hit me that day and I was unconscious for several weeks and they despaired of my life, later on when I come to myself at last, I could remember everything that had ever happened in my whole twenty years of life except my landlord's name, and I couldn't think of it if I was to be alive. That is why I have been in the kind of difficulty I have been in. It is the hardest thing in the world to hunt for somebody if you don't know his name.

I finally though got the idea to go back to the big building where he and I had lived together, but the building seemed to be under new management, with new super, new tenants, new everybody. Nobody anyhow remembered any singer, they said, nor any composer, and then after a time, it must have been though six months from the day I returned to New York, I realized that I had gone maybe to a building that just looked like the old building my landlord and I have lived in, and so I tore like a blue streak straightaway to this "correct" building to find out if any such person as him was living there, but as I walked around through the halls looking, I become somewhat confused all over again if this was the place either, for I had wanted so bad to find the old building where he and I had lived. I had maybe been overconfident of this one also being the correct place, and so as I walked the halls looking and peering about I become puzzled and unsure all over again, and after a few more turns, I give up and left.

That was an awesome fall, and then winter coming on and all, and no word from him, no trace, and then I remembered a thing from the day that man had beckoned me to come follow him into that theater, and I remembered something, I remembered that on account of my landlord being a gay or queer man, one of his few pleasures when he got an extra dollar was going to the porno movies in Third Avenue. My remembering this was like a light from heaven, if you can think of heaven throwing light on such a thing, for suddenly I knowed for sure that if I went to the porno movie I would find him.

The only drawback for me was these movies was somewhat expensive by now, for since I been in jail prices have surely marched upwards, and I have very little to keep me even in necessities. This was the beginning of me seriously begging, and sometimes I would be holding out my hand on the street for three-fourths of a day before I got me enough to pay my way into the porno theater. I would put down my three bucks, and enter the turnstile, and then inside wait until my eyes got used to the dark, which because of my prison illness took nearly all of ten minutes, and then I would go up to each aisle looking for my landlord. There was not a face I didn't examine carefully. . . . My interest in the spectators earned me several bawlings-out from the manager of the theater, who took me for somebody out to proposition the customers, but I paid him no mind. . . . But his fussing with me gave me an idea, too, for I am attractive to men, both young and old, me being not yet twenty-one, and so I began what was to become regular practice, letting the audience take any liberty they was in a mind to with me in the hopes that through this contact they would divulge the whereabouts of my landlord.

But here again my problem would surface, for I could not recall the very name of the person who was most dear to me, yes that was the real sore spot. But as the men in the movie theater took their liberties with me, which after a time I got sort of almost to enjoy, even though I could barely see their faces, only see enough to know they was not my landlord, I would then, I say, describe him in full to them, and I will give them this much credit, they kind of listened to me as they went about getting their kicks from me, they would bend an ear to my asking for this information, but in the end they never heard of him nor any other singer, and never knowed a man who wrote down notes for a living.

But strange as it might seem to anybody who will ever see these sheets of paper, this came to be my only connection with the world, my only life—sitting in the porno theater. Since my only purpose was to find him and from him find my own way back, this was the only thoroughfare there was open for me to reach him. And yet I did not like it, though at the same time even disliking it as much as I did, it give me some little feeling of a resemblance to warmth and kindess as the unknown men touched me with their invisible faces and extracted from me all I had to offer, such as it was. And then when they had finished me, I would ask them if they knew my landlord (or as I whispered to myself, my lord). But none ever did.

Winter had come in earnest, was raw in the air. The last of the leaves in the park had long blown out to sea, and yet it was not to be thought of giving up the search and going to a warmer place. I would go on here until I had found him or I would know the reason why, yes, I must find him, and not give up. (I tried to keep the phrase *My lord* only for myself, for once or twice when it had slipped out to a stranger, it give him a start, and so I watched what I said from there on out.)

And then I was getting down to the last of the little money I had come out of jail with, and oh the porno theater was so dear, the admission was hiked another dollar just out of the blue, and the leads I got in that old dark hole was so few and far between. Toward the end one man sort of perked up when I mentioned my landlord, the singer, and said he thought he might have known such a fellow, but with no name to go on, he too soon give up, and said he guessed he didn't know after all.

And so I was stumped. Was I to go on patronizing the porno theater, I would have to give up food, for my panhandling did not bring in enough for both grub and movies, and yet there was something about bein' in that house, getting the warmth and attention from the stray men that meant more to me than food and drink. So I began to go without eating in earnest so as to keep up my regular attendance at the films. That was maybe, looking back on it now, a bad mistake, but what is one bad mistake in a lifetime of them.

As I did not eat now but only give my favors to the men in the porno, I grew pretty unsteady on my feet. After a while I could barely drag to the theater. Yet it was the only place I wanted to be, especially in view of its being now full winter. But my worst fears was now realized, for I could no longer afford even the cheap lodging place I had been staying at, and all I had in the world was what was on my back, and the little in my pockets, so I had come at last to this, and yet I did not think about my plight so much as about him, for as I got weaker and weaker he seemed to stand over me as large as the figures of the film actors that raced across the screen, and at which I almost never looked, come to think of it. No, I never watched what went on on the screen itself. I watched the audience, for it was the living that would be able to give me the word.

"Oh come to me, come back and set me right!" I would whisper, hoping someone out of the audience might rise and tell me they knew where he was.

Then at last, but of course slow gradual-like, I no longer left the theater. I was too weak to go out, anyhow had no lodging now to call mine, knew if I got as far as a step beyond the entrance door of the theater, I would never get back inside to its warmth, and me still dressed in my summer clothes.

Then after a long drowsy time, days, weeks, who knows? my worse than worst fears was realized, for one—shall I say day?—for where I was now there was no day or night, and the theater never closed its doors—one time, then, I say, they *come* for me, they had been studying my condition, they told me later, and they come to take me away. I begged them with all the strength I had left not to do so, that I could still walk, that I would be gone and bother nobody again.

When did you last sit down to a bite to eat? A man spoke this direct into my ear, a man by whose kind of voice I knew did not belong to the porno world, but come from some outside authority.

I have lost all tract of time, I replied, closing my eyes.

All right, buddy, the man kept saying, and *Now, bud*, and then as I fought and kicked, they held me and put the straitjacket on me, though didn't they see I was too weak and dispirited to hurt one cruddy man jack of them.

Then as they was taking me finally away, for the first time in months, I raised my voice, as if to the whole city, and called, and shouted, and explained: *"Tell him if he comes, how long I have waited and searched, that I have been hunting for him, and I cannot remember his name. I was hit in prison by another convict and the injury was small, but it destroyed my one needed memory, which is his name. That is all that is wrong with me. If you would cure me of this one little defect, I will never bother any of you again, never bother society again. I will go back to work and make a man of myself, but I have first to thank this former landlord for all he done for me."*

He is hovering between life and death.

I repeated aloud the word *hovering* after the man who had pronounced this sentence somewhere in the vicinity of where I was lying in a bed that smelled strong of carbolic acid.

And as I said the word *hovering*, I knew his name. I raised up. Yes, my landlord's name had come back to me. . . . It had come back after all the wreck and ruin of these weeks and years.

But then one sorrow would follow upon another, as I believe my mother used to say, though that is so long ago I can't believe I had a mother, for when they saw that I was conscious and in my right mind, they come to me and begun asking questions, especially, *What was my name.* I stared at them then with the greatest puzzlement and sadness, for though I had fished up his name from so far down, I could no more remember my own name now when they asked me for it than I could have got out of my straitjacket and run a race, and I was holding on to the just-found landlord's name with the greatest difficulty, for it, too, was beginning to slip from my tongue and go disappear where it had been lost before.

As I hesitated, they begun to persecute me with their kindness, telling me how they would help me in my plight, but first of all they must have my name, and since they needed a name so bad, and was so insistent, and I could see their kindness beginning to go, and the cruelty I had known in jail coming fresh to mind, I said, "I am Sidney Fuller," giving them you see my landlord's name.

"And your age, Sidney?"

"Twenty, come next June."

"And how did you earn your living?"

"I have been without work now for some months."

"What kind of work do you do?"

"Hard labor."

"When were you last employed?"

"In prison."

There was a silence, and the papers was moved about, then: "Do you have a church or faith?"

I waited quite a while, repeating his name, and remembering I could not remember my own, and then I said, "I am of the same faith as my landlord."

There was an even longer silence then, like the questioner had been cut down by his own inquiry, anyhow they did not interrogate me any more after that, they went away and left me by myself.

After a long time, certainly days, maybe weeks, they announced the doctor was coming.

He set down on a sort of ice-cream chair beside me, and took off his glasses and wiped them. I barely saw his face.

"Sidney," he began, after it sounded like he had started to say something else first, and then changed his mind. "Sidney, I have some very serious news to impart to you, and I want you to try to be brave. It is hard for me to say what I am going to say. I will tell you what we have discovered. I want you, though, first, to swallow this tablet, and we will wait together for a few minutes, and then I will tell you."

I had swallowed the tablet it seemed a long time ago, and then all of a sudden I looked down at myself, and I saw I was not in the straitjacket, my arms was free.

"Was I bad, Doctor?" I said, and he seemed to be glad I had broke the ice, I guess.

"I believe, Sidney, that you know in part what I am going to say to you," he started up again. He was a dark man, I saw now, with thick eyebrows, and strange, I thought, that for a doctor he seemed to have no wrinkles, his face was smooth as a sheet.

"We have done all we could to save you, you must believe us," he was going on as I struggled to hear his words through the growing drowsiness given me by the tablet. "You have a sickness, Sidney, for which unfortunately there is today no cure. . . ."

He said more, but I do not remember what, and was glad when he left, no, amend that, I was sad I guess when he left. Still, it didn't matter one way or another if anybody stayed or lit out.

But after a while, when I was a little less drowsy, a new man come in, with some white papers under his arm.

"You told us earlier when you were first admitted," he was saying, "that your immediate family is all dead. . . . Is there nobody to whom you wish to leave any word at all? . . . If there is such a person, we would appreciate your writing the name and address on each of these four sheets of papers, and add any instructions which you care to detail."

At that moment, I remembered my own name, as easily as if it had been written on the paper before me, and the sounds of it placed in my mouth and on my tongue, and since I could not give my landlord's name again and as the someone to whom I could bequeath my all, I give the inquirer with the paper my own real name:

JAMES DE SALLES

"And his address?" the inquirer said.

I shook my head.

"Very well, then, Sidney," he said, rising from the same chair the doctor had sat in. He looked at me some time, then kind of sighed, and folded the sheaf of papers.

"Wait," I said to him then, "just a minute. . . . Could you get me writing paper, and fountain pen and ink to boot. . . ."

"Paper, yes. . . . We have only ball-point pens, though. . . ."

So then he brought the paper and the ball-point, and I have written this down, asking another patient here from time to time how to say this, or spell that, but not showing him what I am about, and it is queer indeed isn't it, that I can only bequeath these papers to myself, for God only knows who would read them later, and it has come to me very clear in my sleep that my landlord is dead also, so there is no point in my telling my attendants that I have lied to them, that I am really James De Salles, and that my lord is or was Sidney Fuller.

But after I done wrote it all down, I was quiet in my mind and heart, and so with some effort I wrote my own name on the only thing I have to leave, and which they took from me a few moments ago with great puzzlement, for neither the person was known to them, and the address of course could not be given, and they only received it from me, I suppose, to make me feel I was being tended to.

SHORT PAPA

for Barry Horwitz

When I caught a glimpse of Short Papa coming through the back yard that cold sleety February afternoon I had straight away a funny feeling it might be the last time he would visit me. He looked about the same, tall and lean and wind-burned, but despite the way he kept his shoulders back and his head up he spoke and shook hands like a man who didn't expect you to believe a word he said.

Neither Mama nor Sister Ruth budged an inch when I told them who was out on the back porch, but after a struggle with herself, Ma finally said, "You can give Short Papa this plate of hot Brunswick stew, and let him get his strength back from wherever he has been this time. And then you tell him, Lester, he has got to light out again soon as possible."

"But, Ma," I began, "can't he stay just the night?"

"Father or not father," she began, "after what that man has done to us, no . . . I'll feed him but I won't take him in, and you give him my message, hear? Eat and get!"

But I seen that my remark about how after all it was my own Dad who had come to see me had moved Ma more than a little, for her breast rose and fell like it always does when she is wrought up.

"He'll only get in more trouble if he stays, Lester, and he'll get you in trouble too. I do regret to talk against your Papa, but he is a no-account, low-down . . ."

She stopped, though, when she saw the expression on my face.

Short Papa sat, hands folded, on a little green wicker upright chair before the round green wicker table as I brought him his hot plate of Brunswick stew to the back porch.

"Thank you, Les." He eyed the plate and then took it from me. I can still see the way he ate the fricassee chicken and little bits of lima beans and potatoes. He was most famished.

"You can assure your Ma I'll be on my way right after sunset," he replied to the message I bore from her. "Tell her I don't want folks to see me in town . . . by daylight."

I nodded, looking at his empty plate.

"Your ma has taken awful good care of you, Les. I observed that right away. I'm grateful to her for that, you can tell her. The day I get back on my feet, son, I will see to it that a lot of the things owin' to you will be yours. . . . Count on me."

I didn't quite know what he meant then, but I was pleased he felt I deserved something. Ma didn't often make me feel deserving.

Short Papa got up from the table, loosened his suspenders under his suit coat, felt in his breast pocket as he kept clearing his throat, and then sat down again as he said, "Matter of fact, Les, I have brought you a little something. But first you best take this plate back to the kitchen, for you know how fussy your ma is about dirty dishes standing around."

I rushed with the plate back to the kitchen and on the double back to Short Papa, and sat down beside him on a little taboret which we use for sitting on.

"I want you to promise me, though, you won't lose it after I give it to you," Short Papa said solemnly.

I promised.

"Cross your heart and all that." Short Papa sort of grinned, but I knew he was dead serious and wanted me to be.

"Cross my heart, Papa."

"All right, Lester. Then here it is."

He handed me a great, really heavy gold watch with a massive chain a-hanging from it.

"Don't you worry, now, Les. It is not stolen. It is your great grandpa's watch. All during my most recent trouble I kept it in a safety deposit vault over at Moortown. I got behind on the annual rent payments when I was in jail, but the bank trusted me, Les, and they kept it. I have paid up for the arrears and this watch is yours. It has been in the family for well over a hundred years, you can count on that."

I was not really glad to get the watch, and yet I wanted it too. I wanted also to show Short Papa I was grateful, and so I hugged and kissed him. His eyes watered a little and he turned away from me, and then he laughed and slapped my shoulder several times.

"Keep it in a safe place, Les, for beyond what it's worth, which aint inconsiderable, it's your old Pa and his Pa, and his Pa before him that owned it. Understand? 'Course you do. . . ."

After Short Papa left, I sat for a long time on the back porch listening to my watch tick. It had a powerful beat to it. From behind me I could hear Ma talking with Sister Ruth about the dress they were making for her wedding. Ruth was going to be married in June.

I considered how Short Papa's sudden arrival and departure had made no impression on them. He might as well have been the man who comes to collect the old papers and tin cans. Yet he was Ruth's father, too.

"You take my word for it, Les, things are going to be hunky-dory one day for all of us again."

That was what Pa had said to me as he slipped out the back way in the gathering darkness, and like the ticking of my watch those words kept pounding in my ears.

Ma had made me ashamed of Papa, always reminding me of the many times he had been sent to jail for a short stretch (hence his nickname), and once out, he would only be sent back again, and so on and so forth, but there was now something about the way this watch ticking away in my possession made me feel not only different about Papa and his Pa and his Pa before him, I felt for the first time I was connected with somebody, or with something. I felt I had a basic, you see. But I didn't want anybody to know I had the watch, and I also felt that I would never see Short Papa again, that he had come back to speak his piece and be gone for good.

As a result I felt awful crushed that Short Papa had been entertained so miserly by Ma, being fed on the back porch like a tramp, and then dismissed. But then Ma's attitude toward Pa was hard to fathom, for though she never wanted any more to do with him she never said anything about getting a divorce. She just didn't want any more men around, for one thing, and then, as she said, why go to the bother of divorcing somebody when you was already divorced from him for good and all. . . .

I kept the watch under my pillow at night, and I wound it cautiously and slow twice a day, like he had instructed me, and I never let it out of my sight whilst I was awake, keeping it with me at all times. I could not imagine being without it ever now.

After a couple to three months of this great care with his watch, and to tell the truth getting a little weary sometimes with the worry and guardianship bestowed on it, the polishing and keeping it when unused in its own little cotton case, and also seeing it was hid from Ma, for I feared she might claim it away from me for what Pa owed her, I remember the time it happened: It was an unsteady spring afternoon, when it couldn't make up its mind whether it was still winter or shirt-sleeves weather, and I had gone to the Regal Pool Parlors to watch the fellows shoot pool, for at this time their hardfast rule there was that nobody under sixteen was allowed to play, but you could be a spectator provided you kept your mouth shut.

Absorbed in the games and the talk of the older fellows, before I was aware of it all the shadows had lengthened outside and the first street lights had begun to pop on, and so then almost automatically

I began to lift the chain to my watch, and as I did so I was all at once reminded of another time further back when Short Papa had been teaching me to fish and he had said nervously:

"Pull up your rod, Les, you've got a bite there!" And I had pulled of course and felt the rod heavy at first and weighted but then pulling harder I got this terrible lightness, and yanking the pole to shore there was nothing on the hook at all, including no bait neither. And pulling now on the watch chain I drew up nothing from my pocket. My watch was gone. I got faint-sick all over. I was too shaky in fact to get up and start looking. I was pretty sure, nonplussed though I was, that I had not lost it here in the Regal Pool Parlors, but I went over to Bud Hughes the manager, who knew me and my family, and told him.

Bud studied my face a long time, and then finally I saw he believed me, but he kept asking a few more questions, like where I had got the watch in the first place, and when. I lied to him then because if he had knowed it come direct from Short Papa he would have thought it was stolen. So I told him the far side of the truth, that it was from my Great Grandfather, passed on to me, and this seemed to satisfy him, and he said he would be on the lookout.

Almost every day thereafter on the way home from school I stopped in at the Regal to see if they had any news about my watch, and it got to be a kind of joke there with the customers and with Bud especially. I think they were almost half-glad to see me show up so regular, and inquire.

"No news, though, yet about your great-grandfather's watch," Bud Hughes would generally manage to quip at some time during my visit, and he would wink at me.

Then, the joke about the missing watch having run its course, no mention was finally ever made of it again, and then after a while I quit going to the Regal entirely.

I held on to the chain, though, like for dear life, and never left it out of my grasp if I could help it.

During this period of what must have been a year or two, Ma

would often study me more carefully than usual as if she had decided there was something wrong somewhere, but then finally decided she didn't want to know maybe what it was, for she had enough other worries nagging away at her.

About this time, school being out, and the long summer vacation getting under way, I got me a job in a concession at Auglaize Amusement Park selling crackerjack and candy bars in the arcade that faces the river. They give me a nice white uniform and cap, and for the first time the girls began making eyes at me. . . . I realized that summer I was growing up, and I also realized I would soon be able to leave Ma for good and fend for myself.

On the way to work I would pass this fortune teller's booth early each P.M. and the lady who told the fortunes was usually seated in a silk-upholstered armchair outside, and got to know me by sight. She wasn't exactly young or old, and went under the name Madame Amelia. She was also very pleasant to me partly because she knowed I worked in the concession. One time right out of the blue she told me she would be happy to give a nice young boy starting out a free reading but not to wait too long to come in and take advantage of it, now business was still a bit slack.

I had sort of a crush on a young girl who come in now with her soldier boy friend and bought popcorn from me, and I wanted like everything to find out her name and if she was going to be married to her boyfriend. So I decided finally to take advantage of Madame Amelia's invitation and offer. . . . The fortune telling booth with the smell of incense and jingle of little wind chimes and the perfume of red jasmine which she wore on her own person, the thought of the girl I loved and her soldier friend sort of went right out of my head and vanished into thin air.

I felt an old hurt begin to throb inside me.

Madame Amelia at first sort of flailed around asking me a few leading questions, such as where I had grown up, if I was the only boy in the family, and if I had worked in the concession before, and so on—all just to get her warmed up, as I later found out was the practice with "readers." But then, just before she began the actual fortune in earnest, she held her breast, her eyes closed tight, and she looked so tortured and distressed I thought she was about to have a heart attack, but it was all part also of her getting in touch with the "hidden forces" which was to direct her sorting out your fortune.

Then she got very calm and quiet, and looked me straight in the eye. I stirred under her searching scowl.

"Before I begin, Lester," she said, shading her brow, "I must ask you something, for you are a good subject, my dear—I can tell—and unusually receptive for a young boy. What I would get for you, therefore, would come from deeper down than just any ordinary fortune. Is that clear?"

She looked at me very narrowly. "In other words, Lester, do you want to hear the truth or do you just want the usual amusement park rigmarole?"

"The truth, Madame Amelia," I said as resolutely as I could.

She nodded, and touched my hand.

"You have had two losses, Lester," she began now at once in a booming voice. "But you know only about one of them, I see."

The words "the truth" seemed to form again and again on my tongue like the first wave of severe nausea.

"As I say," she was going on, "you have lost two things precious to you. A gift, and a man who loves you very deeply.

"The hand that gave you the gift which you have not been able to locate, that hand has been cold a long time, and will soon turn to dust. You will never see him again in this life."

I gave out a short cry, but Madame Amelia pointed an outstretched finger at me which would have silenced a whole auditorium.

"Long since turned to dust," she went on pitilessly. "But the gift which he bestowed on you is not lost." Her voice was now soft and less scary. "I see a bed, Lester, on which you sleep. . . . The gift so precious to both the giver and the receiver you will find within the mattress . . . in a small opening."

I do not even remember leaving Madame Amelia's, or recall

working the rest of the afternoon in the popcorn concession. . . . I do know I ran most of the way home.

Mama was giving a big party for her bridge club, and for once she was in a good humor, so she said very little to me as I rushed past upstairs to my bedroom.

Mama always made my bed so good, I hated to take off the hand-sewn coverlet and the immaculate just-changed and ironed sheet, but I had to know if Madame Amelia was telling me the truth. . . . I hoped and prayed she was wrong, that she had lied, and that I would not find the watch, for if that part of the fortune was not true, neither would be the other part about the hand of the bestower.

I searched and searched but could find no little aperture where my watch would have slipped down in the mattress, until when about to give up, all at once I see under one of the button-like doohickeys a sort of small opening. . . . My hand delved down, my heart came into my mouth, I felt the cold metal, I pulled it out, it was my gold watch.

But instead of the joy at having it back, I felt as bad as if I had killed somebody. Sitting there with the timepiece which I now wound carefully, I lost all track of my surroundings. I sat there on the unmade bed for I don't know how long, hardly looking at my long-lost friend, which ticked on and on uncomfortingly.

"Lester?" I heard Mama's troubled voice. "Why, where on earth did you ever get that beautiful watch?"

I looked up at her, and then I told it all to her. . . .

She looked at the tousled condition of sheets, coverlet, and mattress, but there come from her no criticism or scolding.

She held the watch now in her own palm and gazed at it carefully but sort of absentmindedly.

"You should have told me, Lester, and not kept it locked in your own heart all this time. You should confide in Mama more. Just look at you, too, you're growing into a handsome young man right in front of my eyes."

A queer kind of sob escaped from her. . . .

"Where is Short Papa, do you suppose?" I got out at last as she took my hand.

Mama smoothed her hair briefly, then she went on:

"I have wondered and wondered how I was to tell you all these months, Lester, and I see that as usual I must have did the wrong thing where you and Short Papa are concerned. But you realize I learned of his death weeks after the event. . . . And then weeks and weeks after that I heard he had been buried in accord with his firm instructions that there was to be no funeral and nobody was to be notified back here of his passing. . . ."

I nodded, meaning I did not blame her, but kept looking hard at the watch, and thinking there could be no place safe enough now for it, and that it must never part from me again.

"I've always wanted to do what was best, Lester," Mama went on, "but parents too are only after all flesh and blood as someday you will find out for yourself."

She dried her eyes on her tea apron and then touched me softly on the cheek and started to make up the bed, and at the very last to make a final touch she got out her old-fashioned bedspread from the cedar chest and put that over the rayon coverlet.

RUTHANNA ELDER

Dr. Ulric laid much of his insomnia to the fact that he had too meticulous a memory of the subsequent lives of the more than two thousand babies he had delivered in his time. Their histories weighed on him sometimes as heavy as the slabs from the stone quarry.

Dr. Ulric, aged seventy-five, went for a short walk, then encouraged by the mild evening air he passed beyond the confines of the cornfield surrounding his property, and soon stood before an empty frame house with an enormous door, boarded up, frowning at him in the half-light. It seemed, in the outworn phrase, indeed only yesterday that Ruthanna Elder, the one-time occupant of the house, had spoken with the doctor. Charles Ulric returned home then, but all that night, as he moved his head from one pillow to another in his struggle with his enemy sleeplessness, Ruthanna's story kept presenting itself to him like the streamers of northern lights in the autumn sky.

Ruthanna Elder, who had died only last year, had been the prom queen of such and such a year, and after the blow which life had given her at the age of seventeen, she had sat out the next few years on the very front porch in front of the door which tonight had bestowed on Dr. Ulric his sleeplessness. Until only last spring, Ruthanna, slightly bowed from remaining for too long in a sitting position, but looking younger than many of this year's high school graduates, held her head in a way that suggested she still wore the crown of her brief reign.

Dr. Ulric deep in wakefulness remembered now still further back to that afternoon before the graduation ball when Ruthanna had cautiously entered his office where he had delivered babies, removed bullets from wounded men, set bones, pronounced men dead.

"No, Ruthanna, you are not pregnant." The doctor felt he heard his own voice in the country stillness. "But if you worry so, my dear, why don't you marry your young man, Jess Ference, since you're both graduating in a little while. . . . Get married, if you're that worried."

Ruthanna had cried then a lot, but had finally managed to say, "It was not Jess Ference, Doctor. . . . That is why I have been so worried."

"Did you want to tell me then who it was?" the doctor inquired after he had let her cry out more of her grief. She was in no mood to leave.

"It was my uncle, Dr. Ulric." She gave out the secret which troubled her so ceaselessly. "He approached me after he had invited me to his folks' new house where you can see where the river carried off the bridge in the big flood of two years ago. . . ."

Unlike most uncles, the doctor mused, this uncle was two years younger than she, making him fifteen.

The uncle had closed and then locked the door, Ruthanna remembered silently as the doctor watched her uneasily.

"But don't you see, dear," Dr. Ulric had spoken over her thoughts, "you are not going to have a baby. . . . My examination, Ruthanna, has proved that. You did not conceive," he went on to her incredulous face, "from your uncle's being with you. . . . You'll be fine for Jess Ference. . . .

"But why, Doctor, then, can't I seem to give Jess my promise for our wedding day? When it is after all Jess that I have loved since we were children. . . . But no, I cannot, the words stick in my throat. . . ."

"But have you really tried to tell Jess you love him and wish to be married to him?"

"Oh, yes, I think so. . . . But as I say . . . the words stick. It is as if my uncle held my tongue. . . ."

"That is wrong." Dr. Ulric was severe. "You must tell Jess you are free to marry him. And you need not give away what happened with a blood relation. Tell Jess yes. Or tell him no. But you must not vacillate. . . . He loves you too dearly!"

At the graduation ball, Jess's face had blurred as Ruthanna felt him hold her, and she could only see and remember the uncle closing and then locking the door. . . . She loved Jess with all her heart, but why could she think of nothing but the *closed door.*

Her uncle had removed her blouse, and placed his young lips on her untouched breasts. She had melted under his arms like the river freed from ice.

Jess had looked hurt as he had danced with her that night. He had looked like a man who has been slapped with a wet towel. He had always feared from boyhood there might be someone else, but now he was sure.

But there was nobody, of course, her uncle was not Ruthanna's love, her uncle had only taken her, he was not a real uncle after all but a boy, almost a child, although still the first out of all the ones who had wanted her, had waited for her, and who had first possessed her.

Jess had walked away from the dance like a man in a dream to the young uncle's house, the music drifting away now in the distance, for a chance word from somebody had kindled his suspicion into flame.

He had waked the boy after midnight. Jess had asked him if it was true he had loved Ruthanna. The young man, still in the enclosure of sleep, had not denied anything, he had added indeed all the missing or wanted details. It was the details that had done their terrible work, people later said. Had the uncle only told the fiancé *yes* and then said no more what happened later would never have happened.

But the uncle had told it all so lovingly as if he were confiding to a kind brother, a brother whom he loved as much as he had loved Ruthanna. He held Jess's hand in his as he talked, he wept and told him everything, he touched his face to Jess's cheeks, wetting them also and perhaps he added details which were not precisely consonant with the truth in order to satisfy his late visitor.

Jess had stumbled out of the uncle's house at about daybreak. He had walked down to the stone quarry, past Five Creeks, and beyond the glue factory to where the river glided slow and not too deep this time of year. Then he went back to his own house, and got the gun.

Ruthanna had been promised to Jess since he was a boy. It was arranged, you see, their marriage from the "beginning," from, it seemed to Jess at that moment, before their birth.

The young uncle was seated at breakfast, his eyes riveted on the comic section of the Sunday papers.

Jess had walked up to him with a strange smile ruffling his mouth.

The uncle looked up, turned his untroubled gaze and brow toward his assassin-to-be. He had no chance to beg for pardon. Jess shot once, then twice, the bowl of morning cereal was covered with red like a dish of fresh-gathered berries.

Jess walked out with comely carriage to Ruthanna's house. He stood before the white pillars and fired the same gun into his head, his brains and pieces of skull rushed out from under his fair curly hair onto the glass behind the pillars, onto the screen door, the blood flew like a gentle summer shower. Jess Ference lay on the front steps, the veins in his outstretched hands swollen as if they still carried blood to his stilled heart.

HOW I BECAME A SHADOW

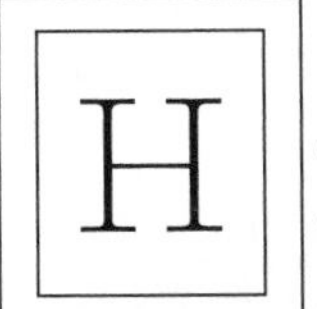

ow I Became a Shadow, how I live in the defile of mountains, and how I lost my Cock.

By Pablo Rangel.

Gonzago is to blame. He said, "That rooster is too good for a pet. He belongs in the cockfight. You give him to me, you owe me favors. I am your cousin. Give him up."

"Never, Gonzago," I replied. "*Nunca.* I raised the little fellow from almost an egg. I never render him to you, *primo.*"

"Shut your mouth that flies are always crawling in. Shut up, you whelp, when I command. That cock is too good for a pet. Hear me. You will give him up, and we will both make money. You bellyache, you say you are always broke, and then when the chance comes to make something you tell your cousin to go hang his ass up to dry. No, Pablo, listen good. The cock is as good as mine because of all the favors I done you, remember. Hear me. I am going to come take him and will fetch you another cock to take his place. Then I will enter your cock at the fight and we will get rich."

"I will not render him," I told Gonzago. "I will keep my pet by me forever. You are not man enough anyhow to take him from me. If Jesus Himself come down from the clouds and said, 'Pablo, I require you to render me your cock as an offering,' I would reply, 'Jesus, go back and hang again on the cross, I will not render my pet, die, Jesus, this time forever.' "

"Ha, Jesus, always Him," Gonzago snorted. "As if He cared about your cock or whether he fights or don't fight. You fool, even your shit isn't brown. You were born to lose. But I will teach you yet. You will not order your cousin about just because you have no wits and need others to watch out for you. . . . Hear me. . . . Tonight I will come for the cock. Hear? Tonight, for tomorrow is the cockfight, and we will win, Pablo. I have been teaching your Placido to fight while you were waiting table at the big American hotel. *Caray*, you did not even notice? See, Placido is ready."

"Ah, so that is why he is so thin and don't eat, evil Gonzago. . . . Never, never say you will take him, though. . . . Look into my eyes, cousin, what do you see there, look good."

"I see nothing in your eyes but stubborn pigheaded pride. Starve to death, why don't you, see if I care. Go with your ass to the wind forever, or die and be dead forever like Jesus. . . . But I will take your cock when I want to on account of you owe me your life, you owe me money for your keep since a boy, you *owe owe owe*!"

"Nothing, Gonzago. I owe you nothing, and won't never give up what I don't owe for. Kill me if you want to. . . . Here is my machete my grandfather passed on to me. Take it and cut me in two, see if I care!"

THAT NIGHT, GONZAGO returned with a big burlap sack with an iron piece that shut over the mouth. He took Placido from his little warm box. My pet gave out piteous little cries as he was grasped. I rushed over to him, but Gonzago had put him already in the sack, and run like the wind and got in his truck and drove off to the cock ring.

I followed on foot. I did not know what I did. I smoked something, smoked it many times. I lost track of time smoking it. Then there I was at the fight sitting in the front row of seats, watching through blue clouds of smoke, not knowing yet one rooster from another.

Then I saw the light of my life come forward, the pet I all alone had raised and whose name I called: "Placido! Placido! *Amor mío*!" I yelled and shouted until the police came and took me outside and clubbed me for kicking them. I fell down on the curb and talked to its cold stones.

After the air revived me, I stole back into the arena. Gonzago stood in the center of a knot of men. "You can have your pet back now." He spoke to me inhaling on a cigar with an end like a volcano. "Over there, *primo*"—he pointed—"behind the piled up folding chairs and the flag."

I went there and looked down on the ground where he had pointed.

At first I see nothing, just earth and a few cigar wrappers. Then I made out his form at last. He was all wings spread on the black soil, but with no eyes. Placido had no eyes! But I knew him still by his gold and red feathers, and his pretty head. But no eyes!

I waited until I got possession of myself, and my heart had quit thundering in my ears. Then I came back to Gonzago. I smiled. Gonzago relaxed. "I invite you to a drink, Pablo."

"Fine," I agreed.

We went to the saloon. Gonzago ordered the best tequila. He paid, he ordered again, the money showered from his hands covered with rings.

When he was feeling his liquor, I pretended friendship and patted him. "Gonzago," I said, "you are a very clever man, and have my good at heart."

"*Gracias, primo*," he said, and he relaxed some more.

"Because of that," I went on, "I want to share again with you. I have another cock you do not know about. A great scrapper and bigger than Placido."

"Is that so?" Gonzago wondered.

"Yes, *primo*, come closer, please, and I will show him to you. This one is a winner. Here, here, look, Gonzago," and I uncovered the little machete I had hidden under my coat.

I cut swiftly like a parcel of winds across Gonzago's unprotected brow. I reddened his eyes with one blow of my machete after another. I cut his eyes to holes like those that were left in Placido's head.

"Placido, *amor*, rest happy, Placido, be avenged. Die, Gonzago, with blind *ojos*, die, blind eyes!"

Then I ran to the mountains where I move like hawks or a mountain cat, or vesper winds. But I keep Placido's feathers against my heart. I live in the defile of mountains. I am called Shadow.

SLEEP TIGHT

Little Judd was about five years old when his sister Nelle mentioned the Sandman to him. Up until that time he had talked and thought mostly about fire chiefs, policemen, soldiers, and of course sailors, because his daddy had gone to sea.

" 'Your daddy is sailing the ocean wide,' " Sister Nelle would sing in a fruitless endeavor to get him to sleep. But that was the one thing little Judd could not do. About dawn he slumbered for a few hours, but during the night, almost never.

Then in despair Nelle had thought of the Sandman and told Judd he would come and put him to sleep if the boy would get quiet and promise not to turn on the radio or play with his watercolors and stain the bedclothes.

"Sandman will come and make your eyelids heavy," Nelle had promised him. "But only if you will be good and lie quiet and still in your bed."

Then Nelle would sing him another song, this last one about the red red robin who comes bob-bob-bobbing along, and Judd would grin when he heard the familiar words.

"Sing more about the robin, why don't you," he coaxed her.

Nelle would sing until she was hoarse, but it only made Judd more wakeful.

"THERE IS NO end to your repertory of songs, Nelle, I declare!" their mother said one evening after Nelle had come downstairs exhausted and pale from trying to put him to sleep.

"I should never have told him about the Sandman," Nelle confessed. "Now he keeps awake on purpose to meet him."

"Don't blame yourself, Nelle, where he is concerned," Mother comforted her. "Whatever we do with regard to little Judd is bound to go wrong." She sighed and took off her apron, folded it, and laid it in the dirty-clothes basket.

Little Judd, as a matter of fact, had thought of almost nothing but the Sandman since Nelle had mentioned him. Yet no matter how much he had questioned his sister about him, Nelle had been unable either to describe his appearance or explain exactly how he was able to put the grains of sand on boys' eyelids. Also, little Judd had wanted to know what sort of a box or sack the Sandman kept his sand in. Nelle was such poor help in filling out these details that the boy became much more wakeful than ever.

ONE NIGHT LONG after his mother and Nelle had gone to sleep downstairs, little Judd heard a strange noise. Turning round, he was sure he was looking right at the Sandman himself, who had crawled in through his open window. He was a tall dark man wearing a sort of Halloween mask, and he had long blue gloves on. There was a large red wet spot on his chest.

He was breathing heavily and every so often he would double all up and hold his belly and say, "Owww."

"Sandman?" little Judd inquired.

The dark man with the mask stared cautiously now at the boy while continuing to make his "Oww" sounds.

"Come on now, mister, give me some of your sand, why don't you!"

The man hesitated for a moment, then came noiselessly over to the boy and sat down heavily on the bed beside him.

"Did you come tonight specially for me?" the boy wondered.

"Yes." The man spoke after brief hesitation. "You can say that, I suppose." He smiled ever so little and began to touch the boy's shoulder, then stopped.

"You're sure you are him, though?" Judd spoke earnestly and loudly.

The Sandman nodded weakly in response, put his finger to his lips and whispered *Shhh.*

"Why don't you give little Judd then some of your sand?" the boy also whispered.

The Sandman started to reply but was halted abruptly by the blaring sound of police sirens outside. His eyes closed and opened nervously as if to convey the rest of his explanation.

But little Judd, who hated the long silence of the night, clapped his hands for joy at the tumult outside. He loved anything that broke the terrible quiet in which he was always tossing and turning and wondering where his father was as he sailed over the shoreless sea.

"I'll give you some sand, little Judd," the visitor spoke out now, "if you'll promise not to tell anybody I am here." Saying this, he stood up with difficulty. "Remember, though, if they ask you whether anybody paid you a call tonight, tell them *only the Sandman.* Hear? Now we'll see about giving you quite a little pile of sand. . . ."

"What is wrong with your chest, Sandman?" Judd questioned, staring at the stranger more closely. All of a sudden, little Judd took the man's hand in his. Then after holding it tightly for a bit, he cried, "Why, see what you have did to my blanket! It looks like you had spilled my red watercolor paints all over it."

The visitor bent over lazily, and his half-opened lips touched briefly the boy's soft yellow hair.

"Now then, little Judd," the man began when he saw how calm the boy had become in his presence. "I will go into that clothes closet over yonder, you see, and I will get you some grains of sand. While I am a-getting them, though, don't you tell nobody at all I am here, dig?"

His eyes fell to where his hand was imprisoned by the boy's grasp. Quickly pulling his hand free, he walked to the closet and opened the door. Turning about to little Judd, he whispered in the softest tone yet, "I will go get you your sand now, Judd."

Below, the front door bell was ringing in alarm, and Judd could hear over that sound his mother calling out, "*All right, all right*," in the same loud provoked voice she used after he had wet the bed and she would cry, "*We can't keep you in rubber pants, can we, I declare!*"

"Yes, Officer." His mother's voice drifted up to him while he kept his eyes fixed on the closet door.

"No, we haven't heard a thing, have we, Nelle?" Mother went on in a soaring, scared voice.

Presently Judd heard footsteps scurrying up the stairs and in no time at all Sister Nelle was peeking through the half-opened door. Meantime, outside, the whole neighborhood had come awake. More sirens and police whistles shattered the air.

"What is it, Nelle?" Judd spoke slyly, still keeping his eyes on the closet door.

Nelle studied him carefully. "There's been a robbery," she began, but then stopped and looked suspiciously around the room. "Someone got shot," she said in a very low voice. "Anyhow, you had best go back to sleep, dear. . . . It's all over." She seemed queer as she spoke, and her eye roved unsatisfied about the room.

Before she could go down again, heavy unfamiliar footsteps reverberated over the threadbare stair treads.

A great man dressed in a blue uniform stood at the door, behind whom, looking white and little, was Mother.

"Everything seems to be all right in here," the police sergeant announced, as if to the room itself. He crossed the threshold and his hand rested for a moment over the hinge of the closet door.

The sergeant smiled then at Judd. "You hear anything, sonny?"

"Just the Sandman," Judd replied in his accustomed sharp tone of voice. Nelle smiled embarrassedly at his reply.

The sergeant and Mother left the room.

"We can't be too careful, Mrs. Bond." The sergeant's voice came to Judd's ears as strong and loud as when he had stood by the closet door. "We'd like to search the yard again and the basement."

Judd heard his mother crying then; Nelle went out into the hall, and her footsteps could soon be heard retreating downstairs. More sirens screamed, coming very close to home, and a man called something through a bullhorn.

"You can come out, Sandman," Judd whispered. There was no answer from the closet.

"Sandman," Judd whispered a little louder. "Come out, and give me some sand. I want to go to sleep. Please . . . pretty please!"

The upstairs was quiet now, but he could hear people moving about down below, and the sergeant was saying something comforting to Mother.

"You needn't be afraid, Mrs. Bond. He is probably a long way from here by now. . . . And our detail will remain here throughout the night. . . ."

Nelle's voice now rose up too: "It's all right, Mother. . . . Please don't cry so hard. . . ."

"Sandman," Judd said out loud.

Just as he spoke, the closet door came open wide, and the Sandman stared, rigid, into the room, but not really looking in the direction of the boy. The wet red circle on his chest had grown larger and covered almost all of his shirt. His eyes looked different also, like little bonfires about to go out.

All at once the Sandman pitched forward, and then, as if trying to break his fall, he twisted and landed face up on the floor.

"What on earth was that noise?" Mother cried from her chair in the kitchen. "My God, don't tell me . . ."

Judd stepped over the Sandman, hurried to the door, opened it, and called down, "It's all right, Mama. I upset the big chair."

"All right, dearest," Mother replied, forgetting to correct him for being awake. "I will be up to see you presently."

Little Judd was the happiest he had been since the day he and his daddy had played Grizzly Bear together. His dad had imitated a fierce bear and then just before he was going to bite him, little Judd had shot his daddy with a toy BB gun, and he had fallen down and lain very still.

Little Judd now went into the closet where the Sandman had been hiding and got his toy gun. He shot the Sandman four or five times. But the Sandman did not play right, as his daddy had. Instead he made strange sounds, which were not too pleasant, and a kind of pink foam formed on his lips, which had never happened with his dad.

Little Judd saw also that the Sandman was very black, and indeed he had never set eyes on anybody that dark except once when a parade had gone by near his house and a large file of dark men and women had shouted and screamed and waved flags.

"Where is the sand you promised me?" little Judd complained.

He looked at the nozzle of his gun and then studied the way the red wet spot on the Sandman's chest kept growing still larger. It was summer and the visitor had very little on except his thin stained shirt and his blue trousers. His feet were naked.

He decided the Sandman had been playing with his watercolors in the closet, which explained the red, or was it he had shot the Sandman so hard he had hurt him with his gun? Whatever it was, it made him want to do watercolors with the wet red that was coming from the Sandman.

"Judd?" he heard his mother's voice from below. "Judd, darling?"

He hurried to the door, opened it softly, and called down *Yes* to her.

"You're sure you're all right, precious?" Judd made kissing sounds in reply and then said, cupping his hands so perhaps only his mother would hear him, "The Sandman has been here."

He heard his mother laugh and put her coffee cup down with a bang.

Behind the closed door, little Judd made a drawing on his watercolor paper of a ship at sea and a sailor looking at the rough waves.

There was so much watercolor red, though, that his paint box was suddenly flooded with it. It was the best watercolor he had ever used, thick and yet runny. No wonder Nelle had talked so much about the Sandman if he brought such good colors to paint with.

After a while, though, little Judd got tired. He had used up all his paper, and then, too, he noticed that the Sandman wasn't making any more paint. Only from his mouth did a kind of pink something issue, but finally that stopped too.

"Sandman, it's time for you to leave. The day is coming, and nobody wants your sand in the sunlight." Little Judd was looking at the orange light streaming through the window. "Sandman, go home," he repeated. "Come back when it's dark and bring me a different color for my paintbrush. . . ."

Little Judd yawned.

It had been an unusual night, he knew, but something was not unusual: he had not slept a wink.

This began to puzzle him, for here the Sandman himself had spent all night with him, and all he had given him was red watercolors.

Again, as so often in the past, Judd felt very sleepy now that day was actually coming. But his bed was too wet with the Sandman's red watercolors.

There was a strong strange smell in the room now, and large black flies had flown in the open window and come to rest on the face and chest of the Sandman. They buzzed and moved their feet in a slithery way, rose in the air, then alighted again on the quiet Sandman.

The buzzing of the flies and the strange sweet smell in the bedroom made little Judd uncomfortable. He felt he was going to be sick. He whimpered a little.

Then he began to realize that he had made a mistake, or Sister Nelle had not told him the exact truth. That is, the black man who lay there so still with the flies swarming on his mouth and chest was perhaps not a real Sandman, for if he was the Sandman, Judd surely would have slept, and he would not have had red watercolors bestowed on him but golden grains of sand.

Then he began to cry very loud. He screamed finally, as he had when he wet his rubber pants.

At last he heard Nelle's step outside the door.

"What is it now, little Judd?" He heard her voice against the closed door.

"I have shot and killed the Sandman," little Judd replied. "He's all covered with watercolors and flies, and I have killed him."

"You try to get some sleep now." Nelle still spoke through the wood of the door. "It's only five-thirty in the morning. . . . Use the potty under your bed if you have to, little Judd."

"I thought he was the Sandman, but I guess he ain't." Little Judd went on speaking to his sister. "I shot him to death with my gun, I guess."

"Use the potty if you can," Nelle told him. Her voice sounded as sleepy as if she had dozed off leaning on the closed door.

"Shall I come in and help you, Judd?"

There was no reply.

"Little Judd!" Nelle cried.

It was then that Sister Nelle opened the door. She stood a long time staring first at the dead man on the floor, then at little Judd, then at the bloodstains on the floor, and all over the many sheets of the watercolor paper. Then Nelle began to scream, at first a low scream, then a more prolonged louder one, and at last, from her astonished countenance, many piercing cries that recalled sirens and bullhorn. Little Judd screamed in response, as if they were singing to one another, echoing one another, as they did together with the red red robin.

RAPTURE

"I wouldn't have known you!" Mrs. Muir spoke to her brother.

"You've grown so tall, and you're so deeply tanned. Oh, Kent, it's really you, then?"

Kent put down his two valises, and kissed her dryly on the cheek.

"You haven't changed much, though, Gladys. The same sweet smile, and sky-blue eyes." He hugged her ever so gently then.

Kent was Gladys Muir's half-brother. He had an extended furlough from the army, where he was stationed in West Germany. Before his assignment there he had been in the Middle East, and before that somewhere in the Pacific. But now, though still a young man, he was a few years over thirty, he was free from his military service at least for a while.

He had been given so long a furlough in order to see Mrs. Muir because the doctor had told him she was not expected to live for more than a few months at the most. Kent, as he studied his sister's face, was not certain if she knew how serious her illness was, and how brief a time yet remained to her.

"Here is Brice," Mrs. Muir said softly as her only son entered the front room of their Florida bungalow. "You've not seen him, Kent, since he was ten or eleven years old, have you?"

Kent stepped back a few inches when he set eyes on his nephew, and his right hand moved slightly upwards as it did when he saluted an enlisted man.

"Here he is at last, your Uncle Kent." Mrs. Muir spoke to Brice as if her brother would not hear her prompting her son. Brice blushed a deep brick red, and looked away.

"Brice has so often spoken of you," Gladys Muir went on. "He has collected all the snapshots of you, and keeps them over his dresser. Especially the photo of you coming out from swimming in the ocean somewhere. That seems to be his favorite of you."

Brice turned his gaze to the patio outside, and colored even more violently. He was then just sixteen and was shy for his age.

"If Uncle Kent will excuse me, Mother, I have to practice my cornet. I have a lesson today," Brice apologized. He almost bowed to his uncle as he left the room.

Mrs. Muir and her brother laughed in agreeable nervousness as the boy took leave of them.

"Brice wears his hair quite long, doesn't he?" Ken remarked as they sat down, and began sipping some fresh lemonade.

Soon they could hear the cornet coming from the garage where Brice practiced.

"Say, he sounds like a real professional."

"He plays with a very fine group of musicians," Mrs. Muir said. "But after his father's death, you see, he left school. That was two or three years ago. He has been working in a restaurant days. He gets up every morning before five o'clock."

Her brother clicked his tongue.

Mrs. Muir observed then how very short Kent's own hair was, though he wore rather long and well-defined sideburns which emphasized his deep-set green eyes.

"He does so much want to be a musician, Kent." Mrs. Muir spoke as if giving away a secret.

"How much have you told Brice about everything, Gladys?" Kent wondered, wiping his mouth from the tart drink.

"Oh, nothing at all. He thinks I am just not feeling up to par."

"I understand," her brother said, looking at one of his fingernails which was blackened owing to his having caught it in his car door that day.

"Let me show you your room, Kent." Mrs. Muir led him up the brightly carpeted stairs. "You'll share the same bathroom with Brice, if you don't mind," she explained. "The bathroom which should be yours has been out of order for a few days. I hope this is agreeable."

When Brice came home from work in the restaurant in the late afternoon the next day, Kent was outside upon a ladder cleaning out the eaves of the roof. Owing to the sudden spell of hot weather, his uncle had taken off his shirt. He had worked so hard, repairing some of the broken parts of the eaves, and also fastening down some loose tiles on the roof, that rivulets of sweat poured down his chest to his bronzed thick arms.

"Need any help, Uncle Kent?" Brice called up to him, smiling broadly.

In answer, coming down from the ladder, Kent ruffled up the boy's thick mop of hair, and grinned.

"All fixed now, Brice, so the water won't run out the wrong way."

Brice avoided his uncle's glance, but smiled continually.

Mrs. Muir observed the two men from inside, where she sat on a new davenport she had purchased only a few days before. She smiled at seeing her brother and son together.

"Brice will be in good hands," Mrs. Muir spoke softly to herself. "Certainly strong ones."

Gladys Muir still did most of the housework, though the doctor had advised her against doing so. She always scrubbed the bathroom immaculately, for she felt Brice liked to see it sparkling clean. On the shelf above the washbasin, Mrs. Muir was accustomed to reach up and take down Brice's comb, in which every day four or five strands of his gold hair were left behind. She would remove the hair, and place it in a small box in her own bedroom.

But after Kent arrived, as she would go in to clean their common bathroom, she observed that there were no hairs now in the comb. The first time she noticed this, she stood for a long time staring at the comb. She lifted it up and looked under it. She felt then, strangely, unaccountably, as if a load had been lifted from her heart.

She found herself from then on waiting, one might say, for the ceremony of the cleaning of the bathroom and the looking at the comb. But with each passing day, every time she picked up the comb it was clean, without one hair remaining.

There was a small aperture leading from the bathroom to a closet down the hall, a kind of register which conveyed hot air from the furnace in winter. The next day, when she heard Kent go into the bathroom, she opened the air register. She was trembling so badly she was afraid he would hear her.

But Kent was completely occupied, she saw, in polishing his boots until they shone like a looking glass. But then, straightening up, she saw him gaze at Brice's comb. He took hold of it with extreme care. He was completely absorbed in looking at the comb which she could see still held a few of Brice's hairs in its teeth.

Kent held the comb for a while close to his mouth, then lowering it, almost languidly, he removed the strands of hair and placed them in his khaki shirt pocket.

Mrs. Muir stole away into her own bedroom, and sat down heavily. She could hear her brother in his own bedroom, moving about. He remained there for only a short time, then he went downstairs, got into his rented car, and drove away.

When she felt her strength return, Mrs. Muir went into Kent's bedroom. She made his bed, and did some dusting and sweeping. Then very slowly she advanced to the dresser and opened each drawer deliberately one after the other. She left the top drawer for last, as if she must prepare herself for what she would find in it. There was a small mother-of-pearl box there. She opened it. At first she saw only the reproduction on its underlid of a painting of John the Baptist as a youth. But in the box itself, arranged in pink tissue paper, she spied a gathering of the gold hair of Brice Muir. She closed the box. There was a kind of strange smile playing over all her features at that moment.

Mrs. Muir felt, she did not know why, the same way she had when her father, the day of her wedding, had held her arm and they had walked down the aisle of the church together, and her father had then presented her to her bridegroom. She had felt at the moment a kind of bliss. She now felt she could give up her son to someone who would cherish him as her bridegroom had cherished her.

But when Gladys Muir began to talk with Kent about her "going," her brother became taciturn and embarrassed, and the serious commitment she wished from him was not made.

The days passed, and Mrs. Muir realized that very little time remained. She knew positively that she had now only days, perhaps hours. The doctor had told her her passing would be so easy she would scarcely be aware of it, such was the nature of her malady.

As she felt then that the time for parting was imminent, she took Brice's comb in her handkerchief so that it could not be seen and joined Kent where he sat playing solitaire in the front room.

He stopped playing immediately she had come in, and stood up in a kind of military fashion. Brice was outside practicing his cornet in the garage, so of course he could not overhear what she might say, or what her brother might answer.

When Kent had put away his cards and was sitting on the new davenport facing her, Gladys Muir without warning brought out Brice's comb.

She saw the look of consternation on her brother's face.

"I want to tell you, Kent, how great a happiness I feel that you are close to my boy. The effort of speaking is very hard for me, as I believe I told you. So I have brought this to speak for me."

A deep silence prevailed.

"Take it, Kent, for I have an identical comb upstairs in my room."

Kent took the comb. His eyes filled with tears.

"You will keep him with you, Kent?" Gladys managed to say.

She was pleased, and grateful, to see how strong her brother's emotion was.

"I don't ever want to leave him," her brother got out. "But do you think he will want to be with me equally?"

"I know he will, Kent. He has a kind of worship of you, and always has. So you will have one another. . . . But what neither of you can know is the great burden that is being lifted from my heart knowing you will be close to one another."

"I will make him my life if he will let me." The uncle spoke in a kind of incoherent manner.

Mrs. Muir was sad she had forced it all upon him in so short a space, but then she saw that no other course would have been possible.

Kent was so blinded by his tears, tears really of joy, he later was to realize, and also tears of so many strange and powerful feelings, that it took him some time to look over at his sister and then to realize she had gone.

At the very moment of his realization he heard the cornet playing cease. He went to the door as Brice was coming through it. As if the boy read the meaning in his uncle's face, he put down his cornet, and threw himself into the older man's arms.

THERE WAS ALMOST no one at the funeral. There was the minister, and a woman who played the organ and who sang one song in a faded alto voice, and then of course the gravediggers and the sexton.

Brice had put on his best Sunday suit, a little too small for him, and a brand-new tie which his mother had purchased for him only last week. Uncle Kent wore his captain's uniform with several bright-colored citations across the jacket.

Kent noticed that Brice did not shed any tears at the service, and he looked very pale. His lips moved from time to time as if he was playing his cornet. They went to a very expensive restaurant later, but neither of them was able to eat very much. Neither Kent nor Brice drank at all, so there was nothing somehow to give them any kind of solace.

"I am going to take care of everything, Brice," Kent told him just before starting the motor of his car. "I don't want you to have to worry about the smallest detail."

It was only eight o'clock in the evening, but Brice said he must go to bed soon as he was due at the restaurant the next morning no later than five-thirty.

"You don't need to work there anymore, Brice," Kent said thickly as he sat on the new davenport. "Unless you want to, of course." He amended his statement when he saw a look of uneasiness on the face of his nephew. "I have enough, you see, for both of us."

"I think, Uncle Kent, it might get my mind off of everything if I did go to work just as usual."

"All right, Brice. But, remember, you don't have to. As I said, there's enough for both of us."

Kent stood up then, and made a motion to take Brice in his arms, but something in the way the young man looked at him caused him merely to shake hands with him and give him a husky good-night.

It began to rain outside, and presently there was a distant peal of thunder, and flashes of silver and sometimes yellow lightning. Kent closed the door leading to the patio. He took out a pack of worn cards, and began his game of solitaire.

All at once it seemed to him he could hear his sister's voice as she showed him the comb with the gold strands of hair.

"She knew everything and was glad," Kent said aloud. "But then, after all, I am his uncle, and too old for him."

THE RAIN HAD wet the top blanket on his bed, so Kent threw this off. He had this small transistor radio and he decided he would just lie in bed and listen to some music.

The rain whipped against the roof and the windows. Kent felt very restless and edgy. His sister's sudden death did not seem real, and he kept seeing her showing him the comb. He could not believe Gladys had meant what she had said, but then what else could she have meant?

He had dozed off when a noise wakened him. It was, he soon realized, Brice taking a shower, and the sound of the water in the bathroom mingled with the sound of the steady downpour, outside, of the rain. He dozed off again, and then he thought he heard someone call. Rising up in bed, he saw that Brice had entered his room. He had no clothes on. At first the thought crossed the uncle's mind that he was walking in his sleep, but then he saw this was not true.

"Can I come in, Uncle Kent?" Brice's voice reached him as if it came from a far distance, and sounded like a small child's in the dark.

"Please, Brice."

"You don't ever drink or smoke, do you. Uncle Kent?"

The uncle shook his head. They both listened to the radio which was playing a waltz.

"May I sit on the edge of your bed?" Brice inquired.

"You're crying," Kent said throatily. "And you're still wet from your shower."

"No, it's from the rain. I stepped out on the porch for a while. I felt so good with the rain coming down on me. . . . But I shouldn't get your bed wet."

"The rain got my top blanket wet also before I turned in," Kent explained.

He suddenly took Brice's outstretched hand in his.

"It's all right to cry in my presence," Kent said, but he had hardly got the words out before Brice threw himself into his uncle's arms. He began weeping convulsively, almost violently.

Kent held him to his chest tightly.

"You're shivering, Brice. Get under the covers for a while at least."

The boy obeyed, and Kent found himself holding him very tightly under the blanket as the boy sobbed on.

Kent all at once kissed the boy on his cheek, and as he kissed him some of the tears came into his mouth.

The sobs began to subside.

"I feel very close to you, Uncle Kent," Brice said. "Do you to me?"

"I do." Kent heard his own voice coming, it seemed, from beneath the floorboards, and unrecognizable as his own.

"I told my mother how I cared for you," Brice said, after a considerable effort, and as he said this he kissed his uncle on the mouth and then let his lips rest there. "She told me to stay with you if you would want me to. She said you loved me."

"If I would want you to!" Kent spoke almost in high anguish, even deliriously.

"Yes, she thought you might."

"Oh, Brice," the uncle stammered, and he kept his mouth against the boy's. "If you care for me," Kent went on, "it will be beyond my wildest dream."

"Why is that, Uncle Kent?"

They kept their lips close together.

"*Why is that?*" the uncle repeated. He kissed him all over the face now.

"You are drying up all my tears," Brice told him.

Then: "I loved you when I first saw you, Uncle Kent," Brice whispered.

The uncle shook his head, but held the boy very close to him. He felt he was dreaming all this. No one had ever loved him before, neither women nor men. He had given up any hope of love. Then he had found his sister's boy's comb full of golden hair, and now he held this boy to his breast. It could not be true. He must be asleep, fast aslumber, or he was still across the ocean and his sister and her son whom he had so seldom seen were far away from him, unknown persons against time and distance.

Then he felt the boy's burning kisses on his body.

They grasped one another then with frantic passion, like men lost at sea who hold to one another before the final breaker will pass over them.

"Is this true, Brice?" Kent said after a while in the midst of such unparalleled joy. "Are you sure you want to be with me?"

Brice held his uncle in his desperate embrace, and kissed him almost brutally on the mouth.

"I said you had dried all my tears," Brice told him. He kissed his uncle again and again, and his hand pressed against the older man's thigh.

"I hope in the morning I will find you against my heart and it will not be just a thing I felt in slumber," Kent said.

He sensed his nephew's hot breath and wet kisses against his chest, and he plunged his thick stubby hard fingers through the mass of gold hair.

Outside, the lightning had turned to a peculiar pink, and the peals of thunder came then more threatening and if possible louder, and the rain fell in great white sheets against the house and the spattered windows.

MUD TOE THE CANNIBAL

A songster by the name of Baby Bundy was accustomed to thrill his church and congregation every Sunday and Thursday in New York by singing anthems, solos, and old hymn tunes. Once in the midst of a long cadenza a dragon fly stole into his mouth and was almost swallowed. Instead of giving forth his next note Baby Bundy exhaled to the congregation's wonder the golden fly, who came sailing straight ahead to freedom.

The dragon fly lived near the lily pond and had for companions midges, golden fish, frogs with blazing green on their coats, and a youthful cannibal named Mud Toe. The cannibal was very doleful because he knew no other cannibals and furthermore it was against the law at the lily pond to eat anything but vegetables. Sometimes the very thought of another vegetable made him scream so loudly the golden fish, the butterflies, and frogs all fled in fear and trembling. The dragon fly, however, who had, after all, been swallowed in church by the songster, was not afraid, for he knew, even if the cannibal swallowed him, he'd soon give him up again. Nobody can enjoy a dragon fly in his stomach.

The dragon fly said, one day, "Cannibal, what is the matter with you, that you mope and scowl and droop?"

"The matter, Dragon Fly, is I know only fish and turtles, and I have to eat sea kale," he complained, "when it's people I long for."

"But you've been living here with us in the lily pond for years now without eating anybody, and look at you: strong, bronzed, with an erect spine and clear eyes! What more do you want out of life, Mud Toe?" (Mud Toe was his adopted name.)

"On the other hand," the dragon fly went on, "Baby Bundy, who lives on the other side of the shore, has to sing for a living in New York (where he swallowed me by mistake), and rides in overage subway cars with people unwashed as midnight and cross as starving tigers. Yet he goes his way summer, fall, and winter, and doesn't give up."

"Then I will visit Baby Bundy and see how he keeps his sweet disposition," the cannibal announced.

Mud Toe went on foot to Greenwich Village, where Bundy lived. His appearance did not startle anybody too much except perhaps a traffic policeman. Yet all Mud Toe had on was a shark's tooth or two, sensibly arranged over his torso.

When the cannibal got to Bank Street, he stopped a boy with scowling blue eyes whom later he was to find to be a thespian.

"Do you know the way to Baby Bundy, the songster?" Mud Toe inquired.

"I do, but why should I tell you?" the thespian scolded. "And besides, why don't you wash your hair? It's full of water lilies."

"I am a retired cannibal," Mud Toe explained (ignoring the personal remark), "not through age, but by law and regulation. I want to visit Baby Bundy to see how he keeps cheerful in the summer, when I am depressed summer, spring, winter, and fall."

"I have just come from Baby Bundy, matter of fact," the thespian volunteered. "And I think he would enjoy at least playing the piano for such as you. He never tires doing so, as far as I can see. . . ."

"Thank you for the suggestion, Thespian," Mud Toe replied, "but you still haven't told me how to reach the songster."

"Go—" the thespian commenced with his mouth tightly closed and his eyes blazing, "go to the big building that overlooks Suicide

Docks, and before you get too close to the water, turn around three times and whistle. The wind will tell you which way to turn at that time."

Mud Toe thanked the thespian and went on his way.

Night was falling when he reached Suicide Docks, and there was no wind. The cannibal sat down on the curb and began to cry. The people about him were so dirty and cross he had no desire to eat any of them. There was no air, the trucks gave out black curls of smoke, and several children were beating an old woman because she refused to buy them frozen fudge bars.

Mud Toe became very homesick for his pond, the dragon fly, and the turtle (whom he had almost married during the cold winter of two years ago).

Just then he heard a piano, coming from above.

"Is that you, Bundy?" Mud Toe cried from the curb.

A window went up on story two, and a brown-eyed young man eating two pieces of chocolate cake yelled down, "Who's taking my name in vain again?"

"It's Mud Toe," came the reply. "A cannibal forbidden to practice his calling. May I come up and see how you keep cheerful in the Good Old Summertime?"

"*Mud Toe!*" Bundy mused over the name. "Why, haven't I seen you mentioned in *Remarkable People You May Have Missed*, the celebrity calendar?"

"No way!" Mud Toe replied in the lingo he had heard near Suicide Docks. "I have lived practically all my life with the dragon fly and the turtle, and a few golden fish at the lily pond."

"Very well!" Baby Bundy consented. "If you don't mind only a brief visit, well and good, for I'm due uptown in half an hour at the studio of the Slavic Queen for an accompanist session, so come up and I'll tell you how I keep happy and cool in the summer."

"I declare! You don't care much for clothes, do you?" Baby B. exclaimed when Mud Toe entered his big studio with the forty-foot ceilings and the five-acre rehearsal rooms. "I guess, though, your physique can stand airing." The songster went on looking at his visitor with careful scrutiny.

"What can I fix you to drink?" Bundy inquired as the cannibal continued on his part to gaze open-mouthed about him. "I have coconut glacé, sarsaparilla shake, and Hershey dream soda."

"I'll take the whole shebang, Baby B., and while I'm drinking I'd like you to play me one of your 'Happy Hour Melodies' people are always talking about."

"I will make you a Hershey dream soda, as it's all mixed and ready," Baby B. proposed, and almost instantly proffered the cannibal a king-size cup of frothy imported cocoa.

"Mmm," Mud Toe panted, "we don't get this at the pond, I can tell you."

"Doesn't surprise me, for prices have never been higher, Mud Toe, yet somehow I go on eating and sleeping in the big town."

"You have lots of room, here, don't you?" Mud Toe went on with his observations of the studio.

"Only enough though for myself," Baby B. said nervously. "I've had my share of roomers and sleeping companions. They just don't pan out for an artist. I have a lot on my mind, and I don't need steady company. It's worse than *lonely*!"

"Well, as it's not getting any earlier out, shall we begin?" Baby Bundy proposed when Mud Toe made no rejoinder to his observation about living by himself. "Gather round the piano, why don't you, and I'll play a Happy Melody."

Seating himself before his grand piano, the songster closed his eyes tightly for a moment, then plunged both hands into resounding, cheerful, ear-splitting chords.

"Oh, oh, oh, and oh!" cried the cannibal.

"What's amiss now?" the songster wondered, leaving off playing.

"I'm only exclaiming with joy," Mud Toe retorted. "Please continue the concert."

The songster then played a number of his famous Happy Songs, one after the other in rapid fire.

What was the piano player's astonishment, though, when he saw the cannibal looking down on him from atop the forty-foot ceiling.

"What on earth, or rather how in heaven's name did you get up there!" Baby B. vociferated.

"I rose automatically," the cannibal tried to explain. "Your songs are wings and have made me fly! I can never thank you enough!"

Baby B. now played a melancholy albeit still sweet melody, and the cannibal slowly descended.

Kneeling at the feet of the songster, Mud Toe cried, "How can I ever repay you for such happiness?"

As he spoke he kissed the pianist's feet hungrily.

"Now, now," the songster admonished uneasily. "No need for excessive demonstrations, you know."

Rising and bowing, the young cannibal said, "May I ask you a favor?" But even as he was making his request, Mud Toe's eyes caught sight of a ticking clock.

"Is that timepiece fast?" the visitor wondered. "Because it doesn't jibe with my dragon fly–turtle sun chart!"

"That clock is about twenty minutes fast, Mud Toe," Baby B. admitted. "I'm a 'latey,' you know, and so have to hurry all day because I have this natural inclination to come late."

"To make a long matter short, Baby B.," Mud Toe began after a great deal of bashfulness and hesitation, "you have made me feel entirely different about life. You have also cheered me up tremendously. I guess I can bear my lot now."

Baby B. lowered his eyes in embarrassed pleasure.

"To go back to the favor I mentioned. Will you permit me to kiss you good and hard as a farewell gesture?" the cannibal inquired. "Please," he said as he saw his host hesitate. "Don't start so. I gave up eating people long ago, though I am still a young man by the lily pond calendar. Only fourteen. Would you mind shaving off your moustache though, before I kiss you, Baby B.?"

"Why, I certainly would, Mud Toe!" The songster spoke with

indignation. "My moustache is part of my stock-in-trade. I'm really quite annoyed you could ask such a favor."

"Don't be annoyed with me," Mud Toe implored. "I'll kiss you right through the hair."

"Well, get along with it, then, why don't you, because I'm due uptown in just a few more minutes."

Baby B. closed his eyes, and Mud Toe bent down and kissed him once gently, then again and again, each time with more force.

"I believe that is enough." Baby B. opened his eyes smartly and looked questioningly at Mud Toe.

"Just one more kiss for the road," Mud Toe coaxed.

"All right, but then stop."

"Thank you, Baby B.," Mud Toe responded, wiping his mouth dry and then kissing him again.

"Ah," the cannibal said. "The dragon fly was right. . . . You have made me feel I can go on living at the lily pond. . . . I think I've changed disposition mostly owing to the Hershey soda, maybe. No, it was your songs, of course! No, it was your forty-foot ceiling! No, it was your kisses! No, it was—"

"I'm sorry!" Baby Bundy interrupted, and ushered the cannibal to the door. "But you'll have you go now. I have to vocalize a bit and spray my tonsils prior to my task as accompanist to the Slavic Queen. . . . But thank you so much for coming, Mud Toe, and thank you also for your compliments! We all need *them*."

"Just one more kiss, Baby B., at the threshold," Mud Toe implored.

"Oh, stop it!" the songster pretended to scold while allowing Mud Toe to take another kiss. "Now go back to your pond!"

And Baby B. closed the door.

The songster stood on the threshold for several minutes, thinking about his visitor.

It had been an unusual afternoon, no question about it, and to tell the truth nobody kisses quite so tenderly as a retired cannibal.

DAWN

It wasn't as if Timmy had made his living posing nude and having his picture in the flesh magazines. Tim modeled clothes mostly and was making good money. But he did do one underwear modeling job and that was the one his dad saw in North Carolina. Wouldn't you know it would be! So his dad thought there must be more and worse ones. Nude ones, you know. His dad was a pill.

His dad came in to New York from this place he had lived in all his life. Population about four hundred people, probably counting the dead.

Well, his dad was something. He arrived in the dead of night or rather when the first streaks of morning were reaching the Empire State.

"Where is Timmy?" he said without even saying hello or telling me who he was. (I recognized him from one of Tim's snapshots.) He pushed right past me into the front room like a house detective with the passkey.

"Well, where is he?" He roared his question this time.

"Mr. Jaqua," I replied. "He just stepped out for a moment."

"I bet," the old man quipped. "Where does he sleep when he is to home?" he went on while looking around the apartment as if for clues.

I showed him the little room down the hall. He took a quick look inside and clicked his tongue in disapproval, and rushed right on back to the front room and helped himself to the big easy chair.

He brought out a raggedy clipping from his breast pocket.

"Have you laid eyes on this?" He beckoned for me to come over and see what he was holding.

It was the magazine ad of Tim all right, posing in very scanty red shorts.

I colored by way of reply and Mr. Jaqua studied me.

"I suppose there are more of these in other places," he accused me.

"Well!" He raised his voice when I did not reply.

"I don't poke my nose into his business," I said lamely. I colored again.

"I can't blame you if you don't." He was a bit conciliatory.

"See here, Freddy. . . . You are Freddy, I suppose, unless he's changed roommates. Pay me mind. I wanted Tim to be a lawyer and make good money and settle down, but he was stagestruck from a boy of ten." Mr. Jaqua seemed to be talking to a large assembly of people, and he looked out through my small apartment window into the street. "I've sent him enough money to educate four boys," he went on. "I could even have stood it, I think, if he had made good on the stage. But where are the parts he should have found? You tell me!" His eyes moved away from outdoors, and his gaze rested on me.

"He failed," the old man finished and looked at the underwear ad fiercely.

But Tim had some good parts, Mr. Jaqua. Even on Broadway." I began my defense, but I was so stricken by this man's rudeness and insensitivity that I found myself finally just studying him as a spectacle.

"There's a screw loose somewhere." He ignored my bits of information about Tim's acting career. "I've come to take him home, Freddy."

He looked at me now very sadly as if by studying me, the underwear ad, the acting career, and the loose screw would all at last be explained.

"See here. Everybody saw this ad back home." He tapped the clipping with his finger. "The damned thing was in the barbershop, then it turned up in the pool parlor, I'm told, and the dentist's office, and God knows maybe finally in Sunday school and church."

"It paid good money, though, Mr. Jaqua."

"Good money," he repeated and I remembered then he was a trial lawyer.

"I should think it would, Freddy," he sneered as if finally dismissing me as a witness.

"It's very tough being an actor, Mr. Jaqua." I interrupted his silence. "I know because I am one. There's almost no serious theater today, you see."

"Do you have any coffee in the house, Freddy?" he said after another prolonged silence.

"I have fresh breakfast coffee, sir. Would you like a cup?"

"Yes, that would be nice." He folded the advertisement of the red shorts and put it back in his pocket until it would be produced again later on.

"What I'd like better, though," he said after sipping a little of my strong brew, "would you let me lie down on his bed and get some rest pending his arrival?"

Mr. Jaqua never waited for my nod of approval, for he went immediately to the bedroom and closed the door energetically.

"YOUR DAD IS here," I told Timmy as he came through the door.

"No," he moaned. He turned deathly pale, almost green. "Jesus," he whimpered.

"He's lying down on your bed," I explained.

"Oh, Freddy," he said. "I was afraid this would happen one day. . . . What does he want?"

"Seems he saw you in that underwear ad."

Tim made a grimace with his lips that looked like the smile on a man I once saw lying dead of gunshot wounds on the street. I looked away.

"He expects you to go home with him, Timmy," I warned him.

"Oh, Christ in heaven!" He sat down in the big chair, and picked up the coffee cup his dad had left and sipped some of it. It was my turn to show a queer smile.

Tim just sat on there then for an hour or more while I pretended to do some cleaning up of our apartment, all the while watching him every so often and being scared at what I saw.

Then all at once, as if he had heard his cue, he stood up, squared his shoulders, muttered something, and without a look or word to me, he went to the bedroom door, opened it, and went in.

At first the voices were low, almost whispers, then they rose in a high, dizzy crescendo, and there was cursing and banging and so on as in all domestic quarrels. Then came a silence, and after that silence I could hear Tim weeping hard. I had never heard him or seen him cry in all our three years of living together. I felt terribly disappointed somehow. He was crying like a little boy.

I sat down stunned as if my own father had come back from the dead and pointed out all my shortcomings and my poor record as an actor and a man.

Finally they came out together, and Tim had his two big suitcases in hand.

"I'm going home for a while, Freddy," he told me, and this time he smiled his old familiar smile. "Take this." He extended a big handful of bills.

"I don't want it, Timmy."

His father took the bills from him then—there were several hundred-dollar ones—and pressed them hard into my hand. Somehow I could accept them from Mr. Jaqua.

"Tim will write you when he gets settled back home. Won't you, Tim?" the old man inquired as they went out the door.

After their footsteps died away, I broke down and cried, not like a young boy, but like a baby. I cried for over an hour. And strange to say I felt almost refreshed at shedding so many bitter tears. I realized how badly I had suffered in New York, and how much I loved Timmy, though I knew he did not love me very much in return. And I knew then as I do now I would never see him again.

THE CANDLES OF YOUR EYES

s late as two years ago a powerfully built black man used to walk up and down East Fourth Street carrying a placard in purple and crocus letters which read:

I Am a Murderer
Why Don't They Give Me the Chair?
Signed, Soldier

Strangers to the East Village would inquire who Soldier was and who it was he had murdered.

There were always some of us from Louisiana who had time enough to tell the inquirer Soldier's story, which evolved as much around Beaut Orleans as it did the placard-carrier.

Beauty Orleans, or Beaut, who came from the same section of Louisiana as Soldier, grew more handsome the older he got, we thought, but he was always from the time he appeared in the Village a cynosure for all eyes. At seventeen Beaut looked sometimes only thirteen. His most unusual feature, though, happened to be his eyes, which someone said reminded one of flashes of heat lightning.

How Beauty lived before Soldier took him over nobody ever tried to figure out. He had no education, no training, no skills. He wore the same clothes winter and summer, and was often even on frigid December days barefoot. In summer he put on a German undershirt which he pulled down almost as far as his knees. He found most of his clothes outside the back door of a repertory theater.

After considerable coaxing and begging Beauty agreed to settle down with Soldier in a run-down half-vacant building, not far from the Bowery.

Because of Beaut's extraordinary good looks and his strange eyes, artists were always clamoring to make drawings of him.

His friend Soldier, whose own eyes were the color of slightly new pennies, protected or perhaps imprisoned Beaut out of his love for the boy. If you wanted to get permission to draw Beaut, you had to go straight to Soldier first and finagle the arrangements.

Soldier would hesitate a long while with a suing artist, would leaf through an old ledger he had found in the same theater Beaut got his clothes from, and finally, after arguing and scolding, would arrive at a just price, and Beaut was begrudgingly allowed to leave for a calculated number of hours.

I don't know which of the two loved the other the most, Beaut Soldier or Soldier Beaut.

Soldier used to hold Beaut in his arms and lullaby him in a big rocking chair which they had found in good shape left behind on the street by looters.

He rocked Beaut in the chair as one would a doll. It was their chief occupation, their sole entertainment. It was an unforgettable sight, midnight-black strapping Soldier holding the somewhat delicate, though really tough, Beaut. If you looked in on them in the dark, you seemed to see only Beaut asleep in what looked like the dark branches of a tree.

Soldier earned for them both, either by begging or stealing. But he was not considered a professional thief even by the police. Just light-fingered when the need was pressing.

Soldier insisted Beaut always wear a gold chain he had picked up from somewhere, but the younger man did not like the feel of metal against his throat. He said it reminded him of a gun pointed at him. But in the end he gave in and wore the chain.

People in the Village wondered how these two could go on so long together. But it was finally understood that Beaut and Soldier had reached some kind of perfection in their love for one another. They had no future, and no past—just the *now* in which Soldier rocked Beauty on his knees and kissed his smooth satiny reddish-gold hair.

"Beaut," Soldier said once near the end of their time together, gazing at him out of his brown-penny eyes, "you are my morning, noon, and night. But especially noon, you hear? Broad noon. Why, if the sun went out, and no stars shined, and I had you, Beaut, I wouldn't give a snap if all them luminaries was snuffed out. You'd shine to make me think they was still out there blazin'."

Then he would rock Beaut and lullaby him as the night settled down over the city.

We knew it couldn't last. Nothing perfect and beautiful has any future. And these two were already overdue in their paradise together. Doom is what perfect love is always headed for.

So then one night Soldier did not come back to that shell of a building they had lived together in.

Beaut stirred after a while in the chair, like a child in his mother's body wanting to be born. Still, no Soldier.

Hunger at last drove Beaut out into the street. Outside, he rubbed his eyes and stared about as if he had been asleep for many considerable years.

"Where's Soldier?" he asked of everybody he met, friend or total stranger.

By way of reply, we gave him food and drink. No one thought to rock him.

As days and weeks passed, the young boy got older-looking, but if anything more beautiful. His eyes located deep in his skull looked like little birthday candles flickering. A few wrinkles began forming around those candlelike eyes. Some of his teeth came out, but he looked handsome still even without them.

All he ever said when he said anything was "Where is Soldier at?"

Beaut stole some reading glasses from a secondhand store in order to go over the ledger which Soldier had left behind and into which his black friend was accustomed to put down sentences when he was not rocking Beaut.

But the sentences in the ledger, it appeared, all said the same thing over and again, often in the same wording, like the copybook of a schoolboy who is learning to spell.

The sentences read: "Soldier loves Beaut. He's my sky and land and deep blue sea. Beaut, don't ever leave me. Beaut, never stop loving me and letting me love you. You hear me?"

Beaut rocked in the chair, singing his own lullaby to himself. He broke his glasses, but managed to read the ledger anyhow, for in any case he had got by heart the few repeated sentences Soldier had put down in it.

"He'll come back," Beaut told Orley Austin, a Negro ex-boxer from Mississippi. "I know Soldier."

One day Orley came into the room with the rocking chair, and closed the door loudly behind him. He looked at Beaut. He spat on his palms and rubbed them together vigorously.

"Say," Beaut raised his voice. Orley bent down and kissed Beaut on the crown of his head, and put his right hand over Beaut's heart, thus testifying he had come to take Soldier's place in the rocking-chair room.

So they began where Soldier had left off, the new lover and Beaut together, but though the younger man was not so lonesome with Orley around, you could see he was not quite as satisfied with the ex-boxer as he had been with Soldier—despite the fact that if anything Orley rocked Beaut more than Soldier had. He could rock him all night long because he smoked too much stuff.

Then you remember that terrible winter that broke all weather records. Usually New York doesn't have such fierce cold as say Boston or northern Maine, though for those from Louisiana even a little taste of Northern winter is too much. And you have got to remember the house with the rocking-chair room didn't have much in the way of a furnace. The pipes all froze, the front windows turned to a kind of iceberg, and even the rats were found ice-stiff on the stairs.

Ice hung from the big high ceiling like it had grown chandeliers.

The staircase collapsed from broken pipes and accumulations of giant icicles.

At the first break in the weather, wouldn't you know, Soldier returned. He had some difficulty getting to the upstairs on account of there was no stairs now, only piles of lumber, but he crawled and crept his way up to the rocking-chair room.

What he saw froze him like the ice had frozen the house.

He saw his place taken by Orley, who was holding Beaut in his arms in the chair, their lips pressed tightly together, their hands holding one another more securely than Soldier had ever dared hold Beaut. They looked to him like flowers under deep mountain streams, but motionless like the moon in November.

"Explain me" was all Soldier was able to get out from his lips. "Explain me!"

When they did not answer, and did not so much as open their eyes, he brought out his stolen gun.

"Tell me what I am lookin' at ain't so," he thought he said to them.

When nobody spoke, he cocked his gun.

He waited another minute in the silence, then he fired all the bullets. But as they flew through the melting air, he saw something was wrong even with the bullets, for though they hit their target, their target deflected them like stone, not flesh and blood.

We have decided that Soldier had gone crazy even before he emptied the gun on the two lovers, but the realization his bullets did not reach flesh and blood caused him to lose his mind completely.

After the shooting he went to the police station and charged himself. The police hardly said two words to him, and took down nothing he said. But they did finally get around to going to the rocking-chair room in their own good time. They must have seen at once that Beaut and Orley had been dead for days, maybe weeks, long before Soldier reached them. No gun can kill people who have frozen to death.

Every day for many weeks Soldier went to the police precinct and confessed to murder. Some of the cops even pretended to take down what he said. They gave him cigarettes and bottled soda.

Soldier lives in a different building now with an older white boy. But every day, especially on Sundays, he carries up and down Fourth Street this placard, whose letters are beginning to fade:

I Am a Murderer
Why Don't They Give Me the Chair?

IN THIS CORNER . . .

When he was 42, Hayes's second wife, like his first, died unexpectedly. She had left instructions that there were to be no special services for her, that she should be cremated and her ashes scattered over the water. The farewell note did not say what water, and her husband one late evening threw the ashes into the river near the docks in Brooklyn. Once they had been disposed of he felt a loosening of tension such as he had not experienced since boyhood. This was followed by a kind of exaltation so pronounced he was nonplused. He breathed deeply and looked out over the dark river on which a small tugboat with green and orange lights was gliding in perfect silence.

A few moments later he found himself whistling.

When he got to his flat near Middagh Street, he opened the seldom-used store room which contained his archery set and his punching bag. He got his boxing gloves out, and punched the bag until he was tired. That night he slept with the deep unconsciousness he had experienced as a soldier on furlough.

It was beginning to get nippy, for they were in late September, and yet he went to his Wall Street job without bothering to put on his jacket or tie.

For some time now, whenever he got off at the Bowling Green subway stop, he had been noticing a young man, almost a boy, holding up a stack of missionary tracts. Today, on a sudden impulse, Hayes bought up all the tracts the boy had for sale. The vendor did not seem too pleased at this unusual generosity, but managed a husky thanks.

The next time he got off at his subway stop, he looked immediately for the young man with the tracts, but when he went up to him, the boy turned away abruptly and began talking with a vendor of Italian ices. Hayes did not feel nervy enough to buy any more tracts.

There was an unexpected killing frost, which was supposed to have set some kind of record, and the next day, shivering from the change in weather, Hayes, as he came from underground, caught sight of the boy with the tracts sitting on a little folding chair. He had no tracts in his hands, and was wearing only a thin summer shirt, very light trousers, and worn canvas shoes without socks.

As he was late for work, he hurried on, but that evening as he left work he observed the young man still sitting on the folding chair.

"Hello," Hayes called out. "Where's your tracts?"

The boy's lips moved fitfully, and then after considerable effort, he got out the words: "I'm not with the missionary society any more," and his eyes moved down to the pavement.

Hayes walked on toward the subway entrance without having been able to make any rejoinder to the boy's explanation. Then all at once before descending he stopped and looked back. The boy had followed Hayes with his eyes. The expression on his face was of such sad eloquence Hayes retraced his steps, but could think of nothing to say. Studying the boy's features he could not miss the evidence that the boy had been crying.

"Supposin' we go over there and get something to eat," Hayes suggested, pointing to a well-known chop house.

"Suits me, but I don't have a dime to my name."

They sat in the back part of the restaurant, which was nearly deserted at this hour owing to the fact that most of their clientele were luncheon patrons.

"What looks good to you?" Hayes went on, shifting his weight in the roomy booth, and watching the boy study the elaborate pages of the menu.

"Oh, why don't you choose for me?" the boy finally said, and handed over the bill of fare to his host.

"We'll have the deluxe steak platter," Hayes told the waiter.

"So that's that," Hayes smiled awkwardly as they waited for their order. The boy flushed under his deep tan, and brushed a lock of his straw-colored hair from his eyes.

When the deluxe steak platters were set before them, the young man kept his knife and fork raised over the still sizzling Porterhouse, as if unsure how to begin. Then after the first hesitant motions, he was eating almost ferociously, his tongue and jaw moving spasmodically.

When the boy had finished, Hayes inquired: "Wouldn't you like my portion?"

"You don't want it?" the boy wondered blankly, looking down at the untasted steak.

"I had a very hearty lunch today," Hayes explained. He pushed his platter toward the boy. "Please don't let it go to waste."

"You're sure?"

Hayes nodded weakly.

"Well, then, if you say so." The boy grinned and began on the second platter. He ate it with even more relish.

"I love to see a young guy with a good appetite," Hayes congratulated him when he had finished.

"How about some dessert? Their pies are all baked here on the premises, you know."

The boy shook his head and put his right hand over his stomach.

"By the way, what is your name?" Hayes wondered bashfully.

"Clark," the boy raised his voice. "Clark Vail."

"And mine is Hayes." The older man stood up and extended his hand, and Clark followed suit. Their handclasp resembled somehow that of two contending athletes before the fray.

"Where do you live now that you're not with the missionary society?" Hayes wondered after they had finished their coffee.

Clark gave a start. "To tell the truth, nowhere." At a long look from Hayes, Clark lowered his eyes and said, "I've been sleeping . . . out."

"Out?" Hayes spoke with something like affront.

A kind of warmth was coming over Hayes. He felt little pearls of perspiration on his upper lip. He wanted to take out his handkerchief and dry himself but somehow he felt any movement at that moment would spoil what he wanted to say. Finally, he forced out:

"Clark, you are more than welcome to stay the night at my place. It's not too far."

Clark made no answer, and his mouth came open, then closed tightly.

"If you are sleeping out, I mean," Hayes went on. "I insist you come where you'll have a roof over your head."

They both rose at the same moment, as in a business meeting where a project had been approved.

Owing to the clatter and noise on the subway they did not speak again until they had got out at their stop.

"I live near the river," Hayes told the younger man.

"YOU HAVE BOXING gloves," Clark cried, picking the gloves up admiringly when they were inside his apartment. "Were you a boxer?"

"Amateur," Hayes colored. "Golden Gloves," he added almost inaudibly.

"I was in the CYO bouts a few times," Clark volunteered.

They both laughed embarrassedly.

"This is a big place you have here," Clark said wonderingly. "And you look out over the water and all the skyscrapers!"

"Excuse me if I take off my shoes," Hayes said. "They pinch."

"You have big feet like me," the boy looked at his friend's feet. He relaxed a bit.

"Want to try my shoes on for a fit?" Hayes joked.

Clark went over to the chair near where Hayes was seated, and picked up one of the shoes.

"Go on, try it on."

Finding the shoe more comfortable, Clark smiled broadly for the first time.

"Try the other while you're at it, Clark."

Clark obeyed.

"Walk around now to see if they feel all right."

Clark walked around the room in Hayes's shoes. He looked as carefree and joyful as a boy who is walking on stilts.

"They're yours, Clark," Hayes told him. When the young man acted perturbed, Hayes walked over to a partly closed door, and opened it fully to reveal inside a whole closetful of shoes.

"Look at my collection," Hayes quipped. "Two dozen pairs of shoes, and every one pinches!"

Clark laughed. "These do fit," he said, looking down at his feet. "But I don't think I should have such expensive shoes."

"Well if you don't, I do." Hayes's voice had a kind of edge in it. At that moment, their eyes met. Hayes's right hand raised, and then fell heavily against his thigh.

"I'm glad you chose to come here tonight," he managed to say. He had meant to say *come home*, but instead changed it to *here*.

Hayes rose very slowly then like a man coming out of a deep slumber and walked in his stocking feet over to where Clark, seated in a big armchair, was looking at his new shoes.

Hayes put his hand briefly on the boy's yellow hair. "I know I need a haircut," Clark looked up trustfully at his friend.

"I like your hair just this length," Hayes told him.

Clark's lips trembled, and his eyes closed briefly.

"You should never have to sleep . . . out," Hayes managed to say.

His hand moved from the boy's hair to his cheek. To his relief, the boy took his hand and pressed it.

"I have only the one bed, Clark. Come on and look."

They walked over to the next room where a four-poster faced them.

"Big enough for four people," Clark's voice came out rather loud.

"Could you stand to share it? Be frank now. If not, I can always sleep on the davenport."

"Sure, share," Clark agreed.

Hayes strode over to a big chiffonier and pulled out from one of the drawers a pair of pajamas.

"Here, Clark, you can put these on. Whenever you want to turn in, that is."

"To tell the truth, that bed looks good to me." Clark sat down on a small stool and took off his new shoes. He yawned widely.

There was a long silence.

"Do you want to change in the bathroom?" Hayes wondered when the boy sat motionless holding his pajamas.

"No, no," Clark rose from where he was sitting, and then as if at a command seated himself again.

"It's just that . . ."

"What?" Hayes prompted him, a kind of urgency in his tone.

"It's the *change* in everything, all around me. From being out there!" Hayes saw with acute uneasiness that there were tears in his friend's eyes.

"Talk about *change*," Hayes began huskily. "Your coming here has changed a lot."

As if this speech of Hayes were a signal, very quickly Clark undressed, and even more quickly stepped into the fresh pajamas which gave off a faint smell of dried lavender.

"Remember, though, if you would be more comfortable alone," Hayes reminded him of his offer to go sleep on the davenport.

Hayes's eyes rested on the boy's pajamas, which had several buttons missing, revealing the white skin of his belly.

"Don't you worry, Hayes," the boy told him. "I'm so dead tired I could lie down in a bed with a whole platoon."

Hayes began taking off his own clothes. He deposited his shirt, undershirt, and trousers on a little chest.

"I can see you was a boxer, all right," Clark noted. "You're pretty husky still."

Hayes smiled, and went to the bed and pulled back the comforter and the sheets under it. Then he helped himself in on the right side of the bed.

"Would you mind if I prayed before I get in?" Clark wondered.

Hayes was so taken by surprise he did not reply for a moment. Then he nodded emphatically.

Clark knelt down on the left side of the bed, and raised his two hands clasped together. Hayes could only hear a few words, like *I thank thee O Father for thy kindness and thy care.*

When they were both under the covers, Hayes extinguished the little lamp on the stand beside the bed.

They could hear the boat whistles as clearly as if they were standing on the docks, and they could see out the windows the thousands of lights from the skyscrapers from across the water.

To his sharp disbelief, Hayes felt the younger man take his left hand in his right, and the boy brought it then against his heart and held it there.

"Clark," Hayes heard his own voice coming from it seemed over water.

The boy in answer pressed his friend's hand tighter.

Hardly knowing what he was doing, as when in the morning he would sometimes rise still numbed with slumber, Hayes turned his head toward the boy and kissed him lightly on the lips. Clark held his hand even tighter, painfully tighter. He felt the young man's soft sweet spittle as he kissed him all over his face, and then lowered his lips and kissed his throat, and pressed against his Adam's apple.

Hayes had the feeling the last twenty-five years of his life had been erased, that he had been returned to the Vermont countryside where he had grown up, that he had never been married, had never worked in a broker's office, and ridden dirty ear-piercing subways or had rented a flat in a huge impersonal building designed for multi-millionaires.

He helped Clark off with his pajamas and turned a kind of famished countenance against the boy's bare chest, and to his lower body.

"Yes, oh yes," the boy cried under the avalanche of caresses.

IN THE MORNING, Hayes realized he had overslept. It was nearly nine o'clock by his wristwatch, and he would never be able to get to the office in time. The place where Clark had slept beside him was vacant, so that he assumed the young man was in the bathroom. He waited, then, hearing nothing, he walked down the hall. The door to the bath was open, the room vacant. The apartment, he knew, was also vacant, vacant of the one he had loved so deliriously.

"Clark?"

Hayes felt a kind of stab in his abdomen, as if a practiced fist had hit him with full force.

After such a night when he had felt such unexpected complete happiness, and when he had felt sure the young man, despite the great difference in their ages, had returned his love—how could Clark then have left him? A rush of even greater anguish hit him when he saw that the shoes he had given Clark were resting under the chair near the closet.

He knew then Clark had left him for good, left him, that is, for dead.

He did not bother to shave or wash before going to work. Several of the secretaries looked at him wonderingly. They probably thought he had been out on a tear. His boss, an elderly man who favored Hayes, was, as usual, out of the office on a trip somewhere.

He finally made no attempt to keep his mind on his work, but stared out at the vast gray canyons of buildings facing him from the windows. Each time he signed some letter or memorandum for a secretary, he would mutter to himself that at five o'clock he would begin his search for Clark.

"And if I don't find him," he said aloud to himself, "what will I do then?"

One thing he saw was certain: if he did not find him, he could not live.

The sudden unforeseen upheaval in his life was just as difficult to understand as if he had fallen under a subway train and lost his arms and legs. He went over the implausibility, the impossibility even of it all, a 42-year-old man, married twice, had taken a young man home, and never having loved any man before, had fallen somehow ecstatically in love, had confessed his love, as had the young man, and then after this happiness, it had all been taken from him. He had been ushered to the gates of some unreachable paradise, and waking had found himself in an empty hell.

IS SEARCH WENT on day and night. Often he did not go to work at all, and he did not even bother to call his employer. He quit shaving and soon sported a rather attractive beard.

He looked crazily and brazenly into the face of every young man who crossed his path, hoping it would be Clark. He wore out one pair of shoes after another. He no longer was aware that his shoes pinched, and taking off a pair at night he saw with indifference that his feet were not only afflicted with new calluses and corns, but that his toes were bleeding from so much walking. Had he seen his toes had been severed, it could not have meant less to him.

"Clark, Clark," he would cry at night. He could still smell the boy's hair against the adjoining pillow.

One night while walking late on the promenade, two men approached him and asked him something. Hayes was so lost in his own misery he paid no attention to them. The next moment he was aware they were ripping off his jacket, and robbing him. After taking all he had they beat him with what seemed to be brass knuckles and then knocked him to the pavement.

He lay there for a long time. He felt his jaw aching horribly, and he noticed that he had lost a tooth. The physical pain he found more bearable than his loss of Clark.

He knew then that he would kill himself, but he did not know what means to choose: the wheels of the subway, jumping from his building, or swallowing countless painkilling pills.

The elderly widows of his building were very much alarmed by the change in "young Mr. Hayes," as they called him. They blamed it on the death of his wife.

The mugging he had received left several deep gashes on his forehead and cheek which did not heal. He did not want to go to a doctor, but whenever he touched the wounded places, they would open and a thin trickle of blood would run down his face. He spitefully welcomed this purely physical anguish. It made his losing Clark at least momentarily less excruciating.

The loss of Clark was equaled only by his failure to understand why the boy had deserted him. What had he done wrong to drive him away when they had felt such great happiness in one another's arms?

In late November a heavy wet snow began falling. Hayes went out only in a light windbreaker, and no hat. He walked to the end of the promenade and then as he was about to turn and go further north down the steep hill on Columbia Heights, he slipped and fell. The sudden sharp blow to his head and face opened his still unhealed cuts and abrasions.

He lay as if lifeless with the snow quickly covering his face and hair. A few persons began stopping and looking down at him. Soon others began to gather.

A policeman got out of a squad car and hurried over to where he lay. When he saw the policeman, Hayes rose on one elbow, and made every effort to get up.

The cop kept asking him if he was going to be all right, or if he thought he should go to the emergency room of a hospital.

Hayes managed somehow to get on his feet, and, shaking off the accumulation of snow, assured the policeman and the onlookers that he was all right. But his eye fell on someone in the crowd the sight of whom almost caused him to fall to the pavement again. There, watching him with a kind of lunatic fear, was Clark.

Hayes moved quickly away from the last of the onlookers and sat down on one of the benches thick with snow. He was as a matter of fact not certain Clark had really been there staring at him. He decided that he had sustained a slight concussion and it had made him imagine Clark's presence. He held his face in his hands, and felt the wet snow descending on his mouth and throat.

Presently he was aware someone was standing close over him. He removed his hands from his face. It was Clark, no mistake.

All at once a great anger took over, and he rose and cried: "Well, what's your excuse?"

When Clark did not respond, he moved close to him, and taking a swipe with his right hand he hit the boy a fierce blow knocking him to the pavement.

Standing over him, Hayes muttered again, *What's your excuse?*

THEN HE MUST have blacked out, for when he came to himself he was again seated on the wet snow-covered bench, and Clark was standing over him, saying, "Can I sit beside you, Hayes?"

"What ever for?"

"Please."

"Well," Hayes snarled, "to quote the way you talk, *suit yourself.*"

Clark sat down beside him, but Hayes moved vengefully away from him.

"The reason I left, Hayes," the boy began, "the reason has nothing to do with you, understand. It's only what's missing in me . . . I wanted to stay—stay forever," he gulped and could not go on.

But Hayes's anger was only getting more intense.

"That's a lot of bull, if I ever heard any," the older man roared. "You missionary people are all alike, aren't you. All nuts. You should all be locked up from meddling with the rest of the human race."

"I'm not a missionary person, as you call it. I never was, Hayes. They took me in, true, but I couldn't believe in what they believed. I couldn't believe in their kind of love, that is."

"Love," Hayes spat out. "Look at me when you say that. See what it did to me. . . ."

Hayes stopped all at once. He could see that Clark's own mouth and jaw were bleeding, evidently from Hayes's blow.

"I have done lots of soul-searching," the boy was going on as if talking to himself. "But the reason, Hayes, I left, you ain't heard, and maybe you won't believe me. See," he almost shouted, "I left because I felt such great happiness with you was . . . well, more than I could bear. I thought my heart would break. And I feared it couldn't last. That something would spoil it. When I first left you I thought I'd come back at once, of course, once I got myself together. But a kind of paralysis took over. The night with you was the happiest in my life. And you were the best thing ever. I couldn't take such happiness after the life I have led. I couldn't believe it was real for me."

"Bull, bull," Hayes cried. He rose, the anger flashing out of his eyes, but as he moved toward the street where he lived he fell headlong and hurt himself on the paving stones. He was too weak to rise too weak also to resist Clark picking him up.

"Hayes, listen to me . . . you've got to let me help you home."

Hayes swore under his breath. Then, as if remembering Clark had been a missionary, he used all the foul language and curses he could recall from his army days.

Impervious to all the insults and abuse, Clark helped him home, holding him under his arms. Hayes tried a last time to shake him off at the front entrance, but Clark insisted on coming up to his apartment with him.

Hayes fell almost unconscious on his bed.

"If you could only believe me," Clark kept saying. He began taking off Hayes's wet clothing. Then he went into the kitchen and heated some water, and put it in a basin he found under the sink.

He began wiping Hayes's face of dirt and blood and snow. When he had finished these ablutions he took off Hayes's shoes and socks. He drew back for a moment at the sight of his naked feet, for they looked as if they had been run over, and at his touch the toes streamed with blood. He wiped them gently, bathing them again and again though Hayes winced and even cried out from the discomfort.

All at once Hayes raised up for he felt Clark kissing his feet.

"No, no," Hayes cried. "Don't humiliate me all over again."

"Let me stay," Clark begged him. "Hayes, let me stay with you."

"No," Hayes growled. "I don't want you."

Hayes could feel the boy's lips on his bare feet.

"You need someone," Clark beseeched him.

"Not you, not you."

Clark covered his friend's feet, and came up to the bed and lay down beside him. He refused to budge from this position, and then slowly without further remonstrance from Hayes he put his head over Hayes's heart, and kissed him softly.

At these kisses, Hayes began weeping violently. Almost like an athlete who has been told he must give up his place to another younger, more promising candidate, he yielded then any attempt to dispute Clark's claim.

Clark removed all of his own clothing now, and held Hayes to him in an almost punishing embrace. Still weeping, indeed almost more violently, Hayes nonetheless began to return Clark's kisses.

Then slowly began a repetition of their first evening of lovemaking, with perhaps even more ardor, and this time Hayes's cries could be heard beyond their own room, perhaps clear to the river and the boats.

"And tomorrow, I suppose, when I wake up, you'll have cleared out again." Hayes said, running his fingers through the boy's hair.

"No, Hayes," Clark said with a bitter contriteness. "I think you know now wild horses couldn't drag me from your side. Even if you was to tell me to leave you, I'd stay this time."

"And do you swear to it on that stack of tracts you used to peddle?" Hayes asked him.

"I'll swear to it on my own love of you," the boy confessed. . . . "Cross my heart, Hayes, cross my heart."

KITTY BLUE

for Teresa Stratas

Many years ago in a far distant country there was a famous opera singer who was very fond of cats. She found her greatest inspiration in talking with her cats both before and after she sang in grand opera houses. Without the encouragement and love of these gifted beasts she felt she would never understand the various roles she interpreted on the opera stage. Her only sorrow was that very often a favorite cat would die or disappear or sometimes even be stolen by a person who was envious of her.

Madame Lenore, the opera singer, was admired by the Crown Prince who at the time of this story was only fifteen years old. He never missed a single one of Madame Lenore's performances and showered her with costly gifts, and after one of her appearances he saw to it that the stage was piled high with the most expensive and exotic flowers.

One day the Crown Prince learned that Madame Lenore had lost the last of her favorite cats. The Prince immediately decided to send her a new one, but he knew this one should be not only the most beautiful cat in his kingdom but the brightest and most gifted.

The Prince scoured his realm looking for a cat worthy of so eminent a singer. He went to over a hundred shops in his search. At long last he found the cat he was looking for in an out-of-the-way bazaar run by a young Abyssinian youth named Abdullah. Abdullah pointed out to his majesty that although the cat he presented to the Prince was only a few months old it already displayed extraordinary mental powers and under his careful tutelage could speak fluently in human language.

The Prince was carried away with enthusiasm for his find and immediately struck a bargain to purchase so splendid a puss.

"There is only one thing I must warn you of, your majesty," Abdullah said as the Prince was about to leave with his purchase. "This cat must not be allowed to keep company with other ordinary cats, but he must remain always close to his human owner and guardian. For in my opinion he is only a cat in his exterior, his soul is that of a higher being."

The Prince was even more delighted with this new information from Abdullah, and he promised he would obey the instructions to the letter, and with that he set out with the gifted cat.

On their way to the palace the Prince was suddenly dumbfounded to hear the cat speaking to him in a soft but clear and unaffected voice.

"My Prince, my name is Kitty Blue," the cat began, "and I am honored that you should wish to adopt me into your royal household. You may depend, your majesty, on my always being a faithful subject who will never disappoint you or leave your royal company."

"Thank you, Kitty Blue. I am most touched by what you say," the young Prince replied. "But unfortunately," he stammered, "unfortunately . . ."

"Unfortunately what?" the cat inquired, for he saw his royal owner was upset. "Please tell me what is worrying you."

"Dear Kitty Blue, the fact is I have promised you to another."

"To another!" Kitty Blue raised his voice. "How can that be?"

"I promised you, dear friend, to the most beautiful and most talented opera singer of our day, Madame Lenore."

The cat said nothing, and the Prince saw that the gifted creature was deeply hurt that the Prince had promised him to someone else.

"I cannot very well go back on my promise, can I?" the Prince spoke in anguished tones.

"I suppose not, your highness," the cat said hesitantly. "But it will be hard to leave your royal presence even for so gifted and beautiful a person as Madame Lenore."

"But I will always be near you, Kitty Blue, and you can always call on me at any hour. Remember that."

The Prince noticed a few tears falling from the cat's wonderfully blue eyes, and he remembered that Kitty Blue had the name he was known by because of the beautiful blue color of his eyes.

Hugging the cat to him, the Prince tried to comfort his unusual pet with many sweet words, but he saw, alas, that nothing he said could console the cat for having to leave his royal protection and company.

The next day the Prince summoned Madame Lenore to the palace to receive the gift he had promised her.

It was a beautiful June evening. The odor of jasmine was in the air, and the sky was a cloudless blue over which songbirds flew in countless numbers, and the many trees surrounding the palace stirred in a faint breeze.

Madame Lenore came accompanied by a young attendant who was extremely devoted to the famous singer and who almost never left her side.

The Prince forbade Madame Lenore to bow to him.

"You are the sovereign here this evening," the Prince said and took her hand in his, "and I shall bow to you."

When they had all taken their seats, the Prince slowly began speaking.

"I have a gift for you, dear singer," the Prince informed her. "A gift such as I myself would be thrilled to accept for my own."

He clapped his hands, and an attendant brought in a great silver box with tiny windows, the top and sides of which sparkled with precious gems.

"Kitty Blue," the Prince said, rising. "Will you now come forth, and meet your new mistress."

"I will, my Prince," a small but clear voice resounded. And Kitty Blue, attired in a handsome suit with small diamond buttons, emerged from the box and immediately after bowing to the Crown Prince advanced toward Madame Lenore and said in perfectly articulated tones, "Good evening, esteemed Madame Lenore."

Madame Lenore was so overcome with surprise and joy at hearing so beautiful a cat address her she came close to fainting. Immediately a servant brought her a glittering glass of refreshment which she quaffed quickly and so regained her composure.

Kitty Blue then leaped into her lap and looking up into her eyes, exclaimed: "You're just as beautiful and charming as the whole world says you are."

"How can I ever thank you, my lord," Madame Lenore cried, turning to the Prince. "You have given me the one gift I have longed for day and night."

There was all at once a clarion call of brass instruments summoning the Prince to leave so that he rose hurriedly and kissed the singer's hand by way of leave-taking.

He then turned to Kitty Blue. "Be good and considerate, Kitty Blue, to your new mistress, for no one except for myself will love you so devotedly. But should you ever need anything, remember I too am your loving friend."

Having said this the Prince bowed low to the wonderful cat and his new mistress and then surrounded all at once by his guards left the room.

Just before he got into his horse-drawn carriage the Prince remembered the warning of Abdullah, and he wrote out a note which he asked one of his attendants to hurry back and give to the singer.

The note read:

> *Under no circumstances, dear Madame Lenore, are you to permit Kitty Blue to associate with common cats. He must speak only to persons such as ourselves.*
>
> *The Crown Prince*

Madame Lenore read the Prince's note carefully several times and afterwards put it away in one of her voluminous pockets. But she was still so captivated by the gift of the wonderful cat the Prince's message of warning soon slipped her mind.

Madame Lenore had never known such a devoted companion as she found in Kitty Blue. Because of his fluency in speaking, there was no subject on which she could not converse with him. He asked a thousand questions about her life and her career as a singer. They often spoke far into the night and fell asleep together in the singer's sumptuous four-poster bed. If Madame Lenore awoke during the night and did not find Kitty Blue by her side, she would call out to him, and then to her relief and joy she would find him at only an arm's length away from her.

Madame Lenore began taking Kitty Blue with her to the opera house. He would wait patiently in her dressing room during the performance of the music drama, and during the intermission the two of them would confer lengthily.

The public and the singer's countless admirers had never remembered her to sing so beautifully or look so stunning as she interpreted her various operatic roles.

It was indeed a new Madame Lenore who appeared before the operatic stage.

The singer gave full credit to Kitty Blue for her resurgence, and she was not ashamed to tell her manager and the conductor of the orchestra that it was Kitty Blue who often coached her in her interpretation of her roles.

She was at the acme of her happiness.

One day an invitation came from the ruling monarch of Constantinople, requesting the favor of her appearing in a series of private performances at the royal court. She was about to accept so important an invitation when she learned from an official of the court that she could not bring any pets or animals.

"But Kitty Blue is not a pet or an animal," she spoke to the delegate of the King.

But the delegate was adamant.

At first Madame Lenore declined the invitation, but Kitty Blue then spoke up to her. "Madame Lenore, your career is your life, and you must go to Constantinople without me. I will be waiting for you here, and you will be gone in any case only a few days or a week or so at the most."

But Madame Lenore could not be consoled. She wept and sobbed, and kept repeating that she could not stand to be without her tried and true companion Kitty Blue.

Finally, at the insistence of her manager and the representative of the royal court of Constantinople, she made the hard decision and agreed to go.

She entrusted Kitty Blue to her faithful attendant, beseeching him to look after her prized and beloved cat.

Their parting was heartbreaking for both the singer and the marvelous cat, and Madame Lenore had almost to be carried out to the ship waiting in the harbor.

Kitty Blue was if possible even more unhappy without the companionship and love of Madame Lenore than the great singer was without her wonderful cat. The young man who was to keep him company, Jack Morfey, treated Kitty Blue kindly but only as he would any cat, seldom spoke to him and never sang to him as did Madame Lenore. True, Jack fed him excellent meals, brushed his fur and changed his suits, often three times a day, but otherwise ignored him.

One day in his lonesomeness, Kitty Blue observed that off the large drawing room was a great window overlooking a spacious garden. From then on the cat took his position always in front of the window to gaze longingly out at all the trees and flowering plants and the butterflies and birds flying endlessly across the sky. He was almost happy then.

Because of his sitting in front of the window so many hours, he attracted the attention of a great monarch of a cat who considered himself in fact the king of the garden.

One day Great Cat strode up to the big window and addressed Kitty Blue: "What are you doing here so close to my garden?" he inquired, and he flashed his coal black eyes with indignation.

Now Kitty Blue had never spoken with a cat before, for he had learned only human language, so for a moment he was not sure what Great Cat was saying, but being so bright he soon deduced what his visitor had said.

"I am Kitty Blue, sir, friend and companion to Madame Lenore, the famous diva."

Great Cat was nearly as bright as Kitty Blue, and he soon had figured out what Kitty Blue was saying in human language.

"I see," Great Cat spoke in a slightly sneering tone. "Well, you certainly have on pretty clothes, don't you, and ribbons besides, and is that by chance a jewel in your left ear?"

Kitty Blue nodded and looked wistfully out at all the trees, flowers, butterflies and dragonflies.

"Would you care to take a stroll in my garden?" Great Cat spoke coaxingly.

"I am forbidden to leave this room, Great Cat."

"By whom are you forbidden, may I ask?" his visitor wondered contemptuously.

"By the Crown Prince."

Great Cat showed utter indifference for this explanation.

"Kitty Blue, think what you are missing. Look out way over there," Great Cat said, pointing with his paw to a wildflower garden in the rear of the garden proper. "Have you ever seen anything so beautiful. And you want to stay cooped up in this stuffy room because some Prince says you must! When we cats all know royalty don't give a hoot about us, and in the first place the Prince has given you away to Madame Lenore, and Madame Lenore herself can't care too much about you since she has gone gallivanting off to Constantinople leaving you behind."

Kitty Blue was so pained by this last remark that two fat tears dropped from his very blue eyes.

"See here, Blue," Great Cat said, "supposing I come by here tomorrow at ten o'clock and by then maybe you will have made up your mind to visit my garden. Toodle-oo."

And Great Cat having given this speech rose loftily and without another word departed.

Kitty Blue could not think of anything but the words of Great Cat, and though he tried to speak with Jack Morfey, Jack paid little or no attention to what Kitty Blue said. Jack confined his attentions to serving Kitty his meals punctually and changing his costumes every few hours. (He had a morning costume, an afternoon costume and finally a sumptuous evening wear suit.)

The forlorn cat kept looking out at the beautiful garden all that day and all evening too, and when night came instead of going to his bedchamber he lay in front of the window and watched the stars come out in the eastern sky as a lazy, red moon rose over the sycamore trees.

He made up his mind then and there he would accept Great Cat's invitation and go for a stroll with him in the garden.

True to Great Cat's promise, he arrived the next day punctually at ten o'clock.

"Well, what is your decision?" Great Cat said in an offhand and curt manner. "Are you coming with me to the garden or aren't you?"

"I would like very much to, but isn't the window tightly bolted?" Kitty Blue said anxiously.

"What's bolted can always be unbolted," Great Cat responded, and putting all his considerable weight against the window pane, he pushed it wide open.

"Coming?" Great Cat spoke in a scolding tone.

Kitty Blue cast one look behind him at his room and the different velvet cushions on which he reclined, and then with a sigh followed Great Cat out into the immense outdoors.

Kitty Blue could not help exclaiming about the marvelous variety of things the garden had to offer. He had never seen such an abundance of trees, shrubs, and climbing vines, or so many birds, chipmunks, and bluejays and crows.

"And beyond the garden, Kitty Blue, are even more wonderful things waiting for you! Why you want to live in that old house crowded with antique furniture, bric-a-brac and thick dusty carpets I will never know."

Great Cat then proceeded to give the younger cat a complete and comprehensive tour, pointing out all the different varieties of trees, bushes, creeping vines and flowers, and drawing attention to the many gray squirrels and last of all to a number of huge crows who watched the two cats with extreme suspicion. And all around them there was a constant moving circle of butterflies, dragonflies and small twittering wrens.

"Excuse me a moment, Kitty Blue," Great Cat said suddenly. "I see a friend over there near the tulip tree who I am sure would like to meet you. Stay here until I speak with him."

Great Cat rushed over to the edge of the garden where a gray tomcat with only one eye and massive jaws and paws had been observing them.

Kitty Blue watched with considerable uneasiness as the two large cats spoke together. From time to time they would both look over in his direction and grin.

All at once Kitty Blue heard someone call him by name. Looking up toward a rhododendron bush, he caught sight of a very pretty mourning dove who now addressed him: "Kitty Blue, if you know what is good for you, return at once to Madame Lenore's house. You are keeping the worst possible company by coming out here with Great Cat and his friend One Eye. They are both bad actors and will get you into plenty of trouble if you are not careful. Mark my words."

The mourning dove then flew up to the roof of an adjoining church where his mate was waiting for him.

Kitty Blue was so frightened by the dove's warning he hurried back to Madame Lenore's house, but not only was the window now tightly closed but an enormous shutter had been placed over the window preventing entry.

All at once a strong even melodious voice said: "So you are the Kitty Blue we have all been hearing about." A young man, dressed as if for a pageant wearing a high hat and a feathered vest with rings on almost all his fingers, was addressing the unhappy cat.

Kitty Blue had barely enough strength to say yes.

Great Cat and One Eye now approached also and began speaking, but the young man severely warned them to be quiet, and better still, be off.

"You alley cats have served your purpose, now skidoo!" he cried. Both Great Cat and One Eye made a great caterwauling until the young mountebank (for this is what he was) threw them several helpings of catnip which the cats greedily seized and then ran off into the bushes.

"Let me introduce myself, Kitty Blue," the young man said, and all at once he took hold of Kitty Blue and sitting down on a bench held him in his lap. "My name is Kirby Jericho," he said, "and I am a long-time friend of your mistress, Madame Lenore. I happened to hear those two alley cats by chance talking about you, for I understand puss language since I am in the pageant and theater business. They brought me straight to you." As he spoke Kirby fondled Kitty Blue gently and then carefully touched him on the ear.

"I don't suppose you noticed, but Great Cat robbed you of your earring and your necklace."

Kitty Blue gave out a short sob when he realized this was true.

"Madame Lenore," Kirby Jericho went on, "has been detained in Constantinople. The young sovereign there has absolutely refused to let her leave for another month or so. Since I am one of her friends of long standing I am proposing you come and stay with me until she returns. Meantime I want to train you for appearing in the theater of Herbert of Old Vienna, who is also a former friend of Madame Lenore."

Kitty Blue was so miserable at having been locked out of Madame Lenore's apartment and of being robbed by Great Cat, he barely heard anything Kirby Jericho said to him, but being in a desperate mood, he reluctantly allowed himself to be persuaded to go with his new protector, for that is what Jericho said he was.

Kitty Blue was considerably surprised to see that a brand new roadster was waiting for them beyond the garden walls.

"Sit in the front, if you please, so we can talk on the way to my studio, if you don't mind," Jericho advised.

Kitty Blue took his place beside Jericho, and in one second or two off they went through the lonely deserted streets on the way to the vaudeville and dance theater, and to what Kitty Blue was later to learn would be a new and entirely different life.

After a while Jericho slowed down and turned to the cat, and after stammering badly, he managed to get out the following: "Kitty Blue, do you realize the danger you were in trespassing in Great Cat's garden?"

Kitty Blue was so miserable and unhappy without Madame Lenore he barely heard what Jericho said. Finally however he managed to say, "I suppose so."

"I see you don't," Jericho sighed. "But let me tell you another thing. Madame Lenore could not have cared very much about you if she up and left you without anybody to watch over you. No, don't interrupt, don't defend her. She is a fickle woman. On the other hand if you will come live with me in the Vaudeville and Paradise Theater, you will find a true home and what's more, a profession. I will teach you to be a dancer and performer, and a guitar player. Doesn't that sound like the real thing now?"

Kitty Blue nodded, but he was so heartbroken to hear that

Madame Lenore was fickle and had deserted him that he burst into tears.

"There, there now," Jericho comforted him and handed him a handkerchief to dry his tears with. Jericho started the motor again, and they were soon across the river and into the backstreets of a district given over to acrobats, dancers, jugglers and other entertainers.

They drove up to a theater ablaze with pink and violet lights, and over the front entrance shimmered a great marquee with the words:

THE VAUDEVILLE AND MUSIC HALL
OF HERBERT OF OLD VIENNA

"Don't be upset that my name is not in lights," Jericho said, helping Kitty Blue out of his car, "it will be one day soon, for Herbert is longing to retire. By the way did you know Madame Lenore got her start in this very vaudeville and music hall? Well, she did, and Herbert was her maestro. They quarreled of course, and Madame Lenore went on to be a famous diva."

Kitty Blue dried his tears and with a great sigh allowed himself to be ushered into Herbert of Vienna's Vaudeville and Music Hall Theater.

Madame Lenore's appearance in Constantinople was thought to be a stunning success by everybody except the singer herself and her manager, a young man from Milan who had watched her progress from her early days. "Something was missing," she confided to him one evening as they sat together in their spacious hotel suite. "Don't tell me I was perfect for I was not!"

"Correct me if what I am going to say is wrong," the manager said, "but, Madame Lenore, strange as it may seem, you miss Kitty Blue. Being away from him has taken something out of your voice."

Madame Lenore sadly agreed. "How perceptive you are, my dear friend. Not only do I miss him but I have had terrible dreams and a presentiment something has happened to him while I have been away."

"I am sure everything is all right with him," her manager replied, "for you left him in the company of your most trusted servant. So don't worry on that score. You are homesick and homesickness is one of our greatest sorrows."

Madame Lenore tried now to look on the bright side, but she noted again the next evening that her voice, despite the rapturous applause greeting her, was lacking in a certain strength and conviction. She knew then how much she loved Kitty Blue and that she could not be happy without him.

After her performance that evening the stage was filled with hundreds of large bouquets and wreaths of flowers of every kind, but their perfume and beauty failed to touch the singer's heart, and her eyes were streaming with tears.

All the way back on the ship she could think of nothing but Kitty Blue and his amazing gift of speaking to her in her own language.

"As soon as I set eyes on him," she told her manager, "my heart will be lifted up and then, you see, my voice will again have all its former resonance and power."

The next day they arrived home, and Madame Lenore flung open the door with fervent expectation and called out the name of the cat.

The young attendant appeared immediately. As she looked at his troubled face, Madame Lenore's worst suspicions stirred in her mind.

"What is your news?" she inquired in a chilled, weak voice.

"Madame Lenore," the attendant began as he helped her off with her coat, "something very upsetting has occurred."

"Is it Kitty Blue?"

He nodded. "Kitty Blue has disappeared," he explained. "We have made every effort to locate him, but he has left without a trace except for the little scarf which he sometimes wore around his neck. This we found in the garden outside." And the attendant produced the scarf which was the same color as the eyes of the cat.

Madame Lenore lay back in her chair, closed her eyes, and shook with choking sobs.

All kinds of dire fears and suspicions tormented Madame Lenore's mind. After realizing Kitty Blue had disappeared without the least clue to where he had gone, the great singer took to her bed, refused food and lived on ice water and an occasional glass of champagne. Within two weeks she had lost so much weight and was so frail she could scarcely rise from her sumptuous four-poster. She canceled all of her appearances to the anger and bitter disappointment of the great Gatti-Casazza, the director of the opera house.

Against the advice of her manager and her friends she summoned many world famous detectives. Only the enormous amount of money the singer promised them prevailed upon the detectives to take a case involving the disappearance of a cat, despite the fact the cat had been the gift of the Crown Prince.

One of the detectives who listened to her story was a more humane and benevolent man than his colleagues who merely had taken huge sums of the singer's money and produced no results.

The detective, named Nello Gambini, listened quietly as Madame Lenore poured out all her sorrow together with the few facts she had gathered about Kitty Blue's last days.

"What you need, my dear lady," Nello Gambini finally said, "is not a detective but a seeress."

"A seeress!" Madame Lenore exclaimed and sat up in her bed for the first time in days. "I think, Signor Gambini, you are absolutely right, but . . ." and her voice quavered, "where on earth can I find a seeress who will not be dishonest and grasping."

"Ah, but there is one, and only one. The difficulty, however," Signor Gambini said, as he accepted a cup of coffee, "the difficulty is Señora Cleandra no longer will see anybody."

"Then why have you given me her name," the anguished singer broke into new weeping.

"Listen to me, dear Madame," Signor Gambini comforted her,

"if I call her she will see you, for I once located her lost diamond necklace."

Madame Lenore smiled.

The famous detective handed her a card with the name and address of the seeress.

Rising, the detective wiped his mouth carefully with a linen napkin and said, "Be sure to tell her that I arranged for you to meet one another and under no circumstances is she to refuse to help you."

Madame Lenore was too ill and weak to go to Señora Cleandra's home, and only after emphasizing it was a matter of life and death did the old fortune-teller agree to visit the singer though, as Señora Cleandra remarked on the phone, it was against her considered better judgement to leave her own domicile.

Señora Cleandra's appearance was astounding. She was nearly seven feet tall and her hands were laden with jewels and a strong herbal odor emanated from her person. Besides this she was so heavily veiled from head to foot one could scarcely see her eyes. She said she would only partake of a raw onion as refreshment, but after chewing thoughtfully on the onion for a while, she changed her mind and said she would take a cup of beef broth.

"And now, dear Madame Lenore, tell me what person so beloved of you is missing, and I will attempt to locate him."

"When you say *person*, dear Señora, you are speaking the truth. Yet I must tell you the loved one, whose absence has brought me to my death bed, is a cat. . . ."

Señora Cleandra hearing who the missing party was stood up in all her seven feet and gave out an ear-splitting shriek followed by a volley of curses.

"Pray be seated, dear Señora," Madame Lenore begged her.

"You have brought me here to locate a *cat* for you," the seeress cried. "Have you no realization of what an insult that is to me, the Señora Cleandra who has hitherto only been a consultant to members of royalty and other crowned heads. A cat! Indeed!"

"Dear Señora, listen to me," Madame Lenore whispered, shaking in a fit of trembling. "Though he has, it is true, a cat's body, he is not a cat but a young Prince I am convinced. He speaks the language of aristocracy and not the mewings of an ordinary feline. And he loves me, and I love him. If he does not come back to me I shall die."

"Have you any spirits in the house?" Señora Cleandra inquired of one of the attendants. "Some eau-de-vie perhaps," she added.

The servant immediately brought the seeress a snifter of the finest brandy, and after sipping the liquor lengthily, Señora Cleandra lowered her veil and, looking closely at Madame Lenore, said, "If he is not a cat but as you claim a Prince, I could extend to you my services. But first I must have an article the disappeared one often touched—I suppose in his case something he held in his paw."

"Bring the Señora Kitty Blue's velvet breeches," Madame Lenore commanded, and for the first time in weeks the singer rose and painfully walked over to the largest chair in the room.

Madame Lenore was about to add some more information to Señora Cleandra about her missing pet when she saw that the seeress had fallen into a deep trance: her head had leaned to one side and the veils about her face had fallen away so that one saw her chin and upper lip were covered with a heavy growth of beard.

The seeress then began speaking in a greatly altered voice: "Your beloved Kitty Blue is a prisoner, dear lady, of the notorious live-animal trainer and pantomimist, Herbert of Old Vienna. Kitty Blue was handed over to Herbert by the notorious rapscallion Kirby Jericho, and your dearly beloved is required to appear nightly as an entertainer and guitarist and is also forced to dance and perform acrobatics."

Señora Cleandra now opened her eyes and adjusted her veils so that her growth of beard was no longer noticeable. She stared balefully then at Madame Lenore.

"You should eat nothing but rare beef for the next two weeks," she advised the opera singer.

"But where, dear Señora, can I find Herbert of Old Vienna?" Madame Lenore entreated the seeress.

"You, a singer, have never heard of Herbert of Old Vienna? Then I pity you."

Señora Cleandra hurriedly wrote out the showman's address and handed it to the bereaved Lenore.

"How much am I indebted to you for, Señora?" Madame Lenore inquired after getting possession of herself and reading again and again the address of Herbert of Old Vienna.

The seeress had moved toward the door. Then turning around she said in a voice as low as that of a bass baritone, "Owe? Are you crazy! Nothing. Do you think I would accept money for locating a cat, whether he is a Prince in disguise or maybe a goblin? Señora Cleandra does not receive pay for locating animals."

She opened the door and rushed out.

Weak as she was, Madame Lenore followed after the seeress and cried, "You must have some recompense, dear lady. Please come back and accept any gift you may desire."

But Madame Lenore was too late. The heavy outer door had slammed behind the visitor and a cold current of air came in from the street, causing Madame Lenore to cough and sneeze.

Madame Lenore was filled with hope on hearing Señora Cleandra's words that Kitty Blue might be found at Herbert of Old Vienna's, but this information also caused her great pain. Madame Lenore now recalled that many years ago she had been a pupil at Herbert of Old Vienna's Ventriloquist and Vaudeville Studio as it was then called. He had been very fond of her and she was his favorite student in that long ago epoch. But they had quarreled violently because Herbert, who was once world-famous in Vienna, had proposed marriage to Madame Lenore. She had refused his suit, and as a result he had become her bitter enemy. She realized that it would be very difficult to return to the Ventriloquist and Vaudeville Studio, especially when her coming was to beg the favor of returning Kitty Blue to her. But Madame Lenore was now only too aware that unless she could find Kitty Blue again she would never recover her health or her operatic career.

Herbert of Old Vienna had already been alerted by Señora Cleandra that Madame Lenore would be coming to his studio and would attempt to abduct Kitty Blue.

Although the singer was heavily disguised the evening she paid her call to the Vaudeville Theater, she knew Herbert who was also clairvoyant would spot her, even if she appeared as a bundle of brooms.

Nonetheless she took her courage in her hand and boldly walked into the small theater and sat in a prominent place near the stage.

A young man dressed in lemon-colored tights was juggling what appeared to be a hundred brightly colored balls, but of course clever use of lights had made one ball appear many. It was easy to believe the young man was throwing countless balls in the air and catching every one with more ease than the best trained seal.

He bowed to Madame Lenore at the end of his act and blew her several kisses.

Next a young girl dressed as a mermaid appeared and again through Herbert's clever use of lights she gave the illusion she was swimming in a beautiful green sea. She too recognized Madame Lenore and bowed low after her act.

Giuseppe Fellorini, the strong man of Herbert's troupe, now came thundering out. He raised one heavy object after another in his brawny arms, including what looked like a grand piano, and a Fat Lady reputed to weigh 500 pounds. He was too proud of his strength however to bow to Madame Lenore and barely would look at her, but instead he blew kisses to the audience which was applauding him fervently.

Then the lights dimmed, and soft if slightly sad music from the cello and the harp sounded. Madame Lenore knew her "prince" was about to appear, and she had to reach for her smelling bottle to keep from fainting.

Kitty Blue dressed in a suit of mother-of-pearl and diamonds came forward with a guitar. He did not seem to recognize Madame Lenore at first, and began strumming his guitar and then sang the famous words:

In your sweet-scented garden
I lost my way.
Your window once full of light
Closed forever against my beating heart,
I lost my way because you had gone away.

But here Kitty Blue's paws trembled and his voice became choked. He had recognized Madame Lenore. He rose from the shining silver chair in which he was seated and cried out: "Madame Lenore, is it after all you? Tell me what I see is true."

Madame Lenore could not contain herself. She rose from her own seat and rushed upon the stage. The cat and the great singer embraced and kissed one another and burst into tears.

"You must come home with me at once, dear Blue," Madame Lenore managed to get these words out.

But at that moment they heard a terrifying voice of such volume that the chandeliers of the small theater vibrated and shook.

"You shall do nothing of the sort, Madame Lenore—for it is you, isn't it? Take your hands off my star performer, and you, Kitty Blue, go to your dressing room!"

It was of course Herbert of Old Vienna.

"How dare you interrupt a performance here!" he shouted in the most terrible rage Madame Lenore could recall.

But she was no longer the cringing young pupil she had been in Herbert's vaudeville and burlesque house.

Madame Lenore almost spat at the great ventriloquist as she cried, "Kitty Blue is mine, not yours. He was a gift from the Crown Prince, and you have no claim on him."

"If you so much as touch this cat," Herbert shouted in an even louder tone, "I shall have both you and him arrested and sent to the Island. You are in my theater, and furthermore you are still facing charges for having run out on me years ago, owing me thousands of pounds sterling and gold guineas. And once you are jailed you shall stay there till you are turned to dust!"

"Jail me? You shall do nothing of the sort, you low mountebank," Madame Lenore cried.

Because she was living in a dangerous city Madame Lenore always carried a pearl-handled pistol. And so she drew out this pistol from one of the voluminous folds of her gown.

Now Herbert of Old Vienna had an almost demented fear of firearms, possibly because both his third and fourth wives had shot him, seriously wounding him.

When he saw Madame Lenore leveling the gun at him, he fell on his knees and burst into an unmanly series of sobs.

Still holding the gun in his direction, Madame Lenore, walking backwards, reached the stage door and then the dressing room. She found Kitty Blue hiding under a player piano. Kitty Blue, hearing the singer's voice, rushed into her arms.

They hurried into the back part of the theater and went out the stage door where fortuitously one of the horse-drawn carriages was waiting for the Strong Man. They jumped in and, as Madame Lenore was still holding her pearl-handled pistol, the driver was too terrified not to obey her and started in the direction of the singer's palatial residence.

Herbert had recovered partially from his fear and raced out after them, but at this point Madame Lenore fired her pistol in the air, and when the mountebank heard the gunfire he fell in a dead faint to the pavement thinking he had been shot.

The carriage was soon rushing away and within minutes had reached the residence of the famed opera singer.

Exhausted from his ordeal, Kitty Blue was easily persuaded to be ensconced in his comfortable place in Madame Lenore's four-poster, but sleep was out of the question. And the singer was avid to hear of the cat's adventures.

But before he could begin, the new servants (Madame Lenore had dismissed all her former help on the grounds they had neglected the safety and person of Kitty Blue) brought his favorite dessert of candied deviled shrimp and strawberries in brandy and anise cream.

He had barely begun to enjoy the repast when all the doors of the chamber were flung open and in strode the Crown Prince who had got wind of the rescue of the cat.

The Prince was nearly as overcome with joy as his friend the opera singer and they all embraced one another in an excess of joyful thanksgiving.

"He was just beginning to tell me how it was he was lost to us," Madame Lenore told the Prince.

"I had forgotten, Your Grace," Kitty Blue turned to his highness, "that I was forbidden to talk with common cats."

"And from what I have heard," the Prince said, "you could hardly have chosen a worse creature to speak to than the notorious Great Cat and his accomplice One Eye, who I am glad to tell you have both been sent to prison for life."

Kitty Blue could not help smiling.

"After Great Cat had robbed me of my earring, I was rescued by a young theater scout sent to locate promising talent by Herbert of Old Vienna."

"And don't I know the theater scout you mention," the Prince was indignant. "Kirby Jericho is his name."

Kitty Blue nodded. "He took me to his training chamber," the cat went on, "and for six weeks I was his prisoner while he coached me and instructed me in the art of guitar playing, elocution and soft-shoe dancing, prior to his turning me over to Herbert of Old Vienna."

The Prince could not help interrupting the narrative here by cries of outrage.

Madame Lenore cringed at the thought of what her beloved cat had suffered in her absence.

Despite his painful adventures and the accompanying pain and suffering they had inflicted on Kitty Blue, both Madame Lenore and the Prince had to admit that the cat's experiences had given him if possible an even more ingratiating and splendid personality, and what is more an almost inexhaustible repertory.

"Before, dear Blue," the Prince expressed it this way, "you were a marvelous companion and a sterling intimate, but having been trained by wicked but brilliant Herbert of Old Vienna and Kirby Jericho, you are without an equal in the entire world.

The Prince then stood up and folded his arms.

"I want to invite you, Madame Lenore and Kitty Blue, to accompany me on an ocean cruise around the world beginning tomorrow at noon. Will you kindly accept such an invitation?"

As he waited for their reply the Prince added: "I think both of you could stand with a long vacation, and this one is scheduled to last for seventeen months."

Madame Lenore turned to her favorite cat for a response.

Kitty Blue fairly leaped for joy at the thought of a world cruise with a royal protector and the greatest living singer, and nodded acceptance.

And so the three of them became during that long sea voyage inseparable friends and companions. And almost every night, at the Prince's command, Kitty Blue would entertain them with the story of his adventures, interspersed with his guitar playing and singing and soft-shoe routine. The narrative of his adventures changing a little from night to night, new details coming into the story, new additions not imparted before, gave the Prince and Madame Lenore such entertainment they never knew a dull moment on their sea voyage. The three of them became the most famous trio perhaps known then or thereafter.

BONNIE

People begin always by asking me about my dove, but what they really want me to tell them about is Bonnie. I think they find it, if not amusing, a bit outside the ordinary run of story. They tell it to others and pass it around. I resent this, but people ask me to tell our story, and I oblige them. So I am to blame if people retell it and maybe laugh behind my back.

I have after all only one story, and it is Bonnie. At first maybe I was ashamed that this was so, but now I admit it, and I don't care anymore what people say or think or how much they laugh.

I married her when I was only eighteen. She was a bit older than me, everybody said. Actually I never thought about her having any age at all, she was so all-in-all to me. It was even more than love, though it was that too, all of it. And I guess I would have loved her if she had turned out to be twice my age, or maybe even not a human being at all.

Our troubles started in earnest (though we had trouble from the very first night together on our honeymoon) when Bonnie began putting on weight. At first I sort of liked it, you see. It didn't spoil her appearance, or her prettiness as far as I was concerned, and Bonnie was the prettiest girl in the world. All the old worn-out phrases described her to a T, "peaches and cream, snow and roses." And her yellow hair everybody always called "spun gold," and so on. Her weight in fact didn't seem to show because of such precious good looks.

But in the end it was her strange hunger for sweets that caused the final breakup between us, not her getting fat. When, for example, we'd pass a bakery, we would have to stop and she would gaze through the glass at the spectacle of the cakes, pie, jelly rolls, cookies and tarts, till once I said more good-humored than angry, "Bonnie, you love sweets more than you do me!"

When it got so bad, and she had put on thirty extra pounds, I said one day as she stopped suddenly to look in a pastry shop, "Maybe, Bonnie, we should see a doctor."

"Maybe you should, Danny," and the way she said "Danny" went through me like a knife because it had the real sound of goodbye in it. I can't explain how one word, my name, as she pronounced it could tell me everything was at an end, but when I heard her say it, I knew.

I knew too she blamed me in her heart for her not having babies.

SO IT WENT on like this for some months. Whenever I would come home, whether unexpected or not, she would be sitting at the big dining room table eating something fattening, a piece of pie loaded with whipped cream or a slice of Sacher torte, caving in with chocolate.

"Bonnie," I said one time, seizing her hand with the fork in it so that I hurt her, "You don't want to put on any more pounds!"

"How do you know what I want or don't want," she retorted, tears in her eyes.

Finally I could hardly recognize her. She was getting on to becoming "circus fat." I moved to the small room down the hall and left her to sleep by herself. I began missing supper in the evening, and there were days I didn't come home at all, but slept in my office in this big firm in the financial district. I didn't have another girl, which was what she thought. The truth is I was still in love with Bonnie, more so than ever in fact, but there was no Bonnie for me, you see. Just this fat woman growing toward "circus fat."

Then I moved out entirely. She didn't put up the least resistance. We weren't going to be divorced even, for how could I divorce a woman whom I no longer even recognized? The real Bonnie was gone. At work I sometimes daydreamed about her as if she had left on a round-the-world voyage.

AFTER A YEAR or so had passed like this the thought presented itself to me that at least a legal separation might be better for us both. I stopped by the old place and rang the bell furtively, almost shuddering to think how it would be. A young man, hardly more than a boy, answered the door. I faltered for a moment, then got out, "Bonnie here?"

He nodded, studying me cooly as if he recognized her description of me easily.

The long wait in the hall made me wonder if she had gotten so heavy maybe he was going to have to wheel her out.

Then I was aware of a presence, and I looked straight forward and saw her. I had to hold my right hand on the doorjamb to steady me. For there she was, Bonnie, but just the way she had looked when I had been eighteen and taken her to dances and drive-in movies. In fact she was a little thinner I believe than when I first began going with her.

"Gosh all get out," was all I could utter and finally, "Bonnie! Bonnie!"

But though she looked just like the old Bonnie I had gone with and had married, so slim and if anything prettier and even more luscious-looking, there was no real look of recognition in her face for me, no greeting, warmth, certainly no welcome home.

"I'm glad you stopped by, Dan," she began icily, while I just stood there, and why not admit it, worshipped her, and kept muttering her name again and again until she cut me short with: "We do want the divorce now after all.

"Since you've been out of a job, I've heard," she went on without letting me catch my breath, "we can pay for it ourselves, can't we, Earle?" She turned to the young man who had greeted me and who now stood directly beside her.

"Oh, I'm going to work again soon in the financial district," I said too unemphatically and soft for them perhaps to have heard.

"Just the same," she continued, "since you've missed so much work, we'd like to pay all the court costs."

"I don't want a divorce," I tried to put some body in my voice, but it came out about as substantial as a whisper. "I may not have any ground to stand on," I was continuing, "but Bonnie . . . Bonnie. . . ."

"I have a good lawyer," she was going right forward, and all the time like a simp I was uttering her name. I couldn't stop saying it, like a man with the hiccups.

Then I saw the stare she was giving me. The leave-taking came like winter sleet. I would hear from them, she said and she added that they had tried to contact me several times earlier.

"If I could only speak what is in my heart, Bonnie," I think I said or words to that effect between the space left by the door closing against me.

THEN THE DIVORCE was granted without my contesting it or replying to the many legal communications which piled up on my desk. Two years passed, maybe more. I became deeply absorbed in my new work on Broad Street and Wall. For a man so at loose ends my rise was perhaps surprising and probably impressed all who knew me except myself.

I worked often fourteen hours a day, the outside world became thin and insubstantial and even when leaving the office I noticed very little around me. My whole life was work.

Yet in the late evening, when I would leave my office, I usually passed a woman on a park bench who held patiently on her outstretched hand a small, beautifully shaped bird which I was to learn later as if in a school lesson was no ordinary pet shop specimen.

Up until then I had never been interested in birds, but I looked at this bird attentively while barely glancing at the woman who held it. In truth I had quit looking close at anybody for some time after my matrimonial fiasco.

But once soon after the very cold days arrived, one day when I was about to pass the bird and its owner, I stopped, as if frozen in my tracks, gawked, stared, was unable to take my eyes off her. The woman holding the bird was Bonnie, but not a Bonnie I believe even her own mother would have recognized.

"What is it, Bonnie?" I began as if there had not been our separation and the distance of time. "Can I do anything?"

She was so thin one could see many little veins in her face and hands and the protuberance of bones. She had not an extra ounce of flesh on her.

"Where is Earle?" I said at a loss as to how to continue.

"Oh, Earle? Remarried." She spoke indifferently, almost sleepily.

"Can I come to see you, Bonnie?" I asked against my own better judgment.

"It wouldn't be a good idea," she replied after a careful silence.

"Remember," I began awkwardly, my voice almost unrecognizable to my own ears, "I'm . . . yours Bonnie, if you want me!" I blushed at those last improvident words.

She cut me down with a look.

EVERY DAY THEN for many weeks I would see her sitting on the same bench under a huge sycamore tree, the bird always with her, each day a different kind of tiny neckband on its throat. I dared not go near.

Then at the beginning of a break in the weather, when sitting out would have been more customary, I missed her. The next day also she was absent, and the day after that, and so on. Several weeks passed without her turning up.

One Saturday when I had to go to work to finish some pressing details of my job, I stopped short. There on the identical bench all alone was the white small bird. I looked frantically. I waited, I forgot about my job. I picked up the bird, and kept looking up and down the street. He was quite tame and made no effort to struggle out of my grasp. I walked over to an outdoor stand which sold bird seed, and bought some to feed him. He seemed in fact hungry and partook of all I could give him. I sat there half the day, waiting, never going near my office, certain she must return for the pet.

That evening I returned home with the bird. I had purchased him a small cage from a variety store around the corner from where I live.

Sunday I went back to work to finish the task I should have performed on Saturday. While looking over my ledger, William Weston, a well-known investigator, happened to drop past and asked me a few questions about some technicality in an area in which I am now becoming somewhat expert. After I had replied to his satisfaction, I hesitantly asked him if he knew of an investigator who could trace the whereabouts of a missing person.

William's face did not change expression and hesitating only a few moments he said he'd be more than pleased to take the assignment himself.

A YEAR PASSED, and he had come up with nothing. I then hired, without telling him, another investigator. It was not cheap, let me tell you, hunting for Bonnie. At last, since not the most minuscule clue came to light, I gave up the search.

AFTER THE END of our hunting, I used to go and sit on the identical seat and hold her pet in my hand, as I am doing today. Nothing, however, came of that either, so far as attracting her to come back to me.

One day a gentleman carefully dressed and wearing only a single eyepiece stopped and asked me if he could examine the bird. He bent over me for what seemed an eternity.

"Would you sell him?" he finally inquired.

I declined frigidly.

"Your bird belongs to quite a rare species of dove," he informed me.

"It wouldn't surprise me it's rare," I mumbled. My present rudeness and lack of interest recalled to me Bonnie's treatment of me.

"Are you aware, sir, of its worth, then?" he persisted.

"I am aware of only one thing," I raised my voice now in the face of his insulting condescension. "This is a dove, as you call him, placed in safekeeping with me against the owner's return."

He stepped back on hearing this and studied me with a curious mixture of disbelief, puzzlement and slight contempt.

After he had gone I held the "dove" gently against my overcoat.

HE HAS GROWN so comfortable with me of late that I have put away his cage in a back closet, leaving him to come and go as if he were in his own great outdoor home.

GERTRUDE'S HAND

Sonny at no time complained about being left out of Gertrude's will. Perhaps he never thought he would ever be remembered by her in any case. Still, everybody was a bit surprised Gertrude had left everything to her cook and companion, a dark-complexioned woman of thirty who appeared to cultivate the pronounced mustache growing above her hard, thin lips. Sonny had been just as devoted as Gertrude's cook, Alda, but whereas Alda had almost never left the house, Sonny had run his legs off for Gertrude on errands of all kinds, had assisted Gertrude in her atelier where she made the iron-wrought primitive sculptures that had given her at the end of her life a kind of local fame. Sonny had gone sometimes even thrice a day to the blacksmith's where Gertrude's sculptures were finally finished. He must have worn out fifty or so boots during his fifteen years' service with the sculptress.

Once Gertrude was gone and lying beneath a very simple headstone in Cypress Grove Cemetery, Alda sat in the same oak chair her former employer had always occupied, moved into the larger, more airy, and better lighted bedroom that was Gertrude's, and from then on cooked very little. Gertrude had been a hearty eater, and Alda, thin and pinched, though with the beginning of a pot belly owing to poor posture rather than overeating, was easily satisfied with an omelet and perhaps some pea or bean soup to eke out the rest of her diet. She occasionally invited Sonny now to these frugal repasts, although in the days of Gertrude he had never been asked to partake of anything at the table, but had once in a while "pieced" on something in the pantry.

Gertrude's distant great-nieces and a nephew had attempted to break the will, but in the end, partly because the will had been drawn up so well, partly because Gertrude herself had written down dreadful criticisms of these far-away relatives, all of Gertrude's not inconsiderable fortune had passed to the bird-like, mustached Alda, whose eyes were never still. (Sonny had once remarked that he wondered if her eyes did not move all night rather than close motionless in sleep.)

Alda was a bit puzzled at Sonny's obvious signs of mourning over Gertrude's passing. He wore a large, almost purple armband immediately she was dead, while Alda made no change in her attire, for she had always preferred in any case black dresses and black hats.

Alda had planned to go to an island off the coast of Georgia shortly after the reading of the will, for the New England winters had come to be a trial to her, and wealthy as Gertrude was, she had insisted on their going on living together in the converted Maine farmhouse. But after Gertrude's death, Alda had had a serious fall and her dream of going to Georgia vanished. After her accident, Alda hobbled considerably, and her doctor had advised her to remain at home in Maine and rest, for she could hardly travel without assistance.

Of course Alda could have called in other people to aid her, but the fact that she had passed from being Gertrude's cook to Gertrude's heir had caused her to look on everybody with slightly different eyes. She distrusted Sonny, but she knew him. She was aware he had expected to be included in Gertrude's will, but he had never spoken of it, and, what is more, went on from time to time to shed tears when he thought of the sculptress's death. These tears were a source of wonder to Alda. She had never seen a grown man cry so much.

Though she was only in her thirties, Alda's fall reminded her that she too might need a lawyer, and improbable as it seemed for her, a woman who had been poor all her life, an heir. She had neither. Well, she could have Gertrude's lawyer, of course, Mr. Seavers, but she had never liked him. He had certainly never been kind to or considerate of her, and at the reading of the will in his spacious, blindingly bright law office he had pronounced the legal words in a kind of fury as if it were the warrant for her arrest.

"Do you understand everything in it?" he fairly thundered at her after he had read it all. "You are the only heir," he had added when she did not respond at once.

"She left Sonny McGuire nothing?" Alda had managed to say in the rather menacing silence as Seavers waited for her to say (obviously) something.

"I told you, Miss Bayliss, you were the only heir. It's a very well-written will," he smiled bitterly.

"I'm surprised," Alda had said. "I can't believe he is to have nothing." She looked though considerably satisfied on the whole and accepted a copy of the will from his broad hands which might have been more comfortable behind a tractor. "You are a very wealthy woman," the lawyer remarked before closing the door on her.

When Sonny did not come by for a week or so, Alda fully realized her predicament. Though she could now walk with a cane, she felt considerable pain in her back and legs. But even had she not had the fall, she realized she would need to see somebody. She had not quite been aware during Gertrude's lifetime that she knew only her. Sonny had not counted then. He had been merely an errand boy. Now she had nobody to think of but him.

His grief over Gertrude's death seemed to have dried up. He never referred to her, and he acted more like a servant than ever under the changed circumstances. With Gertrude he had acted almost as an equal. Sonny was only about thirty-five years old at the time of her death. He looked even younger, perhaps because he spent most of the time in the open air, rode horses a good deal for exercise and did very little hard work of any kind. He lived down the road in a remodeled farmhouse which had been in his family for three generations.

"Would you like to take supper with me every evening?" Alda asked him one morning.

Sonny removed his stocking cap and thought over her statement. Alda fidgeted when there was no immediate response.

"I would prepare a genuine meal for you," she added, fearing perhaps that he thought she would serve only soup and corn muffins.

"If it would make your feet comfortable," Sonny finally said.

"The evenings are pretty long," she told him. He made no comment on this.

After a pause he asked, "Do you suppose I could have the little weather-vane she completed about a year ago? I am pretty fond of it and helped her to make it."

Alda stirred in her chair, and took hold of her cane and brought it in front of her dress. "The rooster?" she wondered. He nodded.

"I don't see any reason why not," she said uneasily. "In fact, I wonder she didn't leave it to you."

"Well, she didn't," Sonny said somewhat tartly.

"Then take it—it's upstairs in the storeroom." Alda gave out a long sigh.

Alda began to cook rather ambitious suppers then. She herself ate sparingly, and sometimes when her hip pained her she partook of almost nothing, while Sonny ate everything in sight, including, one supposed, her portion.

"Was the meal to your satisfaction?" she said one night when they had dined on venison, wild rabbit, scalloped potatoes, Indian pudding, and coffee with thick, farm-fresh cream. He had merely nodded.

"Do you think Gertrude would be surprised to see us mixing socially though?" Sonny inquired.

As there was no reply, Sonny turned around and looked at Alda. She was, he saw, considering the question.

"I don't think she looked down on you socially, Sonny, if that is what you mean," Alda responded. "But she thought of you as a boy. Almost a child."

"But they invite boys or children to supper," he said in a somewhat spiteful tone. Her face became even more impassive.

"I mean, you cook quite different grub for me than you did for her," he commented.

Alda grasped her cane as if she meant to rise, but she actually fell back further into her chair. "Gertrude was a picky eater," she observed. "It cost me a lot of worry and trouble to tempt her appetite. She liked dainty things mostly, and fattening ones too. Towards the end very little pleased her."

"I would enjoy having the same menu you prepared for her," Sonny spoke in a low toneless voice, yet it sounded like a command. "For instance, you would never have prepared venison and rabbit for her, would you?"

"Will Hawkins brought me the venison and the rabbit," Alda replied. "I wasn't of a mind to let it go to waste."

"Would you have prepared it for her, though?" Sonny inquired.

Alda fidgeted. "I would have made her some broth out of it, I guess," she conceded.

"I would be quite satisfied if you prepared the same menus for me as you did for her." He spoke neutrally now, and smiled a little. Her face looked discomposed at the sight of his smile. "Otherwise, I could just drop in on you once every week or every two weeks."

Alda now leaned forward with the cane. Her face had gone white, then flamed into a kind of hectic flush.

"Just tell me what you'd like to eat, Sonny. Then we'd both know where we're at."

"No, no." He raised his voice. "I ain't the cook. You are. And you cooked good for her all these years. I want the same grub you prepared for her. I can eat venison and rabbit with the hunters, but if I come here I want the quality grub or I don't come back."

She looked at his chapped, heavy hands. One of the thumbs was bandaged. As she stared at his hands he put on his mittens.

"I just never thought a man would care for her type of food." Alda spoke slowly, cautiously, and she stammered on: "I have been cooking you meals I thought a man would like."

"Well, go back then, why don't you, to the quality menu."

"I will, Sonny," she said in a sort of prayerful voice, "I'll oblige you," she added, and smiled weakly. He said good night then and went out.

Waiting until he was well out of earshot, Alda picked her cane up and beat it against the heavy timber of the floors. She beat several times, and then she broke into a fit of weeping.

ALDA WAS COOKING supper the next evening when she heard the scissors-grinder's bell outside. She hurried to open the door at once, for he had not come by for some months and all her kitchen knives, not to speak of the axe and hatchet, wanted sharpening.

Flinders, the grinder, was a tanned, wiry fellow of about forty, with lank yellow hair which fell from under his slouch hat, and he had already moved down the road with his wagon and horse when he heard Alda's imperious command.

He stopped the horse and walked back to the fence on which Alda leaned, having forgotten her cane. "You must have missed us last time," she was querulous.

He followed her on back to the kitchen, carrying his whetstone with him.

"You remember where I keep all the sharp-edged instruments," Alda said, and returned to her cooking.

"Where's the fat lady who was here before?" the grinder inquired after he had begun to sharpen her butcher knife on his grindstone.

"Gertrude, you mean," Alda said in a matter-of-fact tone.

"Yes, I guess that was her name." Flinders took up the axe now and looked at it. "Why don't you take decent care of your tools?" he wondered. "You should always wipe these sharp-edged instruments after use; I'd put a little oil on them when you put them away—I told her that."

Alda said nothing. She was making dumplings.

"Well, where is Gertrude?" he inquired testing the edge of the axe.

"Gertrude passed away a few months ago," Alda informed him.

"Was it sudden?" he wondered, taking up the hatchet now and shaking his head over its wretched condition.

"Yes, it was fairly sudden," Alda replied.

He had finished sharpening all the tools and stood waiting to be paid.

"I've forgotten how much you charge," Alda told him, for Gertrude always took care of things like this.

He named a figure, and Alda hobbled over to a little china closet, opened one of its lower drawers and took out her purse.

"I'd appreciate it if you came more often," she had begun telling Flinders when the door opened and Sonny came in. The two men glanced at one another but did not speak.

"Why didn't you let me know your knives needed sharpening?" Sonny said when the scissors-grinder had gone, and he was tucking his napkin under his chin. "I could do that just as well."

"As long as he showed up, I figured he ought to do it."

"Remember I can do it just as good from now on—if not better," Sonny warned her.

"Look here," Alda said, dishing him out some veal stew and dumplings, "I don't like that tone of command in your voice." Her hands trembled as she gave him a portion of lima beans. "I'll do just what I think is right."

"Then do it alone!" He loosened his napkin and threw it down.

"Now, now, no need to get riled, Sonny," Alda spoke quietly. She went over into a far corner of the room and sat down in a cushiony chair whose bottom was beginning to fall apart.

"Ain't you going to eat nothing?" he inquired, staring at his plate.

"Put your napkin back around your neck, and eat, Sonny—I'm not hungry."

"Let me see how he done those knives." He walked into the little back room where all the tools were kept. He lifted up each of them, the axe, hatchet, butcher knives, and so on.

"Well, what is your verdict?" Alda inquired sourly when he did come on back into the room and sat down but with his chair pushed considerably away from the table.

"I can do everything for you," he told her. "We don't need no scissors-grinder."

"Good. Glad to hear you say so," she humored him. "Now eat your veal stew and dumplings."

"I don't like to eat alone," he told her. "Why don't you ever eat with me?" he cried.

"Very well, if it will make you have a better appetite. I will have some."

She laid a plate, knife, fork, and napkin quickly at her old place and sat down with difficulty. He helped her to stew and dumplings. "Ah, ah, that's too much," she protested over the amount of the serving.

"You eat it and shut up," he spoke in surly indifference.

"It is good," she admitted, chewing.

"How do I know you ain't poisonin' me when you don't eat from the same pot," he said at last. "From now on you eat what I eat," he told her, eyes flashing under his hair which had fallen down low. He pushed upward the black forelock.

"What's the matter with you?" Sonny almost shouted one evening after they had had supper together, and as usual Alda had only picked at her food. "I know you didn't care for her that much."

"I'd rather not talk about her," she sighed. "It's too painful. Too painful."

"It's painful also to deal with a silent woman like you. You make me tired."

He set his coffee cup down on the table with a bang.

"Go ahead and break the cup, why don't you," Alda told him.

"Do you feel guilty she left you so much money?" Sonny said in a more conciliatory voice after they had sat there glaring at one another in short little spiteful glances.

"The bequest does bother me, Sonny," Alda said.

"How?" he wondered.

"I came here from a farm, you know. Had no mother and father of my own. The Baylisses who brought me up was glad to be rid of me. Gertrude had come there one day looking for a hired girl, Gertrude had come there one day looking for a hired girl, she said. She saw me and wanted me right away. What did I have to lose? She taught me everything I know about cooking, though I read cookbooks too of course. I occasionally consulted Mrs. Bayliss. But mostly I taught myself. Gertrude was pleased with my cooking, and in a way with my company, though we never talked much."

"Why do you feel guilty?" Sonny wondered now.

"Did I say I did?" Alda wondered. The color had come back to her face, and she looked more youthful. "I am puzzled."

"Why?"

"I don't know what to do with so much money. And another thing . . ." She hesitated a long time until his snort of impatience made her bring out: "I feel like there is nothing left for me to do! I feel my life is over."

"With all that money, over?" he shook his head.

"There's nobody needs me," she almost whined. "I worked for her twelve hours a day. Now what is there to do?"

"Mind?" he asked her, and took out his pipe.

"Smoke away, Sonny," Alda consented.

ONE EVENING WHEN she had shown even poorer appetite than usual, he had all at once thrown down his napkin and said, "How do I know you did not poison Gertrude?"

Alda was so astonished she could say nothing. She remained dumbfounded for some time, and then she began to laugh hysterically. From laughing she soon turned to tears and wept loudly and had to use several handkerchiefs.

He sat gloomily watching her, cold and unyielding.

"I won't go to the police if that's why you're bawling," he said after a bit. He drank a little of the coffee, then spat it out in the saucer.

"That was the last thing in my mind. The very last," she said.

"Oh, I don't think you killed her," he said. Then he got up and reached for his overcoat, hat, and gloves.

"You cannot just up and leave after you have said such a terrible thing," she told him. "Do you realize what you have done to me?"

"You didn't kill her?" he joked, tying his scarf tightly around his neck.

"No, no—I loved Gertrude," she cried, for she failed to note he was not serious. "We were real friends, life-long companions. Don't you see how miserably lonesome I am without her? And that you would even think such a thing, let alone say it. God in heaven! You are an evil, wicked man. Who put such ideas into your head? And why would I want to poison you? You are the only one I can depend on." She sat down in Gertrude's chair and began to weep even harder.

After a while he took off his scarf and unbuttoned his greatcoat and sat down at the table.

"If you put just a little poison in her food at the beginning she would gradually die from it all," he pointed out.

Alda cried harder. "I never expected to be her heir, and I don't really want all that money now," Alda said. "I never knew how to spend money. She handled all the business affairs. To think you would think such a thing of me—oh, merciful Christ!"

"Yes, merciful Christ."

MR. SEAVERS CAME out of his office when his secretary told him Alda Bayliss was waiting to see him. He looked at her coat and shoes in a critical fashion before he said good morning and then invited her into his office.

"I am very busy this morning, Miss Bayliss," he informed her, and he looked at the face of his pocket watch which he already had in the palm of his hand.

"It's very important," Alda began. "I have been accused of poisoning Gertrude," she brought out.

"By whom?" he said with glacial indifference, as if she had said she had been accused of having forgotten to stamp an envelope she had put in the mail.

"Sonny McGuire," she replied.

He snorted by way of reply.

"What am I to do, Mr. Seavers? If he should go around telling such a thing. . . ."

Mr. Seavers put his watch in his vest pocket and shook his head. "What did you tell him when he accused you?" he wondered.

"I denied it again and again."

"I will speak to him about it," he said. He looked at her very carefully then. "He could find himself in serious trouble spreading such a story," he went on, but with no indication he felt she was to be defended from such a charge.

As soon as Alda had left, he picked up the phone and asked his secretary to call Sonny McGuire and tell him to get over to his office as fast as his legs could carry him.

EVERY SATURDAY, MUCH against her will, and only because Gertrude had insisted she do so, Alda would take her weekly bath. She invariably caught a chill after bathing, and felt miserable until Sunday afternoon.

She heard the front door open and then familiar footsteps. Sonny opened the door and stared down at her in the tub. She crossed her hands over her breast and mumbled something.

"Why did you have to tattle on me?" he wondered. He took off his greatcoat and sat down on the edge of the tub. He barely looked at her so that perhaps he was not aware of the consternation and confusion he was causing Alda. Perhaps he hardly heard her cries of shame and alarm and suppressed rage.

"Of course I did not mean what I said. I was only angry. I knew you didn't want to poison Gertrude. And I know you do not care for money. I know all that. Alda," he cried, "look at me—Alda, look at me!" he touched one of her arms held over her breast.

She suddenly went into convulsions and writhed, and a kind of hoarfrost came over her mouth. He threw a huge bath towel over her, picked her up as if she were a doll and carried her into her room. He rubbed her thoroughly with the towel and then laid her down on the bed. "Where's your nightgown?" he wondered, then found it hanging in her closet. He put her in her nightgown and pulled back the sheets and put her between them. Her teeth chattered loudly.

"So I am sorry I accused you."

Alda said nothing. She had in fact become somewhat delirious and moaned a great deal. Occasionally she would look at him as much as to say, "Who are you?" or "Whose house am I in?"

All at once Sonny rose and hurried into the next room. A few moments later she heard the front door close.

ALDA CHANGED SO markedly after he had looked at her in the bathtub that there were times, especially when he had been drinking, that Sonny wondered if some other woman had not slipped into the house and taken her place.

She no longer used her cane, and could walk without stiffness or discomfort. She spent all her time in the kitchen preparing him his "quality" evening meal.

And when they dined in the evening she did everything possible to show her appetite had improved, and she was tasting every dish and morsel that he tasted. "If there is anybody who is being poisoned here," she seemed to say, "I am the first to be poison's victim."

ONE DAY WHEN she felt strong enough, when her grief from Gertrude's death appeared to have dissipated, she dressed in her best tailored outfit, put on a large, almost-never-worn floppy hat, and went directly to lawyer Seaver's office.

His secretary, after having apprised the lawyer of who was waiting, had come out and said he could not see her. She walked past the secretary, opened the door and went directly up to the old man's desk; he, being partially deaf, was unaware for a moment she had entered.

"I want the will changed," Alda said.

"What on earth are you talking about?" he shouted at her.

"Will you lower your voice, Mr. Seavers?" She spoke as she thought Gertrude might have spoken, except of course Mr. Seavers would never have dared roar at her.

"No one can change the will of a deceased person," he cried. "Have you lost what little wits you ever had?"

"I am aware that Gertrude cannot come back and change her will, Mr. Seavers. But I can certainly give away all she has left me. Except the house which I already owned with her and which was mine on her death."

Mr. Seavers put down his pencil and squared his shoulders. He took off his glasses, looked through them and put them back on, and went on scrutinizing Gertrude's cook.

"I want to give all the money to my church," Alda said in a magisterial voice. "And I don't want any discussion. I've thought about it for weeks, and my mind is made up. So much money makes me very unhappy, Mr. Seavers. I won't have it."

He shook his head gravely.

"What is your church?" he inquired at length in a voice which if not kindly was civil.

"The Disciples of Christ, sir."

"But are you certain, Alda!"

"I am certain, or I would not be here. Now are you going to take care of it, or shall I go to another lawyer? Give me your decision."

Mr. Seavers rose then and cleared his throat. "You have changed, Alda. You have changed. I have known you since you were a mere girl. Yes, you have changed."

"It don't matter whether I have changed or not, Mr. Seavers. I hate that money. I will not be a rich woman. I can't stand it. I can't stand being wealthy and have people envy me. I want to be the way I was, and I will be it."

"Very well, if that is your positive last word. But why go to another lawyer? To someone who doesn't know you and never knew Gertrude. Besides, you'd have to go miles to find another. Old man McCready died last week, and he was the only other man practicing law here."

"Then you'll draw up the proper papers, Mr. Seavers?"

"You can count on it, Alda, of course you can."

She stood before him with composed features and almost a haughty angle to her chin. Her gray eyes were for the first time in his memory calm and unafraid.

EVERYONE IN THAT small community soon learned of Alda Bayliss having given away her fortune to the Disciples of Christ. Sonny was of course included among the number who learned of the event.

Alda had told him nothing, had not even hinted at such a decision, such a rash and precipitous turnaround.

"She don't even go to that church too often, and Gertrude used to have to scold her about her lax attendance," Sonny told himself.

He went to Alda's house early on the evening of the news, around five o'clock to be exact, and knocked rather than ringing Gertrude's old silver-throated chimes.

"Come in," said a composed and firm voice.

Sonny took off his hat and stood for a moment on the threshold.

"Close the door, if you please, and don't let in any more draught than already comes through the cracks and crannies of this old house."

"I don't imagine you will want me to come to supper anymore," he began, still standing.

"Why don't you sit down if you are going to say something," Alda spoke in her new, though comfortable tone of authority.

"Will you?" he inquired, sitting down as if the seat of his pants might touch something very hot or very cold.

"Supper always bored me," Alda said. "Cooking for her day after day, you know. Especially with me such a light eater."

"You'll go back to the dainty fare then?"

"I may skip supper altogether," she said. "Now I am free."

"Would you mind explaining that to me, Alda?" Sonny said. "I don't speak sarcastically. I just don't understand."

"The money she left me maybe wasn't enough after all," Alda spoke into her folded hands.

"Would you mind raising your voice?" Sonny said almost penitently.

"I said no bequest could be big enough to repay me for all those suppers I cooked for her. If I accepted the money, I would go on forever being her cook right over her grave. No, I am through with being a cook, through with being Gertrude's heir. I am going to Georgia."

"I'm sorry I walked in on you in the bathroom the other day," he said.

"Well, maybe that was what made me give up the bequest, I sometimes think. As long as I was her heir, as long as I lived under her bounty, people could do that to me. Walk in on me in my bath and have me cook their supper. No, thank you. No thank you, Gertrude."

Sonny stared at her dumbly. She saw the look of both wonder and admiration on his face and flushed under his scrutiny.

"I am happy, if not at ease, for the first time in my life. Not happy maybe, but relieved. That's as near happiness or freedom as I can get. I'm not Gertrude's cook any more. I'm not nobody's. And I will live on dainty fare from now on."

"Soups and salads?" he whispered.

"And an occasional sandwich . . . I'm through with victuals. Let the church worry about her money."

"Would you care for me to come by and do your odd jobs ever, though?" He had risen and was holding his hat by its stained frayed brim.

She picked up a shiny glossy travel folder.

She opened its many pages and maps.

"I'll tell you," she began. "I've been thinking of selling this place and going to one of these islands off the coast of Georgia."

He nodded.

"They say you can live on next to nothing, and the winters ain't fierce like here. . . . This house always reminds me too much of cooking," she added.

"I have to hand it to you," Sonny began again, but she stood up all at once. There was no trace in her movements of her recent stiffness.

ABOUT A MONTH later, towards nightfall, Sonny was eating a warmed-over portion of hunter's stew composed of wild rabbit and squirrel and some not-too-choice pieces of venison, when he heard the tinkle of the doorbell. He started up because nobody had rung that doorbell in a number of years. His friends, and the hunters, walked right in.

"It's you!" he said staring at Alda through the glass partition of the door. "It's you," he repeated.

He did not think to undo the latch and let her in for some seconds. Her appearance was drastically changed, her hair had been cut or shampooed or something, at any rate it looked totally different, and she looked almost younger, certainly thinner, but her face was more wrinkled and drawn. Still, she looked better and more like a woman than he had ever seen her.

"There was nobody to go to," she began after he had motioned for her to be seated on the settee.

He went on eating his stew.

"Do you want some of my supper?" he inquired when she offered to say no more about the reason for her presence here tonight. "It's not your kind of grub," he cautioned her.

"I might take just about a half of what you have on your plate."

He walked out to the kitchen, took a plate off the pantry shelf and served her some hunter's stew.

He was surprised all over again to see her eat it, almost greedily. "They have turned down my gift," she told him.

"Who?" he wondered. Then without waiting for her to reply he said, "I thought you had gone to Georgia to live. You said . . ."

"I didn't like it there. But that's not why I'm back."

He looked down at his empty plate.

"Well," he said gruffly, turning his attention to her.

"They turned down my bequest. The Disciples of Christ," she announced.

He stared at her with that rather imbecilic expression on his face that had always annoyed both Gertrude and her.

"You remember I was going to give them . . ."

"Yeah, yeah, Gertrude's money," he finished for her biliously.

"Well, the preacher and the congregation all voted not to accept it. They felt it would not be appropriate considering the source."

"Considering the source!" He was nearly thunderstruck. He rose with his plate and took it out to the kitchen sink and deposited it there. "What source?" he said coming back into the room.

"Perhaps Gertrude, perhaps me. She was an unbeliever, you know. And they never liked her kind of sculpture, either. They also pointed out I seldom came to church and never worked with the other church members on committees or church business. They have turned down my gift!"

"So you're rich all over again," he said. He had lit his pipe and was engulfing his face and chest in thick smoke.

"Turning down good money like that," he mused.

She began to weep very hard.

"What was wrong with Georgia?" he asked after a while.

"I don't know," she said. "Probably nothing. I am too old to go to a new place but I would have stayed if the Disciples of Christ had kept my money. That was the last straw, their turning down my gift. I feel now like the money is mine."

He rose and went to the window and looked out. "That's some rainstorm coming down," he noted. "You got here just in time." He turned around and stared at her. "Like you planned it that way, didn't you?" He laughed rather hysterically then.

"I just had to talk to somebody. I had my phone shut off when I went to Georgia so I couldn't call you."

"Well, anyhow, Alda," Sonny began shyly now, "let me say, welcome home. It was lonesomer than usual with you in Georgia, let me tell you." He started to move closer to his guest, then stopped abruptly. "I wonder, Alda," he almost stuttered now, "do you think you could join me in a libation in honor of your homecoming?"

"And why ever not, Sonny, for goodness gracious sakes?"

"Well, Gertrude once drew me aside and told me to remember you was brought up never to taste, or allow others in your presence to taste, strong drink."

"Gertrude told you that, did she?" Alda mused, scowling deeply. "Well, look here now, Sonny. That maybe was then, understand, but today is a brand-new day so far as I'm concerned."

Sonny hurried to a little cabinet and pulled out a tall bottle of French brandy and in a trice took up two glasses and poured each of them one-third full of the deep amber drink. Handing her a glass, Sonny said almost in a whisper, "To long life and happiness . . . and let them church folks go . . . you know where."

"Oh, go ahead and swear, Sonny, see if I care." Alda grinned broadly and took a long taste of the brandy. "To your own good health and long life, Sonny, dear friend."

They both smiled comfortably at one another and went on tasting their drinks, and then in the silence that followed they listened with undivided attention to the fury of the storm outside and its pelting the windows in a barrage of sleet and icy rain.

THE WHITE BLACKBIRD

Even before I reached my one hundredth birthday, I had made several wills, and yet just before I put down my signature, Delia Mattlock, my hand refused to form the letters. My attorney was in despair. I had outlived everyone, and there was only one person to whom I could bequeath much, my young godson, and he was not yet twenty-one.

I am putting all this down more to explain the course of events to myself than leave this as a document to posterity, for as I say outside of my godson, Clyde Furness, even my life-long servants have departed this life.

The reason I could not sign my name then is simply this: piece by piece my family jewels have been disappearing over the last few years, and today as I near my one hundred years all of these precious heirlooms one by one have vanished into thin air.

I blamed myself at first, for even as a young girl I used to misplace articles to the great sorrow of my mother. My great grandmother's gold thimble is an example. "You would lose your head if it wasn't tied on," Mother would joke rather sourly. I lost my graduation watch, I lost my diamond engagement ring, and if I had not taken the vow never to remove it, my wedding ring to Will Mattlock would have also taken flight. I will never remove it and will go to my grave wearing it.

But, to return to the jewels. They go back in my family over two hundred years, and yes piece by piece, as I say, they have been disappearing. Take my emerald necklace—its loss nearly finished me. But what of my diamond earrings, the lavaliere over a century old, my ruby earrings—oh why mention them, for to mention them is like a stab in the heart.

I could tell no one for fear they would think I had lost my wits, and then they would blame the servants, who were I knew blameless—such perfect even holy caretakers of me and mine.

But there came the day when I felt I must at least hint to my godson, Clyde Furness, that my jewels were all by now unaccounted for. I hesitated weeks, months before telling him.

About Clyde now. His Uncle Enos told me many times that it was his heartbroken conviction Clyde was somewhat retarded. "Spends all his time in the forest," Enos went on, "failed every grade in school, couldn't add up a column of figures or do his multiplication tables."

"Utter rot and nonsense," I told Enos. "Clyde is bright as a silver dollar. I have taught him all he needs to know, and I never had to teach him twice because he has a splendid memory. In fact, Enos, he is becoming my memory."

Then of course Enos had to die. Only sixty, went off like a puff of smoke while reading the weekly racing news.

So then there was only Clyde and me. We played cards, chess, and then one day he caught sight of my old Ouija board.

I went over to where he was looking at it. That was when I knew I would tell him, of the jewels vanishing of course.

Who else was there. Yet Clyde is a boy I thought, forgetting he was now twenty, for he looked only fourteen to my eyes.

"Put the Ouija board down for a while," I asked him. "I have something to tell you, Clyde." He sat down and looked at me out of his handsome hazel eyes.

I think he already knew what I was to say. But I got out the words. "My heirloom jewels, Clyde, have been taken." My voice sounded far away and more like Uncle Enos's than mine.

"All, Delia?" Clyde whispered, staring still sideways at the Ouija board.

"All, all. One by one over the past three years they have been slipping away. I have almost wondered sometimes if there are spirits, Clyde."

He shook his head.

That was the beginning of even greater closeness between us.

I had given out, at last, my secret. He had accepted it; we were, I saw, like confederates, though we were innocent of course of wrongdoing ourselves. We shared secretly the wrongdoing of someone else.

Or was it *wrongdoing* I wondered. Perhaps the disappearance of the jewels could be understood as the work of some blind power.

But what kind?

My grandfather had a great wine cellar. I had never cared for wine, but in the long winter evenings I finally suggested to Clyde we might try one of the cellar wines.

He did not seem very taken with the idea, for which I was glad, but he obeyed docilely, went down the interminable steps of the cellar and brought back a dusty bottle.

It was a red wine.

We, neither of us, relished it, though I had had it chilled in a bucket of ice, but you see it was the ceremony we both liked. We had to be doing something as we shared the secret.

There were cards, dominoes, Parcheesi, and finally, alas, the Ouija board, but with which we had no luck at all. It sat wordless and morose under our touch.

Often as we sat at cards I would blurt out some thoughtless remark, like once I said, "If we only knew what was before us!"

Either Clyde did not hear, or he pretended I had not spoken.

There was only one subject between us. The missing jewels. And yet I always felt it was wrong to burden a young man with such a loss. But then I gradually saw that we were close, very close. I realized that he had something for me that could only be called love. Uncle Enos was gone, Clyde had never known either mother or father. I was his all, he was my all. The jewels in the end meant nothing to me. A topic for us—no more.

I had been the despair of my mother because as she said I cared little for real property, farmlands, mansions, not even dresses. Certainly not jewels.

"You will be a wealthy woman one day," mother said, "and yet look at you, you care evidently for nothing this world has to offer."

My two husbands must have felt this also. Pouring over their ledgers at night, they would often look up and say, "Delia, you don't care if the store keeps or not, do you?"

"You will be a wealthy woman in time, if only by reason of your jewels," my mother's words of long ago began to echo in my mind when I no longer had them.

My real wealth was in Clyde. At times when I would put my hand through his long chestnut hair a shiver would run through his entire body.

He suffered from a peculiar kind of headache followed by partial deafness and he told me the only thing which helped the pain was when I would pull tightly on his curls.

"Pull away, Delia," he would encourage me.

How it quickened the pulse when he called me by my first name.

Yes, we came to share everything after I told him without warning that bitter cold afternoon. "Clyde, listen patiently. I have only my wedding ring now to my name."

I loved the beautiful expression in his hazel eyes and in the large almost fierce black pupils as he stared at me.

"Do you miss Uncle Enos?" I wondered later that day when we were together.

"No," he said in a sharp, loud voice.

I was both glad and sad because of the remark. Why I felt both things I don't exactly know. I guess it was his honesty.

He was honest like a pane of the finest window glass. I loved his openness. Oh, how I trusted him. And that trust was never betrayed.

I saw at last there was someone I loved. And my love was as pure as his honesty was perfect.

My secret had given us a bond, one to the other.

IN THOSE LONG winter evenings on the edge of the Canadian wildlands, there was little to do but doze, then come awake and talk, sip our wine so sparingly (I would not allow him to have more than a half glass an evening), and there was our talk. We talked about the same things over and again, but we never wearied one another. We were always talking at length on every subject—except the main one. And I knew he was waiting to hear me on that very one.

"How long has it been now, Delia," his voice sounded as if it were coming from a room away.

At first I was tempted to reply, "How long has it been from what?" Instead I answered, "Three years more or less."

"And you told no one in all this time?"

"I could not tell anyone because for a while I thought maybe I had mislaid them, but even as I offered this excuse, Clyde, I knew I could not be mistaken. I knew something, yes let that word be the right one, something was taking my jewels. Oh why do I say my. They never belonged to me, dear boy. I never affected jewels. I did not like the feel of them against my skin or clothes. Perhaps they reminded me of the dead."

"So that is all you know then," he spoke after minutes of silence.

I had to laugh almost uproariously at his tone. "I am laughing, dear Clyde, because you spoke so like an old judge just then. Addressing me as a dubious witness! And dubious witness I am to myself! I accuse myself—of not knowing anything!"

"Could we go to the room where you kept them?" he wondered.

I hesitated.

"No?" he said in a forthright almost ill-humored way.

"It's a long way up the stairs, and I have never liked that big room where I kept them. Then there are the keys. Many many keys to bother and fumble with."

"Then we won't go," he muttered.

"No, we will, Clyde. We will go."

Ah, I had forgotten indeed what a long way up to the big room it was. Even Clyde got a bit tired. Four or five or more flights.

"Well, it's a real castle we live in, my dear," I encouraged him as we toiled upwards.

"You must have a good heart and strong lungs," he said, and he smiled and brought his face very close to mine.

Then I pulled out my flashlight, or as my grandfather would have called it, my torch.

"Now the next flight," I explained, "has poor illumination."

As we approached that terrible door, I brought out the heavy bunch of keys.

"Put this long key, Clyde, in the upper lock, and then this smaller key, when you've unlocked the top one, place it in the lower one here."

He did it well, and we went through the door where of course another bigger door awaited us.

"Now, Clyde, here is the second bunch of keys. Put the upper key to the large keyhole above, give the door a good shove, and we can go in."

He fumbled a little, and I believe I heard him swear for the first time. (Well, his Uncle Enos was a profane old cuss.)

We entered. There were fewer cobwebs now than when I had come in so many months before.

"See all these velvet cases spread out over the oak table there," I said. "In the red velvet large cases were the jewels. Their jewels."

He looked around, and I gave him my torch. But then I remembered there was an upper light, and I turned it on.

He shut off the torch. He seemed in charge of it all and much older than his twenty years then. I felt safe, comfortable, almost sleepy from my trust in him.

"Look there, will you," he exclaimed.

I put on my long-distance glasses and looked where he pointed.

He bent down to touch something on the floor under the red velvet cases.

I took off my glasses and stared.

"What is it, Clyde?" I said.

"Don't you see," he replied in a hushed way. "It's a white feather. A white bird's feather. Very pretty, isn't it." He raised up the feather toward my trembling hand.

A STRANGE CALM descended on us both after Clyde found the white feather. At first I was afraid to touch it. Clyde coaxed me to take it in my hand, and only after repeated urgings on his part did I do so.

At that moment the calm descended on me as many years ago during one of my few serious illnesses old sharp-eyed Doctor Noddy had insisted I take a tincture of opium.

Why, I wondered, did the glimpse of a white bird's feather confer both upon me and Clyde this unusual calm. As if we had found the jewels, or at least had come to understand by what means the jewels had been taken. I say *us* advisedly, for by now Clyde and I were as close as mother and grandson, even husband and wife. We were so close that sometimes at night I would in my bed shudder and words (I was unaware of where they came from) filled my mouth.

Clyde more than the jewels then—let me repeat—was my all, but the jewels were important I realized dimly only because they were the bond holding us together.

That evening I allowed Clyde a little more than half a glass of red wine.

"The only pleasure, Clyde," I addressed him, "is in sipping. Gulping, swallowing spoil all the real delicate pleasure."

I saw his mind was on the white feather.

He had put it on the same table the Ouija board rested on.

"We should see it in a safe place," Clyde said gazing at the feather.

His statement filled me with puzzlement. I wanted to say why ever should we, but I was silent. I spilled some wine on my fresh, white dress. He rose at once and went to the back kitchen and came forward with a little basin filled with water. He carefully and painstakingly wiped away the red stain.

"There," Clyde said looking at where the stain had been.

When he had taken back the basin, he sat very quietly for a while, his eyes half-closed, and then:

"I say we should put it in a safe place."

"Is there any such, Clyde, now the jewels have been taken."

"Just the same I think we should keep the feather out where it is visible, don't you?"

"It is certainly a beautiful one," I remarked.

He nodded faintly and then raising his voice said, "It's a clue."

My calm all at once disappeared. I put the wineglass down for fear I might spill more.

"Had you never seen the feather before, Delia?" he inquired.

The way he said my name revealed to me that we were confederates, though I would never have used this word to his face. It might have pained him. But we were what the word really meant.

"I think it will lead us to find your jewels," he finished, and he drank, thank heavens, still so sparingly of the wine.

I dared not ask him what he meant.

"I think the place for the feather," I spoke rather loudly, "is in that large collection of cases over there where Cousin Berty kept her assortment of rare South American butterflies."

"I don't think so," Clyde said after a bit.

"Then where would you want it?" I said.

"On your music stand by your piano where it's in full view."

"Full view?" I spoke almost crossly.

"Yes, for it's the clue," he almost shouted. "The feather is our clue. Don't you see?"

He sounded almost angry, certainly jarring, if not unkind.

I dared not raise my wineglass, for I would have surely at that moment spilled nearly all of it, and I could not have stood for his cleaning my white dress again that evening. It was too great a ceremony for ruffled nerves.

"There it shall be put, Clyde," I said at last, and he smiled.

HAVE I FORGOTTEN to tell how else we whiled away the very long evenings? Near the music stand where we had placed the feather stood the unused, old grand piano, by some miracle still fairly in tune.

Clyde Furness had one of the most beautiful voices I have ever heard. In my youth I had attended the opera. In my day I heard all the great tenors, but it was Clyde's voice which moved me almost to a swoon. We played what is known as parlor songs, ancient, ageless songs. My hands surprised him when he saw how nimble and quick they still were on the keys. My hands surprised me as a matter of fact. When he sang, my fingers moved like a young woman's. When I played the piano alone, they were stiff and hit many wrong keys.

But I saw then what he meant. As I played the parlor songs my eyes rested not only on him but on the feather. What he called—the clue.

I had suggested one or two times that, now Uncle Enos had departed, Clyde should move in with me. "There's lots of room here; you can choose what part of the house you like and make yourself to home, godson."

Whenever I'd mentioned his moving in up till then, he had always pouted like a small boy. The day we found the feather I felt something had changed not only in me, in the house, in the very air we breathed—something had changed in him.

As I went up to kiss him goodnight that evening, I noticed over his upper lip there was beginning to grow ever so softly traces of his beard.

"What is it?" I inquired when he hesitated at the door. He touched the place on his cheek where I had kissed him.

"Are you sure as sure can be, you still want me to move my things here?" Clyde asked.

"I want you to, of course. You know that. Why should you walk two miles every day to Uncle Enos's and back when it's here the welcome mat is out."

"You certainly have the room don't you," he joked. "How many rooms have you got?" he grinned.

"Oh I've almost forgotten, Clyde."

"Forty?" he wondered.

I smiled. I kissed him again.

The feather had changed everything. I must have looked at it every time I went near the piano. I touched it occasionally. It seemed to move when I picked it up as if it had breath. It was both warm and cool and so soft except for its strong shaft. I once touched it to my lips, and some tears formed in my eyes.

"To think that Clyde is going to be under my roof," I spoke aloud and put the feather back on the music stand.

DR. NODDY PAID his monthly visit shortly after Clyde had come to stay with me.

Dr. Noddy was an extremely tall man, but as if apologetic for his height he stooped and was beginning to be terribly bent so that his head was never held high but always leaned over like he was everlastingly writing prescriptions. This visit was remarkable by the fact he acted unsurprised to see Clyde Furness in my company. One would have thought from the doctor's attitude Clyde had always lived with me.

He began his cursory examination of me—pulse, listening to my lungs and heart, rolling back my eyelids, having me stick out my tongue.

"The tongue and the whites of the eyes tell everything," he once said.

Then he gave me another box of the little purple pills to be taken on rising and on getting into bed.

"And shan't we examine the young man then," Dr. Noddy spoke as if to himself.

He had Clyde remove his shirt and undershirt much to the poor boy's embarrassment. I went into an adjoining closet and brought out one of my grandfather's imported dressing gowns and insisted Clyde put this on to avoid further humiliation.

Dr. Noddy examined Clyde's ears carefully, but his attention seemed to wander over to the music stand. After staring at it for some time and changing his eyeglasses, he then looked at Clyde's hair and scalp and finally took out a pocket comb of his own and combed the boy's hair meticulously.

"Delia, he has parted his hair wrong. Come over here and see for yourself."

I took my time coming to where the doctor was examining my godson, and my deliberateness annoyed him. But all the time nonetheless he kept looking over at the music stand.

"I want you to part his hair on his left side, not on his right. His hair is growing all wrong as a result. And another thing, look in his right ear. See all that wax."

Dr. Noddy now went over to his little doctor's bag and drew out a small silver instrument of some kind.

"I will give you this for his ear. Clean out the wax daily. Just as I am doing now." Clyde gave out a little cry more of surprise than pain as the doctor cleaned his ear of the wax.

"Now then, we should be fine." But Dr. Noddy was no longer paying any attention to us. He was staring at the music stand, and finally he went over to it. He straightened up as much as age and rheumatism would permit.

It was the feather of course he had been staring at so intently, so continuously!

He picked the feather up and came over to where I was studying the instrument he had recommended for Clyde's ear.

"Where did this come from?" he spoke in almost angry, certainly accusatory tones.

"Oh that," I said, and I stuttered for the first time since I was a girl.

"Where did it come from?" he now addressed Clyde in a kind of tone of rage.

"Well, sir," Clyde began but failed to continue.

"Clyde and I found it the other day when we went to the fourth story, Dr. Noddy."

"You climbed all the way up there, did you," the old man mumbled, but his attention was all on the feather. "May I keep this for the time being," he said turning brusquely to me.

"If you wish, doctor, of course," I told him when I saw his usual bad temper was asserting itself.

"Unless, Delia, you have some use for it."

Before I could think I said, "Only as a clue, Dr. Noddy."

"What?" Dr. Noddy almost roared.

Taking advantage of his deafness, I soothed him by saying, "We thought it rather queer, didn't we, Clyde, that there was a feather in the room where I used to keep my grandmother's jewels."

Whether Dr. Noddy heard this last statement or not, I do not know. He put the feather in his huge leather wallet and returned the wallet inside his outer coat with unusual and irritable vigor.

"I will be back then in a month. Have Clyde here drink more well water during the day." Staring at me then, he added, "He's good company I take for you, Delia Mattlock."

Before I could even say yes, he was gone, slamming the big front door behind him.

Dr. Noddy's visit had spoiled something. I do not know exactly how otherwise to describe it. A kind of gloom settled over everything.

Clyde kept holding his ear and touching his beautiful hair and his scalp.

"Does your ear pain you, Clyde?" I finally broke the silence.

"No," he said after a very long pause. "But funny thing is I hear now better."

"We always called earwax beeswax when I was a girl," I said. Clyde snickered a little but only I believe to be polite.

"He took the feather, didn't he," Clyde came out of his reverie.

"And I wonder why, Clyde. Of course, Dr. Noddy is among other things a kind of outdoorsman. A naturalist they call it. Studies animals and birds."

"Oh that could explain it then, maybe."

"Not quite," I disagreed. "Did you see how he kept staring at the feather on the music stand?"

"I did. That's about all he did while he was here."

I nodded. "I never take his pills. Oh, I did at the beginning, but they did nothing for me that I could appreciate. Probably they are made of sugar. I've heard doctors often give some of their patients sugar pills."

"He certainly changed the part in my hair. Excuse me while I look in the mirror over there now, Delia."

Clyde went over to the fifteen foot high mirror brought from England so many years gone by. He made little cries of surprise or perhaps dismay as he looked at himself in the glass.

"I don't look like me," he said gruffly and closed his eyes.

"If you don't like the new part in your hair, we can just comb it back the way it was."

"No, I think maybe I like the new way it's parted. Have to get used to it I suppose, that's all."

"Your hair would look fine with any kind of a part you chose. You have beautiful hair."

He mumbled a thank you and blushed.

"I had a close girl-chum at school, Irma Stairs. She had the most beautiful hair in the world. The color they call Titian. She let it grow until it fell clear to below her knees. When she would let it all down sometimes just to show me, I could not believe my eyes. It made me a little uneasy. I like your hair though, Clyde, even better."

"What do you think he wants to keep the white feather for?" Clyde wondered.

We walked toward the piano just then as if from a signal.

I opened the book of parlor songs, and we began our singing and playing hour.

He sang "Come Where My Love Lies Dreaming." It made the tears come. Then he sang a rollicking sailor's song.

But things were not right after the doctor's visit.

"It's time for our glass of wine," I said, rising from the piano. "We need it after old Dr. Noddy."

A GREAT UNEASINESS, even sadness, now came over both of us.

I have for many years had the bad habit of talking to myself or, what was considered worse, talking out my own thoughts aloud even in front of company.

Dr. Noddy's having walked off with the feather Clyde and I had found in the jewel room was the source of our discontent.

Thinking Clyde was dozing after his sipping his wine, I found myself speaking aloud of my discomfiture and even alarm.

"He is making us feel like the accused," I said, and then I added more similar thoughts.

To my surprise I heard Clyde answering me, which was very unlike himself.

I felt we were in some ancient Italian opera singing back to one another, echoing one another's thoughts.

"I didn't like the way he stared at us with his holding the feather like it was proof of something," Clyde started up.

"Exactly, godson. The very words I was trying to express when I thought you were dozing."

"What does he aim to do with it?" Clyde raised his voice.

"And what does he mean to do with it regarding us," I took up his point. "He acts more like a policeman or detective than a doctor where the feather is concerned."

"You take the words right out of my mouth," he spoke loudly.

"Oh Clyde, Clyde, whatever would I do without you."

"You'd do all right, Delia. You know you would." He picked up the empty wineglass, and to my considerable shock he spat into it. "It's me," he said, "who wouldn't know where to turn if I wasn't here with you. I would be the one didn't know up from down."

"With all your talents, dear boy," I cried almost angry he had spoken so against himself. "Never!"

"Never what, Delia. You know how I failed in school and disappointed Uncle Enos."

"Failed him, failed school! Poppycock! Then it was their fault if you did. Uncle Enos adored you. You could do no wrong in his eyes. Oh if he was only here to tell us about the feather. And about that wretched doctor. He would set us straight."

"Now, now," Clyde said rising, and he came over to my chair, and all at once he knelt down and looked up into my troubled face.

"Does old Dr. Noddy know your jewels have disappeared?"

"I think so."

"You think so?"

"I'm sure I told him when I was having an attack of the neuralgia that they had all vanished."

"And what did he say then?"

"It's not so much what he said, he never says much, it was the way he stared at me when I said, 'All my jewels are gone.'"

"Stared how?"

"As he stared at us today when he held the feather. Stared as if I had done something wrong. As if I had done away with my own jewels."

"Oh, he couldn't think that against you, Delia."

"He thinks against everybody. He feels anybody who needs him and his services has something to be held against them. If we are ailing, then we are to blame. That's what I gather from old Dr. Noddy."

"And now, Delia," he said rising and standing behind my chair so that I could feel his honey sweet breath against my hair. "And now," he went on, "we have to wait like the accused in a court of law."

"Exactly, exactly. And oh my stars, what on earth can he do with a feather anyhow? Make *it* confess?"

We both laughed.

"I can't go to bed on all of this we're facing now," I told Clyde. "I am going to the kitchen and make us some coffee."

"Let me make it, Delia."

"No no, I am the cook here and the coffee maker. You make it too weak. I must stay alert. And we must put Doc Noddy on trial here tonight before he can put us in the witness box and call us liars to our face."

With that I went into the kitchen and took down the jar of Arabian coffee, got out the old coffee grinder, and let Clyde (who had followed me without being asked), let *him* grind the beans.

"What a heavenly aroma," I said when our chores was finished. "And I made it with well water of course, for as old Doc Noddy says, you must drink well water religiously, dear lad."

We felt less threatened, less on trial at any rate, drinking the Arabian brew.

Then a great cloud of worry and fear descended upon me. I did all I could to conceal my feelings from my godson.

The source of my fear was, of course, who else, Doctor Noddy.

I recalled in the long, heavy burden of memory that Dr. Noddy was nearly as old as I, at least he must have been far into his eighties at this time. But it was not his age which weighed upon me. It was the memory of Dr. Noddy having been accused a half century or more ago of practicing hypnotism on his patients. And also being suspected of giving his older patients a good deal of opium. But the opium did not concern me now, has indeed never worried me. He only gave it in any case to those of us who were so advanced in age we could no longer endure the pain of, or the weight of, so many years, so much passed time.

No, what gave me pause was hypnotism if indeed he ever had practiced it. His taking away the feather had brought back this old charge. But my godson sensed my sorrow. He watched me with his beautiful if almost pitiless hazel eyes.

At last he took a seat on a little hand-carved stool beside me. He took my right hand in his and kissed it.

"You are very troubled, Delia," he said at last. He seemed to be looking at the gnarled very blue veins on the hand he had just kissed.

"I am that," I said after a lengthy silence on my part.

"You don't need to say more, Delia. We understand one another."

"I know that, godson, but see here, I want to share with you all that is necessary for me to share. I want you to have everything you deserve."

"I don't deserve much."

"Never say that again. You don't know how precious you are, Clyde, and that is because you *are* perfection."

He turned a furious red and faced away from me.

"Let me think how I am to tell you, Clyde," I spoke so low he cupped his ear and then he again took my hand in his.

"I can see it's something you've got to share."

"Unwillingly, Clyde, so unwillingly. Perhaps though when I tell you, you won't think it's worth troubling about."

He nodded encouragement.

"Clyde, years ago before even your parents were born, before the days of Uncle Enos, Dr. Noddy was charged with having practiced hypnotism on his patients."

Clyde's mouth came open, and then he closed it tight. I thought his lips had formed a cuss word.

We sat in silence for a lengthy while.

"That is why his taking away the feather has worried me."

"And worries me now," he almost gasped.

"My worry over the white feather finally recalled the charge he had hypnotized some of his patients."

"But what is the connection," he wondered, "between a bird's feather and hypnotism."

"I don't know myself, Clyde. Only I feel the two have a connection we don't understand."

He smiled a strange smile.

"We must be calm and patient. Maybe nothing will happen at all, and we will resume our old, quiet evenings," I said.

He released my hand softly.

Looking into his face, yes I saw what I had feared. My trouble had fallen upon him. And so that long evening drew to its close.

For a whole month we could do nothing but wait in suspense for Dr. Noddy's return. Now that I come to think of it, how happy I would have been if there had been no Dr. Noddy! Yes, I do think and believe that had he never appeared out of the fog and the snow and the bitter winds, Clyde and I would have been happy and without real sorrow forever. Dr. Noddy having found the clue, the feather, began to dig and delve, uncover and discover, sift evidence, draw conclusions and then shatter all our peace and love along with our parlor song evenings and Clyde's solos on the Jew's harp. All was to be spoiled, shattered, brought to nothing.

But then as someone was to tell me much later (perhaps it was one of the Gypsy fortune-tellers who happen by in this part of the world), someone said to me, *"Had it not been Dr. Noddy, there would have been someone else to have brought sorrow and change into your lives."*

"Then call it destiny why don't you," I shouted to this forgotten person, Gypsy or preacher or peddler or whoever it was made the point. Oh, well then, just call it Dr. Noddy and be done with it.

"IN OUR PART of the world nature sometimes is enabled to work out phenomena not observed by ordinary people," Dr. Noddy began on his next visit, sounding a little like a preacher.

Dr. Noddy had tasted the wine Clyde had brought him from the cellar even more sparingly, if possible, than was our own custom.

(I had felt the physician needed wine to judge by his haggard and weary appearance.)

To my embarrassment he fished out a piece of cork, tiny but as I saw very distasteful to him.

"Fetch Doctor a clean glass," I suggested to Clyde.

Dr. Noddy meanwhile went on talking about Nature's often indulging in her own schemes and experiments, indifferent to man.

"She in the end can only baffle us. Our most indefatigable scholars and scientists finally admit defeat and throw up their hands to acknowledge her inscrutable puissance."

I looked into my wineglass as if also searching for pieces of cork. Clyde had meanwhile brought Dr. Noddy a sparkling-clean glass. He had opened a new bottle and poured out fresh wine.

"Dr. Noddy was saying, Clyde, whilst you were out of earshot, that Nature is an inscrutable goddess," I summarized the Doctor's speech.

"Yes," Clyde answered and gave me a look inviting instruction. I could only manage a kind of sad, sour smile.

"The feather," Dr. Noddy began again pulling it out now from his huge wallet, "is one of her pranks."

Clyde and I exchanged quick glances.

"But we should let Clyde here expatiate on Dame Nature's hidden ways and purposes. Your godson was known from the time he came to live with Uncle Enos as a true son of the wilderness, a boon companion to wild creatures and the migratory fowl."

Clyde lowered his head down almost to the rim of his wineglass.

"Our young man therefore must have known that nearby there lived a perfect battalion of white crows, or perhaps they were white blackbirds!"

At that moment Clyde gave out a short, stifled gasp which may have chilled Dr. Noddy into silence. To my uneasiness I saw Dr. Noddy rise and go over to my godson. He took both Clyde's hands and held them tightly and then slowly allowed the hands to fall to his sides. Dr. Noddy then touched Clyde's eyes with both his hands. When the doctor removed his hands, Clyde's eyes were closed.

"Please tell us now," Dr. Noddy moved even closer to Clyde, "if you know of the birds I am speaking of."

"I am not positive," Clyde said in a stern, even grand tone, so unlike the way he usually spoke. He kept his eyes still closed.

"You must have known there were white crows or white blackbirds, what some who delve into their histories call a sport of nature."

"I often thought," Clyde spoke musingly and in an almost small-boy voice now, "often would have swore I saw white birds in the vicinity of the Bell Tower."

"The Bell Tower!" I could not help but gasp. The Bell Tower was one of the many deserted large buildings which I had long ago sold to Uncle Enos at a very low price.

"You see," Dr. Noddy turned to me. "We have our witness!"

"But what can it all mean," I spoke with partial vexation. "It is so late, Dr. Noddy, in time I mean. Must we go round Robin Hood's barn before you tell us what you have found out."

"This feather," Dr. Noddy now held it again and almost shook it in my face, "let Clyde expand upon it." The old man turned now to my godson. "Open your eyes, Clyde!" He extended the feather to Clyde. "Tell us what you think now, my boy."

Clyde shrank back in alarm from the feather. "It could certainly be from a white crow if there is such a bird," my godson said.

"Or a white blackbird, Clyde?"

Clyde opened his eyes wide and stared at his questioner. "All I know, Delia," Clyde turned to me, "is yes I have seen white birds flying near the Bell Tower, and sometimes . . ."

"And sometimes," Dr. Noddy made as if to rise from his chair.

"Sometimes flying into the open or the broken windows of the Bell Tower."

"And did you ever see a white crow carrying anything in its beak when you saw it making its way to your Bell Tower?" Clyde's eyes closed again. "I may have, sir, yes I may have spied something there, but you see," and he again turned his eyes now opened to me, "you see, I was so startled to glimpse a large white bird against the high green trees and the dark sky, for near the Bell Tower the sky always looks dark. I was startled, and I was scared." Some quick small tears escaped from his right eye.

"And could those things the white bird carried, Clyde, could they have been jewels?"

At that very moment, the wineglass fell from Clyde's hand and he slipped from his chair and fell prone to the thick carpet below.

Dr. Noddy rushed to his side. I hurried also and bent over my prostrate godson.

"Oh, Doctor Noddy, for pity's sake, he is not dead is he!"

Dr. Noddy turned a deprecatory gaze in my direction. "Help me carry him to that big sofa yonder," he said in reply.

Oh, I was more than opposed by then to Dr. Noddy. Seeing my godson lying there as if in his coffin. I blamed it all on the old physician. "You frightened him, doctor," I shouted.

I was surprised at my own angry words leveled against him. I would look now to my godson lying there as if passed over and then return my gaze to Noddy. I must have actually sworn, for when I came out of my fit of anger I heard the old man say, as if he was also in a dream, "I never would have thought I would hear you use such language. And against someone who has only your good at heart, Delia. Only your good!"

Taking me gently by the hand he ushered me into a seldom used little sitting room. The word hypnotism seemed at that moment to be not a word but a being; perhaps *it* was a bird flying about the room.

"What I want to impart to you, Delia," the old physician began, "is simply this: I must now take action. I and I alone must pay a visit to the Bell Tower. For in its ruined masonry there lies the final explanation of the mystery."

The very mention of the Bell Tower had always filled me with a palsy-like terror; so when Dr. Noddy announced that he must go there I could not find a word to say to him.

"Did you hear me, Delia," he finally spoke in a querulous but soft tone.

"If you think you must, dear friend," I managed to reply. "If there is no other way."

"But now we must look in on Clyde," he said after a pause. At the same time he failed to make a motion to rise. A heavy long silence ensued on both our parts when unexpectedly my godson himself entered our private sitting room. We both stared without greeting him.

Clyde looked refreshed after his slumber. His face had resumed its high coloring, and he smiled at us as he took a seat next to Dr. Noddy.

"I have been telling Delia, Clyde, that I must make a special visit to the Bell Tower."

Clyde's face fell and a slight paleness again spread over his features.

"Unless you object, Clyde," the doctor added.

As I say, the very mention of the Bell Tower had always filled me with dread and loathing. But I had never told Clyde or Dr. Noddy the partial reason for my aversion. I did not tell them now what it was which troubled me. My great uncle had committed suicide in the Tower over a hundred years ago, and then later my cousin Keith had fallen from the top of the edifice to his death.

These deaths had been all but forgotten in our village, and perhaps even I no longer remembered them until Dr. Noddy announced he was about to pay a visit there.

While I was lost in these musings I suddenly came to myself in time to see Noddy buttoning up his greatcoat preparatory to leaving.

"But you can't be paying your visit there now!" I cautioned him. "What with a bad storm coming on and with the freezing cold and snow what it is."

"This is one visit that should not be postponed, Delia! So stop once and for all your fussing."

He actually blew a kiss to me and raised his hand to Clyde in farewell.

I watched him go from the big front window. The wind had changed and was blowing from a northeast direction. The sycamore trees were bending almost to the ground in a fashion such as I could not ever recall.

I came back to my seat.

"Are you warm enough, Delia?" Clyde asked, smiling concern.

"Clyde, listen," I began, gazing at him intently.

"Yes, Delia, speak your mind," he said gaily, almost as if we were again partaking of the jollity of our evenings.

"We must be prepared, Clyde, for whatever our good doctor will discover in the Bell Tower," I said in a lackluster manner.

Clyde gazed down at the carpet under his feet.

I felt then that if I were not who I was I would be afraid to be alone that night with Clyde Furness. But I had gone beyond fear.

"Shan't we have our evening wine, Delia," he said, and as he spoke fresh disquietude began again.

"Please, dear boy, let's have our wine."

We drank if possible even more sparingly. I believe indeed we barely touched the wineglass to our lips. Time passed in a church-like silence as we sat waiting for the doctor's return. I more than Clyde could visualize the many steps the old man must climb before he reached the top floor of the Tower. And I wondered indeed if he would be able to summon the strength to make it. Perhaps the visit thither would be too much for his old bones.

It was the longest evening I can recall. And what made it even more painful was that as I studied my godson I realized he was no longer the Clyde Furness I had been so happy with. No, he had changed. I studied his face for a sign but there was no sign—his face was closed to me. Then began a current of words which will remain with me to the end of my days:

"It's hard for me to believe, Clyde, our good Doctor's theory that it is a bird which has taken my ancestors' jewels."

Clyde straightened up to gaze at me intently.

"Ah, but, Delia, do you understand how hard it has been for me over and again these many weeks to have to listen to your doubts and suspicions!"

"But doubts and suspicions, Clyde, have no claim upon you where I am concerned."

"No claim," he spoke in a bitterness which took me totally by surprise. "Perhaps, Delia, not in your mind, but what about mine?"

"But Clyde, for God in heaven's sake, you can't believe that I regard you as . . ." But I could not finish the sentence. Clyde finished it for me.

"That I am the white blackbird, Delia? For that is what you think in your inmost being."

Then I cried out, "Never, never has such a thought crossed my mind."

"Perhaps not in your waking hours, Delia. But in your deepest being, in your troubled sleeping hours, Delia, I feel you think I am the white blackbird."

I could think of no response to make then to his dreadful avalanche of words launched against me. Nothing, I came to see, could dispel his thought that I considered him the thief, the white blackbird himself. My mouth was dry. My heart itself was stilled. My godson was lost to me I all at once realized. He would never again be the young and faithful evening companion who had given my life its greatest happiness. As he returned my gaze I saw that he understood what I felt, and he looked away not only in sadness but grief. I knew then he would leave me.

Yet we had to sit on like sentinels, our worry growing as the minutes and the hours slipped by.

It was long past midnight, and we sat on. We neither of us wanted more wine. But at last Clyde insisted he make some coffee, and I was too troubled and weak to offer to make it myself.

As we were sipping our second cup of the Arabian brew, we heard footsteps and then the banging on the door with a heavy walking stick.

Clyde and I both cried out with relief when Dr. Noddy, covered with wet snow and carrying three parcels stomped in, his white breath covering his face like a mask.

"Help me, my boy," Dr. Noddy scolded. He was handing Clyde three packages wrapped in cloth of old cramoisie velvet. "And be careful. Put them over there on that big oak table, why don't you, where they used to feed the threshers in summers gone by."

As Clyde was carrying the parcels to the oak table, I saw with surprise Dr. Noddy pick up Clyde's second cup of Arabian coffee and gulp it all down at one swallow. He wiped his mustache on a stray napkin near the cup!

"Help me off with my greatcoat, Delia, for I'm frozen to the bone and my hands are cakes of ice."

As soon as I had helped him off with his coat and Clyde had hung it on a hall tree, Dr. Noddy collapsed on one of the larger settees. He took off his spectacles and wiped them and muttered something inaudible.

For a while, because he kept his eyes closed, I thought the doctor had fallen into one of those slumbers I had observed in him before. My own eyes felt heavy as lead.

Then I heard him speaking in louder than usual volume: "I have fetched back everything, Delia, that was missing or lost to you. And I have wrapped what I've found in scraps and shreds from the crimson hanging curtains of the Bell Tower."

His voice had an unaccustomed ring of jubilee to it.

"Bring out the first package, Clyde," he shouted the orders and as he spoke he waved both his arms like the conductor of a band.

Clyde carried the first bundle morosely and placed it on the coffee table before us.

"Now, Delia, let us begin!" Noddy snapped one of the cords with his bone pocketknife and began undoing the bundle of its coverings with a ferocious swiftness.

I felt weak as water as he exposed to view one after the other my diamond necklace, my emerald brooch, my ruby rings, my pearl necklace, and last of all my sapphire earrings!

"Tell me they are yours, Delia," Noddy roared as only a deaf man can.

I nodded.

"And don't weep," he cautioned me. "We'll have no bawling here tonight after the trouble I've been to in the Tower!"

At a signal from the doctor, Clyde fetched to the table even more doggedly the second package, and this time my godson watched as the doctor undid the wrappings.

"Tell us what you see," Dr. Noddy scolded and glowered.

"My gold necklace," I answered, "and yes, my diamond choker, and those are my amethyst rings and that priceless lavaliere, and oh see, my long-forgotten gold bracelet."

I went on and on. But my eyes were swimming with the tears he had forbidden me to shed.

Then the third bundle was produced, unwrapped and displayed before us as if I were presiding at Judgment Day itself.

"They are all mine, doctor," I testified, avoiding his direful stare. I touched the gems softly and looked away.

"What treasures," Clyde kept mumbling and shaking his head.

My eyes were all on Clyde rather than the treasures, for I took note again that it was not so much perhaps Dr. Noddy who had taken him away from me, it was the power of the treasures themselves which had separated my godson and me forever.

And so the jewels, which I had never wanted in my possession from the beginning, were returned again to be mine. Their theft or disappearance had plagued me of course over the years as a puzzle will tease and torment one, but now seeing them again in my possession all I could think of was their restoration was the cause of Clyde's no longer being mine, no longer loving me! I was unable to explain this belief even to myself but I knew it was the truth.

The next day Clyde holding his few belongings in a kind of sailor's duffel bag, his eyes desperately looking away from my face, managed to get out the words: "Delia, my dear friend, now the weather is beginning to clear, I do feel I must be returning to Uncle Enos's so I can look after his property as I promised him in his last hours."

Had he stabbed me with one of my servants' hunting knives his words could not have struck me deeper. I could barely hold out my hand to him.

"I have, you know, too, a bounden duty to see his property is kept as he wanted me to keep it," he could barely whisper. "But should you need me you have only to call, and I will respond."

I am sure a hundred things came to both our lips as we stood facing one another in our farewell. Instead all we could do was gaze for a last time into each other's eyes.

With Clyde's return "in bounden duty" to his Uncle Enos's, there went our evenings of wine sipping and parlor songs and all the other things that had made for me complete happiness.

I was left then with only the stolen jewels, stolen according to our Dr. Noddy by a breed of white blackbird known as far back as remote antiquity as creatures irresistibly attracted to steal anything which was shining bright and dazzling.

SHORTLY AFTER CLYDE had departed for his uncle's, I had called some world-famous jewel merchants for a final appraisal of the treasures. The appraisers came on the heels of my godson's departure. The men reminded me of London policemen or detectives, impeccable gentlemen, formal and with a stultifying politeness. As they appraised my jewels, however, even they would pause from time to time and briefly stare at me with something like incomprehension. They would break the silence then to say in their dry clear voices: "Is nothing missing, ma'am?"

"Nothing at all," I would reply to the same question put to me again and again.

I had by then taken such a horror to the jewels and to their beauty which everyone had always spoken of with bated breath that even to draw near them brought on me a kind of fit of shuddering.

After I had signed countless pages of documents, the appraisers hauled the whole collection off to a famous safety vault in Montreal.

Then for the first time in years I felt a kind of relief that would have been, if not happiness, a kind of benediction or thanksgiving, had I not been so aware I had lost forever my evenings with my godson.

BRAWITH

Moira went for Brawith at the Vets Hospital despite the fact everybody told her it would not work out, and should he get worse, she would bear the blame for his death. There was no way for him to get well the same people claimed, and all her trouble would go for nothing. But Moira was his grandmother, she reminded everyone, and so she took him home to Flempton where she had a nice property near the copse. The river is close by, and there are lots of woodlands, and the town is only about a mile or so due west on a gravel road not too bad to walk on.

Brawith had been nearly made a sieve of from the war, as people in the hospital said, whether from bullets or an explosion or from both factors.

Brawith seldom spoke. When you asked him questions he blinked and looked at his nails.

Moira did not know how bad off he was until he had been home with her about a week or so, and then it was too late to be sorry. She was to have many a heartache over her decision to take him from the Vets Hospital, but if she sometimes was sorry, she never let on to anybody about what she felt.

Her cousin Keith came in occasionally and shook his head but said nothing and left after a short visit. Brawith's parents were dead and gone so long as to be nearly forgotten. They died long before the war. Moira was Brawith's grandmother on his mother's side. Moira had not known Brawith very well when he was a boy. And now she saw she hardly knew him once he had come to stay; she had certainly not known to begin with he had no control over his bowels and carried a roll of toilet paper wherever he went.

After he was back home with her awhile he seemed to get worse, but Moira would not hear of him going back to the hospital ward.

Most of the time Brawith sat quietly in a big chair remodeled from an antique rocker and looked out over the stretch of woods visible from the back door.

Strangely enough he had a fair appetite, and she spent most of her hours cooking.

"If I have made a mistake," Moira began a letter to her sister Lily who lived ten miles away, "I will not back down now. I will stand by my decision, let whoever say what they may." For some reason she found she could not finish the letter.

Brawith liked to walk to the post office and mail her letters, and so she would write something to her other relatives on a government postcard, and he would take it to the main post office, carrying the roll of toilet paper along with him. It was this habit of his more than what happened later on that drew attention to him. Moira did not have the heart to tell him not to take the roll of paper along, and besides she knew he needed it.

"If he did all that for his country, why can't people look the other way if they see him coming," she wrote Lily.

"Brawith, come in and rest. Take the weight off your poor feet," Moira said to him one hot August noon when he had been to the post office for her. "You're flushed from the walk in the sun!" She tried to take the roll of toilet paper away from him, but he held on tight and would not let her.

After that he always held on to it, whether at the dining table or sitting on the back porch watching the woods, or taking his walks to the post office.

Gradually it occurred even to her that he was slowly oozing from almost every pore in his body, and it was not that he did not think with words anymore, or not hear words, his attention was entirely occupied by the soft sounds like whispers arising from the wet parts of his insides, which shattered by wounds and hurts had begun gently coming out from within him or so it seemed, so that all his insides would one day peacefully come out; so his insides and his outer skin would merge finally into one complete wet mass. Moira began to understand this also, and she was never out of eyeshot of him except when he went on his walks. She did not ever relent then on having taken him from the Vets Hospital. She would not admit it was a mistake and agree to return him back there. No, he was her own, he was the only human being she felt who looked up to her, and she would keep him by her side therefore from this day forth.

Her reward, she always said, came when he would once or twice a week, no more, look up at her and say, *"Moira."* It meant thank you, she supposed, it meant, even love she felt. His soft glossy brown hair and beard, thick almost as the pelt of an animal, were bathed in constant streams of sweat. She would touch his hair at such moments, and her hand came away as wet as if she had wrung out a mop. His hair showed none of the affliction his body had undergone but was, one might almost say, blossoming. His hair and his beard had not been cut in the new fashion of nowadays.

After a few evenings she came to the understanding that Brawith did not sleep. She slept very little herself, but she did fall off toward morning for two to three hours of slumber. The realization he did not sleep at all harmed her peace of mind more than any other fact. She did not regret nonetheless her action. She had this home, and the wide expanse of land around it, and she was his own flesh and blood and there was nothing she would not do for him. Besides she had never wanted him in the Vets Hospital in the first place, but her cousin Keith had arranged that. She had countermanded his action—hence Keith's anger against her.

It had all begun the day when she was visiting Brawith in the hospital just as the sun was getting ready to go down. There was nobody in his ward at that moment but a colored man mopping the floor. She had taken Brawith's hand in her own, and not letting go her hold, she had spoken as if begging on her knees, "Brawith, do you choose Grandma's own house or this place? Tell me the truth." He had looked at her like a small child summoned in the middle of night by fire engines. He had despite his confusion tried to keep his mind on what it was she was saying, and at last after a long pause, he had said: "Grandmother's house," and nodded repeatedly.

Thereafter against all advice, instruction and pleas, against the opinion of the doctors and nurses who had talked and even shouted at her, she had taken him away with her. One nurse had handed her the roll of toilet paper as she was going out the door with him. Moira had been too astonished not to receive it, and as if he sensed her dilemma, Brawith took the roll from her, holding it in the manner of one who would receive a present, and so they went down the long flight of white clean-swept steps into Mr. Kwis's truck and thence to her property.

"I know of course I will be criticized," she finished the government postcard to Lily the same day she brought Brawith home, "but I feel as if I have had this call from the boy's mother and father from on high. And I want to do something for the boy before I go."

She had no more written these last words than she saw Brawith was, as if by means of telepathy, waiting to take the postcard to the post office.

Once in a blue moon Lily telephoned her from East Portage. During these phone calls Brawith was observed by his grandmother to sit down in the rocking chair, and letting the roll of toilet paper rest on his lap, he would rock and rock contentedly. She could see the damp emerging from his scalp and hair even from her position in the next room.

"He has given his all," Moira was heard again and again to retort on the phone to Lily, and as she said these words Brawith looked over at her, and something almost like a smile passed over his blurred lips, for there was never any real expression on his face—all there was of expression must have been kept now in the depths of his insides which nudged and urged more and more to come out, to be released themselves like a sheet which would cover his outside skin and hair.

Her cousin Keith visited her from time to time on the side porch and always insisted the same thing. "In the name of decency at least," Keith would say, "if not of proper care—which you cannot give him—send him back to the Vets Hospital."

"They were giving him nothing," Moira always contradicted Keith.

She frequently looked anxiously within the house when she and Keith talked on the side porch. She heard Brawith's rocking chair going faster and faster.

"He has the right to die with his loved ones," Moira told Keith firmly, and Keith got up and drove off in a fury after these last words.

Coming back into the house, she took Brawith's hand in hers, but he drew it away shortly to place it back on the roll of toilet paper.

His hands were only quiet, actually, when they rested on the roll of paper. The rolls were like a sleeping powder for him she thought. He appeared to sleep with them over his moving chest.

She kept a plentiful store of the rolls in her kitchen closet. They were of varying colors, but Brawith paid no attention to details of this kind.

"Nothing is too good for you, Brawith," she sometimes would speak in a loud voice to him. And, she added in a softer voice, "nothing is too good for my darling."

She felt he heard her, though she was beginning to understand at last that all he heard, all he felt, all he knew was the communications which the vast flowing wet of his insides imparted to him, those rivulets of blood and lymph, the outpouring of his arteries and veins, all of which whispered and told him of irreparable damage and disrepair, and of the awesome future that was to come.

Then one day when all was very still (Moira was somewhat deaf in one ear), when no automobile having gone past for some time, as she was cleaning his feet in a basin, she became perfectly aware herself, despite her own moderate deafness, of the sounds inside himself. She paused for a moment, incredulous, fearful, yet at the same time with an anticipated relief that she could share his knowledge. She listened carefully and she heard enough of the many sounds that were coming from inside himself and which he listened to constantly. All this she was now aware of. Their eyes met briefly, and he gave her a kind of nod, meaning he knew she had heard the sounds and had understood. She held his feet in a tight clasp. That was the beginning of their even deeper closeness.

She moved her cot into his room, and now they were sleepless together in the darkness, as they both listened to his body and waited for the day or perhaps the night to come when the fearful event would take place.

He now never spoke, and she occasionally hummed tunes and songs to him rather than say anything in ordinary speech except an occasional, "That's good, that's very good. I want you to taste this mutton broth."

But the voices of his insides did something to her. She had known it all before, being mother, grandmother but hearing it in a young man's body, a young man who had not had a chance to live as yet, made her incapable to go about her work for a time.

Then gradually she resumed daily tasks, but nothing was the same.

Mr. Kwis, who had helped to bring Brawith home, now delivered the bread and other victuals for their meals, including a few fresh vegetables. He waited on the side porch always for Moira to come out and gather up the provisions.

Brawith tasted all the food she prepared, but spit most of it out in a container provided near the table for this purpose. But his appetite was unimpaired. Whilst he ate, Moira and he both listened casually to the sounds coming from inside his body.

After a time they ceased speaking to one another except when Moira issued commands for herself, as when she would say, "I must wash out all your underthings this evening. And I must think up a new dish to tempt you, Brawith, for my knowledge of cooking's gone from me."

Brawith would nod then and his nods were like a thousand smiles so far as she was concerned.

"It is better here than where you were," Moira often inquired in what was almost a shouting tone.

His eyes studied her mouth, or rather her chin. She repeated her question. Almost as if to answer her, the sounds in his body became louder in response.

They walked out now into the garden, and he stooped down and gathered some of the black nasturtium seeds and held them in his hands. He played with the seeds later that night when he tired of holding the toilet tissues.

As they lay near to one another at night, Moira began speaking aloud. She slept as little as Brawith did, that is, not at all. She said in a voice that was loud enough to carry into the yard by the window, "Brawith, I have been criticized for everything. I am only sorry, though, I didn't come for you sooner. Do you hear? It was the only thing to do, my dear, the only thing. . . ."

After a while his scalp and brow seemed to flow with a thick beady moisture. She often thought she spent most of the time wiping his brow free of the ever-gathering damp. It reminded her of driving in cars long ago before there were windshield wipers, and the snow, rain or sleet fell remorselessly against the car's panes of glass. They would have to stop the car, and clean off the windshield, but to no avail.

"I can't tell you what it means to me," Moira spoke as she wiped his brow often in the middle of night. "Having you here with me,

I was doing nothing before you came," she went on. "Cousin Keith and my own daughter can hardly wait to leave now the minute they arrive here. I've told them all I know. They've heard my same old tale till they gag if I begin even to say what kind of weather we've been having. They've had all of me, but Brawith, you allow me to give you of the little I have for anybody."

Having spoken, she would then wipe his brow until it was almost dry, but then another sheet of the moisture came down, and he was as damp as before.

"My dear grandson, Brawith," she whispered too low for him to hear.

After a long pause she went on, "Mr. Kwis is more interested in what I say than my daughter or son. Certainly more than Cousin Keith."

As his brow became more and more sopping wet the voices inside his body grew more insistent, more authoritative. She felt they were crying out for something withheld from him, and now Brawith no longer swallowed what he chewed and tasted, but spat the whole thing out.

Moira and he sat listening to the dictatorial sounds issuing from inside him. Grandmother and grandson were pushed into a deeper silence as if they sat before a political orator or a preacher of the gospel.

One morning, coming out of a short nap-like sleep, she heard some new sounds arising from the fireplace. She called his name, but she realized now he could barely hear her because the sounds from his own swimming insides drowned out all other sound.

Walking into the next room, she found he had put his head up into the chimney of the huge fireplace. The fireplace was so high she could see his mouth and part of his nose, for he was not standing up very straight.

"Brawith, what is it?" She stooped low in order to look up at his eyes. "Are you more comfortable there, my dear boy."

After a long while he came out from the chimney. He looked

happier, and this pleased Moira. They went out into the kitchen together, and she prepared him his breakfast.

She realized her danger then at last, that is that she had perhaps made a mistake in disobeying the trained nurses and the doctors, in ignoring the advice of her kinfolk. She remembered, too, even in her good friend Mr. Kwis's face, the look sometimes of wonderment if not disapproval.

At the same time she could not go back on her decision in the first place. She felt even more strongly she could not give up Brawith. She studied her own heart, and she knew she had never loved anybody with such complete absorption as she did Brawith. She felt her own insides cried out along with his. Yet she made up her mind to ask him one last time.

Whilst she was mopping his forehead, she pressed his head toward her, and said, "Listen good now, Brawith, for Moira wants to do the right thing. Do you think maybe you should go back to the Vets? Say the word, and I will do what's right."

He did not say anything in reply, and in the silence she began combing his hair which was sopping wet.

"Just say the word, Brawith, and I will do as you see fit."

As he did not say anything, she sighed, for she knew his silence naturally meant he would not wish to return.

"You didn't think that I was indirectly asking you to leave now, did you?" she turned to him. "Heaven forbid you thinking that, Brawith. You're more welcome than sunshine. You've brought so much to me, precious."

After that she knew she would never need ask him about returning.

He would have certainly said something had he thought it was best for his condition to go back to the Vets.

Now for the most of the night, he began standing upright in the chimney of the fireplace, so that after a while she brought her cot there in the center of the big living room to be as near as possible to him. It was beginning to be more unbearable than ever for her, but she could no more have forbidden him standing in the fireplace than ordering him back to the hospital.

The odor from his sickness, however, now discouraged anybody from visiting them. Mr. Kwis himself came only as far as the side door, and having brought them the groceries, he deposited them on a small table and departed. Cousin Keith no longer came at all.

Moira often whispered with Mr. Kwis in the buttery.

"He gave his all, Mr. Kwis, and it's very little I can give him in return for all he has sacrificed, yes siree."

She felt now that he had come to her of his own free will, that she had not prevailed on him to join her here at the outskirts of Flempton, that he had in fact written her asking to join her in her home. She had never known such happiness, such calm, such useful tasks. Mr. Kwis, though he did not come so far into the house to see Brawith, was the soul of understanding. He listened. He understood, unlike Cousin Keith or her son and daughter. Mr. Kwis offered no word of contradiction, no bilious corrective or cold comment.

Brawith now refused to come out of the place he had chosen for himself in the chimney. He spent the entire day and night there. Moira saw that a terrible crisis was coming, yet she did not want to call the doctor or inform the Veterans Hospital. Brawith had promised her he would stay until the last.

Mr. Kwis came when the terrible thing was at its height. Owing to the stench he said he would remain as his custom was on the side porch, and if she thought it advisable he would go for help.

Brawith now began to scratch and claw the brick, but instead of dust coming down from the chimney, Moira saw a sheet of sweat was descending as if from a broken pipe, and this was followed by actual sheets of blood.

Moira begged him to come out of the chimney and lie down on his bed, but the sounds of his body all at once tripled in volume. Even Mr. Kwis heard them from outside.

Occasionally Moira would cry out his name, but the sound of his inside machinery as she thought of it drowned out her words.

At last he foamed at the mouth, and the foam fell down in thick cusps like what comes off cheap beer in the summer.

She felt she must hold him up into the body of the chimney since this was his wish.

Mr. Kwis kept calling from the side porch if there was anything at all which he might do, but she either did not hear him, or the few times she did hear him she was too distracted to reply.

The climax was coming or whatever it was, the end she supposed was a better word. His sufferings were culminating and here she was his only flesh and blood relation to help at this dire moment. No nurse or doctor could do what she was doing, and this thought strengthened and appeased her.

"Tell me, dear boy, if I should do anything different from what I am doing," Moira would cry out, but the sounds from his insides extinguished her voice.

All at once he lowered his head from inside the chimney and pointed with a kind of queer majesty with one hand toward a roll of toilet paper.

She unwound some of the roll and put it within reach of him. Then she saw that without her being aware of it he was naked, but looking again she decided that he still had his clothes on but they had become of the same color and wetness as his skin which breaking totally now exposed his insides. The clothes only resembled his broken skin and bleeding organs. He was not so much hemorrhaging as bursting from inside.

He managed to put the sheets of toilet paper over the worst of the bursting places on his body.

He soon used up the one roll of toilet paper, and Moira now called for Mr. Kwis to go into the buttery where she had put all the remaining rolls, and to toss her one from time to time for Brawith was quickly using them all up.

"You won't have to come much closer to us than you are now," she advised Mr. Kwis. "The crisis, dear friend, is near."

It seemed that Brawith exhausted one entire toilet paper roll almost immediately it was given to him. There were only four left. As he draped his body with the tissues they immediately became red from the wet stuff that was now breaking from within his entire body.

When the last roll was consumed, Moira wondered what would happen.

Then she thought she heard him scream, but she realized that the many noises and sounds which had been audible within his body were moving up now to his larynx and causing his vocal chords to vibrate as if he were speaking. Then she fancied he did speak the one word or part of an unfinished phrase: "*Deliver!*" repeated again and again: "*Deliver.*"

Then like a flock of birds the terrible noise seemed to rush over her head deafening her. She fell, losing her hold on his legs, and as she did so an immense shower of blood and intestines covered her, and his body entirely wrapped in toilet paper from head to toe fell heavily on her.

Moira did not know how she was able to rise and finally make her toilsome way to the side porch where Mr. Kwis was waiting with anxious dread. She hardly needed to tell him her grandson was no more. In silence Mr. Kwis took her hands in his and pressed them to his lips. Then speaking in a faint whisper, he said he would go now to tell those who were concerned that the heavy burden of Brawith's life had been lifted at last.

GERALDINE

Sue and her mother Belle no longer met in person, but Sue called her mother daily, in fact sometimes she called her two or three times in a day. The subject was always her worries over her thirteen year-old son Elmo.

"Now what has he done this time," Belle would sigh or more often yawn.

They had never been close, mother and daughter, and as if to emphasize their lack of rapport through the years, Belle had from his birth taken an almost inordinate delight and interest in her grandson Elmo. She gave him lavish birthday, Christmas, and Easter gifts and of late had begun taking him to the opera. Belle could not tell whether he enjoyed the opera or not, but he paid it a strict, almost hypnotic attention and applauded the singers with frenzy. Then they would go off to some midnight cafe and have a dinner of quail or venison.

Belle had heard of course about Geraldine. In fact Geraldine herself came to be very real to the grandmother. The girl, Elmo's girl in Sue's phrase, had the persistent presence of a character in great fiction, though Belle had never met her. At night, under the covers of her bed, Belle would often whisper "Geraldine" and smile.

"They are idiotically in love, and she is at least two years older than Elmo," Sue would report on the telephone. "They are together constantly, constantly. And their kissing! Oh, Belle, Belle." Sue had ceased calling her mother mother for at least ten years. Although the grandmother pretended to like this familiarity, it piqued her nonetheless. But then she had never ever been close enough to Sue even to correct her.

"*Don't put your foot down*," was almost the only advice Belle ever gave her daughter. "*Let what will be be*. Let him love Geraldine."

GERALDINE AND ELMO came to an evening Sunday supper one day in December when there was a light spitting snow outside. Belle was not prepared for Geraldine's extreme good looks and beautiful clothes. She felt she had opened the door on a painting from some little known Italian hand. Geraldine's eyelashes alone brought a flush to the grandmother's face and lips. The girl's hands free of rings and her arms without bracelets looked like they were made out of some wonderful cream. And then Belle looked round and saw her grandson, not as he had always been on his previous visits but now as a young man with the first show of a beard on his upper lip.

"At last, at last," Belle cried and held both of the young people in succession to her. Tonight she only kissed Geraldine however.

They began going to the opera as a threesome. They attended all of Donizetti's operas that season, and after the opera they went to Belle's special cafe and spent hours there laughing as though they were all of the same age.

THE CRISIS CAME when Sue called Belle at six o'clock in the morning.

"He has had his right ear pierced!"

At first the grandmother thought this referred to an accident of some kind. Only when she was given the explanation that the boy had gone to a professional ear piercer, did she recover from her fright. She broke into laughter at that moment which drove Sue into a fit of weeping, weeping propelled by rage and the revival of the feeling her mother had never loved her.

"No, no, my dear, you must not feel it is a disgrace," Belle advised Sue. "It is the fashion for young boys."

"Fashion, my foot," Sue screamed over the wires. "It is Geraldine!" Then Belle as if in spite began even at that early hour to praise the beauty of Geraldine.

A torrent of abuse then followed on the other end of the wire. Sue told of the girl's excesses.

"They do not show, my dear," Belle disagreed. She is unspotted, unsoiled in every lineament of face and body.

Belle waited with a queer smile on her face while her daughter wept and told of all the shortcomings of Geraldine.

SUE KEPT A kind of "black book" of Belle's "crimes" against her. She considered in the first place that Belle had usurped her place in Elmo's affections. She had taken Elmo away from her as surely as if she kidnapped him, Sue wrote in her black book. She listed other of Belle's crimes as 1) making Elmo fond of imported sweetmeats, such as chestnuts covered with whipped cream, 2) reading him stories beyond his age group, stories which had questionable morality or contained improper innuendoes, 3) late hours, 4) breakfast in bed after a night of attending the opera, 5) imported hairdressing creams which made Elmo smell more like a fast woman than a young boy, and so on and so on. Then Sue would burst into tears. "Belle never loved me," Sue would whisper to the covers of the black book. Never never so much as one hour did she squander on me the affection she showers on Elmo or that bitch Geraldine.

Elmo once called his mother to her face a boo-hooer. That epithet rankled in her heart for a long time. It drove her, as if imitating her mother's largesse, to go to the most expensive women's shop in Manhattan and purchase for herself imported hand-sewn handkerchiefs. Into these she wept openly and with uncontrolled wetness.

I will boo-hoo both of them, she cried. She even thought of taking legal action against her mother. In fact she called a noted lawyer who dealt in unusual family problems. He discouraged her coldly, even warned her to proceed no further. Then he sent her a bill for $1,000.00.

"I have Belle," Sue would often say as she looked out into the garden of her townhouse. "She will outlive all of us, including Geraldine."

"YOUR MOTHER SAYS I act like your fairy godmother," Belle said one late afternoon just before she and Elmo were to go to the opera.

Elmo smiled his strange little smile and pressed Geraldine's hand.

"She doesn't mean it as a compliment," Belle told him. "Are you as happy with me, dear boy, as with Sue?" Belle inquired.

"Oh, a thousand times happier, Belle," Elmo replied. He, too, had fallen somehow naturally into calling her by her first name.

The old woman beamed. "I would keep you forever," she whispered. "And Geraldine, too. Wouldn't we all be a threesome of happy ones," Belle cried. Elmo beamed and nodded, and Geraldine grinned.

"As happy as larks!" Belle almost shouted. She held Elmo in her arms and kissed him on his cowlick. Then she embraced Geraldine.

"You love Geraldine, don't you?" Belle whispered.

Elmo stiffened a little under her caresses, then in a smothered voice said, "A lot, Grandma, a lot."

WHETHER IT WAS the coming of Geraldine or the desecration of Elmo's and Geraldine's earlobes by the ear-piercing practitioner, Belle was hurtled back in time—what other way could she describe it—to her own youth. She examined her own ear lobes and found that the tiny holes put there so long ago were still ready to bear the presence of her own many earrings. And how many earrings she had! Yes, Sue had criticized her on this score likewise. "You have enough earrings to bestow on a museum," Sue had spoken this judgment on Belle not too long ago. "And you never wear one pair of them."

"But I will, now I will," Belle said aloud today. In her older years she often spent whole afternoons and evenings talking to herself. "But what am I saying. They shall wear them also! Geraldine and Elmo. How I do love them, Lord!"

The next evening before the opera the three of them all laughing and giggling and even guffawing began putting on Belle's many earrings.

"Too bad, loves, only one of your ears is pierced," Belle cried, and she showed them herself in full panoply, wearing first a priceless jade set of earrings, then the ancient turquoise pair, after that the diamond, and then to the hush-hush of the young couple, her emerald pair.

"O, may I wear the emerald tonight?" Elmo cried.

"Why, Elmo," Geraldine whispered and kissed him wetly on his mouth and chin.

"Why ever not, dears, why ever not! And Geraldine must not be left out. By no means. Oh, God in Heaven," Belle cried, "how happy I am. I never would have dreamed two people could have brought me such happiness. Never, never." And she held them to her tightly. "And I don't care what Sue thinks, children," Belle cried.

All at once, as if from a cue somewhere, perhaps from the opera house itself at which they practically lived now, they began dancing all three of them as if in some queer minuet. With their new earrings sparkling they might indeed have been part of the ballet of some rarely performed opera.

"The only thing that makes sense is gaiety!" Belle cried, a bit out of breath. "If one were never gay, it would not be worth a candle. One must sparkle like our earrings, children! One must sparkle."

SUE'S CONVERSION CAME swiftly and without warning. She had got used to Elmo's always staying the night—and often the weekend—with his grandmother. In fact Sue began somehow to believe that

Elmo now lived with Belle. True, it had always been Belle's wish of course that Elmo stay—really live with her. And since Elmo never went anywhere now without Geraldine, in Sue's troubled mind she assumed that like brother and sister both now resided with Sue's mother Belle.

Sue kept touching her earlobes. The piercing in both her ears which Belle in fact had supervised some twenty years earlier needed attention. The skin in the pierced holes was beginning to close. "I must have them tended to," Sue spoke to herself. Her tall Finnish butler served her course after course tonight, all of which she left untasted.

She had stared at Jan the same way at the beginning of every meal when he asked "Will Master Elmo be dining?" Sue would look only at his long blond sideburns and reply, "He is still at his grandmother's."

"I must have my earlobes pierced again. My earrings don't go in." She spoke aloud within the hearing of Jan.

But that evening came her realization. Unlike Belle, Sue did not hold a box at the opera. But she kept a seat very near the stage which cost more or nearly as much as Belle's royal box. Actually she retained two seats, but Elmo almost never attended the opera with her.

"For where would Geraldine sit, then?" She addressed this statement also to her Finnish servant.

He could hardly wait until he reached the safety of the kitchen to burst out laughing to the cook. Sue heard his laughter but construed it as coming from his asthmatic attacks. "He wheezes like an animal," she once remarked to Elmo. "If he weren't so tall and personable, I would ditch him."

SHE ARRIVED LATE at the opera but tipped the usher to allow her to go in against regulations when the opera was in progress.

No sooner had she disturbed forty or fifty people gaining her seat than her eyes swept away from the stage to Belle in her box.

"Ah, ah," she cried again disturbing the opera lovers. She had never seen anything so resplendent! There they were, Belle, Geraldine and Elmo, but with what a difference. Each wore earrings, each wore some kind of shining necklace attached to the beads of which was a resplendent kind of brooch. Sue wondered why every eye in the opera house was not watching Belle and her retinue.

Sue wept unashamedly. She never heard a note of the opera. But her weeping refreshed her more than a dive in a cool spring. The vision of her loved ones—for she now knew she too loved Geraldine almost as much as her own flesh and blood—that vision dissolved then and forever her jealousy and rancor. She suddenly accepted Belle, and with her acceptance of her mother she accepted her jurisdiction and sequestration of her son and her son's sweetheart Geraldine.

"Let them love one another," she cried, and falling back against the rich upholstery of her seat she went to sleep.

She was awakened by an usher shaking her. The opera had long been over, every seat but hers emptied. Looking up at Belle's box, she saw it too was deserted, extinct of resplendence.

She was helped out to the street by the usher who summoned her a cab. She gave him an ostentatiously grand tip and sped away in the cab.

"Tomorrow, I will have my earlobes re-pierced," she spoke loud enough for the cab driver to hear. He nodded gloomily.

I wanted to please her, yes, Sue reflected after it was all over, I saw I wanted only one thing, to be Belle's little girl.

THE WORLD-FAMOUS JEWELER was not too surprised as he had been Sue's jeweler for twenty years when he saw Sue enter his private consulting room in the jeweler's shop, a room reserved only for the phenomenally wealthy.

"My dear, you look tired." He helped her to a green French settee. "Shan't I get you something?"

Sue could only nod. He brought her out a dark liquid in a glass so thin it resembled mere paper but sparkled like diamonds. One would have thought he knew she was coming, had prepared for her visit days in advance.

"I saw the earrings in the window," Sue only moistened her lips with the brandy.

"I had hoped you'd come by and look at them," Mr. Henton-Coburn confided.

"I want to please Belle," she brought out. "My husband spoiled me so I wouldn't bother him. Every time he felt I was going to ask something of him I got a gift. They were mostly jewels as you know. He purchased however very few earrings. I will need all the earrings on display."

"But two are spoken for."

She put down her glass, and touched her lower lip.

"But if you insist of course."

"I said I wanted them. I mean I have to have them. I have to please Belle. . . .

"But, listen, dear friend," and she took a noisy swallow of the brandy. "I think" (she placed a finger on an earlobe) "they need piercing again. When I had my trouble, my sorrow with Belle, I all but quit wearing jewels."

"May I?" he inquired and bent over her left ear. Then her right ear.

"What is needed, dear lady, is," and he produced a kind of stiff thread. "I will pull this through with your say-so where the old piercing was, and you'll be perfect for the displays in the window. Oh, my dear, why haven't you been by." He bent down and kissed her.

HER DECISION TO attend the opera then one snowy bitter night with the mercury near zero ushered in what resembled, as she later noted in her book of records, what resembled different ceremonies, a first communion, a wedding, perhaps even a funeral. But it was none of these. It was more—she blushed as she wrote it down—like going to paradise.

She had spent hours on her toilet. She had tried on at least fourteen pairs of earrings.

That night at the opera looking down with his opera glasses, Elmo caught sight of a woman who looked somehow familiar, yet the more he gazed at her the less sure he was it was anyone whom he knew. Yes! Looking again he saw that it was someone who resembled Sue, yet this Sue was wearing the most elegant and ornate earrings he had ever seen anybody wearing.

"Is that Sue?" he inquired of Geraldine.

Geraldine took the opera glasses and looked only a moment, then merely shrugged her shoulders. Elmo stared at Geraldine coldly, and Geraldine returned the stare with a frigid contemptuous expression in her eyes and on her lips.

Belle now took the opera glasses and looked down. But at that moment the house lights dimmed, and soon the overture to the third act began.

Geraldine and Elmo had quarreled. And Belle had become distant, as if her real center of affection now was Geraldine and not Elmo.

It was snowing harder when the three of them left the opera house. Belle looked at Elmo inquiringly as he summoned for them a cab.

"I will not be coming with you, Grandma," Elmo spoke with devastating aplomb. Helping Belle into the cab, he almost pushed Geraldine in after her. Belle was too surprised to protest, or even say anything but "Good night then."

"I am going home," Elmo spoke aloud, his mouth opened wide and received the thick goosefeathery flakes of snow. "It was Sue, I know that with her ears pierced."

"YES, SO IT was you."

Elmo had entered his mother's room on the top floor as he said this. He was so covered with snow, his eyebrows and the hair sticking out from his ski cap white as avalanches, even a few hairs in his nostrils white.

Sue had just in fact put on an even more resplendent pair of earrings as if she was waiting for him to see her so arrayed. When as a matter of fact she thought he would stay on indefinitely with Geraldine and Belle.

"Mother, good evening," he said. He sat down on the divan near her.

She was still too astounded to speak, and his calling her mother further stopped the speech in her throat.

"Take off your wet clothes and put them in the bathroom to dry."

"I can't get over it," he said obeying her and going into the bathroom, a room as large as many New York parlors.

He looked at himself in the mirror. To his astonishment—or was it astonishment really—anyhow he saw that his own earring had disappeared from his earlobe. He touched where it had been pierced.

Coming out of the bathroom, he gazed at Sue. She looked almost as young as Geraldine and yes, admit it, Elmo, he thought to himself, admit it, more lovely.

"Well, Mother," he said again.

"What has brought this about?" Sue wondered. "Shall I wake up Jan and have him prepare us something." Elmo shook his head.

"Geraldine is through with me," he began. He sniffled a bit, whether from the snow or his grief was not clear. "Finished, finito."

"Ah, well, that is what being young brings," Sue said.

"And Belle prefers her to me."

"Oh, Belle," Sue said. Then minding her speech she merely added. "Well, she's old."

"And fickle," he added. "The opera is her lifeblood."

"Certainly the costumes and the sets are. She's deaf as a nest of adders."

"Belle is deaf?"

"And nearly blind."

"How many earrings do you have?" he wondered.

"I'm afraid enough for everybody in the opera."

"Do you mind if I stay with you now, Mother?"

"Nothing you could suggest would make me more happy." Two huge tears descended from her eyes.

Elmo sat back astonished, some wet snow drops falling from his thick black hair. His eyelashes, too long for a boy's as Geraldine had pointed out, sparkled with wetness.

"And you won't send me away somewhere."

Sue shook her head and mumbled, "Never."

"May I kiss you then?" he wondered. He came over to where she sat limp and disheveled for all her jewels.

"Mother, I believe . . ."

"Don't say any more."

But he finished his sentence. "I feel I'm home."

A LITTLE VARIETY, PLEASE

lice Drummond feared the Green Dragon almost as much as she did being late to tea. (Her stepmother always whipped her for tardiness.)

The Green Dragon did not have it in for Alice, but his only pleasure, it is true, was to frighten small girls. He had been wintering in Mountain Gulch and was now rested up for hearty springtime activity.

Alice's stepmother warned her the Dragon was back and would be looking for her in particular, and to kindly practice her roller-skating.

"If you have on your skates, you'll be sure to outpace him," the stepmother assured her. "He's also, remember, out of condition from wintering."

"If I could be sure of that," Alice Drummond whispered to herself. Alice tired so of roller skating, and spring made her sleepy and careless.

MILDRED TERRY, A friend of Alice's stepmother, had a bad fright the day Alice was getting warned by her adopted parent. Mildred had come home unexpectedly from the store and found the Dragon going through her apple bin.

"If you'd written me a note, I'd have set out a bushel or so of apples beforehand," Mildred scolded him. "I don't like you coming in here like a harum-scarum."

She sat down on her best divan, folding and unfolding her handkerchief. The Dragon threw one apple after another upon the floor.

"These are all Northern Spy and of a poor quality at that," he said finally. Then he ate a small apple at the bottom of the pile. "Just so-so," the Dragon remarked between chewing sounds.

"In all my years in Centerville I've never known so inconsiderate a creature as yourself," Mildred cried on. "You've frightened poor little Alice Drummond something awful. She feels you're after her. Are you?"

The Dragon wiped his paws clean of apple parings, and then began picking and cleaning his front teeth with the remains of a rolling pin.

"Why in Sam Hill did you come back here?" Mildred finally said, when she saw he was not going to answer. "Isn't there another place for you to go firecrackering about?" Suddenly the Dragon began to moan and whine almost like a small cat and held his left arm to his stomach. His eyes rolled in his head, and his scales lowered their lights.

"Oh, me and my," the Dragon cried. "I feel on fire. . . ."

Mildred got up and went to the medicine cabinet, and brought out a bottle of essence of peppermint. She poured a few drops in a tumbler and handed it to the Green Dragon, who swallowed it down.

"Mmm, better already," he mused. "Where now does Alice Drummond live . . ."

"You can't go there, Green Dragon," Mildred spoke, still holding the tumbler in her hand. "You must promise me to give up little girls. Think of all I've done for you. I want you to leave Centerville."

"I am going to cure Alice Drummond of being afraid of tardiness," the Dragon said. "You know," he repressed a fiery belch, "that I have never harmed the hair of a living creature. However, even I, if pressed by aggressive fear on the part of my inferiors, will frighten . . ."

"Little girls." Mildred sobbed.

"Little girls!" he roared. "I hate the creatures. Only like old parcels like you." He fondled Mildred against his scales briefly.

"Oh, Draggie, why can't you be satisfied?" she cooed. "Why don't you stay out of sight and live with me then at night. You're so selfish."

"I'll see the Drummond Girl. . . ."

"You'll frighten the poor dear to death." The Dragon smiled. "Oh, Draggie, why can't you let well enough alone."

"MILDRED HAS WARNED me that the Green Dragon is coming to teach Alice a lesson," Mrs. Drummond told her husband that evening. As Alice was only an adopted child of the Drummonds, they were not so frightened as they might have been. Alice had been left on their doorstep six years before, and though they had never wanted her, nobody else would take her, and so she had boarded and lived with them. They were all very unhappy with one another.

"He may be here any moment," Mrs. Drummond said.

"Who?" Mr. Drummond inquired, looking up from his cribbage board.

"I just told you, simpleton."

"Oh, the Dragon," Mr. Drummond replied. "Mae, perhaps it would be better for all if Draggie took her."

"Don't think I haven't entertained the idea," Mrs. Drummond said. "But the principle of the thing is wrong, Corless, you know it is. We'd be criticized by the community."

"Well, warn the girl, and if he comes, I suppose he'll have to take her." At supper the two Drummonds and Alice discussed the contingencies of a visit from the Dragon. Alice cried right through dessert, and had to be taken into the front room and laid on a sofa. She continued to cry until Mrs. Drummond slapped her. Then Alice made little whimpering sounds, and Mr. Drummond cuffed her for making those, and then she didn't know what she might do, and she held her breath until she turned purple.

At that moment the Green Dragon came through the wall and shot his tongue out. He had not recovered from his colic from eating apples, and he sat down in the large fireplace chair and looked at Alice. When she saw the Dragon she began breathing again. The Drummonds tiptoed out into the kitchen.

"I have fallen in love with you on hearsay," Alice began, looking obliquely at the huge animal.

The Dragon's eyes opened wider than usual, and the room became noticeably warmer. "You . . . fallen for me?" he roared. "That isn't in my book." The Dragon loosened his scales and moved his tongue about in his parched mouth.

"I had no idea you would look the way you do. I am ready to go away with you," she went on.

The Dragon looked out the window at the lengthening spring evening. "I am only interested in *scaring* little . . ."

"Why are you pictured so differently by the press?" Alice wanted to know. She paced up and down the room. She could see her stepmother's eyes through the kitchen door keyhole. Her anger against her adopted parents suddenly gave her the courage to go directly up to the Dragon. Her fear of course had left her, and she sat down on the big animal's lap. The heat from his body made her terribly uncomfortable, but then Alice Drummond had been uncomfortable all her life. She threw her arms about him while the great animal shifted on his seat.

"Do you think you could get up long enough to get me a frosty cold drink?" the Dragon inquired.

"Anything you ask for is already yours," the girl spoke like one who talks to herself in sleep. The room was getting absolutely torrid. Mrs. Drummond who had heard his request for a drink was already reaching out from the half-opened kitchen door a glass, which Alice took and gave to the great animal. He drank it off and required another. Then a series of exhausting tasks for the Drummonds began. They brought over 300 glasses to the Dragon, but both he and the house became hotter and hotter.

"You're bringing me the wrong kind of liquid," he shouted at last and threw the glass straight at Mrs. Drummond. "Now get out to that kitchen and prepare a frosty drink, as I told you. . . ."

But the wallpaper was already in flames in the room where Alice was proposing to the Dragon. "Have no fear, Alice D.," the Dragon spoke to her. "If it looks like a fire, we'll exit. But I must have a frosty drink, my dear. You understand that, of course. You have been unhappy so long, dear Alice, and though I could never love you as you require because you are only a little girl still—"

"You will grow to love me," she quoted from a favorite novel.

"Love you? Let me finish," the Dragon said. "I will adopt you, if not love you. For one thing I am perfectly indifferent to tardiness of any kind. You will live in my palatial castle and do as you please. After all, you are as much legally mine as theirs. . . ."

"We've got to leave, Alice," Mrs. Drummond was wringing her hands. "The entire house is in flames . . . the attic's going now, see, look out there . . . it's already fallen on the front yard. We've notified the fire department. Good-bye, Alice, my dear . . . I'm afraid escape is out of the question for you." She had noticed the girl was being hugged tightly by the big animal.

"Good-bye, my dear," Mr. Drummond spoke to Alice. He had on his fireman's hat, as he was a member of the auxiliary fire department. "Good-bye, sir," he said to the Dragon.

"We have nothing to fear from flames," the Dragon told Alice, as she nestled against his scales.

"I've never felt cooler, Draggie, never felt so much at ease."

THE HOUSE BURNED entirely down, and the water from the firemen's hoses quenched the thirst of the huge animal, who had sat on during the entire conflagration hugging Alice Drummond to his scales.

"THEY WERE TWINED together like two lilies," the local press described their position. The townspeople at first understood that Alice Drummond had been burnt to an unrecognizable cinder, and hence Mrs. Drummond had permitted the Dragon to take her off to Green Dragon Lodge with no more feeling than a shrug of the shoulder.

But when all learned that she had not so much as suffered a singeing of one of her curls, everybody began going to Dragon Lodge in hopes of catching a glimpse of the pair.

Whether the Dragon had finally fallen in love with Alice, after being disinterested in little girls except for his liking to frighten them, was not known. But Alice showed by her every movement and gesture that she was hopelessly attached to the Green Dragon. She radiated joy.

MRS. DRUMMOND, IN an interview with the girl who stood between the front paws of the Dragon, threw up to her all that they had done for her. "You were a very expensive child, my dear," Mrs. Drummond said. "You ate your weight in food every other month. We are poor people as a result of having provided for you . . ."

Alice said nothing, and Mrs. Drummond, unable to bear silence when she was having a quarrel with anybody, shrieked in anger and came up as was her custom to slap the girl to sleep, but the Dragon at the moment she was about to strike the girl emitted a kind of steam which drove the stepmother back.

"You're too young to know happiness like this, Alice," she said, on leaving, "and you'll pay for every hour of joy you enjoy with that hideous animal . . . This is good-bye, Alice. I've done all I know I can for you. Good-bye, and may you be brought to a realization of your selfish ways and pay for it dearly." Mr. Drummond who had hidden behind his wife now came out and seconded his wife's statements. "Happiness is much too good for both of you," he said.

"Shall we go on with our lessons in being late for everything, Alice, my dear," the Dragon inquired. "Or would you like a cup of hot turtle soup . . ."

"I am so happy since we ran off together, Draggie, it don't make much difference . . . I want to enjoy all of our happiness to the full while I have it."

She embraced the Dragon, and they went back into Dragon Lodge and had a delicious cup of hot turtle soup.

AND NOW IT was Mildred Terry's turn to come to Dragon Lodge, and complain: "I would be ashamed of myself if I were you," she addressed the Green Dragon. "Living with a spoiled little snipe who never did a thing for a soul. You'll never know the real kind of happiness, Dragon. Never."

The Dragon listened patiently to all Mildred said.

"I could have made a wonderful life for both of us," Mildred tried to go on, but was weeping too hard. "A lot you ever cared about me. I sacrificed my youth for you, and this is what I get. You'll wake up one day, both of you, and discover the kind of person you are living with, and no punishment can be greater than that, none in the world.

"Good-bye, and try to learn from your mistakes," Mildred finished, and disappeared into the leafy streets of Centerville.

THE DRAGON CAME out, green as cabbage. Their luggage was all neatly in a pile about them, and they were leaving now to go to the Everglades to live. There was one tiny place in it, the Dragon knew, which would be lonesome, private, and natural. There they would live out their lives together, never having to care about being late, or indeed early.

"Good-bye, Centerville," they both cried as the Dragon took off, his wings making a great din over the streets of Centerville . . . "Good-bye," Alice shouted, "I won't be back, I'm afraid, or rather am not afraid."

That was the last the Drummonds, Mildred Terry, or Centerville ever saw of them, and after a while nobody believed there had been an Alice Drummond, and certainly nobody believed there had been a Green Dragon. But of course there was, there were. . . .

EASY STREET

Mother Green and her faithful friend Viola Daniels, shut away as they were in their old four story brownstone, at the end of the mews, were unprepared for a sudden change in this unfrequented neighborhood. Big trucks with deafening sound equipment had moved in, men with bullhorns were shouting at other men up and down the street, and the whole area was roped off from access to the adjoining neighborhood.

Mother Green had recently celebrated her 96th birthday, and her companion Viola (she looked on her as a daughter more than an attendant) was some thirty years younger.

Their neighbors spoke of them as ladies in retirement who seldom ventured out into the great city beyond. At the unusual noise and tumult today the two friends stood at the windows in wonderment and incipient alarm.

Then all at once (it was July) a summer thunderstorm of unusual violence struck the neighborhood. Hail and blinding downpour and, as the newspaper called it, "dangerous and prolonged lightning" descended. The thunder was so loud no one had ever heard such peals. It reminded the older men of the sounds of battle and bombing.

The rain continued to come down in unpitying volume, interspersed with hailstones the size of duck eggs.

The two retired ladies drew away from the window and pulled down the blinds, but curiosity tempted them to occasionally peek outside.

What they saw was that all the men and the bullhorns and the trucks and the infernal shouting had ended. The disturbers of the peace could have been swept out to sea, who knows. Except for the unceasing downpour the street was as quiet as an uninhabited island.

It was then they caught sight of somebody seeking shelter from the flood. He was standing under their tiny front porch, drenched to the skin, his clothes so tight pressed against his body he resembled a naked drowned man, and such streams of wetness came over his face he appeared to be weeping in torrents.

Catching sight of Mother Green and Viola, the stranger made frantic gestures in their direction with his dripping hands.

"Open the door for him," Mother Green spoke to Viola.

Viola was taken aback by such a command, for Mother Green seldom if ever admitted anybody inside, and her voice now rang out like that of some woman preacher.

Viola hesitated only a minute. She flung open the door, and the drenched man staggered inside, and whether from being blinded by the torrent or through weakness, slipped and fell on his knees in front of the two ladies.

Streams of water flowed from his sopping vestments.

Meanwhile Mother Green was whispering to Viola that in the little closet off the parlor there was a man's bathrobe left from a roomer who had stayed with them some years ago, and a number of towels.

The stranger was given the bathrobe and towels and was ushered into the "little room" off the parlor. The two ladies waited uneasily for him to come out.

Many things crossed the two women's minds of course. Such as who, in fact, had she admitted to their solitary domain. What if he was dangerous or wanted by the authorities.

When their visitor emerged, Viola let out a short gasp, and Mother Green gave out a sound somewhere between astonishment and relief.

They saw the stranger was, like Mother Green, a very dark African, but he was also very young. His almond-shaped eyes betokened something very like benediction.

He sat down on the carpet and crossed his bare legs. He gave out his name which was Bewick Freeth.

"We were filming out there," he said, and he stretched his right arm in the direction of the downpour.

Neither then nor later did the ladies take in the word "filming." If it was heard at all, it was not understood.

But what made the impression now on the older woman was she heard in the stranger's speech the unmistakable accent of Alabama from where she had come so many decades ago.

Replying to her question if she was right about his speech, Bewick did not smile so much as grin, and all his gleaming white teeth reinforced his good looks.

It slipped out then both Mother Green and Bewick Freeth were from almost the very same section of Alabama, near a small lake, and the name Tallassee was mentioned.

Both ladies could now relax and smile.

Mother Green, at hearing the town named in a peremptory, even a slightly grand manner, urged Viola to go to the kitchen and bring some refreshment.

Bewick smiled at hearing her order and closed his eyes.

Mother Green liked the way he tasted the drink he was given, in small almost delicate sips, nodding his head with each sip as a kind of thank-you.

Yes, she saw she had not been mistaken in him, had not run any risk. And meanwhile the sound of Alabama in his speech brought back to her in a rush her almost forgotten memories of the South she had put behind her.

Looking at him closely, she wondered at times if she was not "seeing things." The terrible storm, his sudden appearance, their reckless admitting of a total stranger—Mother Green did wonder, but she knew she was right. She knew then she must have been meant to know Bewick Freeth.

Viola Daniels listened then as the visitor and Mother Green spoke. Viola Daniels was light-skinned and what Mother Green sometimes joked was that she looked almost more white even than an octoroon, while the more one looked at their visitor his very dark skin stood out deeper in hue.

Mother Green was easy then, not only because of his Alabama speech but the deep darkness of his face, as well as his long eyelashes, and she could sense the sweetness of his breath coming to her in waves.

LATER, MUCH LATER as Mother Green recalled his coming, it was as if they had been expecting him. He had walked in and they had spoken to him like he had been there before. No stranger. Even the glimpse Mother Green got of an earring in his left ear was no surprise to her.

They set aside for him the large front guest room up two flights of stairs. It had not been resided in for some years.

Bewie, as he asked to be called, one day after some time noticing Mother Green's limp, asked if she was in some discomfort from the way she walked.

Mother Green hesitated and fidgeted.

"She suffers from bunions," Viola informed him, and Mother Green stared reproachfully at her.

Bewie in a strange gesture clasped his hands.

"I know the very thing," he cried in the face of Mother Green's displeasure her affliction had been made known.

The next day Bewie instructed Viola to prepare a small basin of mildly hot water to which he added some herbs he had purchased.

Had he not done another thing, his bathing of Mother Green's painful feet would have insured him a refuge with them.

Only Viola looked a bit uneasy. More and more she had a kind of bewildered air.

"What is it, Viola, dear?" Mother Green wondered while Bewie busied himself with some self-appointed task in the kitchen.

"Nothing, Mother."

"You act a little put out," the older woman spoke almost in a whisper.

Yes, she saw perhaps Viola was hurt or maybe just jealous. And her almost white face between Mother Green and Bewie's fierce complexions may have been a cause. She felt in a way set aside. And she wanted more than anything to be close to them, important to both.

Mother Green patted Viola's hand and kissed her middle finger. "It's *all* all right, Viola," she whispered.

AND SO IT began, their life together, Mother Green and Viola and this perfect stranger from Alabama.

He did not tell them what his work or calling was from outside. He only indicated that he would be out from part of the day and perhaps even some of the night.

"It's my present livelihood," he added, letting them know he would have to be absent every so often.

It all seemed unsurprising at least to Mother Green—as in a dream even the unbelievable will be perfectly believable.

He had come to stay with them and they were to respect his absences and his sparse explanations. "It's his livelihood," Mother Green repeated his words to Viola.

THEN, AS THE stranger stayed on, Viola's uneasiness grew. Often she would go to the big hall mirror and look at her own face. She saw that not only was Mother Green closer to him because he spoke in an Alabama accent, but closer likewise because like her his face was the welcome dark color.

"You will always be dear to me," Mother Green said one afternoon when they were alone and she realized Viola was grieving.

Viola tried to swallow her pride and went about as before, caring for Mother Green. In fact, after the arrival of Bewie she was more attentive and caring than before, if that was possible.

But Viola as if confiding to herself would think, "Bewie is everything to her. More than if he were her own flesh and blood."

ONE DAY MOTHER Green acted a little uneasy. "Where do you suppose Bewie goes? We don't as a matter of fact know much about him now do we," she reflected.

"We don't know nothin', you mean."

"Oh Viola, who is he, yes, who is this Bewie?"

Mother Green then held Viola's hand tight in hers.

ONE THING OF course they could not help noticing. Bewie hardly ever returned without he was carrying a heavy package or two.

At the ladies' look of astonishment, he sat down and said in a joking tone, "My wardrobe. In my profession, you have to look your best. And the film people of course insist on it."

Again the word *film* did not register with the ladies. And they were too shy to ask him outright what required so many clothes.

The clothes, or the *wardrobe* to use his term, intrigued Mother Green and Viola. They spent—yes hours discussing all the clothes he was required to possess because, yes, his *livelihood* made them a necessity.

The curiosity became too strong for Mother Green. One afternoon she told Viola she would like to go upstairs to see how he kept his room.

Viola frowned, "Those stairs are steep and rickety. And dangerous!"

"Oh you can come along then and steady me, Viola dear."

Mother Green was nearly a cripple from her bunions, but she must see how he kept his room.

It was more than a big surprise to her.

She opened the big closet door and stared at some brand-new three-piece suits, fancy cravats, big-brimmed straw hats, and shiny elegant high-shoes.

"All bandbox new!" Mother Green sighed and sat down on the easy chair Viola had brought from downstairs.

"What are you doing?" Mother Green exclaimed, for she saw Viola had brought with her the big thermos bottle.

"I fetched us some hot coffee."

Mother Green sipped the steaming brew.

"What did I ever do, Viola, to deserve a child like you."

A little sob escaped Viola, undetected probably by Mother Green.

SO THE MYSTERY of Bewie deepened. Yes, who was he after all, and where did the expensive suits and shoes and ties and gold cufflinks come from.

Yet both Mother Green and Viola believed in him. He did not scare them. Even had he had no Alabama accent, he was one of them they were sure. He was not really a stranger in spite of his mysterious ways.

IF ONLY MOTHER Green loved me as much as she does Bewie, Viola would sometimes speak out aloud, knowing of course Mother Green's deafness would not let her hear.

It appeared to Viola Daniels at times that both Mother Green and Bewie had returned to Alabama to take up again their life in the South and converse in their unforgettable Alabama speech.

Viola sometimes thought about running away. But where could she go after all. She was no longer young. Who would want her. And beside all that she would never have the heart to leave Mother Green.

"Let her love Bewie more than me!" Viola would then say out loud.

"What's you talking about over there," Mother Green would say in a joking voice.

"I hardly know myself, Mother Green," Viola would say in a loud voice, and then the two ladies would both laugh.

It became if possible less and less clear both to Mother Green and Viola Daniels how and why Bewie had become part of their lives. It was especially unclear at times how he had appeared at all. Once Viola almost got the word out, "Like a housebreaker!" but she caught herself from saying it at the last moment. But it would have been true maybe to say an apparition.

"We always knew Bewie," Viola said long afterward.

SOMETHING HAD BEEN on Bewie's mind. Perhaps that's why he was so happy always performing so many tasks for Mother Green. He tidied the place up. He even washed the large front windows. And one evening he insisted on preparing a real Southern dinner for them.

But his presence in the house became shorter, less frequent. Sometimes he did not come home at night. Sometimes he barely spoke to them. He became sad, downcast . . . even tearful. Once Mother Green had heard this terrible sobbing in the front parlor. She didn't know what to do. It didn't sound like anybody she had ever heard. It sounded almost like a heartbeat. She opened the door ever so soft and there he sat slumped in the big chair just crying his eyes out. She closed the door as soft as she had opened it, waited a while, and then called out very loud, "Bewie is that you?" When she went in the front parlor his face was as dry as chalk, and he was composed and looked like always. Yes, as Mother Green kept repeating, "Something is on his mind. Something is worrying him."

SOMETHING, TOO, WAS on Mother Green's mind. She would start to say something to Viola, and then she would stop all of a sudden, or in Viola's words "clam up." She would clear her throat and relapse into silence.

"Do you remember Ruby Loftus?" the old woman broke her silence.

Viola said yes though she was not sure she did remember Ruby.

Mother Green smiled, lapsed again into a brief silence. Then she began to speak hurriedly, "She was what they call a psychic reader. She had second sight. Well, she often read for me. What she got for me was usually mighty interesting if not exactly calming. But what she told me one time happened years ago. Before your time, Viola. She 'read' me, and lord how she read me. She told me that in my later years there would come into my life a wonderful presence, a shining kind of being who would bring me many of the rewards and fulfill many of the promises I had never thought would be mine. It would be harvest time."

Viola closed her eyes.

"That prophecy has come to pass," Mother Green went on. "My reward, my shining blessing has got to be Bewie Freeth."

Up until then Viola had never known Mother Green to offer her strong drink except in case of illness.

Tonight she asked Viola to go to the little cupboard in the pantry and on the first shelf reach for the whisky and then pour out two glasses.

Viola was even less used to strong drink than Mother Green, but she knew she must not disappoint her old friend after she had told her of the prophecy of the psychic reader.

And Viola was as sure as sure could be Ruby Loftus had told the undeniable truth. Sad as Viola was that Bewie occupied so deep a place in Mother Green's heart, a place Viola would never hold, nonetheless, Bewie Freeth, beyond the shadow of a doubt, as if foretold by an angel, had come into the old woman's life a late blessing and a special gift.

MOTHER GREEN WAS so happy when Bewie was around, Viola Daniels later remarked often to visitors. She never did seem to reckon it would all come to a close.

The first night he didn't come home, or rather the first dawn, Mother Green was calm.

"Bewie will be home soon, mark my word," she would smile.

But one day was followed by another. Mother Green would hobble up to where he had his room.

"He'll be back if only to wear his outfits," she told Viola.

"Maybe we should notify the police," Viola said one evening after several weeks went by.

It was the only time Viola and Mother Green disagreed.

"Don't never say police ever again in my presence, Viola Daniels. If you have to do somethin' get down on your knees and pray, but don't say we should call the law."

MOTHER GREEN RELIED on Viola Daniels in so many ways, but principally to keep her straight on time and events. Viola knew the old woman's memory had begun to show the effects of time.

Often Mother Green would inquire, "When was it that Bewie came to us?"

"Don't you recall, Mother. He come on that blusterous July night."

"Which July though?"

"Why, July last, dear."

But in a day or so Mother Green would ask the same question over again.

Viola choked up then with the realization her old friend was beginning to fail, and she could not restrain a tear. She knew Mother Green was only holding to life at all because of Bewie.

"He was her all and everything." Viola would tell of it some time later.

ANOTHER THING WHICH worried Viola was that Mother Green continued to steal upstairs to Bewie's room despite the fact she had such a problem managing the rickety stairs.

At the foot of the stairs Viola would listen. She could hear Mother

Green lifting up his shirts and muttering something like, "Why ain't you come home, Bewie, when you know we miss you so."

Finally though if Mother Green didn't guess at the truth, Viola did. The truth that Bewie Freeth was gone for good.

But yet, if he had gone, his duds and finery was left behind.

Viola herself could not help stealing up the stairs and going to his closet. She took down his silk underwear, his pure cotton shirts, and once while arranging his Palm Beach suit on a handmade hanger, something fell out of one of the pockets onto the floor. The slight sound it gave out falling frightened her almost as if it was a firearm going off.

Slowly she picked the object up. It was a newspaper clipping. And the clipping was rather recent from a Chicago newspaper. Its heading read: METEORIC RISE OF UNKNOWN YOUTH. Her eyes moved on the article! Bewick Freeth who made hosannas ring nation-wide from his two previous films is now the undisputed charismatic idol of the hour. He has never been greater, his success unanimous.

Viola let the newsprint slip to the floor and sat down heavily on one of Mother Green's upholstered chairs. She felt faint, she felt, yes, betrayed, perhaps even mocked. Here he had been with them and never let on who he was. Yes, he had deceived them.

At the same time she felt he had not really lied to them. She knew he must have cared for them, a little perhaps, but, yes, he had been happy with them. He had often said he never wanted to leave, that she and Mother Green were "home to him." And now the clipping.

SITTING WITH MOTHER Green that evening, she was gradually aware the old woman was staring at her.

"Yes?" Viola managed to say.

"You look like you seen a ghost," Mother Green said. When there was no answer from Viola the old woman clicked her tongue.

"You know somethin' I don't know, Viola. You know somethin' and you know you know somethin'."

"Maybe I have found out who Bewie really is, Mother Green. And how come he ain't here anymore I guess."

"If you know something Viola, let's hear it, all of it."

"Bewie Freeth is not like us, Alabama accent or not. He's a famous movie star. What he was doin' here with us, well who knows."

Slowly, unostentatiously, as if handing Mother Green something she had perhaps asked for, Viola handed her the clipping.

The old woman put on her spectacles. She read and reread the article from the Chicago paper.

To Viola's consternation Mother Green, after putting away her spectacles, handed back the clipping to Viola without a word. Was the old woman beginning to fail, beginning not to take in things. No, not at all, Viola was sure. The truth about Bewie, the truth who he was had shocked her into this silence. After a long pause Mother Green smiled a kind of smile that meant, who knows, the dream was broken.

DOING HER EVENING sewing, Viola stopped working for a moment and said, "Mother Green."

"Yes," the old woman answered.

"I come across upstairs in the little store room along beside the games of checkers that old German Ouija board, planchette and all."

Mother Green's jaw dropped, and she reached in her side pocket for her handkerchief and wiped her eyes.

"You don't say," she spoke in a far-off voice. When Viola said no more, Mother Green, adjusting the lavaliere she wore about her throat said, "You mean you want to bring Ouija out then."

Viola nodded. After a silence she said, "I thought, Mother Green, Ouija might explain things to us, do you reckon?"

"You mean Bewie?"

"Yes, maybe."

"Explain him how."

"You said yourself the other evening as we lingered over tea that we can barely remember when or how he came to us."

Mother Green sighed in an odd off-hand way. "And you think Ouija can tell us the why and how of him. And whether we'll ever see him again."

The next day Viola brought the Ouija board out and set it on the card table.

"I declare," Mother Green said.

When they had arranged the board both ladies admitted they hardly dared begin.

"Do you ask Ouija somethin', Viola, now."

They put both their hands on the planchette. It did not move.

"You got to ask it, Mother Green, dear."

Their hands began moving slowly, sleepily after a while.

"No, no, Viola, you ask it."

The board moved jerkily, stopped and then began slowly to move to the letters.

It spelled KEWPIE.

The ladies giggled in spite of themselves.

The planchette moved wildly, then slowed down, then very pokily spelled

LUKY THE DAY HE COME TO YOU
& LUKIER THE EVENIN HE BE GONE
LUKY LUKY LADIES

"Mother Green, whether it's me or Ouija, but Ouija don't know how to spell now, do he?" Viola commented.

"But is he gone forever?" Mother Green asked Ouija. The planchette was still, perfectly still.

Viola began to see then that she should never have let Mother Green know that Bewie was a famous film actor. It was after Mother Green found out that fact that she began going down hill in no small measure. She complained too of what she called the weight of memory.

"After a while," Mother Green spoke in a low voice now to Viola almost as if she was praying, "there is too much to remember. And there is too much of past days to know *when* it happened, and sometimes there is the doubt maybe it did happen or I dreamt it. And the people! All the faces and the talk and the shoutin' from the beginning until now. Why all those years of mine in Alabama alone would take another fifty years to tell you about."

But Viola was sure it was Bewie's absence and his never coming back which pushed her down to what she called the shady side of life. "I'm going down the shady side now" she had once said before Bewie came, and now it had got worse than shady—it bespoke the deep night.

"Where is he?" she would often shout coming out of a dozing spell in her chair.

"Now, now Mother," Viola would respond.

"You don't tell me nothin', do you, Viola."

"Whatever you ask I will tell you if I know," Viola answered.

"I feel I am bein' kept in the dark," Mother Green would mumble.

AND SO THEY spent many evenings consulting Ouija, but sort of dispiritedly now. If Ouija had had one fault, that of misspelling words, now he had a worse fault, he was tongue-tied most of the time. When not silent Ouija stammered.

Mother Green spoke more and more of Ouija in fact as if he was a person, a person sort of like Bewie Freeth who was visiting them but wouldn't be permanent, a kind of transient somebody, yes, like Bewie Freeth had been.

Sometimes Viola wondered if she and Mother Green had only dreamed there was a Bewie Freeth. And Viola often thought Mother Green might be having the same thought.

They were both waiting for something, and Bewie had intercepted the wait, but now that he was gone, as Ouija said, they would have no occupation but to wait together.

VIOLA HAD TAKEN over the tasks that Bewie had performed, bathing Mother Green's feet and bunions in the medicated water, cleaning sometimes the wax out of her ears (though it didn't cure her deafness) and answering the endless query, "Do you think Bewie is ever comin' back?"

Then one day she up and told Mother Green Bewie had been gone for nearly a year, but she was glad for the first time Mother Green's deafness had prevented her from hearing her words.

Viola's sorrow grew as she often confided to herself when alone.

Mother Green seeing Viola's sorrow spoke up sharply, "Viola, Viola, what ails you you are so weepy. What is going on, dear child."

"I didn't know I was weepy, dear Mother," she said trying to smile.

"You miss Bewie, don't you."

But the mention of Bewie brought back to her how Mother Green's memory was playing tricks on her. For she always wondered where Bewie had gone, and she kept asking when he would return.

As many times as Viola told her that Bewie was gone, and would not come back, she saw that Mother Green either did not hear this explanation or having heard it erased it from her memory. For Mother Green, Bewie was a timeless part of their life, and so if he was gone, no matter, he would be back.

THE HEAVENS THEMSELVES seemed to give warning of what was happening, Viola Daniels would later tell people who visited.

Mother Green and Viola heard the sound that was like thunder, only probably closer and scarier. The sky seemed to blossom with many flaming colors which then fell like stars.

Difficult as it was now for both of the ladies to trudge up the long stairwell, they felt they had to find out what the commotion was.

It took Mother Green nearly a half hour to reach the top. How she sighed and groaned, and her bunions were killing her. She would rest on some of the steps before going further.

"I should have brought the smelling bottle, dear heart," Viola muttered, but Mother Green only gave her a reproachful look.

The top floor had great high huge windows. They no more got up there than she realized what it was.

"Fireworks," Mother Green exclaimed.

"It means something," Viola shook her head.

"If that's what you feel, we might consult Ouija."

This time Ouija was not evasive. The planchette began to move as soon as they touched it.

Mother Green came up with a start when Viola queried, "Where's Bewie?"

Ouija responded, "IN THE SWEET BY-AND-BY."

"And what do you mean *by-and-by*, Ouija?" Viola asked as Mother Green stared at the board.

Viola stirred uneasily for she knew Mother Green was alert tonight.

"HE GONE," Ouija responded.

At this, Mother Green sat up very straight in her chair but retained her hand on the planchette.

"Gone where?" Viola raised her voice.

Ouija moved at once.

"GONE TO CAMP GROUND."

"Where Camp Ground?"

Ouija did not move. Viola raised her voice, but the planchette was still, and then finally Ouija spelled again:

"CAMP GROUND."

VIOLA DANIELS' OWN memory was getting almost as bad as Mother Green's, and it wasn't exactly due to her drinking the strong spirits she found in the cupboard. No, Viola's memory was not what it was, say, the day Bewie had arrived.

She tried to remember how she had learned for a proven fact that Bewie had passed over.

Soon after their episode with the Ouija, one day while out shopping, Viola in one of her now common absentminded spells, found herself more than a few blocks away from Mother Green's, in a kind of promenade where there were expensive shops, saloons, and motion picture theaters. She saw that one of the movie houses was draped in black cloth, and there were wreaths and flowers and signs all everywhere. Her eye caught sight of the marquee. She stopped dead in her tracks. She kept reading over and again the lettering:

"YOU WILL ALWAYS BE WITH US BEWIE.
FOREVER AND A DAY"

Viola braced herself and went up to a uniformed man who was in charge of inspecting tickets as you went into the theater.

"Excuse me," she began. The uniformed man looked at her carefully and blinked.

"Tell me if Bewie Freeth. . . ."

He did not let Viola finish but pointed to a large oversize photo from a newspaper. Without her glasses Viola was hardly able to read the print, but finally at least one sentence came clear. Yes, Bewie Freeth was no more, had, in the words of Ouija, gone to Camp Ground.

IT WAS SEVERAL nights later that the first of the gatherings outside Mother Green's house began. They were mostly of young men, some of whom played every so often on a horn, others on a sax, and still others blew on what looked like a little cornet. When they quit playin' they shouted to passersby, "Bewie lived here for your information!"

Viola crept out on the frail front porch.

A smothered shout went up from the musicians.

There was the strong smell of something smoky, and as if it were their final number, each of the players took out big handkerchiefs and waved them at her in token, one supposed in tribute, to their idol Bewie.

Mother Green slept through it and other "live" performances that would take place as a tribute to their hero.

Looking at Mother Green after one of these performances, Viola heard her own voice say, "Lucky you, dear heart, you don't know what this is all about on account of I wouldn't know how to tell you, and I don't understand it maybe any better than you do or would."

"So, he in the sweet by-and-by," Viola said later that night to herself after she had had a shot of spirits in the kitchen.

TIME GOT MORE and more mixed up. After the night of the fireworks there was a long vacant pause in everything.

Viola was the first to say she thought something was about to bring them news.

And this time it was not Ouija who warned them, no it was a ticking sound Viola heard coming from Bewie's closet.

Viola trembled and even sobbed a little. Yet she had to investigate what on earth was making a ticking sound in the clothes closet.

It took her a long time to locate where the sound was coming from. She had no idea Bewie would carry an old-fashioned very heavy, yes, antique pocket watch. Why it seemed to weigh three pounds.

She removed it from his breast pocket. The sparkling gold watch was ticking! After all these—was it months or years?

Later Viola talked with a very venerable watchmaker, oh Mother Green said he must have gone back to the early days after emancipation. Watches and clocks, old Tyrrwhit assured her, like dead people, sometimes would come to life whether by means of a loud noise, or a building shaking, or often because of an earthquake or cyclone, a very old clock or watch, that had not ticked for ages, would all of a sudden begin ticking away. Clocks he assured Viola were imbued with a spirit all their own, and a watchmaker, a good watchmaker, knows the clock has a mind and knowledge superior to the watchmaker.

She took the ticking watch down to Mother Green who stared openmouthed at it and agreed, oh yes it was a sign.

NEHEMIAH HIGHSTEAD ACCOMPANIED by two lawyers arrived in weather even more stormy than the day when Bewick Freeth had entered the lives of the two ladies.

Nehemiah was an elderly black man who wore very thick colored glasses from which there extended a fluttering kind of frayed ribbon. His right hand trembled and he continually wiped his eyes with a large handkerchief from which there came a faint sweetish aroma.

"This is a very strange bequest, ladies," one of the attorneys finally began after looking about from ceiling to floor suspiciously. "Mr. Freeth came to our offices only a few days before his sudden decease."

Viola Daniels' full attention now rested on Mother Green whose face was devoid of expression. Had she heard the word *decease*? And having heard it did she understand it, understand, that is, what Viola had tried to tell her time and again that their Bewie was no more.

"You are the sole inheritors of what is more than a modest fortune. Much more!" the attorney continued.

He waited sleepily peevishly for his statement to take hold of his auditors as a judge will wait before he gives the verdict.

"He also provided for Mr. Highstead to look in on you ladies and be of any assistance as you may wish. Reverend Highstead was an acquaintance of Mr. Freeth from the actor's first days in the city. He is the pastor of the Ebenezer Resurrection Church which is on the other side of town. It would be completely up to you as to how much and to what extent you would request his support."

Viola nudged Mother Green from time to time as the old woman kept closing her eyes and breathing heavily, but the three gentlemen appeared not to notice this.

Finally the second attorney drew out from a Moroccan satchel a sheaf of papers. "If you ladies then will sign here on these dotted lines," he pushed the stiff legal pages to Mother Green.

Grasping tightly the pen he gave her she was able to sign:

Elgiva Green

The attorney repeated the name she had put down, confirming that she was the Mother Green designated in the will. It was, strange to say, the first time Viola Daniels had heard Mother Green's Christian name spoken out loud.

When the ladies had signed, Nehemiah Highstead rose, bowed his head, and asked everyone to join him in prayer.

It went something like this, as Viola recalled it some time later, "We are gathered here today chosen to represent a young man who went under the name of Bewick Freeth, originally from Tallassee, Alabama, who gained brief but almost universal fame as a film actor. We applaud his devotion to Mother Green and Viola Daniels and his generosity in bequeathing these two respectable ladies with his entire fortune. May the Almighty grant us the wisdom that we can administer it with integrity and zeal. We ask thee, eternal Master, to bless us all as we stand here in prayer and supplication."

No one could have foreseen the result of the two ladies coming into what even to wealthy persons would have been a sizable fortune.

Their disbelief they had inherited so much money was followed by a kind distemper and unwillingness to accept their change of fortune.

Ladies from the Ebenezer Resurrection Church called frequently not merely to rejoice with Mother Green and Viola so much as to give them the courage to accept their unbelievable change of circumstance. They also discreetly suggested that some of the money could go to the Church.

Mother Green hardly heard anything anybody said to her. She began to live in many different divisions of time. There were her early years in Alabama, then there were her later years of toil and poverty, followed by her proprietorship of the ramshackle mansion, and then the time when Bewick Freeth came out of the friendless blue and the unknown to stay with her and minister to her needs; then there was the time when Bewick, having left her without a word of goodbye, showered her with wealth.

She sat in the front window of the old mansion she now owned and nodded to passersby. She was the Mother Green then people came to recognize. She would raise her hand in blessing to them in the manner of an old film star herself. Everyone thought she was Bewick's mother. And at certain times of the day she herself may have thought so, for hour by hour her impression of reality changed.

"We missed knowing he was a world-famous movie star," Viola would confide sleepily to the visitors who now dropped in as if Mother Green's house was a sort of gathering place. Mostly young ones came. Crazy about their idol. They wanted to see too where he hung his clothes. But their request to go upstairs was vetoed of course.

The past, the present, the future became all mixed up in Mother Green's mind. Sometimes she thought Bewie was her own flesh and blood. Again he was her hired man. Sometimes he seemed like her grandson. He was hardly ever the famed movie star the world knew him by.

Often out of complete bewilderment and confusion as to what to do, Viola would hold Mother Green's hand and even kiss its worn flesh.

Once after holding her hand in hers for an unusually long spell Viola heard Mother Green say, "He'll be back, don't you believe now otherwise. Bewie will be back here whatever any folk may say he won't."

Viola actually almost believed what Mother Green said. For how could so vital so fresh so overwhelmingly youthful a young man disappear, any more than sunbeams would one day cease to visit this world of sorrow and loss.

IN THIS RESPLENDENT light then they went on with their lives, allowing Nehemiah Highstead and the Ebenezer Resurrection Church to tend to whatever arrangements so immense a bequest had visited upon the two retired ladies.

"I think he was sent," Mother Green often confided to Nehemiah on one of his frequent visits. To Viola's relief she saw that Nehemiah acted as if he agreed with Mother Green. Yes, he was not playacting. She believed the old man too felt Bewie's kind of splendor was not extinguished, would in fact make its presence known again.

From then on Mother Green if not Viola always spoke about Bewie as "amongst the living" and not ever amongst the departed. "He was like her very own," Viola often told the ladies of the Ebenezer Resurrection Church and the steady stream of young visitors who were Bewie's followers.

If for no other reason Mother Green's and Viola's daily lives were made more cheerful, more enjoyable, and yes more sociable. Their long years of lonesomeness and solitary grief (save when Bewie had come to them) was set aside for hours of joyfulness and even quiet mirth.

The church ladies brought from their own kitchens sumptuous repasts for supper, and lighter but even perhaps more enjoyable victuals for lunch. They brought daily fresh flowers and made other arrangements for brightening the premises. They hired at times limousines and entertained the two ladies with little excursions. They even undertook to restore the ruined mansion to its original splendor.

There was also singing, for all the ladies were members of the choir.

And like Viola Daniels they would often agree with nearly everything Mother Green remarked, such as, "Bewie ain't gone far," or "Bewie will be here amongst us again, mark my words."

And so, even had the two ladies not inherited great wealth, the presence of the many young visitors and of old Nehemiah and the church choir ladies made Mother Green's last days, if not quite as heavenly as the fortune teller had foretold, nonetheless *a* peaceable kind of half-light that suggests the growing presence of angels from beyond.

ENTRE DOS LUCES

I write this letter to all my friends in the states to let them know the whole truth about what really happened.

I have been told on reliable report that there is a warrant out in New York for the arrest of myself and my close friend Rico Alonso. You will remember we lived in the same string of rooms together on East Fourth Street, Manhattan, and our landlord was Felipe Parral.

We are innocent of murdering Felipe and of all the charges except burglarizing a pet shop. We did burglar it, but we did not kill Felipe. He was found with his throat cut days after we have run off from him on account of we feared he would kill us. The basis of our fear was that he had gone crazy over the death of his birds, and then the fact that when we replaced the dead birds with the new ones, he thought they had come back from the dead. He has many superstitious fears, or rather he had many. Even though we told him the new birds was stolen and brought to him by us, he would not believe us. He thought they had come back from the other world because of his many sins.

And now since Felipe is dead and gone himself, I will tell you that he once told Rico he had murdered several men in New York.

Whether he told the truth or not, Rico don't have no way of knowing of course, but Felipe swore to him he had killed them. That is why the birds coming back as he thought from hell scared him so. He had many enemies.

TO EXPLAIN OUR situation, let me go back then to how it all happened.

In exchange for a tiny room I had on the top of his building I was to keep his apartment clean, and water and feed the birds (he was so crazy about his birds) and keep their cages clean, but never to let them out. It was a hard task to clean the cages and not let them out, but I was successful until the unlucky day I am now going to tell you about.

His pet birds were not pets. They were more like wild animals, and I don't think they were like any birds people in cities are familiar with. Again, they were like small mammals with a hateful even vicious streak. I was taking care of them while he was in Havana. Felipe why he kept such large birds in such a small space eludes me also.

Felipe eludes everybody, in any case. The room smelled bad no matter how many times one cleaned their cages and aired the room even on bitter December nights in Manhattan. A bad bad odor, what a fellow I knew called fetor.

The trouble began in earnest when Rico who rented the side room from Felipe left his transom open. The birds while I was cleaning the cage as if they seen their chance all rushed up and out through the transom. I called to them to come back as if they were human.

I heard weak but prolonged hoarse cries coming from Rico's room. The door was always locked, and I had been told never to bother the tenant who was said to be recovering from a severe attack of something contagious.

I stood before this firmly locked door and asked if I could come in. For answer only the hoarse cries like someone suffocating to death. I tried the door, it was solidly locked, bolted.

As the cries continued, there was nothing to do but follow the birds and climb through the transom also. I pulled myself through the transom with some difficulty although I weigh only around 140 pounds at that time.

When I picked myself up from the floor in Rico's room, I was a good deal shaken by what I saw. All the birds, they were by the way some kind of crow or ravens, but of a kind Felipe told me not native to the United States, were, it seemed, holding Rico down and pulling on his skin like it was a worm.

He had nothing on at all but he was holding his rosary in his right hand. It was the rosary I later learned which had attracted the birds, but the Rico man thinking they meant to attack him, had struck out at the birds with the rosary, which either alarmed or frightened them, so that they began to pick and claw at him, and as he struck them again they attacked him finally in earnest.

I picked up a broom, and as the birds then turned their anger against me, before I knew it I had killed both of them by striking hard against their heads.

I gazed at them as they lay with their wings spread, their eyes open, their beaks streaming with blood. A little moan came from my mouth. Then I turned my attention to Rico. I was frightened to see that the two birds had badly torn his flesh, and he was crying and near hysteria.

"Let me put something on your cuts, Rico."

"Cuts," he said, "do you call them heridas just cuts."

"Well, whatever." I went to the sink and got a small basin and filled it with warm soap and water, and fetched a cloth from a drawer. I bathed his wounds.

"They have attacked me before," he said, looking down at himself. "Whenever I paid the rent and they were loose they would get at me."

"Let go of your beads," I advised him, "for your hand is badly wounded."

I begun cleaning out the different bleeding wounds on his hand.

"Now let me put some disinfectant of some kind on them," I said. I found a bottle of the stuff and put them on all his wounds.

HOW CAN ANYONE describe our landlord Felipe's anger when he returned and found his pets dead.

We knew he had a vile disposition, but we had not seen anyone gnash his teeth the way he did. The electricity of anger went up into his coal black hair, and each hair raised, as if it was seated in its own electric chair. Froth soon formed on his lips, and his heavily muscled arms trembled like an old man who has suffered multiple strokes.

He could not speak for many minutes, so strong was his wrath.

"What's your excuse," he finally turned to Federico, whom everybody calls Rico, but today he said, "Federico!" Like it was some big curse word he had found written on a wall.

"I was asleep," Rico began, "for I had worked all night."

"That's your story," our landlord said. "Cuentos!" he said in shame "Cuentos!"

"Cuentos!" Rico shouted. "Shit, I worked all night and was dead beat lyin' here with a sore foot I got caught in the subway train the other night."

"I want your alibi, Rico," he said rolling his eyes. "And I want to hear it good."

"I am tellin' you what happened and that ain't an alibi or nothing else, I am giving you the facts of what occurred, so don't foam at the mouth at me like a mad dog, or I'll pack and go."

"You don't leave owin' me five months' back rent."

Now Rico rolled his eyes.

"All right, what's your excuse," Felipe turned to me, leaving Rico thinking about all his back rent, I guess.

"I don't have none, boss."

"Skip that boss shit."

"I was lax."

"You was born lax, and all your ancestors was born lax back to Eve and Adam. So what else is recent?"

"I said I was careless and didn't notice the transom was open."

"What did I tell you about leavin' the cages open."

"I have seen you leave them cage doors open yourself."

"Yeah but me leavin' 'em open, since I'm in my right mind, and you leavin' them open is two different stories, chulo."

"All right, they're your birds and your birds' cage doors. I stand corrected."

"You bet your ass you are corrected. Do you know how much them birds was worth?"

"I suppose ten or twenty dollars not countin' their beaks and claws."

"You should be on the stage," he said coming up close to me. "Look," he said, to me, "I'll tell you what them birds is worth, or was worth. Five thousand a piece on account of they talk, do dances, and wink at you like clowns."

"I don't have that much money to give you for their death," I told him.

"You bet your black dirty soul, you don't. All right. All right. You killed the best friends I ever had." Turning to Rico, he said, "How many times have I told you to keep that Goddamn transom closed."

"I got to breathe, man. I got to have air."

"There's too much air in there, you claimed last winter, from ten thousand cracks in the wall. Now it's barely June, and you say there ain't air. I tell you, fellows, I am a ruined man. I'm through."

THAT NIGHT RICO and I burglared the pet shop. It was easy, because the owner must have forgot to lock his back door. We just walked in, took the covers off the cages, and chose two ravens, I think they was. We wrapped them in a blanket and carried them against us, leavin' the cages behind, and went to Felipe's room.

He was so drunk he didn't hear us come in, didn't hear us put the new birds in the cage.

That night I slept in Rico's room.

There was a knock on our door as we was eating breakfast. It was him, Felipe. We both saw he had maybe lost his mind.

"They're back," he cried. I saw clearly now he had as I say lost his mind. "They're back," he kept sayin', "they're back. They've returned from the dead."

"No, no, Felipe, we replaced them for you."

"Don't lie, hijo de puta, don't lie. The birds come back from the dead. I buried them so good too in a fashionable cemetery in Brooklyn."

He began eating one of our breakfast rolls, famished like, and drank half of the coffee in my cup.

"They went to hell," he went on, "and then they told them down there I missed them so much they could return and take me back down below to be with them again." He began bawling.

Rico and I looked at one another. We're sorry we had burgled the shop and brought him this new trouble, that is by bringing back the dead birds to life we saw we had driven him over the edge. Felipe was crazy.

BUT AS THE days passed, he calmed down a bit. Both ravens spoke Spanish whereas the dead birds only said things like, "Sailors sail the seven seas," or "Put on the tea kettle, dear." But Felipe paid no mind.

One night late while Felipe was drunk, Rico and I packed our valises, and went to the Greyhound station. We thought for quite a while where to go. Then we bought tickets one way for Tulsa, Oklahoma. We felt he would never follow us there. We got stuck for a while in Laredo, then finally crossed the border and headed towards Parras de la Fuente.

But believe me Felipe's death cannot be laid at our door. Though we did wrong by robbing the pet shop we did not kill Felipe. He was found lying in a pool of blood and there was no trace of the birds. He must have somehow made the whole thing come down on himself. It was his way to always carry on and never let a thing rest. "He was crazier than the devil on Christmas," as Rico always says.

Isidro Crespo
Mexico

MOE'S VILLA

The presence of Frau Storeholder at the entrance of Vesta Hawley's sprawling forty-room mansion had always annoyed Dr. Sherman Cooke on his frequent visits to see Miss Hawley. Dr. Cooke was not paying a visit as a physician but, according to the town wiseacre, he came as her suitor of more than twenty years.

Even when Dr. Cooke finally remarried suddenly to wealthy Miss Mamie Resch, he continued his courtship of the only woman he had ever loved—Mistress Hawley, as people in Gilboa often called her.

Frau Storeholder who spoke German with more ease than English spent most of her time, Dr. Cooke was sure, reading the obituary notices in several local and out-of-town newspapers. She often would call attention to a recent death to Dr. Cooke who, however, pointedly ignored her.

"She is like an ill-tempered though usually silent watchdog," Dr. Cooke often remarked of Frau Storeholder to Miss Hawley. "Do you have to have her here, and if you do have to have her, why then can't she sit in her own room rather than station herself like a sentinel at your front door?"

Vesta Hawley would smile at the doctor's observations. "I find Frau Storeholder's presence most comforting," she would reply.

"And her reading aloud to all and sundry from the latest obituary notices?" the doctor complained.

Vesta chuckled at this remark.

"Why should hearing an obituary notice irk you, a doctor of medicine, dear Sherman?" Then Sherman Cooke would gaze at his only love with sheep's eyes.

Though no longer young, Vesta Hawley's hair was of a remarkable yellow color (one had to see it in the sunshine to appreciate it fully), and someone had once compared it to the hue of the Circassian walnut furniture scattered throughout her mansion.

THERE WERE DIFFERENT theories in Gilboa why Vesta Hawley had never married a suitor of such indefatigable faithfulness and ardour as Sherman Cooke. Of course her only previous marriage to Peter Driscoll had been a disaster, and Peter had decamped early on after only a few years of matrimony. And certainly Vesta could have been more comfortable with someone who could help support her mansion and herself. She was always in debt, owing many banks huge sums of mortgage money.

Not only had Peter Driscoll "decamped" but her only son, young Rory (whom she had foolishly thought might one day support her), had run away before he was even grown up.

Rory Hawley had taken his mother's name since there was some doubt Vesta had ever been legally married to Peter Driscoll in the first place.

Vesta Hawley had never bothered to send her son to school. True, the public schools of Gilboa were hardly equipped to teach their few pupils even the essentials of reading and arithmetic. It was believed, however, in any case that Rory had almost never attended classes from his earliest years. His mother pretended to believe he was at school when she must have known better.

Rather than attend school and learn at least to read and write,

Rory often went from his mother's house in the morning to another mansion a mile or more away whose owner was a Shawnee Indian by the name of Moses Swearingen. Moses Swearingen's mansion, called the Villa, although it did serve admirable evening repasts, was more famous for its gambling salons behind the restaurant proper and the number of young men who waited on him hand and foot.

Moses Swearingen himself had taken an interest in Rory when he saw how neglected he was by his mother ("She lived in Cloud-Cuckoo-Land," Swearingen had often remarked after the different scandals which occurred around Rory and to a lesser degree himself).

Moses Swearingen had taught Rory to read, write and cipher, and finally how to play cards.

Rory soon surpassed his teacher in the art of card playing and finally gambling. It was both the boy's salvation and some said his eventual ruin.

Our story begins quite far back, or as we might say, in the era when there were still brawny men who delivered ice from the quarry to residents like those of Vesta and Moses Swearingen. For there was no refrigeration as we know it now in Gilboa, an unincorporated village of nearly 3,000 people. There were as a result icemen and also milkmen, and fruit and vegetable men, and knife and scissors sharpeners. All these came in vehicles drawn by dray horses.

Swearingen himself once said he could not have maintained his restaurant without the icemen and the rest of the horse-drawn vehicles.

Moses Swearingen did not look like an Indian. For one thing he had hair almost the color of Vesta Hawley's, except it was if anything more abundant and of a finer texture. His eyes changed, it was observed, like the tides. In the morning his eyes were almost robin's egg blue, but as the day progressed his orbs became darker, and as he sat overlooking the card players in the evening his eyes were of a fearful black.

A young man who had dabbled in anthropology and who visited Moe's Villa from time to time said that, despite Moses' fair hair, his pronounced high cheekbones were the telltale proof he had Shawnee blood.

Where Moses' great-grandfather came into his fortune and his mansion was never truthfully known. Indeed it has been an equal mystery where his family originally came from.

On the other hand Dr. Sherman Cooke did not resemble at all a family physician in his appearance. He had the chest of an athlete, almost a Samson, and even at an advanced age he gave the impression of a blacksmith or the wielder of a sledgehammer. He had a waist, some of his clients joked, not above twenty-eight inches in girth.

There were some blotches or scars on his weather-beaten complexion. Rumour had it that Rory had attacked the doctor one evening when he saw the doctor emerging from Vesta's bedroom. Some claimed that the boy had thrown a pot of scalding water on the doctor's countenance. Others said Rory had stabbed him with a penknife.

Once, however, the doctor told one of his closest friends he had fallen as a child into a bonfire and was only tardily rescued at the last moment, else he would have perished.

Even more arresting to his appearance was his untamable shock of very black hair, which appeared never to have been cut or indeed combed. And, until at a late age, it was all but untouched by gray. (He laid this fact to his eating foods rich in copper.) In short, Dr. Cooke (he also spelled his name indifferently now and again as Coke) resembled a Shawnee Indian more than Moses Swearingen. And townsfolk often jeered that the scars on the doctor's countenance were inherited from tomahawk wounds.

After the disappearance of Pete Driscoll, they came from far and near. At first perhaps the suitors were curious concerning Vesta's reputed wealth and the fact of course she owned one of the great showplaces of this remote rural area. For the general opinion was that whoever inherited her mansion was set for life. (What no one realized, perhaps not even Vesta Hawley, was that the house, in disrepair since the Civil War, was gradually turning to powder.)

But the indomitable untamable and indestructible suitor was of course Dr. Sherman Cooke of the blotched countenance and unruly uncut unbarbered hair.

It was also whispered that Moses Swearingen himself far back had often paid Vesta Hawley short mysterious calls. It was said he always left the premises with lowered brow and sagging shoulders.

Vesta herself frequently remarked that had she not had so intractable and unteachable a son as Rory, perhaps she would have married. Doubtful, in retrospect. For Vesta loved her own independence more than life itself. And she did not wish to marry for another reason: she wished one day to bequeath her mansion to Rory who she always called her fate and nemesis—as the only means she could make up for her failure as a mother and guide.

"Rory will never be satisfied," she once remarked to some of her gentlemen visitors, "until he sees me lying in a pinewood box on the way to Maple Grove Cemetery. Then and only then can he do exactly as he pleases!"

But Rory as soon as he could talk had done exactly as he pleased, and Vesta soon realized he was as intractable as a tiger cub.

So extensive was Vesta's mansion there were—she claimed—many rooms she had never set foot in.

But in all the rooms she was familiar with there were her clocks. Everyone in Gilboa had heard stories of them, and some lucky people had actually heard them tick and chime. Almost all the rooms on the main floor had at least one grandfather clock. In Vesta's huge bedroom (large enough to sleep a squadron) there were over sixteen clocks of varying size.

The irony of all this collection of timepieces was that most of them had long ago given out, and no matter how Vesta herself and her friends tinkered with them, they could not bring the clocks back to life.

But when none of the clocks kept time at all, and poor as she was or claimed to be, she was able to persuade a famous watchsmith from Toronto, Canada, to come to visit her.

Dr. Sherman Cooke had attempted to dissuade her from inviting an unknown man to her house. He scoffed at her assurance that the watchsmith was considered the finest in the hemisphere.

"Famous or not, you may be in actual peril," the doctor cautioned.

"The invitation stands, Sherman!" and she added, "If you really had been concerned over the years, you would have bought me a proper timepiece."

"*A* timepiece! You would only be satisfied with a hundred! And I am convinced, dear girl, that there is something in the temperature of your rooms which slows down and finally stops all your clocks."

They both laughed after he had made this little speech.

Vesta was more worried over how she would pay the famous visiting watchsmith than under any apprehension he might murder her.

"He was too young, much too young!" Dr. Sherman Cooke later recalled the watchsmith. "It cost me many a sleepless night while he was at her beck and call. And the scamp also fell for Vesta, wouldn't you know—the Canadian watchsmith! Head over heels he was!"

Dr. Sherman Cooke slowly began to understand why Rory had run away from home, if one could call such an establishment as Vesta's "home."

"Rory saw she was not his mother, but a Circe," Dr. Cooke confided to one of his oldest patients who was dying of an undiagnosed illness.

The young Canadian watchsmith had stayed a week and, to give the devil his due, he succeeded in making almost all the clocks run again except one ancient grandfather timepiece.

"It will have to be sent to my workshop in Canada," he told Vesta. "For we would have to repair almost all of its inner works."

Dr. Cooke saw the watchsmith's behaviour (he charged Vesta only five dollars for his extensive time and workmanship) as a kind of repeat performance of all the men, young and old, who had fallen for Vesta Hawley, including even her young son Rory. For the boy, constantly caressed and spoiled, then neglected and confused, had his own inner working ruined perhaps forever.

IT WAS THE schoolteacher Bess Byal who called on Vesta one blustering fall evening when all the countless clocks were by now ticking and chiming away.

Vesta insisted on giving the schoolmarm her best India tea together with fresh homemade Parker House rolls and gooseberry jam.

"Do you realize," Bess said after unwillingly enjoying the repast, "that Rory has not attended school since the first two days of the term."

Vesta's mind was a thousand miles away.

"He is either at the picture show, or when the picture show is not running, he spends the day and even most of the night at Moe's Villa."

"Moe's?" Vesta was evasive and toyed with her grandmother's brooch.

"The very same," Bess confirmed and then swallowing some tea the wrong way, she burst into a seizure of coughing.

"And did the truant officer never talk to the boy?" Vesta inquired with the vagueness and indifference she might have shown had Bess told her of a child's kite which the wind had blown out of reach.

"I'm afraid we have no such officer, Vesta. Ben Wheatley, our truant officer, passed away last year, and the school board doesn't now have the funds to employ another."

"Yes, what is to become of Rory," Vesta said listlessly, and pinched the bridge of her nose.

Bess let the Parker House rolls tempt her again in the face of this absence of maternal responsibility.

DR. COOKE WAS both fascinated and made uneasy by Vesta's many "fancies," as the doctor called her pet pleasures. There was of course her obsessive interest in—as an example—her countless clocks. But her unusual "fancies" extended to many other phenomena.

One evening when the doctor was seated beside her in the velvet settee of the parlour, holding her hand and hoping she would allow him to kiss her, he saw Vesta all at once leap up and go to the large front window, pull back the heavy curtains and bend her ear close to the pane.

"What on earth is it?" he wondered.

"Sh! Listen, only listen."

He heard from a distance a man's powerful whistle.

It was the sound of young men whistling, he learned finally, which created in Vesta Hawley an almost swooning pleasure such as she experienced when she heard the combined ticking of her many clocks.

Yes, she admitted, she found the sound of young men whistling from their powerful lungs as breathtakingly moving as a more sophisticated person might experience hearing a sax or fine piccolo solo.

"Oh, Vesta, Vesta, I will never understand you."

Then there came the day when it seemed clear that Rory had left his mother's house for good, that Vesta noticed Frau Storeholder grasping one of the out-of-town evening newspapers, standing worriedly and hoping to be allowed to tell her mistress something.

"No more obituaries, Frau Storeholder. I am not strong enough this evening to hear who has left us for the other shore! Please!"

"May I read from the marriage announcements of last month," Frau Storeholder was very firm and obstinate.

"But why on earth marriage," Vesta said, and then perhaps sensing at a severe look from Frau Storeholder what was to come, "All right," Vesta managed to say. "Read your news! But only if it is about the living."

Frau Storeholder in her heavy accent read then from a Chicago newspaper that Dr. Sherman Cooke of Gilboa had married Miss Mamie Resch also of Gilboa in a private ceremony.

Vesta made her way to the easy chair and slumped down against its freshly-laundered antimacassar.

"Shall I bring you the elixir doctor left you last week?" Frau Storeholder, having put away the newspaper suggested.

"That may be a good idea," Vesta answered in a voice at least two octaves lower than usual. "Kindly do so."

Sipping the elixir, Vesta muttered to her faithful friend, "I will weigh carefully what it is I must do next."

A bit afraid Vesta might mean an act of violence, Frau Storeholder spoke in her lullaby manner, urging Vesta to take no action until the shock had subsided.

Queerly enough, Dr. Cooke arrived at his usual hour of visiting the next evening, but Frau Storeholder informed him that Vesta was not at home to anyone this night.

"Not at home!" the doctor scoffed and then bore down his Herculean presence past the old obituary-reader and rudely opened the sliding doors which lead to the parlour. There he caught sight of his only love with a hot water bottle attached to her aching head, sprawled out on a fancy ottoman.

Dr. Cooke courageously removed the hot water bottle and took both her hands in his. She was too weak to rebuff him.

"Where is the pain?" he whispered, touching lightly his lips in her fragrant hair.

She tried to push him away, but in her weakness failed to achieve this action.

"Nothing will have changed, dear Vesta. You are my only one. You know that!"

She slapped him across the face, but he noticed this no more than had he felt a fly alight on his forehead.

"I have been in catastrophic financial straits," he began, and Vesta knew this was a sly reference to his having helped her modestly in days gone past.

"And you have moved in bag and baggage with her I am told.

Have you departed your own place where you treated your patients for so many decades."

"My wife has given me her entire first floor for my professional duties," he spoke lamely.

More excuses now followed in a lachrymose delivery.

"The banks would not honor my last request for a loan," he finished, and without her permission he bestowed a kiss on her forehead.

Because she did not repulse him for this action he knew then she probably would continue to admit him to her presence, married or not! But then who could predict Vesta's changing moods?

That night Vesta had a strange dream. It had to do not so much with the doctor, though he flitted in and out of the dream, as it showed Miss Mamie Resch in the action of hiding a collection of gold pieces in what looked like an opening in the wallpaper.

Waking, Vesta could not get the dream out of her mind. She knew of course, as did everybody in Gilboa, that Mamie Resch was not only incredibly rich, but was even more famous as a miser who hid her money in all kinds of secret places.

The next morning Vesta Hawley was consumed with anger and outraged to such an extent she feared she might suffer palpitations for which Dr. Cooke had treated her in times past with tiny little red pills.

Under the pretext she had run out of medicine, she decided to pay a visit to Dr. Cooke.

Yes, Vesta Hawley who almost never left her own residence realized that was exactly what she must do. She summoned one of her "whistlers," a farmer's boy, Stu Hysted, who came at once in his rickety car with tires which appeared to be not so much punctured as shredded. He doffed his hat and bowed low when he saw Vesta come out of her front door and grinned showing his toothpaste ad beautiful teeth.

They rode then not to the Doctor's old lodging but to the imposing edifice of Dr. Cooke's new mistress—the heiress Mamie Resch who else!

Asking Stu Hysted to wait in his jalopy, Vesta strode up the twenty or so steep steps leading to Mamie's front living room. Out of breath more from anger than palpitations, Vesta flung open the door and then all but fell onto an ottoman.

She could hear the doctor's voice coming from the next room, advising a woman patient about remedies for the discomfort of the change of life.

Catching her breath slowly, Vesta surveyed the rather dingy furnishings in the room until her eye fell on the faded rose and gold wallpaper. It did and did not resemble the wallpaper she had seen in her dream. Rising, she walked about the room with its assortment of wandering jew plants and several vases of artificial flowers covered with dust.

Then her eye caught a metallic little something near the floor almost indistinguishable from the wallpaper.

Vesta was so disturbed by the metal's resemblance to her dream of the night before she had the sudden wish to leave the premises. She was afraid, afraid for herself, afraid for her dream.

The sound of the doctor's voice continuing and his patient's long-winded replies persuaded her to stay.

Almost before she knew what she was doing she had knelt down on the floor and touched the metallic protuberance from the wallpaper. Her hand had hardly done so than it came open like a loose door, and she saw inside a kind of passageway in which was located a thick envelope.

She pulled it out. Across the outside was written:

TO BE OPENED ONLY IN AN EMERGENCY.

A kind of anger had almost blinded Vesta to such an extent she had trouble reading the message.

The envelope came open as she held it with trembling fingers. Inside she could make out several thousand-dollar bills.

"Is someone there?" the doctor's voice now reached her.

Like any ordinary burglar, Vesta, putting the envelope in the pocket of her outside coat, waited, breathless, then hearing no one approach, managed to tiptoe out of the room. Outside, she rushed toward her young chauffeur.

"Are you all right," he was saying to her as she sat in the backseat. She was unable to answer.

"Do you want me to call anybody?" he inquired worriedly.

"No, no, Stu," she wailed. "Let's go to my house as soon as you can drive me there."

Stu watched her carefully before he took the wheel and drove off at an almost reckless speed, which may have reminded Vesta of robberies she had heard of from Frau Storeholder reading from the evening news.

DR. COOKE CAME a few evenings later.

"I'm sorry I missed you," he spoke lamely after she had served him with a hot bowl of his favorite soup. "I believe you paid me a visit, Vesta."

Vesta eyed him carefully.

Either Dr. Cooke was the greatest actor the nation had seen, she decided, or else the heavens be praised, he knew nothing of her theft, indeed now made no further mention of her having visited his new abode.

Taking his manner to mean he was ignorant of her deed or that he acquiesced in her crime, she allowed him to give her quick little kisses, with the satisfaction perhaps she was now not only a robber but guilty of adultery in the bargain.

Guilty people, according to popular works on the subject, often keep notes of their misdeeds, recounting in detail their crimes and their methods of performing them.

Vesta Hawley's method was not to write down what she had committed but to confide her misdeed to Frau Storeholder. It was like whispering, she felt, to a tomb.

One of the things about Frau Storeholder which puzzled Vesta Hawley was the fact the old lady's hair had not one strand of gray. Knowing her attendant so well over the years, Vesta was positive she did not dye her hair. And she often recalled, having read somewhere in a book on the occult, that persons who have second sight often keep the original color of their hair until death.

And then began Vesta's confession of her crime.

"My back was to the wall," she began her litany.

Frau Storeholder had never been to an eye doctor but made occasional visits to a drug store where the druggist supplied her with cheap reading glasses.

Frau Storeholder now took off her spectacles and gazed at Vesta without the aid of optics. She gazed as if she had to be sure it was Vesta herself who was confessing to her falling from the path of righteousness.

And when Frau Storeholder removed her spectacles, it meant Vesta could confide anything she wished to her "doorkeeper."

"My back was to the wall," she repeated these words now. "God pity me, Belinda! You know I cannot let the bank take my house away from me, now can you. For where would you go, dear Belinda (Belinda was Frau Storeholder's Christian name and known only to Vesta, though she was like everyone else more often than not to call the old woman Frau Storeholder. But for secret and even damaging information, she always said *Belinda*).

"As you know better than anyone else, I have fought for over a quarter of a century to keep a roof over our heads and in the bargain, my dearest friend, I have sometimes under such pressure stepped over the bounds of the straight and narrow."

Frau Storeholder now toyed with her store-bought spectacles but refrained from putting them on.

Vesta always took this gesture of Belinda's as encouragement to continue.

In any case, Belinda won't remember by morning, Vesta reflected, what I've told her at vespers!

And to whom could Frau Storeholder go if she wished to tattle? The old woman knew nobody now. All Frau Storeholder's friends, family, her near and distant relatives had joined the choir invisible.

And then would such a Christian person sully her lips with what Vesta told her.

"This is what occurred in Mamie Resch's living room," Vesta began in a voice more like that of an opera singer than her usual pedestrian, often mumbling, manner.

"I have as you know for some time been desperate to meet my mortgage payments on my house—our house, Belinda. You would probably say the Prince of Darkness himself showed me the way. I discovered an envelope hidden there. Don't ask me how I found it. I say I found an envelope. I opened it. I thought of my many years of worry and privation, my having lost Rory through my poverty and through my having sometimes overstepped the conventions with my men boarders. I say this woman had money to burn and I had nothing. I took the money. I have it now. Oh, have no fear, Dr. Cooke will see that I return it. You have noticed he continues to pay calls on me, him a married man. Has told me barefaced that he loves only me. So, Belinda, I have fallen from grace!"

Because of the long and dreadful silence on the part of Frau Storeholder after Vesta's confession, Vesta almost wondered if her good friend had fallen asleep, or, what is worse, had a stroke and had died owing to her revelation!

But no, now her Belinda stirred, smiled faintly and oddly enough nodded slowly several times.

The theft of the thousand-dollar bills, Vesta feared, might be the one straw that would destroy their love and friendship. And unless Frau Storeholder actually did not hear her chronicle of dishonesty, at any rate she made no hint of disapproval or even judgement. And as Vesta studied the old woman's features, she saw something in the way her eyes closed and opened and the fact her pale lips became more crimson in the movement of a half-smile that gave her pause.

"My dear Vesta," Frau Storeholder began in a voice entirely unlike her own, a voice a little like that of the preacher speaking after communion or some other of the sacraments.

"We sometimes, Vesta," Frau Storeholder went on speaking in her new untypical voice, "yes, sometimes, dear lady, we must take the law in our own hands."

Astonished at such a statement from a student of Scripture, Vesta waited for Belinda to say more. There was no more!

But when Vesta gave Belinda an eloquent look, and this look took in that Frau Storeholder was smiling almost beatifically at Vesta, she assumed her normal behaviour and began talking rapidly.

"For what would you and I do after all, my dear Belinda, with no roof over our heads, no food on our plates."

As a matter of fact both ladies had often bewailed the fact that the village of Gilboa no longer could afford even a poorhouse for its indigent. The depression had destroyed charity itself! Many of the homeless lived now on the edge of Maple Grove Cemetery.

"She forgives me!" Vesta smothered the unspoken words into a linen handkerchief. "And people wonder, yes Dr. Cooke among them, why I put up with the poor dear. The real question I reckon is how come she puts up with me."

"I lost my boy from trying to keep a roof over his head," Vesta now recounted this episode of her life for the hundredth time.

Yes, Vesta mused, Frau Storeholder must have recalled from her incessant Bible reading that it was the Good Shepherd who forgave the harlots and sinners. It was the Good Shepherd indeed who forgave the thief on the cross and promised he would meet him in paradise. He would have understood also a woman like herself who erred on the side of the law in order to keep a shelter for her loved ones and for those lonely young men who shared the fare of her banquets.

Vesta Hawley had not recovered from her purloining a small fortune from Dr. Cooke's wife when Mr. Eli Jaqua, the principal of schools, telephoned to say he must meet with Miss Hawley immediately.

It was Frau Storeholder of course who took the message and who, disturbed by the urgency of tone of the principal, told Mr. Jaqua she was sure Miss Hawley would of course see him. Vesta Hawley was too ill with a sick headache to quarrel with her faithful friend's agreeing to this unwelcome visit from a man she loathed and despised—Eli Jaqua. (He had according to Vesta bad-mouthed her and her mansion for years.)

"I refuse to see him, dear Belinda," Vesta managed to say taking the hot water bottle away from her face.

When Vesta saw the look of anxiety and disapproval even on Frau Storeholder's face, she added: "Do you talk to the man, why don't you. For, dear friend, you know more about me and my affairs than perhaps I do. See him for me!"

Saying this, Vesta pulled a sheet over her face and head. Frau Storeholder was majestic that day as she sat in the parlour with Principal Eli Jaqua. He noticed it and marveled as he had been marveling at the grand albeit decayed aspect of this once great showplace.

Principal Jaqua was not an old man, but the cares of his calling, the lack of funds for operating a public school in Gilboa and his wearing spectacles all added years to his otherwise rather handsome features and made him appear as a rule often old and tired. Such a face, such a man could hardly be asked as a dinner guest for Vesta Hawley's midnight banquets.

"I believe, dear Frau Storeholder, that you know the purpose of my visit, and I would not have come had the errand been anything but a grave one."

Looking around suspiciously, he coughed then inquired, "When may I see Miss Hawley?"

"She is very ill, Mr. Jaqua, and the doctor has told her she must see no one."

"That ill?" Mr. Jaqua said and looked at one of the many clocks ticking away.

He fidgeted, his mouth moved to say more, then was still, and as he fidgeted even more he colored almost violently.

"Frau Storeholder, let me say this: You know probably more about what the purpose of my errand is today than Miss Hawley herself does, racked in pain as I gather that she is."

Frau Storeholder nodded and agreed Miss Hawley was quite under the weather.

"Then I will say right out what it is. Rory Hawley, dear lady, can no longer be called just a truant. No, not at all."

Mr. Jaqua let this remark sink in before continuing, but regretfully saw no change of expression on Miss Hawley's beloved confidante. She was as cool indeed as Vesta Hawley always was when hearing bad news.

"Rory Hawley," Mr. Jaqua continued, "has gone from truant to deserter, and from deserter to a kind of, shall we say, turncoat to his own ancestry and upbringing. He is a resident along with many other young men who are out of work at Moe's Villa. Indeed he lives there!"

Even this last fierce and even dreadful statement failed to evoke any change in Frau Storeholder's countenance. Had Mr. Jaqua said only, "Rory Hawley is now fifteen years of age!" she would have been just as poker-faced and calm.

"There are worse places for Rory to be, I suppose," Frau Storeholder commented in the icy silence which had taken place.

"I beg your pardon," Mr. Jaqua spoke between his teeth and his eyes flashed under his ill-fitting glasses. "How, may I ask, could hell itself be worse than the Villa. Let me clarify my comment on the Villa."

"I have known Moses from the time he was a boy," she now explained her incendiary statement. "Rory will be provided for—if I know Mr. Swearingen at all!"

"But in a gambling hell, dear Frau Storeholder. A young boy in a gambling hell!"

"Every attempt, dear Mr. Jaqua, has been made to bring Rory back. Miss Hawley does not wish to do more. And time, Mr. Jaqua, if you will allow me to say so, is often the best arbiter of our dilemmas."

"Time—the arbiter!" He gave a kind of sound between a whimper and a groan and rose then, as did Frau Storeholder. "I see, I'm afraid," Mr. Jaqua raised his voice loud enough for perhaps Miss Hawley to hear, "I see and understand that my mission here has not borne fruit. But as a Christian gentleman, let me say I am glad I have put forth the effort."

In the awkwardness which now ensued, Mr. Jaqua, hands trembling, attempted to put on his long woolen gloves. But like his mission, they appeared to resist his best efforts. Finally, pulling off the one glove he had somehow managed to get on, he put both gloves in his outer coat and extended his hand to Frau Storeholder.

She took his very cold hand in her warm one and bowed slightly.

"You may tell our good Miss Hawley," he said at the outer door, "that she shall hear from the Superintendent of Schools with reference to the matter at hand, be assured!"

Fearing Mr. Jaqua might slam the door in the state he was in and perhaps break the rather delicate frosted glass of the ancient portal, Frau Storeholder now held the door wide open for him until her visitor had bowed himself out.

THE NEXT DAY Mr. Eli Jaqua, after his unsuccessful visit to the Hawley mansion, called an emergency meeting of the school board.

Although it was Superintendent Shingles's priority to arrange such a meeting, for some years he had allowed Mr. Jaqua to conduct almost all business without prior knowledge of the superintendent himself. After all Mr. Shingles was over ninety years old and was usually more than pleased to turn over most of his duties to the younger principal. In addition to Mr. Shingles, Bess Byal (the truant boy's teacher) and two other teachers were also in attendance.

Superintendent Shingles was more than a little deaf and inclined to doze off during the sessions which Mr. Jaqua chaired. And for some time the old gentleman was usually completely in the dark about any business at hand.

Today, however, Superintendent Shingles brightened at the mention of Vesta Hawley and then, to the annoyance of Mr. Jaqua, admitted he did not realize there was a son named Rory. He expressed surprise indeed that, in his words, so beautiful, young, and attractive a woman as Vesta Hawley had ever had a child!

Superintendent Shingles furthermore annoyed Mr. Jaqua to no end today by reminiscing on Vesta Hawley's "showplace" of a mansion, and he recalled that some few years past he had often been invited as a special guest of Mistress Hawley to her soirees and banquets.

Finally interrupting Mr. Shingles's recollections, Mr. Jaqua with ill-concealed annoyance asked what measures should now be taken with reference to Rory Hawley, who, among his many wrongdoings, had not attended school for nearly two years and, what was more alarming to the school board, the young man had all but moved in with Moses Swearingen, without his mother's knowledge, in the residence known by the townspeople as Moe's Villa!

"Yes, Superintendent Shingles," Mr. Jaqua now raised his voice, "our young truant Rory is permanently quartered in a rather notorious domicile already referred to as Moe's Villa!"

"But see here," the Superintendent bridled, and he appeared all at once to be bright as a silver dollar, "I have known Moses Swearingen since he was a boy! He is actually a young man of remarkable resources, a former war hero, we must remember, and now the owner of a property called by Mr. Jaqua, Moe's Villa—rather despairingly I fear—a property nonetheless which rivals Vesta Hawley's own mansion but is, if I am correctly informed, worth a great deal more in value!"

Mr. Shingles now wiped his forehead of what was, one supposed, sweat at this unheard-of long speech from him, but noting Mr.

Jaqua was about to interrupt him, the Superintendent continued: "So I believe if I may say so, gentlemen and Miss Byal, that Rory Hawley could be in a much worse place than the name Moe's Villa might imply." Wiping his forehead again carefully, he continued, "May I also indulge in a little local history by reminding everyone here today that Moses Swearingen has exerted every effort of muscle and brain to keep under his ownership the property of the Villa inherited from his great-grandfather, a hero in the Civil War; and in order not to lose this property from taxes and mortgages, Moses, it is true, began to operate a section of his house as a very stylish eating place and also a recreation room (billiards, card playing, I hear). He has hired many young men who have been, through no fault of their own, unemployed! He also defended himself against a bully who attacked him, leaving Moe seriously wounded. Yes, my dear friends, young Rory could be in a much worse situation."

"Yes, my dear Mr. Shingles, how right you are. Rory Hawley could be living in a den of thieves, I suppose."

Mr. Shingles smiled at the pointed remark only because he had not heard a word Mr. Jaqua had said.

The wind considerably taken out of his sails, Mr. Jaqua however managed to resume his role as chairman by saying: "What action then, gentlemen and Miss Byal, are we to take in view of the important information given us just now by Superintendent Shingles?"

Mr. Shingles then, to the astonishment of everyone present, had taken up Mr. Jaqua's gavel and with this gesture appeared to be now in actual fact the Superintendent.

"Let me say at this time, my dear friends and colleagues, that in my opinion we have no jurisdiction over the lives of the person we have been discussing. We are, let us remember, schoolmasters and teachers. What Mistress Hawley does in her private chambers, and Mr. Swearingen does in his, do not concern us. If the Hawley boy has gone to Mr. Swearingen of his own free will, as I understand he has, and if his mother, the excellent Vesta Hawley herself, has made no appeal to outside authority for his return, who are we, as I say, mere schoolteachers, to interfere in the freedom and privacy of these two leading citizens!"

No silence could have been more profound than the dead silence that now followed this speech (indeed had not only a pin dropped but a sledgehammer, no one would have heard it). Mr. Shingles, smiling a bit triumphantly and letting go his gavel, picked up his heavy felt hat and almost slammed it over his ears. And following this singular action, he took from his breast pocket a silver whistle and blew it forcefully.

His private chauffeur, Kurt Bandor, appeared immediately as if from nowhere on hearing the whistle blown and with a rather elaborate and possessive manner led the old man outside to his waiting limousine.

Mr. Jaqua, put in his place, and acting as if he had been slapped in the bargain, crimsoned to the roots of his hair and, for the first time in his tenure as principal, could find nothing to say until after a nervous question from Bess Byal, he managed to utter, "The meeting, Miss Byal and gentlemen, is indeed adjourned; thank you."

As everyone was filing out then, except for Mr. Jaqua, the members of the gathering were astonished to hear all of a sudden from the room just vacated Mr. Jaqua striking the table at which he still sat with Superintendent Shingles's gavel.

Bess Byal, at the sound of the gavel, turned back and stared questioningly at the principal.

"Good night, Miss Byal," he managed to say, still grasping the superintendent's gavel.

ONE FROSTY NOVEMBER evening as Vesta was entertaining some star customers over dessert and mulled wine, Frau Storeholder a bit ruffled entered and whispered in Vesta's ear: "Dr. Cooke says he would like a word with you."

"Tell the good doctor to join us in dessert."

Just then the clock struck twelve.

"Doctor asks a word alone with you," Frau Storeholder added solemnly.

"No, no, no!" Vesta cried. But she got up, dropping her napkin, and excused herself from her three dinner guests and faced the doctor.

"Why won't you come and have some dessert," Vesta scolded. "Don't tell me you won't."

Dr. Cooke knew enough from past experience not to vex her more at the moment. Doffing his heavy coat, he entered the dining hall. The guests were Dave Dysinger, a young man who worked at the greenhouse, Hal Bryer, a minister of the gospel, and Hayes Wishart, who lived off his family's income.

The three guests all rose and greeted Dr. Cooke, who unwillingly, then, and very grudgingly, consented to taste some plum pudding in a heavy sauce. But the pudding, against his will, actually revived him, and he broke gradually into a thin smile and then suddenly grinned and licked the spoon.

The three young men now left, using the excuse of allowing the doctor to be alone with Vesta, though they had been ready to depart an hour or so earlier.

In the parlour, Vesta now sat with the doctor as she yawned and occasionally sighed.

"We have had an unfortunate episode at our house," Dr. Cooke began.

Vesta looked at the folds of her evening gown and lifted the hem which had fallen on her high shoes.

"Episode?" she wondered indifferently. "And who do you mean by *we*?"

"My wife of course," he said deeply hurt, deeply offended.

"You mean Mamie Resch, I suppose," Vesta said as she looked up at the ceiling chandelier and yawned again.

"Oh, Vesta, try to be a little civil at least."

"Civil! After you have broken in on my evening supper and driven my guests out of the house. Civil! And you dare to mention that abandoned creature you now claim as your wife when you are in my house, and uninvited at that! And you barge in after midnight at that! Well, then, why are you here?"

"We have had a break-in, Vesta. A robbery."

"I hope you have informed the authorities."

He shook his head gravely. "That I will never do," he mumbled.

"Then the episode you speak of must be rather trifling."

"If ten thousand dollars is a trifle!" He bowed his head, and they both knew he was "licked."

Vesta rose grandly and touched a tiny silver bell. It brought one of the kitchen help almost immediately. A young man hardly more than sixteen, wearing a kitchen apron much too large for him, entered.

"Fetch the brandy bottle, Theo, and the little glasses, and be quick about it too."

"No, no, Vesta," Dr. Cooke implored.

"Yes, yes, doctor. God knows you need something to clear your brain."

Drinking first one glass of brandy and shortly thereafter another, Dr. Cooke all at once in a gravelly but loud voice exclaimed: "I forgive you, Vesta, and you will never hear me mention the affair again."

His statement only infuriated Vesta the more.

"You have been my suitor now for how long, doctor?"

"Oh, Vesta, please."

"Please, nothing! Answer my question."

"A good twenty years, I expect."

"And during all those difficult years when I wondered day in and day out how I was to meet my expenses, who lent me a helping hand? Who kept the sheriff from closing me down?"

He shook his head and stared into his drink.

"Shake your head a thousand times. The answer is Dr. Cooke certainly did not lend a hand. Yet he had free run of my house. Strolled at will through every one of my floors and my rooms like a baron!"

Here she raised her milk-white arms as if those arms held a rawhide about to fall.

"Yes, the good doctor, as he is known, enjoyed all this great house has to offer, including the upper chamber. Yet did he ever contribute more than one farthing to the upkeep of my regal outlays and expenditures? And then one fine day out of a blue sky without warning, or so much as a hint of what he was up to, he ups and marries a woman who had in twenty years never invited him to any of her skimpy soirees, was indeed barely on speaking acquaintance with him, a woman so desperate for conjugal closeness that it was she, old and unfrequented as the hills, who proposed to him, and he at the thought of Mamie's wealth, our good doctor, grasped her hand as if she had stretched it out to save him from drowning!"

Dr. Cooke, who had seen action, they say, in at least two wars and had won several citations for bravery, now flinched more than when he was under enemy fire. But Vesta, perhaps too disgusted to lay hands on her former suitor, merely groaned and moved her head vigorously until her star sapphire earrings threatened to come loose in her rage.

"If there is a thief anywhere in this blasted town I am looking at him now! And if money is missing, certainly over-the-hill Mamie Resch ought to know what become of it, and who took it."

"I know you took it." Dr. Cooke to his own astonishment was able to get these words out.

Vesta laughed shrilly and so loudly that hobbling old Frau Storeholder entered the room in alarm.

"Sit down, dear lady," Vesta smiled and made a cooing sound at her old doorkeeper.

"I will settle the score, then, Vesta, with my wife," Dr. Cooke said and looked longingly at the bottle of brandy.

"For all you have consumed here, doctor, over the decades and the rolling years," Vesta had begun again, "for all the grub, Canadian pheasant and venison, the roast suckling pig and fatted calf, the sweetmeats and pumpkin royals, and all the other bounty of my kitchen, and certainly the spirits which have flowed for you and only you like the waters of the lake in springtime, for all that, you could never repay me in a hundred years what you have over time usurped from me. For yes, God knows, you have bled me white. And you dare come here at this late hour to accuse me of robbery when I am looking right now at the greatest robber who ever entered any woman's life!"

Rising, or rather tottering to his feet, Dr. Cooke now shouted: "And I tell you I will make it all right with my wife."

"You have no wife," Vesta called out. "Do you mean to tell me you are capable of the marriage rite, you and that old bag of bones, wigs and paint that is Mamie Resch, a crone old enough to be your own mother. Yes, go home now, waken your legal spouse, tell her you *owe* the grass widow, owner of the finest showplace in the state, tell her, do you hear, you owe me at the very least twenty million dollars which no peephole in wallpaper is big enough to hide."

Dr. Cooke was already on his way out, bent almost double, and sniveling and choking from his own effluvia.

Vesta who had threateningly accompanied the doctor to the door and slammed it after him now returned to the parlour.

Had Frau Storeholder ever gone to the theater, she might have thought Sarah Bernhardt had come back to the stage. And for a split second Frau Storeholder did not actually believe she had been hearing the Vesta she knew. She shivered a little. She shook.

Only when Vesta sat down in the best chair in the house and began laughing uproariously did Frau Storeholder return to reality.

"Oh, what a wonderful audience you make, what a divine onlooker, dear Belinda. Yes, you egged me on to one of my finest performances, I do believe. Dunning me for a few thousand dollars when he is in my debt for millions!"

Vesta picked up a half-empty glass of brandy left by her late-hour guest and downed it all in one swallow. She wiped her eyes of the tears which her laughter had brought forth and then sank back limp as a rag against the bolster of one of her antique overstuffed chairs.

For the zeal of thine house hath eaten me up.

Vesta found this verse underlined in an open copy of Frau Storeholder's well-worn Holy Bible.

The verse was from the Psalms, and whether owing to the fact the verse had been underlined with pencil or because of the words themselves, the text appeared to be blazing like hot coals.

Vesta felt the underlined verse was meant for her. She was not sure of its meaning, but she had been aware for some time that Frau Storeholder, if not downright critical of her, was not altogether comfortable with Vesta's behaviour of late.

"Yet what would the poor old thing do without me," Vesta muttered, still gazing at the passage in the Psalms. "Yes, I suppose I do have zeal for my house. It's all I have, and it was all my own people had before me. And, as I've told Frau Storeholder a thousand times, what would become of her if some day the sheriff came and closed the property. Where would she go? Where would I go?"

That evening, after an unusually sumptuous banquet and after every one of the guests had departed, Vesta came into the little parlour reserved primarily for Frau Storeholder. She was sitting in a wicker rocking chair, her eyes closed.

The Holy Bible was still open at the marked passage in the Psalms.

Vesta strode over to where the book lay and deliberately read aloud the underlined passage.

"You are quite a student of Scripture, Belinda," she remarked, turning to gaze at Frau Storeholder.

Frau Storeholder opened her eyes, roused as if out of sleep, brought on in part perhaps by the excellent dinner she had just enjoyed.

"I am afraid I am far from what anyone could call a student of Scripture," the old woman managed to say. She spoke as if she was talking in her sleep.

"Does the verse have some special meaning for you, Belinda, seeing you have underlined it."

"Let me look at it, Vesta." She rose now and came over to stare at the passage marked in the Psalms.

"I'm afraid I don't understand the verse myself," she confessed. "Perhaps that is why it's underlined."

"I was wondering if the verse had some reference to me," Vesta tried to make her voice kind and reasonable, but still it came out rather edgy.

Frau Storeholder now gazed lengthily at Vesta, then spoke up bravely, "I believe *house* here means the Temple of the Lord."

Vesta now took up the heavy tome in her hands and read the passage again aloud in her soaring contralto.

"Isn't the passage, dear Belinda, a pointed reference to someone who worships her *own* mansion?"

When Frau Storeholder did not respond, Vesta put down the heavy book on its stand.

"I'm afraid you think I worship my home more than I do anything else in creation."

Frau Storeholder moved about the room now as if she was looking for something which might explain the passage itself. Finishing her pacing, the old woman sat down in her favorite chair, and again closed her eyes.

"You believe, I feel, that I love my house more than I love Rory, my only child. For he has left me, think of it, just think of it. Zeal, zeal!" She almost shouted this word. "Yes, whatever you say, I am afraid the passage has more than a little to do with me. Say or think whatever you like."

"Vesta," Frau Storeholder's voice came now as distant as if from the banquet room, "we must do what we must do in this life."

"But *eaten me up*! That is a terrible way of putting it. For I do believe the verse has to do with me. With my life."

Vesta could not restrain a few short sobs.

"We should not try to understand Holy Writ, dear Vesta. Let me repeat, the word *house* here means the Lord's Temple, that and nothing more."

"Oh, how I wish I could believe you. I have heard there are many ways of interpreting Scripture of course."

"Don't fret, dear Vesta. It breaks my heart to see you fret."

"And you didn't leave the book open at this passage for my eyes?"

Frau Storeholder said nothing at this point.

"I wish you would admit you did. I think the passage does refer to my kind of worship. A house! It's all I have. My only son has deserted me. And his deserting me has been approved of by the Superintendent of Schools! Think of that. Rory has gone permanently to live with Moses Swearingen."

"Moe's Villa," Frau Storeholder clicked her tongue.

The mention of Moe's Villa drove out then from Vesta's mind the Bible and its verses. All she could think of then was they had taken her boy away from her. Of course she had neglected him, had not paid attention to his needs, to his truancy from school! She was not free of blame, but she had kept a roof over his precious head! Her *zeal* as the Good Book said, had been behind it. And the passage, no matter what Frau Storeholder might say, yes, it was about her!

MOSES SWEARINGEN BELONGED to one of the most respected families in Gilboa. His ancestors went back before the Revolution. And he had, like Vesta Hawley, inherited an antebellum sprawling piece of property which had possibly more rooms than the mansion of the grass widow herself.

Moses had studied to be a medical doctor, but having to work with cadavers had caused him to have such a horror of the profession, he had left school a few months before graduation.

He had returned to Gilboa and settled down. It was said he sometimes practiced medicine without a license, and even Dr. Cooke often remarked Moses knew more about the profession than many a licensed M.D.

But Moses Swearingen's real interest outside of cards, gambling and strong drink, lay—unbeknownst to almost everyone—in the field of psychic phenomenona, which he had studied in the medical school, devouring every book he could lay his hands on.

He felt that he himself had some talent in the field, but he was afraid to go further into this science. It seemed to threaten something very deep in his nature.

Moses, being perhaps the wealthiest man in the county, could afford to hire the unemployed young men to do the hard work about his mansion and run his many errands. But he was always looking in them also for some hint that they might have psychic ability.

Moses Swearingen had noticed for some time the strange behaviour of young Rory Hawley, the neglected child of a ruined marriage.

Everyone in Gilboa knew Rory never attended school regularly, if at all, and was, as they said, a dyed-in-the-wool truant.

The word "truant" kept running though Moses' mind the first time some men in the pool parlor mentioned it in reference to Widow Hawley's son.

One cold winter day Moses spied young Rory wandering aimlessly about the town square. He wore no overcoat or gloves and was blowing his hands to keep them warm.

It did not take many words for Moses to invite him to his Villa, as his property was frequently, though sarcastically, called.

Moses rummaged about the garments in his clothes closet and came back with a thick sweater, two or three sizes too large for the boy, but which would give him the warmth he needed.

But the sweater, Moses soon saw, was not warm enough to keep Rory from a fit of shivering. His lips were almost blue. Moses felt the boy's forehead and took his pulse. Rory began shaking convulsively.

At Moe's Villa bottles of spirits were in evidence everywhere. He poured Rory a few jiggers of alcohol against the boy's resistance but got some of it anyhow down his throat. The remaining drops fell over the young boy's chin and chest.

Frightened at the boy's dangerous condition, Moses carried him up the long antique staircase to the front guest room where there were plenty of goose down comforters, quilts, and pillows.

He didn't bother to remove the boy's clothing, but put him between the thick linen sheets and piled on the blankets and comforters.

A quaking fright took over him that the boy might expire in his care.

He called in one of his hired girls and told her to make some tea. The girl stared for a long time at the unfamiliar guest. Moses had to shout for her to get on with his request.

Moses sat up the rest of the night, unwilling to leave the boy for fear he might perish if left untended. Toward morning, however, Rory stirred and opened his eyes and half-smiled at Moses, then lay back and closed his eyes. A thin stream of blood came out of his nostrils. Moses wiped his nose and mouth delicately of the stains.

Sensing the boy might be conscious, he asked, "Do you know where you are, Rory?"

The boy's eyelids fluttered, his mouth twitched and then said, "General Yoxtheimer's."

Moses was unable to restrain a gasp, for General Yoxtheimer was one of his remote ancestors who had fought the Revolutionary War and in several Indian uprisings. And it was furthermore the General's house where they were now present.

"And who was General Yoxtheimer?" Moses whispered.

The boy thrashed about now frantically, and then shaking his head, managed: "Died . . . the Indians."

"You mean they killed the General?" Moses was barely able to inquire.

No one, Moses reflected, could have known General Yoxtheimer had been killed in an Indian massacre. Even he had only lately learned this fact from a very old history of the Revolutionary period he had found in a library in Chicago.

"Do you hear me, Rory?"

There was no response.

"Do you, Rory?"

"I hear a man who is a card player and gambler."

Moses, to his own embarrassment and chagrin, let out a swear word, and now to his sudden anger he heard a strange laugh come from his visitor.

Moses sat on by the bedside of Rory Hawley, deep in thoughts he would never have thought himself capable of entertaining before.

Everyone of course in town knew that Moses Swearingen was fond of card playing and gambling and had initiated many young men into the practice. But the boy's mentioning the fact of his card playing and betting could hardly be proof of psychic ability, but could be mere repetition of what he had heard in his wandering about the streets when he should have been at school.

"Who let you in on the fact I am a gambler," Moses finally said after a long silence between them.

The silence was broken only after four or five minutes.

"You broke your mother's heart betting away your inheritance."

Having mumbled these words, Rory started up as if coming out of a deep slumber. Rising from the bed, he shouted something unintelligible or words in a foreign language.

Moses groaned and wondered what he was up against with such a boy.

"Who was it brought me here?" Rory now spoke in his ordinary wide-awake voice, and he came over to where Moses sat and seized him by the hand.

Moses was astonished at the strength of the boy's own hand in view of his otherwise rather delicate appearance.

"Who else brought you here but me," Moses snapped. "I brought you!"

Rory stood looking at Moses carefully. And it was then that Moses was convinced that maybe he did not have someone who had second sight on his hands, but a someone at any rate who was different from anyone he had ever known before.

For a while Swearingen wondered if the local authorities might not call on him and demand to know why young Rory Hawley was staying with him.

But as the days passed and there was no visit from "above," he reflected that the village of Gilboa was so bankrupt it could no longer even pay for a police force.

The condition of the boy showed every kind of neglect. His clothing was much too large for him, as were his shoes. And though a handsome fellow, everything about him indicated inveterate neglect. His teeth looked like they needed attention for they were almost black in places. His hair, a beautiful shade of the same color as his mother's (if, Moses mused, she was his mother), was long unaccustomed to tonsorial care, if indeed he had ever set foot in a barber shop. His fingernails were broken and some blackened. From wearing the wrong-size shoes his toenails were discoloured and broken. And under his paper-thin shirt (he wore no undershirt) one could count every one of his ribs.

Moses now ushered his visitor to the kitchen which was nearly as large as Vesta's banquet room.

The cook had left several dishes sitting atop the stove, all ready to be heated.

Moses took the lid off one or two of the pots to see what might tempt his guest, and he noticed with a kind of bitter amusement the boy's nose wrinkled and moved as he got a whiff of the victuals.

Without asking Rory's preference, Moses heated a soup of turkey, leeks, cabbage and potatoes.

He set the dish down before Rory and handed him an oversize silver spoon.

When Rory only stared at the streaming dish, Moses shouted, "Eat."

Rory dove in at this command. Moses grinned, noticing the boy did not bother to wipe his mouth and chin from his dribbling. He was too busy swallowing.

Moses picked up a stiff linen napkin and methodically wiped the boy's mouth.

For the first time then Rory gave Moses a searching look as if he had just now become aware of Moses' presence.

When Rory had eaten his fill, Moses ushered him into a lavatory which like the kitchen was the size of three or four ordinary rooms.

"Sit over here, why don't you," he used his drill-sergeant tone. Rory once again gave evidence that he was about to doze.

Moses opened a drawer and took out barber's scissors and comb.

"I want to untangle that head of hair of yours."

Before Moses had really begun his barbering, he took out from the boy's hair the remains of what looked like briars and petals of marigolds.

Moses clicked his tongue.

Rory, still sleepy, acted entirely indifferent to those ministrations, but occasionally sighed and let his head fall down to his chest.

When the cutting and combing was over, Moses pointed to the wastebasket now full of the yellow tresses.

Moses touched the down on the boy's cheeks.

"Quite a ways from a beard, ain't it," he remarked, perhaps to himself.

For the first time in his life Moses Swearingen felt, if not outright uneasiness, a kind of fearful awe of another person. This was the turbulence he experienced in the boy's presence.

He had taken the boy into his mansion because he saw how needful, even desperate, the young man was.

But instead of having ushered in a child in desperate trouble and need, he found he had taken in a kind of being who appeared barely of this world. And instead of Moses being the master, he was often to have the sinking feeling the boy held the real sway at the Villa.

He recalled then that years ago when Rory could have not been more than three or four years old, he had seen the boy's grandmother taking him for drives in her horse-drawn buggy. The grandmother had always stopped when she saw Moses and would exchange a few cordial greetings.

The grandmother did not look like anyone remotely related to Rory or his mother. She was so dark-complexioned the townspeople often wondered if she did not have African blood. But older residents claimed she was, like Moses, part Shawnee.

One cold December afternoon long ago when the wind and snow

had kept everybody within doors, Moses heard a—it could not be called a knocking at his front door—it was more like the sound of a blacksmith mistaking the door for an anvil. And Moses felt all over again now the same kind of sinking feeling he had experienced at hearing the knocking as when he looked into Rory's blazing countenance.

The late visitor with the fierce knocking was Rory's grandmother. Recovering from his astonishment, Moses greeted the old woman in a blithe manner foreign to his usual brusqueness.

"Sit over here, why don't you, by the fireplace where I've got a bit of kindling going to take the chill off," Moses urged his visitor.

The grandmother did not appear to be cold, but she chose a seat nearest the fire, and a tardy smile came over her lips.

Without being asked, Moses produced a glass with some kind of spirits.

His guest tasted the drink critically, and Moses for a moment thought from her strange gesture she was about to toss the contents into the blazing logs of the fireplace.

Instead she finished her drink, and extending her glass, indicated she would care for another.

"I have had a presentiment," she began at last after they had both listened a while to the crackling sound coming from the burning logs.

When she said no more Moses asked, "And what was its nature?"

"Its nature—who knows, Moses. I will tell you my message though. *You are to look after Rory when I'm gone.*"

"I hope that will not be soon," he spoke under his breath so low perhaps she didn't hear him.

"My daughter isn't capable of caring for even a song sparrow. But you're a different story." She swallowed the last of her third drink and Moses offered her another.

"On that day, and I hope you're listening, Moe. On that day, which may be any day or the next day or never, you are to consider Rory your own flesh and blood."

As a matter of fact until this very moment when Rory took residence in his mansion, Moses had forgotten almost entirely the grandmother's December visit. In fact he had thought the night of her bequest she was perhaps crazy or, who knows, a bit drunk on his cheer.

But now it all came back. He could almost hear the wheels of the buggy and the snorting of the half-tamed horse she kept in her barn along with a half dozen or so other untamed horses.

Again Moses felt a chill come over him as if his visitor of so many years ago had also descended on him with bag and baggage.

He looked up just then and saw Rory staring at him.

Again the fireplace was going just as on the night the grandmother had delivered her bequest.

Rory now took the best seat in front of the fire, and then to Moses' astonishment he heard the boy spit into the flames and, as if in answer, the fire turned a queer greenish color and gave an echoing sound as it ascended the ancient chimney.

VESTA HAWLEY OFTEN found herself weeping against Frau Storeholder's comforting bosom. She sometimes even lay prone on the carpet in front of Frau Storeholder's chair. She was sobbing, imploring even, like a zealot before a number of votive candles.

So carried away in grief was she that an onlooker might have thought Vesta Hawley was drunk or indeed mad by reason of her finally embracing the old woman's feet in her sorrow.

But she was of course neither drunk nor mad. She was consumed with guilt and with homesickness for her son.

Whether Frau Storeholder ever listened attentively any more to this endless unburdening of Rory's mother is questionable. She had heard the story after all so many times. Countless innumerable times.

As if walking in his sleep young Rory often times entered his mother's bedroom and discovered her in the embrace of one of her banqueters or lodgers. The young man of the occasion holding his mother was probably drunk for he did not appear to notice that Vesta's son had entered the room and was staring at his embraces. For one thing Rory's eyes were so swollen with sleep the lover of the evening might have decided the boy was not actually seeing what was transpiring. Was dreaming in fact upright!

But Vesta knew Rory saw, even if he saw in deep slumber!

One morning after he had surprised her with a lover, Vesta was unusually affectionate and lavish to her son. She prepared his breakfast herself: a sumptuous plate of eggs laid by the hen within the hour, a mountain of brown steamed potatoes, cornbread, grits, and gooseberry jam.

Rory ate it all but without showing any appreciation or appetite for what he ate. At the conclusion of his meal, he took up the thick stiff hand-embroidered linen napkin and assiduously and repeatedly wiped his mouth and chin, even going on to wipe his open throat and chest, while muttering something. Tears followed slowly, painfully from his eyes as if those eyes, still flush from what he had seen the night before, were at last letting fall their water in sorrow for all the sins of the world.

As Rory, having gathered up his schoolbooks, began to walk toward the door, Vesta followed him meekly and said softly: "Aren't you going to kiss Mama good morning?"

Rory shook his head.

"Don't you know how much I want your kisses," she whispered.

Rory refused to look at her.

"Say something, or say anything even if it is a curse."

He only shook his head more slowly, more mournfully.

"Do you mean you will never kiss your Mama again then, Rory?"

He grinned unhumorously then, like a gargoyle or perhaps a frog.

"Never again?" she begged.

He only nodded and grinned more fiercely.

She had closed her eyes on getting no answer to her appeal.

Finally opening her eyes, she saw he had departed.

Weeping and between sobs, Vesta told Frau Storeholder the story all over again for the hundredth time.

"Didn't Rory know I yielded to the banqueters and the roomers only to keep a roof over his head, dear Belinda? Oh do say something. Don't be like Rory on that long ago, terrible morning. *Didn't he know I did it for him?*"

Frau Storeholder's own eyes were widening, the pupils a deep black.

"Tell me, Belinda," she began to try to rise but then only fell back on her knees, looking up at her confessor.

"Love is a very jealous god," Frau Storeholder managed to say. She removed her glasses and put them away in their satin case.

"I don't know what you mean, a jealous god. Are you referring to my boy when you speak so!"

The old woman nodded. "Love will not permit or allow for it to be shared. And you, poor child, have shared love with so many, so countless many."

"You are condemning me, unlike the Good Shepherd who forgave the Woman at the Well."

"I am not condemning you, my poor girl. I am telling you what love's commands are. He will never allow his love to be shared with others. In your case multitudes."

"Tell me this," Vesta coughed out the words as she rose from her, kneeling and exhausted, and fell into one of the antique lounge chairs.

"Tell me, Belinda, and do not lie to me. Will Rory then never come back to me, never forgive me, never, oh yes, let me say, never love me?"

Frau Storeholder weakly almost imperceptibly shook her head.

"You are shaking your head like he did! Oh wicked, wicked Belinda. You are pronouncing my doom with that idle movement of your head.

"He will never come back to me, then," Vesta muttered.

Even if Belinda Storeholder had replied then that Rory would return, Vesta would not have heard her.

The final realization came that Rory would not be returning home one cold clear December morning when a young messenger arrived, holding in his hands a stiff white envelope addressed to Miss Hawley in huge Roman letters.

Vesta for a few moments was unable to take the envelope in her hands.

The messenger kept saying, "It's for you, ma'am."

Vesta still hesitating then called Frau Storeholder to come to the door.

She received the message.

"Do you have any change for this young man?" Vesta inquired of Frau Storeholder. One thing about her friend which always amused Vesta was the old woman always managed to have money on her person. The change was hidden deep in a large beaded purse.

Frau Storeholder produced a shiny fifty-cent piece and hand-fed it to Vesta. But when Vesta offered the money to the messenger (he was, she supposed, one of the young gamblers who lived at Moe's Villa), he refused the emolument, uttering an excuse.

"May I leave the envelope now with you, ma'am? Please do take the envelope," the young man now quite flustered inquired.

As Vesta appeared at this moment incapable of taking the envelope, Frau Storeholder received it for her.

"I thank you," he told the old woman and touched his cap. Vesta returned to the front parlour then and threw herself into one of her favorite easy chairs.

Frau Storeholder was still holding the envelope.

"Shall I read you what the message is," Frau Storeholder's voice had a kind of tenderness in it, rare for her.

"I don't know if I can bear for you to read it. At the same time I've mislaid my glasses, so I suppose you'll have to oblige me. I'd just as soon throw it in the fireplace. A message from the kidnapper of my boy! What more can he want out of me!"

Frau Storeholder had opened the envelope with a letter opener and read the few lines contained in it silently to herself.

A very thin smile spread over her lips, and the sight of that smile, feeble though it was, heartened Vesta.

"Read the message, then, Belinda, I am ready!"

Frau Storeholder cleared her throat noisily, a bit like an elocution teacher, and read:

My dear Vesta Hawley,
As cold weather has set in would you kindly send to us as soon as possible your son's heavy overcoat.
Yours most respectfully,
Moses Swearingen

"And is that all it says, Belinda?"

Frau Storeholder replied that it was all.

"I was afraid Moses Swearingen was going maybe to bring court action against me."

"He would never do that," Frau Storeholder assured her.

A heavy silence now intervened. At last Frau Storeholder gave out a great sigh, and Vesta, raising her voice, said: "I have no idea where his overcoat is. The last time I saw it the moths had been into one of the sleeves. The whole coat is probably in tatters. Oh, God in heaven, why am I plagued with such a child, will you tell me!"

"I know exactly where the overcoat is," Frau Storeholder spoke in her most soothing tones. "I once stumbled over a whole row of gold spittoons near the coat."

"Those spittoons belonged to Pete," Vesta reflected. "He chewed and was never without a plug of tobacco, let me tell you. Some time after he left me there came to see me a collector who was interested in one of my antique rockers, but when he saw the spittoons, he wanted to have them instead. I held off from selling them. Seems they are very valuable now."

Not wanting Vesta to begin on her reminiscences of Peter Driscoll, Frau Storeholder interrupted to say: "Let me go and see, Vesta, just what condition his overcoat is in then."

"Yes, go fetch it, Belinda, if there's anything left of it. But why can't that multi-millionaire of a Swearingen buy the boy a decent coat. He's smothering in money, he sweats money!" She took out one of her hand-embroidered handkerchiefs and gave a snort in it which caused Frau Storeholder to flinch, for she found the sound indelicate.

Vesta waited then for Belinda to return. Her long absence caused her frayed nerves to worsen.

"You was gone forever!" she greeted Frau Storeholder when she reappeared.

She was not carrying the boy's overcoat but instead was lugging an unwieldy package.

She almost dropped the cumbersome object on the floor but managed instead to deposit it on a long seldom-used end table.

"What on earth have you brought from upstairs," Vesta wondered, and her temper flared.

"The boy's overcoat, dear Vesta, is all rags and tatters from the moths."

"But where on earth did you lay hands on this package?"

"I found it near his coat. There's writing on the outside as you can see. It's from . . ."

"Yes, from Peter Driscoll," Vesta whined.

Peter Driscoll was Rory's father, though nobody was sure he was actually Vesta Hawley's legal husband. At least there was no record of their having been to the altar.

"But what do you suppose is in the package, Vesta?"

"Marbles, I think," she replied bitterly.

"Marbles!"

"It all comes back to me now. When this package arrived nearly ten years ago, and I haven't thought of it again until today, let me tell you, I only half opened it. And I have never looked into it since. But I thought then it must be marbles. When Rory was a little boy of five or so, he and his . . . Dad" (here Vesta choked on the last word), "they played marbles together on the big carpet. As I say, I peeked into the package when it was delivered, and as I was ill I barely saw Rory in the next few days that followed to inform him there was a package upstairs from his Dad. He had begun even then to keep himself away from me."

"You mean Rory never found out what his Dad had sent him for a present?"

"That's right," Vesta sighed.

Vesta's complete indifference may have given Frau Storeholder the goad to undo the long-forgotten birthday present. Her old heavy-veined hands removed the heavy paper and excelsior which contained the father's gift. She felt a kind of fear nonetheless, exploring the package's interior. Perhaps, she wondered, maybe it was not something like marbles, but—who knows—explosives! But of course explosives was hardly a possibility.

Before uncovering the gift itself Frau Storeholder could not refrain from saying: "And you never looked all the way inside, Vesta, all these years."

"I told you, I peeked, Belinda. And I decided then it contained marbles. But I hated Pete Driscoll so much I didn't want to see what he had given my boy for his birthday. He ruined both of our lives, after all. And so I forgot in time there had ever been a birthday present for Rory! Go ahead, blame me.

"Open the confounded thing up then! What are you waiting for? Can't you see how the very mention of the name Peter Driscoll has brought on a sick headache. But wait a minute. I'm going out to the kitchen and take some of those drops Dr. Cooke prescribed."

Frau Storeholder went on attempting to extricate the birthday present from all the heavy wrapping paper and excelsior.

When the contents were finally exposed, Frau Storeholder at first drew back and gave a kind of stifled moan as if a nest of serpents had been uncovered.

Vesta had closed her eyes, waiting.

Frau Storeholder then drew out from the wrapping paper row after row of its shining contents.

The objects she displayed to a silent Vesta Hawley appeared to be a collection of gems, jewels, precious stones—whatever they were. Indeed their blazing red beauty caused her to gasp, and finally cry out.

"They're not marbles, Vesta," Frau Storeholder spoke in a lofty stern manner such as Vesta had never heard come from her before.

Vesta moved cautiously toward the shining red objects as if they might indeed be dangerous.

"Rubies?" she wondered.

"Rubies?" Frau Storeholder repeated wonderingly.

"Precious rubies, I do believe," Vesta gasped, and tears overflowed her eyes. "What else can look like that, I ask you!"

"But see how many there are of them, Vesta. Just come closer please. Row after row of the same stones or gems or whatever they are."

"I can't believe that's what they are, Frau Storeholder. Precious stones. Oh God in Heaven, what does this mean. *Rubies* all these years up there in that old attic. Let me sit down before I fall down. God in Heaven!"

"Rubies," Frau Storeholder muttered in awe.

JEFF CALDWELL OPERATED the local livery barn. His Dad had run the barn for many years, supplying carriage-drawn horses for the quality to travel short distances in.

Today, receiving a call from Vesta Hawley for a conveyance, Jeff decided to use his old Willys-Knight car. He cogitated long and deep however, wondering what on earth Vesta Hawley wanted a conveyance for, she who never set foot outside her mansion.

Arriving at the Hawley address, Jeff was met by Frau Storeholder at the entrance, holding a large package wrapped in pieces of old quilt.

"Let me give you a hand," Jeff took the package from her, and after eyeing it wonderingly, tipped his cap and asked: "Miss Hawley ain't going too?"

"I'm the passenger today, Jeff," Frau Storeholder had brightened a little at the sight of the young liveryman who had a face that betokened both health and kindness.

Still eyeing the package, Jeff wondered: "And where are we off to, Frau Storeholder?"

She hesitated only a moment.

"Moe's Villa."

Jeff almost lost his grasp of the package on hearing the name of the destination.

Frau Storeholder grinned at his surprise. Had she told him she was going to the disorderly house some five miles from the village limits, he could hardly have shown more shock.

They rode in silence, but after a while Frau Storeholder noticed Jeff was having trouble in not breaking out into, yes, a horselaugh.

Whether by reason of guilt or perhaps a usually hidden generosity, Vesta Hawley had provided Frau Storeholder with a tip of several silver dollars for Jeff Caldwell.

He jumped out after receiving the gratuity and, carrying the package, he proceeded with his fare up the twenty-eight steps leading to the front door of the Villa.

He had to ring a score of times before Moses Swearingen himself appeared in a kind of business suit and wearing a fedora hat.

"Jeff, I'll be damned!" he greeted the liveryman, and then he caught sight of Frau Storeholder.

Mumbling a good day to her, Moses grumbled and bowed in the direction of Frau Storeholder.

Inside they all sat down in the front parlour. Jeff had not bothered to remove his cap and was catching his breath perhaps at his horror that he had conveyed a respectable lady to the Villa.

"When do you want Jeff to call for you," Moses now inquired almost bashfully of Frau Storeholder.

Moses was as a matter of fact more bewildered and uneasy even than Jeff Caldwell over Frau Storeholder's visit, and he kept eyeing the bulky package weighted down in pieces of ragged quilt with increasing curiosity.

"Ah, but you mean I am to remain, Moses?" Frau Storeholder acted surprised that she had more to do here than merely deposit the package from Peter Driscoll.

"Of course you're to remain," Moses sounded almost hurt.

And Moses now to the astonishment of Jeff Caldwell smiled, a smile Jeff had never seen cross the face of the proprietor of the Villa.

"In about a half an hour then?" Jeff said rising.

"Make it an hour, Jeff," Moses told the liveryman, who touching his cap to Moses and again to Frau Storeholder made such a rapid retreat one had the feeling he had disappeared before their eyes until they heard the slamming of the outside doors.

Moses Swearingen now moved his lips awkwardly, but without being able to frame what he was thinking in words.

Finally, crossing and re-crossing his long legs, he got out: "Frau Storeholder, this is such a rare occasion, I can only wonder how I am privileged to have you for company."

Frau Storeholder's own lips now moved also without her being able to reply to his compliment, until the ensuing silence forced her to say, "The pleasure is all mine, Moses." She smiled comfortably now, for after all she had known him since he was hardly more than a boy.

Moses went on staring fixedly now at the package. Seeing Moses' wonder, she exclaimed, "You see, Moses, Miss Hawley and I were looking for Rory's winter coat in answer to your message. The coat, well, is in tatters. But we came across this package meanwhile."

Both Moses and Frau Storeholder now stared in unison at the object in question.

"It seems," she continued, still gazing at the package as if it acted as a kind of prompter, "the package I've brought today was a gift sent ten years ago from Peter Driscoll for his son Rory."

Moses's features moved uncomfortably at the mention of Peter Driscoll.

"Miss Hawley, on first receiving the package sent as I say so long ago, told me she only peeked inside at the time. She thought it was marbles."

"Marbles," Moses raised his voice, and instead of crossing or uncrossing his legs now, he put both his feet down on the carpet with a thud.

"Because you see, Moses, when Rory was a very small boy his Dad and he used to play marbles together on the big carpet in the living room."

Looking up from her recital, Frau Storeholder saw Moses wiping his face with a broad blue polka-dot handkerchief. He was sweating profusely.

"But what was our wonder," she went on doggedly, "when we opened the package up, and it was not marbles at all. It was something else."

"Something else," Moses repeated her last words in a kind of hoarse whisper.

"At any rate, I have brought the gift for the boy it was originally destined for."

She then drew out from her wraps a thick envelope.

"This letter," she pointed at it as if it might contradict her, "it is from Peter Driscoll to his son and was inside the package. I have glanced at the letter," she said guiltily. "I had to know if it might throw light on the package's contents."

Moses Swearingen nodded solemnly.

"My hands, Moses, are not quite up to opening the package. If you would be so kind. . . ."

He gave her an almost accusing look and then left the room to return presently, carrying some heavy shears and a hunting knife.

He grimly, almost angrily, tore open the package.

After nearly reducing the entire package to shreds, he halted just as Vesta and Frau Storeholder had halted the day they had looked inside.

Very slowly Moses began lifting one row after another of what appeared to be, if not precious jewels, certainly gems of some kind.

"And Miss Hawley called them marbles!" he shouted. He laughed. "Did you ever hear gems like these called marbles, Frau Storeholder? I am surprised indeed. These marbles are rubies, or I'll eat my hat!"

He held his right hand now to his eyes as if the sight of the gems had hurt his vision.

Having gazed at the jewels for as long as the sight of such a spectacle could be endured, Moses Swearingen rose unsteadily and began pacing around the room in an agitated manner.

Frau Storeholder looked after him concernedly. She felt puzzled, even sorry for him somehow. It was obvious the sight of what is called rubies was highly disturbing to him—why, of course, she had no way of knowing.

"And then what about the letter Peter Driscoll wrote to his son," he now turned to face her. "Am I not to know the contents of it also?" he wondered, and he motioned with his hand to the gems now exposed to anybody's inspection after their long absence from the sun.

"Oh, the letter," Frau Storeholder exclaimed, and after a flurry she handed him the document.

Before beginning the reading, however, Moses Swearingen gave another long look at the gems as if they required some kind of say-so for him to proceed.

He read aloud, and as he did so Frau Storeholder closed her eyes.

My dear boy [Moses' voice boomed out], *I have had you on my heart and mind ever since I left you with your mother. I did not leave you willingly, always remember that. Not at all. There was no way your mother and I could see eye to eye. And there was no way I could earn a living in Gilboa, especially owing to the great expense of keeping up so large, so oversized a place as Vesta's. So I have been travelling not only through this country but in foreign lands to boot, hoping against hope I could mend my fortunes and come back to see you someday. In place of my coming home, I am sending this special gift for you. Be sure to keep good care of yourself. My own health is not of the best, and I do not know in fact when or if I will be better. Remember, dear boy, how much I care for you and miss you more than I have words to tell you. These little red gems are only a small token of how much I care for you.*

Your loving father, ever
Peter Driscoll

Moses Swearingen handed back the letter to Frau Storeholder with the alacrity of someone relinquishing an object aflame.

He sat down and, following Frau Storeholder's example, closed his eyes.

There was again a long silence during which one could catch the sound of a large green fly buzzing somewhere.

"He is dead, I take it." Moses inquired, his eyes still closed.

"Peter Driscoll? Oh, a long time ago, Moses. Years and years."

Moses nodded and a queer enigmatic smile broke over his mouth.

"I cannot say, Frau Storeholder, that I am happy to have such a possession as you have brought to me today. But I believe since Rory is the one who is entitled to be the owner, it belongs here for as long as he remains with me. Which I hope will be forever!"

He almost shouted these last words, and Frau Storeholder drew in her breath.

At that moment the front door bell rang, and Jeff Caldwell was seen staring at them through the frosted glass of the door.

"Must you go?" Moses wondered.

She nodded.

"There are a number of things I would like to ask you," he explained. He looked over at the gift again as if it were the cause of everything that faced or would face him.

"But I suppose we can arrange for you to come here again," he gave a faint smile.

"Just as you wish, Moses."

She was gone then without another word, but Jeff Caldwell shook

Moses's hand and volunteered something about the change in the weather outside.

Moses sat down then. His eyes tried to avoid looking at the package of jewels. Finally he picked up the letter of Peter Driscoll and stared at the peculiar handwriting of its author.

Then his eye returned again to take in the gems.

A FEW HOURS after Frau Storeholder had taken her leave, Moses Swearingen was taken suddenly ill and retired to his bedroom without having spoken to Rory about the "rubies." Seeing he was going to be sick, Moses had instructed one of his hired men to apprise Rory of the arrival of the package and the letter from Peter Driscoll.

Moses Swearingen's illness was this: he had been in some kind of gunfight years ago when he was a fairly young man. The bullet of his assailant still lodged in his chest or, as Dr. Cooke said, near his breastbone. It was too dangerous to remove the bullet, yet every so often the pain was almost intolerable were it not for the morphine Dr. Cooke was always kind enough to supply.

Today, as if somehow the sight of the rubies had brought it on, Moses experienced the most fearful pain in his chest he could remember.

He was tossing and turning in his king-sized bed even after swallowing a heavy dose of morphine when Rory entered.

Rory had now been with Moses for some months—it seemed years—and the boy had changed. This was brought home to Moses when he thought he saw coming into his bedroom an unknown young man. He was about to cry out when he recognized Rory.

It was not impudence or ill-breeding, Moses recognized, but for some other reason that the boy came directly to his bedside and sat down on one of the heavy comforters. Moses' broad chest was bare, and Rory stared incredulous at the wound.

Then the morphine began to take effect or was it, Moses wondered bitterly, the presence of Rory that quieted his agony.

He was loath to admit that every time he saw Rory he felt a kind of calming effect. This was now especially true.

"Did you inspect your Dad's gift to you?" Moses managed to ask.

Rory gave an almost imperceptible nod.

"And you read his letter to you also?"

Rory mumbled a yes.

"You never told me you had a bullet lodged in your chest," Rory spoke now no longer like the boy Moses had brought home but like a young man.

"Well, now you know," Moses said, and attempted to rise, but the pain began again and he slumped down.

"May I have a look at where the bullet went in?" Rory inquired. He would never have dared say such a thing to the master of the Villa even a few days ago, but today the master was too much in pain to correct or even to notice his breach of behaviour.

Rory touched the place on his chest where the bullet had entered.

"What in the name of . . ." Moses began, then stopped. "I say, what did you do just then with your hand?"

"Just touched where the bullet is," Rory replied.

"The pain has all left me," Moses stared at his visitor. Then after a long pause: "Oh, it was Doc Cooke's dope, I guess."

Rory touched the sore place again, and more little threads of pain appeared to leave Moses' chest.

"What do you do when you touch the place?" Moses wondered. "You must do something."

Rory went then into one of what people called his absentminded "starts." He said no more and indeed acted as if he had forgotten where he was.

"Well, what do you think of your present?"

"Oh, the gems," Rory replied.

"And the letter, too, don't forget."

Rory became silent.

Just then the pain in his chest began again. Moses tossed and turned and groaned. His face was dripping with sweat.

Then, as if it was his turn, Rory touched the hurt place and again all the pain left Moses.

"What is going on?" Moses wondered after the pain had left again, but he was still too out of breath to say more and was sweating profusely.

"I can see the bullet is trying to come out from your . . . hide," the boy remarked.

Moses tried to look down at his chest to see what Rory saw, but the effort tired him, and he lay back on the pillows under his head.

"So you're cool about the rubies from your Dad, ain't you," Moses managed to get out these words.

"Rubies? I guess I have to get used to them," Rory mumbled.

"THE BULLET WILL be working its way out, Moses," Dr. Sherman Cooke told his patient. The doctor had been summoned in the middle of the night to come at once for Moses Swearingen had taken a turn for the worse. Unlike many physicians, Dr. Cooke relished these midnight emergency house calls. He also relished, though he would be the last to admit it, that he got a great deal out of tending someone as unlike any of his other patients as Moses Swearingen.

"I'm surprised at you, Moses," Dr. Cooke was saying as he administered the hypodermic. "You boo-hoo and ki-yi more than any woman. Why, I bet Rory here could stand pain better than you."

Moses smiled a little at this last remark of the Doc.

"By the way, Moe, where are these gems I've been hearing about for the last week or so? For the jewels are in your possession, I gather."

Moses leaned up on one elbow and stared at the doctor.

"Do you know rubies, Doc?"

Rory had been sitting quietly and observing everything. He had found the news that the bullet was working its way out evidently of more interest than the gems.

"Rory," Moses barked, "go fetch the present from your Dad for the Doc to see, will you."

Rory took his own good time before rising and going out of the room.

"I wouldn't have recognized the chap," Dr. Cooke referred to the boy. "You've cleaned him up, got rid of his cowlick, and put some decent duds on him."

Rory entered with the package from his Dad and set it down on the counterpane beside Moses.

"Open up the box and show 'em to the Doc," Moses instructed the boy.

Again Rory hesitated, and then in his own good time took out one of the panels containing some of the rubies.

Dr. Cooke whistled at the sight of them, then chuckled and even slapped his thigh. Moses acted disgusted at the doctor's reaction.

"I almost wish my first wife was still alive," Dr. Cooke remarked, squinting one eye and examining one of the larger of the rubies. "Looks genuine enough. But it could be just glass!" he sighed.

"Glass, my eye," Moses almost roared, for he felt almost free of pain.

"You may scoff, Moe. But my first wife had costume jewels so splendid they fooled even the jewel experts."

The doctor held up another of the rubies to the light.

"And even the greatest experts can be fooled in the matter of precious gems," the Doc added.

"I wager these are the real McCoy, Doc," Moses muttered.

"And what does Rory say to all of this," Dr. Cooke gazed moodily at the boy. Rory looked brand-new to him now, and the gift of rubies somehow made him seem a complete stranger.

"Whatever did Pete Driscoll do to be able to lay his hands on these jewels, will you tell me, Moe," the doctor remarked.

Both men were then silent for they felt an awkward reticence in mentioning the character of Peter Driscoll in the presence of his son.

"Why don't they look like the real thing," Rory blurted out, an edge in his voice.

Dr. Cooke gave a start at the boy's remark for his voice was as new as his appearance, partly owing to the fact his voice was changing.

"Are you addressing this remark to me, young man," the doctor wondered. "Or to your benefactor here?"

Rory made a kind of snorting sound at the Doc's calling Moses his benefactor, then managed to say, "I guess I was asking both of you."

"They're too beautiful," Moses said, and he got up and took a seat in the rocking chair.

"Too beautiful for what?" Dr. Cooke asked.

"Why too beautiful to be anything but glass. I've read somewhere that fine glass imitations or what you called a moment ago costume jewelry can look niftier than the real thing."

Dr. Cooke now gave a snort.

"I must say, Moe," the doctor weighed his words now, "I have never seen anything to match them. But jewels, if they're real, pose a problem, and if they're not real, well, you have something else to worry about.

"But, Moe, I want to go back to the bullet in your chest. Let me look at your chest again."

Before he departed, Dr. Cooke issued instructions both to Moses and Rory.

"Now, boys, the bullet may come out sometime during the night," he told them. "I want Rory here to stay with you, Moe, at all times." The doctor hesitated, blinked, and then went on: "I recommend Rory sleep next to you so there will be no loss of time if the bullet begins to get dislodged. I am leaving a surgical instrument he can help retrieve the bullet with. It's good you have a king-size bed so Rory can have plenty of room as he looks after you. I've left some extra pills also," he pointed to a package on the big chiffonier.

"Rory talks in his sleep, Doc."

Dr. Cooke guffawed at this remark. "I said I want him as near to you as can be in case the bullet begins to come out. You can't dislodge the damned thing alone. Anyhow, hearing somebody talk in his sleep is better than having to sleep next to someone who snores. He don't snore, does he?"

"I haven't heard him, Doc."

"Then let him share the bed with you until the emergency is passed."

Dr. Cooke now rose in all his six feet four inches, and grabbing his little black bag, gave Moses a look which was akin perhaps to a benediction.

"Remember my instructions then," the doctor sternly spoke to Rory. "And don't leave my patient even for a minute. Do you hear? There is a chamber pot under the bed if you have to relieve yourself. Clear? Do not leave him for as much as a split second."

Rory's face was a perfect blank, just as it had also been when Bess Byal had tried to get him to understand long division and common fractions.

"Mind me now, Rory, or you will have to answer to me!"

Rory muttered somewhat grumpily to the effect he would obey the doctor.

THE DOCTOR HAD left one lamp burning near the bed, and Moses began to pile four or five pillows to rest his head on. He motioned to Rory to lie down half a bed's distance away from him.

"I hope you got by heart all the Doc told you," he said and motioned to his chest, which, at the doctor's instructions was left exposed.

Later Moses Swearingen would recall not so much the moment the bullet had emerged as Rory's almost uninterrupted talking in his sleep.

The general subject of his whispering beside him seemed to enumerate Vesta Hawley's roster of lovers, whose names were repeated so often Moses could tick them off by heart:

Carl Gretzinger, soap salesman
Bud Hotchkiss, life guard

Elmo Larrabee, choir director
Joel Sausser, mail clerk
Hal Eoff, Railway Express delivery man

"Will you lay off," Moses would mutter piteously from time to time, begging for silence. He had forgotten if he ever knew that people who talk in their sleep, like sleepwalkers, can never hear what anyone awake and near them says.

"Will you give a guy a break, for Christ's sake?"

He had no more said this than Rory heard Moses let out a war whoop, which he later said would have been loud enough to wake the dead.

Twisting and turning, even frothing at the mouth, Moses tried to turn this way and that, but Rory took hold of him and pushed him down firmly so that he could keep his eye on the bullet hole.

Then as Moses cried out as if a torch had been set afire on his bare flesh, he felt those strong pitiless young hands moving as if to touch his beating heart, and he heard an echoing cry come from the "sleeptalker."

Moses stared openmouthed at the boy who was holding the bullet now in his hand and brandishing it at Moses.

"You mean it's out, Rory?" Moses said in a voice totally unlike his own.

Jumping up, Rory let Moses see the bullet close up as he held it in his right hand.

"Do you aim to keep it?" Moses moaned, and he somehow was able to rise and get out of bed.

"Can't I?" Rory wondered, still holding the bullet in plain view for the sufferer.

"What in hell do you want my bullet for?"

"Well, ain't I earned it by getting it out of you!"

"I say again, what in hell do you want to keep my bullet for."

When there was no answer from Rory, Moses sighed as he sat in his armchair. This time though he was not taking morphine pills, he was drinking right out of the bottle of bootleg whiskey.

"Keep the damned thing if you want to then. Guess you think you earned it, I reckon. Who knows, maybe you did."

"I WAS A fool ever to let those jewels leave my house," Vesta was speaking to Dr. Cooke the next evening after his visit to Moe's Villa.

Frau Storeholder, at Vesta's urging, was also in the same room with her and the doctor.

For one thing, Vesta had observed tonight that Dr. Cooke was if anything more beguiled by her than ever before. His dippy behaviour tonight both pleased and annoyed Vesta. The fact she had "stolen" the thousand-dollar bills somehow—evidently—made him more admiring of her.

He claimed he had come tonight only to report on his meeting with Moe.

The doctor was somewhat appalled Vesta did not ask about Rory.

"I believe Moe thinks the rubies are the real thing," Dr. Cooke was saying.

"A lot such a fellow as Moe Swearingen would know about gems," Vesta scoffed. "I fear they're no more genuine than Peter Driscoll was on the up-and-up. And do you think Peter would have sent his son anything worth even a half million if it had any market value. For you did know Peter Driscoll, didn't you, Sherman?" she shot at him.

Dr. Cooke winced at her tone.

"Of course I knew Peter. Treated him very often."

Amazed at this retort, Vesta wondered, "May I ask you what ailed him that he came to you?"

"His ears were full of wax," the doctor quipped.

Vesta made a sneering sound. Perhaps she hoped to hear her former husband had a more serious ailment.

"You are quite right, Vesta," the doctor sighed and looked at her with longing. "Pete Driscoll would never have sent anything through the mail as precious as rubies."

"But maybe he wanted a place to hide them in," Frau Storeholder spoke all at once out of her deep silence—in fact both the doctor and Vesta thought she had been dozing as usual.

"I never thought of that, Belinda," Vesta spoke almost in a whisper. "Do you think Peter Driscoll was seeking a hiding place, Sherman?"

Dr. Cooke dismissed the idea at first, but then Vesta noticed an expression of doubt, even uneasiness came over her suitor.

"I looked carefully at all the rubies," the doctor spoke now in his professional manner. "They are glass. Fine glass, but in my opinion, only glass. Very good workmanship. Worth something in their own right. But glass, Vesta dear."

The atmosphere had changed suddenly. Doubt was in all their minds, and that doubt had been created by the Doctor himself.

"The whole town is talking about my neglect of Rory," Vesta brought up this topic again. "Bess Byal was over the other day to say everybody is up in arms. But thank God the superintendent of schools will take no action. Yet people think Rory could hardly be in a place more unsuitable for a young boy than Moe's Villa."

"Moe Swearingen may not be a gentleman," the doctor said, "but he is far from being a bad sort. Not a bit of it."

The doctor as usual was annoyed that Frau Storeholder was present. He knew also that she was here because Vesta wished her to be and that she wished her to be here to punish him. And this thought made him more in love with Vesta than ever. Love forbidden is twice as powerful, he mused. And his for Vesta Hawley had never been so intense.

ONE SNOWY AFTERNOON one of the young men who waited on Moses with such faithful attendance that he seemed to be everywhere at once entered the card room where Moses and Rory were playing a card game invented by Moses Swearingen himself.

"A lady is asking to see you," the attendant informed Moses.

"A lady?" Moses wondered sarcastically.

"Mrs. Hawley," the young man stuttered a bit.

Moses dropped his hand of cards and stared at Rory.

"Tell her to wait in the front parlour," Moses said after a pause in which he kept his eyes glued to his hand of cards.

In the parlour Vesta Hawley was seated on a rickety straight-backed chair. She wore a half-veil and large gold earrings. She had only one glove, this on her left hand.

"Yes," Moses said.

"Sit down, Mr. Swearingen." Vesta Hawley addressed him as if *he* was entering *her* parlour.

Moses hesitated a moment, grinned, then sat down on a faded settee.

"I want to speak with my son," she explained, and she fumbled in her purse and brought out a pack of cigarettes and stuck one in her mouth.

"May I smoke," she said although she had already lit her cigarette from a matchbox which she had found on the side table by her chair.

Moses shrugged.

"I supposed you wanted to discuss the gems," he said, and rising he brought her an immense cut glass ashtray.

Then he turned his back on her like a servant who, having given her the necessary attention, is about to leave.

"I do want to see the rubies again, I confess," she blew a ring of smoke toward him.

Turning to face her he said, "But you've already had a look at them, and besides you turned them over to your son."

He walked closer to her now and looked at the burning end of her smoke.

"At any rate, rubies or no rubies, you can't very well refuse me from seeing my own flesh and blood."

"Flesh and blood," he repeated as if he had never heard the phrase before.

"You have no idea how upset this has made me. I never dreamed . . ."

"Yes," he prompted her when she stopped speaking.

"How a man like Peter Driscoll. . . . Well, after all, you knew him, didn't you?"

Moses nodded in mock encouragement.

"I can't believe he could ever have acquired real gems," she spoke with the cigarette tightly between her lips.

"When I first set eyes on them, I had thought, you see, Moses, that . . ."

"That they were marbles!"

"All right. Marbles!" she snapped.

"And do you mean to take them from Rory now if you've decided they're maybe not marbles."

"No, no, no!" she raised her voice and got up and walked around the room, dropping cigarette ashes everywhere.

"The whole thing has really stricken me. Yes, that's the right word for it."

"You've always been very high-strung, Vesta."

"You say that as if it was my fault."

"I only speak from observing you."

"I wish we had never opened the box now. Actually as time passed I had forgotten Peter ever sent my boy a present. I was sure when it arrived it was of no consequence, considering where it came from."

"A present, though, from a boy's dad is usually not something to be put away and forgotten, its value aside."

"I broke out in a cold sweat when I saw his handwriting on the package," she confided, and put out her cigarette in the big ashtray. "After all Peter Driscoll had done to me, after all I had suffered at his hands. But no, I didn't mean to hide the gift from Rory. I was ill at the time, very ill, and by the time I recovered I had all but forgotten about it—until you asked for Rory's overcoat, and Frau Storeholder came across the forgotten gift package in the attic."

Moses consulted his large pocket watch.

"Let me see him, Mr. Swearingen." She was standing directly over him as she said this.

He pointed to the open door leading to the card room.

"Rory, my love," Vesta cried as she entered the card room. She took him in her arms and kissed him several times in rapid succession.

To Moe's disgust he saw a wave of happiness sweep over Rory's face.

"You have no idea how I've missed you," his mother went on. "I can see though that Mr. Swearingen has taken very good care of you. If I had his means, dear boy, I would see you wearing even better clothes than he has fitted you out with. Oh, I am grateful to him, no question about that. We have had hard times together, Moses," she turned now to Swearingen. "Very hard times. I suppose I should have sold the mansion and lived in some little flat somewhere with my boy. Holding on to an ancestral property with no husband to depend on, oh, well, you have heard it all a thousand times I expect."

She wiped her eyes of tears with a delicately scented handkerchief and sighed.

"I have been thinking, Rory, that if the gems are real, we might sell them, and if they are worth a fortune, we could buy back my mansion from the banks and the mortgage holders. Oh, I know some people say the rubies are not rubies," she almost sobbed now. "Tell me what you think, Rory."

"I don't know one jewel from another, Mama."

"Oh, my dear boy, when you say *Mama*, you have no idea how happy it makes me. Rory, your Dad never loved us. He deserted us. Do you think I neglected you on purpose? Think again. I love only you. You are my life, my all. The mansion is only something I have held on to so that one day I could leave it to you. But the mansion has been too heavy a burden for one woman to carry. Now, dear boy, let me see the rubies again, if you don't mind."

"Shall your Mother see your rubies?" Moe said, but there was now little trace in his voice of his usual biting manner and sarcasm.

At a nod from Rory, Moe went into an adjoining room and brought out the box of the jewels and placed it on a long table once used in his own banquets.

Vesta had to put on her glasses which she hated to wear as they made her look, she always said, like an old grandma.

"Oh, oh," she began as the jewels were uncovered. "But, Rory, they look so different from the time I first set eyes on them. Before the box was even opened of course—years ago, and I, merely peeping in, thought they were marbles, agates, maybe, but not worth the powder to blow them up with. Oh dear, now I don't know." She touched one of the gems cautiously. "They do look like jewels of some sort, I reckon. But they're sticky to the touch!"

Both Moe and Rory approached the box of gems and stared. The word "sticky" may have had something to do with their looking now at the gems with suspicion and puzzlement.

"We must call in an expert, Moe," Vesta spoke now familiarly. "You with all your worldly contacts must know of someone."

Moe could not help being pleased at Vesta calling him a man with worldly contacts. He half-smiled.

"There is a Russian, Alexander Oblonsky, or some such name. Met him once in France. Escaped from the Bolsheviks in the nick of time or they'd have beheaded him, he told me. Rich as Croesus and loves to show off his knowledge of diamonds, pearls, and of course rubies. He claims to have been one of the most dependable and faithful retainers of the late Tsarina and that she gave him some of her own jewels for safekeeping.

"You don't say, Moe." Vesta was greatly intrigued. "And we can send for him?"

"We can, but will he come? A busy man, almost a celebrity."

"I suppose he would charge us a fortune then," Vesta complained.

"Not necessarily so. He owes me many favors. I helped him with all the paperwork when he became a Canadian citizen, and then there were other favors I won't go into."

"Oh, Moe, how can I thank you. And he will tell us if the rubies (or whatever they are) have value or not."

"A man who knew the Tsarina and her jewels!" Moe exclaimed. "I should think he would know their value right off the bat."

"And you will send for him?"

Moses thought for a moment and then nodded.

Vesta could not restrain herself from going over to Moses and kissing him on both his cheeks.

It was Rory's turn now to look displeased and disgruntled. But he said nothing. After all, when didn't he recall the time he had seen his mother kissing gentlemen in his presence.

"And, Moe," Vesta ran on, "you do think Alexander Oblonsky, if I have his name right, will come to a small village like ours?"

"If I ask him, I am sure he will. If he is still alive."

"Oh, dear. You think he might not be."

"No, I think he is alive. I heard from him by letter only six months ago."

"Thank fortune, then. Oh, if he will only come and tell us. I will be in your debt, dear Moe, forever."

Again Rory saw with deep dismay that Moe beamed at his mother.

"I first met Alexei when I was a young soldier in France," Moe now began his reminiscences. "I don't for a minute think that is his real name. But I believe he is Russian. The rest of his story, like his name, I don't know whether to believe or not. But he is a jewel expert, we can be sure of that."

"And why don't you believe *all* of his story?" Vesta Hawley inquired.

"For one thing," Moses replied, "though he claims he came into the possession of some jewels once owned by Alexandra Romanov, the Tsarina who died at the hands of the Bolsheviks, he may not have known her at all. Another version that circulated was that he got ownership of these jewels from a desperate Russian émigré in Paris who died shortly after he entrusted Alexei with the royal gems."

"And what become of those jewels," Vesta warmed to his narrative.

"Who knows, Mrs. Hawley, but he must have had some kind of fortune to fall back on in those dark days of exile in France. At any rate shortly after the Armistice, he emigrated to Canada. I have visited him there several times. He claims I have done him many favors, such as help him secure his citizenship. But even that is an exaggeration. I pleased him, I believe, by listening to his stories and believing them. He is very fond of me, and that I believe; but why he is fond of me, who knows? At any rate I have only to call him, and he will come here and inspect your gems. For his life work has been the study of jewels. And who knows, maybe he did possess gems from the Romanovs!"

"But isn't there any expert on jewels who lives closer to us?" Vesta wondered, for the thought of a Russian whose real name and origin was unknown and whose friendship for Moses Swearingen was also suspicious troubled her.

"There is no one any more, dear Vesta Hawley, who can give a better estimate of the worth of gems that Alexei. Trust me for knowing that."

"Oh, I will have to, I suppose. But let me also speak with Dr. Sherman Cooke about this matter."

Moses Swearingen, irritated, now stood and put his hands in his deep pockets.

"Speak to him all you like! Dr. Cooke knows no more about gems than the local blacksmith. Indeed I'd be more inclined to get the blacksmith's estimate of your gems than the Doc's."

"Oh, all right, Moe. You are always, like most men of course, right. Call your Russian then, even if maybe he is a Bolshevik himself."

Moe grimaced on this, and their "confab," as Vesta later called it, came to a close.

LATER THAT EVENING, at home alone with Dr. Cooke, Vesta was tearful and allowed the "good doctor," as she called him, to hold her hand and kiss, in her words, her careworn fingers.

"Oh I don't trust this Alexei Oblonsky or whatever his name is, and I certainly don't want him to be in touch with Rory. A Russian. God knows what he was up to during the Revolution. And he is said to have got hold of Alexandra the Tsarina's jewels! I don't believe a word of it. Oh Sherman, why can't someone from here evaluate these jewels of ours."

Between his furtive kisses, Dr. Cooke managed to say: "I went to our public library after speaking with you the last time. I located a book there on precious gems. A very learned work, also by a Russian, come to think of it. But evidently very rare gems have to be appraised only by an expert. And even experts can be deceived. Especially in the case of diamonds and rubies."

"And so we have called in a Bolshevik to let us in on the truth of this mystery!"

"Dear Vesta, he is not a Bolshevik, I think, or he would not have come to this side of the world."

Vesta smiled and to the doctor's astonishment she gave him a chaste and icy kiss on his cheek.

ALEXEI OBLONSKY'S ARRIVAL in Gilboa by coincidence took place when there was a great torchlight parade on Main Street in honor of the return of a state senator who had served the small town well in his day. The torchlight parade and the brass band which accompanied it had turned the entire community into a noisy resplendent gala.

Alexei Oblonsky himself arrived in a miserable state of health and, as he remarked, he was lucky to have gotten safely to Moe's Villa, for he explained he had had to change trains three times, owing to a snowstorm and the loss of one of the engines.

Moe Swearingen was taken aback when he laid eyes on his Russian friend, for Alexei had changed greatly in the two or three years since Moe had last set eyes on him. His hair was gone nearly white, and an eye disease of some kind afflicted him so painfully he was required to use at intervals several different pairs of glasses and in addition made use of an oversize magnifying glass.

The din of the brass band together with the fact that they all caught flashes of the passing torchlight procession was nonetheless much to Alexei Oblonsky's liking.

"How kind of you to arrange such a reception," he quipped, pretending the demonstration of the torches and the bands were in his honor.

His witticism broke the ice of those gathered in Moe's large front parlour and from then on there was an air of general relaxation and cordiality on the part of everyone assembled in honor of the Russian gem expert.

Alexei's eyesight was not so impaired that he failed to fully take in the invited guests. He was especially drawn to Rory. "What a handsome son you have, Moe," Alexei exclaimed after he had employed different spectacles to view the boy. "I had no idea you have a son."

Moe quickly disabused his visitor of his mistake and gave a brief introduction then to the presence of Vesta Hawley, the boy's actual parent.

Alexei Oblonsky appeared if possible, even more enchanted at meeting Rory's mother. He rose, hobbled over to her, and taking her hand covered for this occasion by countless rings, kissed hand and rings devotedly.

Dr. Cooke was next introduced to the visitor.

"My dear Doctor," Alexei cried with something like glee. "How grateful I am to see a man of medicine, for I have had a journey every bit as slow, dangerous and snowbound as if I were in the vast wastes of my own motherland once more!"

And he took the doctor's hand in a grip so strong Sherman Cooke winced with a pain from the pressure.

Alexei Oblonsky then strolled over to the crackling fire blazing away in the chimney and extended his rather massive hands contentedly against the welcome heat of the logs.

"What a charming place you have, dear Moe," he now addressed the owner of the Villa. "I had no idea Fortune had smiled on you with such favor. And you deserve every one of her blessings."

Oblonsky now took a seat on a sprawling davenport (newly upholstered) and put on a new pair of spectacles and having looked about for a minute or so, removed these and replaced them with yet another pair of optics.

Several young servants now entered and served libations to all but Rory.

Oblonsky smacked his thin pale lips repeatedly as he tasted his drink. Then without warning he rose all at once to say: "May I propose a toast, ladies and gentlemen."

Almost losing his balance for a moment, he was assisted in standing on his two feet by one of the young servers, but this little awkwardness only added to the Russian's self-possession for he turned his momentary loss of balance to his own adroitness and somewhat theatrical poise, and as Moe gazed at his friend, he decided that Alexei must indeed have had some relationship however transitory with royalty.

At this moment, however, the brass band was passing close to the Villa, and Oblonsky was barely able to make his voice heard.

Perhaps he used the uproar of the band as an excuse for his cutting short his toast which nonetheless went something like this: "I am deeply moved and honored by the lavish and cordial welcome extended to a Russian in exile, and I extend my gratitude to the hospitable and distinguished gathering at this matchless Villa."

He put such an emphasis on his pronouncing Villa that everyone perhaps for the first time realized what a superb property their Moe was in possession of.

Everyone now stood and, after applauding, drank the toast.

It was possible in retrospect however that the banquet which now followed all but put in the shade the magnificence of the Villa itself and the background glitter of torchlights and brass bands.

Young servers dressed in gold-trimmed uniforms demonstrated furthermore that Rory was not the only handsome young man present, and Alexei Oblonsky found it necessary all during the eight-course banquet to put one pair of spectacles on after another in order to take in the resplendent magnificence he found everywhere his eyes wandered.

He later told Moe that not since his early days in St. Petersburg had he been regaled with such festivities. As to the banquet itself—with its venison, quail, guinea fowl, wild duck, and, for dessert, its assortment of pies, including of course pumpkin, mince and rhubarb—Oblonsky humbly informed the guests he doubted that even in imperial Russia itself could there have been a feast to equal the one he was now enjoying.

Oblonsky had eyes however not only for the young Adonises who served the feast, but more and more for Vesta herself, who wearing her grandmother's opals, must have stirred the Russian's memories of the royal beauties of his own homeland.

Retiring after hours at the festive board, the guests were next treated to the outpouring of a young men's chorus discreetly distanced from the guests in the front parlour by handsome screens.

It was clear, however, at least to Moe Swearingen, if to no one else, that the guest of honor was a bit listless, even sleepy, after his long train journey through snowstorms, engine problems, and bitter cold and by his nearly regal reception and entertainment at the Villa.

Neither Moe himself nor any of the other guests dared breathe a word concerning the matter of the birthday gift of Peter Driscoll to his only son, the rubies themselves.

After an hour or so of talk and occasional listening to the young men's chorus, it was the Russian guest himself who ventured to say: "And now, my dear Moe, I believe you might wish to have my opinion concerning some gems you wrote me several times about. I must warn you and your distinguished guests, however (and here he turned his full gaze toward Vesta Hawley), that contrary to what my dear friend Moe Swearingen may have told you, I am not the world's leading expert on gems and jewels. I am in this matter only an amateur."

"Nonsense!" Moe raised his voice. "I have it on the word of a number of authorities (he now turned his gaze also on Vesta as he spoke) there is no one at all here or abroad who knows more about precious gems than my excellent friend, Alexei Oblonsky."

Moe rose, and going over to the Russian, embraced him in continental fashion.

In the strained silence which now followed, several young men entered with trays of after-dinner drinks, but Alexei Oblonsky, begging they excuse him, declined any alcoholic beverage.

Moe then rose again to strike a small silver gong.

Almost immediately one of the young "footmen" (as Alexei Oblonsky called the attendants) entered with the box of gems and put them on a long low oak table near the Russian jewel expert.

At that very moment, and as if on cue, the brass band blared forth—concomitant with a sudden reflection of the torches which spotlighted the parlour as if after all both the band and the torches were in direct correspondence with the presentation of the jewels!

And so the moment had arrived, the moment they had all been waiting for so long, the moment in which the value and the future reputation of the jewels were to be established and settled by the greatest appraiser of precious gems to be found anywhere in the world.

The lid of the box was now removed by Moe Swearingen.

A kind of low murmur arose from the onlookers.

Alexei Oblonsky smiled as he almost devoutly studied the gems before him. His smile was followed by a pleasing nodding of his head several times. He took off the pair of glasses he was wearing and substituted them for one of probably greater strength.

His smile had now disappeared and his nodding likewise. He stared at the gems, picked them up cautiously one by one and to the surprise of everyone smelled them. He began to shake his head slowly. Then he would put down a single one of the gems and take up another in his hand.

Then he lay back in the throne-like chair provided for him, as if exhausted, and gave forth a series of short coughs, but his coughing sounded more like a person being strangled. It was a true paroxysm as Dr. Sherman Cooke would later describe it. It was certainly to the ears of those assembled the sound like that of a convulsion.

Dr. Cooke rose and rushed to the cloakroom where he had left his little black bag. He whispered something to Frau Storeholder who hurried out to the kitchen.

The doctor produced a small bottle and spoon, and Frau Storeholder hurried back from the kitchen with a tumbler of spring water.

"Do try to swallow this," Dr. Cooke was heard speaking to Alexei Oblonsky. The gem expert smiled and obeyed. He lay back against the chair's luxuriant backrest and closed his eyes. Then he opened them and smiled faintly to say, "Ladies and gentlemen, it is passing."

Dr. Cooke had ready another kind of medicine from a still smaller bottle, and the Russian tasted this docilely, smiled broadly and wiped his mouth.

"Let me retire to the kitchen with this kindest of kind ladies whom you call Frau Storeholder," Alexei Oblonsky spoke hoarsely but with authority. "I wish to examine one of the . . . jewels [he came near to not pronouncing the last word] where there may be running hot water."

He immediately left the room, carrying one or more of the jewels with Frau Storeholder in close attendance.

Everyone in the room was at that moment too bewildered and perhaps shocked to say anything. There was silence not unlike the silence of the conclusion of Thursday night prayer meeting.

Moe Swearingen thought for a moment of following Alexei Oblonsky out into the kitchen, but something ominous in the gem expert's manner forbade him to do so.

To the relief of all, the Russian returned in a few minutes and entered the room, solemnly chewing something. His hands were empty.

Instead of speaking however at once, Alexei Oblonsky roamed about the room, his fingers clasped behind his back, a patient almost-martyred expression on his old weathered and very careworn face. He resembled to some that evening a professor overseeing pupils taking their final examination.

Then he energetically strode forth to the center of the large room, cleared his throat, and attempted to smile, but the smile changed into a somewhat disturbing thin line, and a deep frown arose between his inflamed eyes.

"I am at some loss how to report the results of my examination," he began, his eyes looking up toward the high ceiling. A few flurries of his cough persisted, but he waved away Dr. Cooke's offering of another taste of his medicines.

"If I may so say, ladies and gentlemen, I have tasted your rubies whilst in the kitchen with my dear Frau Storeholder. I say *tasted* with deliberate choice." He then pointed to his mouth as the receptacle which had partaken of the jewels.

"My dear and esteemed friends all, and my very special dear friend of many years past, the nonpareil distinguished host of tonight's beautiful reception, Moe Swearingen, I cannot tell him and you how anguished I am to give you the verdict, if I may use such a term, the conclusion then, let me say, yes, conclusion is a better word for my examination of the gems."

He raised both his hands then like a preacher who is about to invoke either a blessing or a request for their departing the premises.

"The jewels, dear Mistress Hawley, and dear, dear young Rory Hawley, are not jewels or gems or precious gems or precious stones."

He waited a moment then, half-lifting both his arms.

"They are candy! I repeat, *candy*!"

Alexei Oblonsky then waited, perhaps expecting someone of those who had heard his verdict to say something. There was only a silence as deep as the word eternity itself.

It was Vesta Hawley who broke the silence induced by the shock of the verdict by rising from her place of honor and advancing toward the Russian. But Moe Swearingen intervened and, whispering cautiously something to Vesta, persuaded her not to perpetrate whatever she intended to perpetrate, and which Moe, sensing danger, prevented.

She pushed Moe away from her but then merely stood staring open-mouthed at the Russian.

Hardly unaware of Vesta's having tried to reach him, the Russian now spoke more at length.

"They are very old, these candies. We have found similar confections in the tombs of Egypt. Time and chemistry and perhaps the eggs of wasps are in evidence—who can tell. I am only a jewel expert. Let us say then the vicissitudes of time have turned a box of birthday candies (here he bowed in the direction of Rory), turned them into a kind of sweet cement. Nonetheless some hot water in the kitchen allowed one of the gems to melt so that I could taste it and pronounce my verdict which is, alas, that the rubies are and were sweetmeats. Mummified of course, lost in time, and yet at first glance one is quite understandably pardoned in having thought them jewels of some sort, rubies, say. We have all been taken in, therefore. My first glance convinced me in fact we had before us rubies. We have been hoodwinked, you may feel, dear friends, but if hoodwinked, then by Father Time himself and by no human prankster."

Having spoken thus, Alexei Oblonsky sat or rather fell into the enormous chair he had sat in before, and he emitted queer little sounds that were either weeping, moaning, or perhaps again coughing, which resembled, in the mind of Dr. Cooke at least, almost the sound of a death rattle.

THE NEWS THAT the rubies were not genuine but were, in fact, candy, spread not so much like wildfire through the entire village of Gilboa, but more like the effect of a huge meteorite which, falling, had struck all the palatial mansions of the town.

There was especial sympathy and concern for Vesta Hawley; for everyone had assumed that the rubies would enable her to retain possession of her own mansion and perhaps allow her to welcome back her runaway son, Rory.

Even Moe Swearingen himself was, if not pitied, at least pardoned for his many past deviations from the norm. He had at least, by summoning a famous jewel expert, attempted to establish the authenticity of the gems, even though his attempt had revealed the jewels were bogus.

The scandal of the false rubies even broke into print across the nation, and reporters from New York City and Chicago visited Gilboa and made an attempt to interview Vesta Hawley, her son Rory, and Moe Swearingen. But in vain. These main dramatis personae indeed were as impossible to reach as if they were some kind of royalty and the rubies were genuine.

Though there was no reason for the brass band to play or the torchlights to parade about the town, somehow each evening for quite a while this was exactly what occurred. Young men carrying banners which were illuminated by the torches assembled in front of Moe's Villa and Vesta Hawley's mansion. On these banners one could make out messages such as:

WE LOVE YOU VESTA
COME WHAT WILL

and before Moe Swearingen's Villa another fluttering banner could be deciphered, to wit:

MOE, WE HONOR AND COMMEND
YOU AND YOR VILLA

If before Gilboa had some fame for the renowned splendour of some of its mansions, from this time forward the village became equally famous for the episode of the false rubies.

From then on Vesta Hawley was said to wear only black mourning attire and was seldom or never afterwards seen in public.

A rumour also spread that Moe Swearingen had taken papers of adoption for Vesta's son Rory, but this was never proved, and no adoption evidently ever took place.

Stung as both mother and son were by this whim of Fortune, it was Rory who now began visiting his mother almost every evening for the duration of an hour or so. It is thought she obtained his pardon for never having given him on their arrival the box of candies from his scapegrace father, Peter Driscoll. For, as Vesta was reported having said, according to Frau Storeholder, "Had you and I eaten the candies on their arrival, as I suppose Pete meant us to, think of how different everything else would have turned out."

To meet the demand of the bank and Vesta Hawley's other creditors, Moe Swearingen, who was after all one of the most wealthy men in this part of the country, paid off all Vesta's debts so that she was the sole mistress at last of her mansion.

Did we say Vesta received no visitors except that of Rory? We hardly thought of mentioning Dr. Sherman Cooke in this regard, as he was now not so much a visitor as a permanent lodger at Vesta's by reason in part that his wife, having passed away shortly after the scandal of the rubies, he more or less took his place as a star boarder at Vesta's, chaperoned of course always by the ubiquitous everfaithful watchdog Frau Storeholder.

THE END

NO STRANGER TO LUKE

The first Luke realized that people in town had heard someone was stealing from his mother's kitchen cabinet was when he was having a haircut.

Young Pete Snyder, the barber, holding the straight razor up high and about to shave his young customer's neck, pressed his mouth close to Luke's ear and confided: "I hear you have a thief at your house."

Luke gave a slight shudder not so much at the sight of the straight razor at so close an angle as Pete's pronouncing the word *thief.*

"You don't have any suspicion who it is?" Peter queried.

Luke shook his head, and Pete began moving the razor through the thick suds and around the back of Luke's neck. Finished shaving, Pete took off the voluminous cloth covering Luke and bowed as the boy handed him the fifty-cent piece.

"I hope you catch him, whoever he is," Pete remarked as he opened the door for Luke.

"I DON'T KNOW how Peter Snyder got wind of it," Luke's mother remarked that night at supper.

She was what people in that small town call a grass widow, for

Luke's dad had deserted the family some years ago. Mother was a good-looking woman, still in relative youth.

"Once you open your mouth in this town, Luke, somebody is sure to hear you, and that somebody talks," Mother went on.

Luke fingered the slight cut on the back of his neck caused by Pete's shaving him, and then he winked just then at his younger brother, Vance, who sat always next to him at meals, for both boys were amused at their mother's gift of gab.

"But, boys," she went on, "I have been worried all the same about losing money from the kitchen cabinet drawer. You know I keep all my change for the milkman and the grocery boy in that little cabinet."

Mother then recounted all over again that the thief had taken the money in such a hurry he had failed to close the drawer in the cabinet and had left it to remain open as if to show he didn't care if she knew someone had stolen her money or not.

"But it does begin to add up to quite an amount over time," Mother finished.

"I bet this little tattletale here told the barber," Luke now turned his gaze on his younger brother, Vance.

Vance colored under his summer tan and hung his head.

"Now don't start on Vance, Luke," his mother warned.

"That's right, always take the side of your little favorite," Luke sneered.

OVER THE DISHPAN that night, Luke helped his mother dry the silverware and plates with a tea towel.

"Sometimes I wonder about Dan Schofield," Mother said all at once.

"Dan Schofield," Luke showed real surprise.

"Yes, Luke, your best friend," she added in a kind of sudden indignation.

"Well, I know it sounds far-fetched. You're so fond of him too, I know," Mother continued, "of course Dan comes from a good family. His folks are very well-off," she backed down now a little.

Luke frowned and waited, "You call him my best friend, Mama. But he calls on you and Vance more often than I see him. In fact Pete Snyder once asked if you was going steady with Dan!"

"Pete Snyder," his mother scoffed. "He would say that. Going steady with a boy young enough to be my own son! I declare."

Luke's mother had always pooh-poohed any importance to her going out with some eligible gentleman or other. "A person does get lonesome for the company of someone her own age, and a little company with an older gentleman isn't anything serious. But Dan Schofield, for heaven's sake! What a thing to say!" She laughed uneasily now at her own remark.

Luke was also a little jealous of how his mother always was praising Dan. She pointed out how he could play the piano like a concert pianist, and she recalled he often gave her presents and flowers on St. Valentine's Day and Easter.

"Poor Dan would be heartbroken if he knew we suspected him," Luke spoke somewhat sarcastically.

His mother all at once became thoughtful. She looked critically at the tumbler she had just scalded.

"What is it, Mama?" Luke saw her change of mood.

"The truth is, Luke, the thefts do seem to occur only when Dan has been here."

Luke put down the tea towel and shook his head.

His mother, sensing how upset Luke was, thanked him for helping her dry the dishes and gave him a stealthy kiss.

"We mustn't let on about this, Luke, to outsiders. And after all we have no proof it is Dan."

Mother feared Luke's hot temper, and she recalled the quarrels Luke had always had with his dad. Once Luke struck his father with a monkey wrench during an argument. It had frightened the boy so much he hid all night in the cellar where she found him lying in an old hammock near the furnace room. She had smoothed his hair and let him cry.

Perhaps Luke thought his mother saw he was thinking back now on all the good times he used to have with Dan. Lately, however, Dan had been seeing his younger brother Vance more than he did Luke, and Luke was somewhat jealous of this change in Dan's feelings for him.

Tonight Luke sauntered out on the front porch where Vance was seated. Luke came to the point of what he wanted to say at once.

"What do you make of Mama's fear that maybe it's Dan who has been stealing from the cupboard drawer?"

Just to be contrary, Vance pretended not to have any opinion about it.

"But you see Dan now more than I do," Luke went on, and he sat down on the porch swing beside his brother.

When Vance was silent and pouted, Luke gave him a shove. Vance was afraid of Luke who often "socked" him when they had an argument. And the mention of Dan as a thief frightened him. Then, too, Vance had once dreamed that his brother had killed him, and he had told his mother one day when she was ironing the clothes about his dream. She had put the iron down on its holder and stared at him. "You mustn't put any store on dreams, dear. They often mean the opposite." But Vance could see she was frightened.

"Did you tell Pete Snyder about the thefts?" Luke wondered.

"No," Vance was more communicative now, "all I know is what Mama has already told you. That she found the cupboard drawer pulled open with some of the string hanging out. Her small change was gone. I never said boo to anybody about it."

"And the long and short of it is *your Dan* took the money!" Luke said *your Dan* because Vance and Dan were chums now and often went swimming together in the summer and in the winter patronized the pool parlors or the movies. "I think you know something you're not telling me," Luke went on, puffing on a cigarette. Luke was smoking one of his mother's cigarettes.

Vance could see that Luke did not really enjoy smoking. He coughed a lot while doing so and was constantly removing little bits of tobacco from his teeth. Luke was proud of his white teeth and feared smoking would turn them to be dingy, for his secret ambition was to be a movie star or a nightclub singer. But tonight Luke was nervous and smoked.

"Could it be you know something you're not telling me," Luke went on puffing on his smoke, and he all at once gave Vance a push. Vance could hear the anger coming out from his brother. Luke kept swallowing so hard then in his riled mood that Vance laughed. Vance loved to mock Luke whenever he dared, although he was afraid usually to do so.

"Tell you what," Luke now rose from the porch swing. "I think after all I should have a talk with Dan then," he said, the cigarette hanging out of his teeth in the manner of a movie star he copied after.

"A lot you'll get out of Dan, Luke."

"Is that so?" Luke responded, and at that moment he sounded exactly like their absent dad. And if Vance had told his brother he sounded like his father, he would have beat the tar out of him.

"And think how rich Dan's parents are," Luke spoke moodily.

Vance shrugged his shoulders which annoyed Luke. He felt his younger brother knew a lot more about the theft than he was letting on. His Adam's apple bobbed up and down when he was angry, but this time instead of punching Vance he merely said: "See you keep an eye then on Dan, why don't you."

Luke opened the screen door, then went on inside.

"WHAT IS IT, Luke?" his mother looked up when he entered the little alcove that led to her bedroom. She had put her hair in curlers, and her face was covered with vanishing cream.

Luke had almost never come into her own private room at this hour, and she knew he must be troubled.

"You've been worrying about Dan Schofield, Luke." She wiped some of the vanishing cream off her face with a fancy white cloth.

"As I said, we can't be positive after all it's him," she spoke in a conciliating manner, but she kept her eyes averted from him.

"I thought you told Vance you knew it was him."

She straightened one of her sheer hose from above her high heels and hesitated. "I said it only does seem to happen when Dan comes to see us."

"Is that proof then that it's him?"

"If it is him, Luke, then *why* does he do it?"

"Yes, *why*! Why can't you at least admit for once and all then Mama he's the thief!"

There was a note of real irritation in Luke's voice, and his mother winced because, like his father, Luke had a fearful temper.

"I think maybe you've spoiled Dan," he grumbled.

"Not any more than I've spoiled you and Vance maybe."

"It's true what some people say, for one thing you've always acted like Dan was one of your fellows. Yes, your beaux!"

His mother drew in her breath and was silent. She looked in a little hand mirror and touched quickly where some of the night cream remained.

"I can't understand if it's Dan who steals, *why* he steals, when his family is more than well off; and Dan for all practical purposes has the big house all to himself since his people are gone most of the year.

"I don't like Dan being so thick with Vance, either," Luke shut his eyes as he said this.

"But Dan is no stranger to you! You used to see more of him than little Vance ever does."

"Used to is right," Luke answered hotly. "I seldom see him anymore at all, except of course when he comes to see you!"

"Luke!" his mother spoke in an almost syrupy manner. "The good thing about Vance seeing Dan, Luke, is Dan has been teaching him to swim, and they sometimes go hiking together. Vance is not very popular with boys his own age as you know. Being able to go with Dan has been a good thing for the boy."

"But if he is a thief!"

His mother made a deprecating expression then.

"So then you don't think it matters if Dan steals," Luke sneered.

"Don't misquote me, Luke, and don't go," she asked him, for Luke began to move toward the door. She wiped nearly all the night cream from her face and stood up. "I don't suppose you would want to talk to Dan," she said. "At his house maybe."

When Luke said nothing in return, she went on: "It's a great pity if he steals." She spoke as if she was thinking aloud. "Dan is quite talented in his own right—not only plays the piano beautifully, but is a good dancer. He lost two years from high school when he was in the navy, so he's older than the boys in his class."

When Luke remained silent, his mother continued: "So I don't guess you would want to speak to Dan then."

"About his going steady with you," Luke joked now.

"Oh, Luke, please, that's not at all funny."

"I'll speak to him if you say so, Mama."

"I'll leave that up to you," she spoke icily.

"Oh, I suppose I could sound him out."

"Yes, maybe it would be a good thing if you did sometime." She smiled encouragingly.

Luke sighed on the word *sometime*.

"Maybe it will all stop of itself, Luke," his mother said, and she looked pleadingly at her older boy.

"I'm afraid if he is a thief, it won't."

His mother shook her head. "I suppose you may be right."

Luke bent down then and kissed her on her face, the residue of the vanishing cream and all. They both laughed then that he would kiss her with some of her night cream still on.

LUKE HAD NEVER been inside Dan's house. He had forgotten, if he ever knew, how much larger and more imposing it was than where he and Vance lived with their mother. He almost lost his courage as he stood before the heavy front door with the golden knocker. He rapped, but there was no answer. He was a bit surprised when, as he grasped the gleaming brass doorknob, the door opened easily under his touch.

Inside, Luke was about to leave, under the impression Dan was not at home. Then he thought of the thefts. A kind of uncontrollable wrath gave him the encouragement to remain. He heard some sound down the long, brightly-lit hall. His sense of outrage over the thefts allowed him to walk toward the room where he heard the sounds. He entered a large kind of sitting room which contained a number of upholstered chairs arranged as if for a meeting of some kind. Then he could hear someone singing in the room adjoining.

"Just a minute!" It was Dan's voice.

Again Luke had the wish to leave and forget the whole affair. In his discomfort he had come to the conclusion Dan could not have been the thief.

As he turned to leave, the door to the room, from which Dan's voice came, opened. At first Dan appeared thunderstruck at the sight of Luke.

"Why, Luke," Dan greeted him, "I can't believe my eyes. What a surprise!"

Dan was silent, then stared at Luke for a full minute.

Luke on the other hand couldn't get over Dan's appearance. He had on evening clothes!

Usually Dan dressed (in the words of Luke's mother) in a very casual manner, by which she meant he appeared slovenly. Tonight he resembled a young man out of a fashion magazine. His curly hair was carefully combed (his mother once laughingly called it marcelled). His cheeks were flushed to an extent they appeared almost touched with rouge.

"Take a chair, why don't you," Dan spoke unlike his usual self-assured manner.

Luke almost stumbled into one of the mammoth, cushiony affairs which might have just come from the upholsterer.

Dan walked around the room aimlessly, occasionally glancing at his guest.

"Tell me what I can do for you, Luke," he spoke as if he was addressing a stranger.

Luke shook his head. A sigh almost like a sob came out from him.

"See here, Luke, what is the matter? You look so confounded upset."

Then going directly up to Luke and observing him closely, he all but shouted, "Do you know how pale you are, Luke!"

Luke touched his face with his hand, as if paleness could be checked by touch.

"You're so dressed up tonight, Dan," Luke changed the subject. "Are you going to town?"

"I was going to the dance tonight," Dan mumbled.

Then Dan sat down in a chair rather at a distance from Luke and studied Luke's face. "But I needn't go now you're here!" he finished effusively.

Luke showed surprise at this remark. Then all at once, remembering Dan's comment that he looked pale, he felt all at once indisposed. A thin thread of spittle came out from his lips.

"Let me get you a drink," Dan jumped up and hurried out of the room.

He returned with a bottle of brandy and a glass, and pouring out a shot, he brought the glass directly to Luke's lips.

"Go ahead, drink it," Dan spoke with authority. Luke obeyed.

"Drink all of it," Dan insisted.

Even after Luke drank some more, there was some brandy left in the glass as Luke handed it back to Dan. Dan drank off the residue. Then grasping the bottle, he poured himself a full glass and downed that.

"You're very troubled, you know," he told Luke impatiently, and then all at once smiled a kind of smile Luke had never seen on Dan's face before.

"I'd best be going then," Luke proposed.

"Going! For cripes' sake!" Dan shouted now. "Before you've even told me why you came to see me, you're going!"

"But you're off to a dance!"

"I've already forgotten the dance," Dan replied and gave Luke so eloquent a look the younger boy let out another sigh; and removing a large blue handkerchief from his hip pocket, he wiped his lips assiduously.

"You must have come here for something, Luke. And do you realize you've never bothered to visit me before tonight."

"You never invited me," Luke complained.

"You didn't need an invitation, and you know that! You know you are welcome here more than anybody else!"

"Know! I don't know!" As he said this, Luke looked about the room as if the opulence surrounding him was the reason for his never having been here before.

"I want you to take a little more brandy," Dan spoke with a kind of lofty inflection.

"If you think so," Luke said in a monotone.

"Unless you mind drinking out of the same glass I drank from," Dan laughed as he poured Luke another drink from the bottle.

Luke stared at the edges of the glass; then closing his eyes, he drank it all at one gulp and handed the glass back to Dan.

"What is it now?" Dan wondered softly. "What do you want to tell me?"

"You don't know?" Luke raised his voice slightly.

Dan avoided looking at Luke now.

"Dan, see here," Luke lowered his voice, "Why don't you go to the dance, and I'll be going back home."

"Because I don't want to go to the dance now, smarty. Why should I leave you alone here. Especially since you won't tell me why you've showed up here out of the blue!"

"Are you scared I might steal something if you go away and leave me?"

"What in the hell do you mean by that remark?"

"All right then. Let me ask you. Why did you do it?" Luke had gone very pale again.

"Do what?" Dan muttered between his teeth.

"Took money from my mom! When you're rich as Croesus!"

"Money?" Dan spoke crazily. "What money!" He turned and picked up the bottle of brandy and drank thirstily from it.

"You don't know what money I am talking about?"

"Wait a minute, just wait," Dan said. He passed his hand over his eyes; then blinking, he mumbled something.

"You did take the money, why not say it, Dan. Say it, Goddamn it. Get it off your chest."

Dan kept shaking his head. He ran his fingers through his thick auburn hair and was silent.

"That's why I came here tonight, and you damned well knew it the minute you set eyes on me!"

"Supposin' I told you I don't know why I took the money; what would you say to that?" Dan searched Luke's face for an answer.

"You sure don't need the money, do you," Luke sneered, and he waved a hand at the fancy wallpaper and drapes.

"So go ahead, judge me then! When you've never been through the mill, never had to go through the gauntlet like me. Always safe at home with your mom and little Vance. A real mama's boy, aren't you. Never did anything wrong!"

Having said this, Dan rose and walked aimlessly about the room. Then seizing the bottle, he drank more of the brandy and wiped his mouth noisily with his free hand.

"So look down on me and go to hell!" Dan shouted. "What do you know about life. You spoiled little snot."

"But you did steal the money. Why not say it?"

"You call taking chicken feed stealing? All right. Sure I took it. But not to steal."

"What in hell did you take it for then?" And Luke all of a sudden took the brandy bottle up and, following Dan's example, drank direct from the bottle.

"Ask me the question again, why don't you," Dan growled. "Why did I steal? Ain't that your question."

Luke shrank now at the rage in Dan's eyes and mouth.

"*Why did I steal?* And do you know what the answer is?" And walking over to Luke, he took both the boy's hands in his. "The answer is: I don't know if I was to be shot why I took it." Going more closely up to Luke, he slapped him sharply across the face. "You good people!" he shouted. "You make me sick."

"What's being good have to do with you stealing, will you tell me that," Luke said as he touched the place where Dan had slapped him as if the blow had given him something he stood in need of. "You sure didn't need the money, did you? A rich boy like you," and Luke snorted with anger but kept touching the place where Dan slapped him.

"For your information I am the poorest son-of-a-bitch who ever lived. It's you and Vance and your mother are the rich ones, but you are too spoiled and pampered to know it! I am dying of my own poverty! Dying!" As he said this Dan approached Luke again so closely Luke covered his face as if he expected a new blow.

Dan pulled Luke's hands away from his face.

"You and Vance and your mother have everything, everything I don't have and never will have! You have one another for one thing. You live in a real love nest. Don't interrupt me, or I will slap you to sleep! You three lack nothing in my eyes."

"And you stand there and tell me you don't have a lot!" Luke rushed to the fray. "All this luxury," and he waved his hand at the chandeliers and the fine molding of the walls.

"What do I have? Less than nothing. My mother hasn't got ten minutes a year for me. I'm not even positive she's my mother. I don't think I ever heard her call me *son*. My dad, if he was my dad, was never home. Spent all his time, before he shot himself, at the races trying to rake in more money. They meant zero to me, and I never even meant a zero to them."

"But what's all that got to do with your thieving!" Luke cried out as if he saw another blow coming.

"Thieving!" Dan jumped up as if a hot iron had touched him.

"What do you call it, taking money from my mother's meager earnings!" Luke drew closer to him.

All at once Dan became quiet, thoughtful. "I always left a few quarters and fifty-cent pieces from what I took."

"And what good did that do you, then?"

"Now you're getting to it, ain't you. What good did it do, yes. Let me tell you something," Dan advanced again as close as possible to his visitor. "I don't have a clue as to why I took the money in the kitchen cabinet. All I know is you and Vance and your mom have everything. As I say, you live in a love nest! That's right, a love nest! You have each other. And I have nothing and never have had anything and won't never have anything in the future."

Luke stared speechless. His mouth was filled with half-swallowed brandy, and as it overflowed to his chin, he began to wipe his face with his handkerchief. Dan grabbed the handkerchief from him and began to wipe the boy's lips carefully and then silently handed him back the handkerchief.

"I always hoped I would have the three of you for my own friends," Dan said looking up at the ceiling. "I thought you would share some of the love you had from each other. But you didn't have none to spare, did you."

Luke now held the handkerchief awkwardly in his hands, staring at it as if it was something that had a pulse.

"You are the only family that I ever had," Dan spoke so low his words were nearly inaudible. "But, as I say, I soon realized you didn't have nothing to spare for me. So it was, I guess, *then* I began to steal from you. I did so 'cause I wanted to have something from you, I guess. Something I could touch and feel."

Luke covered his eyes with his hands. Dan stared at him fixedly; then going over to Luke he pulled his hands away from his eyes.

"I want you to watch me as I testify against myself, do you hear." The sternness of his voice made Luke gaze at Dan in a kind of hushed desperation. "I have kept all the small change and some loose strings that happened to be in the drawer in a little hiding place of my own. I wish somebody loved me enough to steal them from me! But nobody loves me. Nor ever will."

"My head is swimming," Luke mumbled, but perhaps Dan did not hear him.

"Anyhow, I was planning on leaving town even before you came here tonight. So when you go home, Luke, you can tell your mother I will never come to your house again. You can all sleep peacefully from now on. I won't trouble your domestic bliss! Will you tell her?"

Luke had wanted to tell Dan that if he left town after what they had said tonight that he would not be able to bear it. He felt he could almost fall to his knees and beg Dan not to leave. He wanted to say he would feel somehow lost without him. He walked toward the door.

"I don't know what I'll say to her," Luke said, after the silence between them.

"Before you go, Luke may I ask one last favor of you."

"What is it?" Luke turned to stare at Dan.

"Will you grant me the favor?"

"Yes I will," Luke practically shouted.

"Let me kiss you."

Luke advanced toward Dan in the manner of a sleepwalker.

Dan waited quite a while before slowly, chastely, even icily kissing Luke quietly first on his mouth then over each of his eyes. Dan then broke away and rushed into the next room and closed the door.

WHERE WERE YOU so long?" His mother was waiting up for him.

"Where's Vance?" Luke wondered.

His mother went up to him just then, "Do I smell liquor on your breath?" she asked. When there was no answer she said, "Vance is asleep upstairs."

"I hear tell Dan is leaving town," Luke said, and sat down in mother's favorite chair. "Maybe for good."

"Did you have a talk with him?"

"No."

"Are you going to?"

"No, Mama, I'm not. I don't see what the point would be now if it's true we won't be seeing him for a good long time. It ain't likely he'd admit to anything now anyway."

She shook her head. It was the thought Luke was drinking which occupied her mind.

They both sat there then in complete silence.

"It's so very late, Luke, I will bid you goodnight. Don't stay up too much longer then. Do you hear, Luke."

Luke nodded.

His mother blew him a kiss and went toward the front stairs.

But then coming suddenly back into the room, she said looking nowhere in particular, "If Dan didn't steal the money, who did then, Luke, I ask you?"

"The wind, Mama. The wind."

REACHING ROSE

Mr. Sendel in his late years spent almost the entire evening in his favorite saloon, seated in an imposing manner on the center barstool from where he could survey very close to Richard, the bartender, all that went on. After a few drinks which he sipped very slowly, Mr. Sendel would gaze absentmindedly at the telephone booth nearest him.

Then giving another taste to his drink, leaving it more than half full, he would make a rather stately progress to the booth, partly closing the door. He would take down the receiver and hesitantly begin speaking into the mouthpiece.

Actually Mr. Sendel was talking only to himself. He would talk for several minutes into the silent phone, explaining how worried he was and how despairing it was at his time of life when all or almost all those dear to one have departed.

Opening the booth door wide, Mr. Sendel would stroll back to the bar and finish his drink. Feeling the eyes of others fastened upon him after a while he would again leave to go back to the phone booth.

He was convinced that nobody suspected he was in the booth talking to himself. Not even the bartender who was smart suspected it, he consoled himself.

Mr. Sendel always went through the motions of dialing the number, however, to throw anybody off the scent who might be watching, and then he would begin speaking again through the black opening of the phone. As he spoke the cold blackness of the mouthpiece warmed up slightly, throwing back the smell of the liquor he had drunk, the tobacco fumes, even perhaps the smell of the dental work he was always having done.

As he talked into the phone he felt, if not quieter, more of one piece, whereas when he sat at the bar he would often feel like a pane of glass struck by an invisible hammer and so about to crash, not in one piece, but all over, so that the broken glass would fall into shimmering and tiny silver particles to the floor.

Mr. Sendel now talked to prevent himself from collapsing like glass into smithereens.

When Mr. Sendel first began going to the telephone booth he had talked only to himself, but this had never really satisfied him. First of all he no longer had anything more he wanted to say to *himself*. He was an old man, and he did not care about *himself*; he no longer actually wanted to exist as he was now. Often as he sat at the bar he wished that he could become invisible, disembodied, with just his mind at work, observing. He wished the painful husk of ancient flesh which covered him would be no more, that he might live only remembering the past currents of his life. Perhaps, he reflected, that was all immortality was: the release from the painful husk of the flesh with the mind free to wander without the accumulated harvest of suffering.

Later when he would go to the telephone, he would pretend to talk with people whom he once knew, but after a while he tired also of this pretense. The people he really cared for were all dead. They had all been gone for many years. He realized this for the first time when he was in the phone booth. *"They are all gone,"* he had said into the mouthpiece. *"All of them."* He had sat there for a long time after that, thinking, the mouthpiece unspoken into, the receiver lying in the palm of his hand like a wilted bouquet. Finally a man had tapped on the pane of the telephone booth. "Are you finished?" he asked Mr. Sendel somewhat anxiously. He had looked at the man a moment, then nodded slowly, and turning to the mouthpiece he said, "Goodbye then, dear."

He saw that the man in his hurry to get into the telephone booth did not notice anything unusual in his behavior.

He went back to his place at the bar and ordered another brandy.

IT WAS THE next evening things came to a head.

"What I like about you, Mr. Sendel, is you are always busy," the bartender greeted him. "You always have something on tap. That's why you look so young."

He looked at the bartender without changing his expression, despite the surprise which he felt at such a remark.

"Isn't that true, sir," the bartender asked him hesitantly.

"You really think I look occupied?" Mr. Sendel wondered in a tone rather unlike himself, perhaps because for the first time in that bar, for the first time perhaps in many years, he had made a comment about himself.

"You look completely . . . well, in business," the bartender finished.

"Thank you, Richard," Mr. Sendel retorted.

Then as Richard looked peculiar at him, he said, "I *am* terribly occupied," and bartender and customer both laughed with relief.

"I admire you, sir," Richard said.

"And you know what my estimation of you is," Mr. Sendel winked.

Richard was one of the few persons whom Mr. Sendel actually *knew* any more. Everyone else, somehow, was somebody you talked generalities with, but occasionally he and Richard managed to say some particularity that made up the little there was of meaning.

Usually after exchanging one of these particularities, Richard would move on to another customer, but today something impelled him to stay, and not only stay, but to question or rather to comment.

"Sir," Richard spoke somewhat awkwardly for him. "About the phone calls."

Mr. Sendel's mouth moved downwards and his pale brown eyes flashed weakly.

Seeing his look, Richard said, "It's so wonderful."

Mr. Sendel was vague and unhelpful.

"What I mean, sir," Richard continued suddenly lost as he had never before been with his old friend, "it's wonderful you have so much to . . . tend to."

Then seeing the old man's look of distant incomprehension, he continued, "For you to be so alive at your age is, to me, wonderful."

"Thank you, Richard," Mr. Sendel managed to say, and his old warmth and vivacity rushed back, so that the bartender was moved almost to tears.

"Richard," the old man began, "have one drink with me, why don't you," and he handed the bartender some bills.

"For you it will be all right," Richard said, grinning awkwardly.

Richard began to pour a drink for himself from one of the nearby bottles, but Mr. Sendel tapped imperiously and pointed to a large, seldom-used flask. "That one, Richard."

The two men drank then to one another.

Outside the sound of a saxophone drifted over to them, and both men exchanged looks. Richard tightened the string of his apron.

Mr. Sendel wanted to look at the phone booth nearest him, the one he always used, but he did not.

"Of all the men who ever come in here," the bartender said sleepily, "you're the finest," and with a special gesture of his hand, he moved off and out of the presence of the old man.

Mr. Sendel stared after him. He was not sure what Richard had meant exactly, as he thought it over, and his pleasure at Richard's friendliness turned suddenly to anguish and fear that perhaps the bartender knew something. He had not liked his mentioning the telephone. And the more he thought about it, the more worried he became. *Richard should not have mentioned the phone*, he repeated to himself.

Then the thought came that perhaps Richard did *know*, that is, that there was nobody on the wire, and that he had *no* business whatsoever, that there was *nobody*, nobody but Richard and him. Bartenders, like Delphic oracles, are naturally defined by their very profession as anonymous. They administer haphazardly and are Great Nobodies by reason of their calling.

"He could *not* know," Mr. Sendel said aloud.

He was surprised as he heard his own voice and, turning around, was relieved to see that nobody had heard, not even Richard.

He could NOT know, Mr. Sendel spoke almost prayerfully.

He thought how terrible it would be if Richard did know. There would be nothing left of his world at all. His mind had never before dwelt on the exact components of that world before, but now, at a glance, he saw everything just as it was: his world was merely this bar, was Richard, and most important of all the telephone booth; but all of them went together, the booth and the bar and Richard could not be disassociated.

He paused before the thought of all this.

If Richard knew, there would be nothing.

The thought—so simple and so devastating—completely unnerved him.

And now a second disturbing thing occurred to him. Tonight he had not telephoned. He had barely looked at the phone booth, and he knew that Richard was, after their conversation, waiting for him to do so. Richard expected, had to expect, him to phone.

And all at once he feared he could not go to the booth. And quite as suddenly he felt sure that Richard knew. He must know. Why would he have brought it up otherwise. In all the years he had been coming to the bar, Richard had never made so much as a sign that he saw Mr. Sendel go to the telephone booth, but tonight—perhaps Richard was growing old too—he had wanted to show comradeship, show pity, sympathy, what you will, and he had, Mr. Sendel saw with horror, destroyed their world.

The thought that all was destroyed came to him now with complete and awful clarity. Not only had Richard always probably known, but he had always kept the knowledge to himself, had told nobody. Perhaps he had nobody to tell, but then to whom could one tell such a thing, a thing as insubstantial as the mind itself.

"He knows," Mr. Sendel said aloud.

He sat with his brandy whose delicate aroma suddenly resembled the faint perfume of flowers he had smelled many years ago in a room he could barely remember, perhaps forty years had passed since he had even thought of that room. The room was real, but its occupant was lost to him.

"And what does he expect me to do?" he said to himself. He was suddenly a prisoner of decision. He could not act, he did not know what to do next, he did not know what was expected of him.

He managed once or twice to look back at the phone booth, and as he did so he fancied Richard saw him from the far end of the bar where he was talking with a young man who was said to come from Sumatra.

Mr. Sendel could only sit there now with the brandy, hoping that his tired mind would give him at last the plan that he must pursue and the method by which he might extricate himself.

He saw weakly and with growing nausea that the final crisis that is said to come with old age had struck hard, peremptory, unannounced and with full authority. And he had not even the strength to drink.

Then forcing his hand which trembled badly, he gulped down the entire brandy.

With an unaccustomed energy and a tone never before used with him, he clapped his hands and shouted, "If you please, Richard."

Richard stopped talking with the young man from Sumatra and came over to his favorite customer, but as Mr. Sendel stared at him he could see that in the few minutes which had passed Richard had changed just as fundamentally as he himself.

"Is this your best brandy?" Mr. Sendel wondered, and his voice resembled the whining complaint of men in hospitals.

Richard watched him.

"I'll get you the best," Richard spoke vaguely.

"And what would that be?" Mr. Sendel asked, as though he no longer knew what words were being put into his mouth.

Richard pointed to a bottle near them both.

"Of course, of course," the old man said.

"This should make you feel less tired," Richard said.

"Tired?" Mr. Sendel was loud and worried.

Richard poured, not speaking for a moment.

"Aren't you a bit, sir?" he wondered.

Mr. Sendel observed the change in his bartender. Richard was all at once like a stranger. The change was complete, terrifying. And even this stranger whom he would have to go on of course addressing as Richard, this stranger seemed to have already joined the many passed-over voices to whom he spoke on the telephone. He could actually, he felt, now phone Richard.

But he knew that his bartender was waiting for him to say something, and a daring, even foolhardy plan crossed his mind.

"I've lost my most important telephone number." He was intrepid and rash and looked boldly into the face of his bartender.

"A telephone *number*," Richard wondered, and Mr. Sendel was sure now that the bartender *knew*, had known perhaps from the beginning.

"I've lost it."

"A local number?" Richard was cautious, quieter than he had ever been before.

Mr. Sendel hesitated. "Yes."

"Can't we look it up for you," Richard's voice was nearly inaudible.

"Oh no," Mr. Sendel was calm now, deliberate, as though the offensive had passed to his hand. "It's something that can wait. Only it's irritating, you know."

"But we could look it up," Richard ignored the mentioning of irritation.

"But I can't remember her first name, and her last name is so common," Mr. Sendel told him.

Richard blinked rapidly.

"Maybe," Mr. Sendel began. "Maybe if I just went and sat in the phone booth there," and he turned and motioned toward it, wanting to be sure Richard saw which booth he meant. "Perhaps both the name of the lady and the number will come to me."

He saw that Richard's eyes narrowed under these words, and he was now more sure than ever of Richard's knowing. A fierce anger made Mr. Sendel's temples throb. He felt he hated Richard, that he hated everybody, and that he was ridiculously trapped.

"I think I may recall her number if I sit in the booth," Mr. Sendel confided weakly, looking into his glass.

Wiping the bar dry with a long cloth, Richard spoke softly, "Call on me if you need anything, Mr. Sendel," and he went off like an actor who has finished his lines for the evening.

Mr. Sendel sat on, his rage and despair growing, but a feeling of strength was returning after the frightening weakness he had experienced at his first suspicion of Richard.

Sipping his brandy, he tried to think what he must do next. He could not sit here of course all night, and it was imperative that he go to telephone.

At the same time he was not sure he would be able to reach the booth, a realization which wiped out once and for all the thought that his strength was being restored.

Suddenly, however, a thing happened then as though a message had been written in letters of fire over the bar mirror. The aroma of the brandy and the perfume of flowers in the forgotten room merged, and he could now *remember*—that is, the bridge to the past was visible, and he could, he felt, cross into that room of an obliterated time. He need not stay where he was.

He left the tip on the bar, for he believed he would not be back, not tonight at any rate.

"Not with the bridge ahead," he said to himself.

He waited after he had got off his seat at the bar, then walking stiffly but he thought well he advanced toward the telephone booth under the silent gaze of everybody in the room.

Then miraculously he remembered the number! Effortlessly, clearly, completely!

This time he put in the coin meticulously, loudly.

He dialed slowly and effectively the number which he knew tonight would bring him closer to the forgotten room.

He waited.

He closed his eyes now because he knew that if they watched him, if they had watched him all those years, it did not matter tonight because he had *remembered*.

"Is Rose there?" he said with the quiet and satisfied tone of a man who knows that the answer to his question will be yes. He waited.

"This time, Rose, nothing kept you," he began, and she laughed. He had forgotten what a complete joy her laugh was.

"I have something," he said smiling, "that will amuse you. I found a counterpart of you somewhere. I found part of you, my dear, in a most out-of-the-way place."

She spoke now quite at length, and he realized how tired he was, for he could not hear all of her words, and he found himself almost nodding over what she said.

"This has, my dear, to do with your special perfume."

"Which?" she said in a rich contralto voice, "For I have so many!"

"Which but the one you always wore in the music room, of course," he said.

There was suddenly no answer.

"Rose, Rose!" he called.

Then after a wait he felt she was again on the line.

"I thought that we had been disconnected," he cried, happy to know she was there, was still listening.

"It's been so long since I got even the slightest whiff of your perfume," he went on.

She said something witty and rather cutting which was so typical of her.

"You won't be offended if I tell you your perfume is in French brandy!" He laughed. "Of course it's the best . . . the best Richard has to offer."

His hand involuntarily went up to the door.

"Rose," he almost cried, for there was a discordant hum now on the wires. In dismay his hand pressed against the booth door. It was, he saw, with horror, locked. Someone had locked the door!

He did not want to alarm Rose, but kept his hand tightly pushing the door, struggling against it at every conceivable point to measure the extent of its being sealed and locked against him.

"My dear, is everything all right otherwise," he inquired in his desperation.

He waited for an answer.

"Rose," he cried.

The phone slipped from his hand as though it had turned to a rope of sand.

His head fell heavily against the pane of glass which all at once broke sickeningly into scattered bits and fragments.

He remembered at the same time his old, long-standing fear:

Struck by an invisible hammer.

A blinding crash shook the telephone booth.

He stretched out his hand to grasp something, anything, but his fingers felt nothing, not even air.

"Mr. Sendel!" came Richard's voice from very far off.

"Mr. Sendel! Can you hear what I am saying to you?"

Mr. Sendel did not reply.

EARLY STORIES

All archival material, the Early Stories were collected posthumously and never submitted for commercial publication. They represent Purdy's growth as a writer.

Introductory Note

The use of variant and distinctive forms of English, including American idiom, is a characteristic of Purdy's work. The author's grammar and structure upend the ordinary, posing editorial challenges. In "Dr. Dieck & Company," for example, the term *wive*—a word unusual to contemporary readers but used in the King James Bible—is likely intended. (Purdy himself had done a preliminary edit of the story.) The final text adheres to the author's multilayered, if unusual, vernacular. The difficulties are purposeful: Purdy said, "I think I learned early on that the only subjects I could deal with were impossible. That is, they were impossible to write because they were so difficult; if I chose an easy subject, I couldn't write it because it wouldn't mean anything to me. So nearly all my stories are based on 'impossible' subjects." (*Critique: Studies in Contemporary Fiction* 40, issue 1, 1998) The continual evolution of increasingly impossible subjects, the idiosyncratic speech patterns, and the nonconforming structure that Purdy begins to work with in these stories (written in a period in which his own impossibilities included the isolation of his life while teaching in Appleton, Wisconsin; awareness of a wider world that contained figures such as Gertrude Stein; and the frustration of not being published or recognized as a writer himself) set the pattern for the style for which he would become known.

A CHANCE TO SAY NO

dedicated to Carl Van Vechten

Written between 1935 and 1939 during the period Purdy was a student at Bowling Green College.

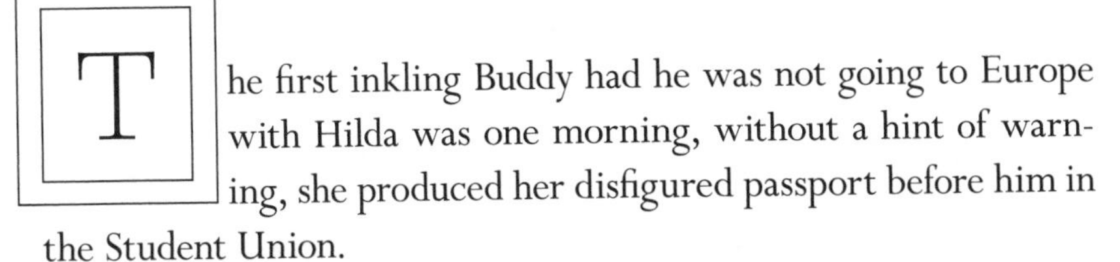

The first inkling Buddy had he was not going to Europe with Hilda was one morning, without a hint of warning, she produced her disfigured passport before him in the Student Union.

They had planned their trip together for nearly four years—ever since they were freshmen, and the sight of her passport, savagely torn, with the photo missing, left him entirely wordless. He felt almost as though she had disfigured herself.

"You'll have to send for another passport right away," Buddy told her.

"But I don't mean to!" Hilda said, laughing. She was in wonderful humor.

They sat right by the window where she could wave to her friends who passed, and as she said she didn't mean to, she waved to a girl.

"What do you mean *you don't mean to*," he said. He had been eating a dish of chocolate-marshmallow ice cream, and now he pushed it away quickly, nodded to the bus-boy, who with the rapidity of a walk-on in a play, took the dish from him.

"What did you say?" Hilda asked suddenly, bringing her attention from the window.

"How are you going to get to Europe?" he said.

"I'm using Corinne's passport. My sister Corinne's," Hilda told him.

"Look, have you gone bats or what," he picked up the pieces of passport and stared at them. "What in hell did you *tear* this with?" he inquired.

"Don't be tiresome," she said. "Seriously!" she exclaimed, and she looked at the window now.

"But Hilda, I mean," he began, and his voice was suddenly like that of a man of forty.

"I told you what I'm going to do," she said. "Stop nagging."

"You can't use Corinne's passport," he said. "It's against the law."

"My own sister's? Why I look more like her than she does."

Hilda finished her lime-ade, and smiling at the bus-boy handed the glass to him.

"You have really gone bats," he told her.

"You say that much too much," she replied.

"Why we could both get into terrible . . ." He stopped because he saw that there must be something he didn't know.

"You don't want to go to Europe, then," he said, unconvinced that this statement had anything to do with their situation.

She looked at him. "Why of course I *want to*," she said, and she sounded very sincere. "I'm dying to. I've *waited* four years!"

"Of course, I know you are crazy," he told her. "I wouldn't want to go with you if you weren't. But I don't think we should take on the whole United States Government."

"Oh it's only the passport people," she replied. "And it's only Corinne. If they arrested anybody, they would arrest her, for Pete's sake."

"Then the whole trip's off, you mean," he said without any expression, as though he had read this statement on the table. "Three,—four years of planning," he said in the same expressionless voice, and then, with a bit more force: "What do you think I'm going to tell my folks?"

"Tell them anything you like," she said.

His wounded look brought up something like attention in her and she began to talk a little more. "You see, Buddy, I couldn't *bear* that photograph of me in the passport, for one thing. It made me look like our French teacher or something. About 100 and a permanent virgin. I couldn't appear in European capitals with that photo."

"But you could have another made."

"And the boat sailing in three days," she said.

He admitted she was right.

"We planned this trip ever since we were freshmen," he repeated this bit of knowledge. "And now that we're engaged too and all," he said, looking up from the bits of her passport.

"But if you cared anything at all about me, you wouldn't *care*," she said. "You're just afraid is all. I don't know what you're afraid of, but you are. And I hate you for it. I just hate you for it."

"For the love of mud," he said.

"Oh how tiresome," she replied.

"Well," Hilda said, after a pause during which she had watched him for some sign of decision, and she stood up, still watching him lazily. "I hope you'll come to your senses," she said. "Let Corinne worry. She deserves to."

Suddenly her eye lighting on the remains of her passport, she seized the pieces quietly and tearing them in even finer pieces, left them with him.

"For the love of mud," he said again. His face went a terrible red as though she had thrown a chemical in his eyes.

He sat there in the deserted student union trying to think of what to do, and finally he decided he must see Hilda's mother. Corinne was in another city, and he couldn't just let the whole thing rest here. Picking up the pieces of her passport, he walked out of the building, and headed for Mrs. Wormley's.

BUDDY TOLD HILDA's mother about her daughter's not wanting to use her own passport, and he found not too much to his surprise that Mrs. Wormley was almost as unaware of the nature of law as her daughter. Mrs. Wormley had purple fingernails today, he noticed, and her hair was close to a certain shade of purple also. She was too nervous to sit down during their talk and kept looking out the window.

"I'm expecting a special delivery letter," she told Buddy.

He nodded.

"How about my daughter," Mrs. Wormley said finally, half-turning to him. "Let her use her sister's passport. You know she looks more like Corinne than Corinne does."

"Could I have a glass of water, do you suppose?" Buddy asked her.

She looked at him a short while before answering. "Of course you may," she said at last, and she pulled on a cord.

"Bring the young man a glass of *cold* water," she told the maid who entered.

"You see," Mrs. Wormley said, still not sitting down, and repeating her thought, "Hilda looks more like Corinne than Corinne does. Always has. You've met Corinne, haven't you," Mrs. Wormley wanted to know.

Buddy nodded.

"We just can't go then, I guess," he said when he had drunk the water.

"Well that's up to you, of course," Mrs. Wormley told him. "Quite up to you . . . But I don't see why you should cross Hilda in a small thing like this . . . You see, you're engaged to her now, and that makes a bit of a difference . . ."

"I know I'm engaged, of course," he told Mrs. Wormley.

"You're *both* engaged," Mrs. Wormley said. "Remember that." She looked out the window again. "I can't understand why that letter doesn't come," she said.

"Are you sure it's coming?" he said, and he immediately regretted saying this. He didn't understand somehow what his own statement meant. But Mrs. Wormley did not seem to mind at all.

"I'm not sure of a thing," she said. "I've so much to worry me!"

Finally she sat down, but the moment she did so she noticed a runner in her right hose, and she let out a soft cry of disbelief.

"I try not to intervene in my children's lives," Mrs. Wormley said after a pause.

Buddy nodded.

"You see," she went on, "since Hilda has been thirteen I have tried to make her make all her own decisions. Now if she does want to use her sister Corinne's passport, I won't interfere."

Buddy drank a little more of the water, and pulled out a package of cigarettes.

"You smoke in here, don't you?" he said, a bit unsure why he had made this statement also.

Mrs. Wormley stared at him. "Why we smoke everywhere in my house," she said, and she seemed, he thought, quite puzzled at this. She was going to say more, he could see, but instead she got up and looked out the window.

"Hilda will simply have to make up her own mind," Mrs. Wormley told him. "I won't do a thing."

"I CAN'T go with her!" Buddy suddenly almost shouted at her.

Mrs. Wormley looked at him carefully.

"I CAN'T!" he said, this time shouting.

"Well, there you are," Mrs. Wormley said. "I suppose she'll go anyhow."

"On Corrine's passport?"

"Oh you always come back to that," Mrs. Wormley said.

"If her father were only alive," Buddy finally expressed a wish.

"Mr. Wormley never interfered in our way of doing things," she said, but with her mouth so close to the wall near the window Buddy was not sure he had heard her.

"If *somebody* could only tell her!" Buddy cried.

"But you're still only in college!" Mrs. Wormley said.

"But what has that to do with passports?" he said, more hysterical than angry now.

"You're so serious, you see," Mrs. Wormley told him. "You

shouldn't be when you're in college. You should have fun. Why is it you don't know that?"

"Your daughter is going to be arrested or something, Mrs. Wormley."

"Oh come now," she replied. "What ever brought you to such a conclusion."

Buddy got up, he wanted to leave the house at once, but he was somehow too dizzy, actually dizzy, with confusion to know whether he could manage to get out of the house without stumbling over something.

"You'll just have to tell her no then, Mrs. Wormley," he said, ready to leave.

"No to what?" Mrs. Wormley wondered vaguely.

"No to Europe," he said. "No to everything."

Mrs. Wormley nodded. Then, walking behind a large vase of flowers she said: "Well she'll be disappointed, of course," she said as though perhaps she saw things clearly at last. "But she'll get over it!" she finished, more like herself again. "And you will too."

Buddy stared at her, puffing audibly in the room.

"And maybe she didn't *want* to go, poor dear," Mrs. Wormley said thoughtfully, as though at last she had had the time to consider the question. "She's had to wait you know all through college!

ON HIS WAY out, Buddy found a postman ready to ring the bell. The postman was holding a special delivery letter.

"She's ready for you," Buddy shouted at the postman, who stared at Buddy's face with grave surprise, and Buddy feeling he must look very peculiar, headed on back to the student union.

DR. DIECK & COMPANY

Though this story was written in 1986, it reflects the "lost decade" (between 1946 and 1955) when Purdy taught at Lawrence College in Appleton, Wisconsin.

Dr. Dieck was the big frog in that literary pond, Irene reminisced. Among so many college professors who have been divorced by their wives, he remained oh for so long so long unsmirched. But at last Dr. Dieck himself fell. Rather, his wife fell first. She was like the wive in that old American comedy about a woman who had a mania for keeping her house clean. She also would not allow anybody to raise his voice. Silence and cleanliness were Clara's gods. Her husband did most of his work in the faculty men's club, or huddled into that tiny narrow hateful office of his. He so seldom appeared with her in public, he used the excuse of his literary studies. There Clara was at home endlessly cleaning. The women who came in to help with the housework wore pinched white faces, they would, it was commonly thought, have preferred to help the lumberjacks rather than work for her. She seldom kept a housecleaner for more than six months. And it was Wisconsin you know oh yes, where though much less dirt than in New York where we are today, still the paper factories brought in considerable dirt. He joked that he spent an hour a day cleaning his feet before entering his residence. I will explain that he ran back and forth to his classroom as so many of those college professors did at that period. To school, home again, clean your feet, to school, home again, clean your feet. Wisconsin has heavy snows beginning almost with the falling of the petals of the last roses, and not ending until the first crocus is buried in a drift of heavy white. And in summer of course the damp earth clings to one's feet. He wiped then as he had in the snow and sleet. Dr. Dieck I often thought was essentially a wiper. I can remember him wiping his old-fashioned stick-pen after he had dipped it in the ink well. He had old-fashioned habits. They said he wore stiff wing collars long after they were in style . . . He wore high-shoes for many years . . . Gradually he moved into a new decade after the decades in question had passed . . . He was always a generation removed from the present, yet since he moved, he did not quite remain in his own period.

Dr. Dieck wrote novels about people whom he knew, but he was ever careful of sparing feelings, and when his books were published, his readers paid him the supreme compliment of not recognizing themselves in his pages. In fact, as the President of the college once remarked, nobody had ever finished one of Dr. Dieck's novels except the students in his creative writing class. Some of these, however, it was learned later had not finished his books.

Writing stories and novels in his spare time, which, owing to a pull he had had with the administration, he had nothing but spare time, and taught almost not at all, much to the disgruntlement of the other faculty members. Yet he was busier than the most weighted down members of the faculty who were on special committees, inspected the dormitories, attended football banquets and the like. Dr. Dieck did, as they said, nothing but his spare time, and his wiping. He was ever on his way to Main Hall, or on his way back, and even when he arrived at the old building erected in 1838, he wiped his feet dutifully there, on a welcome mat, though no one was expected to do so, and the students, one observed, if anything, always anointed their feet with extra mud or snow before entering the hall.

As Dr. Dieck went through the corridors (his own office he had kept on the third floor because of memories and perhaps superstition) he was not above listening in on some of his colleagues' lectures, especially the history professor, a Roman Catholic whom he disliked intensely.

But Dr. Dieck was not a confirmed eavesdropper. Observing others, listening, took too much time from his writing, and it was after all writing, and not people which interested him. He had admitted this himself, and his enemies had confirmed it.

As Dr. Dieck wiped and wiped his feet, Mrs. Dieck grew, it was known, more and more punctilious, clean, particular, as the ladies said. Nothing was clean enough. Dr. Dieck's face was always scrubbed to the irritating of a large mole on his cheek to such an extent he finally had to have it removed.

It was the removal of his "cleanliness" mole (his wife could determine by it whether or not his face was as clean as it should be) which many said led to his downfall. The removal of the mole, no question about it, changed the expression and perhaps the actual meaning of his face. He looked younger and more vacant, but more interested suddenly in life.

Shortly after the mole came off, he began to cease wiping his feet at the entrance of Main Hall, the humanities classroom building. He wiped more perfunctorily too at home.

It was rumored that Dr. Dieck had found another person than Mrs. Dieck. It did not come as an actual surprise to the college, which while ostensibly Methodist, entertained a rather wearisome number of adulteries, divorces, and varied extra-marital relationships, including faculty men who fell in love with young unmarried bachelors. Everything went on in Wisconsin in microcosm therefore which goes on say in New York.

Dr. Dieck, therefore, everybody said, at the age of 50 had fallen in love, or, the same thing, an unknown "party" had fallen in love with him. The shade in his office was now frequently pulled, and he took to making tea in his office, much to the annoyance of Mrs. Dieck who felt he could not "keep house" well in his own study in Main

Hall if he took to "cooking" and eating there. Dr. Dieck surprised her to the point of tears here by overruling her command, and told her he would do as he pleased with reference to his own office, and in his rage, Mrs. Dieck heard—to her disturbance—heard him wiping his feet savagely under the dining room table, where they had all arguments. She never rose in time for breakfast.

The knowledge that Dr. Dieck was in love, or more properly, had a lover became known instantaneously and as it were was carried ubiquitously to town and gown. Everybody in Stapleton knew it. It was recalled suddenly angrily (where before it had been recalled gaily) that Dr. Dieck had once called Stapleton the Kotex empire of the world. It was of course the center for papermaking.

Everybody talked about nothing but Dr. Dieck's new love, and nobody knew a thing. The lover was said of course to be a student. Married women were satisfied it was a co-ed, while unmarried men, bachelors on the faculty asserted it was a football player interested in poetry.

His mole was gone, he was developing untidy habits, and he was already classified as a common adulterer. Dr. Dieck had fallen, but whether he lived in the decade of the time or not was of small moment, for no one was impressed by adultery, even if it was only with a boy. The news was simply that Dr. Dieck had fallen. That was enough. He no longer wiped his feet, his mole was gone, everything had changed.

Mrs. Dieck did not at once know her husband's reputation was changed. Perhaps because her own seemed to continue as it was. She was known as a maniac for housekeeping and this was as final for her as a tombstone erected over her, while Dr. Dieck had been a literary celebrity, and this fame was now overshadowed by his rep as an adulterer at 50. A keeper of rendezvous, a lover in short.

Mrs. Dieck learned of her husband's activities only by the merest chance, for she did not attend many of the social functions of the college or the town, and where a choice was to be made she always chose the town. She had gone to the faculty wives' tea, and had heard, from her station in the powder room, Mrs. Wickham tell the whole thing to Miss Perrins. The last sentence which had drifted to her through the wall was "Of course Tessie (Mrs. Dieck) doesn't know." The meaning of that sentence was then enhanced by one which followed. "It's good she has her house to keep her busy with."

Mrs. Dieck's hands stretched out now as if cleaning a window, and catching herself in this pose, she realized that there was some connection perhaps at least in the ladies' minds with her incessant housecleaning and Dr. Dieck's fall.

The change with regard to public opinion concerning Dr. Dieck was total and very rapid. Methodist though the college community was, there was not the slightest moral condemnation of Dr. Dieck. There was, somehow, only relief that he had been found human and probably common, and that there was no longer any need on the part of anybody to regard him as a literary figure, a literary critic, or a literary anything. No one again need try to pretend they had to read his books, which nobody in power had ever praised, and almost nobody unless under compulsion had ever read.

As one senile lady said, "Dr. Dieck has entered seventh oblivion."

Her remark was quoted up and down the town.

So absorbed was Dr. Dieck at this time, that he at first did not notice the changes in his wife, that she now spoke little, ate almost nothing (these changes or his not noticing them could be explained in that she had never eaten very much in the first place and he had seldom listened to anything she ever said in any case).

But his real awareness that something had come over Mrs. Dieck came when one evening he had upset by some kind of "lucky shot" such as might happen in a bowling-alley both the cream pitcher, the petit point coffee pot, and a tall pitcher of molasses (dessert) which was, it must be admitted, wrongly placed, at least for Mrs. Dieck. There on the imported linen ran rivers of cream, coffee, and molasses. As he gazed at the destruction he noted the similarity of it all to what nurses might face in a hospital bed.

Normally Mrs. Dieck would have given three brief cries, and

then pushing herself away from the table would have gone into the kitchen and wept hysterically; Dr. Dieck would have followed her to the kitchen sink, begged her to overlook his fault, she would have refused him forgiveness, gone upstairs, and not appeared again perhaps for a week, meanwhile delegating his being fed to the ladies in charge of the college dormitory cafeterias. Tonight, however, Mrs. Dieck said nothing for a moment. Her silence imposed silence on him. At last, however, with a deceitful gay laugh, she had said blithely: "We'll send the tablecloth to the old lady by the river."

Dr. Dieck did not know to whom she referred.

Strangely enough, it was Dr. Dieck who began silently weeping, great tears the size of hazel nuts rolling down his cheeks.

"Strain," Mrs. Dieck said sibyl-like and rose. She did not leave the room, however.

"I know everything, Dick," she then made her statement.

"I expect so," he wiped his face now.

"Who is she?" Mrs. Dieck asked. Then wiping a strand of hair from her eyes (a few weeks before a strand of hair falling over her eyes at the dinner table would have been quite impossible), she waited.

"I beg your pardon, dear," he said. "Ah!" he brightened, "you mean the old lady by the river. I was about to ask you. Don't know any laundress down by the river, though when we were children do you remember—

"Don't change the subject," Mrs. Dieck warned him. "And don't tell me who she is."

"Well, dear, you're even over overwrought than I am. I can't understand how I've stained your tablecloth in this thorough way."

"I suppose you are planning a divorce," she asked him. "It would be a natural thing to plan at this time . . . But if she's a student . . . My god, you can't be sure it will last, Dick. Well, the children are nearly grown, so we've completed ourselves there!

"Do you want me to get the divorce or shall you get it?" Mrs. Dieck inquired.

"Clara, my dear, will you explain all this to me," he cried, removing his spectacles. When Dr. Dieck removed his spectacles, especially now that he no longer had his mole, he was to say the least totally unrecognizable.

Mrs. Dieck's open-mouthed astonishment now had nothing to do with the charges of adultery and immorality, clandestine vice, hypocrisy, deceit. She was openmouthed only because she frankly did not recognize him.

"My dear, you're unwell."

"I'm well well well!" she shouted.

Going up to him and narrowing her eyes, Mrs. Dieck said with breathless caution: "Are you, my dear, really the man I married."

There was doubt in her voice, anguish in her heart, and as she knew the beginning of something mental.

"Look all you want, my dear."

He had pushed his chair back from the table, and allowed his arms to drop. He noted his own posture, and recalled with great nausea the fact that he resembled a man whom he had seen on trial in town a few years back for manslaughter. It had been a boring trial, but the man on trial had interested him if only for the fact he looked totally guilty and totally too weary to defend himself. He understood the man now completely. He was obviously on trial and did not feel any spark of energy to defend himself.

She sat down about two yards away from him, near a large wandering jew.

"I first heard about it at the faculty wives' tea."

"Everything is discussed there. I'm aware of that."

"Of course I would be the last to know. Wives always are."

"Come, come, Clara, my patience and my time are running out."

Without warning he lifted up one of her hand-painted china cake plates and threw it against the wall.

The outrage snapped the tension in the room, and she could weep now with some mild comfort, but without, he could see, any shock or concern for the priceless plate. (Aunt Clayburn)

"You admit then you have a lover," she said, examining the broken pieces of china, from her chair.

"I don't admit any such god damned thing," he scoffed.

"The ladies were certainly sold on the truth of it."

"I wish I had the nerve to have a lover. I might have been a better writer."

It was the first time she ever heard him admit he was anything short of an eminent, and important literary figure.

The shock of his self-deprecation quieted her.

Here then my dear is heaven and hell and if Dr. Dieck's mysterious lover was unknown even to himself, there was not the slightest doubt in the mind of Clara Dieck that this lover existed, albeit it was only the cool pressure of a co-ed's hand, unfelt, unseen by poor Dr. Dieck. The years and years he had lectured before co-eds, both in the day of his mole and today without that mark of distinction, surely (she saw this at once) there must have been many a co-ed who languished over his charm, his knowledge, his then literary eminence, now for sofaras he was concerned gone forever.

"Then you've lost your fame!" she cried.

"Clara, will you listen to me for the only time in your life."

She surveyed the ruins of her dining room.

"I never had any literary reputation," Dr. Dieck said. "I am what President Dorsey said before he left the college."

"I can't remember a thing President Dorsey ever said when he was here or prior to his departure or since his departure and death."

"President Dorsey said to me just before he himself was dismissed by the board of trustees, 'My dear Dieck, you're not known, believe me, fifty miles beyond our campus here.' "

"What did President Dorsey himself know fifty miles from home."

"I'm afraid I don't know the answer to your question," Dr. Dieck told his wife. He rose. He did not deign to look at the tablecloth or the broken hand-painted china plate.

"You deny then you have a sweetheart, a lover, whatever they call such things today . . ."

"I have nobody," Dr. Dieck said. "You may have a divorce anytime you wish," he added.

"But I don't wish one. I thought you wished one. I thought you had a lover."

"At fifty, my dear. A lover. Where are you sending the tablecloth to be laundered," he said.

That then was his last word, that there was no lover. And to tell the truth, to present the truth, no lover was ever found. *But*, the effect on our characters was the same: Mary Jesus Joseph. We are and have of a right ought to be free and independent Kotex empires, and we come we come and can only therefore come. We come and the Kotex empire then is safe . . .

Dr. Dieck perhaps, as some wag said, had a lover and did not know it. Ladies and faculty wives especially are seldom wrong. Mrs. Dieck, Clara, died with the surety of true knowledge that one pale April evening he had yielded to the blandishments of a co-ed. Nothing could shake her from that belief. She died another man's wife of course, for shortly after Dr. Dieck bespattered her tablecloth and mashed her hand-painted china dish, she sued for divorce. He did not contest it.

Shortly after the divorce, while lowering a shade in his office, Dr. Dieck fell face forward upon the carpet which he had received among his mother's effects.

He had died, the doctors and coroners (one office) said instantly. His secret of course went with him.

"No one," as President Dorsey said, "ever read Dr. Dieck except under compulsion, meaning under his personal supervision." After his death, nobody read him except, oddly enough, Mrs. Dieck. Who was then Mrs. Webb Stuart. After the death of Dr. Dieck and her second—her illegal marriage, as she often bitterly called it, for her second husband, left her, under disgraceful circumstances, she began reading all of her first husband's works. She found them as tasteless, as boring as the most "persuaded" of his co-eds, but they became with her something of a drug. She had to go on reading him. He was, after all, all she ever had. And she thought by reading him to discover perhaps if he had had a lover.

THAT'S ABOUT ENOUGH OUT OF YOU

Written circa 1955.

"I did something I don't know what for," Pete told his mother. "I didn't want it and knew I didn't want it, and I didn't like it."

The old woman seemed to understand. She cleaned the kitchen thoroughly tonight, gathered up the waste food and put it carefully in the garbage pail, and put this outside of the room. Then she began to wash her hands in the strong disinfectant soap Pete always had on the sink.

"Do you know what happened?" he asked his mother.

"Just so you didn't kill anybody," the old woman replied.

"No, none of that. But why do you suppose I did something I didn't want to do," Pete wondered, as if to himself.

The old woman stood there listening. "She's not young," the old mother said.

"She's not anything," Pete said.

"Well if nobody was hurt," the old woman said . . . Then, "you won't hear anything about her again, unless you go there," the woman said.

"That's just it," Pete said, "what if I go there again."

"Do you plan on marrying," she wondered.

He made a gesture of deprecation with his mouth. "I don't like her and I don't hate her," Pete said. "I don't want her, I don't ever want to see her again. It just happened was all, and why did it have to occur that way do you suppose . . . I knew the way she . . ." He stopped, and the old woman looked at him.

"Well for heaven's sake forget it. And at my age what am I listening to it for. She must be common or she wouldn't have let you."

HE WENT TO the tavern and found George Diamandapolos and told him. George didn't really listen, he had had a good many already at the bar, but finally he said, "Let's go into the back room then, let's talk in there."

"NO, IT DOESN'T surprise me too much," George said after a little while, "not too whole goddam much it don't."

"Why would I do that to her . . . I told my old woman too I did it."

"You told her," George wondered. "Well you're crazy Pete."

"And I'm afraid I might go over there again," Pete said.

"Well, the old gal is probably expecting that," George said.

"I believe you," Pete said, and he was terribly pale, "I believe you."

"But don't go," George said suddenly and he was pale now too.

"Don't go?" Pete echoed.

"That's right," George said, and he finished his whiskey . . . "Don't!"

"I don't want to go," Pete said. "I don't know why I did it. She was so old too. But when she looked at me, George . . . Say are you listening."

George grunted.

"When she looked at me, I could tell she was thinking how *desirable* I was, she made me feel . . . feel superb like . . . SUPERB like," Pete said . . . "That's why I did it."

"Well it wasn't rape anyhow, that's all your old woman meant too when she didn't make no fuss . . . But imagine telling your old woman you . . . *raped* her."—George said raped anyhow.

"I raped her," Pete echoed dully.

"She thought I was everything, that's why I did it," Pete began again.

"Well you're not," George said, "You're not much. I've seen all you've got and you're nothing. Christ."

"Look, George, look what do you think I let her for."

"You let her," George laughed. He was very drunk.

"What do you think I let her let me," Pete said.

"I don't understand now," George said.

"You don't have to," Pete said. "You don't have to understand . . . Listen," he said, and he held on to George now. "She was almost my first woman, she felt like my first woman," he said to George. "Do you follow me."

"Don't pull on my shirt," George commanded.

"Go to hell," Pete said.

"I said don't pull on my shirt and I mean it. I don't want my shirt mussed."

"George," Pete began again, "you tell me why did I do that to an old woman," he began to cry now, and George calmed his own anger down.

"I don't know why you done it," George said. "Why don't you forget it."

"I'm afraid I'll go there again," Pete said.

"Well it don't matter does it if you do or don't. You didn't kill nobody."

"That's what my old woman said," Pete said.

"Well then that's the truth for both of us," George told him.

"But I don't want old women," Pete said. "I'm a *young* man."

George stared at him.

"Ain't I?"

"You're young enough I guess," George said.

"But I don't want old women, then," Pete went on.

"Well there's a whole batch of young ones just everywhere," George told him. "Just crawling with young ones."

"Look here," Pete said, getting up, and he pulled on George's shirt, but George didn't say anything. "Maybe I don't want young women."

"Then that's your funeral," George replied. Pete put his hand on his and George pulled it off his shirt.

"George I believe you hate me," Pete said.

"I told you not to pull on my shirt," George explained again. Then without waiting he said, "What's wrong with an old woman. Maybe you're old enough for an old woman. She's got money probably."

"I can't answer your question," Pete said incoherently.

"Well don't try if you can't. I don't need no answers."

"You lie," Pete said.

"I what." George wondered.

"You lie, you lie . . . I don't need no old woman, and I can get all the young ones."

"That's what I told you," George said, getting up.

"All right all right," Pete said . . . "I'm not going back there either."

GEORGE DIDN'T SAY anything. He was staring straight ahead now into the front part of the saloon. He was thinking of something else.

"Are you thinking about Greece," Pete said. He always said that when he was drunk, and George laughed.

"No," he replied.

"What are you thinking about then," Pete said, and this question was always just as inevitable as his first one.

"Women," George laughed.

"Well quit it then," Pete said.

"Why should I," George said.

"Because it don't get you nowhere . . . They're all the same . . ."

"Shit," George said.

"They're all *all all* the same," Pete said, his head resting on the table now. "I tell you, they drain a man."

George said, "Shit." again, and then said no more.

"I might go back and see that old bag," Pete said. "I might teach her something."

"Your trouble is you're crazy," George said. "You always stayed home, near your old mother."

"I was in Korea," Pete said.

"Your old woman wrote you though," George said. "That's why you don't know nothing. You're always waiting for your mother. You need to go to hell. All men go to hell."

"I saw Korea."

"You didn't believe it," George told him. "You didn't believe Korea."

"I saw Korea," Pete said, and he got up.

"Sit down, god damn you."

Pete got up and pulled on George's sleeve and suddenly George had hit him.

"That's good," George said, surprised at himself, looking down on the floor at Pete where he had knocked him. "I say, that's good . . ." "I should have hit you a long time ago. You piss me off."

"Why would you hit a friend," Pete said.

"You make everything complicated," George said. "Then I get complicated. It's this country maybe or maybe it's the world, but it's all complicated up and you make it that way by talking and talking about this old woman or that young woman and that old mother. Stop all of it," he commanded. "Stop it or I will kill you."

"I believe you would," Pete said staring at him, raising himself on one elbow.

"Well don't believe me, then," George sat down and drank a little more.

"I won't believe you then," Pete said.

"Well shut up," George told him. "Shut up and keep shut."

"Tell me what to do," Pete begged him.

"I ain't your father. Go away," he told Pete. "Go away go away."

"I don't know what to do."

"Don't do anything," George told him. "Rest. Or should I knock you again."

Pete crawled up to where George was sitting. "I can't make up my mind about anything. Maybe you're right and I should have gone to hell."

"Don't pull on my cuffs like that," George said. "It makes me nervous."

"Tell me what you're thinking about," Pete said.

"Women," George echoed.

"Why do you think about them."

"It comes automatically," George said. "I just see women everytime I sit or rest or work or anything. Women just appear."

"I just see myself, I guess," Pete said.

"Well that's your trouble," George said. "You finally said it, I guess, what's your trouble. I'm a woman crazy man, I see women all the time."

"I just see myself." Pete sat up and began drinking again.

"You should have gone to hell."

"I should have died in Korea," Pete said.

"Well rest more," George said. "Let life take you, that's for the ones that don't or wasn't in hell."

"What?" Pete said.

"Take life as it comes. Don't see yourself, see women, see life."

Pete drank steadily of the whiskey.

"George," he said, "you are a GREAT man."

"I'm just a man and that makes me seem different," George said.

"That's true," Pete said, "You're a man and I just see myself when I think."

Then George did not say any more.

There was a silence at the end and they both felt rested, they felt calm, they felt perhaps the morning was coming with a good deal of comfort and that the day following the morning would be a success.

TALK ABOUT YESTERDAY

Written circa 1956.

Percy Fairfield is a bartender at the Music Box Lounge outside of Chicago, and he has had nearly a thousand different jobs. Every time you sit at the bar he will tell you this is his last night at the Music Box, too, because he can't take it any more. Then if you listen, he will begin to tell you about himself and what has happened to him, and if you nod your head a little and frown he will think you are interested, and he will begin to tell you about Madame Sobey and her penthouse and the spiders. That's all he really likes to talk about, and though he has had these thousand jobs, and is always going to quit the one he has, I think he has really come to his final *lighting-place*, and the Music Box is it, and the story is the one I have mentioned.

The way I first heard him tell it was a woman asked for a drink called a *white spider*, and Percy shuddered, and after he mixed the drink, he pretended to shudder some more, and because I was looking at him and he didn't *feel* busy, he began telling this story. I think it took him three hours, and during all that time he mixed a good many *white spiders* and lots of other drinks, most of whose names I had never heard before.

"I have always hated spiders," Percy Fairfield said, "but the place that was the most full of them wasn't any place you would expect them to be at all. It was the most elegant and famous place probably in this city, and I worked there. You've heard of Madame Sobey (she wasn't any more French or Madame than I am) and her penthouse. Her old house was *full* of spiders. None of the bug powders or sprays or anything had the least effect on them. The only thing to do was in the evening when they seemed to be running around more than other times get out the broom and knock them down on the floor and squash them. No matter how many you killed, though, that way, the next night there seemed to be just as many or maybe even more of them than the night before. And so the massacre went on.

"Madame Sobey looked at her TV machine a great deal of the time, and of course she knew every minute there was spiders up there, but she said her penthouse was made so old-fashioned there was nothing you could do about fixing the screens in the windows right and so they just came in all the time and lived with her there, along with the starlings, the ants, and the occasional droves of may-flies and wasps.

"She almost welcomed winter, she said, because she hated so many forms of insect life. But spiders she hated almost as much as I did. She said she woke up one night and one was biting her on the eye. Her eye did swell up a great deal, and she said she thought she would call the doctor maybe, but then nothing serious happened and she forgot about it. She had me go around, though, everywhere spraying, even though that didn't do no good, and killing them with the broom. I don't believe, though, she ever got to hate them like I did.

"Once a young bird fell down the chimney into her house and though it was dead she screamed all afternoon. She said things had got much too much for her in the house, and she missed her husband after all, who had just divorced her on the grounds of their not living together as man and wife.

"Madame Sobey told me that she liked colored people much better than white people and that was why she hired me. She said she wanted me to stay with her to the *very end*. She loved to say that over and over: *to the very end, dear heart.*

After she would say that she would usually get up and say, 'Well, it's time to go to the doctor.'

"'Now you keep the house up while I'm gone,' she would say, 'and if the delicatessen people come, you let them in, but you mustn't entertain, Per- (she started to say *Percy*, but I had forbid her ever to use that name) and—FAIRfield!'

"I didn't feel Fairfield sounded good up there either, but I hated Percy as a name and as I say made her call me Fairfield.

"Madame Sobey didn't pay me money because she said she hadn't collected any alimony in so long from her husband, who was, she said, living with the rottenest woman in Chicago down on the South Side, where they both belonged.

"'You don't know what I've suffered,' Madame Sobey used to tell me, 'at the hands of that *weasel* alone.' The weasel was the woman. I couldn't tell you in a public place like this what she called her husband.

"'Don't entertain any of your friends now,' Madame Sobey would say, putting on her last year's furs. 'That's the only rule I have to enforce,' she said. 'No visitors. You know,' she went on, 'I'm not well and my doctor doesn't even want me to see my own friends. And you know what happens when you bring *yours*, Fairfield.'

"'I do,' I told her, and I did. Every time I ever brought any of my own friends she would get drunk and want to dance with them. They didn't want to dance, but out of respect for my job, they would do it. She would have danced to the middle of next week with them, if they hadn't give out. They didn't have all those fancy medicines and drugs in them like she did. I don't know how old she was, due to her wearing the *Mask of Youth* makeup on her, something she put on early and that lasted most of her waking hours. Once I saw her with the *Mask* off, and she looked not so much older, as all pinched up like a monkey. She saw my look and tried to explain her appearance by saying she had put on her night cream by mistake and it made her look like another woman.

"'Listen to the records, Fairfield,' she told me, 'if you get lonesome, or turn on TV or call up those different numbers on the telephone, you know. I often do that when I'm lonesome. There is a telephone number for religious guidance that is awfully interesting; and another for serious trouble or desperate situations; then you can call the Weather Bureau and find out what kind of weather we're going to get, and there's the time of the day, of course,—all those things you can get by calling a number on the telephone. But don't go out of the house, as I hate to come back to it empty, and you know now, Fairfield, that was one of the reasons you were hired, to always be here.'

"'Yes, Madame Sobey, I know,' I would say, and then she would always say right back; 'Call me Madge. It sounds more relaxed and we have so much time to spend together anyhow.'

"I knew there was not a chance that I would be with her *to the very end* like she was always saying, and like I was already her husband or something.

"She always drank enough for a pirate before she went to this doctor. She said she couldn't think up anything to tell him unless she was crocked.

"'What are you being treated for?' I asked her, straightening my new uniform before the mirror.

"'Oh, Fairfield, for heaven's sake!' she said. 'I don't have to tell *you*.'

"'Well you're awful sick, I guess, if you have to go every day,' I told her.

"'I'm not getting anywhere with him,' Madame Sobey said. 'Of course, my former husband pays for it all or I wouldn't go near. I just hate myself, though, for going.'

"'What's wrong with stopping, then,' I asked her.

Madame Sobey smiled and smiled when I said that. I don't think she *could* laugh due to an operation she had had for her face, but she smiled terribly hard to show she was laughing. Then she got serious immediately, so fast, you know, it looked like a curtain fell on her smiling face, and this new mad old face showed at you.

"'I told the doctor about *you*,' she said.

"'That you had a colored servant,' I said in a kind of a mean voice.

"'Oh, I didn't mention your color,' she lied. 'Goodness, what do you think I am . . .' She stopped a moment or two, and then smiling again, said, 'He thought it was a good idea.'

"'What was?' I wondered.

"'You being here with me,' she said.

"'Well, you can't live all to yourself all the time,' I told her.

"'That isn't why he liked it, though,' Madame Sobey said.

"'Why did he then?'

"'Why, he feels you're good for me just now for one thing . . . You know all the *others* up here *stole*.'

"I didn't wonder they had because she wouldn't pay you and yet she wanted you to sit up with her at all hours and talk; due to her having been in the nut-hatch so often she didn't for some reason ever like to be alone, and just TV, the radio, and the phonograph all going at once as they often did wasn't enough: she had to have the living breathing flesh of men around her or she got just wild.

"I didn't see how the doctor knew I was good for her or honest or anything, because how did she know I was going to be good for her or honest or anything. Yet every day she came home from the doctor, and she went damned near every day, and she had all this talk to tell me about how he knew everything.

"'Well, is this here doctor a spiritualist or something,' I said one day when I was tired of hearing about how he knew everything.

"'Fairfield, Fairfield,' she said weary-like, reaching for her earrings on the lamp stand—she took on and off her earrings all the time as she was so nervous from trying to quit drinking. 'Oh dear,' she said. 'You *know* what kind of doctor he is without my telling you.'

"'He sounds like one of those spiritualists, Madame Sobey,' I persisted.

"'Please, can't you say *Madge*,' she begged.

"'My doctor thinks you're prejudiced against white women,' she said suddenly, and I wanted to laugh out loud but I kept on sitting there just as though I couldn't care less about everything.

"'I told him I just didn't think so,' she added, kind of crafty, and awfully weak-sounding, I thought.

"'Oh, I don't know *what* I'm prejudiced against,' I said, *crafty* right back at her, and I laughed and let her see all my teeth then because she did compliment me more on my teeth than on almost anything else. She saw my teeth and smiled.

"'Fairfield, I appreciate you I bet more than anybody else ever has,' she said finally.

"'Thank you, Madge,' I told her.

"'You're a fine boy,' she said in a voice as sad as at a funeral.

"'I wish I knew what I was going to do, though,' I told her.

"'Oh, Fairfield,' Madame Sobey said. 'You know you always have a house here. I wish you wouldn't act as though you were—well, as though you had to leave.'

"I thanked her with my teeth again, and she said, *'Don't leave!'* She acted very upset. 'I'm used to you, Fairfield, and I want you to stay.'

"I wanted to tell her about her not paying anything, but I think she had got all that by telepathy waves because she cleared her throat and said, 'I've put by several bonds of mine with you as beneficiary, Fairfield.'

"When I just stared at her thanking her with my eyes, she said, 'In case I should die, Fairfield, you would have those bonds.'

"I thanked her and she said, 'They're not large, but they would make you comfortable at a later date.'

"I couldn't help laughing, it was something, I think, about the word *comfortable*, I guess: I couldn't think of me being *that* ever, and she laughed a little bit too, which, come to think of it, was kind of odd because she *couldn't*.

"'Fairfield, should we watch TV,' she said, and I told her, 'Why don't I go out and bake a pineapple upside-down-cake or some Danish bread, you know, the *sweet* kind . . . You see, I had worked as a pastry cook, and she loved pastry, but she was trying to cut down on sweets, and didn't like to eat hardly anything at all. If she had cut down on her liquor she could have eaten ten or twelve upside-down-cakes and still had a lower calory count, but she just wouldn't give up the old juices.

"'I would rather you just sat here,' Madame Sobey said after I proposed baking the pastry to her. 'I don't like to think of you,' she said, 'out there in the kitchen working when it's so late in the day.'

"She saw how disappointed I was, so she said, 'All right, Fairfield, if you want to go out and bake something.' She was awful put out and I knew she would begin to drink now she was alone for a few minutes.

"'Why is it so few people will sit down and just talk with a person,' she said.

"'People don't want to talk to me really because they fear I will bring up the tragedy of my divorce!' she said to me.

"She had told me about her last divorce several million times, and I don't think any new facts were known even to her own imagination. But I knew—eventually—even if I made the pineapple upside-down-cake *and* the Danish bread, she would tell me all about her husband and how he had run off with a tart.

"'Why do men *prefer* those women,' she would begin on that topic, and I would say, 'Oh, it is a mystery!'

"'What's so mysterious about it?' she always answered me, and then we were off on that. She cursed her husband up one end of the South Side and down the other, and then she began on that tart he had married, and she cursed her to the doors of hell and back. She said they were both diseased and that was why they acted that way.

"This disease they had, I gathered, was one that infected every organ and nerve, and was especially bad in the centers that controlled their animal nature and their reasoning power. She said they were actually, though, queer for disease, and for that reason, diseased as they undoubtedly were, they thrived on disease and would outlive her.

"She told me how much she hated especially the tart and how she was going over to their big old modern-style glass house and mash that front big modern window that was nearly twenty feet across and about as many high.

"'You'll cut an artery,' I warned her laughing.

"'Don't advise me, you cheap clown,' she said suddenly, and that was her signal to begin. First some mild drink like Dubonnet, which she said wasn't liquor, then bourbon, then gin, and then the big race to the finish with vodka.

"But by the next afternoon she was sobered up enough to go back to her doctor (though she always had to drink some more to get there) and hear how he knew everything she had been doing anyhow, and that encouraged her to go home, talk to me, and start her life all over again from there.

"After I made her her cake or Danish bread in the evening, she would eat just a little to be polite, and then she would always *always* say, 'I bet you think I'm prejudiced against you, don't you?'

"'What for?' I always said.

"'Well, I think you think I am,' she said.

"'Everybody's prejudiced,' I told her.

"'Not me!' she said.

"'Well, I bet *I am*,' then, I laughed.

"'You don't like me, is that it?' she said suspiciously. She had begun on the bourbon now, and was pretty well through her second installment of that.

"'Why don't you drink with me,' she said. 'Is that *your* prejudice?'

"'Uh-huh,' I giggled.

"'Nobody will drink with me,' she confided.

"'I know,' she went on, 'I may not be promising now, but people have treated me awful bad. Nobody would ever know I was a white woman if they read my life story.'

"'Well, you're rich anyhow,' I told her. 'You've got *that*!'

"'Rich,' she coughed out the word. '*You're* rich!'

"I laughed: What am I rich *in*? Outside of being *black*,—all of a sudden I had said *that* without even knowing I was going to.

"And then, bang, her other face came down over her and she looked as mean as a snake at me: 'You're trying to insult me, aren't you,' she said. 'You're trying to pretend I'm prejudiced,' she moaned.

"'No, I'm not,' I soothed her. 'I said I was the prejudiced one!'

"She stared at me. 'Let's talk about something pleasant,' she said.

"'We neither of us know the same pleasant things,' I said to her.

"'Don't be smart,' she said, 'just because you're prejudiced against me, and don't be witty!'

"Then she was sorry and she got up and kissed my hair.

"When she was drunk enough she called it wool, but usually she was sober enough to say flax, or silk, or something.

"'I don't have a chance with you, do I,' she often would say along about eleven o'clock at night just before she left the gin to begin on the vodka.

"'Madame Sobey,' I said,—'excuse me, *Madge*, I'm too tired, I've been cleaning this old house all day . . .'

"'The spiders keep you busy,' she said.

"I nodded.

"'Can't we do anything about them spiders,' I asked her.

"'No,' she said. 'You know we can't.'

"'Aren't there companies that come and get rid of them for people?'

"'Oh, I suppose,' she said. 'But I couldn't stand men up here poking around. After everybody's been reading about me in the newspapers, especially.'

"'You could wear a mask,' I laughed.

"'Yes,' she sneered.

"'Or an artifical head!' I said.

"Oh I did laugh on that, an *artificial head*. I kept laughing at that, and all of a sudden she had thrown the bottle right at my mouth. It knocked out two teeth. I was too surprised to be mad.

"I went right into *her* bathroom and looked at the damage. Them two teeth were completely out.

"She come running after me still holding her drink and asking me to forgive her.

" 'I'll call a doctor,' she said.

" 'Huh-huh,' I said. 'He would recognize you from the newspapers.'

" 'Don't be mean," she cried.

" 'I'm not mean: I'm bleeding.'

"She patted my cheek. 'Come into the front room, please, when you've got yourself doctored up.'

"She went out and I could hear her after a while crying in the front room.

"All banged up as I was, I couldn't help feeling sorry for old Madame Sobey.

"I went back on in and I was thinking that in a way it was true what she said, that everybody had everything but her. She was a woman who had a good deal and she wasn't really old or ugly, she just never felt *satisfied*. There was hardly a moment of the day when she was ever *satisfied* with anything or anybody.

"And most people, you know, just maybe one hour or one half hour or maybe only five minutes feel some tiny little bit of satisfaction, but Madame Sobey told me herself, both drunk and sober, that she never felt any least teeny bit of satisfaction, and she felt, she said, like every damned thing in the world had been permanently screwed for her, like it had all been planned wrong before she even got here. And so she never slept unless she took drugs and she said even they made her have all-night nightmares.

"That is why sometimes I am almost sorry I left her, and run off. I think she really meant what she said about me staying with her *to the very end, dear heart*. But being she was a white woman, I couldn't tell.

"Anyhow that was a phrase I have often thought of since working for all the various and sundry people I have worked for, and I don't think she really did care about me being colored. But she busted so many of my teeth and she hurt my head so much throwing bottles, and then she was just like a tiger, even when she didn't keep bothering me with her kissing and hugging, she just looked at me like a big old hungry tiger and when she wasn't doing that, she was talking all night about what a big old criminal her husband was, and what a big old tart he had got married to, and I honestly felt more sorry for her than almost any human being I have ever seen or talked to.

"But nobody can live with a tiger or spiders, either. And sometimes it seems to me that the spiders were the chief reason for me leaving her big old beautiful house. Every time I see a spider or hear about one, I bet I see and hear something different from anything anybody else does."

THE PUPIL

Written in 1956.

The boy from Havana watched the civics teacher, who was also the coach, with steady unflinching gaze. Whether it was in gym class or in civics, the boy gazed almost without ceasing, even when the teacher stared boldly back. In civics class the teacher noted that the boy, who was a good artist, was drawing his picture. The teacher was somehow not displeased, yet he felt that he should say something to the boy about it. It was his first teaching assignment anywhere, and he did want to do the correct thing, so he said nothing, and the boy continued to gaze and draw. The boy from Cuba was furthermore well-liked by all the students and teachers, and his attention to the new teacher was not hostile, it was almost, the coach thought, *reverent*. He would never say such a word to anybody if he had to describe the boy's behavior, but *reverent* was, he knew, how the boy acted. The boy's attitude toward him was not only reverent, it was more: it was, he knew, *worshipful* also.

After the first few weeks of school, a kind of silent understanding had been established between pupil and teacher. They often found themselves gazing silently at one another when the others were doing their written work. And during gym class, when the teacher would throw the basketball to someone near the pupil, they would often exchange long looks.

The teacher was perhaps not clearly aware that when he was at the school his eye always sought Gonzalez, and Gonzalez' eye was always already on him. Once the man had automatically smiled at the boy and the boy had smiled a full resplendent smile in return and had nodded slowly. The coach had at that moment noticed that the boy resembled him very much. They both had light brown curly hair and long eyelashes, and their fair skin was covered with pale brown freckles. The boy was slim and lithe and the coach, five or six years older at most, had the same body, but thicker and heavier from the muscles he had consciously and assiduously gained.

At night when the coach was at home with his wife and small daughter his eyes dimmed with the exhaustion of teaching, settled slowly on his memory of the boy's gaze.

THE HEADMASTER HAD wanted to be especially friendly with the coach. Coaches who could teach well, the headmaster told him, were extremely rare, and he wanted to hold on to him.

"Is anybody giving you trouble?" the headmaster wondered.

"Gonzalez," the coach said mechanically and without hesitation.

"Gonzalez!" the headmaster was astonished. "The late consul's son?"

"No, no," the coach amended at once, but without the force of denial which might have been expected. "He gives me no *trouble*." A deep blush spread over his face and his open throat.

The headmaster sighed with relief.

"I wondered," the headmaster cried. "A wonderful lad!" he went on musing. "Talented! Cultured! Knows everything."

"That is what I meant," the coach said lamely. "He is so talented in everything."

"Is he good in gym class?" the headmaster wondered.

The coach thought a moment.

"Perhaps you could give him special attention," the headmaster said. "His father was very wealthy and would have liked to have his son have this extra attention."

The coach nodded.

"I will begin tonight," the coach said after a pause.

"Well, you don't have to begin that soon," the headmaster laughed, surprised. "But I'm glad you like Gonzalez, coach. His family extends quite a bit of financial support to the school, you see," he spoke with relief.

The two men shook hands.

All the way down the hall the coach, who hardly remembered now having spoken to the headmaster, kept thinking of Gonzalez' gaze. He felt slightly dizzy. He had never thought about a boy before, he dimly knew, but of course he had never taught boys before. He had never taught. It was the excitement of teaching, he knew. His uncle, who had once been a teacher, had warned him how strenuous and exciting it would be. *You will be terribly upset at first*, the uncle had warned.

He was not so much upset, he knew, he was rather *taken over*, he felt.

He stopped in the school cafeteria and drank some milk with the other teachers. He could feel, he believed, a wave of popularity gathering around him. He was extremely popular, and this was, he knew, a fact as easy to recognize as one recognizes he is tall and strong. The coach was immediately liked by everybody. He had a presence which attracted all as though he gave out light in darkened rooms.

As he drank the milk he talked with the mathematics teacher about Gonzalez, and then turning to the other teachers who were listening he explained to them also about Gonzalez.

The civics class was the last class of the day and as though he were now sleepwalking the coach walked up to Gonzalez and tapped him. The other students had all gone, as though they had melted away in time, and as though also in a dream he and the boy were alone together in the classroom. Outside one could hear the students opening and shutting their lockers prior to their leaving the building for their homes.

"You need extra help," the coach said, and he expelled his breath as in an exercise, and a deep blush extended itself over his face and neck.

"In what, sir?" the boy spoke quietly to the coach as from a distance.

"Well, in gym . . . or English," he said.

The boy laughed. It was so obvious he needed no help there.

"What are these," the coach said after a moment looking at some drawing paper which the boy was holding.

The boy showed him. They were drawings of the coach, and the coach showed his astonishment only after his pleasure at seeing his likeness.

"You like to draw," the coach said, and his eyes clouded as though they would now close.

"You're not angry, sir," the boy said calmly, and of course they both knew the coach was not angry.

"I would like to make a full length drawing of you," the boy said as the coach continued to hold the drawings before him.

"A nude, I suppose," the coach said. Perhaps he had meant to make this remark witty, but it sounded merely calm and practical, so that the boy replied:

"That would be best, of course, sir."

The boy spoke now as though he were on a moving vehicle, the expression on his face gradually receding and blurring as space came between them.

"Well, if you wish it, you may," the coach said still looking at the drawings.

"Where would I sketch you, though," the boy wondered.

The coach's face was very pink now, but he spoke with cold insistence, as though his being sketched were the one thing now he wanted most in the scheme of things. "The shower room would do, wouldn't it. That room just before the showers, that is."

"Oh, the old football room," the boy laughed. "All right."

"Whenever you wish, then, Gonzalez," the coach shook hands with him.

"You have the perfect build for a study I have been making," Gonzalez said, but suddenly he blushed too. "It's called The Evening of Adonis."

A bell rang in the corridor.

"When do you want to draw me," the coach said looking at his watch.

"Oh any time."

"Since you have your drawing tablets with you now," the coach said.

"I couldn't tonight, sir," the boy said, and his eyes seemed suddenly in their warmth to have changed color.

The coach remembered a time when as a boy he had swum far out beyond his depth and could feel the fatigue and cold of the water closing over him, but he refused to give up the still distant goal, and continued swimming. He felt this same iciness and suspension of breath now, this dizziness, as he went on with Gonzalez.

"What night do you want me then?" the coach continued.

The boy thought. "Tomorrow night, sir, you see there is nobody in the old football room then."

"That is so," the coach said. "Tomorrow is Friday."

"All right then, Friday after classes," the boy said. They shook hands again.

The coach stood there after the boy had left and the feeling of dizziness came and went over him.

Several times that evening his wife had to repeat questions put to him.

"The work of teaching is hard for you," she said, just before they went upstairs to bed.

The next day a kind of controlled dizziness took possession of him. He kept saying all through the classes that today was Friday. In the gym classes of that day he had taken off all his clothes but his jock strap, while he instructed the boys in the use of the "horse." They seemed to accept his nudity as not unusual, and he seemed to look on his own action as necessary in testing his way for what was to come later here. He went down into the shower room with them after the class and carefully took off his clothes and bathed slowly in the showers so that each successive boy could not miss him there.

At the noon lunch with the faculty several of the older men teachers had to put questions to him many times before he heard them.

My first teaching position, yes was the usual answer he seemed to hear himself giving to every question. *No I have never taught before.*

He did not see Gonzalez that day until civics class which was just forty-five minutes away from the day's end.

Today, Friday, he noticed that Gonzalez did not draw him or gaze at him, though occasionally his pencil came down on the paper as though he had sketched one line of the coach's face, but it always came up immediately again. They avoided one another's gaze.

As the class came to an end, the coach, his face drained of blood, kept one of the other boys after class, talking to him about the bicameral system of legislation which, the boy said, he now understood, but which the coach continued to explain to him.

Gonzalez, however, sat down in the front row with his calm Latin face watching the coach.

When the boy went out the coach turned to him questioningly.

"All ready, sir?" the boy said.

The coach stared. "Why, this is Friday," he said weakly, and he knew he was very pale.

As they went out and down the hall together the coach looked about as though he might find one of the faculty members or a student who would at the last detain him. The coach felt now, as he had felt from the beginning, the power of the boy, and the inevitability of their walking down the hall together. His dizziness returned again.

Everybody in the building seemed to have gone. It was nearly five o'clock, even the janitors had disappeared. A feeling of listening silence presided everywhere.

They went into the small sweaty room that led to the showers. The coach sat down heavily on the long gray bench before the lockers. He put his hand out and touched his own locker.

Gonzalez sat down on a chair and began arranging his drawing tablets.

"You don't feel like it maybe?" Gonzalez said, silently laughing.

"I always keep my promise," the coach said professionally, his mouth pale.

The boy nodded.

The coach began taking off his clothes, slowly at first and with a kind of forced, somber quality, then more quickly. He had stripped off everything but his jock strap, which he had kept on since the gym classes today. He took this off slowly, snapping the rubber of it over his legs at the last.

Gonzalez was calm, collected, critical. He squinted.

"Move over here, now, sir, and we will make this a complete drawing."

"Put everything in," the coach said almost bitterly, threateningly, but the boy did not appear to hear him.

"I'm going to turn on this other light," the Cuban said, and the room was flooded with a kind of gold luminescence.

The boy suddenly let his eyes come fully open under the thick lashes.

"You've made this your life, haven't you, sir," the boy said.

"What?" the coach said suddenly, tensing.

"I mean building your body."

The coach stared at him.

"It's obvious you have modelled every part of yourself, like a sculptor."

The coach smiled. He had hardly known this consciously perhaps, but it had, of course, been his life. The boy had merely told him what he had done.

He began to feel strong now again, his dizziness passed, and he was calm with the boy. He knew too that everybody had left the building. They were alone here with their male knowledge.

"I would like to sketch you very carefully," the boy said.

"Do anything you like," the coach told him.

The boy looked at him, and then began to draw.

He drew for some minutes without saying anything.

"Tired?" the boy said in his adult manner, commanding and yet obedient to the coach.

"A little," the coach admitted.

"You hold yourself a little too stiff," the boy said, and laughed.

The coach laughed too and looked down briefly.

"Relax," the boy said.

"All right," the coach said.

"Hold your arm up just a little, like this," the boy told him, and went on drawing. He drew some more in silence.

"Now you *are* tired," the boy said.

The coach nodded and sat down on the gray bench to rest. The boy went on correcting his work.

When he looked up the coach was staring at him as he had never quite even done in the classroom, and they both suddenly looked at one another with the knowledge that the barriers of others were no more. They both registered their customary blush, the blush they had exchanged with one another for these long weeks.

"You are unusually and beautifully developed, sir. Perfect for the artist who wants to sketch," he said, and his lips and throat revealed their dryness in his voice.

The coach nodded to thank him.

Then to cover his terrible excitement, the coach reached for his jock strap and threw it roughly over his middle.

"You don't need to do that, sir," the boy said hoarsely, and all the nervousness which the coach had experienced earlier in the day came now to him.

"It must be the heat in the room," the coach laughed awkwardly.

As though hypnotized the boy put down his drawing tablets and then glided over to the bench.

The coach sat there helplessly, as though suddenly ensnared by the development he had given his own body.

"I haven't seen anyone else so perfect," the boy said. "I had suspected you might be, but I did not know."

He touched the coach on his chest.

Giving him a look that resembled an exhausted animal in a net the coach lay back on the bench, his hands loosely hanging down. His face and body were covered with a deep rose that seemed to come as though hot burning clothes had been laid upon him. His penis bobbed wildly, throbbingly as though it too suddenly sprang for release, and with its struggles forced him back on the bench. He was the image of prey, capture, helplessness.

The young boy merely sat there now watching him.

The coach looked up at him imploringly trying to raise his head. Tears, whether of helplessness, rage, fear, or love descended his cheeks.

The boy put both his hands on the neck of the coach as if to hold him down now, and then his own head fell slowly upon the man's chest, and he opened his mouth on one of his nipples. The man gave out now great sobs of an emotion impossible to define. The boy's breath was like something from a terrible concentrated tiny furnace and brought the red blush of unexpectedness to a flaming crimson on the man's body. The boy's lips descended now slowly and heavily.

The coach now felt imprisoned, lost, forever changed, and that in his change he had grown a white hairless tail from his backside and that this tail, another agent of his imprisonment, along with his penis, was thrashing powerfully but impotently on the rough floor, wounding itself, wounding him, splitting open something inside himself.

As the young Cuban tasted his flesh, his tropical appetite long depressed by the North American dryness suddenly revived, and brought to his mind the thought of his long famishment. His mouth opened like the jaws of a beautiful but mythical monster, and brought itself down upon the organ of the coach.

Suddenly neither of them could bear any restraint.

"Tear me," the coach implored in the agony of a man who must command a friend to slay him.

The Cuban nodded.

"You don't understand," the coach cried, breathing as though near death. "Wound me, wound me!" the coach cried.

The boy continued his passionate embraces.

"Tear me!" the coach cried. "Let me see how I can stand the pain."

The Cuban's head, with its thick intwined locks, fastened securely to his organ like some great revolving planet of the heavens, was suddenly lifted and the eyes which had pursued the coach all those long weeks stared at him. "I can't hurt you, sir."

"If not there, then here," he cried, and he pointed to his chest.

The boy turned back to his embrace.

"Tear me before you bring me," the coach cried.

Suddenly he struck the boy. "Obey!" he cried.

And he brought the boy up to his breast, and made as though to crush his neck.

As he crushed him to his chest the boy fastened his teeth tightly into the coach's chest bringing easily from it blood and a kind of foam from his saliva that resembled milk. The coach sighed with release and pushed the boy's head now down to his organ again.

"Bring me now," the coach said.

WHEN THE BOY had at last disengaged himself the coach rolled onto the floor writhing still, his imaginary white tail still twisting in the dust and sweat of the young men he had trained, his seed and blood alike flecking himself and the floor.

The Cuban bent down over to him now and as though exacting his own price began to kiss the coach's mouth, which the coach surrendered to him in totality.

"I was your first," the boy wept, "your first."

The coach kissed the words as the boy said them.

FINAL STORIES

Written during his lifetime with the aim of putting together a final collection of short stories, these texts were approved for publication by the author before his death. This is their first time in print.

VERA'S STORY

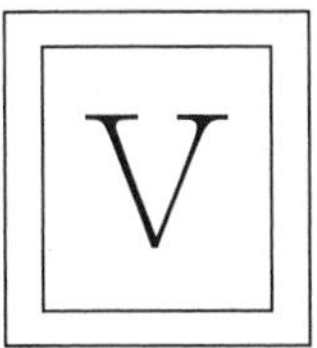

era had hopes of course, though her life had few hints of her ever coming into better fortune. "When my ship comes in," she whispered, or let out a cry of despair.

She often laid all her bad luck on her former husband Will Patterson, but maybe who knows it was all in the realm of Destiny. Her boys usually remembered her as she toiled over the dishpan or stood behind the ironing board tending to their countless shirts and underwear. She loved her housework for as she told her close friend Ada Coe, "What would there be for me had I not my domestic housework?" Once however she did take a job selling dresses located within walking distance of her home. She was popular with the salesmen and the customers as well as the store owner, Bud Turley, who advised her to give up housework and become the first lady of gowns and dresses. But Vera was not cut out for selling dresses.

"The thing about boys," she opined, "is even when hardly half grown they up and leave you." And so no more shirts to mend, no more socks to darn. And so the ironing board was seldom in use, and the kitchen had no more gas for cooking. Her house inherited from a great-uncle had at the very least 30 rooms, and so Vera took in lodgers who did not require their shirts to be mended or their missing buttons to be replaced.

Then there were the evenings when elderly suitors dropped in, perhaps because she dwelt in such a mammoth mansion. These gents were too old for Vera but she loved to be admired even by oldsters. And they always came with a gift or bouquet or a box of Irish linen handkerchiefs, "For me to cry on," Vera would joke. "But marriage with an elderly bloke? Not on your life! Remember your last marriage, Vera Cowick." They enjoyed her cooking too, and her witty conversation, but even they sensed they bored her after a stint. They smelled rejections from her yawning and the endless lapses in the conversation.

Her life was slow now *like molasses in January* or sort of sleepy *like watching the woodbine spinneth*—sayings she had heard from her great grandma. For since long ago Vera could boast she came from quality.

NOT A DAY went by that Vera did not hear from her mother Minnie Mae and her stepfather Ab Nisley who had married Minnie after the death of her first husband Judson Otis. Minnie Mae had grudgingly supported Vera's divorcing her husband Will Patterson who had been the cause by his bad investments of ruining the fortunes of Minnie and Ab Nisley.

But as a grass widow, Vera had found there was no other path open to her but to take in boarders and roomers in her mansion. As Vera toiled now in her kitchen she dreamed of the dim possibility that there was somewhere the right fellow who would rescue her. When she heard a young man whistle the sound revived all her dreams of romance. A man's whistle made her feel that life was after all worth living.

Life would maybe not be a bowl of cherries but maybe the zephyrs of a June day. But the sounds of whistling had got scarcer with the war. She often herself tried to whistle as she did the dishes or ironed one of the young roomers' shirts. In vain nothing came from her sad pipes. The sound resembled a bird that has no mate. "Silence is a loud voice," she told a neighbor woman. "And puts a pallor to your cheeks. Silence is meaner than a slammed door, or a wet firecracker. Life is no picnic and the worst is perhaps to come."

"Such depressing thoughts," Minnie would tell her daughter.

"But what can a grass widow do with not one red cent in the bank, Mother? You tell me."

"Well you said a while ago, Vera, you read the tea leaves and they give you a good reading."

"Yes, I know dear that often when I have taken a nap or snooze in my chair a bit I feel better, that good fortune is on its way."

"Yes, I know, I know." Minnie now appeared to look on the gloomy side.

"Yes, fortune telling will say the moon is made of green cheese. Or you will win the lottery, just you see. No darling," and now she called her mother by her first name as she often did, "no Minnie what I've got to do is work even harder, roll up my sleeves and quit this sniveling."

"Very well, Vera." Minnie spoke now of something that had troubled her with Vera for some time. "I'd lay off those imported cigarettes if I was you," Minnie said. "If I was you I would chew some Juicy Fruit gum. At least it will sweeten your breath and not stain your teeth as do the tobacco leaves."

"Let me have some little pleasure no matter how harmful in the long run. Or let me have my dreams or the tea leaves why don't you. Or let my heart beat a little faster when I hear some young guy who knows how to whistle. You can have your Juicy Fruit gum, Minnie. But hearing a whistler or smoking a cigarette ain't going to make me have to pay the piper."

THERE WAS ONE subject on which mother and daughter did not agree. Did not agree at all. That subject was Vera's former spouse, Will Patterson, or as Minnie insisted on the appellation, Billy. The very sound of "*Billy*" made Vera nauseous. But even more than her ex-husband Vera loathed and hated Will's own mother, Kate Patterson. She had opposed Vera's divorce suit against her son Will and had even written to the judge of Common Pleas Court to give him more reasons not to grant Vera a divorce. Kate Patterson must have known that her son had caused nothing but sorrow and had destroyed her own fortune not to mention the ruin of the fortune of Minnie Cowick. But Kate continued lauding her son anyway whilst blackening the name of her daughter-in-law. And Minnie to Vera's mind, yes, Minnie was ever too lenient with regard to Will.

"Mother, Mother," Vera would often say, "now how can you defend a man and his insolent mother Kate when you know Will brought your own daughter to such misery and sorrow."

"Vera, Vera." Minnie would smile. "I will defend you to the last breath I draw. But see here, Kate is aware of her son Will's follies in business. She blames herself for having spoiled her youngest boy."

"Very well, Mother, have it your way, but for pity's sake don't call him Billy instead of Will in my presence."

Minnie laughed outright then at such a remark until Vera lit one of her imported cigarettes. Then Minnie, sniffing the pestiferous air, would again level her criticism of the terrible weed nicotine. Then both mother and daughter would smile, and Vera would bend down and kiss her mother.

"A mother will always love her own flesh and blood." Minnie would turn now to crocheting a doily. The two women would then turn their attention to Vera's eldest son who had run off to the great Babylon New York City to become an actor, and later a star on Broadway, and all thought of Kate Patterson and her spoiled son, Will, was laid aside.

"You always say, Mother," Vera began, "that I did not put my foot down on Rick's stage ambitions. You must know that there was no pressure I did not exert to keep him at home until he was ready to brave the Metropolis and ruin his health, his mind, and his self-respect. An actor, Mother. Do you not know the kind of lives those madcaps lead?"

Minnie had to agree with Vera on this matter though she knew much less about "thespians" than she did about Kate Patterson's having spoiled Will for his own business follies and stubborn misjudgments.

"Rick has inherited his father's temperament," Vera concluded. "It's in the Patterson blood."

Minnie nodded and proceeded with her crocheting.

IN HER REVERIES Vera often went back to her own early girlhood when Will was courting her. It was the age of cuspidors also called spittoons. They were everywhere: private homes, banks, restaurants, wherever. She remembered them now because Will was known as a Mama's boy. He did not smoke, drink, and certainly never chewed tobacco. He also was fond of manicuring his own nails. His one masculine pastime was his love of guns. Rifles especially. Yet he did not like to kill bird or beasts. He shot at targets only.

"Did your divorce lead you to smoke?" Minnie once said. Sometimes when Vera lit a cigarette she recalled the expensive cuspidors.

"Somehow, if I had one of those gold spittoons I'd be in the money," she would think. "No, I haven't any cuspidors to sell and be rich."

She would remember Mrs. Hennings, a lovely housekeeper, but her spouse was a mean old German fellow who couldn't keep his mouth without a plug of tobacco. The whole downstairs was full of spittoons. How did dear Mrs. Hennings stand it or stand her hubby?

She would then go back to her own husband. "I wonder what got into Will to squander all those fortunes. How long ago it all was, our loss of fortune. Yes as long ago as spittoons and corsets and bloomers. And gold toothpicks."

CLIFFORD SHRADER, THE youngest son of old Dr. Shrader and the last of his line, his father, mother, and eldest brother Jack all having passed into the "Great Beyond," to use Clifford's expression for it, Cliff then could find nothing more entertaining than to listen as he stretched out in a hammock to the goings on in the Patterson ménage. Cliff was very much on the side of the besmirched divorcée, Vera. He adored her. He winced and coughed (he was a heavy drinker) as he heard his heroine being burned at the stake by mother Patterson and her unmarried daughter, Cora. They spared no calumny against Cliff's favorite gal, Vera. Cora, whom Cliff once called "that withering blasted remains of last year's bittersweet," was especially vindictive against Vera. It was actually Vera's beauty which galled Cora the most—she, who was plainer than a warmed over tea. Cora would have given anything, Cliff chuckled, to have half the good looks of maligned Vera. And in the fray against their sister and daughter-in-law one could hear a hidden but strong admiration and jealousy. There was no sign or shortcoming the Patterson women could level against Vera. She was as guilty as an adulteress, a loose woman and perhaps a would-be murderess.

After listening for an hour or so Cliff would saunter back into his ancestral digs and help himself to a brandy or some special French wine. He would then laugh until the tears streamed down his once handsome face. "If only I could have Vera for my sister," he would chortle. "And were I fetching enough myself could be her sweetheart." But gradually mother and daughter would run out of ammunition to level against the already nearly consumed Vera Cowick, for the two ladies refused now to give Vera her married name, since married to Will she was no longer thanks to Judge Duncan who had granted her a divorce because the silly old Justice to quote the Patterson ladies had himself fallen under her spell and thus had broken the highest legal sanctuary by giving Vera her freedom. And what freedom! She was now said to operate a rooming and boardinghouse where the most outrageous carrying on was nightly in progress. How many young men or older gents had lost their reputation spending a night under the roof of the temptress and siren that was Vera Cowick, the grass widow?

Now that Will was "no longer a married man," in the phraseology of Clifford Shrader, Will had dropped in very often to chat with his neighbor of so many years. Will, however, disapproved of Clifford's drinking. Will himself had never indulged in the habit of drink or even cigarettes. Clifford on the other hand not only had grown to be a heavy drinker but he had never cared much for Will's impeccable lifestyle. Or rather he at this time had never known about Will's own womanizing. Furthermore Clifford had always cared deeply for Vera. They often spent hours together when Vera was still married to Will, and Clifford could see she had made a mistake in her marriage.

When he was not drinking Clifford acted as house detective in a nearby city. Once while on duty there and when he was not in his cups Clifford had been astonished to run into Vera accompanied by a rather suspiciously good looking young man. Vera however acted as the great innocent when she ran into Clifford. She introduced her male companion without any bashfulness. Clifford launched into a conversation with them. The young man turned out to be not as bad as Clifford had first thought, and Vera's pleasure in knowing someone so much more to Vera's taste made Clifford happy he had happened upon him. He promised Vera by winking and clasping her hands that he would never tell Will of the occurrence even though Vera was no longer his wife. For Will still tried to see her and learn about her and hoped one day to—who knows?—remarry her.

But now the years had passed and Clifford was seeing Will more than he cared to, but in such a small town who could Clifford know as easily as he could his next door neighbor Will Patterson? On this occasion Clifford had been drinking more than usual and Will had never seemed such a bore. Without Cliff's meaning to, he let the "cat out of the bag," in his kind of phrase: he told Will he had seen Vera while about his work as a house detective, seen her with a man as handsome as a movie star. Immediately Clifford regretted he had said this.

Will lapsed into a fit of sour displeasure. "You drink too much, Cliff," he finally managed to say.

Irritated by this remark Cliff said, "And you were hardly the gentleman dear Vera could ever have been happy with."

Will suddenly broke into tears. Without asking Will's invitation, Cliff brought him a small glass of brandy. But Will, ever the Sir Galahad, refused the drink. This angered Clifford even more and the two engaged in angry and inexcusable badinage, as Cliff later realized, which almost ended their shaky relationship. But Will never forgave Cliff and Cliff never forgave Will for refusing a brandy. "A drink might take some of the *holier than thou* manner you show the world. I think Will you must be hiding something from us. No one could be as pure as you."

CLIFFORD HAD MADE a beeline to Vera's rooming and boardinghouse shortly after his visit with Will. Clifford was more than welcome at Vera's. A short while ago he had defended Vera against the calumnies of Ruth K. Stevens, head of the W.C.T.U. and a friend of the local mayor Jeff Groves. Mrs. Stevens had reported to the mayor that Vera was operating a house of ill fame. Although the Mayor did not believe a word of the old harridan Ruth K., he nonetheless sent one of his subalterns to scold and revile Vera. Vera had told of her fear of scandal and had called on Clifford to see the Mayor. Clifford, despite his being known more as a heavy drinker than one of the city's front families, at once had a conference with the Mayor, who actually despised Mistress Stevens. The affair was settled. The Mayor happened to know that both Ruth K. and her husband had been involved in some shady financial deals. When the Mayor summoned the old Stevens woman he had threatened her with the thought that a lawsuit might be instituted against her despite her piety in the W.C.T.U. She never again brought problems against Vera.

As a result of this rescue and Vera possibly owning the right to operate a rooming house, Clifford was a constant caller at Vera's. Not without some uneasiness on Vera's part, but drink had so debilitated poor Clifford he could be no problem to Vera no matter how many visits he was now allowed. In fact Vera loved being adored and even worshipped by Clifford. Nothing pleased Vera more than someone who could burn a candle at her shrine and yet expect nothing in return.

Today Clifford brought news of his visit with Will. "I am afraid," he began his recital of the visit with her former spouse, "I was a bit under the weather when I sat down with Will."

Vera knew that the reference to weather was of course inebriation. She patted Clifford's hand gently which made him shed a few grateful tears. Then "the beautiful charmer," in Clifford's phrase, prepared him some delicious tea and home made sweets. Again Clifford wept, and Vera herself was in a kind of Seventh Heaven at being cherished so greatly and at no cost to her own safety.

"Why can't I take you away from this?" Clifford motioned to the walls and frayed furniture of her rooming house.

"Clifford, dear friend," she answered him, "You would soon like everybody else tire of me."

"Tire of you!" He wiped away a fresh number of tears. "I would sooner die than give up my love for you."

To be loved, to be worshipped. Vera thought over Clifford's plea to her. But if Vera was beautiful she was also a sharp student of men. She knew marriage with Clifford would be an even greater shipwreck than her marriage with Will had been. No, the situation the way it was pleased her more than marriage. To be caressed and flattered, laughed with and worshipped, with always the gift of an envelope of money.

TO MANY PEOPLE's surprise Clifford Shrader became a frequent visitor to Vera's house. Everyone wondered what this meant. There were many suitors she could certainly have chosen instead of Clifford. Of course he was very wealthy, but then there was no one who did not know of his drinking to excess. What no one knew is that Clifford had learned enough from Doctor Jack Shrader, his brilliant brother whom he often assisted in his medical practice. But was Clifford's knowledge of medicine the cause of his frequent visits to Vera?

Due to her growing uneasiness over her own health Vera had gone to several local physicians. She had no idea until then that her malaise was her going through menopause. Vera had never dreamed she would ever grow old. People who did not know her often mistook her for a lost teenager. Eternal youth was what Vera expected. To her added horror one young MD gave her some medicine which she discovered contained the urine of mares!

Drinking a wee bit of brandy one day with Clifford her tongue became loosened. Her state of health and her sorrow that she might be facing if not old age gloomy middle age let her confide in Clifford. On this special visit he was a sober judge. "If only Dr. Ray still had his practice," she almost wailed. "He also paid special house calls for me. He has retired to his old country home in Gilboa."

"But, Vera," Clifford spoke brightly, "I happen to know he sees his patients there in Gilboa."

Vera was so relieved to hear this, she almost rose as if to give Clifford one of her special kisses.

"I know Dr. Ray through my dear brother Jack. And if you will allow me to get in touch with him I know he will see you in Gilboa or for all I know he will come here. But I will drive you to see the doctor."

"You would do that, Clifford?" Vera pretended he had agreed to a difficult even impossible assignment.

"For you, Vera, I would do anything to chase away your sorrow."

Clifford came over to Vera, took her hand in his, and for the first time kissed her in a manner so resolutely Vera burst into one of her most resounding laughs.

"But isn't Gilboa a bit of a trip, Clifford?"

"You know better," he proposed such a statement. "I have Jack's darling car now. Gilboa is only a half hour from where we are."

"My eldest boy, Richard, used to go there, come to think of it."

"Richard went to see the doctor?" Clifford wondered.

Vera caught the alarm in Clifford's voice.

"Oh, it was not serious." She spoke also with a kind of perturbation.

"You know as well as I the kind of company he kept before he went to New York."

Everybody remembered Richard as a stage-struck young man who finally had achieved a modest success on the stage.

DR. RAY'S THREE story house was nearly invisible by reason of a massive wild ivy and a small forest of oak and elm trees which further made the edifice nearly hidden from view.

Clifford did not bother to knock and helped Vera into the waiting room.

As if he was expecting them, the doctor came out and took Vera in his arms. He was a man who had watched his own health so carefully except for his Havana cigars that he could have passed for forty instead of advanced old age.

"You are in good hands I see," Dr. Ray took Clifford's hand.

Leaving Clifford in the anteroom, Dr. Ray drew up an antique overstuffed chair for his guest.

"Is it about Richard?" he began.

Vera immediately flushed and took a hand stitched handkerchief from her purse as if she perhaps meant to stop the beginning of tears.

"Richard is as far as I know, dear doctor, well in New York circles of theater."

Vera almost babbled as she spoke of her own ailment.

"I wish most of my women patients, Vera, looked as well as you," the doctor said.

Vera a little rattled told the doctor of her malaise (a word the doctor had used in times past with Vera's health). Vera had always found Dr. Ray capable of putting her completely at ease. She felt now a wonderful kind of drowsiness. And it seemed to her that she was telling the doctor all the years of heartache and sorrow which her life had been ever since her marriage to Will.

"The last time I was happy . . . ," she heard her own voice as if someone else was speaking in her stead. On and on came her torrent of words.

The next thing she remembered the doctor was speaking again with a voice which calmed her even more deeply. After some other questions and answers, the doctor brightened, and opening a door to an adjoining room in no time at all came back with a small box which resembled a gift rather than something from the pharmacopoeia.

"I never, well almost never prescribe drugs when there are herbs that cry out to be taken by my women patients."

Vera now daubed her eyes at the doctor's mentioning herbs and not medicine.

"You will find these little herbals the very thing you will be happy with."

Vera thanked the doctor again and again. She felt already better than she had in weeks.

"If you need more of these little fellows," he said and touched the herbal box he had given Vera, "please let Clifford bring you again. But I say this that without a doubt you may not need to see me as your doctor but as a friend from times past."

Grateful for anything the doctor could give her, Vera again broke into sobs, and then just as suddenly into tears, more refreshing than if she had been caught in a small spring shower. She all at once saw she was with Clifford who ushered her into his car. Vera felt so much more in good spirits that Clifford could not help telling her she looked the picture of health by whatever the doctor had given her. And Clifford helping her in his car began whistling to Vera's added gratefulness. The doctor had been of such benefice.

"You look better already," he said. He touched her hand and pressed it as they reached Vera's house.

THAT EVENING VERA undid the costly package. The doctor had explained several times he had given her an herb, not an ordinary medicine. Sitting alone in her own room, she took two of the herbs and drank them down with some spring water drawn from her well.

To her wonder within five or ten minutes she felt the discomfort which had plagued her for many months leaving her entirely. She picked up the package of herbs and wondered if they would tell her what she had taken. There was no written explanation of their name.

LATE THAT EVENING long past her usual hour of retirement, Vera sat alone. But now as if she had entered the room to be with her she felt the presence of her mother.

"Minnie," Vera spoke aloud.

As a young girl she had been allowed at times to call her mother by her Christian name. But it seemed now to Vera that Minnie herself had entered the room. It was then Vera could at last realize that she had only been happy when she lived the carefree and even paradisiacal life with Minnie. Everything else—her marriage to Will, the disaster he had brought to Minnie and her, her being the mother of three ungovernable boys who had brought even more sorrow to her than their father Will—her life then as now was a sea voyage that knew only storms and near shipwreck.

And now having swallowed Dr. Ray's herbs, she was again the young girl with Minnie in a timeless region of some unknown world but the only world she had ever been happy in. One of her young roomers awakened her, Neils Laferty. His fresh youthful face was not unwelcome. Neils asked her permission to postpone paying her the rent past due for his room.

Vera told him not to spend a minute worrying about the matter. He looked rather skeptical at her reply then smiling, he took her hand in his and kissed it.

YOUNG AND HANDSOME as a youth, Will was also as pure and unversed in passion as a high school boy. Cliff had discovered his neighbor when he had shown Will some of his secret and prized books of pornography albeit the kind done by the greatest Italian artists.

After he had perused these burning portrayals of lust and passion, Will had become afflicted with a nasty headache and, at Cliff's suggestion, had lain down on an antique sofa. It was then Cliff administered for the first time his imported coffee. Will's headache, if not entirely dissipated, was banished in part so that Will could sit up instead of lying prone. From then on like a youth seeking forbidden pleasures, Will would venture again in Cliff's mansion to peep at the unspeakable and taste again the caffeine known only to wealthy sybarites.

Word soon leaked out that Clifford had escorted Vera to Dr. Ray's mysterious sanctuary. Will Patterson struggled day and night not to visit Clifford in order to get news of Vera. But in the end, shamefaced and lame, he rang the front door bell of the Shrader home.

Cliff answered the bell with a broad smirk. He would have bet money of course that Will would yield to temptation and present himself to Cliff. Cliff knew that Will never drank strong drink. He also once offered his friend a cup of English tea which he turned up his nose at after sipping a couple of teaspoons of in the words of Will "dishwater." Will's only vice Cliff remembered was his love of coffee which he liked to drink black. But he seldom was able to find any coffee which deserved the name of caffeine. Cliff had gone out of his way then to procure some expensive Colombian coffee which he now brewed to celebrate Will's yielding to temptation.

As Will drank one cup after another of the steaming black luxury, Clifford cold sober studied his guest. Will looked even younger, he believed, than his lost darling Vera. His hair was only partially gray and he did not weigh more than he had weighed as a twenty-five-year-old man. He stood six-foot-three in his stocking feet and his eyes which Vera once described as the color of robin eggs blue, sparkled like a youth looking for an ideal love.

Today Will, now assigned devotee of the forbidden, managed to get out, "What on earth did Dr. Ray find Vera ill of?"

Clifford took a long time replying and had a small glass of imported brandy after asking Will's permission to so imbibe. "I could not help hearing what your dear girl Vera and the doctor were saying."

Will sat up a bit straight, and his mouth opened hungrily. But Cliff was in no mood to yield to Will's eagerness to know why Vera had gone to the good doctor.

"Your wife," Clifford used the noun on purpose, "though it is impossible to believe, is going through the change of life."

"Change of life?" Will spoke with total disbelief. "Impossible."

"I would have thought so too, but in one of Vera's conversations with me she was overwrought, and told me her other doctor had prescribed a pill containing mares' urine which is known as a palliative to one going through change of life."

Will fell back again on the sofa as if his good friend Clifford had shot him. "Our Vera, like any ordinary woman, is menstruating."

Will, unversed in so much of life's ordinary transitions, gagged slightly and he shaded his eyes. Clifford was immediately at hand with another cup of steaming strong restoring caffeine. Will was barely able to say thank you. From then on Clifford and Will Patterson were if not bosom friends, closely knit in forbidden secrets.

AFTER LEAVING CLIFFORD and his long bewildering recital of Vera's visit to old Dr. Ray and her facing "change of life," Will found himself in such a state of nerves, he had no thought of doing anything but taking a long stroll. Going to his lonely bachelor's hall as he called home now was unthinkable. He was also wondering if Clifford had not put something stronger than coffee in the drink Clifford had carefully prepared for him. Will felt both excited and in an angry, irascible mood. Before he knew it, he found himself standing in front of Vera's rooming house! From the front rooms he could hear a myriad of voices, laughter, and a mixed chorus of hilarity. He felt as shut out from this happy conviviality as if he was a beggar or a common tramp. Before he knew what he was doing he had entered the house of joy.

Coming toward it at that moment was Vera bearing a heavy tray of refreshments. Vera did not see Will bearing down on her until she had bumped with force against him. The steaming supper spilled in all its richness and heat against his jacket and stiff collar. Both Vera and Will looked at the damage wrought with a kind of horror. He heard her call out as she might have years ago, "Will!"

Finally collecting herself, he heard her voice. "Will, sit here on the settee while I call for some help for us."

Will was "so far out of it," in his phrase, he hardly realized that a young woman from the kitchen was helping Vera take care of Will's ruined suit and his brand new tie and collar.

Will felt Vera's hands move over him so that this closeness made him even more if possible beside himself.

HOW LONG THEY sat side by side with Vera lamenting the damage to his clothing, Will hardly knew. The last word however he heard come from Vera was in a cordial note. "Will, you are always welcome here on Friday when we have our Friday summer special."

The next thing he was conscious of was he was walking in a labored gait—where he didn't know.

"That damned coffee," he said aloud. "Cliff put something in it, I'll be damned."

It was too early or too late to go to his own gloomy digs.

All at once as when he had happened on the supper in progress at Vera's he saw he had come upon Bide a Wee, Spirits and Ales.

He stumbled in and was greeted by the owner bartender Hal Jaqua, who tried to conceal his amazement that Will Patterson, known as a spoil sport and teetotaler, had entered his disreputable abode.

"Will, Will, what'll it be?" His cordiality would have melted an iceberg. Will, now helpless for the events of the day and evening, slumped down on a barstool.

"Coffee?"

"Coffee be damned!" Will responded. Looking at the bill of fare in great red letters, Will almost shouted, "I will have brandy."

Jaqua's Adam's apple rose and fell convulsively. He put a nice glass of French brandy before his guest. Will raised the glass, bowed, and swallowed the entire draught in one swallow.

ADA COE, AFTER a career of giving piano lessons to the ungifted from the coffers of wealthy parents, found she had a more rewarding gift as a psychic consultant. Beginning modestly, she soon found she had more people seeking psychic advice than her years at the pianoforte. Everyone, she once remarked, is dying to know the future; men, women, even children.

Vera was no exception. A few days after Will's unscheduled appearance at her Friday gala, Vera could think of nothing else. She even wondered if she could possibly forgive Will's past behavior and take him back, divorce or no divorce. But having called her mother Minnie for advice, Minnie had warned her that to go back to a man who had ruined all of those he touched would be the act of supreme folly.

This advice from Minnie sent Vera therefore to seek the good word from Ada.

Ada's prices had soared since she taught piano lessons to ungifted youngsters. She now dwelt in a rather expensive three-story mansion, and had undergone some kind of beauty treatments so that on entering her studio Vera did not at first recognize her. She recognized Vera immediately and knew Vera would be a perfect consultant to the unknown hidden powers of the psychic.

First of course Ada insisted on Vera's drinking two or three cups of Japanese tea. Both ladies were impressed by the changes in Vera's own change in perception, and her willingness to hear what the unseen powers had to say to her.

Ada insisted they both close their eyes for a few minutes and inquire if the great powers were ready. They were more than ready as the unknown spirits saw in Vera a perfect seeker of the mysteries.

Unlike many psychics Ada enjoyed her work. Nothing inquired of her bored her. She felt an immediate electricity when hearing Vera's anguished questions. For one thing, should she consider remarrying Will? For another, if she did not soon marry one of her suitors, how on earth could she continue to keep body and soul together in view of the rising cost of the present world of dollars and cents?

"You must never dream of giving up your boarding and rooming house," Ada began after another cup or two of tea.

This rather mundane message from the occult dampened Vera's spirit. She had expected something more of the unseen.

"Ah, but listen, dear heart," Ada scolded a little. "Your house for wayfarers is the ideal meeting place of one who can be your all-in-all."

"And where is he?" Vera wondered crisply.

"There is a rather young gentleman, I see dear Vera, whom you have not as yet come to know. And your rooming house is the exact site he will be drawn to. Make no other plans until you meet him. Is that clear? No other plans."

But Vera, ever practical, wanted to know when this prince charming might be expected.

Ada closed her eyes again, for nearly five minutes.

"I see the number 5 and 7; five days perhaps or more correctly five months."

Vera went back into a trance of anticipation and wishfulness. "I see," she said after a long wait during which Ada offered her a tiny sweet probably also from Japan.

Whether it was the tea, the sweet, or the message, Vera suddenly felt uplifted, or inspired—even hopeful.

Both ladies rose at the same time, perhaps propelled to do so by the psychic forces themselves.

But when Vera offered to give her seer a crisp bill, Ada having noted the denomination threw up her hands and said, "Not one cent from you, my dear girl. Absolutely nothing. Perhaps later."

Vera however was somehow disappointed, as if not to give the psychic reading something was perhaps to nullify its promise, its seriousness.

At last, after more protests Ada accepted one of the bills now offered and kissed it gingerly. It was this kiss of the money that somehow restored Vera's faith in the mysterious psychic reading.

DAYS, WEEKS PASSED and Vera heard nothing from Ada Coe. Going through some old clippings one afternoon Vera discovered a little book published by an obscure "New Thought" semi-religious organization. Leaping through the book Vera came across a sentence that Ada had once spoken to Vera some time past. "Nothing is ever lost," the sentence read. Vera had never forgotten this statement. She was not sure what the words meant, but she was sure they were from some great wisdom and the words meant something, Vera was sure, for her present spiritual darkness.

She plunged again into her work as the operator of a boarding and rooming business. She was often surprised at the sighs that came unbidden from her. A deep depression had overtaken her. She had come to the realization that Ada's psychic pronouncements were probably no deeper than fortune telling. At the same time Vera still believed in Ada. Why, she did not know. And the crowning bit of wisdom, that "nothing is ever lost," kept recurring to her mind.

ONE DAY A special carrier arrived at her house. For a moment Vera felt the unfamiliar messenger was bringing some bad news. He asked her to sign document after document, and to Vera's bewilderment she saw the package had come from Morocco in Africa.

She took the package inside but did not open it for a few hours as her business required her immediate attention.

It was not until that evening and after her boarding house was closed that Vera was able to open the package. Inside was what looked like a kind of legal document. Vera went to her own room to get a pair of stronger glasses. She did not like to use glasses while operating her boarding house. The glasses made her look older, she feared.

She was grateful now that she had the spectacles on. The legal document was a check. She could not believe she was reading the figures correctly. But after reading and re-reading the figure she saw that she was being given an international check for twenty thousand dollars. The donor was Dan Schofield whom she had known some years past. He was a close friend of her youngest boy and Vera had always feared Dan was not a proper companion for her son. There had been rumors Dan had led a dissolute life and was even arrested at one time in Chicago. But she had always liked Dan despite the rumors. She had done him many favors and had listened to his own sorrows and problems. Now all her kindness was being rewarded. However, looking more carefully at the accompanying papers, she read to her shock that the donor Daniel Schofield had died in Africa a month or so past and the money had been sent to Vera as part of his will.

A tempest of tears now followed. She would have given anything to have Daniel among the living, and the money he just had bestowed on her caused her no happiness, no joy. She spent that night weeping and sleepless. She felt she hated the money, for somehow she felt it had deprived her of Daniel himself. That night she was so racked with pain she took a strong sedative which she did not like becoming used to. But her sorrow was such, the pill failed to give her peace or rest.

THE GIFT OF the money, far from making her as happy as she should have been, made it so she could neither sleep nor eat. At times she wanted to return such a sum of money. She remembered Daniel Schofield's "shady" past.

At last she decided to call Minnie and ask her advice. But here again she came against another problem. Her former husband, Will Patterson, by reason of his business mistakes and perhaps even his deliberate carelessness in his dealings, had ruined Vera's mother and her second husband Ab Nisley. Minnie had forgiven Will, to everybody's disapproval including that of Vera, but Ab Nisley harbored a grudge against Will which no time could erase. When Ab had decided to marry Minnie after the death of Judson Otis, her first husband, he was not unaware that he would be marrying a wife of considerable, even resplendent wealth. But soon after their marriage, Minnie's foolish reliance on Will's financial involvements had ruined Minnie and her new husband Ab Nisley.

For this reason Vera did not wish to approach Ab for advice, although Minnie insisted she do so.

There was another reason Vera did not wish to see Ab Nisley. Even after his marriage to Minnie there had been some scandal about Ab's "friendship" with Hat (for Hattie), an incredibly wealthy heiress. There was another qualm. Ab had made no secret he was very fond of his stepchild, Vera, and especially her beauty.

But Minnie's insistence Vera see Ab, and her own illness from worry over receiving the request from young Schofield, prevailed.

At last the day arrived, with Vera in even worse health than usual. She had forgotten how young her stepfather still was as he entered. She had not forgotten, however, the scandal concerning Hat Eoff and Ab, though later his innocence was established. Ab was a skilled engineer and had helped Hat understand what repairs were needed in her lavishly expensive electric car.

Ab's first words to Vera broke the ice when he asked Vera if she might prepare him a cup of her best coffee which he had tasted at her kindness once before.

Stepfather and daughter warmed up to each other after three cups of the dark brew and some angel food cake. The presence of Ab began to drive away Vera's blues, aided and abetted by the strong coffee perhaps.

"You should invest the money, dear Vera," he concluded his advice. "Keep this in mind. Never touch the principal, do you hear? Never! And, never see people who under the guise of friendship want a loan however small. You must hold on to every cent. Remember what Will Patterson did to your mother and me. Don't see him!" he almost thundered. "For we know he visited you recently on one of your Friday galas."

Vera agreed, but her agreement was tinged with guilt. Her stepfather, she later thought back to that night, was too handsome for a father, step- or blood related. But his advice, yes she would follow it. She would not follow her mother's folly and be ruined. But, despite her good intentions, her series of headaches did not abate.

WILL HAD NOT completely recovered from his visit to Vera's Friday gala and his having gotten a bit drunk afterwards when he received a long distance call from one Isham Cosalas, a perfect stranger to him. Mr. Cosalas said he was in the vicinity of Mr. Patterson's home and that he had been entrusted with a book of memoirs written by Rick Patterson, Will's son who had died some years ago.

Will distrusted the call and the information, but he grudgingly agreed to see this person. Will and Rick had never been close and had many upsets. Will had disapproved of Rick's life as an actor and now he expected nothing but trouble from this unknown call with a foreign name.

Mr. Cossalas, however, made a favorable impression on Will. He sat down and told of his mission. After Rick's death in New York he had left Mr. Cossalas some of his own precious items, including what was known as Rick's Memoirs.

After a few short bits of conversation, Mr. Cossalas gave Will the handwritten book of Rick's memoirs, a small book in fine leather of perhaps 100 handwritten pages.

Will took the book gingerly and leafed idly through some of the pages.

"I must tell you, Mr. Patterson, that this book contains information which my own father would have difficulty reading. For this reason you may refuse to accept the book."

Will flushed. Mr. Cossalas saw at once Mr. Patterson was in a bind. Whether he accepted the gift or refused it, he would be in trouble.

Nonetheless, after the departure of Rick's Greek friend, as if fate itself had brought this punishment on Will who would be the first to admit he had not been a good or loving father to his son, he read every word of this monstrous confession. Will had been, as his son pointed out, a dreamer, a selfish and self satisfied man who cared nothing about other human beings were they decent and smug like himself or wild, immoral and out of control like his eldest boy Rick.

Will became so ill after reading the book he had made a hurried visit to Clifford, who kept a storehouse of medicine he had inherited from his doctor brother.

Clifford was so upset at Will's appearance he hurriedly administered a medicine—probably morphine.

As Will slept, Clifford read the outrageous confession of a young man who had fallen not among thieves, that would have been perhaps a kind fate, but young men of the most twisted dangerous kind.

Much more worldly than Will, and conversant with many different kinds of men of which he was a secret one, Clifford, himself, was so shocked he also partook of a strong drug to calm himself.

The next day—for Will had spent the day and the night with Clifford—Clifford was able to ask if Vera should be given what Clifford now called: "The Memoirs."

"Vera!" Will cried. "Do you want to kill her? Isn't it enough what the book has done to me?"

"I only asked, Will, for what we are to do?"

"You have asked. And I have answered."

"What are we to do then? Burn it?"

"Do you think even flames will be able to burn such a document?" Will almost shouted, then feeling his weakness he lay back muttering.

"Shall I keep it for you?"

"Keep it?" Will rose up a bit from his position on the couch. "Where on earth could we keep such a thing?"

"Come, come, Will. There are worse things in the word than what happened to poor Rick. Be a man!"

"Worse things? There are no worse things. And Vera must never know any of it."

"I have known young men who have done worse things, and they had a loving father in spite of their downturn. They lived to tell their story and their father stood up for them and helped to cure them."

"My son though is dead and I can see you think I am to blame for his fall and his death. Very well then, I am, and was, to blame. But my body is not made of steel and I am ready to die."

"Not as long as I live, Will. I mean to see that you live."

"You are in for a task for a Titan."

"Not a Titan, Will. A human being who knows we are all flesh and blood, neither demons nor angels. You will live and I will see you do so."

At that Will burst into such a paroxysm of weeping that Clifford helped administer another "antidote" to such passionate grief.

While Will Patterson slept under heavy sedation in an adjoining room, Clifford idly leafed through Rick Patterson's memoirs. Clifford noticed that Will must have missed a section of the book, or else his horror had dimmed his eyesight. There was a page or two in which Rick mentioned that his Mother and Clifford had visited him during his last weeks of life.

Putting aside the memoirs Clifford mused on what he must do next. He felt for one thing that Rick's mother should be given the memoirs. She had, after all, gone to see her boy, to see one who, according to the verdict of society, was dying under the virus of the most infamous disease yet known, a disease more commonly recognized as the infection of young men of a dissolute life.

Clifford Shrader might congratulate himself as being of a more venerable and respected family than the Pattersons. But Cliff's own life had been nearly as infamous in some respects as poor Rick's. He had missed, by mere chance, having to pay the penalty of his own derelictions. But noble family ties or not, Cliff had one thing in his character that many pious folk fail to be given. Cliff, whether by his inheritance, or more likely because he could sympathize fully with the outcasts, like the Christ, could help lift the fallen; while respectable men like Will Patterson, a church member and elder, could not embrace his own dying boy or tell him he loved him. Vera had been equally fearful of how her only son was dying. But something in her rallied at the last and, accompanied by Clifford, she had gone to the frightening shelter reserved for those who were not allowed in respectable hospitals. She had sat for hours beside her boy, helped by Clifford's giving her, finally, one of his secret palliatives.

Now the question for all of them was this: Should not Vera be given her boy's memoirs? Clifford believed she should and she must. Where he had received this notion, who knows? But, though not a believer in orthodox religion or perhaps any religion except his willingness and even zest in lifting up the fallen, he believed a mother should read what her boy had suffered.

After a day or so, Will Patterson was able to sit up and converse. He could not as yet eat any solid food and was obviously very fragile.

Despite this, Clifford insisted he read the pages he had overlooked in the memoirs. Will did, and oddly enough reading them gave him a kind of rallying energy.

Handing back the pages to Clifford, Will said, "Let Vera read them if she wishes. After all, Clifford, if she had the kindness to visit our son, I see it is right for her to read what he wrote in his final day."

Clifford stared at Will. He felt he was seeing something like a conversion for one whose heart had been so cold.

They said no more that day, but Clifford insisted on Will's remaining as his guest until his strength returned.

The collapse of Will Patterson from an unknown ailment was likened to the fall of a great oak tree in the forest, according to Clifford Shrader. He had called Dr. Ray when Will became seriously unlike himself, and Clifford waited patiently while the old Doctor made his examination. Dr. Ray's diagnosis which Clifford listened to silently was both less serious and, in a way, more alarming. The doctor said Will was not suffering from life threatening sickness, but, on the other hand, he would not be able to be his old active self, at least for a while. "Will needs rest, much rest, but not in a hospital or other hospice. No, no that would finish such a man off." Then Dr. Ray made the most unexpected suggestion of all. "Will should go stay at Vera's. I have already spoken to her about it."

"Vera's!" Clifford almost roared. "Are you serious?"

The doctor smiled and nodded.

Clifford sat down and caught his own breath.

"And you actually got her O.K. for such a plan?"

"Oh, yes, but already Ab Nisley and Cora Patterson have expressed disfavor. Cora on the grounds Vera is running a disorderly house, and Ab Nisley of course because he regards Will as the architect of his and Minnie's ruin. However, I spoke alone with Minnie and she approves of Will returning to the woman who was Will's wife."

Clifford was much too overwhelmed to be his old jovial self. He had little opinion for a while as to Will's going to stay at Vera's. He had hoped, he told the doctor, that Will would remain with him.

The doctor smiled. "If Will were not so ill I would agree. But the Will we knew," Dr. Ray continued, "that Will is no longer with us. I hope and pray he will return to his old self. But meanwhile the loving care of his former wife, and the spaciousness of her huge mansion, are ideal for a semi-invalid like Will."

"Semi-invalid?" Clifford almost shouted.

"For now that is," the Doctor attempting to cheer Clifford up who saw himself deprived of the Will he had so long known.

"Semi-invalid," Clifford muttered.

"But, Clifford, our Will is alive. And, there is no one who can care for him like Vera. And, to mention something mundane, she is now quite wealthy in her own right."

Clifford barely heard Dr. Ray after his terrible pronouncement.

"And I will be able to visit Will at Vera's?"

"Of course, Cliff, your visits will cheer him up. But you will have to change your own behavior now when you do see Will."

Clifford felt this was a dig at his fondness for drink. He sighed and said he would do everything in his power to encourage Will to get back his strength.

The thought of Will returning to Vera was, for Cliff, beyond his wildest imagination. Yet he was glad Will could be looked after in her mansion rather than see his dearest friend in some medical institution.

IT WAS ALL arranged then, as Clifford later described it. Call it sleight of hand, or whatever. Only the Doctor could have arranged Clifford carrying the memoirs of Rick, so if it were lost or miscarried, a real disaster would be laid at his feet. And the Doctor sent Will and Clifford with his blessing to Vera's. Oh, yes, she had been warned, and like many people who know they are facing some unavoidable and perilous crisis, Vera was already apprised either by the Doctor or by her own feminine second sight that she was to receive her boy's sentencing of her, and second of himself. She was almost calm.

Clifford gazed at her as he ushered in Will. Vera gave Clifford a look he would never forget. And Will was as calm as if he was in a drama for which he had memorized all the necessary speeches, intonations and gestures.

Vera seeing his weakness ushered him into one of her mammoth easy chairs. He sighed gratefully and closed his eyes. Then slowly relaxing all his facial muscles, Will uttered the one word, "Vera."

She had accepted without his noticing it, had taken the memoirs from Clifford as if it were a great door leading into a room they had not seen previously. A maid entered then bearing a tray of refreshment.

Yes, Clifford told his friends later, it did remind him of communion in the long ago days when he took communion.

Vera moved the memoirs now against her quiet face as if she was fanning herself against a sudden unforeseen rush of fiery heat.

"If you gentlemen will bear with me," Vera muttered, and she gave Will now an anxious but encouraging look.

The gentlemen were not able to gaze at her then. They whispered to one another now as if in church, a church at which they had long ceased to attend.

A clock somewhere in the recesses of the old house chimed pitifully.

The men hardly dared gaze at her, except in furtive almost guilty glances.

How much time had passed? An hour, perhaps, or longer. At last, Vera rose then and with steady step, everything about her calm and steadfast, she handed the pages back to Clifford, as if his friendship for Rick and her merited his keeping what her boy had written, as if such a document belonged to a kind but responsible stranger.

Dr. Ray had once told Will that women in his view were usually stronger than men when family tragedy struck. "For women," the Doctor went on, "are the ushers in of life and very often the presiders over a loved one's passing."

She had now stood the test of her boy's terrible volley of words, not so much words as a firebrand of what he felt was truth: the failure of his parents to understand his lament at having no one in his short life to partake of his anguish and their failure to prevent his death.

"You will stay of course?" Vera gave Will such a desperate beseeching, how could anyone least of all Will refuse her welcome? Vera mentioned the name then of the Doctor and Will nodded, meaning of course it was the Doctor's wish, the Doctor's insistent advice that the time had come for Will to come home; to come, that is, to Vera. That Rick's memoirs, then, were a passionate invitation for Rick to bring the two parents back to where they belonged, to keep Rick also at home, after his terrible life in the Babylon of New York. In death he needed to join them now, away from his years of shame, madness, and suffocation.

But Clifford rose now and in an almost incoherent manner of speaking said he had something to bring to their attention.

Both Vera and Will stood up now and wondered what Clifford

could mean. He pointed to a door leading to a dusty back stairs. Something awaited them, they realized, something was there they had lost account of but their faithful friend Clifford knew was there waiting now to be brought out to the light.

Yes, it was the toy rocking horse, Rick's rocking horse, that changed everything. And Clifford Shrader, who had remembered seeing Rick's toy rocking horse in the unused staircase, brought the toy out now.

The expression on Will's face was like the sun breaking through a massive thundercloud. And Vera too, who must have forgotten having put Rick's favorite toy in a never used stairwell. Vera held the rocking horse close to her as if the favorite toy of her son might speed away now and leave her.

But she remembered then that Will was no longer as absent as Rick. She stood over him then, Will that is, the once absent husband now returned, who was sitting as to rest at his own hearth, and held the rocking horse close to his face. Again, as if the sun had at last burst forth for Will, he took the rocking horse from Vera and held it, not trembling now but firm. Vera welcomed Will then as if he too had come from as far away as his son.

Clifford then relieved the parents of the horse, no longer a toy but a messenger from their boy wherever he might be, and who was looking down on them.

ADELINE

Master Bruno, in his extreme old age, was accustomed to going to a little frequented tavern called La Fonda near the East River. There, he could relax from his work as a famous artist, in which he was still engaged despite his many years. No one spoke English at La Fonda. Bruno's ignorance of foreign tongues, together with his appreciation that the patrons were unable to recognize him as the famous artist that he really was, helped him to relax there.

But what drew him to La Fonda even more was the presence of a very young girl whom everyone called Adeline. In all his years as an artist, he had never glimpsed any one of such unsurpassed or unspoiled beauty. Her crown of golden hair was her chief appeal to Bruno. It made him think of the sun at noon in all its unblemished glory, only rivaled by her cerulean eyes of equal splendor.

Bruno tried not to draw attention to his rapture on the part of the coarse and rough and ready patrons of the lowest strata of society. But he soon was made aware that the often drunk and pur-blind patrons had only attention for their own coarse grained mates who were unaware both of his existence and that of Adeline. Bruno could therefore feast his eyes on her without drawing any others' attention to his rapture.

ADELINE WAS THUS from then on not a young kitchen menial but the reincarnation of a goddess forced by Jupiter to reside on earth for some disobedience to the god himself. Coming home then to his ramshackled living quarters for Bruno's genius though recognized in some quarters had not secured for him a living standard much unlike that which Adeline herself had been obliged to live in as a peeler of potatoes and scrubber of the worn linoleum floors of the tavern.

At home Bruno would make one drawing after another of the goddess so that he felt they made his home shine also like the noon sun. Bruno's detractors and the money men of the art world while conceding that the old man has true genius, nevertheless pointed out that genius or no, he had limited himself to only one subject—that of youthful feminine pulchritude.

BUT THEN BRUNO's sketches of Adeline in his cramped little atelier came to an impasse. He needed a live model, and could no longer rely on his memory of Adeline. But would so young a girl be persuaded to come to his own premises. He had overheard one evening that the owner did speak a little English, and Bruno could speak a garble of his own Italian and Spanish.

One evening, when the owner appeared more free from his duties, Bruno inquired of him how old Adeline was. The owner fidgeted a little whether from his lack of English or his fear of something else. Finally Bruno thought he heard the word *FOURTEEN*. But owing to his own partial deafness this ended his colloquy for a while. If she was that young would he be able to invite her to his studio? But when the owner had said fourteen Bruno heard him say quite plainly, despite his being hard of hearing, that *he* is fourteen.

A few days later Bruno got his courage up again and spoke to the owner in a mixture of Spanish and English.

"Would you permit Adeline to come to my studio sir?" and Bruno showed him some of his sketches. The owner looked very pleased and shook the artist's hand.

"Any time you wish him to come to your studio will be alright—any day after he is through here."

Again Bruno heard Adeline referred to as *he* but he had heard the owner, in times past, mix up pronouns when he tried to speak English and Bruno's own deafness perhaps was also a factor. But permission was then granted. The divine Adeline was coming to his studio and the owner received some money for the permission to be granted.

"And Adeline's age?" Bruno said again.

"Forget that," said the owner as he counted the money again. "You are a gentleman and a famous artist."

And so Adeline was to come to his studio despite her fourteen years, and Bruno seemed to hear again *his* fourteen years—Bruno was sure it was because of his being hard of hearing.

ADELINE'S ARRIVAL AT the studio brought a certain disappointment to the artist. She did not look so pretty in the sallow light of his room. And to his further chagrin he thought he saw a faint appearance of what looked like hair about her lips but he blamed it on his sight in the poor light. Her golden hair and cerulean eyes were still unspoiled to his own eyes.

"So you are going to pose for me," Bruno began. But Adeline had caught sight of his drawings and sketches of his past models. She took down several of the sketches. Her glance widened as she noted the models, young women, had posed without any clothing at all. She looked up then and the artist's and the girl's eyes met briefly. But Adeline began to speak. Bruno was troubled now at hearing her voice which seemed to be hoarse and broken like that of a youngster whose voice is changing.

"And I am to not wear clothes." Again Bruno was caught at Adeline suddenly able to speak to him in his own language.

Waiting until he could think of what to say, Bruno now more than Adeline seemed to be speaking as if in a language not his own.

"Only if you wish to," he got out. "Clothing or no, Adeline."

The name *ADELINE* as he spoke seemed at once to puzzle her as if the artist had mentioned someone whose name was virtually unknown to either of them. She began then removing her little outer garment. He turned away for a moment to put on stronger glasses and, his fingers trembling, he had difficulty adjusting the glasses.

But when he turned to look at her, a low sort of cry escaped his lips. The person standing before him seemed someone he had never seen before. He stepped back and held on to the chair by the large half open bed.

"What is it, sir?" She advanced alarmed toward him. Bruno gave one shaking stare after another. A young man, not Adeline, was gazing at him with a face troubled and that of a young man. Trembling, Bruno motioned to her to bring an unopened bottle of brandy. Adeline's training at the tavern came in handy. She had seen many others who had got unsteady or were even ill. Adeline or rather the now young man standing before Bruno helped him to several swallows of the brandy from the bottle itself.

Bruno was getting back his composure, only slowly.

"You are not angry?" the young boy now spoke.

"Not angry." Bruno said. "But," he went on, "you are not Adeline then."

The person who was no longer Adeline replied that he was also a young man, or at least Bruno thought the old Adeline said this.

Probably neither Bruno nor the young boy who had replaced Adeline would have been able to explain what happened next. Bruno later explained to his friends that the young man who was once Adeline saw that the artist needed someone to help him over his spell of dizziness and virtual helplessness.

LATER, AWAKING FROM a deep slumber Bruno saw oddly enough, not to his surprise, that the young man had removed the artist's outer clothing and then tucked him into the huge bed, a bed which could have found room for four people instead of the artist and the young man. They had slept together the whole night, Bruno realized as the first streak of daylight came into the room. And so, as if by something like magic, there was no Adeline but a young man who was a valuable house mate and something of both a nurse and even a physician.

ADELINE NEVER RETURNED to the tavern. The new model for Bruno became one he had never dreamed of using as a model. When Bruno had recovered his strength, he was engaged in literally hundreds of sketches of a nude young man with a fair share of muscles but who could also boast a crown of golden hair, now trimmed a bit, but still capable of flooding where he stood with a radiance like the noon sun.

IN HIS ART Adeline was now both a young girl and a young man and this became for Bruno his final and greatest creation, the two were one and the one was two. The one was two the two were one.

BIBLIOGRAPHY

PUBLISHED STORIES BY JAMES PURDY

"A Good Woman." *Creative Writing*, (January–February 1939).

"You Reach For Your Hat." *Prairie Schooner* 20 (Spring 1946).

"The Sound of Talking." *Black Mountain Review* 5 (Summer 1955).

Don't Call Me by My Right Name and Other Stories. Published by Osborn Andreas, Andreas Foundation, Chicago. New York: private author-published imprint with William-Frederick Press, 1956.)

"A Good Woman," "Cutting Edge," "Don't Call Me by My Right Name," "Eventide," "Man and Wife," "Plan Now to Attend," "Sound of Talking," "Why Can't They Tell You Why?," "You Reach for Your Hat"

63: Dream Palace: A Novella. published by Jorma Sjoblom, Allentown, PA. New York: private author-published imprint with William-Frederick Press, 1956.

"You Reach for Your Hat," *Mademoiselle* 44 (March 1957), published as "You Reach for Your Wraps."

63: Dream Palace: A Novella and Nine Stories, London: Victor Gollancz, 1957. (James Purdy's first commercially published book.)

"63: Dream Palace," "A Good Woman," "Cutting Edge," "Don't Call Me by My Right Name," "Eventide," "Man and Wife," "Plan Now to Attend," "Sound of Talking," "Why Can't They Tell You Why?," "You Reach for Your Hat"

Color of Darkness: Eleven Stories and a Novella. New York: New Directions, 1957.

"63: Dream Palace" Color of Darkness," "A Good Woman," "Cutting Edge," "Don't Call Me by My Right Name," "Eventide," "Man and Wife," "Plan Now to Attend," "Sound of Talking," "Why Can't They Tell You Why?," "You May Safely Gaze," "You Reach for Your Hat"

"About Jessie Mae." *The New Yorker* 33 (May 25, 1957).

"Cutting Edge." *Evergreen Review* 1, no. 1 (1957).

"Night and Day." *Esquire* 50 (July 1958).

"The Lesson." *Texas Quarterly* 1 (Winter 1958).

"Encore." *Commentary* 27 (March 13, 1959).

"Mrs. Benson." *Commentary* 28 (October 19, 1959).

"Everything Under the Sun." *Partisan Review* (Summer—July 27, 1959).

"Daddy Wolf." *New World Writing* 17 (1960).

"Goodnight, Sweetheart." *Esquire* 54 (October 1960).

"Sermon." *New Directions in Poetry and Prose* 17 (1961).

Children Is All (ten stories and two plays). New York: New Directions, 1962.

Short stories: "About Jessie Mae," "Daddy Wolf," "Encore," "Everything Under the Sun," "Goodnight, Sweetheart," "Home by Dark," "Mrs. Benson," "Night and Day," "Sermon," "The Lesson"

Children Is All (ten stories and two plays). London: Secker & Warburg, 1963.

Short stories: "About Jessie Mae," "Daddy Wolf," "Encore," "Everything Under the Sun," "Goodnight, Sweetheart," "Home by Dark," "Mrs. Benson," "Night and Day," "Sermon," "The Lesson"

"Scrap of Paper." *Evergreen Review* 11, no. 48 (August 1, 1967).

"Mr. Evening." *Harper's Bazaar* 101 (September 1968).

"On the Rebound." *New Directions in Prose and Poetry* 23 (1971).

"Lily's Party." *Antaeus* 13–14, Special Fiction Issue (Spring–Summer 1974).

"Summer Tidings." *Esquire* 82 (December 1974).

"Some of These Days." *New Directions in Prose and Poetry* 3 (1975).

"Short Papa." *Antioch Review* 34 (Summer 1976).

"Ruthanna Elder." *Barataria* 4 (Fall 1977).

A Day After the Fair: A Collection of Plays and Short Stories. San Francisco: Five Trees Press (private author-published imprint with Note of Hand, NY, 1977).

Short stories: "Lily's Party," "Mr. Evening," "On the Rebound," "Scrap of Paper," "Short Papa," "Some of These Days," "Summer Tidings"

"How I Became a Shadow." *New Directions in Prose and Poetry* 36 (1978).

"Summer Tidings." *Granta* 1: (New American Writing) (Fall 1979).

"Sleep Tight." *Antioch Review* 37 (Winter 1979).

"Rapture." *Second Coming* 10, no. 1–2 (1981).

"Mud Toe the Cannibal." *Bomb* 7 (1983).

"Dawn." *Christopher Street* 8, no. 1 (February 4, 1984).

"The Candles of Your Eyes." *Christopher Street* 8, no. 5 (June 5, 1984).

"Rapture." *New Directions in Prose and Poetry* 50 (1986).

"In This Corner . . ." *Christopher Street* 9, no. 7 (1986).

The Candles of Your Eyes, and Thirteen Other Stories. New York: Weidenfeld & Nicolson, 1987.

"Dawn," "How I Became a Shadow", "Lily's Pary", "Mr. Evening," "Mud Toe the Cannibal," "On the Rebound," "Rapture," "Ruthanna Elder," "Scrap of Paper," "Short Papa," "Sleep Tight," "Some of These Days," "Summer Tidings," "The Candles of Your Eyes"

The Candles of Your Eyes and Thirteen Other Stories. London: Peter Owen, 1988.

"Dawn," "How I Became a Shadow," "Lily's Party," "Mr. Evening," "Mud Toe the Cannibal," "On the Rebound," "Rapture," "Ruthanna Elder," "Scrap of Paper," "Short Papa," "Sleep Tight," "Some of These Days," "Summer Tidings," "The Candles of Your Eyes"

63: Dream Palace: Selected Stories 1956–1987. Santa Rosa, CA: Black Sparrow Press, 1991.

"Color of Darkness," "You May Safely Gaze," "Don't Call Me by My Right Name," "Eventide," "Why Can't They Tell You Why?," "Man and Wife," "You Reach for Your Hat," "A Good Woman," "Plan Now to Attend," "Sound of Talking," "Cutting Edge," "63: Dream Palace," "Daddy Wolf," "Home by Dark," "About Jessie Mae," "The Lesson," "Encore," "Night and Day," "Mrs. Benson," "Sermon," "Everything Under The Sun," "Good-night, Sweetheart," "Some of These Days," "Mr. Evening," "Lily's Party," "On the Rebound," "In This Corner . . ."

"Kitty Blue." *Conjunctions* 18 (1992).

"Bonnie." "*Village Voice Literary Supplement* 38 (February 9, 1993).

"Gertrude's Hand." *Antioch Review* 51, no. 3: Annual Fiction Issue (Summer 1993).

"The White Blackbird." *Conjunctions* 20 (1993).

"Brawith." *Antioch Review* 52, no. 2 (Spring 1994).

"Geraldine". *Open City* 6 (1998).

Moe's Villa & Other Stories. London: Arcadia 2000.

"A Little Variety, Please," "Bonnie," "Brawith," "Easy Street," "Entre Dos Luces," "Geraldine," "Gertrude's Hand," "Kitty Blue," "Moe's Villa," "No Stranger to Luke," "Reaching Rose," "The White Blackbird"

"No Stranger to Luke." *Antioch Review* 59, no. 1 (Winter 2001).

Moe's Villa & Other Stories. New York: Carroll & Graf, 2004.
"A Little Variety, Please," "Bonnie," "Brawith," "Easy Street," "Entre Dos Luces," "Geraldine," "Gertrude's Hand," "Kitty Blue," "Moe's Villa," "No Stranger to Luke," "Reaching Rose," "The White Blackbird"

UNPUBLISHED STORIES BY JAMES PURDY

"A Chance to Say No." (circa 1935–1939 during the author's time as a student at Bowling Green College)
"Dr. Dieck & Company." (composed in 1986, but reflective of the author's "lost decade" while teaching at Lawrence College in Appleton, Wisconson, 1946–1955)
"That's About Enough out of You." (circa 1955)
"Talk About Yesterday." (circa 1956)
"The Pupil." (1956)
"Vera's Story." (November 1999–February 2000)
"Adeline." (October 2003)

ACKNOWLEDGEMENTS

A great deal of effort went into preparing this collection, from researching background information and devising an accurate dating process to unearthing archival material and determining its chronological arrangement and presentation.

I would like to extend my warmest gratitude to the people who have supported and aided me in the process of selecting, researching, and editing this collection, including Robert Weil and William Menaker at W. W. Norton & Company/Liveright; Pamela Malpas and Michelle Montalbano at Harold Ober Associates; John Wronoski and Chris Shultz at Lame Duck Books; the Beinecke Rare Book and Manuscript Library at Yale, Nancy Kuhl, Tim Young, and the reading room staff; the Harry Ransom Center at the University of Texas at Austin, Andrew Gasky.

Additional assistance and creative support was provided by Nathaniel Siegel, Jason Hale, and Ian McGrady.

Scholar Michael Snyder, PhD, helped to set forth correct and long-missing biographical information, permitting an understanding of Purdy's creative process and development in the context of his full body of work.

Among those whose research assisted us were Paul W. Miller,

PhD; Marie-Claude Profit; Parker Sams, retired editor of the *Findlay Courier*; Martin Kich, PhD; and Joseph T. Skerrett Jr., PhD.

Finally, Dennis Moore, who formed the James Purdy Society; Todd B. Vance; Bill Troop, a close friend and colleague of James Purdy; Cory MacLauchlin, whose article "Genius in Exile" appeared in *Vice*; J. W. McCormack, whose reflections on James Purdy appeared in *Tin House*; and John Waters, who provided the introduction to the collection, are thanked for their contribution to the process of reintroducing Purdy to a new readership.

—John Uecker, literary executor for James Purdy